The Common Wilderness

By the same author:

THE COMMON THREAD
A Book of Stories

The Common Wilderness

by Michael Seide

FICTION COLLECTIVE

First edition

LCCN: 81-071646
ISBN: 0-914590-74-x

ACKNOWLEDGEMENTS

Thanks are due to the National Endowment for the Arts for a grant to
complete this work. I am also deeply grateful to Bernard Malamud for
his most generous contribution towards its publication.

Published by Fiction Collective with assistance from the National Endowment for the Arts, a federal agency, and New York State Council on the Arts.

Typeset and designed by Open Studio in Rhinebeck, NY 12572, a non-profit
facility for writers, artists and independent literary publishers, supported in
part by grants from the New York State Council on the Arts and National
Endowment for the Arts.

To Katharine

The Common Wilderness

1.

Afraid to go, afraid not to go, was that characteristic of a man who believes himself to be a hero in the making? To ask himself that was to answer himself this, certainly not. Joe frowned at the cardboard on which he was listing the stock. By this time, barely with trouble, it was finally close to three o'clock of the usual everlasting Saturday, and soon there would be no more work to stretch out, and the peculiar business of hanging around for nothing would begin, and if ever he was going to do it, now was not the time to flinch or flutter. He searched the shelves for the next row of gown boxes to list. For anyone who is so fainthearted as to allow himself to be squashed beforehand, no matter how prettily or politely it is accomplished, is an absolute idiot, at least according to Mr. Colish, so that, just to give an example, when Joe said to him, "I'm sorry, Mr. Colish, but it's impossible to get that Gimbels out today," Mr. Colish would rear back and roar, "Why, that's ridiculous, nothing is impossible."

Perhaps. But where did Joe want to go? Or as the saying goes, where did he want to creep with his crooked feet? Simply into the chicken coop Mr. Colish called his private office where, with all the nerve and nobility of his twenty-second year, Joe would say the impossible, and create a sensation. Yes, into that curious room, far from fancy, but close and electric enough with Mr. Colish in it. There was a peachy thing there, a chair, of which Mr. Colish was passionately fond because he could rock in it, and revolve, and rock in it. And a couch there of once-red leather, and above it a curtained peephole a clever foot square, and he could step on the couch and peek right into the showroom, and see if the buyer who had barged in was one he did or did not want to see. And a desk, naturally, on which there steadily diminished a pile of white scratch pads and a beheaded lot of yellow No. 2 pencils, for doodling was a dandy cure for whatever ailed him, particularly when the idea was to draw a daisy round a dollar sign, then link it to another petaled morbidity with the momentous initials M. and C. Great fun for the near great. Still and all, it was almost three o'clock already.

Or exactly a minute of, according to the time clock, but who should be coming in at last, and up the front way too, from delivering a couple of easy cartons to the American Express right downstairs, but Frankie, call him assistant shipping clerk and he cock-a-doodle-doos, so gay with his nose like a pickle, shaking the guts out of the receipt book, doing an imitation of a tap dancer doing an imitation of Pat Rooney, son, imitating Pat Rooney, papa.

"Hey, hey. How am I doing? Okay?"

"Lousy," Joe laughed.

"Lousy?" said Frankie. His two left feet dribbled to a halt. "And I thought I was getting it."

"Oh, you'll get it all right," said Joe. "You'll get it good if you don't stop fooling around this way. Let's have the receipt book."

"Aw," said Frankie. "Say, you know something?"

"What?"

"I just rode up with the boss."

"For crying out loud," said Joe. "Look what you did to the book."

"He was smoking a cigar."

"Who was?"

"The boss. I just rode up with him."

"You're crazy. He never went down, so how could he come up?"

"You want to bet?" said Frankie. "I'll bet you anything you got."

"Pipe down," said Joe. "So you rode up with the boss. So what?"

"Nothing. Only he wanted to know what you were doing."

"Um," said Joe. "That was very nice of him. And what did you tell him?"

"Nothing. I said I didn't know."

"Didn't know?" said Joe. "What do you mean you didn't know?"

"I didn't."

"Mean to say you didn't know I was taking the stock?"

"Oo yeah," said Frankie. "That's right. I forgot."

"You forgot."

"Honest. And then he said to tell you he wants to see you right away."

"How do you like that?" said Joe. "Why didn't you say so in the first place? Hey, see that rag?"

"Huh?" said Frankie. "Where?"

"There."

"This one?"

"No, dummy, that one. Grab it."

"Okay," said Frankie. "I got it."

"Good. You think you'll remember you have it in your hand? Look at him, he's grinning. What're you grinning about?"

"I'm not grinning," Frankie smiled. "You are."

"Go on," said Joe. "Start wiping those shelves."

"Okay," said Frankie. "Where do I begin? Here, Joe? How's right here? Okay, Joe?"

"Yes," said Joe. "Anywhere. Anywhere at all."

So Mr. Colish wanted to see him right away. Good. Clown the second, though of course of a finer clay and color, how amusing that for once, instead of ordering it around, he had been forced by fate to help cut the pattern of a coincidence favorable to the opposition, namely Joe. So in a way Mr. Colish was asking for it. And he was going to get it. And he was going to learn that not everyone would always remain of a size to fit into the palm of his hand. This time it would be no ordinary conference about the advisability of staying a little later in order to get out a shipment capriciously declared to be rush, but a truly solemn and magnificent clash in which at last he, Mr. Colish, would be the listener rather than the loud-mouth. And this was going to happen in his very stronghold. But then such a reversal of form would be enchanting anywhere, anywhere at all.

A row and a half more to go, just the small stack of miscellaneous styles, but there was no hurry now. "Stop fluffing the dust in my face," he yelled at Frankie, then coolly continued to scrawl with large and

3

masterful figures. And then all of a sudden this, he happened to glance at himself from inside out, and he, who was always such a strict one, found himself pleased with what he saw, a properly charming boyishness of weight and height, proud neck, back excellently poised, and except for his apron of pressing cloth slightly smudged along the thighs, and for a film of dust on hair so straight and neat and glossy it had become famous for being untoyable, altogether cleaner-looking right up to his very brown eyes which were large enough to be compelling whether shy or tender or fierce. From him, as Little Bee was once heard to remark, there was never any smell. Even if she was at least half in love with him like all the rest, still it was very sweet of her to say so.

"Frankie, you sonofagun. What're you trying to do? Kill me?"

Quickly, eleven-twelfths of a dozen of that dog of a step-in they could never get rid of, and all finished.

"Okay, dopey. Come over here and help me open up the returns."

Frankie leaned forward as if to get a sign, nodded, straightened, carefully wound up, and chucked the rag past Joe's ear like he was pitching a sharp-breaking curve.

"Hey," said Frankie. "He said right away, Joe. Aren't you going? You better go."

"Easy, boy. Let him wait."

To turn from the winning ways of the brand-new for a moment, tailor-made or edged with lace, embroidered by hand or machine, in colors of maize, blue, white, peach, navy, and pink freshly packed, what could be more drab and indelicate than the return of an item a woman has already worn underneath? Really now, some of these tantalizers in silk underwear all over America ought to go and hide their hides in shame. However, even if Frankie, who knew no tricks, said something like, "She sure must've peed in this one," to handle the soiled and faded sight of what had once been next to nakedness could be fascinating, if done in a dainty sort of way. One can blush as well as bleed internally, at a peculiar stain on a step-in, and with a little hike of the imagination go all the way from the inauguration of intimacy out of mere fingering to, well, to the limit, to the finality of the very dirty word beginning with the letter f, further than which there is no need to go. "In pieces," said Frankie, tossing a pair of pajamas on the pile, "couldn't wait." Joe smiled. Give her credit. Give them all their

4

money back. He cocked his head like a supercilious millionaire. He was feeling very generous today.

"Frankie," said Joe, clapping him resoundingly on the back, "I think you're a stinker. But you know what?"

"What?"

"I think I'll let you go home."

"Yeah?" said Frankie. "No kidding?"

"But you're a stinker, you know that, don't you?"

"Sure, sure," said Frankie. "You mean it, Joe? I can go now?"

"Sure," said Joe. "But I said go. Not crawl all over me."

"But how about the boss, Joe? Suppose he looks for me?"

"Don't worry," said Joe. "I assure you he'll have other things to worry about. Go on. I'll take care of it. Get going."

Which goes to show how ungrateful some people can be. Or so Joe was playful enough to muse for Mr. Colish as he removed his apron. Without being taught out of any book, just by hanging around those sly fakers who think they are smart because they shave more often, some kids can work in a factory a surprisingly short while, regardless of what quaint or flimsy article is riotously manufactured in it, and it immediately becomes apparent that the snotnoses have come to regard the factory as a prison, permanently, a prison from which they so often dream of making a file-in-the-cake kind of escape. Such stupidity is beyond belief. For who does not know, silly idea of being a captive to one side, that here in this factory you make a living? Besides, once released, where can the fools go? Home, all right. So they go home. So how long can they rest at home? God in heaven, he is a witness, if only they would realize that the factory, their second home, is their real home, in which they are allowed to spend their most frisky and fruitful hours, and get paid for it in the bargain. Stupid, stupid. Mention sense, where do you find it nowadays?

It is found. Taking a deep breath before taking the first step to face Mr. Colish in his private office, Joe declared himself to have it. It is found all at once, never to be entirely lost, by those who are so grasping about life that they become gifted with this sense of a power raised to such a magic that it seems to be able to see through and beyond the dark and thick and spiked wall which every lie, modern or medieval, builds round itself as a blinding fortification. But what kind of talk was that? It hurt to be so abstract. What is this phenom called the

5

truth? Too often it acts as candlelight acts, becomes finicky and flickers, blurring what a moment ago had been so bright and original a decision. And then where are you? Lost again. So it is back to the mines for you, brother. Chased along a howling tunnel and caught neatly from behind by the strangely kind and sneaky bogeyman of hope-despair, and his crew of nameless little masked underlings. Stop that thrashing. Here. Give him back his precious hat. Now grab his arm. And boot him out of here.

"Come on, come in," said Mr. Colish irritably even as Joe was knocking.

Joe did so, and carefully shutting the door, walked over to stand before the desk behind which Mr. Colish was drawing gigantic check marks in the air with one hand, and dexterously blowing his nose with the other.

"Where were you?"

"Working," said Joe.

"I thought I told your boy to tell you to come right away."

"He did."

"So why didn't you come?"

"I wanted to finish."

"You wanted to finish?" said Mr. Colish. "Next time don't finish. Come. How much have we got in stock of that 911?"

"Three dozen."

"And 1221?"

"Two."

"Not enough. Skip it. Who the hell does she think she is, calling up the last minute? Her credit's no damn good anyway."

"Mr. Colish."

"These small-town buyers, they can all go and jump in the lake."

"Are you busy?"

"What?" said Mr. Colish. "Why?"

"I wanted to talk to you."

"Talk to me?" said Mr. Colish. "What talk to me?"

"Can I sit down?"

"Sit down?" said Mr. Colish. "What for?"

Funny that such a simple request should instantly change an autocratic look into a fearful one, but understandable, because one, it meant he might be asked to surrender a peewee part of his fortune, and two,

6

when someone sat down with him, Mr. Colish had to descend to the level of speaking as man to man, and that was where he was weakest. So looking elsewhere, he stuffed back his handkerchief, crushed out his smouldering cigar, and said, "Make it Monday, Joe. How about it?"

"No."

"Can't it wait until Monday?"

"No, Mr. Colish."

"You're sure?"

Joe was sure.

"Well, then," Mr. Colish sighed. "All right. Sit down. Now. What's on your mind, Joe?"

"I'm leaving."

"You're what?"

"I'm leaving my job."

"Wait a minute. Say that again?"

"I'm quitting my job, Mr. Colish."

"Quitting your job?" said Mr. Colish. "What is this? A joke? You're crazy? You don't feel well?"

The phone rang as if on the moon. It was queer as an echo in the silence where they sat with enormous googoo eyes, looking comically alike, caught as twins in a cataleptic stare at each other. And kept ringing until Joe managed to lift the correct finger and with it indicate first the phone, and then Mr. Colish. Who obediently groped for the receiver and fumbled it gently to his ear. At which Joe began to rise.

"Hey," said Mr. Colish, with a crash like drums. "Where do you think you're going?"

Joe sank down.

"Hello?" said Mr. Colish. "Hello? Who? Miriam? Oh, you. Well, speak up, for God's sake."

Of all the cuddlesome creatures, the boss's wife, what a lay, so beautifully stacked in front and behind, what was it that had once so treacherously flickered out of her birdbrain when Joe was there to hear it? Something like, "You're too soft, Max." Yes, that was it. "You're too easygoing. Don't be a fool. Don't let them look at you that way. You have to put the fear of God in them. Do you hear me, Max? The fear of God."

But dear old God, if indeed he is to be feared, has at least been very

7

wise in one thing, he has created what can sometimes be a greater fright than himself, that is, a certain kind of woman who is all body, so much so that it is quite as dreadful to seize as not to seize her. So far the workers of the world have not been able to unite against her. One day she appears in the guise of a meteor to flash and crash herself down on the earthiness of a Mr. Colish's lap. One sees that if one happens to be Joe and bursts into the showroom in search of a sample. Takes it all in greedily, popeyed at the sight of the very prim mouth of Mr. Colish sucking on the side of her neck as he claws at a breast more than a mere handful while his eyes, like a stallion which simply must, flash and roll wildly. Yet how casually her own legs are crossed. She is amused to see a squirt blushing. Rattles him further with a wink. Then scares him away when she makes with her lips, boo. Two weeks later, she is Mrs. Colish. For almost a year now. Married before, she is a springy twenty-eight to her second husband's susceptible forty-four. Sometimes Mr. Colish seems to forget and is fresh with her as with his silk boy, but it fools no one, her least of all. He was late to come to lust. And she took him with her eyelids.

"So take some aspirin," said Mr. Colish. "You never had the sniffles before? I can't. No. I'm not alone. A bum did what? Insulted you on the street? You're dreaming. All right. So I believe you. Hang up. I'm really busy. No, not now. Yes. As soon as I can. Yes. All right, darling. Yes. Goodbye."

He stuck a finger in his ear before he knew what he was doing.

"But why, Joe?" said Mr. Colish, flinging out his arms. "You want more money? So all right. So I'll give you two more dollars."

"No," said Joe. "That's not it."

"What is? You haven't got another job?"

"No."

"You're not thinking of getting married or something?"

"No, no."

"Then it's settled," said Mr. Colish. "You get two more dollars."

"Oh, no," said Joe. "I'm leaving, Mr. Colish. I mean it."

"But why?" said Mr. Colish. "What is it? Tell me."

"Because I'm very unhappy here."

"Unhappy?" said Mr. Colish. "How do you like that? Am I happy? Who the hell is happy? What kind of an answer is that?"

"It's true."

"So it's true. So what? So now after six good years with me you

8

want to go out and starve? You'll starve. You have no idea what's doing on the outside. You'll die, I tell you."

"Yes," said Joe. "Six good years. And where am I?"

Nowhere, from beginning to end, nowhere. Yet the memory of how it all began brings back little or no bitterness. If ever there is time, it would be interesting to discover why. It began at nine o'clock one night when that famous rascal called death slouched in to do the Bellinsons dirt with a fatal case of galloping consumption, and through the half-paralyzed mouth of Mamma, had clearly uttered, though it was Sunday, these first curious words, children, your Papa is dead, quick, you must leave high school. Curious then, but it has happened to others before, and will happen to others again. Anyway, it is a cinch for a star pupil to become a hustling bus boy, and a few weeks later to make the jump to errand boy, by the grace of Mr. Colish, because it promised advancement. Sheik, they called him, so slick was his hair. And he was so bashful.

Well, now, perhaps there was no reason to bitch at first because, aside from the pleasure-giving of bringing money home, it was honestly a life of marvelous fun and edification. Why deny it? It was like being entered in a race in which the runner must, and surprisingly could, set a new record every day. Remember and smile. To win against time years ago was to experience a great laugh of joy way inside. And later what amounted to a crazy one when, after being upped to shipping clerk as a reward for inevitably making his sloppy predecessor look as he helped him as slow as a milk-wagon horse, the sheer mathematical fact of so many more dozens lugged out each day was the singular cause for a pat on the back, and this is true, even a handshake once. What was the use of talking? The boy was absolutely out of this world. Mr. Colish used to bring in buyers from all over the country to watch the Brooklyn exhibitionist at work. Talk about being fast. He could tie up a package in the time it took the snappiest of them to say hello. A delightful boy. Look at him go. And so cute. A whiz. A whirlwind. And so sweet. And this went on for years. And the faster the flattered cuckoo went, the more dizzily he seemed to be revolving in the same old place. It had to dawn on him. One bright day he suddenly stopped dead and looked around in a daze and began to wonder. What is this and why? And kept wondering. And still wonders.

"Oh, now, wait a minute," said Mr. Colish. "If I think I know what

9

you mean, you're absolutely wrong, Joe. I've always treated you right. You know that. You know how much you were making when you first came here. Remember?"

"Twelve dollars."

"That's right. And how much are you making now?"

"Thirty."

"Well? So what's wrong with that? Believe me, for a young boy like you, that's doing wonderful."

"There you are," said Joe. "That's the trouble. You'll always think of me as a kid. Be honest, Mr. Colish. You know there's no future for me here."

"No future?" said Mr. Colish.

"I have to go. I must."

"What go? What must? Didn't I try to make you a salesman?"

"It's no use," said Joe. "I must get out of here."

"Stop it," said Mr. Colish. "You talk like a fool. Somebody's been talking to you? Who's been talking to you? You say you must go. Go where? You think you will find a place to go? No, Joe. There are no more places. You must believe me. There is no more. My heart drops when I think of this terrible depression. You don't know what it is yet. You don't know."

"It's all right," said Joe. "I'm not afraid. I'll get along."

Depression. There it was again. Never did a fairy tale have a more obnoxious word for a title. Depression. Of course it appears daily in scare headlines. Yet why is it the dictionary at home does not define it in the sense it is used? What is behind it all? Just what is it the conspirators are trying to say through the medium of this freshly invented journalistic fiction? That insecurity is here to stay with or without a job? My god. Anyone who does not know that, or who believes that no one in this shattered and selfish world is privileged to starve, will please step down and go to the bottom of the class. Which is worse? If it is a case of conditions inside versus conditions outside, which is to come out gaily on top?

But such thinking is itself an example of the kind of nonsense that has become prevalent. The truth is there is only a ghost of a chance of coming out on top. As for doing so gaily, it shows a tendency to be flippant, to insist on laughing a little in between crying a lot. But be serious and agree. The depression is no myth. Yet how can it seem real to one who has not as yet been taken in by the grim and sightless passivity of the persuaded? If the depression is like a red light which will never change to green, what is the use of waiting? Better to break the law. If freedom of choice, the very idea of which is the rouge that tints the illusion of individuality, is ruled out forever, it may be fine and dandy for some of the people, but then none of the people would ever really become either a definite coward or a definite hero. And if one can never be a hero, what is the use of living, just living?

Precisely at this moment, Joe had nerve enough to feel sorry for Mr. Colish, who appeared to be so completely baffled by these answers which were no answers that he could not decide whether to throw a spotlight on his eyes to show contempt entirely or merely fury.

"It's what I feel, Mr. Colish. I can't help it. I know it all sounds silly to you. But that's the way I feel."

"Silly?" said Mr. Colish. "It's stupid, Joe. A Jewish boy to be so stupid? It can't be. You're the best worker I have. You I know I can trust. Fine. But you think you're indispensable, Joe? No, sir, absolutely not. With me no one can be. I don't have to tell you that."

"Sure," said Joe. "I know, I know."

"Otherwise I'd have to go out of business tomorrow. I'm thinking of you, Joe. I like you, Joe. I want you to stay with me. I want you to have patience. I want you to trust me like I trust you. Tell me honest now. How can you be serious when you tell me you want to go?"

"But I am, I tell you."

"It's ridiculous. Listen. I've heard plenty of things in my lifetime, but this I don't believe. No, sir."

"That's funny," said Joe. "But why not? Hasn't anyone ever quit before?"

"Here?" said Mr. Colish. "No, sir. Never here."

"Really?"

"Absolutely. Never in my whole ten years in business."

"Well," said Joe. "I never heard that before. You mean to say I'm going to be the first one?"

"That's right," said Mr. Colish. "If I let you."

"If you let me? How can you stop me?"

"Oh," said Mr. Colish. "What I mean is. It's ridiculous. You won't do it. I know you won't."

"But I will," said Joe. "That's just what I've been trying to tell you.

11

Look, Mr. Colish, I tell you what. If you're interested in keeping the record clean, you can fire me."

"Fire you?"

"That's right. Say in about two weeks from now. How's that?"

"But why should I? I should fire you?"

"There doesn't have to be any reason. No one will ever know. I'll just say you fired me."

"A comedian," said Mr. Colish. "You surprise me. How many times do I have to tell you? As long as I'm in business, you have a job."

Joe was not sure, but did he really hear something? A faraway sound. A kind of boom-boom. Outside the factory? No, closer. As if right in his head.

"Yes, I know, Mr. Colish. But I don't think you understood me. All I meant was that you should."

"You hear it?" said Mr. Colish.

"Yes," said Joe. "You too?"

"In the street?"

"Is it?"

"I think so."

"Yes," said Joe. "It must be. Look, Mr. Colish. What I meant was that if you could only."

Mr. Colish jumped up, beaming with recognition.

"Sure," he said. "It's in the street all right. Come on, let's look."

Joe sat where he was. What a time for that man to become like a kid again, as ravenous for a look at what he was sure was outside as for an all-day sucker, and any color at that. So excited was he that he forgot the window would never yield unless he pushed with all his might on one side only. Plenty of color rushed into the back of his neck and into his ears, offering a rear view of his shoulders jerking up and down as if he were well into a dance which struggles to show how wild and hysterical everyone is in these shaky days.

"Don't sit there," said Mr. Colish. "Come over here and help me."

The window was flung open. Strictly from the left up Madison Avenue came a miniature parade in what at first seemed a little storm of celebration. At the intersection of 29th three men in shirt sleeves were caught in the act of trying to push a stalled Ford out of the way. The man at the wheel had his bald head out, frankly cheering the men on. But the parade engulfed the machine, ran in a ragged stream on either side, and out popped a drum majorette naked to the thighs. Her strut was fantastic. She twirled a gleaming baton from hand to hand, then tossed it terrifically high into the air. It was not caught. It clattered boldly down the street, rolling towards the curb, from which a tiny old lady stepped off and with a clever kick sent it flying in the wrong direction. The bandsmen rushed on. Two wore uniforms freshly mismatched and two were in decent street clothes. The man with the bass drum was the sole show-off and walloped away as if hired by hell. The cornetist was so exasperated that he could be heard trying to reach heaven by means of a single heartbreaking underpaid blast. The clarinetist kept wondering why his very timid squiggles should make him sound like he was gargling. The trombonist played it safe by calmly spitting. A lanky tomboy with a very clean face had now picked up the baton. And the drum majorette was chasing her.

"Now what in the hell is this?" said Mr. Colish.

He meant what came next. Joe leaned so far forward as to risk his precious neck in an effort to make it out from the fourth floor. It was a banner of blue. It said something in gold letters. But the cross or crazy men who held it by the poles at either end insisted on loping along in turn so that the banner would always be shrewdly crumpled. As long as they were in sight, they never caught up with each other. Just the same it seemed to proclaim an anniversary, but whether the 50th or the 80th, whether of an organization or an individual, fraternal or commercial, wet or dry, flourishing or flat broke, remained a mystery. Next came a face so crooked in spite of its perfect teeth and all the rest out of Hollywood that, as it enters the memory, it not only never leaves it, but immediately assumes a dominant position as if it, and it alone, were the personification of what are so well known as the darker moments of life. The instigator himself. Stunningly hatless in the April chill, he waved his hand and wooed the world with his grin. A woman with piano legs and a black straw hat was courageously plucking at his coat sleeve and pointing north and south in an obviously violent attempt to get him to give up and go home and soak his feet. Everyone watched grimly from window or sidewalk as he shoved her as a husband shoves his wife. Behind him in close formation marched a single row of exactly eight unhappy men. No one else belonged to the parade. At the corner of 30th these men quietly turned west and sneaked off down the street. A policeman appeared in the gutter and began to shadow the instigator and the banner bearers and the band as they continued to riot up Madison Avenue. They did not know they had been deserted.

"Do you know what it means?" said Mr. Colish.

"No," said Joe. "I don't know what it means."

They retrieved their heads. They shut the window. They stood there, reviewing with each other's eyes what they had seen.

"See that?" said Mr. Colish. "See what happens to people?"

"I don't get it," said Joe.

"They go crazy. It's the times."

"It was so silly."

"They don't know what they're doing any more."

"It was just like a dream."

"You listen to me," said Mr. Colish. "I'm telling you."

"Telling me what?"

"You think you're smart. You think you can eat up the whole world."

"Oh, no," said Joe. "That's not true."

"You think now you know it all. But I'm telling you, Joe. You listen to me. You'll see. They'll eat you up first."

"I don't know what you're talking about, Mr. Colish. I never said anything like that."

Mr. Colish began with the middle drawer.

"Let me look. Maybe there's some bicarbonate."

"You're absolutely wrong," said Joe. "When did I ever say anything like that?"

"Oh, sure," said Mr. Colish. "I'm foolish. I look. Do you think I would find any? I could kill somebody."

"I'm going, Mr. Colish."

"All right. But think it over."

"I'm going."

"We'll talk some more."

"In two weeks."

"We'll talk some more."

So it was a deadlock again. But by this time it was clear that the man with the heartburn was troubled in the head as well. So why bother to answer him? So go, Joe. But before going, assume this final pose, lean forward ever so slightly with the heels together and incline the head,

14

as a duelist to his opponent after a brief engagement in which each has been barely pinked. So yes, that is exactly what he did do, he bowed, and with some real grace too, luckily remembering from his favorite actor, Ronald Colman, how to shade his smile so that it was easy to see that here at last was a person with the proper amount of assurance and manliness. It was funny. It was all done without a band or a banner. Yet the whole world was a witness.

2.

To be seen is imperative. The dreamer as he dreams in the open air makes sure he is seen. The stage on which he prances so proudly can be bare, can be dim, but all seats must be taken by those who recognize him easily, and at the end the hand clapping must be so terrific as to raise hallelujah with the hair. The boo is definitely not allowed, is punishable. And even the most genteel razz can be shattering. So that his life, which until then had gone nicely round and round, suddenly snaps like a bottom belt, and all the cuteness goes kerplunk out of him. Then it is that he calls on his mamma and papa not to shout, not to get excited, but just to smile and throw out the lifeline, as a last resort. But for Joe this, of course, is unthinkable. The magician in him is still wonderful. He says so himself. He is still much too fiercely young to be other than deft. And cunning. He knows, or so he thinks, he has his audience in the palm of his hand.

He thinks he is lucky. Why? He thinks he is lucky because he had received a favor in the form of a vision. Because of which it would naturally be absurd at present to believe that any amount of argument, no matter how cool or hectic, could move him to change a decision made so dramatically, under the influence of what has just now been mentioned.

What is a vision? Of what is it made? What makes it so precious?

Can it be bought? But why go on? For even the possessor of it like Joe, or one possessed by it like Joe, though he says he most certainly knows, will fail to fix it in mere words, and like a defective will call desperately on his hands for help, will get mad as he claims he has it on the tip of his tongue. But why bother him? Let him have it. It makes him so fearfully happy to have it. He has his fun. For instance, when he sees a streetcar, he is astonished because he seems to be seeing it for the first time. Or an orange. Not to speak of the miraculous visibility of a cigarette or a fingernail. Most mysterious. For all of six months now, Joe has the habit of watching himself where he mentally sits. The cause of it all, his lamb, his pet, his vision, which is of life and is life, can be amazing, can be sexy, can do a little cancan. It makes him stand up with the most embarrassing expression. He does not know where, but he feels he must go places. He is so plainly eager, so wondrously keen, so ready to go. But he does not know where.

A fact which does not faze him. If he makes these half-remembered trips, this time from private office to packing table, with faltering determination, he does manage as yet to emerge encouraged and exult-ant somehow, as if he had swum that river and climbed that moun-tain. After which it is not too surprising that, at such a fresh and lively moment, he likes to act grateful and goes through the ritual of greet-ing the concrete under his feet. And then advances to pure generosity, altogether in love with the grandeur of blessing, even if the recipient is only a redheaded shrimp like Kitzel, the silk boy, who staggers over to salute him, totally bowlegged under a load of rayon.

What Kitzel actually said, first scattering the stuff he had been barely supporting all over the table, was, "Gee, Joe, but you sure got guts."

Joe smiled as he surveyed him down to his belt.

"Excuse me," said Joe.

"And I bet you got it too," said Kitzel, and snuffled.

"I may be mistaken," said Joe. "But I think you're losing your pants."

"Oops," said Kitzel, and remedied the situation. "Hah, Joe? I bet you got it. He likes you. I bet you did, eh?"

More than merely fond of money, incessantly tormented by the very elusiveness of it, Kitzel meant it when he said he hated the fickle stuff. Yet he simply refused to look other than haggard until he got,

18

not movie-glib millions, but a real-life thousand or two or three, honest, Joe, not a cent more. He still had his nerve at twenty-seven. But to be teased so at that tired age was terribly unfair. Think of it. Once he had an actual father and mother. Once he was the younger of two self-devoted children. Now he asks, what does a guy have to do to get somewhere? Be the first-born? Why, once he even went so far as to go to night school to finish high school so that in time he could go on to be a mechanical draftsman or anything that required he abide by some rule of design. And where did it get him? He studied and rushed around and studied, until he found he could no longer see straight. So he went and got himself married.

"Kitzel, my boy, you don't know it, but you're excited again. Now calm down and tell me. What did I get? You mean my pay? Which reminds me."

"Naa," said Kitzel. "You know what I mean."

"I do?" said Joe. "Say, who's got my pay anyway?"

"Sure," said Kitzel. "Stop your kidding. I saw you. I watched you go right in. Christ, I took one look at your face, and I said to myself, goddamn it, I bet you all the swollen bellies in India that guy's going to ask for it."

"You took a look at my face?"

"I said, ha. I said, boyoboy, if he gives it to him, he'll never get away with it, he'll have to give it to everybody else too."

"I wish he would," said Joe. "Whatever it is. You took a look at my face?"

Twitching an eye, likewise a chin badly cut on the bias, Foxy Felix, the head cutter, strolled over, armed with an awl and a yardstick against a possible raid by the boss. "Got a match on you, Joe?" His were flatly and transparently the tactics of a sophisticate whose know-how has been mostly derived from dirty streets with running gutters. His moustache dated from his fifteenth year. He has more than once hinted that when he fathered a boy and a girl with the bewildered help of a clumsy harried little woman who wanted to be absolutely naked when he did it unto her, he made believe he was peering down the slit of some other wrinkled blouse, more full-blown and heavy with a fragrance not of this earth. To be really liked, he had only to relax, but he was too unsure and chickenhearted to control his tricky mind. The one frontal characteristic about him was his mania for betting on a horse right on the nose. He felt safer with those black bits of sen-sen. "Look, kid, you haven't got a cigarette on you too, eh? I'm fresh out." Quite dumb about giving thanks, he stored the favors in his vest pocket, then aimed an ear, ever sensible of the benefits resulting from vigilance, over the rampart of his shoulder. "So Joe? Tell me."

"What?"

"How're things?"

"Okay."

"Anything new?"

"Nope."

"Wait," said Kitzel. "Don't listen to him."

"Look, Kitzel," said Joe. "Why are you hanging around? Why don't you stop bothering and take your junk off my table?"

"He was just in the private office," said Kitzel. "Did you know that?"

"I know it," said Felix. "What happened?"

"He won't tell."

"Why?"

"Ask him."

"What's up, Joe?" said Felix. "Anything happen? What's the dope?"

"Dope," said Joe. "That's a good word. Thanks. I'm going to use it soon for somebody I know."

"Now don't get sore," said Felix.

"Imagine a guy?" said Kitzel. "Why won't he tell us? Haven't we got a right to know? Don't we all work together?"

"Quiet," said Joe. "There's nothing to tell."

"I don't believe it," said Kitzel.

"I don't either," said Felix.

"That's all right," said Joe. "No one is asking you to believe anything."

"Aw, now," said Felix. "Why don't you get off your high horse? Why don't you spill it? You can't tell me nothing happened. You were in there too long."

"Hey," said Joe. "Watch out with that thing."

"Huh?" said Felix. "What's the matter?"

"That yardstick," said Joe. "You almost poked my eye out."

He turned to the pencil sharpener and inserted a pencil which did not need to be sharpened, and cranked. Turned his back on them entirely. The whole trouble was with his face. It was not a bad face as far as faces went, but it did not go far enough, that is to say, it always gave him away. Digusting. He threatened it even now as any kid who squeals is threatened, oh, you wait, wait until I get you alone. He meant at home. He had a beautiful place to get it alone at home in the bathroom mirror. Only there could he speak to it like a father who tries to be both firm and gentle with what is after all his very own. Of course what he wanted it to do was wrong. He wanted it to be a faker. Its funny expression just grew and grew. It seemed so stupid, so completely unable to understand why it should wear a mask which would make it look less alive in order to make it look less foolish to other fools in a world which rarely made sense. So it broke him down. And actually made him laugh. And he would have to say, ah, well, life may be a bitch and life may be a bastard, but it is kind of short and sweet at the same time. So let us be us. Let us try to get there just as we are with just what we have as ours, shall we?

They had not budged.

"You still here?" said Joe. "Why don't you all beat it?"

He hated to see them look so hurt.

"Ah, now," said Joe. "Look, fellas, why don't you be nice? Why don't you believe me? I assure you it has nothing whatsoever to do with anybody in this place but me. Why are you shaking your head? Can't you take my word for it?"

It was Kitzel who was so busy with this business with the head. To which, while he was at it, he thought it would be amusing to add a very peculiar smile. With the astonishing result that he unknowingly turned himself into the wax head of a gypsy fortuneteller cozy behind its dome of glass at a penny arcade, a big glossy boneless head which has been wound up to shake itself from opening to closing time in a constant mocking tremble of, I know you like me to tell you a lie, but you will have to tell me the truth whether you like it or not.

Joe smiled as he slapped him on his slack upper arm.

"If I were you," said Joe. "I'd stop that instantly. That's a good boy. You don't want to scare the hell out of me, do you?"

Nor did Little Bee. Though she did come out of nowhere to clutch at the back of his shirt to keep from crashing to the floor because as usual she had failed at the last moment to say whoa to her feet, her disgraceful cloppers as she herself was quick to describe them.

"Whoops," said Joe, tickled as he steadied her, but had to say, do you mind, before she realized she was still hanging on to what she had ripped out, what at her thirty-three years of age, and already an old-timer in her department of lace, ought to have been as mentionable as her own starched and superior pea-green smock.

"Oh, dear, dear," said Little Bee. "Look what I've done."

"No, no," said Joe. "Please." He recaptured his shirttail and adroitly tucked it back in. "Don't you dare say it. You hear me? I'll kill you if you tell me you're sorry."

She had never told him, she thought no one sensed it, but he knew that nothing infuriated her more than the eternal necessity for saying she was sorry for having a body which, like a banged around indoor baseball, had so little bounce or balance to it. She was so squat she was going to sue the city, as Frankie put it, because the city had built the sidewalk too close to her behind. A real interferer was Felix who kept quizzing her thus, "Why don't you hook yourself a man and get hitched, kiddo?" Somehow her blush helped him to imagine what it would be like to have a kind of beer barrel in bed. Her big joke was that the only reason she did not drown herself deep in her bathtub up to the brim was that it would be a shame to liquidate her one fleshy pride, her cute symmetrical nose. But what she hourly wanted to know was this. Why could she never be other than furious, and therefore sweat so much? Why her fate to be most active and articulate with her armpits? She more than suspected she might be dreaming, but she had to believe that only cash and more cash would finally compound the deodorant. So she fought to save her money. The beloved stuff with which one day she would marry a suddenly noseless someone. O sweet lord on high, Joe crossed his fingers for her, may that sucker come sniffing around soon.

"That's me," said Little Bee. "That's just like me. Did I hurt you?"

"I'll say you did."

"You're joking."

"I'll never be the same."

"Oh, you," said Little Bee. "Look. See what I got?"

"Ah," said Joe. "So you're the one who stole it."

"No, you silly. Don't you trust me? That's why I was coming. Miss Golschman gave it to me to give it to you. Honest, Joe. Take a look. It's still pasted down, isn't it?"

"Is that his pay?" said Kitzel. "Hah, Bee? Is that his pay? Wait. Don't give it to him."

"Now, now," said Joe. "Behave yourself."

"Yeah," said Felix. "That's a good idea. Don't give it to him."

"What's the matter with them?" asked Little Bee. "You owe them money or something?"

"I owe them nothing," said Joe. "Give it here."

"Oh, no, you don't," said Kitzel, and snatched it.

"Hey," said Little Bee, and snatched it back.

"Ah," said Felix, as he snatched it.

"Well," said Joe. "How nice. You're sure I'm not disturbing you? I want you all to have a good time."

"Not me," said Little Bee. "You don't mean me, Joe? Oh, you Felix you. Give it right back, you hear me? Make him give it back, Joe."

"No," said Kitzel. "Don't be a fool. Don't give it to him until he tells."

"You," said Little Bee. "You shut up."

"Shut up yourself," said Kitzel.

"Well, Felix?" said Joe. "You heard the little lady. Hand it over. Let's have it."

"Okay, okay," said Felix. "Here. Take the lousy thing."

"Listen to him," said Little Bee. "Since when is money so lousy to you?"

"Sure," said Felix. "Swell. You can have your goddamn raise. Who the hell cares?"

"Raise?" said Big Bee. "What raise? Who's getting a raise? What's going on here?"

Joe sighed as he pocketed his pay.

"Jump right in," he said. "The water's fine."

He was sarcastic of course, but really he did not mind its becoming the more the merrier. He sat himself down on the packing table, and as he did so, Felix and Kitzel inched closer as if better to stand guard. Such meddlesome and mystified boobs all. He sat on his tin-covered seat as on a throne amid the grinning rolls of rayon, and against the rules, lit an arrogant cigarette. Their eyes popped. His own boss of his own soul. Majestically now, he blew the smoke out of lips beginning to smile, then flipped his hand at them as if he were confronted with a couple of jesters, freshly inviting them to bicker or lark, as it pleased them, but they better be good, or off with their gawking heads.

23

But his reign almost came rudely to an end when Big Bee tried to flick the cigarette out of his hand, partially muffed it, caught a fat spark on a finger, and at once set up a howl. "Ow, you burned me." She would play with fire. Designer, and designing woman, no doubt it must have been when her cheeks first began to crumble that she changed her push into a pat, her strongest touch into the weakest kind of a tickle, favoring for this job the most feminine finger of each of her freckled hands, the pinky. Well, all right. Even if it was a horrid modification, still it made sense, for it simply meant she wished to appear girlish, or more clearly, still young and flushed and inventive enough to merit big money. "All right, wiseguy," Kitzel would challenge Joe, "let me hear you sneeze at seventy smackeroos a week." The others also periodically drooled over this most enviable of pay envelopes in the place. But Joe had yet to train himself to wet his lips. For look what else she did to safeguard her salary, and this she enjoyed doing a bit too much, at the end of every day, with a simper shockingly perfumed, she bounced her buttocks over to the boss to entertain him with her impersonation of a devoted stool pigeon. Mr. Colish never knew how awful he looked in that daily huddle so passionate because he never knew that he listened to her with a sneer. Yet he took in all she told him.

"Isn't he terrible?" said Big Bee, hating Joe so affectionately she was unable to decide which of two things to throw at him, her tiny snot-damp handkerchief or the pattern of a pajama leg.

"Why?" said Little Bee. "I don't think so. Why is he so terrible?"

"Raise," said Big Bee. "Who did I hear say raise? Someone said raise."

"She's always calling him terrible," said Little Bee.

"Me," said Felix. "I did."

"Thanks," said Joe. "I need someone to stick up for me."

"So?" said Big Bee. "Go on. What takes so long? Tell me."

"It's Joe," said Kitzel. "We're sure he's asked for it. And got it. But you know him. You think he'd tell us?"

"Oh, no," said Big Bee. "Why, that's wonderful, Joe. How much?"

"You know what?" said Joe. "I've come to the conclusion that you're just about the silliest people I know. Sometimes you make me laugh. When did I ever keep anything from you? It's been just the opposite. Let's not talk any more about a raise. Believe me, there's no such animal."

24

"Oh, shit," said Kitzel.

"Goodness gracious," said Big Bee as she punished Kitzel with a delicate but definite slap on the cheek. "You are a dope. You frightened the life out of me."

"Then what in the hell were you doing in there so long?" said Felix.

"Really, now," said Little Bee. "Why don't you stop bothering him? You heard him. No raise."

"No," said Joe. "No raise. But something much better than that. For me."

And he gave a little shiver. And clop his heart tried to fly, but flopped all over itself as simultaneously each in the company popped out with a truly major exclamation. For once there was a charm about these beggars now so thoroughly shaken out of their boredom, of tell us, and another clop and a clop again, but please be sweet and do not spin it out. How obvious it is, even to a young squirt, how swift everyone is to snatch at the chance to share in the secret of exaltation. The tongue then forgets the taste of occasional bread and butter. How good it is to see this return to the original innocence of the listener whose eyes are simple again in their rise and shine, and whose breathing in the face is once more shamelessly audible. The mask is thinner than anyone thinks. What is it that so shyly peeps out? Perhaps more than merely that primal eagerness to believe at last in something that is about to be said. But what could that be? Go thou and do likewise? Could that be the message? That crucial failure of words? He now sat up as erectly as he could ever sit. Quite suddenly a poor stiff. They could see he was dying to say something, but he threw them his cigarette to step on instead.

They drew back as if the bitter thing would bite them.

"Do I have to get up?" said Joe. "Step on it someone. Bee?"

"Aa," said Felix. "No one's your slave. Step on it yourself."

"Oh, no," said Joe. "I musn't."

What did that mean? But what else but meaningless could he be when he felt how right they were to dislike him? He had to do something in a hurry. He turned and beckoned to Angelina, knowing exactly where she was stationed. She tiptoed over at once. He pointed. She obediently mashed the smoking butt. She saved his face.

"Ah," said Joe. "That's a good kid."

Was it because of the crucifix? She was such an enigma as she dangled on her indivisible breast this holy necklace, this cool emblem of her belief. Skinniest lamb Jesus ever heard from, the entire skin of her visible face miserably pimpled, she was positively lovable nevertheless. Because she was a packer who could pack and pack all day without once using her frail outside voice to tell anyone how vigorously she was getting along inside, Mr. Colish, who specialized in sacrilege with his hawking and hacking at her with his rush-order generalship, believed she was the perfect worker, that is, a dumb, resigned, but conscientious beast. She had a boy friend with terrific Italian good looks who waited for her downstairs each Saturday, and who was equally a riddle because he always strong-armed her off her feet with a smacking kiss. She seemed to understand that so much virtue will sometimes break out into a rash. Yet tell Mr. Colish how she felt she did, and she was very cute about it, she did it by injecting into her eyes, usually no darker than daylight-blue, a glow of exasperation so pink, it was comic, her innocent idea of a dirty look. But then the Bible too is full of indignation.

"It's not fair," said Kitzel. "I have to say it myself. It's just not fair."

"Oo," said Big Bee. "There he goes again. I can't stand it. Where did you learn how to yell that way?"

"From you," said Kitzel. "Where did you think?"

"You know what I say?" said Felix. "I say let's go. He's just trying to take us all for a ride."

"Joe?" said Little Bee. "You had your mouth open, but nothing came out. Don't be so aggravating. Tell us what it is."

"I will," said Joe. "I'm sorry. I want to, Bee, but you think it's easy? You'll only laugh at me. It sounds like nothing. You'll only be disappointed. I tell you what. Angelina? You come over here. That's right. Scream if I bite you, but let me whisper it to you."

"Whisper what?" said Angelina. "It'll tickle."

"No," said Joe. "Maybe a little. Now bend down."

"Be careful."

"Tell them," said Joe. "Tell them that I'm quitting my job."

She said, "I'm quitting my job."

"Tell them not to look so flabbergasted. It's true."

She said, "Don't look so flabbergasted. It's true."

"In two weeks."

"In two weeks."

"This is no joke, Angelina. I mean it."

"What?" said Angelina.

"I mean it," said Joe.

Angelina faced him with a frown to see if he was serious.

"It's true, Angie. I mean it."

"Oh, no," said Angelina. "Who's going to help me now?"

Little Bee began to breathe through her mouth.

"This is," said Little Bee. "No. No, Joe. You can't do this to me."

Big Bee sagged into forty-three.

"You quitting, Joe?" said Big Bee. "Is that what you said? How can you do that? You can't do that. We need you here, Joe."

"What are you saying?" said Joe. "Why do you say that? Go on. All of you. Get away from me."

But of course, being women, they crowded in to cling all the closer with a heedless and selfish tenacity, boldly bearing down upon his bark instead of recoiling and fleeing from it. This sudden clinch was the feminine limit. How could a mere preliminary boy, trained in the gym to be a clean and smooth boxer for his first fight, contend with these ring-wise professionals who knew how to sneak in a blow stiffly below the belt? But then it is common knowledge that some women do not have to be taught how to have these traitorous reactions. Their small cries of unreasonableness, oh, they would miss him so much, the place would never be the same without him, come naturally to them. They make use of these poison-tipped arrows brainlessly. They breathe most freely in bondage. The nice ones or the spiteful ones, they are what is called all too human, roaming the streets and clogging the subways in a paralysis of caution, missing the point altogether. Only a man who is a dead weight himself can call them delightful. The death of the heart may follow upon desertion. But this dear or that darling, why must so many of them be such timid obstructionists? Why will they not let the people go?

"For chrissakes," said Joe. "Take your hands away. You make me feel so silly. I don't know what the hell I'm saying."

"But why, Joe?" said Little Bee. "I don't understand it. What's got into you? Don't you like us any more?"

"No," said Joe. "That's it. That's exactly the reason why. I hate the whole lot of you."

"You never told us," said Angelina.

"But where will you go?" said Big Bee.

"You seemed so happy all the time," said Angelina.

"What will you do?" said Big Bee.

"That's right," said Joe. "Go on. Keep asking me questions. See how far you get."

"Joe," said Little Bee. "Don't get nasty. Please."

"I can feel it," said Angelina. "He really doesn't want to go. I can see what's going to happen. He's going to change his mind. He'll stay."

"He must," said Little Bee.

"Of course," said Big Bee. "We'll make him."

"You'll make him hell," said Kitzel. "What a nerve. I've been standing here and listening. You women make me sick. Why don't you leave him alone? Come on, give him air. Where do you come off trying to tell him what to do?"

"Well," said Big Bee. "And who could this be that's speaking?"

"John D. Rockefeller," said Kitzel. "Who do you think? Just step aside a minute, will you? Do you mind? I don't know why you're doing this, Joe. I'm not asking any questions, see? But I'd like to shake your hand."

"Why, sure," said Joe. "I'd be glad to."

Never had he seen Kitzel in such a state before. "Put it there," said the new Kitzel, stepping forward theatrically to shake the hand of a hero of his own world. Shook it, honestly and truly shook it. And then what did he do? He immediately stuck a paper clip in his mouth, and stood at attention, looking like just before the battle, mother, his hair a bonfire of enthusiasm, his eyes grown to revolutionary size. He said no more. Simply used his head like a bird tearing out a worm. He was amazing. His joy was so public. But wait. He did say some more as he waved his fist way above his head. "At such a time," he said. And once more. "At such a time." What had happened to the heart of this piker? No longer as cranky and emaciated as the others all around him, it thumped a new tune, a fat and jolly tune of logical desire to celebrate this declaration of independence, this awesomely foolish act he now recognized as one which had long squirmed in secret in the backyard of his own brain. So he had to cheer, it was the least he could do. This was a classic. There must not be a single question to spoil it.

"For crying out loud," said Felix. "What the hell's all the fuss about? If he's crazy, do you have to be crazy too?"

28

"Crazy?" said Kitzel. "What do you know about it? I bet you wish you could be crazy like that."

"Shit," said Felix. "Nuts to the both of you. You think I'm going to be a sucker and hang around and watch you two make love to each other? Not me. I've had my bellyful."

He stalked off all contorted with disgust.

"What does he know about it?" said Kitzel. "And you call him Foxy. What do you know about it? You're all like me. Why don't you admit it? You're jealous. You're afraid."

"Oh," said Big Bee. "You kill me. Absolutely."

"Good," said Kitzel. "Marvelous."

"You're so funny," said Big Bee. "I'm ready to drop dead. Did I ever tell you?"

"Drop dead," said Kitzel. "Terrific. Let me make you laugh some more."

"You little stupid dope," said Big Bee. "Get away from me."

"Hey, now," said Kitzel. "Don't push. Who do you think you're pushing?"

"You hear me?" said Big Bee. "Are you deaf or something? I said, go on, get away from here."

"Listen to that," said Kitzel. "Look who's calling me a dope. You're a dope yourself, you louse. You think I'm a baby you can chase me like that?"

"All right," said Big Bee. "You asked for it."

She slowly raised her hand and smacked him squarely on the mouth.

Holy silk underwear, had it really come to this? The whole goggling bunch watched the paper clip fly out as their astonishment froze in mid-air. For a moment each trembled slightly in a twisted stance, like children playing the statue game.

"Oh, god," Angelina managed to begin to pray.

"Bee," barely breathed Little Bee.

"You hit me," said Kitzel.

"So I'm a louse, am I?" said Big Bee, already sorry as she sprang forward to smack him blindly with the heel of her hand.

"Ow," said Kitzel. "Are you crazy? What are you doing?"

"I'll fix you," said Big Bee.

29

"Jesus," said Kitzel. "What's the matter with you? Do you know what you're doing?"

"Once and for all," said Big Bee. And trapped by sheer momentum, she hauled off and whacked him full on the same sore spot. "That'll show you. Once and for all."

"Bee," said Angelina. "For godsakes, stop it. How can you be so cruel?"

"Oh, wait," said Big Bee. "Wait until I tell Mr. Colish. I'm sick and tired of you, you stinker. I'll have him throw you out of here. That's what I'll do."

"Why?" said Kitzel. "What did I do? I didn't do anything."

"Oh, you poor thing," said Little Bee.

"Mother of god," said Big Bee. "You see what's happening? Nobody respects me any more."

"Tell," said Kitzel. "What is there to tell?"

"Everybody," said Big Bee. "Everybody's getting fresh with me lately."

"If she tells him, I'm sunk."

"Ah," said Big Bee. "My rotten life. My poor rotten life. Everybody picks on it. They pick and pick on it."

"Oh, now," said Little Bee. "When did that ever happen?"

"You see?" said Big Bee. "You see?"

"Please," said Little Bee. "Stop it. Stop making it up."

"Everybody," said Big Bee. "Everybody is against me. You watch. You'll see. One of these days, I'll just string myself up. And that'll be the end of me."

She turned and fled with a final tragic fluff of her hanky.

"What a statement," said Little Bee. "Now I've heard everything."

"Is that blood on me?" said Kitzel. "Is it possible? Can she get me fired?"

"No, no," said Angelina. "You musn't worry. She won't tell. She won't do anything."

"You were here," said Kitzel. "You saw it all. What did I do to her?"

"Nothing," said Little Bee. "That's the trouble. Come. You better go wash your mouth."

"Ah," said Kitzel. "Why does such a stupid thing have to happen to me? I'll lose my job if she tells. The bastard. He always listens to her."

"She won't tell," said Angelina.

"She will," said Kitzel. "I'm sure of it."

"Oh, no," said Little Bee as she helped Angelina lead him away, leaving Joe all alone. "Don't worry. I'll talk to her. She won't say a word. I'll kill her if she does."

A roll of rayon clattered off the table. Imagine what his surprise must have been when the instigator discovered he had been deserted. The banner missing. The drum majorette running off like a coot. And now the band stalled in a snarl of one sour note squiggling after another. Oh, those cross and crazy men. He made the black straw hat bounce as he tried to shake the guts out of her. But then the policeman interfered. As usual there was a crowd of curious people available. The cause of it all began to bluster, protesting that he was an American, that he knew this country like the palm of his hand, had once been robbed in Toledo. But the policeman continued to scribble in his summons book. And as he did so, he said, You were the cause of it all. You can if you wish blame your wife or your country, but it is you who must accept the responsibility. So here. I would advise you to set your alarm clock carefully. For now you must answer for your crime to the judge early Monday morning. Whereupon the instigator paled and slumped to the sidewalk, rolled over on his stomach, and began to beat the pavement with his fists until they bled.

Such a funny story, children. No, no more, you charming little nose pickers, this is the end. For the baseball season opens with a bang this month. Slowly now and with something like a smile Joe softly dropped the curtain on his one-act play of free associational nonsense. Why is it that uneasiness of culpability was gone so soon? And instead present a pleasure derived purely out of a sense of power? But why bleached hair on the back of the hand? Or a certain amount of aching teeth in the gums? Who wants to know? Here is a superior fact, not one of the clowns had dared to kid around with him, the boss of his own bellinsonian soul, the prime mover. Who does not know it? The satellite who is too hasty is always in danger of becoming the fall guy. Yet what a pity that of all those comedians so candidly unconscious it should have been Kitzel who had been seriously, if not hysterically, aware of what was what and why. So do him a favor, be kind, take care of the rolls of rayon he has left behind.

"Hey, there," that real black man Georgie Lee exploded with a cross-country boom from no more than fifteen feet away. "Wake up."

31

Joe hopped a mile off the table.

"Christ almighty," he said.

"I frightened you, huh?"

"You sure in hell did."

Georgie roared. His cleaner teeth flashed. A solidly built porter with a shaved head in which some college education had been poured, he stood his ground in his own territory where he was semipartitioned off, where he was ordered to stay, and roared. The door of the men's room was flung open to show that his foul day's work was done. He beat the handle of his broom against the screen. He was so delighted he made a hole in it.

"George, you sonofagun. How long have you been standing there?"

"Oh, long," said George. "Long."

"Did you hear?"

"Oh, yes. I heard."

"Did you see it all?"

"Oh, sure. The whole shooting match."

"No kidding?" said Joe. "I didn't see you. Were you really there?"

"I sure in hell was."

"And you watched it?"

"Free country," said Georgie. "You looked good, son. How do you feel?"

"Oh, fine," said Joe. "Fine. Didn't you see? It was funny, wasn't it?"

He paused to probe the future with his lively eyes.

"But wait," said Joe with a sort of swagger out of self-mockery. "Leave it to me. I promise you, boy. It'll get funnier and funnier all the time."

3.

Such is sometimes the spunk and immodesty of a youngster, his own clean word for his own condition of just beginning to crawl, who is on the point of becoming a complete illusionist, but checks the desperation and bravura of his recklessness by reminding himself to laugh, and to laugh at himself first, and so bring himself down to earth. Where it is so different. Even if there it does seem to Joe, addicted as he is to the art of prediction, that once something is known, it is known for all time.

After all. Who in these days of sudden damnation can be curious any longer about that meager idea called heaven? If heaven is all rosy, and if on earth there must be every half-hour the good try to pinch a little color into the wizened cheeks of the soul, what on that silly floor upstairs can compare with the fantastic delicacy and rigor of what is real on the ground? Not to speak of what everyone keeps way under ground so religiously. But there it is. Whenever an ignoramus thinks he is thinking he begins to confound heaven and earth, becomes baffled by the tame and the familiar, cannot even comprehend a smoking butt, or an awl, or a simple crucifix. So finally takes refuge in calling himself a dumb ox, and laughs.

Has he therefore come to believe that everything is so funny? He really has not. He is what is known in the trade or the family as a fine type boy. And as such he is merely in a fix. And that is? The trouble now, as he watches himself live up to his promise by carrying Kitzel's rayon to its proper place, is this, why should there be so many short steps after such a great stride? Thinking of it, his becomes the burlesque indignation of the sole passenger. It is a farce. The plutocratic steam is up. The signal screams full speed ahead. The gigantic tub of a groggy ship heaves and groans and boils, but does not budge an inch. What the devil is wrong? He slams the stuff down. Does this mean that there can never be any true movement in the world any more? Since the first telling, wherever he had been, instead of having been set free to drift and stray if he so wished, he had found himself forced to sit as stiff as a popsicle on a stick. Good, yes, but still merely a boy, bound to be playing, twirling the little globe of his miniature world on its frozen axis, fascinated to find that the faster he spins it to make the green lacquer on it drunkenly gleam, the more does it become breathlessly motionless. A potential nut. Why does he allow himself to become spellbound by such an imponderability?

Just about the fairest question so far. And rather fancy. For he had actually used the French word for why which is pourquoi. But it might suggest that he is less vulnerable to the compulsion or the bewitchment or the seduction of that which is less ethereal, of that which has more sensible weight. Not true. Not if it has the shape of a girl of eighteen who is marvelous in her hip-and-breast substantiality. Rosalie. She cuts across the alerted eye of his mind with none of the phony daintiness of a vaudeville nymph but with the plain sidewalk-tripping informality of her name, at last a sensible contact, a welcome relief. Yet he hesitates to make a dash to her, who often wears a pink or blue ribbon of shoulder-strap thinness in her hair. For she is no flimsy entanglement. She is his belly-to-belly love with clothes on, his dreamboat she insists, his honey, his french-kiss. Sounds flattering but foolish, but so she insists, and becomes his foil and antagonist. He begins to walk to where she works. Someone even now must be taking a look at his face. He slowly traverses a shaft of serious afternoon sunlight. He is the only cloud on this cloudless day.

But what would be the color and the climate of the public face of his little sweetheart, as she insists as said before, enclosed as she is at her switchboard? He saw her before she saw him. She was busy at the box which would take it into its head to flicker in a brief contagion of

34

amber lights of three incoming calls. He watched her. She was a corker. She flipped the jiggers up and down, managing the simultaneous business like easy always does it. She had no telephone intonation of laugh or voice. Which was why, strangely enough, she seemed like a pushover on the line, the most subtle kind of a flirt, the kind the boys would call a gal who knew her onions, one with whom they could talk plain turkey. And so it did seem, for aggravatingly enough, her sparkling sex was in her there to stay. Yet if she gabbled, she claimed she finally gagged at what she could read was cooking in their gory minds. Local or long distance, the tramps were always trying to get between her legs. Not like her honey, that funny one, who fondled her as if to find in her, what? That was the perennial question in her grey-blue eyes of medium size. Even when he touched her not, his to her were the hands of a hunter who seemed to be searching for, what for heaven sake? But Rosalie was not Rosalie for nothing. She was no wishy-washy type of a flowering kiddo. She was not afraid to challenge this incitement, this mystery she really loved.

The lobby was empty. He went through the swinging gate and laid his hand on her shoulder just like a detective.

"All right," said Joe. "The jig's up."

She immediately removed her headpiece.

"Hi," said Rosalie. "What did you say?"

"I said you talk too much."

"Me? When?"

"Just now. I've been watching you."

"You have?" She rested a corner of her active lips against his hand. "But you say I'm dumb. You say I can't talk."

"You can't. It's true. All you are is a pretty little you know what."

He removed his hand to wipe it with his other.

"Thanks for the bath," he said.

He began to motion to her encouragingly.

"Up," said Joe.

"What?" said Rosalie.

"Stand up."

"What for?"

"You'll find out."

He took hold of her, dovetailing her nicely against him. As her lipstick-vivid lips began to approach his in a frank initial pout, he

35

studied the slow pale-blue surrender of her eyes very solemnly. He kissed her the way he wanted to kiss her, without haste or passion. Her adjustment was shaky, then firm and splendid. Soon pain of unusual peace made him shiver slightly. Thin and hopeless was the twilight. Holy holy was her mouth.

He felt her beginning to flame. He faded out.

"Oh, you sonofagun," said Rosalie, and clung to him.

"Cut it out."

"Why did you stop?"

"These lousy walls have eyes."

"Who cares?"

"Hold it now," said Joe. "Where do you think you're creeping?"

"There's no one here."

"I said, hold it. I didn't come for this."

She drew back a bit to get a better view of him.

"Ho, ho," said Rosalie. "Tell me again. Maybe I'll believe it."

"Honest," said Joe. "Let go. If you let go, I'll tell you something."

"Tell me what? It's not about the parade, is it?"

"No, no."

"Because I saw it too. Mr. Sackman called me to take a quick look from the showroom. Wasn't it a dilly? I almost died laughing."

"Look," said Joe. "I don't mean to be rude. But you think you can keep quiet a second? I never saw anything like it. Tell me something, will you?"

"Uh-uh," said Rosalie. "Here we go again."

"Was your mother ever frightened by a phonograph needle?"

"Only once," said Rosalie. "Go on, tell. I promise. I'll be quiet."

"Okay, then," said Joe. "I'll tell you. I went and broke my shoelace."

Of course she laughed. She was so glad of the chance to kill herself laughing. He allowed her to carry on alone as she overdid it, her face hidden in him, and all of her heaving. Now once again he had time to notice the banality of her brown hair in its bob which had no trace of high light or curl to it. She was poor. She barely kept herself in order. What then distinguished her from other babes of the same age? Her warmth which was the animal heat of mere humanity? Why was he planted here with this particular one? He honestly wanted some old know-it-all to tell him. Why had he become this much blended with a girl by the name of Rosalie Heller whose compact mind often seemed so attractive, and yet so very fathomable? Was he then so sure of his own superiority? He was not. He began to pat the hair on her head with the watered tenderness of a man who is so afraid to be thought a snob that he must visibly reach out and take hold of that which is after all no less snotty or sorry-looking than his own high and mighty soul.

"Okay," said Joe. "That's enough. It wasn't as funny as all that."

"I swear," said Rosalie. "I'm crying. Only you can make me laugh this way. I'm kind of cuckoo. I love to laugh. You know why?"

"I've often wondered."

"Because it means I'm happy."

"Really?" said Joe. "Hey, now, let's have no more of that. Stand up on your own two feet."

"I'm trying to tell you," said Rosalie. "I'm weak."

"Now don't get cute. You want to hear what I have to say or don't you?"

"Oo, yes," said Rosalie. "I'm so sorry. I forgot all about it."

"You would."

"I didn't mean to. Go ahead now. I'm listening."

"Hooray," said Joe. "Now look, kiddo. Is there a calendar around here?"

"Not lately."

"Then get one. And a red pencil too."

"What for?"

"I want you to put a big circle around this day. I want you to remember it."

"Why?" said Rosalie. "What's up?"

"This is it, Rosalie. This is the day."

"What day? For heaven's sake, what's it all about?"

"I'll tell you later."

"The hell you will. Now. Tell me now."

"Later."

"Now."

"No," said Joe. "Let's get out of here first."

"Shoot," said Rosalie. "Your mouth."

"My mouth? What mouth?"

"It's got goo all over it. Watch it. Here comes the little corporation."

"Mr. Sackman," said Joe.

He whipped out a handkerchief in which he had been frankly blowing his nose all day and with it rubbed at his mouth too freshly tainted with her barbaric brand of lipstick. And at once became angry because he always rebelled against the need to be so fast about it.

"Goddamn it," said Joe. "Why do you have to slap it on so thick?"

"Now, now," said Rosalie. "Don't complain. You know you like the taste of it."

"The hell I do."

Mr. Sackman waddled over with an armload of samples.

"Rosalie, dear," he said. "You busy?"

He winked at Joe with both of his bleary eyes through which could be seen that loosely connected heart of his long ago unscrewed for lack of love. Like anything not housebroken, it was liable to leak at any time and form a puddle so forbidding that even Joe jumped. It made Mr. Sackman so sad. He tried to contain himself, to be frigid, to be unfriendly to flies. But it was no use. For he was a strange kind of a man, if not incurably not a man at all, who pretty near died each time he had to listen to the oversweet intonations of his salesmanship in his territory of New England. When back he came from a trip like a bouncing ball, he found his wife as he had left her on the mattress with the inner springs, as cool and unruffled, and as bounceless as ever. She was remarkably free of hair. She was like a hole in the wall. Or so he had once confided to force himself to sound like a man among men. For such a slip he deserved to be goosed. Not altogether dense about others, what did it avail him to play so dumb about himself? If a little tolerance without spit here and there, then never respect or compassion, not a bit of it. He was much too easy to laugh at, this fat little fairy of forty who often wished himself dead.

"Of course," said Rosalie. "I am always busy."

"Sure, sure, did I say no? I mean now, right now. Are you doing anything? Look. See all this. New prices all of a sudden. The tags have to be changed. It'll only take you a minute you're so quick. If I do it with my shaking hands, I'll never catch the train."

"You'll catch it," said Rosalie. "There's plenty of time."

"Rosalie. Darling. Look into my eyes. I'll miss it. You know me. Be a sweet girl. Change these for me, eh? Please? Pretty please?"

"But Mr. Sackman, can't you see? I'm getting ready to go home."

"Home already? What time is it? I tell you what. What did I do with my pen? I lost my pen. I'll write you a check. I'll pay you overtime from my own personal money."

"A check," said Rosalie. "You're funny. Ask someone else, Mr. Sackman. Go on. Someone else will be glad to do it for you."

"Someone else? You hear that, Joey? Who's my friend in this crazy factory? I could die first."

"Here," said Joe. "Give it to me. She'll do it. Here, kiddo, catch. What the hell. Help out the man."

"Well," said Rosalie. "Thank you. You're sure you're not straining yourself?"

"Sit down," said Joe. "That's right. See that? That's what I like about her. She always listens to reason."

"Reason," said Rosalie, already plucking at the tags. "I'll give you reason right away. If you don't shut up I'll throw it all right back at you."

"Thanks, Joey," said Mr. Sackman. "You're a dear boy."

"Don't mention it."

"Your boss should be like you. Aie. I'm telling you. Have we got a boss. I never saw a man so excited. Why does he yell at me? Is it my fault? Did I tell you what to do?"

"Oh," said Joe. "So he told you, did he?"

"He says he sees me talking to you. So what? So I like to talk to you sometimes. So it means I put the bug in your head? Shake your head. That's right. Tell him the next time. I'm Sackman. I wish everybody luck from the bottom of my heart. But I mind my own business."

"I know," said Joe. "Of course you do."

"And I wish you luck too. You think not? You think I'm like that cruel man? Ah, what's this? Look, Rosalie, my pen. It was all the time in my back pocket. Of all places. No ink in there I hope? But don't you worry, Joe. I'll talk to people about you. If Sackman can help, he'll help. You have my absolute word for it."

"Help?" said Rosalie. "Why should he need help?"

"If he needs it, he needs it. Why not?"

"Why not what?" said Rosalie. "I don't understand. What's he done?"

"She doesn't know?" said Mr. Sackman.

"Rob a bank or something?"

"You didn't tell her?" said Mr. Sackman.

"No," said Joe. "Not yet."

"Uh-uh," said Mr. Sackman. "Well, then. It's been a nice day, folks. I'll be seeing you."

"Mr. Sackman." Rosalie jumped up. "Come back here. Mr. Sackman."

"Let him go," said Joe. "He won't tell you anything."

"Then you tell me. What's wrong? I want to know."

"You will. It's nothing. Finish up. I'll see you later."

"Hey," said Rosalie. "Where do you think you're going?"

"Later," said Joe. "I'll see you later."

"Oh, you stinker," said Rosalie. "Come back here."

"I forgot," said Joe. "I have to do something."

"Liar," said Rosalie.

"I'll be back," said Joe. "Don't worry. I'll be back."

"Coward," said Rosalie, as he fled into the factory.

"Oh," said Felix. "So there you are. What's the good of you coming now? I've already closed most of it myself."

"That's all right," said Joe. "Take it easy. You'll live longer. I'll take the windows along the machines. Okay? We'll make it quick. Don't worry."

So then the idea is not to raise the voice also and increase the racket thereby, but to make it behave itself within the middle register where reason is more likely to rule and be recorded. Tears and tantrums belong to a bygone age. Disorder of commotion ought to be peculiar to a machine only, as in this area of the operators which is ruthlessly in a riot from Monday through Friday. Even right here. To what purpose have the rage and the passion been expended? Peace is as expensive as ever, and ever more mysterious. Everyone is so furious for it in or out of a smock, but no one can sit still long enough to learn the secret of its manufacture so that, when the power is switched off, it may drift down at the day's end with the light-bright solemnity of the fall of snow. He tried to shoo it away. As each window is closed, up drifts a dispassionate puff of dust where the needles have already jabbed out most of the breathable air. The machine heads suffocate beneath their tilted hoods. All the tin bins are banged in. This is no empty playground, as Mr. Colish thinks as he wishes away Sunday, here where the glass is glazed and the silly silk waits to be stitched. This is more like a tomb when it is shut tight. All the toilworn think so, but they will be sucked in again on blue Monday, bored on Sunday with the limp drama of life on a last day off, feeling like fools. But he, he was different, he was Joe. He was sure he had memorized the location of the nearest exit for the last time.

"Boy," said Joe. And this time gave the down button a real good push. "Am I glad this day is over."

"Yeah," said Rosalie. "Me too."

"Well," said Joe. "So it speaks."

For it was the first word out of her since he had come back all dressed for the last lap home.

"Now don't get smart," said Rosalie. "Fix your belt. It's twisted."

So was her mouth.

"What's eating you?" he said.

Suddenly the same thing boiled in both of them. Hate. He gave her such a look out of his red face, but she took it without flinching, so pale and ladylike, turned her rigid head so that all he had left to contend with was a profile absolutely cold to the idea of having dialogue with a worm. The old silent treatment with a curl of the top lip. It struck him as funny to see her step away as if she had nothing better to do than to listen for the ascending hum of the elevator. She was so strictly an amateur when she tried to act. Some day soon, it seemed inevitable at this savage moment this side of the spill of blood, he would very calmly break her head, and thus for once profoundly disturb the constantly maddening slouch of her soul. She would be so surprised.

"You," she lashed out at him. "You of all people. I'm surprised at you. I couldn't believe my ears when Mr. Colish told me. I was so embarrassed. I was sorry I called and asked him. I didn't know what to say."

"Oh," said Joe. "So you called and asked him."

"I never expected him to tell me anything like that."

"You couldn't wait, could you?"

"I felt so ashamed. You mean to say you don't know? he said. How should I know? Did you tell me? Why didn't you tell me? You should've told me the first one."

"I see," said Joe. "So that's what's bothering you. I didn't tell you the first one. I swear. If I don't get a headache today, it'll be a miracle.

41

Come on. Here's the elevator. Or is it? What the hell. Why doesn't he open up? Hey, Karl. Hey, dopey. Open up in there."

Here was another boob who insisted on blocking the way. The door slid back with a crash just as it was about to be kicked. The screwball displayed the hairy apparition of his dome, then a hand which twiddled all of its fingers luringly. It was an act of faith to travel with him. He grinned in every muscle as he sealed them, looking as if he were locking them up for life. He belonged in a circus. With all the goodwill in the world, he loved to give heart failure. His best trick was to climb the cables with the twitter of a monkey in fright. Some original fool had hired and boxed him in, yet he vowed he would one day get himself fired. But the more fresh and familiar he got with the big bosses in the building, the more fond they became of their performing bear. They thought it was a pity on him. Rosalie slapped his hand away. Denied a feel, he produced an umbrella. He wanted to swop. Who had a sled? He swore it was snowing outside, fat flakes, with three good feet of it packed in the gutter. Who would like to go bellywhopping? They said not today, so he rammed down the switch, and began to recite a very dirty limerick. Down he bounced them, and finally out, all at once drawn and miserable to see how anxious they were to leave him. He rose up on his toes and shouted, "You goddamn prisoners." They had to make believe they did not hear him. "You stink, you bastards, all of you." They felt mean and guilty, but glad to escape.

It gets worse and worse every day. It is folly to believe there is solace in a cigarette. This is indeed a dark brown and brutal age in which the abysmal fury of the underling is in the ascendant. His fumbling hand has become a claw and there is fishiness of nicotine in his eye. Perhaps the sky is lucid. Though why a cloud in the shape of a fist? Perhaps this street is rational. Though there is always a car in a stupid rush to shatter its tranquility. But the laugh of a little guy with a moustache is pencil-thin, hysteric and improbable. It is no exaggeration. Every one who passes by has been plundered, first of cradle wholesomeness, then surely of all ensuing equilibrium of the inner sort until the sucker gets the staggers out of which he erupts viciously. It is true. No fooling. The people are more than potentially off their nut because they are in so deep there seems to be no way of getting out. The major emotion is fear. What can stop them from fizzling out? What self-inspired go-between can set them up in another alley? Not Joe. Count him out. His breathing is quick, but very private. He is still in hiding. He attempts to steady himself with the aid of good old Rosalie's arm, and her pink little plausible ribbon.

"Hell," said Joe. "Don't be angry. What's the sense of being angry? There's enough trouble in the world."

"My philosopher," said Rosalie. "You're just as crazy as he is. Why don't they lock him up? He and his filthy mouth."

"Dirty words," said Joe. "So what? Where's your hand?"

"Now don't start dragging me."

"We'll miss the light."

"Who cares? I'm in no hurry."

"Come, come, let's not be so dainty."

"Joe, please, don't make me run."

"Ah," said Joe. "Made it. What're you afraid of? You look damn good when you run."

"Do I? I'm so glad."

"Yipes," said Joe. "Did you see the make-up on that one?"

"Where? Hey, what're you trying to do? Muddle me up?"

"Too late."

"Oo, are you clever."

"Oo, are you dumb. Shame on you. Why don't you be like me? I say the hell with it all."

"That's nice," said Rosalie. "And what does that mean, the hell with it all?"

"It means just that. What do you think? Do I have to draw you a diagram?"

"I wish you would. I mean it. I'm dumb. You know that. Just tell me why you're quitting all of a sudden. That's all I want to know. Why?"

"Oh, christ," said Joe. "I can't, Rosalie. How can I tell you? It's not all of a sudden. Why do you say all of a sudden? You know how I feel about it. A guy just does what he has to do. That's all there is to it. I can talk to you from today until tomorrow. Either you understand it or you don't. That's the way it is with such a thing."

"I see," said Rosalie. "So that tells me everything."

"What else can I say?"

"So now I'm supposed to know why?"

"Aw," said Joe. "Give me a chance. Let me think for a while."

"There," said Rosalie. "See that dog? I bet you think more of that mutt than you do of me."

"Aw, now, wait a minute."

"But that's all right. I don't care. Who cares? Do what you want. What does it mean to me?"

"Aw, come on," said Joe. "Don't be that way. Why do you want to be that way?"

This was silly. This was sad. But it was her privilege all right. Hunched and hatless as she was, she strode beside him with such hauteur it made him wonder, though he hated to feel so estranged, who was she impersonating now with such heartless impeccability? If he was smart, but he was afraid, he would quietly but firmly detach himself from this relative peanut, this hinderer barely average in height, but so dangerous nevertheless because of curves on her conspicuously proportionate, who had made him toss away his address book, though actually he kept it hidden, who had come to believe, so much did the idea of possession haunt her, that now he was forever in her custody. Not every trip to the subway can turn out to be this jolly. She tore open her bag, but only for something into which she barely blew. She had her whip so well concealed. Not every man can have as an escort a trainer who compliments him by using neither gun, nor leash, nor legs of a chair. Ought he then to give out with the roar of a lion who knows he is losing? She knew he was following her down the downtown stairs. Or ought he to be more modest and merely yip and nip at her flying heels?

"Wait," said Joe. "Wait a second. I have a nickel for you."

But she was not to be bought off so easily. No, not Rosalie. With a poke of a peeling wand on which she still had payments to make, she had switched herself into the semblance of a princess of the old school whose first duty was to be deaf to the presumptuous babbling of this commoner who trailed behind her. Bless her cute little temporary daydream. She flounced up to the change booth to break her own dime, but if her movements were majestic, they were also so tight that in scooping at the nickels, darn it, she dropped one. But she was not dismayed, made no dive for it, hardly glanced at it wobbling around somewhere, because she knew that he, the name of the faithful retainer momentarily escaped her, would dash to pick it up for her, which he did. Hardly ever had the 28th Street station of the Lexington

44

Avenue I.R.T. been witness to such goings on. He ventured to doff his hat with a sweep that raised the dust of a century of white stockings and no long pants, and kind of hustled her through the turnstile and well onto the platform, bending over her with such extravagant concern that she blushed. But let everybody look. He wrapped his arms around her, and was about to say as he squeezed to make her grunt at least, that this was no way to play the fool, beautiful, with such vengeance, when a loco train on its last legs rumbled in, positively screeching at the idea that peace could ever be declared between them.

And now came the liberation in the train where he weaved in to find them seats side by side. To sit was to sit. Nothing else. Simple to pinch a subway clamp on the mouth. His tiff with Rosalie, who had made it seem so fabulous, could now be suspended. He sighed. Now he could languidly wave so long to his most fickle possession, his soul, that snaky protoplasmic seeker of hello, could tilt a bit the too-vertical stance of his crisp and critical mind, could slouch and blink, and wearily survey the human equation as it slumps and sways under artifical light.

How dim. The heart goes out to one, is withheld from another. The memory may be more tricky than tenacious, yet when the faces of yesteryear are recalled, they still seem to retain a radiance so ruddy and circumfluent. Never mind the children. Even in these sour new days they do not need the music of a merry-go-round to make them twinkle in the aisles. It is these bigger ones. Whereas at one time there used to be many decidedly dumb-but-happy faces, today each seems so much like each in this, to enter a train means to park the smile under the seat with the chewing gum, means to leave every quiver of aspiration, if not all hope, far behind. They have become such copycats. Each seems to have developed a similar idle tyrannical eye behind which he yells blue murder, though of course he remains diabolically dumb, disgusted, clawing at a cuticle, incapable of being tickled any more by any character of any comic in any newspaper. Poor everybody. What makes this sleeper awake in time? What makes the wheels go round? There are no straphangers yet, but when they come, they will not come playfully. Coming or going, everyone looks like Rosalie, who looks stunned as if her future had received a foul blow.

But then in tripped a trio of girls at the next stop. Their high-school noise seemed a charming refutation. Their bubble of the present was enormous. When they bounced their little cans down opposite, the nicest kid was in the center. Their broad-brimmed Saturday hats for going out for more formal-like fun kept colliding. Their tiny faces squealed cohesively. They were such a sweet dominaton with their sharp apple-biting teeth and the astonishing lucidity of their dewy eyes. The imp in the center opened the book in her lap at the place where she had found it. The others tore at her to have another look. She let them. It made such a dear scene as cheek to cheek they spelt it out purely with their lips. Delicately now, screw, was that the word? How they goggled as their giggles coiled round the naughtiness sparkling on the page. That chippy called life, when first it begins to palpitate where it is beginning to burn, it wears a skimpy plaid skirt to hide the trembling of its thighs, and is not ashamed, so pitiful it is, to show its baby knees where like a dimple the ignorance of the flesh is fading.

At 14th Street a few of the nickel nursers fled, but a fresh bunch rushed in, including a hefty woman high in her descending years who tried to squeeze in next to Joe. He shrank as much as possible to make himself scarce for her sake, but she kept squirming in an effort to slide in the whole of her buttocks, plainly furious with him. He was surprised to be so singled out. But then, as he sized her up in a second, he guessed that she was just another one of those unfortunates who have been so long harried by the hound of unhappiness, who have become so fantastically spent and bloodless in the chase that they must always seize and suck on someone in revenge, so he decided to grin and bear it. Nevertheless she began to mumble. It was amusing. She said, raising her voice a notch, that it would certainly do him no harm if he tried to shove over a bit. He examined his sardine existence, and shrugging his shoulders, smiled right at her as he asked, where? Then he ought to stand up like a gentleman, she said, and let a lady have a decent seat who had been pounding the pavement all day long. But from where he was sitting he could see that she was sitting, so here was her chance, let her rest quietly, if at all possible, okay? At this point it was well worth it because it made Rosalie speak to him for the first time since in the street because she was curious to know, to who was he speaking to, to who, it sounded kind of nasty there. It was nothing, he shushed her, nothing at all. But the bitter antagonist on his other side was far from through. She leaned over to regard them both shrewdly, and then said something which Rosalie could not completely catch, it was a question about their being, but which so astonished Joe that he withdrew from her as far as he could, refusing to answer.

Lucky it was Rosalie's stop at Spring Street.

"What was that?" said Rosalie. "What did she say?"

But Joe only shook his head as he ushered her out of the train.

"I didn't get it," said Rosalie. "She said we were what?"

Joe had to laugh as they paused beside a pillar.

"Goddamn," he said. "Wasn't that a lulu?"

"What was?"

"People are funny all right. So help me. I don't understand them. You know what she said, Rosalie? This'll kill you. She said, 'You two are Jewish people, aren't you?' "

"Jewish people?"

"Right. Can you beat that? As if that explained everything."

"And you let her get away with it?"

"Get away with it. What could I do? There was nothing I could do except ignore her."

"Ignore her?" said Rosalie. "I would've scratched her eyes out."

"Oh, no," said Joe. "And be as bad as she is?"

Rosalie stared at him as if he had just been introduced.

"You know," she said. "Sometimes I think there's something wrong with you. What are you smiling about? I mean it. First you quit your job. I never heard of such a crazy thing. Where did you get the nerve to do it? Then all of a sudden you're like a rabbit. You sit there and take it."

"Bravo," said Joe. "That's a wonderful speech. Shake hands."

"Oh, go away."

"I didn't know you had it in you."

"You aggravate me."

"I'll vote for you any time."

"Everything's a joke with you."

"You want tears?"

"No," said Rosalie. "Sense."

"All right, then," said Joe. "I'll give it to you. Be a good girl. Do yourself a favor. Go upstairs now and take that bus and go home."

"Don't be so anxious to get rid of me."

47

"How about it? And eat. You'll feel better."

"No," said Rosalie. "I think I'll just stay right here."

"Stay here?" said Joe. "What for?"

"Why not? What difference does it make?"

"What do you mean why not? You can't stand here. You have to go home."

"Home," said Rosalie. "I hate it. What am I going to do home?"

"Oh, hell," said Joe. "How do I know? Why do you ask me such stupid questions?"

"Stay with me."

"I can't."

"Don't leave me."

"But I must. I promised the boys, Rosalie. You know that. It's all fixed up. I can't back out now."

"But what about me?" said Rosalie. "I'll go crazy if I have to stay home."

"Then go to the movies or something."

"No. Not alone. You stay. You go with me."

"I can't," said Joe. "I just told you."

"If you go with me, I'll pay for myself."

"Holy mackerel," said Joe. "How did we ever fall into this?"

"I'll even pay for you. How's that?"

"Look," said Joe. "Who's aggravating who now? Why must we stand here like dopes and talk this way? I swear I'll go nuts myself if you keep this up. What's the matter with you? You know I have to go. Why can't you be nice about it?"

"Okay," said Rosalie. "You don't have to yell. Go on. Go. Who's stopping you?"

"You are," said Joe. "I can't leave you like this."

"Oh, yes, you can," said Rosalie. "You can leave me. Don't make believe you can't. I know you now. You don't give a damn what happens to me. What do you care? You only care about yourself. You're so selfish I hate you. Go ahead. Here's your train. Take it. I don't care. But you'll see. You'll be sorry. You'll see."

The doors opened. The doors closed. The train waited for no one. It went. The drunk who had been sprawled out on the bench in a splendid agony, incessantly in contortions directly beneath his battered hat as if he were struggling to rediscover his nomadic face so far-gone in

48

its daytime binge, slowly rolled over and fell flat on what he was looking for. Joe winced and took a step forward, but decided to butt out of it. Let him lie there in his more independent and endurable position.

What did she mean? Did she mean he was going to witness her final disappearance? Or would it be his? If sincerely so, if it so suited her, let her stand there and shrink against the pillar and compile her threats. The next train must be his. If pity was the glue, then he was determined to become unstuck. Still there were his hands crammed in his pockets, he noticed how they ached, they wished to slip themselves inside her coat and cleverly caress the jut and bulge of her, and so defeat and undo him entirely. Yet how could he leave her like this? The mystic lashes of her eyes thinned in retreat, her fever-red lips, the ailing hollows in her cheeks, she often attained this cruel look of sickliness, for by herself what was she behind her rosy skin but scattered and plain, and lonely, and loneliness was to her that cold rumpled horror, an old hag in a crouch, munching the nits she picks out of her tangled hair, which only love-making, even if it be merely an experiment in the art of holding hands, could assuage and chase away. Somewhere there must be someone who can remain alone for one single night without once shivering. A man without a neck stepped on the scales, and with the use of an ordinary penny, profited to the extent of a double-take. He was shocked to learn how much of a burden he really was to those who really loved him.

"Rosalie. Look at me. I said look at me. Why don't you stop making up things and let me go? Why do you want to be so terrible?"

"Because you are. Because you don't love me any more."

"Love," said Joe. "Don't be silly."

"You don't. Don't you think I can tell?"

"Wait a minute," said Joe. 'You're not going to start weeping, are you?"

"Don't worry. I can tell. I know."

"Because if you are, I won't stand for it."

"You're running away from me."

"Running away from you? That settles it. You don't know what you're talking about any more. Rosalie, I'm asking you. For the last time. Are you going home or not?"

"Don't bother me. I told you."

"I hear a train coming."

"I'm not going."

"I'm taking it, Rosalie."

"Take it. I'm staying right here."

"I see," said Joe. "So that's final."

"Yes," said Rosalie. "That's final."

"Okay, baby. You win. Stay here and look foolish. Have a good time. And look me up when you're a little older. I might like you a little better then."

And he wheeled away from her. And he stalked to the edge of the platform. And the train blew dust in his eyes. So he slanged and swore at it. But the ragged clod of his fury was like an artificial flower, rootless, theatrical in color, brittle as any false stem in its lurid resemblance to the true and traditional green of a thing growing, so it cracked just as the door hissed behind him. The weakling, he would not clutch at strap or pole, but had to turn and give his love the satisfaction of a last look as the train carried him away. Her ankles were insolently crossed where she leaned. If she had stuck out her tongue at him, he would have smiled. But even the set of her head which moved in following his flight seemed fixed in a deathlike immobility, and her clearest eye was like an icicle, and she returned his stare of pity and anxiety with no sign that she would ever relent, go home, see him again on Monday. He did not care what she thought it meant. He shook his fist at her.

4.

Perhaps it is the truly passionate man, or the budding philosopher, if his name happens to be Joe, who is most likely to bungle whenever he bumps against what he defines as a basic stupidity. Maybe it is because he is too ambitious. Imagine. He wants always to be direct and simple and tender and sane. That most of all, sane. That of course is so outlandish a notion that it immediately calls for handcuffs, or better yet, a strait jacket. For such a one as he, hissing at his hecklers like a cornered cat, can infuriate and hex those who have become corrupt by becoming complex. Behold. There he is on the loose, a living contradiction of himself, grim with his goodbyes and harsh with his hellos, forever having to reject what the rest accept, abused and disabused, speaking to them like a little brother in their accent, but never able to impress upon them his own. If he hollers let him go.

Incredible. The blindness of those who believe that every step alone is a step away. Trust is the last thing tendered. Foolish and hard-boiled to the end, with her empty belly dead set against the breadbox, did she cry a little after all? And cough? Her late cold had left her with a hacking cough. And spit a bit? Then powder the pockmark on the side of her nose? This is how the earth turns so magnificently for him who is merely so-sorry-dear, who sniffs while he circles around, though he be miles away, the Rosalie to whom in his bungling he has given a bum steer, and the heartless goodbye of his fist in her face.

So he rides, and then he walks, and even talks to himself, very much alive. But of his journey he remembers nothing, for the next thing he knows he is running up the stairs to the second floor of the four-storey building where he lives in apartment 7B in that laughable borough of Brooklyn. He is sure his trip has been but a trifle in time, and not spectacular, but he is enchanted to feel so very much different, if not considerably older, as if the little wheels by faith and the big wheels by the grace of God had whirled in him so fast that he would never be the same, tonic revolutions which left him neither dizzy nor distraught, but decisive, and more intensely balanced on his toes, and altogether anxious all of a sudden to get into the house. He began to take the stone steps two at a time, then tried for three, fickle to all else but speed. His final leap on his landing almost bowled the freckle-face over.

"Jesus," said Joe. "I didn't hurt you, did I?"

He held her a moment while she shook her head with the extravagant wobble of four years going on five.

"See," said Thelma, showing him what she held in her hand.

"A ball," said Joe. "Say, that looks like a good one."

"Afraid not. It doesn't bounce."

Sadly she handed it over for him to see. She was the odd little number from next door who was not to be treated like a toy, or tossed in the air and tickled. Thelma was her name. It made everyone lisp. The startling maturity of her mouth might suggest that she already knew the score, but how could that be? She was far too tiny for that with her toothpick legs, and her half-grown teeth haphazardly spaced, and her one treasure, her elliptical eyes of green which never blinked. But she was no monster. She had her own troubles.

"Hell," said Joe. "It has a hole in it. That's why."

"I know. My father washed it. He found it. I'm lucky to have my own ball. Can you paste it? I'm sick a whole week."

"What?" said Joe. "Not because of this?"

"No, here," said Thelma. "In my throat."

"Oh. That's too bad. I'm sorry to hear that."

"Yes. And now my father. You know why?"

"He must've caught it from you."

"Oh, no," said Thelma. "He tells lies. My mother says so. She yells to him get out of the house. He's a good man, but he sleeps."

"What's wrong with that? Don't tell me. I know."

He reached down to smooth her hair of many colors. Her skull felt as crushable as her own bleached ball with the bad hole in it. This frail product of a father, once a baker or candlestick maker or what difference does it make, who had time now to poke in the gutter for loot among cigarette stubs and eggshells and an occasional lump of dog grunt, and of a mother, incipient fat of her marriage neatly flexed in her house dress, her voice tuneful, but sacrificed in the street to her shyness, who had begun to yap at her good man behind the peeling walls because, how she hated his mean jobs, but hated his joblessness more, because the last pair of long stockings for the kid was torn, and no money coming in for corn or crisco or cotton drawers, and no crumbs even for that cockroach, see it crawling on the chair, there, this iridescent bone of a Thelma, do not ever take away her daily bread, but give her also a taste of honey on it once in a while, or else do not try to feed her at all. If her generation is not humored, it will cause trouble. It will lose its patience. It will talk too much. It will scream. It will go looking for blood.

"But he does," said Thelma. "You know my gramma? She gives him money."

"Look, Thelma. That's very nice. I'm glad to hear it. But you mustn't tell these things."

"Why?"

"If your father knew, he'd be very angry."

"Why? Is it wrong?"

"Don't act so innocent," said Joe. "I don't know if it's wrong, but it's not exactly right either. I'll explain it to you sometimes. Just don't tell."

"I shouldn't?"

"Believe me, it's better that way."

"But I like to tell you. It's a secret."

"A what?"

"A secret."

"Oh," said Joe. "Well, all right, then. If you have to tell somebody. But nobody else. Understand?"

"Yes."

"Good girl."

"So can you paste it?"

"This thing? Naa. Throw it away. I tell you what. Let's see how much I got. Will you do me a favor?"

"What?"

"Here's fifteen cents. Go down and buy a high bouncer."

"No."

"Don't tell me no."

"My mother says never to take."

"Wait a minute," said Joe. "I'm not giving you anything. I want you to buy it for me. For me. Understand?"

"Oh."

"Oh, is right. So take. Now don't cross the street. Go on the corner."

"I will."

"And listen. If you want to, you can stay down and play with it."

"I can?"

"Sure. I wouldn't trust anybody else. But you can hold it for me. Okay?"

"Oh, yes," said Thelma. "Can I stay long? Can I stay long?"

"As long as you like. Only I'll break your head if you go in the gutter. And remember, that ball's mine. When I ask you for it, will you give it to me?"

"I will, I will."

"Good," said Joe. "So that's settled."

She began to hop up and down, clinging to him.

"Oh, boy," she said. "You know what?"

"What?"

"I love you, I love you."

"Naturally," said Joe. "Go on now. Scram."

When the boy scout entered the house, he found two of his nearest and dearest, since he was feeling so mellow, not in the kitchen, so small it could be put in a pocket, but in the living room which had more space for spoofing, his sister, Helen, seated on her legs on the couch, his mother, Mamma, on her feet as usual, with the teapot with the broken spout for watering the plants in her hand, both frowning at this emissary of the devil because he had barged in with such a bang.

Questioners, if left alone, they inevitably slid back again to relive certain sad moments of the past, refusing to forget how once they had been humiliated, be it by dearth or death, forever baffled by the most ordinary fact that life, that straight and lovely, could by a sudden twist become cracked and crooked. Yet they never wept, so stubborn were they, ashamed to be pursuing this silliness but determined to make it say uncle, though it never did because someone was always breathing too loud, and they were disturbed, and still there was no answer. A family failing. On which he had lately begun to slam the door. Against their brooding, he pitted his rudeness, the virtue of his noise. For by this time it ought to be clear to everyone concerned that any dream of space and peace can never flourish in the four rented boxes of a home where the collective spirit is tempted to droop like a bedraggled mop left to lean head down in a dusty corner. So lights, camera, shoot it. He stiffened into the angular salute of a wooden soldier. Then scaled his hat at Helen's head and was delighted to see it stick there.

"Hey," said Joe. "Did you see that?"

Helen had to smile.

"Thanks," she said. "That's just what I need for my headache."

"Did you see that, Ma?" said Joe. "Did you see how I did it?" He snapped his fingers. "Just like that."

"Tricks," said Mrs. Bellinson.

"You said it. Hey, don't take it off yet. Doesn't she look cute? Come on, Ma, you try it. I bet you can do it too."

Mrs. Bellinson shook her head hopelessly.

"Still a child," she said. "He compares himself to me."

"Try it, try it."

"No," she said. "Not with my old hands."

"Ah, yes, your old hands."

He threw his coat like a bundle on the furthest chair.

"You're young," said Joe. "Like a spring chicken. Don't you think I know? You're strong, I tell you. Like iron."

"Sure, sure," said Mrs. Bellinson.

"Look," said Helen. "You may not know it, but there's a closet in this house."

"Is there?" said Joe. "How nice. So?"

"So go hang your coat up."

"Later," said Joe. "There are more important things to do."

For one thing, to do what was never done in this house except on some high and solemn holiday, to kiss his mother as his mother, and not as his foremost and most eloquent advocate before God, with good instinct, with honesty, and with pleasure. But it was difficult, for she saw it coming, and he had to be clever to catch her clean and bloodless cheek, but she kept struggling, making a face as if he had poisoned her, and ploop, a gulp of water came out of the teapot to splash him.

"Fool," said Mrs. Bellinson. "Look what you made me do."

"Holy mackerel," said Joe. "What happened?"

"Ach," said Mrs. Bellinson. "To be so crazy."

"I'm all wet."

"Good for you," said Helen.

"This is lovely," said Joe. "Look at me. My number two pants."

"Your number two?" said Mrs. Bellinson. "Quick. Take it off. I'll press it."

"No, Ma," said Helen. "Don't you do it. Next time he won't get so fresh."

"Fresh?" said Joe.

"Stupid," said Mrs. Bellinson. "You hear me? Come. You'll catch cold."

"You," said Joe. "You know what I'm going to do, Mrs. Bellinson? I'm going to sue you."

"Sue me, don't sue me."

"You're a holy terror."

"Go change."

"Why did you push me?"

"He stands there," said Mrs. Bellinson. "You see? Tomorrow he'll be sick."

"Don't worry," said Joe. "I don't get sick so fast."

"And then who will suffer? Me, of course."

"Uh-uh," said Joe. "Did you hear that, Helen? There goes that word again. We ought to fine her a nickel every time she uses it."

"A dime," said Helen.

"What is this suffer?" said Joe. "Why do you love to use that word so much?"

Mrs. Bellinson raised the teapot threateningly.

"Don't touch me," she said. "I'll spill you from head to foot."

"Now, now," said Joe. "Behave yourself. Be a good kid."

"American children, they make fun of me."

"Fun of you? Oh, no, Mamma. Just the opposite. There's no one

56

like you in the whole world. Don't you know that? Shake hands."

"Oh, no," said Mrs. Bellinson. "Not today."

"She doesn't trust me," said Joe. "She's right. That's the trouble. She's always right. Where's Abe? Did he come in yet?"

"No," said Helen. "What did he say, Ma? Is he coming home?"

"Is he coming home," said Mrs. Bellinson. "Another one. He comes and he goes. Does he ever say?"

"He'll be home," said Helen. "What time is it, Joe?"

"I don't know," said Joe. "Jesus. I'm suddenly pooped. Move over and let me flop down."

Strange how he had almost forgotten he had a definite thing he just had to tell them. He stretched himself out with a sigh beside his wide-awake sister, murmuring a sibilation on sleep, how sweet it would be, to slip into sleep. She smiled to see how loosely he surrendered to his sudden weariness, then placed his hat over his face, making it soft and dim for him. What would be the very safest way? Whiff of a warm and peculiar smell, season of effluvia of his own scalp and hair, he ought not to play at peekaboo with that real old gal necessity, ever a stiff pain in the neck, or with a drop of his jaw, drowsily concoct a white lie out of the genesis of a chocolate dream, but say what he had to say outright, brutal as that may be.

Still he rested in that hazy in-between of the before and the after, thinking was there a slice of store cheesecake in the house, or a lone bakery doughnut, powdered, or a book perhaps which would tell him how to eat and not sleep his way through an italicized event in the history of this close but ordinary family. Or an onion roll. His feet, they were killing him. He closed his eyes entirely. They asked him frankly if he were dead, and receiving no answer, ignored him as if he were, turning unsuspectingly to some other subject. No, there was no good way of telling them, none, not one which could have mercy on their present without panic, on their tolerable now of canary-yellow curtains for the kitchen window, or on their higher chitchat about Skulnick, that apostate of a cousin.

He was going to marry that girl. It was a scandal. Samuel Skulnick at thirty-four, a gloomy foreign-born boy, had called his mother an old bitch for the purple curse with which she had lambasted his love a little too obviously a natural blonde, and had told her in her own mixed language that she could go and stand on her head if she thought it would help, but as for him, he was going to listen to the knock-knock of his heart wherever it may disgracefully mislead him. To his father also he had raised his hand. And had chased them both out of his dusty and failing dry goods store. Shocked by this side of the story, as women who had always been meek before the choleric God of their forefathers, Mamma and Helen could not understand how Skulnick could be so terrible. But was he really? Joe did not think so. And so he would try to tell them in a moment.

Rash as it might sound, what was it but the stale and stuffy nonsense of the synagogue hullabaloo all over again where, in a mishmash of souls yowling for attention, everyone, if he thinks, thinks by the book, and by a book which neither God nor the least of his angels has ever claimed to have written? Love is love in any religion. God says so. God is no nut. He is the architect of the afterworld known down below as heaven, logically looks a lot like Santa Claus, opens the gate himself, is always welcoming, always. So one day Sam dies, waits for his wife to do the same, then together, as man and wife should, they make the climb. God when he sees them booms out in his joy, Come in, Skulnick, come in. Yes, sir, says Skulnick. Thank you, sir. But, sir, how about Daisy here? Can she come in too? Sure, says God. What a question. But she is not Jewish, sir. Not Jewish? says God. Jewish, Jewish. It sounds familiar. Where on earth have I heard that word before? But come, Skulnick, let us not waste time. Bring her in. You know me. I am crazy about people who are genuinely fond of each other. Seen any snakes lately? How are all the kids?

Helen tipped his hat off his face with an excited elbow.

"That's it," she said. "That's just it. I've been thinking about it. Suppose they do have children, Mamma? What then?"

"More cousins," said Joe, struggling to sit up straight.

"Then?" said Mrs. Bellinson. "Then the real trouble will begin."

"You said it," said Joe. "Especially if they're all girls."

"Wiseguy," said Helen. "Where did you come from?"

"I've been here," said Joe. "I've been listening."

"Aie," said Mrs. Bellinson. "An only son. And always such a devoted one."

"Sit down, Mamma," said Joe. "Why is it you never sit down? Have you made a bet with someone?"

"And now so mean," said Mrs. Bellinson. "How will they live

58

without him. Both so sick and old. Who will support them now?"

"That's easy," said Joe. "Hate will do it, Mamma."

"Hate?" said Helen.

"Sure," said Joe. "They will hate him. And they will hate her. And they'll grow fat on it. If you ask me, I think they're both silly."

"Well," said Helen. "Just like that, eh? What are you trying to say? That you're on his side?"

"No," said Joe. "I didn't say that. I'm on nobody's side. But I like Skulnick. There's something about him that I like."

"What, for example?"

"Oh, hell," said Joe. "I am on his side. Here's a guy who wants to live his own life and right away everybody tries to stop him."

"Please," said Helen. "Whatever you do, don't yell. Live his own life. Sure. Who says no? But that's not the point at all. Is it, Mamma? What that fool wants to do is wrong. You don't think it's right, do you?"

"Me?" said Joe. "I told you. It doesn't matter what I think. All I know is that if Skulnick wants to marry a shikseh, that's his business. What does she look like? Does anybody know? The guy has a perfect right to do whatever he wants."

"Ah," said Helen. "Now there is where I don't agree with you at all. What do you mean do whatever he wants?"

"Why not?"

"No, sir. I'm sorry. That's kid stuff."

"I beg your pardon," said Joe.

"Nobody's that free."

"Are you calling me a kid?"

"I'm not calling you anything. We're not talking about you, are we? Though it wouldn't hurt you if you were a little older."

"Like you?"

"Then you'd know. Then you'd find out that you just can't go around doing whatever you want without considering other people."

"Really?" said Joe. "Is that so?"

Helen suddenly laughed, then tapped him once on the back of his head.

"Look at him," she said. "He's angry."

"Don't be silly," said Joe, ducking as if he expected to be tapped again. "Why should I be angry? Only I would like to know one thing.

59

Why is it you still think I'm a baby or something? Mamma too. All right. Maybe Skulnick is a fool. But at least he's doing what he wants to do. And for that I must say I respect him. That's just the way it should be. If you want to do something, and you think it's right, you go ahead and do it, without asking anybody."

Helen was amused.

"You know," she said. "I've heard you talk this way before. And you know what I think? I think you're talking through your hat. Sure. Of course. It's easy to have nerve for someone else. But let me tell you something. I bet you would never do what Skulnick is doing. Or anything like it."

"Oh, you don't think so, do you?"

"No, sir. I know you wouldn't."

"In that case," said Joe, and stopped.

He was smiling queerly.

"In that case, what?" said Helen. "Go ahead. Say it."

"In that case, you're in for a shock."

"I am?"

"I'm afraid so. I quit my job today."

"You did what?" said Helen.

She stared at him, her face and neck at once terrifically red.

"Now look here, Joe. If you're kidding me, I'll kill you."

"Oh, no," said Joe. "I mean it. Today. Just like that. You see?"

"You're crazy," said Helen. "Mamma, did you hear? He's crazy."

"Okay," said Joe. "Maybe I am. But next time."

"Shut up," said Helen. "Shut up. Don't you dare talk to me."

She snatched up the Daily News and ran directly into the bathroom and made the house shake as she locked herself in with a crash, but certainly not for the purpose of poring over the pictures of a triple collision of cars or of a double suicide, but to think it over, to say my god, to slap herself, and try to be reasonable, and push down the bitter pill he had suddenly given her to swallow.

"Goddamn it," said Joe. "That's the first thing she always does. She gets all excited."

Mrs. Bellinson appeared to be looking for something behind her, then as if she had found it, slowly sat down on the tip of a hard chair, and cradling the teapot in her lap, tried very quietly to digest this latest disaster.

"I don't know what's the matter with her," said Joe. "Right away she tells you to shut up. You can never talk to her."

But what was he grumbling for? Only the guilty are likely to grumble. Or those who try not to be timid for once, so talk and talk, but soon realize that they sound absolutely ridiculous. On the contrary, said his pride, inventing hastily, that big and black-looking bird which these women of his had watched with their heads low as it teased them, banking lazily to the left and then to the right in the suspiciously cloud-free blue of the sky, had at last decided to swoop down, and lo, it was not a vulture to dread or despise, but an eagle, fully grown, and fierce to its last feather, and terribly fascinating. Why, all was natural, all as it had always been. It was the chronological truth. He was the baby of the family. And they remembered him from the days of the diaper when his squalling meant that he had a will, but not as yet a mind of his own. Though later they were quick on the trigger when it came to defending him as not the freshest, but the cleverest kid on the block, but a kid, adorable, but as a kid, how convenient and wonderful if he could always remain that way. And now look how he had piped up. Where had been their eyes that they had failed to see that he had been lanky for years in his long pants, had learned how to shave without bleeding, smoked his pack a day, sneered at the clumsiness of his elders, applauded his own grace, knew grief, poker, pain, exaltation, and the slimy why and what for of a condom? He opened his eyes at this and smiled. He better be careful. He made it sound as if to come of age was to arrive at some shady and minor pleasure. Odd how even the truth can seem a bit tricky. But there it was. He was no longer that happy-go-lucky pure one who did not seem to care if it was his fate to be permanently subordinate. This they must know. They must take or leave it.

But one look at Mamma, and yes, it was the worst moment today for this jaunty anarchist, this composer of juvenile ultimatums. Good for him. Whatever serves to smack a little sense into anyone who is too cocksure is good for him. He had to apply the preventive exercise of taking a deep breath and swallowing, else he would have, well acted just like a bawlbaby. Because it was not fair. Because she refused to look furious. Because she did not tear her hair or make a motion to tear his. Because he could see he was not listed in her black book, or would ever be, because she had never had one. How strange. The clock on the

61

rickety bureau ticks for her benefit too. How unlucky to have a mother who was so different, who was so old-fashioned, so full of the stern and monumental dignity of the imported brand as to be submissive and discreet, and if sorrowful, then sorrowful as one who suffers with and for, never against. What is to be done with her? She is such a poor American, though she has been told that America is hers also, such a mild citizen, acknowledging the police, but considered queer because she will not, like the others, allow herself to become mussed in grabbing for gold, or any other article lying around loose. Another socialist. She votes. What is it, Mamma? What was she dreaming of? She looked too good to be true. Of the dour and dingy years under gaslight? Of good old God in his problematical mercy? Of something perishable? Of someone already dead?

Fair were the fields of the farm in Poland where she was born and where she ran around like a peppy little peasant in a smock among the chickies. The sun too drank out of the river. And in the forest was where the devil dwelt. The absentee owner of the land did not interfere. And her father was the overseer. Nine children made a merry lot, knit by primal blood, by barley and oats, by fractures, by candlelight prayers, by death by drowning or by fire, by wild flowers, and frequent kisses. It was immense. By the silky beard of her father, in spite of pogroms near and far, it was breath of wine and wisdom and warmth. What is it about the color green? If it is absorbed in childhood, it seems to highlight the vision forever after, perpetually washing it clean. And then a man came and married her. Talmudic, but with town ideas, and exactly of the same height. The old couple danced, but as promptly fell into a frenzy of lamentation when the new man said he must take her away. Live with us, cried the old couple. But he took her to Brooklyn, god knows why. The letters crossed the ocean in bunches. What are rooms to the back? And a soda of ice cream? And a combination sink and washtub? And trains high in the street? Come back, the old couple cried. Mamma wept at night. But Papa rushed into business with a crony who cheated him. Out of his element as a gambler, the hat store swindle killed him, that is to say, he lived, but hardly a peep out of him until he died, righteously monopolizing all the guilt, peaceful only when he could keep his family poor. The wallflower is gone. Who remembers him now? If the dead are called upon to take a bow, it is Mamma's Papa and it is

Mamma's Mamma who step forward gracefully, shapeless in black, but alert and holding hands as if waiting for the flute to announce the first figure of an extemporaneous dance. It is the teapot she treasures that does it. It constantly wets the memory. Flesh of the lost and forsaken on the window sill. The green that is left. Stuck in pots with saucers to match of shy and assorted sizes. The fern. The rubber plant. The cactus and the onion.

Not a move out of her. Nothing. Not a single move. How deeply the mind must be imbedded in that marvelous head, the skull supreme, the meek attendant hair combed in a classic curve against it, the widowed shell of an ear half-exposed, and at the end, a convolution at the back of an invisible bun. Take a breath. How far it must travel when her eyes are in such a fierce paralysis behind the bifocal glasses. There is no computing the hazards of contemplation. How bitter must be the resistance, that of the redskin occurs, of its taut and bony face of a Sioux or a Mohican. Time and its chemistry of change. The guess to be made is obvious. Nothing can touch or move her now as it could still touch and move him because her biology differed, attacked as it had been year after year by a series of organic insurrections until it has had this scientific result, life is over. Now she knows. It is the final wisdom. There is no tricking her out of it. She has had enough. There is no more to learn. The sparrow may have its passion for pecking, but it is only a bird, frenetic, often electrocuted. The chatter of leaves. The traffic jam in the heart. Bees sting. Children are in action. Do the stars cry? Does the moon show surprise? O go away from me. The darker it gets, the better one sees it all. Life is a runt, discourteous, a misfit. Take it away. Death. Now there is a good thing, a place where peace is polite, and sleep has enormous space, and the soul is at last aristocratic.

Meanwhile there is the body. What is there to say of such a royal and resolute abandonment of the ball in the last quarter of the game? The body is a booby trap, full of the explosive rubbish known as memories. The stands rock. The referee, a fat boy in a shirt like peppermint stick candy, toots on his whistle furiously. Is Mamma deaf? Her teammates gape at their star player. The score is tied. The crowd is up on its frozen feet, murderously blue in the face. There was only the tincture of coffee for supper then. And when the gas mantle burned out, it was not to be thrown away because the powder it made could polish silver. But Mamma coolly ignores the whole shebang. What does she deserve for deserting the bloody game like that? The world will say a spanking. If the world only knew. What a crucial and cockeyed winter that was.

That winter, winter of the creepy episode in the sky. They were living then on Sutter Avenue, in the ancient and bubbling neighborhood of Brownsville, in a two-family house of rat-infested and stuccoed misery when again there was a banging on the door to pay more rent, but the man was mad, always trying as he did to get blood out of a stone. His name was Edelstein, and he was the landlord, and he lived beneath them on his palatial first floor, while beneath him was his profitable shoe store. Mamma was bewildered, she pitied him, but Papa, whose chest had temporarily caved in, was a terrible patient. He was hopeless. He wanted to kill. That a man should so torment them in their poor and broken years. It was really the limit. Even tubby Mrs. Edelstein thought so as she pleaded with her hulk of a husband. Jacob, she cried, what are you doing? I am ashamed. The whole block knows. What is money? Poison when you got too much. Put a radiator in one bedroom at least. They will pay you later. Think of God, Jacob, think. She used to sneak upstairs, the asthmatic appeaser, with something hot in a small aluminum pot hidden under her apron, some tasty peace offering cooked on gas, for she had a gas stove downstairs, but it choked her. Leary of her conglomeration of comparative luxury, tears scalded her eyes as she tried to tell them. Flour for choleh? I have flour for raisin cookies too. I mean it. I have a new kitchen set. Bamboo. Come and see sometimes. I have steam. I have electric lights. What else? But do I enjoy it? To the devil it belongs. How can I enjoy it when mine Jacob makes you live like this? Mrs. Bellinson, you are so good. Have pity on me. Move. You will die here this winter. Please. Jacob will give you the money for it. I promise you. I will tear it from him. Move. Mamma tried to soothe her. But Papa turned to the wall. Later the city relief sent them a ton of coal. One middle of the night, Abe was the first to smell the smoke, and shook them without screaming, and they helped Papa to the fire escape, and they all scrambled to the roof to save themselves in their shameful underwear. The burning old stock in the cellar certainly made a stink. When a fireman with an axe in his hand climbed in to look for the Edelsteins, he found no one, for no one had slept at home. That did not smell so good either. Really, it was the limit. Murderers, cried Papa.

The three little Bellinsons were uselessly little, of lower-grade dependency, joyously erupting in the street, sullenly subsiding in the house, except for Helen with her chin-trembling, her floor-scrubbing compassion, and her mother-mimicking gentility. But she was also highly critical of the family crisis, so she too would snarl and hit back. It was extraordinary how often the kids tried to cripple each other that winter, and how difficult they were to pluck apart. Abe and Joey were a pair. Abe said Joey should do it. And Joey said Abe should do it. And so of course neither of them did it much in the beginning. But one time they came upon Mamma gasping horribly as she lugged up that daily pail of coal. That decided them. They used the secret handshake. They would alternate. Coal is black enough, but what can equal the pure sunlessness of hate below the age of double figures? At first Edelstein suffered the little children to struggle for it with both hands through the cellar in the street, everybody sees us, Mamma, everybody, but then one day he padlocked the iron door, changing the route of their humiliation, and they had to stagger through the trap door in the store itself, spilling lumps on the polished floor, and it was so much longer to carry, and there were strangers now to pity them, properly seated customers, some just looked away and coughed, while others simply stared, startled sight-seers all, with one shoe on and one shoe off.

The arrogance of boys who are underfed, they are positive that no one can match the puff of their pride, or the pathos of their susceptibility, or the glamour of their wounds. They are so tensile and thin, given to delicious fits of supernatural shivering. Lord, the excitement, the excitement. They waited for it at the living room window, peering through poorly smoked bits of milk-bottle glass. My heart is in my mouth, said Joey, huddling up to her. Mamma smiled and tried to fold him in a wing of her shawl and said to swallow it, little fool, but she too was strangely moved. The long-suffering snow on the rooftops looked frightful. One man alone stood in the middle of the gutter, pointing at the sky, like the moon, utterly losing his manners. Oh, they suddenly cried, crowding together to look, seeing it chewed, expecting an explosion. They gazed in awe at the serene and infamous

65

avidity of the moon. Dark and darker, Mamma, dear, look, and how cold, and how funny, feel it, this eerie loneliness of the heavens which quietly descends on the earth. Joey, little fool, he shuddered as he vainly listened for trumpets. What a bafflement. The sun had not raised a finger. The sun had submitted without a sound.

Was it this then? See the interventionist. He slips back into the present as glibly as he had slipped out. He feels fine. Was it this wisdom then that Mamma had absorbed, the wisdom of the sun when it is totally eclipsed? The sun may be a salient member of the universe, but it is no less obedient to its laws. It may toy with the earth, yet is itself only a magnificent dot. It does not holler nor does it bang when it is momentarily obscured. What an imperial confidence it has in the knowledge that it will sunburn its cohorts again.

He ran his hand through his hair. People must try to understand each other. They must. Mamma sits there, a victim of her quiet appearance, almost sepulchral a careless observer thinks, shrinks from her, floored by what seems such a fuliginous humility. But who knows? Mamma may be a luminary instead, actually incandescent, possessed of an inner radiance that will never fade. Pullets of the world, let us be fair. With this puny exhortation, he rose at last to stretch, the bright and bullheaded cogitator, otherwise known as a wiseguy, who had heedlessly pulled up the window shade on the shame of that year. And to what purpose? Everybody is laughing. Of course. Everybody knows it is never any different. Be it this year or that year. The anguish is always the same.

"Goddamn it," said Joe, holding out his hand. "Another one, Mamma. Look at it."

"What?" said Mrs. Bellinson, responding as he had hoped. "Where?"

"A paper cut. See it? Right between the fingers."

"Ah."

"It hurts like hell."

"Go. Put on iodine."

"I will. You're not mad at me, are you, Mamma?"

"Mad?"

"I hope not."

"No."

"That's good," said Joe. "I'm glad. Somebody has to be my friend."

66

Mrs. Bellinson smiled at her youngest and most innocent.

"Yes," she said. "I'm your friend. Go, friend, put on some iodine."

"I can't. Helen's in there. I'm hungry, Mamma."

"Ah, yes," said Mamma. "Of course. And here I sit."

"Sit, sit. Did I ask you to get up? I can take myself. Just tell me what."

"No," said Mamma. "You'll never know. Come. You'll wash in the sink."

"Wash?" said Joe. "What for? All I want to do is eat."

"Eat, sure. But first you wash."

"After."

"First. Come, pig."

"Pig?" said Joe. "Is that what you think of me?"

"Ah," said Mrs. Bellinson. "You better not ask."

She was right. He could see that at once. He better not. Through the strained green pea soup, he was the goy who struck the match to light the gas to warm it, through the quarter of cold chicken which had the white meat and the wing, through slices of tomato and leaves of lettuce salted on the side, through the applesauce and its touch of cinnamon, he said nothing, but sensibly used his mouth for what it was originally intended. He ate heartily. For on this day at least and as yet, it seemed ages since a wrong swallow, satisfaction of hunger had few if any furtive or bitter connotations, but was rather a pleasant necessity, and a calm experience at the end of which, if there was bliss, it was as finely woven and functional as the twenty-year-old tablecloth with tassels. It was sweet to be crumbling his own bread. Came the tea to wash it all down. He was full. No coffee cake or blueberry jam. He waved it away. He would just sip, he said, and smoke like a lord in between.

Helen came in and sat down opposite him.

"Well," she said. "Don't you look satisfied. How about you, Mamma? Did you eat yet? I bet not."

"I'll eat," said Mamma. "Don't worry about me. You want soup?"

"No," said Helen. "I'm not too hungry. Some chicken maybe."

"Chicken's on the table."

"Wait," said Helen. "Will you look at that? What's the matter with you, Mamma? Why must you always be washing dishes in the middle of a meal?"

"It saves time."

"Time. It makes noise, that's all it does."

"Foolish. Can it be done without?"

"Please," said Helen. "Don't argue with me. I feel bad enough as it is."

"Ach," said Mamma. "Did you ever see? She never lets me do a thing."

"She's right," said Joe. "Come on, kiddo, sit down."

"Sit down," said Mamma. "All right. If it makes you so happy, I'll sit down."

"That's the way to talk," said Joe. "Throw away that dish towel."

Helen stared at him.

"I must be dreaming," she said. "Did you say I was right?"

"Ah, well," said Joe. "It slipped out. But then, when you're right, you're right. Didn't you know? Sometimes you can be very smart. And sometimes."

"I can be smarter?"

"Oh, no," said Joe. "Just plain dumb. Especially when you lose your temper and tell me to shut up."

"Oh, that," said Helen. "I'm sorry. I couldn't help it. This chicken's really good, Mamma."

"Good?" said Mamma. "Certainly. Why shouldn't it be? I pay the best prices, don't I?"

"Prices," said Helen. "It's how you cook it. And you know how."

Joe tried to stare at her as she had stared at him.

"I must be dreaming," he said. "Did you say you were sorry?"

"Wiseguy," said Helen, but had to smile.

How she pleased him at that moment, pleased him so much he had to hide it under cover of fiddling with his cigarette. A sister is a sister. So they say. A sister is a girl, usually, to be treated as such, that is, to be squelched, else she will elevate herself to equality with her brothers, for such is the nature of the female, to be grasping, to be vocal, to be insidious, to dream of power beyond the dynamic breath of her perfume. It may be interesting sometimes to inquire into the sex of the soul. But a sister may be a Helen too. And that is the crux of it, that is what makes a man say hooray. True, she still titters like a schoolgirl at the slightest trickle of blood, but she never faints, and some men do. Her boy friend, Louie, that pipe smoker with his very fresh City College B.A., when first he laid eyes on her at a party, said to himself, here now is a compact and sensible entity, then said it to her in these very same big words. When she asked for a translation, please, and promptly received it, she laughed and said that he may touch her, she was real. That was it exactly. He came thereafter to touch her frequently, as a judicious wanderer might, as a free-wheeling orphan who enjoyed the clemency of a lone aunt, to ask her to listen to him theorize, risking her temper as well as her tact, disturbing her more than he realized.

The ruthlessness of what men call knowledge, replete with ructions of individuality, with scorn for sacrifice, with declarations too damn dry that consideration for others would ruin her. Then the kissing. It ends in that. It begins with talk, but it ends in that chaste and charming game in which the hands of the contestants, if neither is coy, are never slapped or told to stop it. So it goes healthily on and on, until all at once the most gentle play of lips seems to result in a profound displacement of loyalty. Yet this was hardly more than a wistful complication when compared with that pain common to all people, the pain of partial surrender. Ah, that independent one. She would not be rushed. She would stand up abruptly in the midst of a session to smooth her dress and to fix her hair, and to beg her baffled Louie to go home, you educated boob, go home. For how could she cling to her precious dreams of order, of a world clean and cheerful everywhere, when clinging to him meant clinging to him unto dishevelment? But then she was adorable. She would sit down again.

Helen raised her knife.

"Our baby," she said. "The hope of the family. Should I kill him now, Mamma?"

"With that?" said Joe. "Don't be funny."

"Or should I wait?"

"You better get something sharper."

"It'll do. God. Isn't it going to be beautiful from now on? How are you on polishing apples, Mamma?"

"Excellent," said Joe. "I can recommend her."

"You can?" said Helen. "Well, that's good. Tell me now. Is it true? Or is it just a rumor?"

"What is?"

"I've heard you're going to dust off your fiddle and play in the backyards."

"Me?" said Joe. "Oh, no, how can I? All the strings are busted."

69

"There," said Helen. "You see what I mean? That's just what beats the hell out of me."

"What does? What is it now? Honest, Ma, I can't keep up with that gal."

"The way you can laugh."

"Oh, that," said Joe. "I know what you're thinking."

"You must have something up your sleeve. What is it? Is it another job?"

"No," said Joe. "Absolutely not. No such thing."

"Then what are you up to? Do you really know what you're doing?"

"Of course I do," said Joe. "Are you going to talk to me like all the rest? I thought you were different."

"What?" said Helen. "You too?"

"What do you mean, you too?"

"That's all I've been hearing lately. I'm different. You must've been talking to Lou. You know what I do every time he leaves me? I look myself over very carefully to see if I have four eyes or six legs or something. I mean it. When he gets on that subject, he scares me. Different. I'm beginning to hate that word. You know what I think? I think that all the trouble in the world is caused by people who are different. I mean by those who think they are."

"Now wait a minute," said Joe. "Don't look at me like that."

"You," said Helen. "I'm afraid you're just another one."

"Oh, no, Helen, you're wrong."

"You're twisted too."

"You're way off the track."

"All twisted up. Like me. Right now. But at least I admit it."

"Ye gods," said Joe. "Are you listening, Ma? Maybe you can straighten us out. What in the hell are we talking about?"

"Yes," said Helen. "What? It's a good question. That's the way it's become in this family. We talk and we talk. But do we ever say anything? You're right. We used to understand each other. But now? My name's Helen. What's yours?"

"Mine is stinky. Who cares? This is really very nice. What's been happening to you anyway? I've never heard you sound so sad."

"There comes a time, sonny. You'll find out. You begin to have reasons."

"Reasons," said Joe. "What reasons?"

70

"I'll write you a letter."

"You mean my quitting?"

"Don't do it, Joe."

"Don't do it?"

"Listen to me."

"But I've already done it."

"Then back out of it somehow."

"I can't," said Joe.

"What can't? Do it. Just do it."

The door slammed, but no one heard it.

"Holy mackerel," said Joe. "Why are you bothering me? You know it's done. And that's all there is to it."

"What's done?" said Abe. "What the hell's going on here?"

His intrusion was elaborately casual. His softened hat was shoved back on his head. The short dead end of a butt was stuck to his lip. His slouch was the lean and relaxed and contemptuous slouch of a hoodlum gracefully leaning in a darkened doorway. His big and candid eyes of a baby could easily blaze. Tough, the guy was tough, clever with a cue stick, had a highly educated left, threw a hard ball, had speed to burn, could roll them bones. Who did he think he was trying to fool? No one but himself, of course. Others could see that when he laughed, how it delighted Mamma, he laughed with his whole face, boyishly purifying for a second the thin and bitter mug of a man who has taken an oath to become separate. And all because he cared, not a little, but too damn much. Precisely what had happened to bring on this firm intuitional rejection of his of the rot that seemed to rise to his ankles everywhere? As soon as he sat down. Just when was it he had first discovered that he was an absolute stranger in the world, incapable of allegiance or partisanship? No one knew. No one dared ask. His liberty had to be total, else he would snarl, ready to kill. Or it had to seem so. He had to be free to follow his faith in his actual legs, in the pride of their positive action, in their obstinate investigation of a mountainous and macabre city he did not fear, but hated. Was he delicately picking a lock somewhere? Was he seeking revenge? Would he soon commit the crime that would clear up everything? Such lovely questions. Of course it was Joe who asked them. He would. He was getting very fresh lately. But what was certain was this, every institution in the land may topple, and every inhabitant in it may die, if Abe

71

was indeed without faith, he was nevertheless faithful. He was careful about his job in a silk house. And he never failed to come home to sleep. A real tough nut to crack. He was like the last member of a patrol who knew relief would never come, yet continued to stray and to search, but the key to bliss, to release from passion, to the recovery of his innocence, was never where he looked, was lost, would never be found.

"Ah," said Helen. "Wait until you hear. You'll like this. Go on. Ask him. You talk to him. I can't any more."

"She can't," said Joe. "Don't worry. She's been doing all right so far."

"See it?" said Helen. "He's just like that wall."

"Hello, Ma," said Abe. "Are you in this too?"

"Just like that wall," said Joe. "That's a hot one."

"Well?" said Helen. "He's waiting. Why don't you tell him?"

"I'll tell him," said Joe. "Don't rush me. I'll tell him."

Abe flipped his butt into the open garbage pail.

"This sounds very important," he said. "Or is it?"

"Oh, it's important, all right," said Helen. "He's quit his job. How do you like that?"

"Uh-uh," said Abe.

"Isn't that beautiful?"

"Well, what do you know?" said Abe. "What happened?"

"Nothing," said Joe.

"Nothing?"

"Nothing at all. I just quit."

"You just quit, eh?"

"Today. I gave notice. That's all."

"Aha," said Abe. "I see. And how do you feel otherwise?"

"All right," said Joe. "I mean it. I'm all right, Abe. I really am. I mean it."

But the waverer, he said so much more with his eyes, and said it so much more eloquently, that Abe could not resist it, had to believe him at once.

"Okay, then," he said quietly. "That's all I wanted to know. Is that all there is? Can I go now?"

"What?" said Helen. "What's going on here? You mean to say you're going to let him get away with it?"

72

"Get away with what?" said Abe. "Do you know? If you don't, then leave him alone."

"Leave him alone?"

"He knows what he's doing."

"Knows what he's doing?"

"I do," said Joe, jumping up. "I mean it. I really do."

He almost turned the table over. Abe had to duck down a bit because he did not want to laugh, but Helen comically collapsed and called to Mamma for a painkiller, midol or aspirin, quick. But a clumsy guy can also be an excitable liar without knowing it when, suddenlike, he flies into a romantic flurry of affirmation, leaping to his feet in what he feels is truly a divine frenzy of defense, only to find that he is not, as he imagines, soaring to heights in a spacious courtroom, but bruising his elbows in a mere hole of a kitchen where two is one too many, is a crowd. The facts around a man are terrible. They shrink him down until he fits into the trap of his apparent, and therefore laughable, size. A mean surprise. Who is it, if it is not the devil, who can block the road so craftily? At the same time, he must give a big boom-chick-a-boom for circumambulation. For is it not written in the manual that if one cannot go straight through, then one must go around? The dunce who obeys this regulation distinguishes himself. Or at the very least makes his getaway. So out and around then, he threads his way, with his enlarged and plaintive eyes and his sad elongated neck, feeling changed again, though again nothing had been settled, acting gay, crying out gangway, his next stop the bathroom which is so everyday, certainly, yet there is where fresh spunk is magically generated. He claimed he had to get clean. The boys would soon be coming.

Having traveled this far, must he travel further? Naked in a cloud of steam, he dipped his toes in the tub of water, a torment, terrifically hot the way he liked it. Not for a while. Please. At last he stood in it, then sank to his knees, and holding on, began to settle backwards slowly, and shut his eyes, and floated, and allowed himself to faint a little, who could see? O go, go away from me. Softly in a whirl, as a god in his ascension, puckering, white as Camay soap the weariness, and crinkly blue the towel of the sky, plucking at a single string, piercing music, the water troubled, the trouble below, the trouble. O what is this grief? A bubble, it rises out of the ancestral mist, and when it breaks, the heart breaks with it. Will it be so in paradise too? Nonsense. Take

73

fifteen cents. For the sea has no shore. And in it death is soundlessly cascading. O day of deliverance, day of uneasy elation. Is anyone standing? Please sit down. His head rolled to one side. His mind fell, and in falling, heard a bell languorously clang-a-langing. See the joy in his soft sleeper's smile all sex. O lord. O lady of hourglass enticement with her pink successive faces and her admirable flounce. Her wrist tinkled as she waved. With a slight bounce of her curious breasts, body heat of her mouth in tidal engulfment, with a whisper of her name, and of all her names, consenting, she crept upon him slyly, and slowly raised her skirt.

5

So that is the tune, is it? But then everyone must merrily agree that a
woman is not a biological betrayal, but is for a man the loveliest of all
lures, an advance on the lollipop, is a confection infinitely more con-
founding, to be tongued and to be tumbled, while driving home to
her, as she resists, the sweet idea that Saturday night is sad unless it
turns out to be a saturnalia. For some of the silly ones do resist. Does
anyone know why? Why, traces of definite antagonism can be detected
even in those known as dogs, as the boys so brutally label them. What
a fuss the floozies make, and this includes the babes who simply
because they look zoftik look more like a sure lay, with their do not
touch me here, and do not touch me there, and their tiny screams of
terror in the dark, and their crazy wriggling in the wrong direction.
Ask Joe. It is no after no after no. Until suddenly it is yes. For those
horrible animals called men.

So it is yes. So is it any better then? Sometimes it is actually worse.
For what is the consequence of such a sheer accident? An immediate
demand for a ring with a diamond in it, to be followed by, but ask Joe
again, when a guy is at a certain age, his sex has as much desire to
function within marriage as a dictator has within a democracy. So
then. Who is far more dangerous than the broad who can be too easily
tossed on her tail? Why, the one who is respectable of course. For she it

is who will only too stubbornly deny herself the frolic of full and final penetration, declaring it to be a sin. There is a word. Preferring death to defloration, she pants and puffs with her partner in preliminaries only, transmitting to him, through her spit flowing so freely, not a venereal, which is bad enough, but a spiritual disease, which is ten times worse, the disease of guilt, another gruesome word.

Nonetheless here is Joe dressed in his best, and anxious to get going, hardly that finicky about fun at his enviable age, saying as he goes, that if sex is so dizzy and does go loop the loop, that is its nature, in Brooklyn as in Borneo, adding, in order to bribe his nerves, that there can be fascinating angles about a girl as well as tormenting curves. An intellectual already. The truth is she better be something like a sizzling blonde for a change, that blind date, a tricky kid who knows just where to titillate, to knock his eyes out literally.

"I think she is," said Dave, as Joe and Eddie piled in after him onto the lumpy front seat of his brother-in-law's jalopy of a Buick famous for the rear axle which screeched so loud it was enough by itself to scare the pants off any pedestrian, so throw the croaking horn away. "What did Honey say about her, Eddie? Is Joe getting a blonde?"

"What?" said Eddie. "Goddamn this door. I can never close it."

"Bang it," said Dave. "What're you afraid of?"

"I'll bust the glass."

"Bang it."

"Hey," said Joe. "That's my leg. Let me get that shift between me."

"Okay?" said Dave. "All set?"

"Let her rip," said Eddie.

"Wait," said Joe. "Maybe we better get out and walk. I don't like the looks of this thing. How long has it been dead?"

"Dead?" said Dave, vainly stamping on the starter. "That's a nasty way to talk about Becky."

"Yeah," said Eddie. "Good old Becky. She's got double pneumonia. And she's down to her rims. But she'll get us there."

"Where?" said Joe. "The graveyard?"

"Quiet," said Dave. "Have respect. Watch how I talk to her. Come on, Becky. This is your Davie talking to you, darling. Becky? Becky, wake up. Becky, you little." She shuddered. "Hah." She sputtered on the choke. "Catch it, baby, catch it." She backfired. "Ah, ah, careful now, sweetheart." She squealed as he mercilessly shifted her into first.

"Ow," said Joe. "How did I get trapped here in the middle?"

76

Eddie nudged him.

"Don't look now," he said. "But I think she's moving."

"Holy mackerel," said Joe. "You're right. She is."

"Sure," said Dave, sending her off with a deafening roar. "That's my Becky for you. What a chariot, what a chariot."

"Ah," said Joe. "You said it."

It was odd how this nonbeliever laughed at her as affectionately as Eddie and Dave. If a thing can still go, let her go. Man alive, look at that thing struggle against death by piecemeal destruction. Foot brake so loose it was useless, the last spring in her wrecked, shimmy of her left front wheel decided, she wobbled down Winthrop in East Flatbush, the dear old dippy thing, as dislocated in her guts as this night so twinkingly current, pie-eyed, weaving along, like a guzzler tanked to the gills, through the consternation of her electrified public and of her clanking sisters in distress, but making it amid her hiccups for the main street Sutter down Brownsville way where various mutts in relays scuttled after her, yipping madly in acclaim. Watch it now. A dirty snotnose flung a decayed banana peel and deftly crowned her. Joe had to applaud, but Dave, he swore he would get that stinker on the way back, and wiggling the wheel, almost climbed on the sidewalk, a cowboy chasing after a terrified jaywalker, an innocent cat. Eddie had half of him hung out, pleading with Joe to look at the can on that one, and the knockers on this one, jesus, if only three, just three of them, would throw their lovely carcasses into Becky in the back, they would soon find out what they, the pick of the female population, had so long been so foolishly missing. The shift Joe clutched between his legs trembled in his hands. He grinned. He was with the boys again. Back way back went his head. He was positive he never told himself to do what he now did, but he sure heard it when it came tearing out of the tunnel of his throat. It amazed him. Life, left to itself, had defined itself as a howl.

"Did that come out of me?" said Joe. "Did I do that?"

"It wasn't your grandmother," said Dave, clapping him solidly on the thigh.

"Or your grandfather," said Eddie. "That's the old zip. Let's have it again."

"Right," said Dave. "Give out. We'll really wake up this old neighborhood."

"Out," said Joe. "Out at last."

77

"Did you hear that, Eddie?" said Dave. "I told you the schmo still had some life left in him."

"You're sure?" said Eddie. "Let's see." He began to pinch the subject under discussion wherever he could. "Hey, he jumps. Maybe you're right."

"Sure I'm right," said Dave. "Didn't he just say something?"

"Yeah," said Eddie. "Something like ouch, wasn't it?"

"Then that settles it," said Dave. He reached across to shake hands. "Hallelujah, brother."

"Hallelujah."

"Our Joe's alive."

"Just about."

"Think we should tell him?"

"Hell, no," said Eddie. "Maybe he's better off this way."

"Hey," said Joe. "Watch out for that kid."

"Kid?" said Dave, coolly steering with two fingers. "What kid?"

"Christ," said Joe. "That was close." He slid down, then abruptly up again. "Wait a second now. You two trying to be wiseguys? What's been going on? Who's been burying me?"

"You," said Eddie.

"Me?"

"Yeah," said Dave. "Who do you think? Tell us all about it, sonny."

"Tell you what?" said Joe. "Speak English, will you?"

"Come on," said Eddie. "You know what we mean. Spit it out. What's the kid's name again?"

"What kid?"

"Listen to him," said Dave. "He's stupid all of a sudden. You know what kid. The kid you're going to marry."

"Marry?" said Joe. "Me?"

"Hey," said Eddie. "What're you trying to do here? Jump out?"

"You guys are off your nut or something?"

"That's right," said Dave. "Go on. Shove me. Did you see that? I almost massacred that old geezer there with the umbrella. Say, it ain't raining, is it? What the hell was he doing there with an umbrella?"

"Whew," said Joe. "Look at me. I'm sweating. Mamma mia. Please, fellas, don't scare me that way again. If you want to know the truth, you guys will have six kids apiece before I ever get married."

"Really?" said Dave. "What color?"

"Albinos, you dumb ox, what else?"

"So?" said Eddie. "So where've you been? What do you do Saturday nights? Every time we ask you to go out with us, you say you can't, you're busy. Busy with what?"

"Oh," said Joe. "Nothing important. Just research."

"Research?" said Dave. "I'll be damned. Is that what you call it now?"

"Nuts," said Joe. "Now I got my arm stuck. How about you, Eddie? Can you get to your cigarettes?"

"I'll try," said Eddie. "That is, if you stop breathing."

"Light me up one too," said Dave. "So it's research, is it? Well, well. When's your next lecture, professor? I tell you what. Why don't you bring that piece of research down the clubroom some night? We'll watch. Maybe we can learn something."

"Watch, hell," said Eddie. "Where's the fun in that? Here you are, grubber. Pass it down. We'll join in. We're sociable."

"Now, now," said Dave. "Leave us not be vulgar, Eddie. Thanks. Is it lit? This is a nice kid he's teaching. I can tell."

"Teaching?" said Joe. "Hey, where's mine?"

"It's coming," said Eddie. "It's coming."

"Yep," said Dave. "The man's hooked and he doesn't know it."

"That's what you think," said Joe. "Well, thank you, son. What did you do? Go around the block for it?"

"Ah," said Dave. "So you do know?"

"I do?" said Joe. "What? Oof. You still smoking these lousy Luckies?"

"Do you mind?" said Eddie. "It just so happens I like them."

"That you're hooked," said Dave. "Take the cotton out of your ears."

Joe stared at him a second and in that second it came to him.

"No," he said. "It can't be true. Are you serious? You mean to say you're worried about me?"

"Well," said Dave.

"You too, Eddie?"

"Well," said Eddie.

"I'll be a sonofagun," said Joe. "How do you like that? This is amazing. I'm touched, fellas. I really am."

"Aw," said Dave. "Cut the baloney."

"I mean it, Dave. You think I'm going to pull out and leave you all flat?"

"It sure in hell looks like it."

"It does, eh? Well, you're wrong, bub. You can take my word for it. This baby is still in circulation. Yes, sir."

"So's your ashes," said Eddie. "Why don't you try again? Maybe this time you can get it in my mouth."

"Is that mine?" said Joe. "I'm sorry. Wait. Don't brush it. Blow."

"So what do you think?" said Dave. "Think we should believe him?"

"Sure," said Eddie. "Why not? He's here, isn't he? Sitting right between us."

"Yeah," said Dave. "Right between us. Which reminds me, Eddie. Don't we owe him something? The mug."

"What?"

"You know, you know."

"Oh," said Eddie. "That. Yes, sir. We certainly do."

"Then quick," said Dave. "Let's give it to him."

And they did, a sandwich, a fist on either side of his face.

But he could take it. Old Joe there, he always could. Remember the trouble they had with him all of fifteen years ago come June when, as a shrimp of six on his very first foxlike appearance on the block between Sackman and Powell on Sutter, they had felt him out with their knuckles? Pow. Enough to make him spit blood. What he did was fight back so fiercely, being two years older, they towered over him, that two days later Eddie's mother, on her return from Kruger's grocery with a large schmaltz herring, a pound of onions, and a small bottle of vinegar, had the fantastic pleasure of catching the three little interns intently poking their forefingers plump into the vicinity of Ettie Weinstein's crotch from next door as she lay stretched out rigidly on the leather sofa, with her bloomers down to her ankles, and her flimsy dress well over her forthcoming face, for she loved the operation, but still in tight braids at twelve, she could not bear to watch it. Routed with a rouse from mine house, bummers, they tore after Ettie for the penny apiece she had promised them, but they never got it. Just the same it had been a pure collective effort. Which was the beauty of it. For what else in the world is it that makes shy boys in floppy knickers feel secure, that glues them together so well in their quivering, that gives them for groundwork a lifelong memory in common? The policeman in them may guard it carefully, but every now and then it does manage to sneak out in a charming and rudimentary blush. The bummers and their roots. How sensibly they cling to them.

Hail, cried Joe to Joe, since who else would listen, to these three survivors of the original Secret Six whose double es they stealthily carved to look like strokes of lightning proudly seated wherever there was woodwork in the hallways of the old tenements, beginning with the banisters. Moish became a muscleman, resisted a conscientious cop, and had his head pretty well flattened by his own billy on his first and last holdup. Jake got the shakes in the middle of a heat wave, so the lodge doctor prescribed a pill which precipitated a delirium, so brilliantly switched to the same panacea in a liquid form, and that did it. Jake lost his shakes. And his curiously illogical health and life altogether. And then Al. His death was altitudinal. He stalked a stray pigeon at twilight, flew at it round a skylight, and at twilight fell right off the roof.

Strange how the memory does sometimes stumble backwards stupidly. For of course these deaths actually occurred in reverse order. It was after the funeral of each that the survivors, charter members only, held a mystic confabulation. Simple definitions of death resulted, mostly arithmetical. Like the minus sign, death was, that schoolbook device pitilessly capable of reducing any given number no matter how grimly it tries to retain its self-sufficiency. At this the remaining digits, in whose cellar was it near the coalbin, wept a little when the candle went out for little Al, little Al. Yet death was like the zero too. It was something. It was nothing. It was a symbol badly drawn in the violet air of that which once existed, but now exists no more. Or more harshly, after blowing the nose, it was like the decimal point which perpetually demands it be carried over, why? At the next powwow, an angrier huddle for Jake on Eddie's stoop on Sackman on a windy night, when why was used, it had a capital doubleyou. Now death was the plus sign as well, sign of the itching palm, of steady and selfish appropriation. If it is given a finger, watch out, it will take the whole hand. So why cry? Why not be bitter instead, and vigilant, and dry-eyed? And thus for once death may be defeated, that damn rotten bug in the blood. The third time, they took a long walk to Betsey Head Park, and on the way, they decided that death was more like a

81

grey round eraser for ink, for had not Moish, sloppy in his splash as a blot on society, been roughly, but lawfully rubbed out? Here they glanced at each other, wondering why they smiled. Such a conceited triplet of brotherhood now in their teens. Here for the first intelligent time, they began to discuss that irresistible subject the soul, touching upon its secret growth, its groaning, its shape, and its means of locomotion. They found a bench near the handball court. It was a frosty evening with a scintillant moon in an eighth of a slice with a lone attendant star frisky beneath it. Who was that laughing so, lucky to be alive? They leaned forward eagerly to make out who were those girls, how old and how many, on the bench across who seemed to be laughing themselves to death so musically. And as they looked they saw that the path betwen them was paved.

"My pals." Joe curled up his lip, too proud to rub his jaws. "That was a nice dirty trick, that was. What comes next? A hotfoot?"

Eddie laughed as he poked him in the ribs affectionately.

"Same old Joe," he said. "Hates to be touched."

"A delicate boy," said Dave. "Always was. Hey, we forgot to ask him. How's the old bank roll, Joey?"

"Flat as a pancake."

"Don't give us that."

"I mean it. You can stop making eyes at me right now."

"The truth," said Dave. "Out with it."

"Okay," said Joe. "You want me to show it to you? I've got five bucks to last me a whole week."

"Five bucks," said Dave. "Okay, we'll take it."

"The hell you will."

"I mean. You know what I mean, Joey. We may need a little extra tonight."

"What for? Aren't we taking them down to the clubroom?"

"Well," said Dave. "You tell him, Eddie."

"Oh, no," said Eddie. "Tell him yourself. It was your idea."

"Well," said Dave. "It's this way, Joey. We thought we'd take a little ride out in Long Island. You know. Just for a change. There's a joint I know with no cover charge. What the hell. We give the dames a sandwich and a beer, and we're big shots. Know what I mean?"

"Perfectly," said Joe. "Just stop the car and let me out of here."

"What did I tell you, Dave?" said Eddie. "I told you he wouldn't go for it."

82

"Shut up," said Dave. "And hold on to him."

"Well, well," said Joe as Eddie embraced him, their noses almost touching. "Is this a proposal, sweetheart? Or just plain robbery?"

"Aw," said Dave. "Come on, Joey. Be a pal. Just say you'll lay it out if you have to. There's a tankful of gas. Eddie has two bucks and I have a buck and a half. Maybe it'll be enough."

"You have?" said Joe. "Okay, gorilla, you can let go of me now. Where did you guys get so much money all of a sudden?"

"So much?" said Eddie. "Are you trying to be sarcastic?"

"Don't tell me you guys are working?"

"That's right," said Dave. "Get funny. This is a good time for it."

"What're you getting so sore about?"

"You really want to know how we got it?" said Eddie. "It's very simple. I killed my mother for it. And Dave killed his."

"I believe it," said Joe. "How else? So why in the hell don't you hold on to it? Make it last, for chrissakes. Why spend it all in one night this way?"

"Look," said Dave. "Let's forget it, okay? We're not talking about millions."

"Right," said Eddie. "That's enough. I don't like this conversation. Let's have your butt, miser, I'll get rid of it."

"Stone Avenue," said Dave. "We're almost there. So who cares? So it'll be the clubroom or nothing. Say, how's that cousin of yours, Ed?"

"Which one?"

"The one with the trick moustache. The one who broke his leg. Doesn't he live around here somewhere?"

"Oh," said Eddie. "That one. He should break his neck too."

"He never paid you back, eh?"

"That's what I mean."

"Christopher," said Dave, wheeling Becky into it, but cutting the corner close to avoid a bonfire of egg boxes kindled by kids who were grimly plunging through or gleefully sailing over it. "Hey, hey. Did you see that? So help me, nothing changes. We used to do it too. Remember when Fatso's hair caught fire? For crying out loud. Don't look so sad, Joey."

"Who's sad?" said Joe.

"Don't worry," said Dave. "Your money's safe."

"Who the hell's thinking of money? Money. You want what I got? All you have to do is ask for it. You know that."

"You mean it?" said Eddie.

"Certainly. When did I say no?"

"Well," said Dave. "That's more like it. What did I tell you, Eddie? I told you he'd come through."

"Sure, sure," said Eddie. "But I still don't like it."

"You like it, you like it."

"Now those bimbos will be expecting it all the time."

"Don't be such a kvetch. They know, they know. This is just for tonight. And it's a beautiful night. Look at the bastard thing. I tell you what. Let's go in singing. Hah, Joey? What'll we sing?"

But Joe had to shake his head.

"Jesus," he said. "It doesn't take much to make you guys happy, does it?"

Should it take more then? Certainly. Take any imbecile. Even he would know that. So wait a minute. So what reason had he to burn so inside at their half-ass blitheness, to sound so scornful of this tendency of theirs, which is perfectly natural in young and old alike in a state of emotional starvation, to snatch with such careless delight at a hunk of stale bread with a live worm in it? The great provider. Could he feed them out of that fabulous loaf of a lick and a promise? It is said that the more one eats of it, the less is it consumed. A promise for which, like sheep appointed to be slain, men and women by the billion have been sacrificed in vain long before he, that miserable crumb, had ever been born? Never mind answering. It must be true. The most disgusting worm of all is not a worm at all. It happens to be the man who is a killjoy.

To show how strict and honest he was, Joe glared at this insolent particle of himself to which he instantly assigned the most venomous and ugliest face he could think of. By all that is precious and proud and holy, what is there to cheer about in the fact that his two best friends who flanked him had suddenly become like the birds, the sappiest of creatures with their suspicious little peck and their stiff and greedy little hop, always so ecstatic over a thimbleful of birdseed that they have to sing, anything, what should they sing?

What then is the wish of the world? In one sentence now. The wish of the world is that joy be prevalent. But it is such an old weary mournful wish by this time. And why? Because of the momentary tickle, because the people keep saying yes to it cringingly, saying please, just for tonight, feverishly scratching in each other's armpits, and elsewhere, forcing sensation, swoon, and the belly laugh until they cry real tears. It is terrific how they can make each other cry. Who has so maligned pride that a man is ashamed to feel it? He trembles when he feels it. He would be magnificent if he would show it. But he falters. And the shame, it doubles when he has to swallow it down. So again it is yes to the tricky and tinsel enchantments. Again he allows himself to be lifted only as high as the Ferris wheel at the carnival can creakingly lift him. No wonder the stars look down at him so mockingly.

But now it was time to tumble out. And the stars were left to gossip among themselves. And Becky to cool off at the curb. And there were steps to be climbed. And a Rifkin doorbell to be rung. And how do you say it? It was like being saved by the bell. For even a baby mind like Joe's can feel that it has deepened the wrong dimple when it has furtively had its say in byplay, when it has too long detained itself in a parenthetical sneer which obviously tried, but fumbled and failed, to equate the cosmic with the terrene, the worm with its abode in the apple, the plug with its socket, the hand with its predestinated pocket, and, and other idiocies of similar extent and contestability. So seeks for a fresh alignment through the manipulation of materiality, shirt, tie, hatbrim, and fly. And as a last touch, the most cunning of all, five imaginary fingers quietly efface the latest crease of mischief, already an antiquity, reserving the space for a futuristic one, for one of fizzy and flippant merriment.

"Come in, boyiss, come in."

Cried the father of Honey and Belle, Mr. Rifkin, looking like a real schlepper in his rumpled vest, and acting like one as he dragged Dave, then Eddie, then Joe, into the foyer with a jailer's cruel and half-crazy grip above the elbow, and sonofagun, it really hurt.

"Well, thanks," said Dave. "I love you too."

"Ha," Mr. Rifkin snorted, herding them forcibly into the living room. "A joker from the old country."

"From the new one too," said Eddie. "How's the ulcers, Pop?"

"You hear?" said Mr. Rifkin, appealing to Joe, with scorn and savagery. "Pop he calls me. Smelling of diapers. Ah, you boyiss today. Wait. The stomach will turn over for you like it turns over with fire for me. You working?"

85

"He's got a job," said Dave. "If that's what you mean."

"Ah," said Mr. Rifkin. "Good."

"Now you like him, eh, Pop?"

"Wonderful, wonderful. And his Mamma, she calls him something, no?"

"Sure," said Eddie. "But let's keep it clean."

"Joe," said Dave. "Joe meet Joe."

"How do you do?" said Joe.

"A pleasure," said Mr. Rifkin. "I like your name."

"Thank you," said Joe. "I like yours too."

"Bums," said Mr. Rifkin. "You see? This is what I call a gentleman. Take off the coat. Sit down. You hungry?"

"Oh, no," said Joe. "Thanks."

"Then you'll drink. You'll drink, hah? I got good schnapps? Wait. Look at me. Let me see the face. Aha. Good, good. God takes care of you. The same name like me, but like me you don't look."

"No," Joe smiled. "Not yet."

"Ah," said Mr. Rifkin. "You hear? This is a boy."

As distraught in his delight as he had been in his crushing dourness, he lunged for the cut-glass bottle of schnapps on the mantelpiece, and with Hasidic abandonment, plooped out four snifters hazardously full to the brim. "Drink, boyiss. You are all sons of mine. Drink." They clinked glasses, they grinned, they spilled it, the loafers, they tossed back their heads in a reckless imitation of their fresh father, and tried to gulp it down like men, but it was fiery stuff, and they gagged. "Cough, cry, let it burn. Come here, come here." They submitted to a second round, welcomed the third. Pools formed in the polar region. Midnight whimpered on the top of the world and exploded. And the flightless penguins reeled. And likewise the elbow benders. With fiddledeedee of facial foolery, with passion, the pupils of their eyes awfully round with fraternity, they pumped the hand of Pop, aching with affection.

"Children," said Mr. Rifkin. "What can I say to you? Will you listen? Have I the mouth for it? Has it ever happened once that God should say to me, 'Joseph Rifkin, fool of mine, take your time, you push too much, stop your sweating, you have a thousand years yet.' Where is the spittoon in this house? Sure, laugh, why not? You want to laugh some more? See the pants I wear like in vaudeville? When I put them on I suffer. When I take them off I suffer. I suffer. You know Abraham Golschman? He works by me on the next machine. Six fingers he's got on one foot. Six, five, why be ashamed? It's foolishness. He dreams. He tells me. You know how he talks to God? You shouldn't hear it. 'Mr. Chairman,' he spits he is so excited. 'I want you should fix a mistake. Did I ask you to be so good to me? Why me with six, and even a murderer with five? It's a scandal. I'm a good union member, no? I pay my dues, no? So? You have a committee on cripples, no? So? Tell them. Show them. Give them a push. Make them fix the mistake.' You hear? Abraham is not afraid to tell me. Listen to this. God puts down the cigar. God makes a face. 'Ach,' he cries, 'he comes to me like a headache. Abraham, Abraham, I am disappointed in you. Why do you bother a busy man with such nonsense? Do I bother you because you say I have to look like you? Come, go home. You like schnapps? Drink it. Your children have no respect? So take out the strap. Spank. Knock down the bosses. And remember this, Abraham. I am God. And God never makes a mistake.' Hah? Did you hear? Did you listen, children? He said good, no? Ah, here comes my missis. See? She brings you strudel. Eat it, my sons, and don't ask me why it comes. Or why, after you lick your lips, the world will still be bitter. Fannie, come here. Fannie, give me your sweet mouth."

With the grace of a true kitchen goddess, with the serenity of a woman who really knows, having really seized her man behind the many social masks of his quick-change artistry, with pure bridal-night shyness because of the company, she retained the plate of strudel to obey him, agitated object of her delight, offering him the sweetness he so implored with glowing eyes, shaping it for him with a subtle thrust of her lower lip, seasoned, childish, serpentine. Angel, missis, passionate babe. It was such a surprise for Joe to see with what a kiss the wiry but wobbly gaffer kissed her, with such gentle homage, home-made.

"I'm next," said Dave.

"I ask you," said Mr. Rifkin, the lucky. "Could I live without her?"

"God forbid," said Mrs. Rifkin. "Bite your tongue. Joseph, what do I see? What is it you have so tight in your hand?"

"Me," said Dave. "Me now."

"Hah?" said Mr. Rifkin. "What hand?"

"Shame on you," said Mrs. Rifkin. "Dr. Grauer should see you.

Come, put down the poison, and go and sit down. Before you fall down."

"Goddamn it," said Dave. "No one listens to me."

"So?" said Mr. Rifkin. "So all right. So I'll fall down. So you'll pick me up, no?"

"Yes," said Mrs. Rifkin. "I'll pick you up, all right. But first, believe me, I'll step on you a little. Aie, don't squeeze. Tell me better. Who is this new boy?"

"He?" said Mr. Rifkin, with an elaborate wink at his half-drunk namesake. "No good."

"Joseph."

"Plain no good."

"Joseph, please."

"What, please? Please. If you open your eyes, my innocence, and take one look, you will see. He is a boy who does terrible things."

"Shah," said Mrs. Rifkin. "You are terrible yourself."

"Hey," said Dave. "I like this."

"Yeah," said Eddie. "Go on, Pop. You're right. Give him hell."

"Ach," said Mrs. Rifkin. "If this is a joke, I don't like it. Joseph, please. Look how his face is changing."

"Excuse me," said Joe. "Do you mind if I sit down?"

Whose little whose-this was he? Now the fools will make a fuss. Is it proper while one is woozy to kiss at impalement time? So plump is this sympathetic she. Mother, pin a rose on this parthenogenetic son, celebrate his sudden nausea and his sudden shrivelment, put an end to this comedy of tangled paternity.

Loosen his tie, Mr. Rifkin cried, it must be something he ate, what is it he has eaten? The curds of his words when he said terrible, terrible. The tactless palpation of this multiple man, accidentally shrewd, why blame him? Quickly now, while there is a moment yet, while they are fluttering around to prevent a faint, consider the response, so whacky and extravagant, of the so-called soul, to dignify it with a name, to this joke, said the wink, make no mistake about it. Yet it had quailed. Just think of it. It had dared to act with such cowardly independence, refusing to be kidded, falling all over itself in its anxiety to confess a crime he had never committed, implying so outrageously that what he had done this afternoon had been a kind of a terrible thing.

This thing, this soul, grow something on its surface it ought as long as it continues to live, flowers preferably, be it sweet william, mock orange, or rattlesnake weed, random choices out of the book on flowers swiped from the Liberty Street Library, or whatever is romantic but real. Right. But it ought never to shake like a frightened accessory after the fact, else it will excite a morbid growth out of guilt, fungus, and become a freak, with a sixth finger. And that would be awful. For who is there who knows, even God does not encourage the legend, where it can go to get itself fixed?

"Ah," said Mr. Rifkin, still loosely punctuating with the same potent bottle, unstoppered. "Look. His eyes are returning. He's smiling. He's all right. Now he'll be all right. You see, Fannie? How many times do I say it? Never stop so quick. Give the boy one more drink and believe me."

"Christ," said Dave, bending down with angry breath to warm his friend's queer faraway face. "What in the hell happened to you? I've never seen you this way before. You looked as if you were dying."

"Where's his glass?" said Mr. Rifkin. "What dying? You talk. You know what you're saying? Dying. No, boychickul. Die he won't. Not so fast. He has plenty to suffer first. The glass. What happened to it?"

"Joseph," said Mrs. Rifkin. "It seems to me a man of your age."

"Can't take it," Eddie mumbled, bumping into Dave.

"What?" said Dave. "Uh-uh. The show's not over yet. Here comes another one."

"You know?" said Eddie, sure he was blinking at someone he recognized. "That's a matter with him. Can't take it."

"Really?" said Dave. "Amazing. Did you figure that out all by yourself? Hey. Don't look now, but your knees are buckling."

"Where?" said Eddie. "I beg your pardon. Are you talking about me?"

"That's the idea," said Dave. "Now you're getting it. Where do you live when you're sober? You know your name?"

"Alphonso Marmaduke," said Eddie. "Trying to be a wiseguy? I'll drink you under the table any time."

"Oh, yeah?" said Dave. "So tell me. Why is it? Every time I crawl under, I find you there first."

"Sure," said Eddie. "That's right. And you know why?"

"No," said Dave. "I'll bite. Why?"

89

"Because I'm looking for you, that's why."

"Oh, yeah?"

"Yeah."

"Yeah," said Mr. Rifkin. "You hear that, Fannie? These are boys with brains? In America when they have nothing to say, they say yeah. Yeah? Yeah."

"So," said Mrs. Rifkin. "So in Odessa it was something else. Has all the knowledge crept into your head? Ah, boyiss, I must say it. You insult me."

"Yeah," said Dave. "That's right. You're absolutely right, Mrs. Rifkin. You see, Eddie? You see what you've done?"

"Me?" said Eddie.

"You. You heard what she said. Come on, now, apologize to the lady."

"You're crazy. I didn't do anything. Did I do anything, Mrs. Rifkin? What did I do?"

"No, darling," said Mrs. Rifkin. "Do something you didn't. It's what you don't do. Here I stand for an hour with the plate. And still you don't eat."

"Well," said Dave. "It's about time."

"Hey, hey," said Eddie. "Nice of you kids to show up. We sure appreciate it."

"Hello, there," said Belle, Dave's heartache, the dark one. "Did we keep you waiting?"

"Oh, no," said Dave. "Only a couple of hours, that's all."

"Still sarcastic," said Belle. "Isn't he sweet? I'll fix him later. What was all the racket about? What's been going on here?"

"Yes," said Honey, Eddie's heartquake, kid sister by a year, the fairer one, but solid, man, just as tantalizingly solid everywhere too. "We're dying to know."

"Naturally," said Eddie. "Aren't you always?"

"Echo," said Honey. "Are you still here? If you want to live, be quiet. Really, it sounded just like a revolution. We could hear you all the way from the bath, I mean the bedroom. Couldn't we, Lee?"

"Murder," said Dave. "And who might this lovely creature be?"

"A blondie," Eddie cried. "Hey, Joe. Where are you?"

Paging the problem child who of course was where he was since he could be seen, that is, he was certainly there, yet somehow the ques-

90

tion still was, where exactly was he? He felt he was both very near and very far, as if he were simultaneously seated in the front row of the orchestra, and in the last of the balcony, in a curious snarl of coexistence, in the wrong theater. But is that so unusual? Think of the fantasia, more rococo and weird, whether it winds up in a cellar, cathedral, or synagogue, which the brain concocts, say in twilight sleep when it is only half trying, so to speak, and his bitched ambiguity of a metaphor, slightly alcoholized, seems bloodless and blah in comparison.

What is the matter with a person who always feels so displaced? Such uneasiness of not belonging, of wishing to escape, is just too catching for comfort. Too much is too much. Let him not have so much contempt for the chin music of the ordinary criers in life, tympanists, tyros of the second violin section, meek feeders and foils, who gladly act as such for each other and for the sake of the superior instrumentalists, who act instead of react. He ought to be told. Someone ought to tell him that he is a sap who is satanically blind to what is stamped so sacredly on the stub of his ticket. Terrible may be what it says there, but it is true, so let the aggravating cuss face it. Other people he will never really know. And no other place.

Grateful always for the possibility of any kind of self-propulsion, he rose to his feet to stop this picking and picking on himself, so as to be introduced to Lee, to give this gal the once-over, to encounter her lips so thoughtlessly popular, and imagine with unfailing optimism first a playful feint at, then a serious unbuttoning without a hitch of whatever was in the way of getting at her boobies of the right size, her thighs so tight, her pubic hair, her cleft, chink, her hypothetical cranny.

"Stop it," said Belle. "Do you want to embarrass her?"

"Oh, more," Eddie grinned. "Much more than that."

"See?" said Honey. "I told you they were bums. In case you're interested. That was Eddie, no less."

"And I'm Dave," said Dave. "Aren't you lucky, kiddo?"

"Oh, sure," said Belle. "She's been waiting for this all her life. I don't mean to be inquisitive. But who's your friend there with the fancy scarf?"

"Scarf?" said Dave, as everyone turned to look. "What scarf?"

"Hey," said Eddie. "How did that get around his neck?"

91

A dish towel of all things.

"Don't look at me," said Dave. "I didn't put it there."

"Me neither," said Eddie.

"Father," said Belle. "How many times have I asked you."

"Me," said Mrs. Rifkin. "It's mine. I had it in my hands. How can that be?"

"Don't worry," said Joe, removing it and folding it carefully before returning it to her. "It's clean, it's clean."

"Forgive me," said Mrs. Rifkin. "I'm ashamed. It's you, Joseph. You see what you make me do? You and your excitement."

"What excitement?" said Mr. Rifkin. "Ridiculous. Nothing is wrong, Fannie. I assure you. On him it was a perfect fit. How many times what? Did you hear what your daughter called me? As soon as company comes, it's father, father. My high-school graduate. What is it, teacher? Papa isn't good enough for you?"

"Of course it is," said Belle. "Why do you always twist things around? What I meant was, of course you're good. That's the trouble. You're too good sometimes."

"And that's bad?"

"It isn't good. I mean it."

"So you mean it. So now you think you've said something?"

"Ach," said Mrs. Rifkin. "Even on Saturday. Will there ever be any peace in this house?"

"Ah, now," said Belle. "That's not fair. Admit it, Papa. Do you ever take care of yourself? As soon as someone comes into this house."

"He can never get out of here," said Dave.

"Yes," said Honey. "Come on, Belle, you'll argue with him later."

"My name's Joe," said Joe to Lee. "I hope you can hear me."

"Oh, yes," said Lee. "I'm used to such a racket. Isn't it hot in here?"

"What?"

"I said, they're cute, aren't they? Gee, I hate blind dates."

"Me too," said Joe. "But not this time. If I may say so."

"Well, thank you," said Lee. "You may certainly say so."

"Arguing," said Belle. "I wasn't arguing. What did I do with my compact? I was just trying to."

"Yes, yes," said Dave. "We know. We know who's boss around here. Come on, baby, take my word for it, you'll never look any better. Kiss your slaves here and let's get going. How about it?"

"Oh," said Honey. "We kiss enough. Come on, lightning. Goodbye you two."

"Whoa," said Eddie. "Look at her. Before you couldn't get her out. Now she's pushing me. Mrs. Rifkin? So long, Pop. Thanks a lot."

"Bye, Ma," said Belle. "Pa?"

"I'm here, I'm here."

"You'll go to bed early?"

"Yes, yes," said Mr. Rifkin. "Go, darling, have a good time. Watch your sister. All right, so kiss me too. You have your key? What? Yes, boyiss, yes. I hear you. Goodbye. Go already. You hear how many times they have to say it?"

"The same to you," said Mrs. Rifkin. "Don't mention it. Call again."

"Call again," Mr. Rifkin muttered wearily. "Don't call again. They're doing me a favor? Fools. All of them. What else? Do they know what they're doing? You think they know where they're going?"

"Joseph, please. They can still hear you."

"But they go. What hear me? Can't you see? They run out so fast, in a minute they'll be in Jerusalem. Why do you stand there looking so chopped down? Ah, they forgot the strudel. Well. Come, Fannie, if we are wise, we'll obey. Let us go where the children are always sending us. Let us creep into bed. Old rags. What else are we? Let us try to sleep. And when we wake up, if God is willing, maybe then we'll know why it is he has made us all so foolish."

What is left behind is left behind. It is no longer fashionable to dissolve into tears at what one hears. Forgivably demonic is the age at which every day is thought to be discovery day, every kid a Columbus. Compassion for the middle-aged bent and crankiness will last as long as it takes a second to tick. Most assuredly, great is the world, and this is its epitome, the rifkin-man, the humanist whose nature is a jungle which even a mind like a tiger is at last afraid to explore, combustible, monodic, carrier of regret and restlessness, mingler revolted by his mingling, wearily quick-witted about children who are engaged in the same old cockeyed quest, which is as tough on the heart as it is on the feet, forced to wave them on with the back of his hand, whether in the process of their search they be sanctified or damned.

Well, then, Joe had to ask. Who can be like the oak or eucalyptus? To name only two. Who can be arboreal enough to grow, as they seem to do, with such steady enthusiasm? Hardly any one. Almost no one at all. For what man is fixed? Above him is the mountain of his dilemma which he must not only climb, but transcend, and transcend not by climbing, but by contemplation. But the nitwit chases around in circles, in the rank vegetation of the foothills, in pursuit of his own tail. Talk about the circus. And then, with the clownlike alertness of a mongrel, he skids to a stop. He has sniffed something.

Beyond the basic odor of her date-night cleanliness, it made Joe wonder, what is it she uses to make her smell like that? She seemed to think it was much too soon, but since Becky was only a business coupe, it had to be two in the front, and four in the back, so Lee made herself small and slid in expertly to sit on his lap. A smell verging on the semisweet, like a decent little blossom which is shy, if not virginal, yet keeps bashfully signaling. Maybe, he said, it would be far better if, instead of trying to bore through him with the point of her elbow, she simply put her soft spare arm around his neck. She proceeded to do precisely that, but why did he now say, thank you? Why, said he, for smelling so nice. Oh, said she, really? Such a compliment. So inducive that she allowed most of her authentic weight to relent, thus giving bright-eyes, who certainly did not resist it, a real gratuitous feel of the solid rise of her, he certainly knew what, so that it rested in a fine, since it was so forgetful, coalescence of their barely separated, silly, she giggled when he whispered it on purpose as if it were a dirty word, but it was not perfume, that was not it, it was, was he listening?

He was all ears. Oh, so then. Scented soap, powder on the post-bath pink, a sneezing cloud of it, puffed into known pits, and mentionable hollows and very private crevices lavishly, reason why it lingers, and yes, what else, and a bit of brilliantine on her hair. What was that? Oh, now, she had heard that one before. What did he mean where had she been all his life? To come out with it so suddenly. After all, what did it really mean? It did have a nice sound to it, true, and as a line it was not too bad, and god, how many fall for it, why was he smiling? Oh, so yes. So as she was saying. No, it would not be fair to figure in the lipstick. That was all she used. Honest. Did he believe her? He barely pressed her where her buttocks began. He believed her.

Hard on that wheel. Ridiculous to slow down for a curve. What ensued is what is known as a pile-up. Girls when they get rumpled get nicer and are easier to feel. But they fail to see it, or pretend to, and castigate and complain in colors which could be cooler. Oo that unspeakable lunatic, that batty creature up in front, was he out to murder them? Quiet, Joe shocked them, but yell it twice he did, for they were dizzy dames, and damn silly at that. Belle turned around to inspect this curiosity, frankly anxious to know if he was often seized this way, or was it only by appointment? Go tell her. Even if he could, she would never understand for all her native cleverness, why he should have this sudden and mysterious revulsion of feeling for her, and for all others of her kind.

For what in Belle's life so far, so creditable, so open-face, had happened that could explain to her what was her luck, and his misfortune? Why is it he must always be asking why of everything, and she hardly ever? She had a brand-new mouth to burn in the memory. Her eyes are like animals. Her breathing is bold. She thrusts out a pair that is priceless. She is perfect for it. She is fresh earth. She is a sorceress on the double, drastic, out like a light, demiurgic. She is disgustingly healthy. Her hair flies. She dives in as confidently in the middle of a movie as in the middle of a sea. Only get her seats together, which row is no worry, and off she floats. It is most amazing. See what a plunge she takes, pure capitulation. She will know the end before she will get to know the beginning, yet she will gawk at the beginning, and gasp, as if she had never gazed at the end. Whatever the picture, it is rarely more than a crude variation of what she has wept at before, but her nose runs again, of what has goosed her so often, but again she roars, and wets herself once more. Learn from her. She is so sensible. Though it be arbitrarily edited, a tease, she swallows what she sees just as she sees it, as she sucks the caramels down her utterly captivated craw.

What is that rushing sound? Stop cranking a second and listen. Six wishful high livers on the lam for the wilds of Long Island, there is something they have forgotten, and they better remember it. Time. It is time they have forgotten. They have forgotten how it whirls on like a gigantic film, spectacle after spectacle, implacable creation, original dead pan, weirdly and endlessly unreeling.

"That's enough out of you," said Eddie.

"What?" said Honey.

"You're talking too much."

"Are you addressing me?"

"No, babe, take it easy. I mean my friend here. What's he been saying, Lee? Anything?"

"Saying?" said Lee. "What do you mean?"

"Has he been talking?"

"Why, yes," said Lee. "He's been talking."

"Don't give me that," said Eddie. "You mean, you've been talking."

"No, really," said Lee. "He's been talking. He's been talking all the time."

"Thanks," said Joe. "You're a sweet kid. Lean back a little, will you? What were you saying there, peasant?"

"I was saying you're a ball of fire."

"In what language?"

"You slay me," said Eddie.

"That's an idea," said Joe. "Shall we arrange it?"

"See?" said Eddie. "That's just what I mean. You hear how he talks? He must be breaking in a voice for somebody. That's not Joe. What's up? What's eating you anyway?"

"That's easy," said Joe. "I know that one. Guys like you."

"No kidding, now," said Eddie. "I mean it. You ought to take something for it. Castoria. What babies cry for. Don't laugh. It'll loosen you up. It'll bring you right back to yourself."

"What self?" said Joe. "Look, sonny, if I'm bothering you that much, just let me know, will you? And I'll make myself scarce. Just like that."

"Now, now," said Eddie. "Don't get your bowels in an uproar."

"What bowels? Why the hell's this guy needling me for? Does anybody know?"

"I do," said Honey. "It's very simple. Isn't it, Lee?"

"It is?" said Lee. "What is?"

"Why, you know," said Honey. "They're just trying to show us how much they love each other. That's all."

"Well, well," said Joe, smiling gently at her spangled image in shadow, an image altered by her goodwill into one of such positive and homespun animation. "Aren't you the clever one? Do you mind telling me? Is that your real name?"

"Which?"

"Honey."

"Oh," said Honey. "That. No. But I would like it to be."

"I agree," said Joe. "It fits you perfectly."

"Thank you," said Honey. "Just for that you deserve to know the real one. That is, if you promise not to laugh."

"I won't."

"Well, then," said Honey. "It's Hannah. Isn't that awful?"

"Awful?" said Joe.

"But it's not my fault now, remember that. It was given to me."

"But that's a beautiful name," said Joe. "It's from the Bible, did you know that? I don't see how you can say it's awful."

"Well," said Honey. "That's just it. It's so."

"So what?"

"So Jewish. You know what I mean."

"Jewish?" said Joe. "Are you serious?"

"She sure is," said Eddie. "Can you imagine? I boil up every time I hear it."

"Stop boiling," said Honey. "Who's talking to you?"

"I am," said Eddie. "I'm talking to myself. Do you mind?"

"Not at all," said Honey. "If you're that crazy."

"So I'm crazy," said Eddie. "At least I'm something."

"Oh, sure," said Honey. "But what?"

"You'll find out. Don't be so anxious. And your lovely friend there. I tell you what, Joe. I'll lay you two to one her name's not Lee. Go on. Ask her."

"Gosh," said Honey. "Did you ever hear anyone so fresh?"

"Ask her," said Eddie. "Go on. You'll see. I bet you I'm right."

He was. Her real name was Leah, not Lee.

"Well," said Joe. "This is really funny. Say. Does anybody here know when we get there? Hey, Dave. Look at that one-armed driver. So you have a real name too. Tell me, Lee, were you born here?"

"Where?"

"Here. Right here in the United States."

"Oh," said Lee. "Oh, yes. I was lucky that time."

"I see," said Joe. "And otherwise?"

"What do you mean?"

"Skip it. So that makes you a real American, I suppose. I mean. It makes you an American first, and then Jewish. Is that right?"

"Certainly," said Lee. "Don't you think that's true?"

"Don't ask me," said Joe. "I'm asking you."

"Say," said Honey. "Are you a mockie?"

"No, dear," said Joe. "Don't get frightened. I was born here too."

"But I wasn't," said Eddie. "So what does that make me?"

"What?" said Honey. "You weren't born here?"

"Didn't you know?" said Joe.

"No," said Honey. "He never told me."

"My," said Joe. "He's sure in a pickle now, isn't he?"

"Why?" said Honey. "Why didn't you tell me?"

"Because," said Eddie. "You never asked me."

"Just the same," said Honey. "You should've told me."

"So all right," said Eddie. "So now I've told you. So what? You think I give a damn whether you like it or not?"

"Who said I don't like it?"

"So fine," said Eddie. "So now you like it. So what in the hell does that make me?"

"Yes," said Joe. "Why don't you tell him, Honey? Can you answer him? What is he? Do you know?"

On this side of the ocean or that, the subject of what a man is, here Dave took time out from his cozy double duty of driving his Becky and coupling his Belle to inform the squabblers in the back that they were on the right highway at last, the Merritt, and that the inn, he begged their pardon, that the joint, Grassy Point or some such crackpot designation was just a piece down the road, and here he laughed, for piece, he was sure they knew, was a delightfully equivocal word. The subject has always been a touchy one. Born in one place, fated to croak in another, what difference does it make when a man, or his original frantic ancestor, has first been forced to cross over? Do the fishes remember? Storm-tossed toddler on surprising sea legs, ship-card saying he was Eli Lapolsky, had pocked and measled, in Russland, was two going on three, he saw that all the passengers in their second-class chairs were retching and rolling in agony, but not he. His earliest recollection, he swore it was his earliest, and swore it rapturously. Yet where a man originates, through no fault of his own, has become a red speck, a crying shame, a stigma much too foul, corny, and crucial, and way too uproarious for so many of those who have been conceived and cradled here, right here in the United States, the jokers. Jesus, what a way to be heaved into this world.

Jeweled accretions of the memory which can be as talkative as a

Fourth-of-July punk for a penny once a kitchen match is put to it to make it sparkle, the hiss of seltzer water is what this only child, Eli-Eddie, remembers next on the very day of disembarkation, like a key sound scissored out of a momentous flash dream in which the opening of a door is first seen, the brilliance of it. Yet what a groggy bundle of opportunity it seemed to a man its stupefied mother called Sam. Just think how this pants presser, Pa, had sweated to save the dough he had to have to bring this googoo-eyed dud of his over. Sam the man, who fondly caressed its deloused head, and tried to force its blue lips open at 16 Powell Street in Brooklyn, where else, so that it too might feel a bit the sizzle of celebration, for think of it, think how queer, this kid now was this man's entire fortune in America. The little kid puked. The little kid, how he did cry when hardly a second later, as it seemed, he was kicked in the behind, as accurately as it could be done by a native to a greenhorn.

The little mockie wept because he was afraid of his brutal enemies in the street, because the festival of the new land was denied him. So forlornly, like a sequestered knight, he found a final hiding place, under the washtub, where day after day he plunked himself silly on an old European chamber with an old European spoon, sustained in his siege by the constant sight of his mother's sturdy legs, in love with her who would ever be his one passive, work-convulsed, but invincible servant. After a twitch of time, the merest, he could spit back the dirtiest words in the English language. So naturally he was asked to play follow-the-leader first, then a quick hide-and-seek as a breather, and for the final test was ordered to fling himself, the deliriously willing sack, into seven straight games of Johnny-on-the-pony. He passed. Then Pa pushed him, Pa with his precious first papers for citizenship hidden deep in the side pocket of his jacket and secured there with a diaper pin, right into 1A of P.S. 150 with a lie, swearing that the kid, who at that time was remarkably undersized, was six when he was barely five. O the felicity of it. To unclasp his hot little hands, and stand, and raise his right hand, and say after Miss Brady the pledge allegiance to the flag. Daily and failing, all over the land, this is the titter, the tiny music which is meant to immortalize this country, and all for which it stands.

So who then is better off? If he, Joe, is told to go back where he came from, though he is already there, where the devil can he go? He can go.

He can hotfoot it to Hades. And that about covers it all. But if Eddie is told to get lost, he suffers from no confusion on that score. He can promptly pick up his woebegone chin plastered to the floor. He can sail, fly, or swim to it, or crawl, but he can reach it easily after all, a village which seems like a sketch of a mound, swiftly but softly indicated, in pink, populated by a thousand or so hazy souls, a hundred or so hazy miles north of Petrograd. Though they do say it gets very cold there.

"Whew," said Joe, his finger rummaging in his collar for air, his back raked by a volley of jazz delivered by a five-piece band, an arrogant combination, and scatterbrained about the seasons too, for it kept shrieking at him to button up his overcoat simply because it happened to be the prevailing whine, the unctuous petition of a popular ditty of the day. "It sure is nice and hot in here, isn't it?"

"God, yes," said Lee, fanning herself with a tattered menu, her blinkless eyes lost to him as they pursued, and sized up, as he was amused to see when he looked, a tall blonde tuxedo-clad show-off who successfully larruped the other leaders, his rivals all, fouling up the floor with his fancy steps, trying to be original.

"Nimble," said Joe. "And so pretty too."

"Ain't he?" said Lee. "Say, what's the name of that movie star again? I have such a head for remembering sometimes. He looks just like him, doesn't he?"

"Just."

"Who?" said Honey, charmingly jerking her head every which way like an alarmed chicken. "Who does?"

"That high jumper there," said Joe. "See him?"

"Where?" said Honey. "Show me."

"There," said Joe. "Mr. Blondie. Know who he is?"

"Who?"

"The Prince of Wales. Incognito."

"Incog what?" said Honey. "You're kidding me."

"How did you ever guess?"

"Hey, Dave," said Eddie, nervously picking at the crust on the cap of the ketchup bottle. "What's the story? Do we pay them? Or do they pay us for coming here?"

"Listen to him," said Dave. He shook a few grains of salt into his palm. "Another wiseguy." He touched his tongue to it. It was not sugar. "You've been in worse places."

"When?" said Eddie. "Remind me. I dare you."

"I don't know," said Belle, spreading apart a hairpin, then twisting up the ends to render it cleverly into something like spectacles. "I don't think it's so bad here. Here, love, put it on your nose."

"Like hell," said Dave. "I look funny enough as it is."

"You're telling me? What I mean is. At least we can dance, no? I mean to some live music for a change. That's something, isn't it?"

"For you?" said Dave, snaking his arm around her waist. "For you, my love, it's sometimes everything. Tell me, twinkletoes. Give me one good reason. Why do I like you so much?"

Her smile instantly became as a twin to his.

"Because you can't help it," she said.

"That's no reason."

"Because I'd kill you if you didn't."

"Ah," said Dave. "Maybe that's it. A real killer. I like the way you act tough in company. Did you hear what she said, Joe? She thinks I'm afraid of her."

"Who isn't?" said Joe.

"Of her?"

"Of any woman. They're all holy terrors."

"Well," said Belle. "What've we got here? A woman hater?"

"Nuts," said Eddie. "Who's that poking me?"

"Me," said Honey. "I just wanted to know."

"What?" said Eddie. "That I can still feel?"

"The waiter's here."

"Is he? That's nice."

"Can we eat? I mean. A little something? Is it all right?"

"Sure," said Eddie. "Why not? You can order anything you want. Up to a dime."

"A dime," said Honey. "Is that all I'm worth?"

"Oh, no," said Eddie. "Far from it. You're worth all the money in the world. Only it just so happens I haven't got it."

"Still angry," said Honey. "Can you beat that? I don't see why you should still be so angry. Please, now, why don't you cool off?"

"I will," said Eddie. "Don't worry. I will."

"What's with them?" said Dave.

"What'll it be?" said the waiter.

"That's love for you," said Belle. "Ain't it grand?"

"I wouldn't know," said the waiter. "I only work here."

"Ah," said Dave. "One of the boys. Beer for everybody. Scratch it down. Who wants a sandwich?"

"He doesn't," said Honey. "He's been eating. He's been eating me up alive."

"Now, Honey," said Belle. "Let's not keep it up, please?"

"That's all right," said Eddie. "Let her get it off her chest."

"You," said Honey. "You keep my chest out of it."

"I wish I could," said Eddie. "But I'm afraid I like it too much."

"Bull's-eye," said Dave.

"Sounds like a real happy family," said the waiter.

"It is," said Dave. "That it is. What kind of sandwiches you got?"

"Since you can't read, I'll help you out. All kinds cheese, ham, salami, ham and swiss, bacon and eggs."

"That's it," said Dave. "Make it bacon and eggs. They'll all have it. They won't know what they're eating anyway. You think you'll bring it tonight?"

"For you?" said the waiter. "For you especially. I'll even bring you a piece of pickle with it. Real sour."

"Quite a guy," said Dave as he watched him shuffle off. "Must be from the old neighborhood. A familiar mug, isn't it?"

"Familiar?" said Joe. "You mean sharp. He had it all over you that time."

"Go on," said Dave. "He wasn't all that good, was he? Hey, now, wait a minute. You're not laughing at me now?"

"I sure am," said Joe. "I like the way you're enjoying this."

"So what?" said Dave. "So what if I am? A new thing he's bringing up. There's no law against it, is there?"

"Hell, no," said Joe. "Not as far as I know. You don't think I'm criticizing you, do you? Look. Want me to let you in on a little secret? I'm enjoying it too. I like anything that turns out to be a real picnic like this."

And with that he rose to his feet as if he were deftly flinging aside a voluminous cloak, a dream, lined with satin of poppy red, as if also he were further denuding himself of a helmet into which the unseen hand of a retainer had stuck a single fluffy plume of an ostrich, rose to his full height, and bowing with a chuckle of exaggeration to that slender chick at his side whose eyes were mainly a gloss of blue, valentine eyes he had yet to fathom, asked Lee point-blank if she would condescend

102

to be clutched and whirled, to which she answered, and her pout was gorgeous, that it was about time he had asked her, she had been wondering.

What the hell, what the hell. This is becoming so clear. There are different emotions which are differently numbered, like on a carnival wheel, and there is always a man in a derby, a barker to spin it when all the nominal bets are down, and the colored bulbs, they blink as if they were breathing for the breathless, and as chance would have it, look at where she stops now, at tenderness, Joe. He begins to swing around. He looks. Of space in which to turn there is very little. But her palm is cool in his. He has sensibly waited until the wild ones on the platform had begun to wobble, to drool, subsiding with a groan into a saxophone moan of a waltz, its lyrics an ooze, rock bottom of sentimentality, but a waltz, to which to dance was still to do so with some dignity. With much of the warmth there is in pride, here she suddenly has to confess, three silver loving cups has she already won for her talent for social dancing in the past, the junior, for what she unblushingly declares to be an absolutely senior dexterity. Amazing, said Joe. With the same partner, dear? Oh, no, said Lee, with a different one each time. As her hair tickles his nose, with his lips closing in on her ear lobe, a six-footer smacks into him from behind just as he is about to nibble, to humor, to bless her. They had to hold on to each other so awkwardly, it made them feel as if they were already absolute failures in life. It seemed a strange moment for them to stumble.

"This is dangerous," said Joe, steering her so prudently now that they were just about dancing on a dime. "They'll cripple us if we don't watch out."

"Clodhoppers," said Lee.

"My, what a big word."

"Football players."

"That's better."

"Really," said Lee. "They ought to keep such oxes off the floor."

"Oxen."

"That's what I said. You know what happened to my girl friend once? And the thing is she's no dope about her feet. I mean they're trained. Hefty as she is. You know where it happened? What's the name of that dinky ballroom on Chester and Pitkin? It happened right there. The gorillas. She fell right on her, you know what. But right on it."

"Really?" said Joe. "Did she bounce?"

"It's no joke. She couldn't sit for a week."

"Well, then," said Joe. "Why dance? That's what I always say."

"Come again?"

"What sense does it make when you can be doing something else? I don't get it."

"But it's fun."

"Fun?" said Joe. "Don't tell me this is your idea of fun?"

"Why not?" said Lee. "What's yours then?"

"Ah," said Joe. "So you want to get personal?"

"I mean it," said Lee. "What do you do for kicks? Stay home and read books or something?"

"Sometimes. When they're open books like you. I see you're wearing armor. No fun in that contraption, is there?"

"No," said Lee. "This time you're right. I won't argue with you. It's just the opposite. It's torture. You don't think I really need it, do you? You know what everybody says?"

"I'm dying to hear."

"I have a figure just like Jean Harlow's."

"You have?"

"Don't you think so?"

"I'd have to get a good look first."

"Stop acting," said Lee. "You're not blind. The only difference is I wear a, you know what."

"A corset?"

"Girdle, silly."

"Ah, but she doesn't, is that it?"

"Oh, no. Not even."

"Panties?"

"I'm sure."

"Well," said Joe. "In that case, there's only one thing to do."

"Really?" said Lee. "What?"

"Get you in the movies."

"Me?" said Lee. "In the movies? You're crazy."

Movies, it was the word of words, the prime dazzler, pistol shot of the unattainable, swishy tissue paper equivalent in the 20th century of the holy grail for which she would steel herself to kiss a leper, at least once. When he said, why not, when he said that, when he said it was foolish for her not to fight to go where she could strip down freely, for was this not, he asked her, the land of opportunity where the shoulder strap is endowed with the unalienable right to slip, and keep slipping, she kept saying he was crazy, that it was good to talk about it, oh yes, but where would she get the pull? And was she good enough? What did he think? Was she really good enough? If he said yes then he was, then of course, he was crazy. But it was naked to his eye that she was panting for a lie, that she prayed he would become even crazier.

"Besides, think of it," said Lee, carried away, already face to face with a camera. "Think how it would scare me. Jesus. Can you imagine how it would scare me? Every time I think of it I get like."

"Excuse me," said Joe.

"Like jelly inside."

"I hate to interrupt you but."

"What's the matter?"

"The fairy coach has disappeared."

"Huh?"

"And there's no more music."

"Oh," said Lee. "Did it stop? I didn't hear it. When did it stop?"

"A long time ago."

"Then, then why are you still holding me?"

"I don't mind," said Joe. "Believe me, this I can do all night."

"Oh, you," said Lee. "Come on. Everybody's looking."

She giggled as he escorted her back to the table.

"Gee," she said, instinctively pouring herself a glass of beer out of the pitcher as soon as she sat herself down in the wrong chair which once had been warmed by him. "That was funny there, wasn't it? Oo this stuff is nice and cold. What was I saying? Oh, yes. It's funny sometimes what can happen to you when you get to talking. You never know. Once a gang of us were having sodas. Where was it now? I forget. Anyways, there I was sipping away at that straw. For hours I tell you, and you know why? I found out later. All that time I was talking those rotten kids were pouring. Huh? Shove over what? Oh, I'm sorry. Did you want some?"

He poured himself a full glass and downed it in one gulp. It was always such dry work listening. To a brook. Now what is a brook? A brook is a swatch of liquid material which nature, as it twitches, flips down like small change, is universally known to be smaller than a river

105

or creek, and has only one tiny duty to perform, to babble. Setting aside such a dashing definition, where have those normal hours gone when one's own conscience seemed to purl as sweetly? Fabulous or fatuous, certainly there used to be such a time. Once all were in tune, and tuned in to it, calmly listening. It seemed so then. There were searching questions asked. And there seemed to be substantial replies. She wants to sit this one out. But please consider now the newfangled, the tormenting assertion of the mouth, its static, its bombilation, its fantastic digressions, its utter selfishness. All on the Lee side of listening. Who listens to the listener now?

"You did what?" said Joe.

"I smacked him I tell you."

"Smacked him?" said Joe. "Who?"

"That poor kid. Didn't you hear me telling you? Like I said, it was on a Saturday night. I was just coming down. I remember I was wearing my new dress with the sash and ruffles for the first time, Ma had to pick up the hem, she did a wonderful job, when suddenly he grabbed me in the hallway downstairs. It's always so dark there. You know. I wanted to scream, but I couldn't. All I could do was to keep smacking him. Mamma. Such a crazy look in his eyes."

"Whose eyes?" said Joe. "Who are you talking about?"

"Teddy. From downstairs. I just told you. I mean it. I never saw hands move so fast in all my life. Imagine him trying to muss me up. It was disgusting."

"Well," said Joe. "I don't know about that."

"And then all of a sudden he stopped. Thank god, I said to myself. You have no idea how lucky I was. And then. I don't know what made me do it. It wasn't necessary. He was just standing there like a dummy, he was really a nice kid, believe me, and smart in school, with his head down. His hands too. Like they were broken. I know I shouldn't have done it, I know it, but I just couldn't help myself being so excited and all. I spit in his face, I'm ashamed to tell you, and whacked him right on the ear with all I had. He almost fell. I was surprised myself. I shook my finger at him, just like I'm showing you, and told him that the next time I'd have to call a cop, I'd have to, did he hear me? Oh, no, it was enough. I tell you I couldn't walk in or out of the house without him running after me with his tongue hanging out a mile, telling me I was poetry, that I was beautiful like Helen from somewhere, that he loved

106

me with all his being, and even more, and all that kind of junk. Twice I just had to go down and tell his mother to make him stop it. He was only fifteen. She could control him. Her poor little orphan. Sure. But you think it helped? All she could do was blow her nose in her apron. She even began to call me names. Imagine. You saw what happened. It was in all the papers."

"What papers?" said Joe. "Look, kiddo, I'm afraid I'm a little lost here. Do you mind beginning again from the beginning? You just said something happened. What happened?"

"Why, he killed himself."

"Killed himself?" said Joe.

"That's right. That very same night. Took the gas. Put his curly little head right in the oven. You don't know his old lady, do you? Well, comes Saturday night, she doesn't give a damn, she's got to go to the movies or she'll die. The movies. That's her whole life. So he was all alone in the house. The poor kid. He left me a note. I'll show it to you. It's in my bag somewhere. Begging me to forgive him. Swearing he was going to love me beyond the grave, or something like that. I'm surprised. Didn't you read about it in the Daily News? It was in the Mirror too. Didn't you even see my picture there?"

"Hey, now," said Joe. "Wait a minute. What kind of a story is this?"

"It's the god's honest truth," said Lee. "I swear it. You can ask Honey here. She'll tell you. Hey. What are you eating there?"

"A sandwich," said Honey. "What do you think?"

"A sandwich?" said Lee. "Are the sandwiches here already? That's funny. I never saw them come. When did they come?"

"While you were killing him," said Joe, lighting up a cigarette without once removing his eyes from her. "You never see anything, do you?"

"What?" said Lee. "I didn't get that."

"That's all right," said Joe. "I didn't expect you to."

"Huh?" said Lee. "Oh, well. I don't know about you, but I'm starved."

"Goody, goody."

"Um," said Lee. "It looks terrific, doesn't it?"

All pearly were the choppers she bared a second before she plunged them into the bacon fried with eggs into a cake overlapping, tearing off a sizable half-moon, chewing it blissfully like a truly adept and

107

unabashed destroyer of flesh, like such a frank lover of it that it was clear she did not care whether it was tasty or tender or not, whether it was mingled with fat or lean, or interlarded with lettuce, or smeared with butter, or impounded in her quaffing mouth with beer, or merely with spittle, or a whitening paste of bread.

"What's the matter?" said Lee, poised to devour her second half. "Aren't you going to eat?"

Joe shook his head.

"No," he said. "I'll just watch you."

"Don't be silly," said Lee. "It's good."

He pushed his plate until it clunked against hers.

"Then take it," he said.

"You mean that?"

"I'll have it notarized."

"Wait a minute," said Honey. "That's not fair. Give me half."

"Oh, no," said Lee. "Why should I? He gave it to me, didn't he?"

"Sure," said Honey. "But you don't have to be such a pig about it, do you?"

"A pig," said Lee. "Look who's talking."

"Come on," said Honey. "Hand it over."

"Okay," said Lee. "Here. If you want it that bad."

"Thanks," said Honey. "Thanks for the fingerprints."

"His pickle," said Belle. "Has anybody touched his pickle yet?"

Were these the baby monsters Mr. Colish meant when, with the heartburn scorching him alive after witnessing that booby parade, he had warned him that he would be consumed if he scorned their union and drastically seceded, that it would be the likes of them who would consume him first? Very possibly so. Both funny and faithful, Eddie and Dave banged their plates and begged him not to be so cool about letting them touch his, easy, now, men. There must be better jokes somewhere. So let us not roll in the aisles yet.

The fanfare startled him. But he immediately smiled. For it seemed to him that this raw flourish, this fresh assault mostly drum had been born out of an umbilical sympathy of the band with his own high-handed and hoity-toity nose. He screwed his chair around to watch. The lights did not dim. Out dashed an eyesore. So like a passion flower was his paper boutonniere that he must tattoo the air in his transit with hand kisses and trace in addition telepathic ones out of

108

eyes shockingly magnetic. Plastered to his peruke with a fresh layer of grease paint caked over the cracked one he had slept in, he pitched his voice as high as the average shriek in a petticoat to greet the ladies, and the drips they had dragged in with them, the dear brutes. What was with him? Some men will imitate a dog to make a dollar. This one, he made like a pansy, and so well, he might as well be one.

So bring on the girls. Anything for a change. And give them a great big hand, the usual, please. Chorus of miscellaneous tits and navels, haggard eight, garbed as fairies were never, the eight comrades, each gripping a wand tipped with a rhinestone star, one broke off and fell, and griping in general about a great day not coming, they brought it on themselves, their goatlike legs assuming delight, their nipples full to false bursting. What a bust. It was yoohoo and yipee out of a boorish customer who swore he recognized one, look everybody, his gramma. Of the eight, four had fangs, so they bared them. Has-beens are not lucky, are they? If they were, they would cease to feel, would then be deaf to the aspersions, to the scurrilities of a dunce. As it is, in this, their boiling trouble, their frisks and leaps were executed as if to pipes and timbrels unheard, so cripes, they completely lost the beat. So they tried to form a line to see if they could somehow, impromptu-like, kick their way out of it together, but some kicked to the left, as some had to do, and others to the right, and right here another paying original motioned wildly he had enough, give those lumpy legs the hook. So they broke ranks and ran off. So it is back to the apple stand, sister, to flaming bunions, to further stoning, to surreptitious vomiting in the toilet sink. These days, these days. What is it that does not cataclysmically turn over in these days of gruel on gruel, and insufficient grace? What did this clot of cheapskates want for their two bits? More blood?

So all right. So why not. So out comes Yvette, baby, the blooming stripper. All eyes scuttle like mice over the bouncing section, the juicy-looking pumpkins of her body to which a slinky evening outfit cunningly devised to be dropped in a jiffy still clings, while this lady in red prances around in vassalage to her elementals like a very proud pussy, there is a naive question to be answered, to wit, how does she manage to live through the day? Around her Cleopatra orbs especially, she looks so anciently dead. Can it be she does not hear how they howl at her to take it off? She stares and acts as if it is in one ear and out the other. Has she then only sawdust upstairs? What about that fagot left out in the rain, that charred stump of hers, her mythical brain? Is it permanently impaired? In order to be a firebrand in the flesh, has she so neglected it that it has silently smoked itself out? Yet watch how. Watch how, in spite of all, instinct directs her so perfectly to incite the coolest imagination to flare up, to feel hot in the pants, how this heiress of the historic seven veils sheds the modern versions one by one, how she highheels it this way and that, never still to shield, to let them peep at her mile-high paps, fat crease of her powdered fanny, how suddenly, to wow them, she rips off her gauzy loin cloth, and stands revealed.

Insufferably green and shiny is the mascara on this cock-teaser in her grimy fig leaf as first she wiggles, then she thrusts, bringing it closer, pumping and pumping her hips, and crash, she bumps it, she bumps it right in his face. O baby. Why deny it? This is the real stuff. Come to think of it, what does a ballerina do that it is thought to be so beautiful? She is a pallid verb. She pirouettes, disciplines her ecstasy to such a remarkable degree it is aimless, noiselessly straddles the idea, twitters when seized with the animal in her, keeps translating a frilly dismay and fright, throws her whole soul into flight, and if she has orgasms, has only dainty ones, off stage. He jumped up. He found himself on his feet. The drums were murderous like Yvette's twot. Do it, do it. Hey, cried his tablemates. Wait a minute, they cried. Where could he be going, right in the middle of this?

Why, to tear his honey, his own Rosalie no less, out of her tear-stained sleep, perhaps, or her still turbulent, or her finally tedious, sleeplessness. Fortunately he had the right change. He held the door of the telephone booth partly open, while he waited for his call to go through. When the ringing began, he shut himself in, and counted. Death rattles, in the middle of the seventh ring, a screaming midget intervened with a hundred hellos, first choking, then juggling the receiver for at least an hour, without exaggeration. There was a noise like mayhem, with the weekly murder in view, in that merry hangout for bummers, in that sloppy candy store, across from her sullen house, right on the corner which was as sacred as it was sullied to every scuffler belonging to it.

"No, no," he began to shout. "I'm not saying hell. I'm saying Heller, you dope. Want me to spell it out for you? What? Well, then, close your damn door there, and you'll hear better. Okay now? What? Of course I'm still here. Where the hell do you think I would go? Yeah, that's right. It's right across the street on the second floor. I said the second. Got it now? Yeah, Rosalie Heller. Oh, so now you know who I mean. You're pretty smart, aren't you? What? What do you mean what do I want? Call her to come down, stupid. And make it snappy. What? Sure, I'll wait. Jesus. There's a brilliant kid for you."

No doubt in days of old, a knight-errant was bolder, and luckier with the lance at piercing an enchantment, of fairly plundering of its life a dragon with a fiery tongue a league long, or a two-headed giant with garlic on his double-breath, or a whole lake of moiling crocodiles, or a mere East Side kid of insignificant stature, with a tough muzzle, stuffed ears, and an impenetrable head. Or was this nothing-comes-easy true for everybody today? He was listening. But not a decent word could be heard in answer, only the sea hum of the receiver which seemed to draw him downwards into the mortification of an aquarium, with indirect lighting, so that any idle bozo could flatten his nose against the glass to gawk at him as if he were a gaping, soundless, tail-propelled fish, the perennial sucker.

Fishy Pinkus. Somehow he remembered. That was his name. For he had been a fishman, with a scaly song in him too in his sober days. Rosalie had seen it all from her perch at the window. She had told Joe. That day Mr. Pinkus, a dumpy neighborhood drunk, had laid himself down like a log against the lamppole, the bay rum working nicely in his belly, his cold nose clogged, snoring away at the sky which, in its confusion, was full of scattered clouds rather than random benedictions. Now it so happened that all the littler boys on the block were attracted to Fishy's serenade, and they gathered around him. After a while, when they had ascertained, by standing on his stomach, that Pinkus was not dead yet, they were so put out that the biggest among them declared that he was tempted to pee on him. No sooner dared than done, and the hand-directed jet was dispatched with derisive skill out of the classic stance. Soused and doused as he was, Pinkus, feeling warm all over, struggled to sit up, to the queer pubescence of the pleasure he felt, and at last did so, looking like an odd ocean creature washed ashore on a tropical beach, with eyes like pin points in his sheepish map. The kids had a fit. They scalped his bliss. What was this on him? Piss?

111

Oh, summer carp and yellow pike, the detestable life that was his, with what could he wipe himself, with what? He seemed almost like a man as he wept. Oh, it was so heartbreaking, Rosalie said, that she flew downstairs in her plain housedress, without thinking. The kids ran from her. What the hell was it her business anyway? Please, Mr. Pinkus, be a man. But even when she managed to help him to his feet, he was inconsolable, so in desperation, she said, here, here is a quarter, feel better now? God knows how it came to be in her pocket. Stop it, stop it now, she had to say, for he was trying to kiss her. Is it guilt? Is it out of fear of being accused? Or is it solely for the sake of self-exaltation that coins are placed on the eyelids of the dead? If he could not kiss her, then he swore he had to do a dance for her. She backed away. For this, he yelped like a man who is plumb loco, this was the easiest quarter he had ever made, that nothing, he begged her to join him in a jig, nothing had ever come easier. She just ran away from him. What else could she do? She simply went back to find another soft chocolate, and to finish painting her nails.

"Ah," said Joe. "So there you are."

But she could hardly hear him through the crackles.

"Hello?" she said. "Who is this?"

"Me," said Joe. "Don't you recognize my voice?"

"What?" said Rosalie. "You'll have to speak a little louder."

"I am goddamn it."

"Get away, you tramp."

"What?"

"Not you. He keeps banging on the door. I'll kill him. Hello? Who did you say you were?"

"I didn't."

"Who?"

"I said it's me, Joe."

"Oh," said Rosalie. "Joe. Where are you? I'm so glad. Are you all right?"

"What?" said Joe. "Damn it. Now I can't hear anything."

"I said there's nothing wrong, is there?"

"Oh, no. Why should there be? I was just thinking of you, that's all."

"You were what?" said Rosalie. "You sound like a million miles away."

"I am," said Joe. "I'm way out here in the wilds of Long Island somewhere."

"Long Island?" said Rosalie. "What are you doing there?"

"I'll be damned if I know. I didn't pull you out of bed, did I?"

"Oh, no," said Rosalie. "I wasn't sleeping. I was reading. You know. That book you gave me. I'm surprised at you."

"You are? Why?"

"Because it's so dirty."

"Don't be silly. What's dirty about it?"

"All them words. My, my. I didn't think they allowed it."

"Well," said Joe. "The truth's the truth. What can you do about it?"

"Yes," said Rosalie. "But which truth? That's the point. Are you having fun? Who are you with there?"

"Oh," said Joe. "You know. Eddie, Dave. You know."

"Is she nice?"

"Who?"

"Yours."

"Oh," said Joe. "She's kind of interesting."

"That's good."

"You know something? Men kill themselves over her."

"Really?"

"I mean high-school boys. Smaller trophies, you know. I meant to ask you. Has it ever happened to you? I understand it's very romantic."

"Romantic," said Rosalie. "Huh. Don't worry, my boy. You're not getting away with it so easy. I still think you're a louse."

"At least you're thinking."

"I mean it, Joe. Like today with Mr. Colish. When I think what you did, my god."

"What?" said Joe. "Hello? Another goddamn dime. I better hang up. It's costing me. Wait a second. When I think of it. Boy. How can one guy be so dumb? I'm telling you. If only I could feel just one thing at a time. And know what I was feeling. Christ. What a relief that would be. You would see me jumping for joy. But you know me. I'm like, you know what. I'm all over the place."

"But why?" said Rosalie. "Why should that be?"

"Why," said Joe. "That's another question."

"It seems so simple to me. Have you got a cold? You sound like you have a cold. You haven't got one of your headaches, have you?"

113

"No, no."

"You're like a baby too sometimes, you know that? You never care what you do. Why didn't you stay home? Why do you go out when you feel this way?"

"Because I like to give myself a hard time, that's why."

"Then go a little further," said Rosalie. "And get on your horse and come see me tomorrow."

"No."

"I'll talk to you like a mother."

"That's what I'm afraid of."

"Like a sister then."

"What for? I already have one."

"Okay, then, I'll force myself on you. Like a sweetheart. How's that?"

"Great," said Joe. "Only you know. When I say no, it's no. You know why I hate to come to your house on Sunday."

"Don't worry. I'll get rid of them somehow."

"Please, Rosalie. Why do you want to make a pest of yourself?"

"A pest of myself?" said Rosalie. "Ye gods. Like you say. I ought to have my head examined. What's got into me anyway? There's at least a million guys chasing after me, and I let you kick me around this way. But, oh, boy, you wait. One of these days. I'm warning you. I'm going to leave you flat."

"On this world which is so round. Aren't you clever?"

"But flat," said Rosalie. "You'll see."

"I'll see you on Monday. That's what I'll see."

"Goodbye."

"Always threatening."

"Didn't you hear me? I said goodbye."

"There's no talking to you, is there? What do you want me to do? Get gooey with you?"

"Why not?"

"You want me to say I love you?"

"Do you?"

"Yes, damn it."

"I love you too."

"Good," said Joe.

"Without the damn it."

114

"Better yet," said Joe.

"I do, Joe. I really do."

"Fine," said Joe. "I'm glad to hear it. Now we can really say good-bye."

O love. O bucking bronco. Where are the tenderhearted? Is every tenderfoot of a listener-in truly disturbed? If Joe must say goodbye, why must he say it in such an abrupt and brutal way? See with what rhetorical strides he makes the return trip to his table, this rascal inbitten and unripe, this rogue who is, in this attenuated chapter of his life, wholly in the clutches of the rambling and the picaresque. How now? Has he not an ounce of romance in him? Does he not assign to love the sound of a muffled cooing behind an ivy-clad wall? Does he wait upon the tinny bell in the tower? Is it for him that it rintintins, that the clapper begins its cool dry kissing? Does he unlatch? Does he tiptoe? Does he climb the brick? He does not, and will not tamper with the latticework, or tempt the too-willing with a mere card of lace, or lavaliere, or appear seriously in long hose, or utter that nanny goat quaver, or lend his fleetness to any such lily-white excursions where love is that much flummery, where the truth about it, like his sandwich, is playfully smutched before it is shamelessly devoured.

What then is love? What is it really? A melange of sacred and lunatic connotations? A martyrdom? A universal hangover? What has caused its sanctity to strip a gear? What has thrown its good strong spine so out of kilter? Intravenous injections of the submissive tang of berries? Merely the insincerity of the screwy language which everyone is taught to tie to its tail? Love itself is lovesick. And its frantic signaling goes on and on, with all sorts of lanterns, flags, and oscillating arms. The poor dear thing, who will be the first to save it from its tin-can existence?

"Not me," said Joe. "You've got the wrong guy."

"Wrong guy, hell," said Dave. "What were you trying to do? Run out on us?"

"Look, my friend," said Joe. "Let's get this straight. When the hell did I ever do anything like that?"

"Never," said Dave. "But the way you've been acting lately, who knows?"

"The way I've been acting?"

"Where the hell were you so long?"

115

"I went to make a call. Is that okay with you?"

"Ah," said Dave. "So that's it. So tell me now. How's the dear little thing?"

"What thing?" said Joe.

"I'm really interested."

"I just had a little business there, that's all."

"Ship ahoy," said Dave. "There she blows again. Did you all hear what he calls it? Bejazus, I sure would like to take a peek at that little business of yours."

"You will."

"When?"

"When, he says. What's the use of showing a bum like you? You wouldn't see it if it was right in front of your nose."

"Say," said Lee. "He's not going steady, is he?"

"I don't know," said Eddie. "You better ask him. All we know is he's sure going. Steady or otherwise."

"Well," said Joe. "What am I supposed to say to that? Oh, yeah?"

"I didn't know you had a girl friend," said Lee.

"You got nothing on me," said Joe. "I didn't know it either."

"Well," said Honey. "I can tell you this, Valentino. You almost lost this one."

"Really?" said Joe.

"That's right," said Belle. "You really missed something. You should've seen that gink go to work. I thought for a second there he sure was going to beat your time."

"Gosh," said Joe. "That would've been just awful."

"Oh," said Lee. "Don't listen to her. It was nothing at all. If he wasn't so high, he would've never had the nerve to come over."

"The blonde boy?" said Joe. "Was he pie-eyed?"

"Oh, boy, was he."

"That's too bad," said Joe. "Somebody ought to tell him. He'll spoil his good looks if he keeps that up."

"But how did you know?"

"Know what?"

"That it was him."

"Oh," said Joe. "Who else would it be? I remember. I had a lot of fun watching him while we were in that jam on the floor. He was trying so hard to give you the eye, I thought any minute he'd drop dead, or have a fit or something."

"Did he? I mean was he? I mean I didn't know that."

"You sound sorry."

"Me?" said Lee. "Don't be silly. Why should I be sorry?"

"Well," said Joe. "Who knows? He might've been the answer to your dream."

"Oh, my," said Lee. "You don't really like me, do you?"

"Don't like you?" said Joe. "How can you say that? Why, in another minute, I'll be crazy about you. That's what always happens, doesn't it?"

"Ah," said Lee. "That's not fair. Now you're making fun of me."

"Hey, Joe," said Eddie.

"Yes?" said Joe.

"You want to see something clever?"

"Here?" said Joe. "Is that possible?"

"Come on, Honey," said Eddie. "Show him that cute trick of yours with the fingers."

"No," said Honey. "I know him. He'll think it's dumb."

"No, he won't. What're you talking about? Don't say you know him when you don't. Come on, sweetheart. I'd do it myself. Only you know me. I'm sure to kill it."

"Well, well," said Joe. "What do you know? They're friends again. Now I'm sure I'll be able to sleep tonight. You see, kiddies? It never pays to get angry, does it?"

"We weren't angry," said Honey. "Not really. Were we, Eddie?"

"Naa," said Eddie. "I don't even remember what it was all about. Come on, kiddo, do it again. Maybe he'll break out into a smile."

"Look," said Joe. "You're very kind. All of you. But if you're down to doing tricks with your fingers, I have a suggestion to make."

"What?" said Eddie.

"Let's get the hell out of here."

He raised an autocratic finger for the check, as if to prove he was the only one qualified to become the boss of the show, and only he could terminate this gross happening in their lives, this gruesome stay of theirs at Grassy Point Inn.

They sure gave it to him with the glares as they groped again for the same positions in the same old car. Somehow the whole soulful group resented the shabby physical fact of Becky as a clearly shameful change of scene. The car was bad because it was springless, because it squealed and rattled, and otherwise sinned. The car was good because it made a

117

wind. With his lap burdened as before with Lee's solid biscuits, Joe sniffed frankly to show them what to do, fresh air, men, breathe it, snuff it in. But they merely sniffed at it as if to say, it is all yours, son, you can have it. So the weatherman had been right in his bold prediction for tonight. It had become decidedly cooler.

What is it that makes us so perverse? Think of the middle of the night. It is then that we begin to know what we really are, what we really long for, and how wildly we wish for it. The contrapuntal cat, cowering in the courtyard, wails with us, stretching its whiskers, performing on a purer gut. The moon serenely guards the fishbones. The toilet is flushed for us next door. There are other angry noises. And a sudden scuttling. And more and more, as we use both hands to hold off sleep which threatens to throttle us, we deepen the plot, we perfect it, evil us, and with a final twist of the bedclothes, we kill. We mercilessly annihilate each other.

Hey, said Joe. He had to try to get around them somehow. Look at that glorious sky out there. But still they snubbed him. People are cut to a crude pattern. People collect. People pile on each other rudely. But the moon is decent, exemplary disc, tactfully exercising its magnetic pull at a distance. And no matter which way the big dipper swings, it remains a polite and heavenly formation of stars. And no one in this freewheeling country is more privileged than the man who is able to commune so perfectly with such dandy things.

But communion with the celestial, if carried too far, distracts a man from his boyish desire to compose his body upon the earth in a sybaritic posture alongside a girl whose mind has quietly edged out of the harbor and sailed away, whose rib-covered heart tugs at its anchor, divinely prepared to receive its full quota of pleasure, and whose instinct, without fret or undue frivolity, is ripe to roll over for that ordinary and extraordinary frolic of the flesh, be it where the sea adjoins, or where the land intrudes.

Now it so happened that Becky suddenly stalled at the last red light she had to obey on Sutter. Whereupon Eddie and Joe were ordered to creep out and push her. And they had to do it for almost a whole block and a half before Becky came to herself again, acknowledging their valiant efforts to revive her by backfiring violently in their faces. They cheered like mad as they scrambled in again. And some of the ice was broken. And some of it was smoothed away.

Thus simple souls combine to cradle hands and skim along together for the sake of their common safety. And since the Rifkin house was now only a matter of a minute or so away, Joe flattened himself on Lee, boldly reversing their positions, asking her to make believe he was her baby. She groaned under his novel weight, what a bony child, but tried to make him more comfortable, smiling at his childish strategy, freeing a hand, quick with mother instinct, to pat and pinch his approaching cheek. He made various contented noises as he nuzzled in her neck. She complained he was tickling. He slowed down the next second as much as he could before he brought his blame-seeking lips, which had traveled so intelligently over one side of her face, to rest very lightly on her sinfully full and fully sustaining mouth. He felt how well it knew how to fasten itself to his, and against his to flutter.

Hello, little house, sang the Rifkin sisters, grateful and childlike ritualists. Shack so memorable with so much risibility beneath its skin of wood, sheltering that iron bed on which both had been born, bounced so neatly out upon a giddy and adoring world, see how old-fashioned, see how asleep. Giggling behind a web of fingers and lifting their shapely legs to an infectious height, they led the rest onto the porch, shushing them all elaborately, acting as divining rods to locate three wicker chairs on which they could tangle and creak for a sweet little session of gitchy before saying goodnight, dear, sleep tight.

She pushed his hand away from there once. She pushed it away twice.

"Ah, well," said Joe, frankly making a nest for his head on her chest where it was softest. "I like you anyway. At least you're nice and warm."

"That's your fault. What time is it?"

"Who cares?"

"Ah," said Lee. "That hurts, you know that?"

"Where?" said Joe. "Show me."

"Listen to that dog. Is he sick or something?"

"I bet you're the youngest in the family."

"Look," said Lee. "You musn't. Give me your hand."

"No big brothers I hope?"

"You want me to be afraid of you?"

"God forbid."

119

"Then give me. Let me hold it."

"Okay," said Joe. "Here. Anything to be sociable."

"Honey told me that Eddie told her you work on a newspaper."

"I do?" said Joe. "On which corner?"

"You don't?"

"Hell, no. I'm sorry to disappoint you, kiddo, but I'm just a plain old shipping clerk, that's all."

"Oh," said Lee. "That's all right. I'm not disappointed. I had an idea it was only a line. You know something? I'm a pretty good book-keeper."

"Gosh, what do you do with all those buttons?"

"And I know a little steno too."

"Do they all work? Or are they mostly decoration?"

"You think you can get me a job? At your place I mean."

"Me?" said Joe. "Get you a job?"

"You see?" said Lee. "I'm not ashamed to ask. I'd ask a street cleaner if I thought it'd do any good. My father thinks I'm dumb or a cripple or something. He won't even look at me any more. He had it good once. His own business. In woolens. Now he has to grub for someone else. For practically nothing. I suppose that's my fault too. You know what he wants now? He wants my kid brother to take out working papers. My mother fights with him about it all the time. Where's your place? I mean. I hope it's a big one."

"Jesus," said Joe. "You have no idea how funny this is."

"I'd take anything, Joe. I really would."

"Ah," said Joe. "It's not really all that bad, is it?"

"Will you ask for me? Will you find out?"

"Say," said Dave. "What are those two mumbling about?"

"Leave them alone," said Belle.

"They bother me."

"Me too," said Eddie. "I can't concentrate."

"Quiet," said Belle. "You want to wake my father up?"

"He's quiet," said Honey. "It's those other two."

"Yeah," said Eddie. "It's annoying. Ask them to speak a little louder. Maybe we'll be able to hear what they're saying."

"Now, look," said Belle. "Don't be so nosy. They're all right. You just go back to what you're doing."

"With pleasure," said Eddie.

"And me?" said Dave.

"The same goes for you too."

"Let's go in the house."

"No."

"Why not?" said Dave. "I'm sick of this. What's so precious about the house? Is it any different than the clubroom? A couch is a couch."

"Are you off your nut?" said Belle.

"What are you afraid of? We can be quiet."

"Shut up. And don't you ever talk to me about the house again, you hear me?"

"Okay, boss, okay."

"There's a friend for you," said Joe.

"Who?" said Lee.

"Belle."

"Oh."

"Did you hear that?" said Joe. "She's trying to wish me on you. That's a laugh. How about your father's place? Have you tried the agencies?"

"Oh, sure," said Lee. "Every day."

"And now you're trying me. Holy mackerel."

"Why not? What've I got to lose?"

"Christ almighty," said Joe. "I tell you, kid, I'm the bottom of the barrel. It's no use."

"Why? Can't you do anything?"

"Where do you live?"

"Can't you even try?"

"Come on," said Joe. "I'll take you home."

"Oh," said Lee. "You don't have to. I'm sleeping here."

"Good," said Joe. "In that case. Look, you're not angry, are you?"

"Oh, no. Why should I be? I have no right to bother you."

"Sure you have."

"No, no, I understand."

"But you have," said Joe. "Goddamn it, can't you see? It's me, Lee. I have no right to be so helpless. Do you mind? I'd like to get up."

"Why? Just because I asked you?"

"No, no," said Joe. "That's not it at all. Let's break it up. I've had enough for one night."

"Well," said Lee. "That's a nice way to leave me."

121

"I'm sorry. It's just that. You heard Dave. I'm getting sick of this too."

"Sick of what?"

"This. This fooling around. This waste of time."

"Waste of time?" said Lee. "What did you expect?"

"Everything. Of course."

"Oh, now, look."

"What's the matter?" said Joe. "Didn't you ever hear anyone say that before?"

"You're terrible, really. Where did you ever get the idea I was such a pushover? What a nerve. What did you expect me to do the first night?"

"What you might do the second. What's the difference?"

"What's the difference?" said Lee. "Listen how he's insulting me."

"I am?" said Joe. "Then I apologize."

"You better, believe me."

"Of course," said Joe. "Why should I want to insult you? You're a good girl, Lee. I know that. Either way, you would still be."

"Please," said Lee. "I don't want to hear anything more about it."

"Right," said Joe. "I agree."

"I hear enough about it as it is. Wherever I go. Day and night. Honestly. I'm disappointed in you."

"That's all right. You're not the only one."

"Really," said Lee. "I thought you were different. Is that what you think too? Is that all I'm good for? Talk about being disgusted. Is that the only reason why I was born? Are you like that nutty kid too?"

"That's right, Lee, give me hell, give me hell."

"My god," said Lee. "Why is that damn dog howling?"

"Where?" said Joe. "I don't hear it."

"I'm trying to remember," said Lee. "I'm sure I've been nice. Haven't I been nice to you all evening?"

"You've been a doll."

"Then why does it have to end this way? You're smart. Tell me. Why is it nothing good ever happens to me? Why is it always happening to somebody else? Oh, I know. You don't have to tell me. I know what's going to happen now. I'll never see you again."

"Maybe," said Joe. "Maybe not. Who knows? Why worry about it? Maybe tomorrow you'll meet a gentleman instead of a bum. Pray. That always helps."

"Oh, sure," said Lee. "I'll pray all right. But it'll be for you."

"Thank you," said Joe. "I'll always be grateful to you for that. Oops. Up we go. Don't fall now. Your pocketbook, my dear. Why do you look at me that way? I wasn't going to steal it. Don't look so sad. You're lucky to get rid of me. Okay, fellas, this is it. Look at that. She won't even shake hands with me. Ah, well. I'll just have to try to learn how to live with it. What can I do?"

Pernicious worser half, habitual transgressor against all hoary transactions and rectitudes, collect the boys and scoot, twirl again the fickle weathercock of the imagination, that gilded rooster with the hackles up, crowing against the female winds, frozen in iron as it is, defiantly. But like each and every wronged one, and deserted one, this lost one, Lee, will prey upon his mind with the shy and mysterious movements of the badger, and the more he pleads innocent, the more will she be transformed into raw and malefic conjunctions of bird and beast, grow the brow of a frog, the great claw of the lobster, the distensible gular pouch of the pelican, the incombustible toe of the salamander, be toad, viper, spider, cockatoo, and cockatrice, and no warning, glide in and out of the foggy orifices inside with the sinister composure of a swan. The nerve of whatever. Was there ever such a screwy animal? The moment he suffers a revulsion, he has to spit it out upon this rocky pellet of a world, pelting it good before it could pelt him. As if this whole whimpering globe were on its knees, begging him to give it his tortured and loathsome contribution to the woeful history of its ululations and ailments, and the fabulous zoology of its guilt.

"You know something?" said Dave, the moment they found themselves alone. "You sure can be a polite bastard. You know that, don't you?"

"Oh, sure," said Joe. "I have no use for any other kind."

He paused on the sidewalk to peer down the street.

"Let me see now," he said.

"Christ," said Eddie. "You sure gave that kid a real good going over, didn't you?"

"Yeah," said Dave. "What the hell did you have against her anyway?"

"Oh," said Joe. "Nothing unmentionable, I assure you. How about this ash can here? Would you fellows like to join me in a very necessary little operation?"

123

"Gosh, yes," said Eddie. "I've been holding it in so long, I'm ready to bust."

"Aie," said Dave. "Now that I think of it, it's been killing me too."

"Then gather around, boys," said Joe. "Hey, not so close. Let's try to keep dry if we can. Now if anyone comes along, you guys know what to do, don't you? Whistle."

The ashes absorbed a great deal of the noise.

"Jesus," said Joe, buttoning up. "I feel like a new man."

"Sure," said Dave. "You always do after you make a woman bawl, don't you?"

"Hey, hey," said Joe. "Look who's talking. You're just dying for me to tell you all about it, aren't you? Well, son, I'll tell you what. You buy me a good hot pastrami sandwich, and I'll give it to you straight. How about that?"

"Right," said Eddie. "I'm for that."

"You are?" said Dave. "Then you pay for it."

"Okay, okay," said Eddie. "You're not scaring me. All you have to do is get us there. If that goddamn jalopy of yours will ever make it."

"Don't worry," said Dave. "It'll make it, it'll make it. I can tell you one thing right now. It's got more sense than the both of you put together."

"Listen to that," said Eddie. "What's he so sore about?"

"Wait a second," said Joe. "You sit in the middle this time."

"Come on," said Dave. "Get in, get in."

"Yes, sir," said Joe. "I'd be very glad to do so, sir. It sure is nice to hear so much love in a voice."

So the prying is not over yet. So this squeezer, Dave, this dumb and self-elected judge, bereft of robe, mace, periwig, gavel, or glasses, was driving him as furiously as he could straight to Dworkin's, a sawdust-strewn oasis in the dead of night, as if he had decided to hold court there, with a mustard pot for inkstand, and greasy lips for hear ye, hear ye. What gall there was in that, that Dave too should imagine he was his keeper, that he was strong enough to stuff Joe into a mirthless cell of spiceless morality as smooth and tight as a sausage skin. It is a fact. The habit of living is long, but longer yet is the yen for persecution. That never seems to rest.

Strange how the store lights resist. They have become so peculiarly yellow. They are like city nerves in the flesh in their idiotic loyalty to wakefulness, and the drowsier they get, the more hectically they seem

124

to blaze. With no pity for what is replaceable, Dworkin greets the three old customers with his changelessly dewy grunt. His fingers like frankfurters are curfewless. He frankly advertises his obscene apron and his fat-obsessed belly beneath it. His face is as hard as knucklewurst from munching on his own provisions like a clever Maccabean. He fills their orders with evil ease and vast suspicion. It is past two in the morning, and no one is next. He folds his arms and watches them eat with eyes the color of the slithery marble of his table tops. When will a bull say boo to him? Or she who snores in the back room on a cot, his bulldozed wife? When will time say when? When will Clarkson and 93rd see the last of him?

These sullen and expendable brutes, present company not excluded, they are enough to give a normal body the staggers, as they relish the glut of a hot dog with sauerkraut on top of a hot pastrami sandwich. Blindman Dave, blunt coadventurer, reduced to a venial killer-diller tonight, he scorns the sugar bowl to squeeze a thick slice of lemon into a second glass of tea, pondering the while, agitating the concoction with his spoon, waiting for his pals to speak, so that he could lace it into them with a wholly embittered tongue. Who would believe that he is devoured by a lust for which he would gladly swallow his gutturals, knowing well what they symbolize, and even the skin of little mice and flies? Thick-lipped and thick-lidded, who would think that the dazzling picket fence of his teeth has long been in the grip of a glorious service, that of nibbling at any handy tit of sufferable size? Sweet allayer of the quotidian fits of the famished other sex, his mimic battles with some of the dim victims have been monstrous, but he will always hark back to the harlotry of the recumbent moments which have been devoid of such a shameful din, which had been more hushed, more sanitary, and most of all more saccharine.

"Tell me," said Joe. "You think you'll ever amount to anything?"

"I beg your pardon?" said Dave.

"You think this goddamn night will ever end? Who wants a cigarette?"

"Me," said Eddie. "Since it's for nothing."

"Hell," said Dave. "Let's have one too. Maybe I'll get a little pleasure out of it."

"Pleasure," said Joe. "Now don't tell me. Let me guess. Where did I ever hear you say that before?"

125

"I always say it," said Dave. "Trying to be funny? I always say. Why the hell not? At least it's something to live for."

"Terrific," said Eddie. "The man's positively brilliant tonight, ain't he?"

"And so disgusted," said Joe. "Look at that puss, will you?"

"Sure," said Dave. "Sure I'm disgusted."

"That's the ticket," said Joe. "Now you're talking. What in the hell took you so long?"

"Because I was trying to be kind to you, that's why."

"Look, son," said Joe. "Why don't you get wise to yourself? You're a big boy now. How long do you think you can go on fooling around this way? Answer me that."

"Well," said Dave. "Listen to Papa talking. First he ruins the evening."

"Who ruined what evening?"

"And now he's going to give us a lecture on it."

"Hell," said Joe. "It was ruined before we even got started."

"Aw, now," said Eddie. "Why don't you guys cut it out? It wasn't that bad, was it? We had some fun, didn't we? What the hell. We always manage to have fun, don't we?"

"That's right," said Joe. "Talk yourself into it, sweetheart. As for me. Watch me raise my right hand. I swear off. I've had enough of this same stupid business over and over again. Maybe I'm wrong. But there must be something else a guy can do on a Saturday night. And I'll be damned if I don't find out."

"Swell," said Dave. "Let us know when you do. Who left this puddle here? But I can tell you one thing right now."

"Tell, tell. I can hardly wait."

"You'll find yourself in bed all alone with yourself one of these days. That's what you'll find out."

"Really?" said Joe. "Then I look forward to it."

"Do that," said Dave. "Prove to us you're really off your rocker. It'll make us all feel very happy. Except the women, of course. Ah, by the way. You said you'd tell us. What happened between you two on the porch?"

"Nothing," said Joe. "Absolutely nothing. I just asked her how about it, and she said no, that's all."

"What the hell did you expect?"

126

"That's what she said. Damn it, now that I think of it, it was a damn good idea. Think of all the time I saved. Who's got a pencil here? I must make a note of it. Congratulate me, boys. I just thought of it. I got myself a new policy."

"It'll lapse," said Eddie. "Don't worry."

"In the pig's eye," said Joe. "From now on, it's either yes or no. Just like that. What do you think of it, men? It's not exactly original. But it sure makes sense, no?"

"Ah," said Dave. "That's the way it goes. All my hard work gone to hell. You dirty rat. Is that what I taught you?"

"No, master, just the opposite. But you can take that, that diploma of yours and stick it."

"Thanks. I'll try to find room for it."

"Yes, sir. I'm graduating anyway."

"Good," said Dave. "Wonderful. But to what?"

"To what?" said Joe.

He looked around sharply, shifted, shoved himself back from the table, scratched his head, and suddenly grinned.

"Well, now," he said. "There you got me."

They roared. They pounded each other and pointed at him. What a comedian. Their laughter was extreme, as crazy and prolonged as the laughter in a dream when, just before the end, the terrific deadlock it has so beautifully built up is suddenly shattered, and the tears come, as their many tears came now, out of gratitude, and not out of spitefulness or derision. He knew they were laughing at him as people laugh at a clown they love, a clown they mimic, and remember ever afterwards affectionately.

Wavering wiseacre Joe, what is it now? His heart beats so he can hardly breathe. He is sure that if he lets them see what he feels, he is lost. What can be done for them? What can he do? Materialize, Moses, make with the thunder. What can be done for these ignorant sufferers if they are stubborn, if they scowl at charity, if they say to it, screw? What can a little guy do?

He can do more than shiver. He can have his fantasies too. Alone and unafraid, dressed in the breezy regalia of a cowboy, a softy in sombrero and chaps, he holds the reins loosely, his six-shooter full of blanks, on a proud pony which cakewalks down the cobbled street. It is obvious that its aim in life, like his, is to become like God. Where are

127

the people? Do they think they will make him believe he has stumbled on a ghost town? He smiles as he halts. He throws down a silver dollar to probe its sound in the lemon-colored sunlight. It rings true, an irresistible calling card. The pony rears as three emissaries march out. There she is, a solid pip in the altogether, flanked by dwarfs. He is surprised. He had expected giants. He doffs his sombrero as she confronts him, but does not dismount. Is it Miss Adversity he has the pleasure of addressing? Or is it Madam?

Suffering cats, says she, here is a bold and handsome stranger. Madam, forsooth. He must be one of the loco ones, the ones she loves best, those who come so well-heeled that they can afford to enjoy her to the limit. Come, she cries, though it be Sunday, and a day off, it is still lunch time, so hop off. Nay, he is careful to blush, she mistakes him. He has merely come to see, not to touch. He is merely passing through. At which one dwarf catches hold of the horse's tail, and the other its bridle. Is this a game, Miss? Fools, she yelps, his pistol. And before he can clap his hand over it, she is waving it languidly at his nose. Sorry, Junior, but when blandishments fail, force must step in, force which is the father of us all. Thou art indeed a pippin, Miss. Zounds, rumor has not maligned thee. Hast thou a match on thee, mayhaps? Thee and thou me later, she replies. And no shenanigans now. Man must be ennobled. He need not pout so nor ask why. And it is a truism, which is sickening to hear by this time, that only a visit with her, Adversity, can do that certain little trick for him come rain or shine.

Ho, says he, so it is sickening, is it? So she calls it a trick, does she? Might he presume to inquire? He does so with calculated irrelevancy. Is her backside as fetching as her face? The dwarfs cackle. She blushes. Listen to the boychick. He slaps his saddlebag significantly. Piecework, is it? What is thy price, thou hoyden? For thy sole and exclusive possession on a ninety-nine year lease, and no cozenage. Be quick now, name it. Duty compels her to empty the pistol. But it is she who staggers. A murrain on thee, she howls, thou practical joker. Who art thou? Art thou him again? Him whose hash was settled a thousand and nine hundred and thirty-two years ago with two slabs of wood and four nails? He laughs. He begins his incantation. And lo, the dwarfs go rolling over the stones, Dave on top of Eddie, and Eddie on top of Dave. When they regain their senses in Brooklyn, will they

128

know just why they must be jubilant? Will time poultice their abrasions, and freedom their lumps, yet leave them as dispirited as before? But one thing at a time. A saviour must concentrate on his saving. So, lo again, Adversity, caught off guard, brilliantly naked as she is, finds herself hoisted on the saddle behind him, and off they go lickety-split.

What makes her cling to him so cooperatively? Villain, she hisses. Yet sucks on his neck. Kidnapper. Yet fumbles professionally for his fly. Ow, he cries, lay off. That one like her should turn out to be such a hot number befuddles him. He checks the puzzled pony when he should be digging the spurs into its hide without mercy. Coward, she whispers unbearably. Creeper. What art thou doing? Hast thou lost the way? And the reason? Mother of God, he cries. What about the boys? What will they say? But the reins are in her hands now. It is downhill all the way. Yipee. Or wouldst thou have it yoicks? Smile, thou sad trifler. Hast thou the makings on thee? Art thou still game? Art thou breathing yet, marplot with the dark eyes? Thou hast called down the thunder. Listen. The boss growls. Thy fantasy shudders. Thy reward, baby? Dost thou still drool for it? O be quick then. Tell me. Behind which bush will it be?

Whew, they were dabbing at their eyes, and otherwise monkeying around with their handkerchiefs, when something happened which slowly paralyzed them with astonishment. With the queerest look they had ever seen limned on his face, this loony pal of theirs had abruptly launched himself from his chair, had lunged for the door, had opened it, only to close it, had turned swiftly with his ears cocked as if for a trumpet call, and apparently hearing nothing, had muttered something to himself, and had then ambled, there was no other word for it, back to his seat into which he simply sank, shaking a long no out of his head, and out of his lips an invective, a kind of meek one which sounded like sonofagun, or was it Santa Maria?

"Holy mackerel," said Dave, his snot-rag clutched in his hand like a ball he was about to throw. "Is this guy nuts or something?"

"Hey, there," said Eddie. "Wake up. Wake up there."

"Huh?" said Joe. "What's the matter?"

"What's a matter?" said Dave. "You hear that? He's asking us yet. Maybe you got a fever. Or crapped in your pants. How the hell do we know?"

"Kitzel," said Joe.

"Who?" said Eddie.

"He's always having trouble with his pants."

"Who is?"

"Kitzel. He works with me."

"He does?" said Dave. "That's very interesting. Reach over and feel his head there, Eddie. He must be burning up."

"And catch what he's got?" said Eddie. "Not me."

"Catch what?" said Joe. "Goddamn. It was really funny. I must tell you all about it."

"Sure," said Dave. "Go right ahead. But first, you tell us. Do you know what you were just doing?"

"What?" said Joe. "Wait a minute. I'm trying to remember. Now what in the hell was it he said to me?"

"Who?" said Eddie. "Kitzel?"

"No," said Joe. "Who's talking about him? I mean my boss, Mr. Colish."

"Mr. Who?" said Dave.

"Ha," said Joe. "It really is funny sometimes how you forget things, isn't it? I mean, I'm trying to remember now what he said to me, but I'll be damned if I can. Well, anyway, I can tell you one thing. I'm sure I told him. I'm sure of that all right."

"You are?" said Dave. "What are you sure of? You want to bet me something, Eddie? I'll bet you two to one he doesn't even know now what he's doing."

"Shh," said Eddie. "Give him a chance. Let's find out."

"Don't worry," said Joe. "I told him. He knows now. He knows."

"Knows what?" said Eddie. "For crying out loud. Say it this time, will you?"

"Sure," said Joe. "Didn't you know? I'm quitting my job. That's right. Ah, boy. You should've seen his face. I honestly don't understand it. What in the hell goes on in this world? Why should he be so surprised? Why can't a guy."

"Hold it," said Dave. "Hold it now. What did you just say?"

"That he was surprised. Why is it everyone is always so."

"No, no," said Dave. "You just said you were quitting your job. Is that what you just said?"

"Sure," said Joe. "Didn't I tell you?"

"Holy mackerel," said Dave.

130

"I thought I told you."

"This is the best one yet."

"That is, I meant to. What's wrong now?"

"My god," said Dave. "You know something, Joey? It's a damn good thing we know where you live."

"Ah, so you don't believe me either, do you?"

"Now, now," said Dave. "Take it easy. You mustn't get excited. We'll get you to bed somehow. Don't worry. Cripes. I sure got something bubbling in my stomach now. I was thinking. Maybe we'll step down to the clubroom afterwards. How about it, Eddie? I don't feel like going home yet, do you?"

"No," said Eddie. "I'm not sleepy either."

"Sleep," said Dave. "Another pain in the ass."

"So he didn't do it," said Eddie. "So he's giving us a ride. So what?"

"Ah," said Joe. "What's the use? You see what I mean? Two more goddamn fools."

"Sure," said Eddie. "A joke's a joke. But that last one, Joe. Really, it was a little bit, you know."

"That's right," said Dave. "Now you're telling him."

"Now look," said Eddie. "Who's talking to you?"

"Tell him," said Dave. "Maybe he'll listen to you."

"Ah, now," said Eddie. "Why don't you shut up?"

"Look at him," said Dave. "You know what his trouble is? He thinks he's smarter than anyone else."

"Thinks?" said Joe.

"He thinks he knows it all."

"You're damn right," said Joe. "How can I help it? All I have to do is compare myself to you."

"See that?" said Dave. "What did I tell you?"

"Suckers."

"Come again?" said Dave.

"You're all poor suckers, all of you."

"Oho," said Dave. "And you're not, eh?"

"I wonder," said Joe. "Do you guys know what's happening to you? Do you really know? Go ahead now. Go down that stinking clubroom. Go bury yourself there. You think I care? Aie, my head. I tell you. It really hurts. You idiots. How many lives do you think you've got? You think you've got a thousand years yet? Ah, boy. I'm telling

131

you. You'll be coming to me one of these days. That's right. You can laugh now. But I'll know then. I'll know what's what. You'll see. You won't be able to help it. Like lost sheep. You'll come crying to me to ask me which way to turn and what to do. Ask me? You'll be begging me to tell you. You watch. You'll see."

6.

Time may, or it may not, skip a heartbeat thinking of it. It may scuttle away from the sight of it, like the daft and emblematic rush hour it is often imagined to be, or it may simply remain seated, so that the proud calligraphy of its profile may be admired, with one passive paw raised like the ampersand thus: & - sign which sees nothing, yet seems to know it all. Or it may be that stylized eye which looks awful whenever it sees an additional soul, in a sort of buglike maneuver, try to force itself through a tiny crack into the future. Before going any further, would not this be a good time to ask the birds to come out and cheep more lucidly, if not more gaily, between the syllables?

Confound his innocence, confound it now and always. He and his possessive case. Quite nimble at deception by nature, he foists it on the first slow-thinking sucker he meets because he, Joe, has misbehaved, and knows it, and so must have something quick to sweeten his existence, that is, something in lieu of an answer to that question which is not his only, that question which is beginning to be piped so pathetically by so many everywhere, do I still belong to you, world, do I? What? No more talk of owning it, only of belonging to it?

Trample on the roses, and throttle the nightingale, if the war-waging begin to quack, and the murderous to quake, how is anyone to know what topsy-turvy item will be tossed at him next? Indeed when a man regards the mollycoddle of today with his supersubtle life of a lunatic, with his neurotic concern with the shadow instead of the substance, with his bloated penances, interior and personal, he is pricked by nostalgia for the singular brutality of the past which can be measured, weighed, and dissipated, for the olden days of the roysterer with his red cheeks and his smouldering soul which was never easily bruised or easily made to feel sorry. It may not be wise to praise so a pagan interlude. But Joe might well drop his head and suck his finger as he tries to assimilate it. How significant it is, and typical of him too, that his brilliant venture of yesterday should seem to him today like the fuzzy invasion of a caterpillar of a clean and communal wall onto which it had quietly crawled, and as quietly clung, another hairy affair, cockily baking in the sun, musing on its metamorphosis, feeling so sure of itself, and so safe.

And yet? What was it that suddenly convulsed it? Why did he have to have that outburst which betrayed his innocence? And made him feel so ashamed that it was he, himself, who brushed himself off? They were impatient words, deformed by captiousness as of old, a dinky boast of watch and see, which revealed to him the measure of his own buffoonery and bluffing. Who can say? Perhaps there is a world elsewhere, a world in which such a blunder is nipped in the bud by an earlier visitation of angels. If so, why not persuade the whelp to make a safari in search of it? Perhaps all he has to do is trust his nose and he will find a bone with more gristle on it, and stranger air with which to refrigerate the heart, and a quincunx of trees in a grove where he can fool more with flowers and less with prickles, where he can get rid of his fleas, and his distemper, and scabless at last, lift a leg, and learn finally how a man differs from a dog.

Sign of a sty this morning, was it an omen? But by noon it had disappeared, as well as those private moments of prayer, panic, and wrath, and the usual blues which clot a Monday. Which even a ridiculous original can sweat out in work, since even he knows the efficacy of the physical kind. So all praise to his manual dexterity, and a snicker at least for his final observation of the morning which went like this, yes, if you listen, you can hear that everybody is ticking, that's for sure, yet not a single one of them ever tells the right time. And so it went. To be more solidly replaced by a vision of a Spanish omelette, a hot plate special already steaming in his mind as he tore across the

134

street for the Nathan & Mitchel Cafeteria with Kitzel and Frankie, and Hymie and Felix hardly lagging behind. The first to pluck a green check, since they switched the color on him every day, out of the machine which snitched on him with a bong as he did so, in a new scientific effort to keep him on the straight and narrow. For with two checks, here is the way it works, have coffee and Danish punched on one, and as high as a steak dish with mushrooms and French fried on the other, and pay for the pittance of the first with a straight face, the trick being to get those two checks first, which was not as simple as it seemed, the upshot of which personal and present failure was that before he knew it, he had allowed himself to be the last of the gang to be served.

Now what kind of a selfish reversal to meekness was this? Was it something premeditated? Had it been caused by a glance from the cashier's petty head with its static permanent wave to the electric clock hung ticklessly behind her, and enticing him to it with the suavity and correctness of its naval observatory time? That such a clear turn of the mind, as pardonable as the twist of a wrist, should seem so enigmatic. But to deal with Joe is to be jolted every now and then by these tiny seismic shocks of insignificance. For the more unnatural and inconvenient, and time consuming it is, the more impulsively will he declare the arbitrary moment to be the inevitable one, the one in which he has decided he must severely chasten and discipline himself.

So there. So now he silently despises his most valid hunger and disdainfully keeps it in check, allowing himself to be shoved and mauled and shouted down, the goon, refusing to grapple with that hydra which calls itself the public in today's lunch hour crush. Sometimes his kind of defiance can be a dilly. He scorns their theory of the survival of the loudest and follows his own of catch her eye and gently does it, which it will eventually, of course, but right now, what does it get him? A hand which creeps into his pocket. Hemmed in as he is, he tries to discover whose it might be, and when he encounters the cool set expression of the pickpocket's face, what does he do? Nothing but shake his head as he smiles directly at it in two ways, first, to show surprise that he should be chosen as a victim, and second, how amused he is that anyone should covet two keys on a ring, tobacco crumbs, and the stub of a movie ticket. Recanting, and philosophically enough, the thwarted hand retrieves itself to try again some other day.

135

Another incident, another omen? If the meek inherit the earth, though it is difficult to imagine what they could possibly do with that particular object once they clamp their provincial claws on it, they will instantly become relatives, and as such, will try to steal it from each other. It will be absolutely the last revolution. The policeman's whistle will shrill perpetually.

Peep, peep. Joe imitated a Cadillac horn to warn the throng he was coming through. His loaded tray was his football. He imagined he was a quarterback with swivel hips who knew how to slip through the smallest hole to reach his goal which, in this case, was the very last table in the rear, roughly preempted each day by the same old bunch for the same old reason, to exchange banter and compulsive boasts, especially after they had depleted their coffee cups and dredged their soup bowls to pile them all on whatever blue plate had been desecrated, though their hunger demanded such a splurge daily, a true meal with all the trimmings, it was not often they could borrow the price of it, or had also tried to trip a trim ankle, in passing, or bum a cigarette from a bus boy, or salt the sugar, or sugar the salt to show they were full of extracurricular gumption, and superfluous wind and beans.

The seats against the wall were best, but now they were all taken. As Joe sat down on the vulnerable side, Kitzel was the one who winked at him. As for the others, they barely glanced at him as if he were a stranger, or, so it seemed to him, as if he were becoming one, which seemed even worse. And it was all done so naturally. He ate. He had to eat. Now how could the dust and heat of their table talk increase without him? How could they continue to make bets without his hypothetical millions? Or without him still seem so witty, and so obscenely so? Was this an omelette he was eating? Or was it straw? Odd dish, fresh intimation at every bite, he took note of each tasteless mouthful as he exercised his jaw in their air, and in their air, he breathed. How generous of them to allow him to hang on to the periphery of their clique by the usual eyelash. Camaraderie so often falsely exalted, his former position at the very heart of it had shifted to the rim inexorably. It was plain now. He was building his own barricade, and behind it now, ever since Saturday, the bad moments were beginning to multiply.

To listen to them is to note. What awful lies they tell. They are contesting now for the new finisher hired today, for her kewpie doll lips, her perfectly muscled butt, her black staring eyes, her stiff and separated lashes. Whose is she to be? A hack-knife into the liver, Indian givers all, giving with one hand, and taking away with the other. Doubt is what will form that peptic ulcer. And in the loose eyes of the law, the innocence of the transgressor is no excuse. They agree she may be syphilitic. Frankie has his mouth wide open for flies. He wonders at these men, his admirable elders, who seem to know how to exploit women other than their wives. Kitzel passes around the chiclets. Joe also takes one. As he chews, he is aware that he is posing as a man who is in a sad decline.

It is such a little vanishing pleasure. He ought to flirt with the wisecrack as they do. And as they do, greet Georgie as if he were a prime example of a vaudeville nigger who, lacking white brains, is expected to lick his plate as if it had been permeated by the spirit of quail on toast instead of two stale and skinny frankfurters. Where is that old thunder of ethical condemnation? Where is the sneak who spits on the preacher? Into each life a little prejudice must fall.

Hymie is a cutter. Hymie is a refinement, a simpler simple simon. Still the snippet of an idea does flutter semiannually, and always with great distress, in the vast empty arena of his size seven and three-quarters skull. In short, he is thought to have the brain of a bird, though there is no bird in Prospect Park Zoo, for one place, which can match his biceps, or his lachrymal nature, or his squawking against his natural enemy, Felix the Fox, his immediate boss, a cleverer one who loves to annoy this bull with the German haircut, as he calls him, this tearjerker who feels most alive when he feels most infuriated. If one has an enemy, and the need to have one is universal, it is fun to have him face to face. Just to hate, and just to be afraid, is wrong and a rotten fate. But how sweet almost, and delicious, and cherishable even, it becomes when fear and hate can be shared by tossing them around in a free-for-all kind of togetherishness. Is there a toddler or a teenager in this crowded classroom who can think of anything more charming or more brotherly?

"Me," said Hymie. "I can."

"Sure, sure," said Felix, who sat beside him, yet never turned to look at him when he spoke. "Who's for getting some water? Georgie?"

"I'm eating."

"You're the nearest to it."

137

"I'm eating."

"Sure I can," said Hymie. "I can tell you. I've been watching it. Christ, I can remember when this place was really mobbed."

"What?" said Felix. "More than this?"

"Sure," said Hymie. "Much more."

"Geh. You see things like you stretch silk. All cockeyed."

"Oh, yeah?" said Hymie. "So tell me this. Where's that snake who used to sneak in here?"

"What snake?" said Felix. "Listen to this, men, he's off."

"You know who I mean. That guy who always had his mouth to your ear, making like a bookie. And that schlang, Maxie, who could whistle. What about him? And Berkman who used to wear those big bow ties? Does anybody ever see him? And that shrimp who used to eat yeast for his pimples? What the hell was his name? And yeah. That crazy truck pusher, Kalinsky. Where is he now?"

"Kalinsky," said Felix. "Right. I remember him. Wasn't he the guy who used to brag about the size of his dick?"

"I heard he's dead," said Kitzel. "Squashed against a wall or something."

"Naa," said Frankie. "I still see him around. Hold everything. Who wants to buy a raffle? Huh? I got it right here."

"Well?" said Hymie. "Why don't you tell me? What's happened to all those guys? Why don't they ever come in here?"

"You win a watch," said Frankie. "And a chain too. Hah, fellas? It's only a dime. That's all it is. Who'll be the first to slap it down?"

"The first?" said Kitzel. "I won't even be the last."

"Just look at it," said Hymie. "Just look around. See what's happening? I'm telling you. In another few months this place'll be so empty, you'll be able to run a dance in here."

"Listen to him," said Felix. "He's selling tickets for it already. A schlub. I didn't even know he could dance."

"Sure," said Hymie. "I can dance."

"Then dance yourself right out of here, will you? What in the hell are you bothering me for? You got spring fever or something?"

"Hey, Joe," said Kitzel.

"What?"

"There's your brother over there. See him?"

"Yes," said Joe. "I see him."

138

"Aw," said Frankie. "Come on, you guys. Don't be so cheap. It's only a dime. If I don't sell fifty, I get kicked right out of the club."

"Good," said Kitzel. "Tell them I'll help them. Any time."

"Sure," said Hymie. "I know. You think I'm sick in the head, don't you?"

"What the hell," said Frankie. "Nobody's going to buy? How about you, Georgie? I got a feeling you'll win. You once told me you won, didn't you?"

"Okay," said Georgie. "Get me a cigarette first."

"That's the stuff," said Frankie. "See that? There's the only real guy around here."

"Spring fever, shit," said Hymie. "It's more like winter for everybody, that's what it is. And that's what it's going to be from now on. Every minute. All the time."

"That does it," said Felix. "That finishes me. Hop around and get me some water, Frankie, and what the hell, I'll buy one too. Anything not to listen to him."

"Oh, boy," said Frankie. "That's the ticket. Now I'm doing business. Who else before I go? Hymie? How about you, Joe? Need some water too?"

"No," said Joe. "Just some fresh air."

Is it so good then to feel so alone? It is not so bad. Or to go out into the street again and pause near a doorway where lambs do not gambol or the lilacs grow, and catch the wistful little wind full in the face, and look up to see a family of four clouds, and wonder why they submit so pompously to being fleeced, and why, if the mind is so cocksure as it suns itself, should the heart remain stubbornly wicked, and scoff at such a spectacle? Yes, that too is good, that something in him should know that if Joe folds his arms across his chest and stands there with his feet apart like a conqueror who has this second been crowned that he is suffering from a common tic called delusions of grandeur. So that he may well ask, why? Why is it that these clowns who clog the street do not tumble in adoration at his feet? Or that Maisie Dubrow, the floorlady, who limps by, says hello without noticing his wings or his halo? His answer is a boy's answer. They are blind. But he can see. The sense of his own uniqueness and invulnerability blinds him so that he does not see any of the cars which swerve and just fail to kill him as he jaywalks arrogantly across the street.

139

Thus nature, a master chef, can churn ice cream for the ego out of simple air and sunshine, and force the fire-eaters and high-steppers of each generation to swallow it greedily each spring at least, as if it were manna for the soul and not that mishmash so necessary to insure the giddy survival of the flesh. Such old stuff. Such a partial statement at which he has to smile as he stations himself near the entrance of his building. For after all, the youthful joy of his soul in its own individuality is as real to him as that particular sneeze which is caused by breathing in a pinch or more of the peppery snuff of the sun. Certainly, if the soul is a contraption, it has not been rashly built out of a few old ripped cards, goose feathers, and broken book matches, and has its own pledges and avowals to make, and to break, and its own endless trials, and enthusiasms, and its own bold lies to tell. What has it to do with the inherited caution and hesitation of the heart? This is its time to crow independently. This is its heydey. It may be a nuisance, but it will aspire, even if it does not have an olive jar of pennies in back of it or six or seven dimes in a piggy bank. The very tires sing of its fearlessness and the possibility of its failing. This reasonable Joe-soul, he views it so ironically, and tries to train it to be sensible and remember that if ever it does succeed, its success will merely be that it will fail in its own peculiar way.

Such a thought, trite as it was, made him look so gentle and obliging that when a Postal Telegaph boy bounced up on the sidewalk with his bike to park it, he did not hesitate to ask Joe to keep an eye on it, how about it, bud? Joe slapped the handle bar and begged him to be easy, he would guard it with his life. Three women he did not know were felicitating a fourth he was sure he did not know either on her tremendous luck. She was going to quit work and have a baby. The vestal delight of the three was such that it seemed they were about to have it with her. An airplane droned overhead as if it were bored, as if it too had overheard.

Ho, hum. What newspaper does not know that its readers will be more fascinated by the taking away of a life than the giving of it which at best is so mere and mimetic? Yesterday, according to a little item in the Times, a babe of two months refused to be shushed, wailed so long and insistently that finally its mother, in a marvelous fit of rage, just stuffed it entire into a live stove. Whether she subsequently warmed her hands over that crackling good fire was not revealed, but when she was told she was a murderer, she protested, and swore by her saint, a very minor one, that her lambkin was so much better off now, that if once she had heard it mew on earth, she could now hear it bleat in heaven where its diaper will never have to be changed, she was sure of it. So sure, said one man to the lapel of another, should we all be. Said the other, we should, say it and believe it, the missis will live and laugh and bring light yet into the house again. All people die. But must it always be from a cataract operation on the eye? Yes, said the buttonholer, how right, if she lives, I promise, I buy her something. And if she dies? sneered the other, suddenly tired of it all. If she dies, said his leech, then it will cost me. I will have to bury her.

Jiminy, what a pair of gams on that one. What accident brings such a ritzy-looking dame so far downtown? She wore a dark orange pillbox hat with a dotted veil, and pigskin gloves to match, and a raglan coat blowing open, and a frankly nippled blouse of beige, and seams on her stockings terribly straight. Is she naughty when she kisses? Does she refuse to use her tongue? Is she as stern and distinguished as she looks? She clip-clopped by him with a kisser on her like ice, as if she had never shared a quilt, or plumped up the pillows, or suffered a sheet burn on her royal behind, this faker, as if, now really, as if she hated to excite this world so full of oglers for such a red and nasty reason. He smiled ambiguously. If only she had a bike. He would have loved to watch it for her.

The boy came out briskly to reclaim his two-wheeler, offered gum, accepted the refusal without any fuss, crammed three slices into his mouth, said thanks clearly enough, and streaked away, simple, responsible, eupeptic all the way. Joe watched him whizz around the corner. Gone now. But would this be the boy who would bring him a merry and revolutionary message some day? The sight of Rosalie coming was a shock. The sun was in her eyes. He stepped back into the shade. Why should it frighten him sometimes when he sees her, when he sees her and has to think of her as his?

To love. Give in order its forms in several colors, search like a sonofagun for a more immaculate conjugation, relinquish none and do not surrender to any. He loved. What did he love? How was it clothed? With sister's shoes resoled and dyed blue, with a hand-me-down cloth green coat with a musty collar of plush, with a utility hairdo, and a useless hatlessness, with patched panties once flashy and

141

a clashing shade of brassiere, and with the doubtful blessedness of looking benign and little in all of it. And yet, whenever she mourned the appearance of her working outfit, her weekend one was as weak for other reasons, he asked her angrily not to speak of it, as if unknown to himself, he was perpetually struggling with a subliminal preference for the insidious blankness and ornamented malignancy of the clothes dummy. She beamed when she spied him. Her legs actually twinkled. She sought for his eyes with a desire so direct that apparently she failed to see that a button on his coat was split or that his knitted tie had begun to unravel at the knot or that the pesty sun had brought out the provoking rain stains on his hat. How strange then that the love which is critical should have something crooked about it and should constantly seem like a crime.

"Hey," said Rosalie. "That's not really your face, is it?"

"I'm afraid so," said Joe. "It's a new thing. It comes and it goes."

"Then let it go. It'll never win a beauty contest. Wow, I'm telling you. I sure had a tough time getting away."

"I know," said Joe. "She wasn't hungry, but this is what she ate."

"Oh, no," said Rosalie. "That's not it. I'm not that rich. I just got into an argument. Why don't you stand in the sun?"

"It hurts my eyes. What argument?"

"Oh," said Rosalie. "That Big Bee. I swear. I'll never eat again where she eats. What's wrong with that woman anyway? It always comes out of a clear blue sky. My, what a nice cool hand this animal has. Maybe you can tell me. What makes her try to boss everybody around lately?"

"Because the miseries have suddenly got her. She's a real case."

"I'll say."

"I'm so glad you agree. Let's go in and sit down."

"On such a gorgeous day?"

"That's the trouble," said Joe. "All this fresh air. It's killing me."

"I believe you. You already look half dead. Bend down a second. Is my face red?"

"Where?"

"I mean. Am I getting a little sunburned?"

"Don't be whacky."

"I must get sunburned. My mother is always after me. And she's right. I sure could use a little sun."

"I thought it was money."

"That too. Ah, remember me last summer?"

"How can I forget? I never saw such blisters. You and your rotten Coney Island."

"What blisters? Did I have blisters? I mean my tan. Didn't I look good in it? I looked good then, didn't I?"

"If it makes you so happy, yes."

"Well, now, don't strain yourself."

"Come on, nature lover. Let's go in and squat."

"Okay," said Rosalie. "But this time, please, don't drag me."

"Sorry," said Joe. "But I need the exercise. Oops, watch that swinging door. Damn it, I must say. I sure envy you, kiddo."

"You do, my love? Why?"

"The way you can be happy. For no reason."

"For no reason?"

"For absolutely no reason at all."

"Why," said Rosalie. "You're a great big dope, you know that? Haven't you heard yet? I'm in love."

"Ah, yes," said Joe. "I forgot all about that."

"You forgot."

"I mean," said Joe. "You know what I mean. I was thinking of something else."

"That's right," said Rosalie. "Be a gentleman. Grab the best seat. Sit down first."

He jumped up.

"What the hell's the matter with me?"

He pulled her down beside him.

"How much time have we got? Say. Maybe I'll ask you something. Why not? Maybe I'll just come right out and ask you."

"Ask me what?"

"No, no, not yet."

"Look who's red now. Where did you get such big eyes?"

"Let's just first sit a while, okay?"

"Okay," said Rosalie. "I'm willing. Let's just sit."

To assure him that he was free, if he so wished, to fumble for the apocalyptic in their humble position, she placed her hand over his which he had placed on her knee, thus paying with her sympathy for her passage with him in his wanderings, strangely proud of him because he was capable of thought, even if his thoughts did often carry him away from her so foolishly. Ah, how often, yes, but not this time, this time it was not true. He actually shook his head. But his was, and so all at once, such an anguish of appreciation, that he felt it would be sacrilegious to enter into the initial stage of stuttering about it, even that, that all his words would seem as fake as the marble of the pink walls of this lobby, and as inelastic and opaque as the step on which they sat like orphans, more stone, like a couple of beggars who seem insufferably crushed, yet aggravatingly enough, remain so well-behaved. No doubt she was more civilized than he when she curtsied to the whim of the gods which had willed them this spot, when she said it was plainly theirs and so could be called ours, idealizing it without plaguing herself about it one bit.

It made him wonder. If time topples all pillars, then love erects them wherever it plants itself, being so confoundedly eager and able. And blind? If Rosalie is in love, if the man says, has love then, with one of its infamous scratches, permanently impaired her vision? How humbling then to realize that her nearsighted vistas of a future with him, that all of her hopes for him, each of them firmly grounded on these same stairs, were far superior to the supposed airiness and breath of his visual flights, and deeper somehow than the depth he imagined as terrifying of the hole he had dug in a deserted nook of his mind in order to secure what is positively silly, a picture of himself as he will be when he is a ghost. His fragrant jailer, all she had to do was sigh and, by her breathing which became funny, show him what she craved, and the clay of his nebulous longings crumbled about him.

Take her then and make an end of it. Or chuck her away altogether as if she were really an untouchable. For she has that terrible nerve of the simple soul which is always profoundly humiliating to resist. To curb and check her forever because she delights in him, can that ever seem glorious? Has it ever seemed so? Challenging bit of jail bait, sixteen and a half years old, when first she joined the chorus at Colish, the very first thing she did was to outstare him. He knew then that he had to run away from her. But fast. And that was almost a year and a half ago.

Is there still a little axiom tucked away somewhere which says that mere propinquity can succeed at last in linking a girl who is pure with a boy who is perverse? If so, let no one resurrect it here. Or be too

144

quick to seize upon this blarney about the invincibility of daily near-ness, how it draws together, and tangles so and knots that it appears to be the only reason why finally the so-called sage mounts the apparent ninny. Or vice versa. What difference does it make? On the contrary, here is an example of an encounter, common enough, yet fabulous each time, which is as naked and naughty at the first glance as it will be at the last. What of this is invalidated if it is true that an animal can reach the same far from unpleasant conclusion with one quick sniff? But then, who cares about such inept comparisons with furred or feathered creatures, be they foxes in a bush or owls on a branch, who have their secret meetings, who stealthily conjoin to act out their painful moments of passion? Concentrate rather on this particular Joe, with his own coat of many colors, this shattered specimen of a man who, according to his sorry version of it, has had the misfortune to collide in the daytime with what he itched for, dreaming that it could happen to him only at night. Anyway, he ran. And she was hilarious.

Pepper pot, seductive dumpling, high-breasted brat, he could kill her for that, for her flush, her public glee. The more he stiffened and squirmed and snarled at her, the more she exulted. She knew she would snare him. It was ordained. Swinging her legs as she perched on his packing table, she made him work around her and closer to her until he saw red, and had to lift her bodily right out in the open, and carry her off as far as he could, and set her down rudely, and warn the little witch, but warn her of what?

Easy now. Sing him no songs of a siren like Cleopatra, who still floats down the river Nile on her monotonous barge, hazy tantalizer, let the eunuchs squeal as they fan that ember of concupiscence, that pinpricking immortal bored with lust whose historic charm depends too much on silks, chalks, condiments, potions, and paintpots. She is a reek, a shimmer, a slithering in a man's mind, no more. Why should he be such a romantic mutt? Why should he magnify these mystic sinuosities, this oriental languor and fustiness? Why should he try to revive the grand manner just to declaim about such an obscure and dusty fragment of desire when he has had to grapple with a temptress more formidable by far, Rosalie, an American kiddo who has simply flowered out of an ash can on the Lower East Side?

Rose, of all the Rosalies, the Rosaliest. For months on end she paraded before him, showing him everything. He could easily see that

145

to bite into any part of her person would be the same as biting into the absolute. He swore he would never. But all of a sudden, she would sneak over to tickle him, then step back to duck the swing he took at her, and pull her dress tight, and ask him to please look and tell her if she was getting too big there. It was tempting, but he never spanked her. One day as he passed the dressing room, he heard her laugh at the mention of his name, then boast to the other girls that, as wonderful as he was, she was sure she had him going, she could tell he was weakening. He waylaid the giggler then to swear that if he ever heard one more peep out of her like that, so help him, he would strangle her. She offered him her neck. He pushed her. If to push her was to touch her, what could he do? He had to push her away. For she was much too compact for him, too vital, too real.

Such too-ing was as good as oo-ing. He knew he would always envy, and curse, the mongrel who would finally mount her. As for him, he confessed he was afraid. What was his fear then? His fear was such a young and simple one. He was afraid he would be overwhelmed by that one thing too early in life, that by annexing, he would be annexed, that it might suddenly turn out to be the last twinge and the final tumult of its kind. And all for a little piece of tail. The wiseguy who wenches where he works often sees his phase of dancing around cut short with a stumbling waltz at his own wedding. Pale now, what is his prize? A horseshoe of anemic flowers. Giant and sanguinary dreams of a love which is wild and unbelievable, again they perish at the altar. Why not then follow that policy which is so punctilious that it reserves all the various acts of pouncing and panting for the after-work hours only when the appetite is most anonymous, or if pressed, can leave behind him a false second name?

Damn the hide of this bouncing baby, if she had a scheme, she boldly announced it, while all he could do was to back off and try to make himself scarce. She began to delay his incoming calls by demanding that first he exchange with her a word or two of babble as crude as baby talk. All that accomplished was to increase his vocabulary of insulting names to call her. Soon she was ringing him on her own. Repeated and irresistible intrusion of her tonic breath, she forced their voices to mingle intimately over the wire, extracting from him pompous lectures on the nature of good and evil, on the sin implicit in her flaming impulse to fling herself on him, on the merits of patience and reason, on the contempt he had for her overeagerness to be fingered, on her stupidity in believing that he was out of the ordinary, on his firm resolve to hold out against her appearance which he was frank enough to describe as a natural disaster. Her laugh reached its crest, then began to break. She absolutely refused to believe it. What was going on here? He seemed to mean what he said. This crazy man of iron, he began to make her look foolish, as if she were really a child who, for her own rare amusement, had been clopping along allegorically in her mother's shoes, vainly chasing after her fleeing father's face painted on a balloon. For he held out. For exactly eleven long months, he did hold out against her.

Surely the worms, whose charm is not altogether inconsequential, quarrel less when they crawl on each other, wriggling under and over, or do not speak of it at all. Further, it is monstrous to assume that they can ever be puffed up by pride, since they have never been known to perform a lucky act of levitation, and so cannot be accused of looking down with withering contempt, with whatever serves them for a nose, upon the comparatively less inspired and lumpish, that is, upon their fatuous companions, their fellow devourers. But of course with a he-man like Joe, there it is quite different. That is to say, it was. For on the basis of what he had not done, he did something that was ridiculous. He fell head over heels in love with himself, tumbling very far every which way. True, he still condescended to wear his apron, but only as a lord would, with a sort of haughty finesse and forbearance, often shucking his disguise to flabbergast the squirts around him, especially one, with his icy comments on their cringing manners and their empty ways. The result was that they began to snub him back. And she began to look awful. The whole proud and mettlesome frame of the rambunctious filly began to sag. It was really a cruel situation.

Saltless eater of his shrinking flesh, of all the maddening sights to see daily, brazenly slouching by him with a livid nose and a rigid eye as if she were deader than dead, as if she were a ghost practicing to be a ghoul as well, gathering material to compose a nightmare for him which would be so forked and cyclonic that it would jab and whirl and whip him for what he had done to her, he and only he. God almighty, what could he do? He had to exaggerate it all because she did. She. She. He just hated her. But collect his bones in a number three carton and bury them in his own backyard, just when he thought his hate

147

would swell forever, his surprising heart suddenly went out to her, floating towards her tipsily. She was so delighted, she almost wept. Her smile became dangerous. He was not that blind. He could see. But he talked to her and talked to her until one day, as they sat on these legendary stairs, she quietly took his hand and brought it to her mouth, and that was how she scuttled him, how this bright boy, the carefree swimmer, finally sank.

"Oh, you dirty dog you."

"Who?" said Rosalie. "Me?"

"You fat little fever-giver."

"Fat?" said Rosalie.

"You nemesis," said Joe. "So now you're mine. So that's the way it has to be, is it?"

"Excuse me," said Rosalie. "But that's my leg you're squeezing."

"What leg?"

The avenger smiled without relaxing his grip.

"I thought I was much further up than that," he said.

"Ow. So help me, Joe, if you give me another blue mark, I'll."

"You'll what? Okay, okay. Don't hit. What the hell. A guy has to try to show he's boss sometimes, doesn't he?"

"Oh, sure," said Rosalie. "Aren't you going to give me one?"

"Give you what?"

"A cigarette, stupid."

"Oh, I'm sorry. I always forget you smoke."

"Only yours, dear."

"Wait," said Joe. "I sniff cocaine. Would you like to try that too?"

"A match, mister."

"At least hold it like a man."

"Fooey," said Rosalie. "I really hate the stuff. You think I should get a holder? Did I ever tell you what happened to my sister once when she tried to get fancy? What did you mean when you said so now you're mine? You never said that before."

"That's all right," said Joe. "Don't let it worry you. There's a lot of things I've never said before."

"That helps. Another funny answer."

"Funny? What's so funny about it?"

"Look, Joe."

"What?"

"Can I ask you something?"

"Sure, why not?"

"No," said Rosalie. "Let it go. I'm sorry. I can't."

"Now don't die on me. What is it you want to know?"

"I feel sick."

"Throw it away then."

"No," said Rosalie. "I'm not talking about that. I mean something else. Don't laugh now, but I'm going to tell you something. I don't think I really like it. The whole thing is making me sick."

"What thing?"

"Oh," said Rosalie. "You know. This stupid love business."

"Yow," he suddenly seized and drew her back. "Watch out."

"What's the matter?"

"Glickman," said Joe. "I don't want him to see us. Sick of it? Did you say you were sick of it? You're improving, you know that? All right. Turn your face away. I understand. Sure. Why shouldn't you be sick of it? Don't you think I know? Here you are waiting with your tongue sticking out. And I'm still fooling around. But I warned you about that, didn't I?"

"Foo. A lot of good that does me now."

"I told you. I would go so far with you and no further."

"It's driving me crazy. I shouldn't say that, should I?"

"Why not? You'd be a liar if you didn't."

"Honest," said Rosalie. "I'm so ashamed of myself. I just can't think of anything else."

"Don't be ashamed. We all think about it. Day and night."

"Oh," said Rosalie. "This, this. This sex, sex, sex. Who invented it anyway?"

"Careful now," said Joe. "Your ever-loving God is listening."

"You mean the devil, don't you?"

"Now don't be that kind of a virgin. Or whatever you are. Look. Let me ask you something. You still like me, don't you?"

"Of course," said Rosalie. "What a question."

"Then all right," said Joe. "The hell with it. Let's get hitched and hop right into bed."

"What?" said Rosalie. "Get married? Just for that?"

"Sure," said Joe. "Why not? Why be afraid to think about it that way? Let's say it's for that reason to begin with. For your sake. Okay,

okay. For mine too. We all have to get married sometimes, don't we? So all right. So it'll be you to me and me to you. And that'll be that. How about it? What do you say?"

Frankie charged in on them like a pocket-sized bull.

"Ah," he said. "So there they are. I knew I'd find you here. How about it, folks? Hurry, hurry, hurry. Get them while they last. Only a dime. The tenth part of a dollar. Come on, you millionaires. Get your money up."

"Get my money up?" said Rosalie. "Why, you little pest. If you don't get away from here, I'll murder you. What do you mean jumping on me that way?"

Frankie stepped way back.

"What's a matter with her?"

"Can't you see?" said Joe. "She loves you. She wants you to live."

"Gee," said Frankie. "What did I do? I didn't do anything."

"Ah," said Joe. "You see? You've hurt the poor kid's feelings."

"My god," said Rosalie. "What's he bothering me for? Do I have to think of him too? Hey, you. Come here."

"It's only a dime," said Frankie.

"What is?" said Rosalie.

"This raffle. You need a watch, don't you?"

"A raffle," said Rosalie. "Can you imagine? Okay. Give it to him, Joe. Lay it out for me. And don't start calling me sweetheart, you hear?"

"I won't," said Frankie. "I won't. That'll be two, eh?"

"Two?" said Joe.

"Well, well," said Felix. "How about that? He's hooking them too."

"But not me," said Kitzel. "I didn't fall for it. See that, Hymie? I told you I'd be the only one."

"More company," said Rosalie. "This is so unexpected."

"Ah," said Felix. "My dear Mrs. Astor. And tell me, if you'll be so kindly. How's the old lovelife lately?"

"Is somebody talking to me?" said Rosalie.

"I swan," said Felix. "She gets prettier and prettier every day. Remember what I said, honeybunch. Just let me know when you get rid of this goofus here."

"I must be dreaming," said Rosalie. "I'm sure I hear somebody talking."

"Hey," said Hymie. "You guys staying here? I'm going up."

150

"Go ahead," said Felix. "Who's holding you?"

"By the way," said Joe. "Nobody's holding you either."

"What?" said Felix. "You mean to say we're not wanted here?"

"That's right," said Joe. "Think about it when you're gone."

"Okay," said Felix. "I get it. Come on, Kitzel. Like they say when the first shovelful hits them smack in the face. Life, my brethren, she simply must go on. With or without us."

"Brilliant," said Joe. "Ain't he?"

"Say," said Frankie. "What did you give me, Joe?"

"My god," said Joe. "You still here?"

"Was that a whole quarter you gave me?"

"Right," said Joe. "You have to give me a nickel change, get it?"

"But I haven't got a nickel."

"Then you'll owe it to me. Go on, now. Scoot upstairs and start packing. Whew. A fine body of men, aren't they?"

"But how would we live?" said Rosalie.

"Oh," said Joe. "We'd live. Since when has that bum been calling you honeybunch?"

"How?" said Rosalie. "On my pitiful salary? Don't be so good to me."

"Look," said Joe. "Who's been talking to you about money?"

"Or does it mean you're staying? Does it mean you're staying, Joe?"

"Hell, no. What gives you that idea?"

"Then what're you talking about?"

"Why," said Joe. "I told you. I'm just trying to give you a chance to sleep with me. Isn't that what you want?"

"All right," said Rosalie. "You guessed it. That's exactly what I want. So then? When does it come off? Come on, now, tell me. When?"

"When you marry me. Didn't you hear what I said?"

"Just when you're quitting?" said Rosalie. "Don't make me laugh. You know that makes it impossible. Is that why you're asking me?"

"Of course," said Joe. "I had it all figured out."

"I bet you did."

"I knew you wouldn't have the guts."

"Ah," said Rosalie. "Why didn't you say it? All you had to do was say it. And I would've said yes right away."

"Say what?"

"That you love me, you idiot."

151

"Oh," said Joe. "That. Okay, then. I love you. Will you marry me?"

"What time is it? There's no sense in being late now."

"You didn't like the way I said that, did you?"

"I don't know about you, brother, but I still need my job."

"Goddamn it, Rosalie. What do you want? You want me to melt at your feet? You want me to become your one and only grease spot? Is that what you want?"

"I want you to leave me alone. You hear me? From now on, just leave me alone."

"The hell I will."

He was almost floored by an incredible shriek.

"Fire," Karl screamed, clawing at the wall. "Run for your lives, you rats."

"Of all the crazy bastards," said Joe.

"Oo, mamma, I'm burning up, I'm burning up."

"Ah," said Joe. "I sure in hell hope so."

"Hello?" said Karl, snuffling into an imaginary receiver. "Let's hear you loud and clear now. Is this the frigging morgue? I got two bodies for you. Yeah, that's right. Rosalie the Ripper. And Joe the Gyp. What? No. Shit on a check. Send cash."

"Jesus," said Joe. "Come on, Rosalie. This is more than I can take."

Karl rattled a real pair of dice.

"Shoot the works," he said. "Who fades me?"

"Rosalie?" said Joe. "Hey, now, what's this? Are you crying? Ah, no. Why do you want to do that for?"

He put his arm around her.

"He scared you? He scared you, didn't he?"

He turned on Karl.

"You crazy sonofabitch. Don't you ever know what you're doing?"

"Hah?" said Karl, intensely puzzled.

He took a step nearer.

"Why, she's crying," he said. "The little lady's crying."

"Well," said Joe. "Hooray for the idiot. He finally sees something."

"But that's all wrong," said Karl. "I never make anybody cry. Tell her, Joe. I was only trying to make her laugh. That's all I was trying to do."

Dark as he was, he had become very pale.

"Now, look," said Joe. "Don't you start crying on me."

"Golly Moses," said Karl. "Tell her, Joe, tell her."

"Okay, okay," said Joe. "Take your hands off me. Your bell's buzzing. Can't you hear it? Come on, Rosalie. Stop it now. He's not here any more. See? Was it me? The nut really scared you, didn't he? Are you all right now? How about walking up? That's a girl. Now you're doing it. Was it anything I said? Tell me. I can't remember. What did I say? Tell me. You'll tell me, won't you?"

But she did nothing of the sort as he continued to insist like a stubborn mule, appealing to her so clumsily, and all because he hesitated, like the comical love-maker that he was, to accept her tears as a tribute to his unaccountable charm, if not to his congenial power, straining instead to make a dishonest mystery of it, as if its true explanation rested in some hyperborean niche, in some blue hollow on the unreachable side of the moon.

The leaves will rustle in June, and again the rains will harangue the pavements in April, sounds self-appraising, fatalistic, all outgoing and world-wide. But he shall stomp through the nagging calendar of his days, with its red ones and its black, the iron clappers on his heels sharply confessing his distress, and whether he turn timid or turn wild, or be civil or boisterous, only he shall hear it as it should be heard, and possibly one other.

What a funny tale of an arm against a body. In the name of all, he reached his around her, anxious to give his lust the more exalted name of compassion. His what? She stumbled. He snorted like a bull as he seized and kissed her. She kissed him back savagely. At it so blindly in a tigerish renewal of the rapacious life between them, how could they know that their guilty ape, Karl, had crawled out of the elevator, had bitched his furious climbing of the cables between floors, had tumbled seven and a half flights, and had broken his back in too many places? How their faces flamed as they slowly toiled up the stairs to the fourth in a union as close as that of bride and husband. Sweet spirit, comfort them. They were taking the path of all promising criminals.

7.

Many a homely court convenes in its carnivorous way, after a Monday night dinner of such dairy dishes as milk soup of corn strained to its essence, croquettes of salmon with butter-fried bits in it of ordinary onion, Bellinsonian potato salad of a pure white cheerfully dotted with green pepper, natural spinach for the vegetable-loving ladies, and the more meaty asparagus out of a can for the men, coffee freshly percolated with an option to it of pound cake, to discourse and decide on the deficiencies and merits, the ascensions and flops, of the latest dead one.

Perhaps it was a cave man who was the first gossiper. Imagine such an antediluvian mystic with his coarse hair hanging over his eyes, and the fur on his chest singed by the flames of a disorderly fire, making that marvelous leap from an animal grunt at death to a metaphysical growl, thus becoming the first to say goodbye to the thing, and hello to its idea. And no doubt it will be a similar lout, composing himself in the rubble, who will be the last to convoke a family to hear him out on the same subject, a sulky and resentful one like Joe, with his gory story of a body divided in the middle, and his cross-eyed wonder why these decent hearts who politely listen are not instantly severed by it.

For the dewy kids and splashers, for the elderly and the marooned, as it was at the beginning, so will it be at the end, that concussive busybody, that derelict apostrophe known as death will always remain, even under the brightest of bulbs, blurred to the vision, and dry as chalk to the touch. But for our tough guy here, touching is never enough. He wants to seize it, and seize it with all his might, and freeze it to his bones, whirling round with it in a rattling good dance in the dark as well as in the light. Another darktown strutter, wildly snaking his hips. See how the stretcher is always ready for every golden and emboldened boy who goes hopping after that immense flirt, mentioned above as death, with the gayest of intentions, with the ungovernable kangaroo of his mind, that flicky little pogo stick.

"Whoa, now," said Abe. "Where are you jumping? Stick to the accident. Then we'll all know what you're talking about."

"Throw me the matches," said Joe. "That's the stuff. Let's have another cigarette. So it's consumption we'll get. What's finally going to happen to this world? They say it's going to blow up. What's the delay? The world. Who really gives a damn. Look. If I burn my finger right now, ow, you see? I yell. All I can think about is my own poor little finger. That's how much we care. That's how much we really give a damn about anything else."

"That was very cute," said Abe. "You mind doing that again?"

"Yow," said Joe. "It's wonderful, isn't it? Here we all are. Thanks to Mamma here, we've had us a damn good dinner. We feel swell now. Why shouldn't we? Soon we'll all be going to sleep. Who dreams the most around here? Or snores like a crosscut saw? A night more or less, a little bit older, the chances are, we'll wake up, here we'll be again. I'll rave. Helen will watch the door. You will keep disappearing through it. And Mamma will have the privilege of watching and worrying about it all. Hah, Ma? She won't talk, but she knows. It's all such a marvel and a miracle, ain't it?"

"Damn him," said Helen. "Where did he learn how to talk that way?"

"I think," said Abe. "I'll go somewhere and shoot a little pool. Very quietly."

"Wait," said Joe. "Don't go yet. I'd like to ask you something."

"One more strike, kid, and you're out."

"What do you suppose would happen if I went down now and stretched myself out in the gutter?"

"Hooray," said Helen. "He's beginning to know where he belongs."

156

"You think anybody would care?" said Joe. "You think they'd even stop? Naa, they're all much too busy. You know how busy they are. By god, they wouldn't even take the trouble to roll me over."

"Well," said Abe. "I don't know if they'd roll you over, but they sure would shovel you away."

"And burn the shovel afterwards," said Helen. "My dear brother. I hate to interrupt you. But may I bring something to your attention?"

"Absolutely," said Joe. "You will anyway."

"You flick those ashes on the floor just once more, and there'll be a dead one right here in this living room, understand me?"

"You hear that?" said Joe. "How does she do it? Even when she talks about ashes on the floor, she has such a sweet voice, hasn't she?"

"The sweetest," said Abe. "And so full of authority too."

"Well, well," said Helen. "So now it's two against one, is it?"

"Hates to interrupt me," said Joe. "Another brave one. Boy, does she squirm when she hears certain things."

"Look," said Helen. "Is somebody paying you to do this?"

"It's an old, old trouble."

"Or is this a new sickness with you?"

"It's tough enough trying to say anything."

"Ah, well," said Abe. "Maybe munching on something will help. Is there any fruit in the house?"

"And even when you do," said Joe. "Nobody wants to listen. But nobody. All of a sudden they get deaf. They begin to look around to see how they can make themselves scarce. And more comfortable. Except that one there, of course. Look at her. Why don't you relax, Ma? There's a back to that lovely chair."

"Come here," said Mrs. Bellinson. "Let me look at your finger."

"What finger?" said Joe. "Oh, that one. It's okay, Ma. I really didn't burn it. I was only making believe."

"I said, let me see it."

"All right," said Joe. "Here. I told you it was nothing, didn't I?"

"Fine then. Helen."

"Yes, Ma?"

"There's a bowl in the icebox."

"I know," said Helen. "Let that apple eater there get it."

"There are bananas in it too."

"Oh," said Helen. "Well, then, in that case."

157

"Ye gods," said Joe. "Our mother in all her glory. Why are you so pale, Mrs. Bellinson? I stole a folding chair from the place for you, didn't I? Why don't you take it and go down with it in the street sometimes? The sun's been out every day for days now. The sun. Remember? It's yours too. Honest. It belongs to you as much as it does to anybody else. Which way are you looking? Didn't you know that?"

Hobbled mares, handicapped kids braced against the blackboard, walled-in forgers and arsonists, traffic violators carrying white canes, state-supported blacks on a chain gang, strumpets on their soiled mattresses, bisexual hunter of the toilet, rickety handy men wrinkling the earth with their rakes, the convulsive captain in the pilot house, chickens in the coop, various old goats, they know it. And the monk in his cell knows it too. And this Mamma or that. Is it a fact that the more absolute the sovereign, the more is he paralyzed? For God comes in here, and the hint of his dazzling and capitalized light. Misdirected ray, and out of order, it visits the heretical skin of the gadabout to make him look like bronze, but leaves the bones of the utterly devoted ones to bleach. And faith is said to be a sunny thing. Pagan sons who wish to live longer and closer to the center of the savage source, will unfurl their tiny flags of insurrection, and use force to set their mothers free to sit before a great exterior door, dignified matriarchs, their prayers spent, their powers abbreviated, their true work done, sadly enshrined in the smile of a fresh baby, an abdicated motherhood crocheting useless doilies for a reprimanding sun.

"Yes," said Mrs. Bellinson. "The day will come."

"Oh, sure," said Joe. "It always does, doesn't it?"

"It will soon be over."

"What will?"

"Then I will rest. Only then."

"Rest," said Joe. "There's a hot one. You're talking about the grave again, aren't you? But how do you know? Maybe once you get in there, you'll be too scared to rest. Where do you get all this information anyway? Does a little fairy come and tell you? I'm around. I don't hear anything. Or do you get bulletins direct from the nearest cemetery?"

Mrs. Bellinson smiled.

"If you'll take your heavy hand away from my head, maybe then I'll be able to tell you."

"Uh-uh," said Joe. "What's this in the air? I think I'm beginning to smell God. Heavy? What do you mean heavy? Feel that touch. Light as a feather, isn't it? As a matter of fact, I was talking to him myself the other day. Boy, did I lace it into him. I really thought I had him going. But you think he answered me?"

"He will."

"When?" said Joe. "When I'm deaf myself? A God with wax in his ears. He ought to go see a specialist. Ah, I'm sorry. I didn't mean that, Mamma. I respect the old boy. You know that. Just the same, what's the deal? How do you get to first base with him? Do you have to go out and buy a whole ox with horns and burn it? What are the magic words you have to say over it? That's a honey of an idea. To sacrifice. Or maybe you have to learn how to whistle in a certain way. I ought to ask Cousin Ethel's canary. Or maybe it's better to give him the silent treatment. That can be a wow sometimes. Or is some kind of a sudden noise really the best? Come on, Ma, here's your chance. If you know, now's the time to tell me."

"A baby," said Mrs. Bellinson. "He wants to eat God like Abie eats an apple."

"Excuse me," said Joe. "Could you let me have a little pail, lady? I understand God spends his afternoons in the orchard. My god. I mean. Suppose when I'm looking, he pops up in a cherry? Or I find him in a single wild strawberry? That would hardly be enough to go around for everybody, would it? Gosh, what do I do then?"

Mrs. Bellinson laughed.

"You will do," she said. "What I said. You will eat it. But say a blessing over it first."

"Ah," said Joe. "That I'll do. That much I remember. I'll show him he's not the only one who thinks he's a gentleman. Ah, Mamushka. Did I ever tell you?"

"What?" said Mrs. Bellinson.

"I like you," said Joe. "Honest. I really do."

"The sonofagun," said Helen. "Look how he plays up to her."

"And you know why?" said Joe. "It's selfish, Ma. I mean it. Who else would stand for it? I know. Don't think I'm so blind. I know I'm developing a big mouth."

"You said it," said Abe. "Another mystery."

"Here," said Helen. "Close it up with this. Maybe it'll stop growing."

159

"A whole banana," said Joe. "Do you see what I see, Ma? She's giving up a whole banana. Hey, where are you going?"

"Downstairs," said Mrs. Bellinson.

"What for?" said Joe. "To buy something? Let me go. I'll go for you."

"No," said Mrs. Bellinson. "I'm afraid. You're too good to me."

"Ho, ho," said Joe. "Know any other jokes? Hello? Where did she go? How do you like that woman? A real magician. Now you see her, now you don't. Amazing. And so damn independent too. Wait until she comes back. I'll pin her down once and for all."

"Oh, no," said Helen. "Please. No. That's enough for tonight. Have pity on us, will you?"

"Let him rave," said Abe. "You know how it is when your best friend dies. What do I do with this garbage, dear? Didn't you bring a plate?"

"Best friend?" said Joe. "I hardly knew the guy."

"Then what in hell are you so excited about?" said Abe. "I'll use the ashtray, okay? An accident is an accident. What's the sense of bawling about it so much?"

"Accident, hell," said Joe. "He asked for it."

"Really?" said Abe. "And what do you think you're doing? You're asking for it too, aren't you?"

"Me?" said Joe. "What do you mean?"

"Now don't get so goddamn red."

"Red?" said Joe. "Who's red?"

"Relax," said Abe. "We don't have to talk about it if you don't want to."

"That's okay," said Joe. "I don't care. Why not? I know what you mean. If quitting my job is asking for it, then I'm glad. I really am."

"Good for you," said Abe, and turned up his sceptical eyes to follow the crazy flight of a fly, a comparable exhibitionist which proceeded to perform a series of impossible stunts on the chandelier and on a ceiling lately calcimined. Joe watched his brother watching it, anxiously waiting for more. Great was his doubt suddenly, as great as his gladness before. Callow and captivating little beast with its diseased and microscopic mark, Helen ran into the kitchen to arm herself boldly with what could promptly kill it.

The future, like the fly swatter to the fly, is an object of supreme

160

invisibility. To fumble for its shape in the conic, the rectangular, or the cylindrical, is to be infatuated with nonsense, which its victim, winged or otherwise, always greets, the moment before it is squashed, with the extremest surprise. Heartless bringer of one thing surely, it conveys its message of inevitable extinction through every human lip and eye. It can be an awful crusher. Watch it. But the more Helen wildly swiped at the pest and missed, the more Joe began to root for adroitness, cunning, and consummate agility. There is no escape. It will die. But if it had ever feared the future, would it have ever dared to fly?

"I'm crazy," said Joe. "Maybe I'm absolutely off my head. But if everything ends in the same way, there, whack, what is there to be afraid of?"

"Did you see me?" said Helen. "I sure got that one, didn't I?"

"Since you're asking me," said Abe. "I'll tell you. You can get hurt, sonny. Real bad."

"Hurt?" said Joe. "How hurt? What? Where?"

"Oh," said Abe. "Just keep it up and you'll find out. Careful, brother. I warn you. Be smart. Pick on someone your size. Or someone smaller. Like Helen here. Maybe then you'll have a chance."

"Oh, indubitably," said Helen. "Which reminds me of a certain wiseguy with down on his cheeks and stars in his eyes who wanted to go fight City Hall. And collapsed on the first step. You know that story?"

"Someone my size," said Joe. "Someone smaller than me. What are we talking about? A prize fight or something? All I know is that this job of mine, job, and only job, is not what I want. That much I know. And you know what else I know?"

"Out with it," said Helen. "The suspense is killing me."

"I know. I can feel it in my heart. There must be something else."

"Really?" said Abe. "What? Where?"

"Ah," said Joe. "Now you're mocking me."

"No, no," said Abe. "I'm serious. Talk. Give us some idea."

"What idea?" said Joe. "How the hell should I know? I'm just beginning. But you can bet all the money you got on one thing. I'm going to find out. Even if it's the last thing I ever do."

"That's sweet," said Helen. "The sooner the better, is what I say."

"Jesus," said Joe. "Just think. Think how happy I'll be the day I do.

161

You see that? I'm already high just thinking about it. So what if I lose an arm? Or get my head split open? Or fall flat on my face finally? So what if everything I say sounds as old as the hills? The hell with being different. Who says I have to be? I'm me. I'm new. If we're alive, we're all absolutely new. That's right. Catch it from me. Get excited. Show a little imagination. Think about it, think."

Cluster of blood, of the four old cardinal humours, violent spade-calling, the passionate laying on of hands, the realistic kiss, the unimpeachable upshot of the traditional fit which rocks every guinea pig of a recruit who volunteers for an experimental grafting of the shrouds and ratlines of his soul onto the mast of life, of being positive of bliss without positively knowing why or wherefore, are each, and are all, fresh and massive sincerities.

Once again. A nimbus quivers about a new figure, a subtler wingspread and more sweeping symbol for today, the nighthawk of happiness. Once the dawn-provoked soothsayer cackled of a quest after the quintessence of light, and the drowsy tinkle of a hand bell was itself the sound of a sunnier myth, and when the sun set, men went to sleep, and the darkness would say to itself sadly, this is a piggish and pigeon-toed time. As yet incommunicable, and still oddly commingled, now the big-bellied intricacies of the night have been affixed to the simplicities of the day, some of which are defunct, and others sinfully diminishing, and the excitement over the result is extremely modern, and the accelerated mind of many a man has already begun to search for images of scary and opulent complication. What was once thin is now so much thicker. Gothic tremors, alcoholized ghosts, the abandoned tails of tributary jokes, the dissonant shadow of the bat, the forcemeat of jazz, the skin-breaking nip of the rat, are tinier elements invading the realm of what is called happiness, crowding it fine, flawing it magnificently. Just once more now, and be done with it, formerly it was easy on the eyes to watch the theological claws of a more priestly bird, soothingly white, scratch its neat circle of hosannas in the heavens. Season then followed season. But now, when one mighty cycle of a depression gives way to another, each vision is double-faced, and the profane and unreasonable side is uppermost, and a man is wise if he burrows in the darkness, for there is where he will find the light.

That is, he hopes so, this shuffler Joe, who bruises the delicate

162

concept of wisdom, lazily patterned as he is after some clumsy light-bringer of the past, fast developing into a fanatic for mood, peeling his banana with a fierce acceptance of this slippery act, and of all the predictable others he will be forced to perpetrate, and in turn, to endure.

What a bore. The self alone cares about its selfhood, and is constantly driving it into a corner in order to repossess it, and when it does, it seems so terribly whimsical about becoming itself again, if only because what it really is, when it is entirely itself, is only Joe. So pleased to come full circle in his foolishness, very much aware of the welcome back he deserves, he anticipates his Helen and his Abe, and with a smile as sardonic as theirs, acts as their spokesman in saying, ah, if only it were possible to get rid of him as he so often wishes to get rid of himself. Parable and paradox, the truth is no longer interesting unless it is twisted.

The related occurrence and influence of happenings galore, if somewhere an ant, defier of the piecemeal way, is propelling hillward the immense body of a moth, here the shot icebox door is banged sharply, and Mamma reappears, and her somewhat bemused appendages of children, these temporarily quiet fractions, become instantly alert when they see how clear and complete is her indignation. The previous clink of glass had told them it was two quarts of milk she had bought from the grocer, Landesberg, that famous windbag. But what they covet most, though they are truly fond of their snack of fresh milk before going to bed, is what money can never buy, such as a purer vision of appreciation or disgust, or of overwhelming despair, which Mamma so often brings back with the potatoes, sour cream, or cornflakes, but of which she can rarely force herself to speak, from these daily journeys outward with an irrational dollar to shop for a grain of significance in what people blurt out or insinuate, or in what they can ever hope to gain by trying to shame and cheat each other. She must tell them? Ach, she sighed, all right. She will try her best to tell them. But they must not judge or blame. They must only listen.

"Well," said Joe. "Thanks for reminding us. It would be terrible to forget we were still babes in the woods. Though it's funny. I don't drool any more. I wonder what that means?"

"Different every second," said Helen. "Ye gods, he sure tries hard enough, doesn't he? You think he really knows what he's doing? Gosh,

163

Ma, you should've heard this son of yours when you left. He became so hysterical, he scared us stiff. Come to think of it. What was it all about anyway? Do you remember, Abe? Ah, yes, happy. He was happy. Slap-happy, that's what he is. You watch, Mamma. He'll never let you get in a word."

"I can wait," said Mrs. Bellinson.

"I really wonder," said Joe. "Does anyone here even catch on?"

"Catch on to what?" said Helen. "Hey, now. You're not wiping those sticky fingers of yours on that doily, are you?"

"That I might have a mind too."

"Besides your tongue?" said Helen. "Don't make me laugh."

"And that when I listen," said Joe. "And I listen, all right. Everyone should listen like me. I have to think too at the same time. Maybe I haven't got the words for it yet. But don't worry. They'll come. Maybe I was only a pair of ears once. But that's all over now. You better get used to it."

"Maybe so," said Abe. "But do you mind if we don't try? Hold it now. Let me ask you something. That is. Before you leave the stage for a while. By request. You ready? Will you please tell me what in the hell makes you think everyone's so damn interested in you all the time?"

"Me?" said Joe. "When did I ever say so? Is that the way I sound?"

"Easy, boy. Don't look so upset. It's all right yet. We still like you."

"Like you?" said Helen. "We simply adore you. Now. What were you saying, Mamma?"

That there was once a rotten apple. Is that all? Strange how now this does seem to be the gist of it. And that there the lonely Macintosh lolled, the last of a crate, still hoping to be sold and at least partially eaten. Little kids at school smile the way her children smile. They smile at her as if they have already heard every story that has ever been told. Wait. So yes. So there it was, a most pathetic object, and as such, plain applesauce for the sentimental, whether they be subtle about it or not. And that means? How can she know as yet? Oh, this dreadful confusion of schemers indoors, and triflers abroad, can her puzzled ones guess just how each resembles each? Why, in this, that each has been known to pray for his own destruction. She shows them her hands. Empty. Yet how is it they still hold everything they have ever held? But not the apple? She will excuse them if they laugh. For to say of an apple that it hopes, that it knows it is without virtue until it feels

164

it is actually being devoured, is to show a childish passion for fantasy and the inconceivable. How true it is again. Where there is much talk, there is much foolishness. Dear children, please, be patient. When an old groping heart struggles to say what it really feels, try to understand, try to suffer its crazy impossible speeches.

It is me, it is me, it is no one else. They may be blood of her blood, but she must disown them if they do not hiss at her for dominating the story, and killing it as a tyrant is killed for the killer's glory. Down, down with the front-running ego, that horned and crested screamer, causing the utmost mischief, trampling the truth into dust. Sometimes it is good to get excited. And think herself funny. Has she ever told them? When she tries to scrawl her name in her own broken English lettering, she smiles, and the grave comes into her mind, and she sees a monument which, as soon as it is unveiled, begins to lean forward, and on it is a dash separating the dates, faintly chiseled, and that will have been her mark on life. A conceit which cheapens life as it vulgarizes death. They can frown at her, but surely it has helped them to listen less to her, and more to what she is saying. So good. So now she feels so much better. She is rid of herself. Now she can begin.

Oh, that grocer's itch. When did Landesberg first put out to sea in his cockleshell store? Clogged or running, he keeps torturing the great big garages of his nose. Ask him why, and he will answer, what other happiness does he have in life? Thus he tries so bitterly to cover over every one of his fresh scabs and bleeding troubles. Such as his weighing hand smashed in Canarsie in a rowboat, this chronic quinsy throat, his mortgaged fate like a stale cracker, to have a hooky player for a son, an accidental only one, with the register picked open many a morning, and so much of the silver profits gone, and a hideous kvetch for a wife, a defeated poodle with her uncombed despair knocking against his head in bed, peeping at his rounder eye from out her individual horse blanket, a free loaf of tip-top bread to anyone who can tell him where that particular animal had come from, if the creative stinkers in the street had a jingle about Landy the Bandy, who never gave candy, Old Mr. Iceberg, the little bastards, they were so wrong, for every man has feelings, and certain true ones which can plain kill him if they show.

All schnooks, what do they know? In they creep, his so-called customers, in their basic business of buying to eat, and when he says

165

money, they say, what? What is what? Never mind pay him later. He shows them the back of his cheese knife as they cleave to his canned goods. Drop it, he yells, or you lose a hand. So they turn stiffly to leave him with a vision of their matching rage, shuffling back to their dim burrows to let the cold water run, and gulp down five more glasses of it on credit, and put their bloated heads together, and who do they blame for it, Mrs. Bellinson? Me, me, only me.

Hungrier fools, their miserable builds, character like cottage cheese, his own grandmother, they were sure she would never die, but as long as she lived in the old country, and she lived to ninety in Pinsk alone, lived all her life each day on hardly more than a single potato with eyes, and a blind herring bone. Patience of long ago, sour and crowded, its stony wisdom impacted in the jaw of time like his wisdom tooth, let them pick at that, this horrible crop of grubbers, and he in turn will gladly burn all their bills, and dream as they do of eating of the fruit too. Mrs. Bellinson, one of the smart ones, bless her, does he have to tell her why he too is beginning to eat less and less? And who is this new dumb bitch now? Look at her. A woman can be a headache as big as the world, standing there with only an apple in her hand. Poverty of a colder region, she looked to him like an Eskimo, bundled in the illusory squatness of her rags, a stranger with the remotest eyes and the yellowest cheekbones, inflaming him at once by asking him in no voice at all, how much?

It was a terrible dumb show, children, for when he indicated five fingers, she merely opened her other hand, and showed him her three cents. He stared at her with all the autocratic rage of a Moses. Who is this backsliding blockhead? How dare she bargain with such a sick man? He stiff-armed her furiously with two commands, first to replace the shrunken symbol, and second to uproot her lopsided feet right out of the store, understand? Hushed story lovers of mine, if only that woman had whimpered before she obeyed, this endless tale would have ended here with a sigh, but she obeyed him so perfectly that pity rattled their foolish mother, just as they see her, and she cried, here is a nickel, tyrant, let her take that apple with her, let her take it, let her go.

What a mistake, what a sin it is, to make a man feel so ashamed, reducing him to the grass-crunching bafflement of a tethered animal which he is not, stealing from him so impulsively his own proud

166

chance to prove there is something faintly human still sputtering in him. All were punished now by the awful silence. Never had she seen a cornered mind race around so madly to free and redeem itself. Not so fast, he suddenly cried. Did his dear Mrs. Bellinson believe she could make like an angel with a nickel only? Cook eggs are brown, and use eggs are white, and mercy darts through shark-infested seas, hooray for the rainbow-colored lady, the most likely fish to praise, but a man is hated when he is practical and fierce, when he visits the strongest of the weak with his reddest emotions. He swiped with his forefinger at the unholy condition of his nose, and down went the whole huge fist on the counter to give it an infernal blow. Here, Mrs. Bellinson, here is the price he fixes now and today to pay for the cheapest pair of wings, such a monstrously clever woman as his dear Mrs. Bellinson would surely know how to clip them to herself, a dollar, Mrs. Bellinson, pay him one dollar, for that apple, and he will throw in the rust and dust of that stupid cow of a woman too. Oh, think of this tremendous challenge, children, and try to guess. What did their poor blundering mother do?

"Why, you spit on him," said Helen. "That's what you did. The nerve of that man. Did you ever hear anything like it?"

"Spit on him?" said Abe. "No. Maybe you would. But not Mamma."

"Sure she would," said Helen. "Why not? Don't try to show me you know her better than I do. I saw how mad she was when she came up. Did I say spit on him? Why, spitting is too mild. He ought to be strung up and riddled full of bullets."

"That's right," said Abe. "Be tough. Act like a woman. Hack away."

"Bang, bang. You know what? I would've taken that woman right out to another store and bought her a whole pound of apples. And then I would've dragged her right back to that monster and said to him, see? So much for you and your one rotten apple. I would've fixed him all right. I would've even picketed him afterwards."

"Picket him," said Mrs. Bellinson. "Is that how you were listening?"

"A dollar," said Helen. "Imagine. Boy, if it was me he was fooling around with, he would've certainly whistled for it. No, no. Don't tell us, Mamma. I don't want to know. If I hear that you just stood there and gave it to him."

167

"Yes," said Mrs. Bellinson.

"What?" said Helen.

"Yes," said Mrs. Bellinson. "I just stood there. I gave it to him."

"Ye gods," said Helen. "And you mean to say he actually took it?"

"Yes," said Mrs. Bellinson. "He took it."

"Ah," said Joe. "That's the stuff. You did absolutely right, kiddo. What a way to top him. That was exactly the way to fix him."

"Hey," said Helen. "Watch where you're flinging your arm. Did you ever hear? I'll be damned if I'm going to let him get away with it. Look, Ma. Give me half of what I get and I'll go right down to him. Just say the word. I'll get that dollar back for you or bust."

"May God forgive me," said Mrs. Bellinson. "Are these my children? Or are they somebody else's idiots?"

"Idiots?" said Helen. "You think I don't understand what happened? So okay. So you gave it to him. That's calling his bluff. That much I like. But what I don't get is, why should he keep it? That's what I don't understand. Why should he be left with all the gravy?"

"The hell with it," said Abe. "Why get into such an uproar about it? Let the old bugger choke on it. That's what I say. Wait a second now. There was something I wanted to say. Now what in the hell was it?"

"Another one," said Helen. "Did you ever see so much confusion all at the same time? A little more of this and we'll all fall asleep. What's wrong with us lately? Why do we fumble around so much? You tell us, Mamma. You started the whole thing. Tell us. What does it all mean?"

"Goddamn it," said Abe. "I know there's something we're leaving out. What is it we're leaving out?"

"Oh," said Helen. "Not much. Just about the rest of the whole world. Including our bugeyed genius over there. JoJo the listening man. At least he has enough sense to keep his mouth shut. Or does he? Uh-uh. Hold everything now. The sun is rising."

What did he have in his fist? A smart aleck with his head at an odd angle, with his old creaking shoes on, he walked over to his mother, gently placed a dollar bill in her lap, and bowing just once before he about-faced, quietly changed his seat to a chair with meager stuffing, and a stiffer back. How straitlaced he looked, and they, how solemnly and totally astonished. He took an open look. Smiling would not do it. He dared to look again. And suddenly began to laugh.

"I beat you," said Joe. "Admit it. I beat you all to it."

"A maniac," said Helen. "I'll knock him over the head right away. What's he trying to do? Make us look foolish or something?"

"The sonofagun," said Abe. "That he certainly has. Let me see now. Who can break a five for me around here?"

"Oh, no," said Helen. "You're not going to pull the same stunt, are you?"

"Or maybe I have enough change."

"Hey," said Joe. "Look what she's doing. She's throwing it on the floor. Holy mackerel. My last buck."

"Ah," said Helen. "Good. I'm glad."

"And I was going to ask her to give it back to me double."

"You were going to do what?"

"No," said Joe. "Don't go, Mamma. Don't go yet. You musn't go this way."

Mrs. Bellinson hesitated. She shook her head.

"What way?" she said. "What is it that's eating away in you? Why are you always so afraid?"

"Ah," said Joe. "Listen how bitter."

"Right away you tremble. You think you can buy me. You had to make a sacrifice. A child. You had to make believe I was God."

"God?" said Joe. "When did I ever say you were God?"

"But don't worry," said Mrs. Bellinson. "You're young yet. You'll forget. When you go to bed, you'll have no trouble falling asleep."

"Wait a second," said Joe. "Give me a chance here."

"Leave your job. Don't leave your job. Only don't play any more tricks on me. Understand?"

"Jesus," said Joe. "There it is again. The way everybody here takes it. It'll end up by killing me."

"Don't touch me. What is this? Am I the only exception around here? Can't I be bitter for one day?"

"I know, Mamma, I know. You don't have to tell me. I understand."

"I'm sorry," said Mrs. Bellinson. "I'm not angry with you. I'm angry. What I see, I see. And sometimes what I see, I say like a fool. And I forget some other fool might be listening. Is it cool outside? You think I will need a sweater? This is funny. How is it I'm wearing my right glasses? No, no, sit. Don't follow me. Talk. You have plenty to talk yet. I will go now and sit by the open window like a cow. I won't bother you. I will just sit there and look out. And sit there. And look out."

169

Because he has plenty to talk yet. Enviable phase of her more solid and spacious age, cleared of patched memories and silly impulses, she will slip into her merited place, her one small opening on to the world, where no one will goad her, and prop her elbows on the sill, and angelically survey the idiotic rumbles and stumbles, the appallingly gay and reckless panorama of his processional rebeldom, and see him she will in whatever she sees, in a world as cramped and delimited as the head of a pin. He had to bend and pick up what she had thrown away. As poor as ever, and as ready to bawl, he knew somehow that he had plenty to pound yet, to inch himself along, ruining toy cymbals, and bashing in baby drums. It was true. He was definitely a primitive and pinhead as yet. He felt so blue. He had to sneer.

"Well?" he said. "Now what? Where do we go from here?"

"Out," said Abe. "And this time, so help me, I mean it."

"Hooray for you," said Joe. "Let me know if you find anything."

"Absolutely," said Abe. "You can depend on me."

"That is," said Joe. "If you know what you're looking for."

"Look," said Abe. "Whatever you do, don't mumble. Do me a favor. If you have anything to say, say it. I don't like this mumbling business."

"Out," said Joe. "It's become a terrific thing. Every time you pick up your head, somebody's running out. Why? What is there that's out that's not in? What?"

"You for one thing," said Abe. "Where's my hat? Now what in the hell did I do with my tie? Damn that rag. I'm always leaving it around somewhere. I'll tell you what I'll do for you, sonny. If anything crops up, I'll send up a flare. How's that? Does that satisfy you?"

"Kitchen," said Helen.

"I beg your pardon," said Abe. "Are you addressing a dog?"

"I said," said Helen. "Your tie. I saw it in the kitchen."

"Kitchen?" said Abe. "How did it get there?"

"You planted it, brother. With your own dear hands."

"Dear, dear," said Abe. "It's all a circus, ain't it? You never know what you do until you do it, do you? Silence in the courthouse. Two pair of eyes full of flies. I mean, lies. It drives me up the wall sometimes. How did I ever get mixed up with this group? Is this the riffraff our dying country is looking for? Ah, well. Toodle-oo, you all. If I get a chance, believe me, I'll trade you both in for one good laugh."

"A deserter," said Joe. "That's what he is."

"Oh," said Helen. "These nights. These awful stupid nights."

"He's right," said Joe. "We're too damn serious."

"You hear me, Joe? What in god's name do you do with them?"

"Say the hell with them," said Joe. "What else?"

Who now? Who he wanted to know? Who was that first earnest ass? Who was that original cock of the walk who flew to the forefront, muscle-bound with suppressed fears between the ears, and squawked of life as it increases, of life as it advances, and as it grows older for each solemn rubberneck, increases immensely in interest and splendor? What then is the height of felicity? To lick a stamp in a pagoda? To bleed a perpetual plum? To ride herd on a saint? To chortle while another chokes? Icings, goulash, and the usual confetti, where is that preposterous pig of a hustler who first raved of a jamboree for one, his own mouth crammed with rich mash of strawberries, while the populace gawked, and allowed its maw to be stuffed with sour oats and prudent wheys?

"Was it a thistle we used to blow at to tell us the time?"

"A what?" said Helen.

"Ah," said Joe. "I wish I had a better memory."

"Stay here," said Helen. "Don't run out on me."

"It seems like a million years ago."

"Let's just sit here and look at each other."

"I could go down to the clubroom."

"Listen," said Helen. "Did I ever tell you about that vegetarian I work with? I wish you could see her."

"I thought you said just sit and look."

"She keeps trying to learn how to whistle. It's pathetic. What do you think it means to her? If I had nerve enough, I'd ask her. Anyway, the other day right after lunch, Zenobia, that's her name, take it or leave it, comes rushing up to me at my desk with two enormous cookies in a paper napkin. Pushes them right under my nose. There's a beauty for you. Would you believe it if I told you that mop of hers is already coming out in bunches? And she's hardly thirty yet. The things you see sometimes. It's enough to make you scream. Anyway, before I get tangled up too much in her long braids, I was full enough as it happened, so I said to her, thanks, Zennie, just the same, but I couldn't possibly. Then I'll have to throw them away, she says, huh, everyone is

171

so particular today. And goes into a long megillah about her old lady with the chin whiskers, the way she talks about her, it's a panic, who had her nose lifted after which the boy, there was once a little rooster in that group of hens, screamed the first time he saw her in her new disguise, and bango, there he was on an oiler in the navy just to run away from this cuckoo mother of theirs who could be so damn dumb as to pack such cookies in her lunch. Look at them, she says. You know I don't eat meat, Helen. Meat? I said. I looked at her. Here we go again, I thought, calling up Bellevue. That's right, she says. Can't you see it? Here's a cat. And this one is a chicken, isn't it?"

"Whoa, now," said Joe. "Wait a minute."

"So help me," said Helen. "I should die right here on this spot if I'm lying to you. She wouldn't eat them. They were shaped like animals."

"Jesus," said Joe.

"Isn't that a riot?"

"Fantastic. You and your powder-puff factory. That's something too. That really is. How can you stand it working there?"

"I don't," said Helen. "I sit."

"Taking dictation from that hairy hippo. What's his name again? Something like Smolnick, isn't it? Or is it Bulnick? Ye gods, Helen, you belong there like I belong in."

"In heaven, I know. Goddamn it, Joe."

"What's the matter?"

"I'm disappointed in you. I thought you would really laugh."

"What?" said Joe. "What are you talking about? I laughed. Didn't you hear me?"

"Sure," said Helen. "One lousy little squeak. Be careful the next time. You might strain yourself. Or was it me? I know. I bet it was me. It always happens. I must've left out the postulate or something."

"The what?"

"The postulate. Don't you know what a postulate is?"

"Ah," said Joe. "Our good friend, Louie."

"What's so funny about that?"

"The real philosopher."

"Now he laughs."

"Him I like. When's he due next? Is he still the one and only?"

"No," said Helen. "I mean, yes, I suppose so. I mean. As much as there can be one. The way things are."

"What was that last?"

"He's fine, damn it. Is that what you want to know?"

"Hey, now."

"I'm sorry," said Helen.

"That's better."

"I didn't mean to bite your head off. It's just that I hate to be asked."

"Sure," said Joe. "I know how it is."

"Oh," said Helen. "He's all right. As a matter of fact, he's so fine it's a crime he can't be even better. Or be what he wants to be. Whatever that is. Do you think he has a chance? Do you know anyone who's ever going to give it to him? All of a sudden. What am I? he says. Did you ever hear such a question? I could kill him. You are what you are, I tell him. You can yell all you want while you live. But you will be what you are until you die. Shoot. You think I know what I'm talking about? But I tell him anyway. Ah, the men these days. What do they think they have to be? What am I that I can creep into his bones? Or he into mine? What? What's this soul he's always moaning about? If he has one, I have one too, haven't I? So then? Does it mean I have to carry on like a nut about it?"

"Look," said Joe. "I don't think you understand."

"All right, then, you tell me. Why should he get paint on the seat of his pants? There is always a sign. He knows his letters. Or forget to button himself in front like a baby? Or dip his tie in his tea? He floats. He's forever swimming away. How can I handle him when all he does is read the Bible and blesses me and makes the sign of the cross every time he sees me for two, three weeks? He's sweet enough as he is. Who wants him any sweeter? Or buries his excited nose in some crazy little book, and then tries to tell me with an expression he's borrowed from some half-crippled wiseguy, Schopenpopover, that women are to blame for everything. You know what I do then? I laugh. I know how much it hurts him, but I can't help it, I laugh right in his face. You should see the tears come into his eyes. I feel like a murderer. Oh, the sunny day he comes to me without a book under his arm. You know what I would do? I'd shake his hand. Yes, sir, I'd congratulate him. I'd say to him, son, today you are a man with your hands free. Now. What are you going to do about it?"

"The poor guy," said Joe. "How did he ever get mixed up with a tough baby like you?"

"But you think that day will ever come?"

"Who knows?" said Joe. "You can always hope, can't you?"

"Oh, sure," said Helen. "I can just see myself sitting around and waiting. I'll be grey by then. And he'll be blind. And we'll both be paying you peanuts to push us around in a wheelchair."

"And by god," said Joe. "I'd do a damn good job too. Even after I lose my hands. Honestly. I don't understand it. What's aggravating you anyway? What is it you want? To twist him around your little finger? Okay, then. You're a woman, aren't you? You know what you have to do. Cry. That's right. Why don't you ever cry? You never cry, do you?"

"Don't kid yourself."

"I mean," said Joe. "I mean when he's around. It works, Helen. Believe me, I can tell you. All you have to do is drop a tear or two, and take my word for it, you'll have him flopping down on his knees right before you."

"Don't be silly. Who wants him there?"

"You do," said Joe. "Even if you don't know it."

"Ah," said Helen. "Please. Don't try to be such a wiseguy. What do you know about such things anyway? If you ask me, you're in a nice little fog yourself. You rushed home tonight with a cockeyed story about your local elevator man getting killed or killing himself, which was it? Another poor sucker dead and gone. Why? You say he asked for it. What was he asking for? To leave this fascinating world way before his time? I don't believe it for a second. All you nuts. You're all chasing after something that isn't there. It just isn't there, Joe. I mean it. So stop looking for it. What's happened to Mamma?"

"You know where she is."

"My god," said Helen. "Are these still my legs?"

"What isn't there?"

"The good old American dream. Or some such rot. How should I know?"

"Listen how ignorant all of a sudden."

"Ah," said Helen. "It's good to stretch. You never take your eyes off a person, do you? God, if I'm bad at this, you're a million times worse. What do I really know about you? Do you ever tell me where you go? Or what you do? Or what's moiling and boiling in you? Why should you expect me to tell you everything when you tell me absolutely

174

nothing at all? A real sphinx. No wonder everybody wants to run away from you."

"I can see," said Joe. "This is my day for getting my lumps."

"Yes," said Helen. "And tomorrow it'll be my turn. If you'll excuse me now, I think I'll go and annoy Mamma for a change. How about pulling up stakes and joining me? Aw, come on. Look at me. Don't sit here all alone like that."

"I won't," said Joe. "Go ahead. Don't worry about me. I'll come. Maybe later. I don't know. Maybe later."

Queer, straggling night of disagreement so oddly amiable, that home rocks, in which one member says, solemnly winking at death, that her day will come, while another, with angry looks of come-hither at that elusive thing which no one as yet has been able to call anything but life, says, and how hopelessly he says it, that his will never come, never. He struck a match to a cigarette like one who knows he is doomed to be dumb just when he most dearly wishes not to be so. His sigh exploded in one huge puff.

Smoke began to billow where he had already begun to talk to himself. Of what in particular, if one must know? Of howling time when the moon is at its plumpest? Of sprinkling away his silence as if it were refined sugar, every heart a sour-milk cake? Of the calcium value, and the daintiness, of his bite-size despair? Of a dippy scheme to dabble in the formal art of minstrelsy, and become both end man and interlocutor, and joke himself, as either one, into squeals of disrobement and roars of confession?

Certainly, and more to the point, it is the hero as faultfinder, screamingly defective himself, who will often find himself fondling an opposite number who is not exactly top-hole or untouched by human hands, who will be shocked when he realizes, will hastily drop that one and as quickly pluck another, tearing the girls apart as if they were no more sensitive than daisies, until he demolishes a whole field, finds a petal in his hair, feels dazed, becomes so afraid he will remain single and apart that he swears he must salvage something in the form of someone from out the innumerable odd sticks and imperfect annuals, so promptly flops on his knees, scratches around feverishly, and finally comes up with. Rosalie.

Rosalie. What a find for the books, perpetually enchanted as he is with what he botches, may he have all the possible benefits of her, from the lydian sting of her lips to the mischievous twitch of her tussie, but keep the news of her existence from his mother and sister he must, though for his sake they might not be so severe or strict, until he no longer considers his Rosalie to be his off again and on again, his one mistake, his casual misprint, his ambivalent bust. In the meantime, there she is, and there he is, and there they are together almost as one. And it does sound so nice. And it does seem so simple. And yet, what would Mamma and Helen think of him? What would they say if they knew what he was at and what he was up to?

Does anyone really care? Does he? Where are the keener troubles? Where are the braver men at war in remote and exotic places who are so much more exposed and miserable than he? What is this indecent dream with variations he suddenly remembers and must live through again, a dream based on the everyday and inescapable season of rutting? How dull it is in the metropolis when only doors are crashed, and dunces are surprised in the act of doing something preliminary on their knees, appealing to each other to get with it, feeling like dogs, and failing. Others have fainted more gracefully. This is odd. That bedroom had eight walls. When the intermission lights go on, the sun is shining at midnight, and the April breeze questions his shirttail which is sticking out. Enter the eighteenth century, hoofbeats and halloos, the pastoral huddling, the rosy ones flushed out of a bush, parted for the nonce, thwacked and cursed roundly. Please. Spare him forever that moment of agony just before awakening. Was that the squeak of a mouse? Such horrid thinking out of school can ruin a man. Where is everybody? Is there anything cool to drink in the house?

He stumbled into the kitchen to settle for a glass of plain sink water, and be thankful for that. Sweet are the uses of the interval. Objects rebel at last and reappear. They are consoling and urbane. Merely to gaze upon the savings-bank calendar tacked to the side of the broom closet helped to put the quietus on him. A picture there was, a rural scene, the rakish comb of a cock on the loose, smudge of sienna for leaves, a hound nosing in the ground between the empty shafts of a buggy, a thin column of smoke skywards tending like a question mark, the chimney red, the shutters green, white is the cottage of her dreams as she stands in the doorway, proudly surveying, though faded and featureless, her own, her native land.

"She is too what?" said Joe.

He knifed his way into their conversation as if it were his inalienable right.

"Hey," said Helen. "What's all the shoving for?"

"Well," said Joe. "You asked me to come, didn't you?"

He forced his chair into a commanding position between them.

"Okay, now?" said Helen. "You're sure you're comfortable?"

"Just a little bit more. Ah, that does it. Hey, Ma, look. It's me again."

"It makes me very happy."

"Gee," said Joe. "It sure is a nice evening outside, isn't it? Ask me now. What am I doing hiding in this damn house?"

"Oh," said Helen. "Just proving again you can be very impolite. You know that?"

"Sorry," said Joe. "I didn't mean to interrupt you. What was that you were saying? Who is too soft?"

"Claire," said Helen. "I was telling Mamma. Ow. How many elbows have you got?"

"I don't know," said Joe. "I haven't counted them lately. Claire. Let me see now. Ah, yes. That's your skinny friend, isn't she?"

"If you mean just the opposite," said Helen. "You're absolutely right. Though it doesn't show much on her, does it? I guess it's because she's so tall. Anyway, as I was telling Mamma. As big as she is, and good-natured, she's certainly throwing herself away."

"Really?" said Joe. "Is there someone strong enough to catch her?"

"A weasel," said Helen. "Wait until you take a look at him. God, I'm telling you, the way some people come popping out of the ground. All of a sudden there he is, Peter the pumpkin eater, the hungriest little tramp you ever laid your eyes on, one of his stories is that he was once a radio operator on a steamer for the sake of his asthma, hanging on to that poor big lummox for all he's worth. What does that fly-by-night think Claire is? An aerial or something? If you're laughing now, wait until you see him. He's got a face on him like a busted clock, I mean it, and eyes like broken glass, and a nose a pig would be ashamed of, and a mouth that hangs limp like a rubber band, and what do you think ever comes out of it? Static. That's all. Day and night. Oh, it's not so bad yet when they're both sitting down. Though even then he looks like a green little mouse, chewing on her ear. But once they stand up, holy mackerel, he's such a nothing, she actually has to reach down if she

177

wants to plant her elbow on his head. Honest. I'm not exaggerating."

"Claire," said Joe. "If I have the right one. I never knew you liked her that much."

"Of course I do," said Helen. "She's one of my very best friends."

"That's it then. Listen. If Clark Gable himself came to take her away."

"I'd talk about him in the same way? Oh, no, Joe. That's where you're wrong. If there's anything I hate, it's being that selfish. No, no. It's just that I don't think he's good enough for her, that's all. Like a damn fool, I did try to tell her once. But you think she listened? I tell you. I simply can't believe it. How can anyone with such clear blue eyes become so blind all of a sudden?"

"Practice."

"It kills me," said Helen. "It really does."

"Oh, hell," said Joe. "Let the poor thing dig her own grave. Maybe it's more fun that way. Besides, you have to give the guy credit. At least he was smart enough to pick her out, wasn't he?"

"Yes, damn him. It should've been you."

"Me?" said Joe.

"That's right," said Helen. "Didn't you know? She had an awful crush on you."

"You're cuckoo," said Joe. "I hardly ever spoke to the girl."

"Okay," said Helen. "The next time she comes, try whistling at her. Just for the hell of it. See what happens."

"Hey, now," said Joe. "Let's not get too silly about it. She's a nice kid and all that. And she may be in a tough spot. But who isn't? I got my own troubles."

"What troubles?" said Helen. "Don't be a fool. Where will you ever find anyone who can be so sweet and stubborn at the same time? She's just the kind of girl you need. Especially you. She would know how to sit down on you. But hard. You'd stop all this flying around god knows where. You'd begin to know where you are in this world. And what for."

"Helen, dear. You're off your rocker, you know that?"

"No, I'm not."

"But I'm trying to tell you. It's absolutely impossible."

"No, it isn't."

"But it is," said Joe. "Why don't you listen to me?"

"Ah," said Mrs. Bellinson. "Look. There she is."

"Who?" said Joe. "What? Where? You don't mean Claire?"

"There," said Helen. "Can't you see? That woman standing there."

What an expression. Caught in the middle, he began to shrink a bit into himself at this curious hostility directed so pointedly at him as they plunged into their bitter recital of their blown up Einstock story, marvelously fused before his eyes into a mythological composite as harsh and ruthless, as quaintly antagonistic as the Furies. They were talking at him as women so often yammer at what they believe to be the unconscionable brute in the male. He knew as he listened that he had to let them hate him, since it seemed so necessary that they should.

Certainly he, Joseph Bellinson, to give his title in full, dashingly rigged out in his new maroon suspenders where his even newer thumbs are hooked, snapping them at the world as if he were showing off the comparable buoyant and solid color of his own irrepressible youth, he no doubt, snugly established as he is between an arrogant common sense on the one hand and a stern and weary wisdom on the other, is himself the best living example of that selfish heartbreaking resolution in the romantic man to lead his own life, as he calls it, while poor plain Mrs. Einstock there, she must shut up like a clam in accordance with her first vow never again to exchange the time of day with anything in the shape of a human being, and with her second, to stand upstairs by the front window and downstairs in the doorway of her brother-in-law's shoe repair store, with his own existence as bootless in spite of his scrupulous prices and his enormous noble brow, and without ever changing her wrap-around corduroy skirt, freeze as completely as she could, a crumpled arrow pointing nowhere.

Aw, now, who were they trying to kid? Who could have told them all that? Certainly not that Gloomy Gus whose gnarled left hand was notorious for extracting the most inexcitable nails from his trouble-hammered mouth. Oh, be quiet. Let this boyish grumbler first suffer pregnancy five times in a row without issue, and then maybe he would earn the right to rip into and abort their talk. It was Solomon Einstock, that master house painter, who really knew a thing or two, especially where babies came from, so he proceeded to congratulate the tender area each time with his most clever hooks and colossal haymakers, because when the future as it swells decides to get fresh with the great stuttering Einstock, no mere mental blocks or empty

179

paint buckets for him, he had the will and the know-how to wind up properly and plaster it. Of course there was much screaming and retching on her part in the process thereof, but the instant she dropped her pelvis and fainted, off he toddled like a giant teddy bear to soak his hairy mitts in pickle juice to harden them the more, grinning from ear to ear at a nasty job exceptionally well done.

And how, said Joe. And not only that, watch those ashes, he was willing to bet his bottom dollar the guy had a third bloodshot eye like a setting sun from which he could drop his crocodile tears, and a long forked tongue in C sharp minor, flickering in and out of a second hallucinated head, or whatever else would help them round out their picture of a truly terrific monster of hearsay. Aha, so as they were saying, since he was so sure he had made his point, they were quite content to let him sit on it, when Mrs. Einstock began to have an epileptic fit every hour on the hour, Solomon the Great, he had it way up to here, so shifted his attack upward, and in five minutes flat so rearranged her features that all of a sudden he had a fresh funny face to raise the hackles on him to a new all-time high. It was only then Mrs. Einstock dimly remembered what a butcher knife was for, so one fine day, she hid herself behind the door, holding her weapon high above her head like a perfect statue, waiting for hours for Solomon E. to come thundering in.

And killed him dead when he did? Ah, would that she had, or had at least slashed his mug to ribbons, but she barely nicked him twice where it would not show. Twice, said Joe. Well, now, that makes it all so nice and accurate. And what about his collar button, ladies? Since they spoke as if they were actually present at this particular brawl. Did it give him a blue mark in the middle of his throat before he managed to disarm her? Oh, absolutely, they said. And what was even worse, the horror's hair was decidedly mussed up. Like this, said Helen, as she tried to show the slippery sceptic just how. Though it must be said that Solomon himself kept his head, as he used the laces out of his own shoes to tie her hands behind her back, and tossed his old army overcoat across her broken shoulders, and sort of half-led and half-carried her in and out of a taxi, honey, straight to his brother's store where he deposited her like an old pair of pumps to be repaired.

What is this with the wobbly world that nothing in it ever seems to work out for what is known as a woman? Where is the last fiery center

180

of true consideration and concern in a Joe-conceived universe of brutal galaxies of gas and cold indifferent dust? Hecky set down his claw hammer like a blind man to unbind his sister-in-law's hands. Such a soft and pale infraperson, as he slowly rubbed her wrists to erase the stigmata, he wondered if it would help if he belled her, or had her shoeless right foot stretched, or simply asked if she had a first name, since she had advanced so rapidly for him from a mere rumor to a crushing reality. She surprised him by saying it was Lena out of Einstock, as if to raise a last smile with her last word. Following which, as said before, she began to stand upstairs and downstairs.

And this, said Mrs. Bellinson, this is how we get used to everything, and while the nails and the hair keep growing, the heartache remains the same unswallowable size, and there is nothing in sight to hold on to, nothing. Yes, said Helen. And yet like idiots, we still look, and we still wait. How wise then is Solomon, in spite of his being lame, he has left himself nothing as precious as his Lena to part with, and that passion he had to divide a baby is almost dead, as he hacks at his hard salami instead, and his stale rye bread. What band of gold? What saffron veil? If there are polly seeds to crack, and a wild western to be seen, that old bull's memory will live in a cloud of dust, and his mind will rust as he munches, but his piebald eyes will gallop away, a horseman with the hiccups, an outlaw whose heart will never fail him.

"And you know why?" said Helen.

"No," said Joe. "You tell me."

"Because he hasn't got one," said Helen. "That's why."

"Wonderful," said Joe. "Marvelous. I don't know how you do it, girl, but that's the most brilliant finish to the cockeyest fairy tale I ever heard in all my life."

"Careful, now. Mamma's in this too, you know."

"Can you imagine?" said Joe. "I had to ask for it yet too. Tonight of all nights. Who the hell wants to hear about such things?"

"Then do me a favor," said Helen. "Go peel an apple. And I'll eat it."

"No, sir," said Joe. "I'll be damned if I believe it. There never was such a guy."

"Really?" said Helen. "Who was Karl then?"

"Who?" said Joe.

"Karl. That elevator boy who belonged in the circus. You told me he was dead, didn't you?"

181

"From head to toe. Completely."

"Okay, then," said Helen. "I believe it."

"Fine," said Joe. "He'll sure be glad to hear that."

"Though as far as I am concerned, he never existed. So there you are."

"I am?" said Joe. "Where?"

"Oh," said Helen. "Wait. People are going to ask the same question about you some day. Don't back away. I mean it. It's going to be a riot. I'll say to them, hey, did you hear about Joe? And they'll say, who? And I'll say, Joe, my brother, did I ever tell you what he did one day? Of course you'll have to imagine me telling them first. I don't think I'll ever have nerve enough to do it. And they'll say, go on, what kind of a story is that? And I'll say, honest, it's the truth, don't you believe me? And they'll say, get out, there never was such a guy, I don't believe it. And I would have to say to them, you're right, I don't believe it either."

"Believe it," said Joe. "Don't worry. You'll believe it when I sock you right in the eye."

"Don't be silly. The last time you tried that, you got yourself a real bloody nose."

"Me?" said Joe. "You're crazy. What bloody nose?"

"Don't you remember?" said Helen. "You must've been about nine or so. You were trying to grab something from me. Now what was it? Oh, yes. That silver pencil with my initials on it that Uncle Willie gave me for my birthday. And when you made a fist, I laid into you with my elbow. Accidentally, of course. You sure howled like you were dying that time."

"What silver pencil? You were lucky if you had a wooden stub with an eraser on it."

"Oh," said Helen. "The night we found you under the bed crying your heart out. You couldn't have been more than three or four. You were so cute. What a sweet little face you had. And your hair was almost blonde. And you were terribly knock-kneed. You were sleeping then with Abe in that middle room without a window. It was the queerest thing. How did you ever manage to get under that folding bed? We almost tore you in half, dragging you out. We kept asking you. Are you cold, sweetheart? What is it? Are you afraid? Were you dreaming? What hurts you? Tell us. But you couldn't. All you did was cry so, we all began to cry with you. That was the funniest part of all. You remember?"

"I don't like this," said Joe. "What is she trying to do to me?"

"But now," said Helen. "Now it's different. Your legs are straight. Your hair is brown. You're not afraid to open your mouth to anyone. You're stringy. You're tough. You have no more blood to lose."

"A machine," said Joe. "Where does she get it all? Doesn't she ever stop?"

"Or brains for that matter. As for us. I agree. It's no use. We're only women. We're soft. There's no hope for us. We have such tender skins. We get red. We go pale. We wear buckets under our eyes. We need special food. We're always puckering up. We're just too goddamn wishy-washy, aren't we? You see? I don't mind helping you out. Maybe we'll get through quicker this way."

"Goddamn it," said Joe. "You don't have to give me such a spiel. We can end it all right here if you want."

"Quiet," said Helen. "Somebody's yelling."

"You're damn right," said Joe. "It's me."

"No," said Helen. "I mean outside."

"Where?" said Joe.

"Take a look."

"Hey," said Joe. "It's Thelma. How are you doing, kid? What's up?"

"Can you chew nails and spit bullets?"

"Can I what?" said Joe.

"I'm playing," said Thelma.

Her head was reared back at a painful angle, her face in comic perspective to the puny rest of her as she began to parley thus with her patron so high up on the second floor, short-waving her reeds, projecting her perfect tonsils, shrieking across the immense distance between them, as if she were the earth supplicating the moon with which it is said to be so much in love.

"You are?" said Joe. "Hooray. Now the whole block knows it."

"I didn't tell them."

"Says you."

"What are you doing up there?"

"Why, I," said Joe. "I don't know. Did you hear that? I have to report to her."

"Tell her the truth," said Helen. "Tell her you're playing too."

"All right," said Joe. "I'm playing too."

"Really?" said Thelma. "Can you come climbing down on a rope?"

"You little tramp," said Joe. "You know what time it is? What are you doing out so late?"

"I have to tell you," said Thelma. "I'm eighty-six years old."

"Is that a fact?"

"I'm a real grandmother."

"No kidding? Since when?"

"Since I was four years old."

"Well, now," said Joe. "There's something that makes sense. At last I'm getting the real dope on something. Hey. What are you putting in your mouth?"

"A peach stone," said Thelma. "I'm cleaning it. Can you make it for me?"

"Make what?"

"A ring."

"A ring?" said Joe. "Out of that? Oh, sure. See me on Sunday."

"What time?"

"Thirteen o'clock."

"Oh," said Thelma. "I can't. I'll be dead by then."

"Yep," said Joe. "There's no doubt about it. You're heading straight in that direction all the way. Go on, now, go to bed. While you can still feel your way."

"It's almost black," said Thelma. "Can you see it?"

"Yes," said Joe. "I can see it."

"See what?" said Helen.

"The ball," said Joe.

"What ball?" said Helen. "Move over a little bit."

"The one I bought her."

"You bought her a ball?"

"I gave her the money for it."

"You gave her the money for it?"

"Now look," said Joe. "It's bad enough to have one little wiseguy mimicking me."

"Hey," said Thelma. "You're not looking at me."

"You hear that?" said Joe. "Another little prima donna."

"You know my mother?"

"Which one?"

184

"She can't breathe."

"Oh, my god. There she goes again. What do you mean she can't breathe?"

"She can't," said Thelma. "She burns a powder."

"Must be asthma," said Helen.

"Oh, sure," said Joe. "Listen to her. I want you all to listen to her."

"And then," said Thelma. "You know what?"

"Go on," said Joe. "Spill it, dear. What've you got to lose?"

"My father cut his finger off."

"He did?" said Joe. "That's nice. It means he loves you."

"You want me to bring it to you now?"

"His finger?" said Helen.

"No," said Joe. "She means the ball."

"See me?" said Thelma. "I bounce it, I bounce it."

"Swell," said Joe. "Now bounce yourself right along with it, okay?"

"I can keep it?"

"Aie," said Joe. "There it goes. I knew it would happen."

"Look at it," said Thelma. "It's rolling away."

"Don't stand there. Run after it."

"I will," said Thelma. "I will."

"No," said Joe. "Not in the gutter. Thelma. Hey, you. She doesn't hear me. Holy mackerel. Two cars coming."

"Wow," said Helen. "Look at that devil go."

"I can't," said Joe. "Where is she?"

"Across the street."

"She made it?"

"Easily."

"Oof," said Joe. "Thank god. That's it, little breeze, come right in, I sure can use you. Whew. Staying home like this can be hell, you know that? What are we doing anyway, lounging around here at the window like three bumps on a log? What's the point? What are we looking at? What in the hell's there to see we haven't seen before? What?"

To see for himself was to scan the city night sky first, with its usual jagged silhouette of roofs for horizon, the reddish glow of a shopping street to the west, and higher, the soft intimation of semipossible stars and the vague crescent of a rising moon already on the wane, before lowering his jaded eyes for a sweeping view of the booby inhabitants of this one short brave block. The blinkers do seem to be on them. A

185

buffalo nickel, a sliver of charcoal, a worn whisk broom, the brass statuette of a bull, each is an object which transmutes itself into a weapon the instant these shadowy stumblebums seize it in their alchemical hands. Such clever citizens, somehow they know that to be armed against a neighbor is the one sure way of making their static lives actually jump with the most violent sense of penny insecurity and insignificance.

Meanwhile they play. They do seem to be playing with each other. The April evening is so teasingly mild that it has tricked a great number to perambulate in their halloween faces. The consciousness of the drama of their bold appearance, after such a long encouragement of the skin to retire more closely to the bone, is seen in their every lazy and lagging step. Some of their shredded bedding has been hauled out to air on the fire escape as if it had been appointed to shed many of their surplus memories of soiled dislocation and despair.

Swoosh, follow the leader, skid on one leg, zigzag as he does, leapfrog over an egg crate, wham, the cracked plate glass of an empty store crashes, and twelve monkeys fan out in flight, beautiful to watch. But the thirteenth, a pair of pigtails with much of her white thighs showing, is rooted to the spot, so charmed is she with the musical tinkle. Two senior contestants, almost as brittle, squat on a doorstep, supporting a checkerboard on their knees. Their heads touch. Their love is like a terrier with loosened teeth. Palpitations amidst their palsy, at no great distance from them, in the arena which the corner lamplight circumscribes, a freshman in a crew neck sweater wrestles with a lusty chick who must show her panties if she means to flout him, but so cleverly does she squirm, that soon her buttocks are insinuated firmly in the region of his groin. But if it suits him as it pleases her, and seems to be so much fun, why does he act as if he were suffering? No less crafty or heated are the neo-guerrillas who have fashioned two swords out of waterlogged wood and two cocked hats out of shiny wrapping paper. They slash away at each other for no plunder at all, until the loser bawls, and the winner, like all conquerors who somehow become aware that their victories are sinful, enjoins every part of his body to apologize.

At the very brink of the curb, leaning over as if peering into a pool, stands a young girl, violet and slender, holding her hands peacefully at her sides. As fortunate as frisky, a kitten trots out from behind a

186

herring barrel just in time to gaze in awe at the nymph as she begins to puke with the utmost daintiness, generously donating the whole of her supper of sardines to this brawling world they both so fear and adore.

Is this the nectar which confers immortality? He shut his eyes upon the scene with all its shifting pantomimes and sorties, without emphasis on the number, a simple animal in his simplest act of renunciation, and sped down an easier incline somewhere in his derivative mind, clutching at the imaginary hood and hem of the holy escapist from whom he was sure he was descended. If this fraction of the world is not his, which is then? The steaming jungle where the tawny leopard snores? The island upon which the lawless anchorite bathes not? Any court of a kingdom of exquisite deportment, of the stately minuet of the mind by blazing candlelight? A surrealistic cliff of ice in the blue antarctic on the way to Little America? Or in cruel Virginia where the creepers twine?

Dog of his heart's desire, distracted retriever, if his chair is his winged chariot, where does he fly but downward to bury his nose in the entrails of the earth where he may yet sniff out some final excitement? For he is a clod who catches himself listening closely, not to that harp which hints so delicately of an accessible heaven, but to that griping sound a goat makes, because it reminds him of the quaver, the very transport itself, of intolerable hunger and tribulation. Others hear choir singing in a cloud, and are fatally attracted to it. But this natural enemy of every version of the hereafter is charmed by a sigh or a cough, and if an election horn is honked, cloop goes his curiosity as he uncorks it. To haunt the haloed footsteps of a Jesus, to invent breathless journeys at the most acute angle just for kicks and a sip of ambrosia, these are merely the signs of a reasonable madman. But how pompous is the prize sap who shoulders a toothpick, and beats on his own eardrums, and makes a military advance upon crumbling bastions of blood. His doom is already dated. His common world is tangled in the weeds of the here and now. It lies in ruins beneath his eyelids.

Joe slapped himself on the forehead.

"What the hell's wrong?" he said. "What's the matter with me anyway? Why can't I sit here and be quiet like everybody else?"

Helen stared at him.

187

"You were saying something? I didn't hear you say anything."

"Ah," said Joe. "For two cents I'd cut my throat and be done with it."

"And for another penny," said Mrs. Bellinson. "You can cut mine too."

"It's a deal," said Joe. "I always intended to take you with me."

"Goody," said Helen. "Gee. Imagine having the whole house to myself."

"Not really," said Joe. "There'll still be Abe, you know."

"Oh," said Helen. "I can take care of him."

"Aha," said Joe. "But not of me? Is that it?"

"Impossible," said Helen. "He hates himself too. But you. You got him beat a mile."

"Yay," said Joe. "The winner and new world's champion. And I didn't cheat, Ma. I did it all fair and square."

"With his arm around her shoulder," said Helen. "And smoothing down her hair. Charming, charming."

"Ah," said Joe. "You're so right to be jealous. Tell me little girl. Whose land is this? Have you lived here very long?"

"Our bum to be," said Helen. "Our lord high executioner. You can't fool me. There's something biting you, isn't there?"

"Well, yes," said Joe. "It's either you or the first mosquito of the season. I can't tell which."

"Fluttering around like a bat. Buzzing in my ear like a bee. There's no telling what a man so busy will do next. How about obliging me with a real good finale? Say like, yes, like diving headfirst right through this window."

"Ah, boy," said Joe. "You can't scare me. I'm ready, I'm ready. Me for the open road. How about it, Ma? Two little pillowcases will do. You a bundle, and me a bundle, and away we go. Who says there's anything keeping us here? We didn't sign a contract with God about it, did we? If the guy doesn't like it, let him sue us. Why should we wait until we die before we go looking for a better world? We'll start absolutely clean. If you get tired, I'll carry you. You don't weigh much. If you get hungry, I'll knock on the first door. All they have to do is take one look at you. And they'll give us everything they've got."

"Knocking on the door," said Helen. "Reminds me."

"How do you like that?" said Joe. "It's really funny. Every time she gives you the cold shoulder like that, she makes you feel like you're hardly born yet."

"I wonder," said Helen. "Did I ever tell you about the man with the egg?"

"Oh, no, you don't," said Joe. "You're not going to change the subject on me this time."

"I'll never forget it as long as I live. What a fool I was. I guess that's why I never told it. It was late on a Sunday afternoon. There was Mamma and me in the kitchen. I know Abe wasn't there. He wasn't with you, was he?"

"Abe with me?" said Joe. "When? Where? When's the last time that happened?"

"The kitchen," said Helen. "Yes. Mamma and me. I remember I was threading a needle for her, she'll just have to go and get her glasses changed no matter what it costs, when all of a sudden we hear a knocking on the door. We looked at each other. Who could be knocking? There's a bell in plain sight out there, isn't there? Aw, I said, it must be those Feldman kids fooling around again. But three, four times, it really got me mad. I ran to the door, pulled it open, and there he was. He was so close to the door, he fell right into my arms. He let me hold him up a second. A man of some kind. Very tiny. No hair on top. And a noisy breather with his mouth hanging open. I set him up on his own feet. I said, excuse me, are you looking for somebody? Why, yes, he said, he was looking for Mamma, he claimed he was a relative. I don't know why, but I took pity on him. So I said, all right, sir, come on in. Very polite, wasn't I? He came in. I brought him a chair from the living room. He sat down very quietly with his hands in his lap. I don't know if I can describe him. You know how it is with some people? They seem to be equipped with all the features, but they work like lightning in every direction so fast, they haven't got one face, they've got a million. You remember, Ma? Wasn't he a strange one?"

"Well," said Mrs. Bellinson. "He was poor. He had suffered."

"That's right," said Joe. "You be nice, Mamma. Stick up for your relatives."

"Relative?" said Helen. "He wasn't a relative."

"No?" said Joe. "Then what was he?"

"A dried-up little peanut," said Helen. "I could've turned him over

189

my knee and spanked him if I wanted to. As a matter of fact, that's just what I should've done. What a bluffer that man was. He had so many troubles, it was impossible to believe him. Every time he turned up his yellow eyes, he killed off another one of his kids. Six or seven, just like that. One swallowed a lump of ice and got pneumonia. One tried to beat a caboose across the railroad tracks. One choked on a lead soldier and died in battle. Don't laugh. It was a real slaughter. And then. Where do you think his wife was? You guessed it. In the hospital. For twenty-seven months. Got caught in some kind of explosion. He never explained what. And then it came. It always does. He begged us to do him a favor. Guess. I bet you'll never guess what it was."

"Oh," said Joe. "A small loan. Say two or three thousand?"

"No," said Helen. "Something so simple."

"I know," said Joe. "He wanted to use the bathroom."

"No, no," said Helen. "Stop trying. You'll never guess. But first, let me ask you. Where's the nearest hospital around here? Kings County. Right? And that's at least a mile away, isn't it? So how come he lands way up here? Well, anyway, as he put it, a wife's a wife, especially when she's the only one you have. And when she's cooped up in a ward so long, and forced to eat the slop they feed a charity patient, how can you blame a man for trying to bring her something fresh to eat once in a while? And with that, what do you think he does? He pulls an egg out of his pocket."

"Ah," said Joe. "The egg. I had forgotten about that."

"Please, he says, could we boil it for him? Boil it for him? I said to myself, my god, what kind of people do we have in this world?"

"Hell," said Joe. "If that's all it was, you were getting away with murder."

"Absolutely," said Helen. "Of course. What did it mean to us if we boiled it for him? So we boiled it for him. As soon as the water started clacking, his tongue stopped. Maybe he was embarrassed. So we made believe he wasn't there. He said she liked it kind of hard-boiled, so I gave it a full five minutes, and then I spooned the damn thing out and put it on a saucer to cool in front of him. Still not a peep out of him. So I turned away and began to talk to Mamma. About when Venus is going to be in conjunction with Mars, and is kale a good vegetable when cooked with carrots, and so on, and so forth. Pretty soon I heard a sound. I turned around. He was cracking the shell. I said

190

to him, what are you doing? He said to me, see? It was all peeled. He took a bite. I jumped up. He took another. I reached over. Mamma pulled me down. He popped the rest of it in his mouth and ran. I screamed after him, I hope you choke. I ran out and yelled down the stairs. You hear me? You idiot. I hope you choke."

"Ye gods," said Joe. "That's a lulu, that is."

"I felt like such a fool. You have no idea."

"Cripes," said Joe. "I must remember this. Who can I tell it to?"

"Disgusting, isn't it? The second headache since Saturday. It must be the beginning of the end. I guess I'm falling apart."

"Aw, now," said Joe. "Don't be silly. Without some pain, how would you know you're alive?"

"Oh, sure," said Helen. "So all right. So go around and knock on all the doors if you want to. But I'm warning you now. Don't come around and knock on mine. Think twice, will I? I'll be thinking a million times before I ever lift a finger to help anyone again. Ouch. I wonder if it's true what I read the other day. Does aspirin really affect the heart? What's that kid doing out there?"

"I've been watching," said Mrs. Bellinson.

"Who?" said Joe. "What kid?"

"Thelma," said Helen. "That's your little girl friend out there, isn't it?"

"Hey," said Joe. "What's she doing with that kitten?"

"Kicking it," said Mrs. Bellinson.

"Kicking it?" said Helen. "You mean plucking it, don't you?"

"Children," said Mrs. Bellinson. "Murderers."

"I'll be damned," said Helen. "She's kissing it now, isn't she?"

"Look again," said Joe. "She just threw it in the gutter."

"This is awful," said Helen. "What's the matter with us? Are we paralyzed? Why don't we get up and do something?"

"It's no use," said Joe. "She's out to kill it."

"Kill it?" said Helen. "I'll give her kill it. Get out of my way."

He was wise to grab her around the waist. All in one breath, she gave one great tug, and with one great yell, she really blew her top, and that did the trick. For Thelma jumped as if she had been whacked on her bottom. She dropped the cat, and in her own scintillating way, she blew too. The kitten knew at once what to do. Mauled as it was, and bruised to its bones, it crept as fast as it could to its cell behind the

191

herring barrel, enriched with a fable to tell its future cronies. A wonderful noise had rescued it.

How ineffably sad. In the heart of every terror sits a tiny delusive seed of faith. Who is to be blamed for trying to preserve it this time? None other than Helen the lioness beside him, with a thorn in her paw, maudlin as she is not, and scarcely liturgical, this wrathful darling of a sister of mercy to those who are attacked, as well as to those who do the attacking, tossing her hellenic head at such gothic rot, one moment thinking only of what hurts her, the next roaring impulsively because a naive little beast has outrageously exposed itself to prolonged pain and extinction. How indignantly all of her still trembles. How admirably she glares at her brother as if he were that particular animal. Does that disturb him? Not at all. He prefers to be quietly amazed, and gazes at her, and this is what makes her look away, with a smile which is like a canto in praise of her unbridled sense, her catholic folly, her sweet and infrangible simplicity.

Cowering saints alive, has it come down to this? If he must kiss them both in such a spill-over of appreciation, as he feels he must, should he clap his hands, and cry out loud, next year Jerusalem? Ripple of aversion, primeval dread, planetary strides away from mere streets, if the antlers of the noble elk were questioned, what would they say? Or the terrorized whiskers of the woodchuck, its ratlike head too abrupt in its movements, giving itself away? Or the cowardly slits the hyena calls its eyes? They would say, see the terrible infant, he takes the scrape of a roller skate for a forest murmur, and froth of spilt milk on the curb for oceanic foam, so bewitched is he by this mere fleck of loving-kindness, this surge of plain sentiment, this poorest human wonder.

An ark of animals, all twitch their tails and chew the cud with him. Time has been too short for his designs. Mortified lights in several windows wink out. Sagging house doors slam like raps of a gavel. One last mother calls for her shadowy offspring to come slinking home. Sights and sounds of gradual retirement, of what do they warn him? Of sinning while sitting down? Of pitch-darkness which people share as inescapable punishment? Of a new master passion out of free enterprise, greedy love ending in selfish murder? When the world ends, will the last merrymaker chuckle, will he say, thinking, thinking is what did it? That may turn out to be true. But what will he do if

192

he still wishes to be chummy? He will be torn between kissing and killing, as all have been torn before him, but there will be no one left for him to kiss or kill. Here is a pretty thought. Joe is so happy to have had it. He feels he can rise now and pledge allegiance with his own hand over his own heart. At last he knows he has himself become the number one fool he can laugh and marvel at, and look down upon and pity.

8.

As with him, so with us all. Who now is there who can as gaily disconnect himself from his own self-entangling concerns, and like a demented one-man mutt, lollop after this reflective flyabout who takes so long to advance that it begins to seem like a retreat, and pitilessly track him down as an avenging spirit might tail a minor evildoer to ruffle him up and inflict confusion, and by sleight of paw or the like, do a trick with his Tuesday, and compose it so that it will turn out to be no mere matter of plums, marrow, or roses?

Into the nearest black hole slips another humpbacked question mark. Simply by proposing it, the unanswerable seems that much easier to answer. As crude and gullible as so many are, how can anyone tremble for him because he seems to promise to become that valorous chief player everyone constantly dreams of, that mighty gyrational performer who would assault all of the eighty-eight notes of experience with his tentative layman fingers, and make that king of instruments yield and kowtow to him? Yet as of now, the timid attitudinizer, the truth is he is merely plucking at its white derisive teeth as if with a frail matchstick, tinkering with the black notes mostly, soft-pedaling it until it can hardly be apprehended in all of its incessant dazzle and clanging ramifications.

Easy does it now. Even if easy does not do it. Not any more. If the soul cannot be discovered in the fabric of the flesh, then look for it beneath the bone. That is his song this morning. He intones it. Drowsy revivalist, partial sleepyhead, why is he so pleased with his cheerful little earful as he cuts into Madison Avenue, an earlier bird, worming his way to work? Are there great scads of glory for him just ahead? Hardly of a much. Only as ever the distinct possibility of being sinfully late. Part of that indecent universal tension, that dumb morning panic from which even a most purely intentioned Angelina is not exempt. As one morning this month, when her terrier leaped to lick her face, it suffered a massive arterial stoppage. It is clear that compassion alone is vastly inferior to a single dose of digitalis. Angelina had to let her Mopsy die rather than be late. It was the delay it caused, not its death, that became the cosmic event. Is it permissible for a Roman Catholic to burn a penny candle for a pup? Punctuality in business has always been a holy thing. Profanely ticking off a prayer to it, Joe stepped into the elevator to find himself alone with a new operator, a pliant old ox caged of this morning, whose hand shook dangerously as he jolted him skyward.

Within four risky seconds, here is how the gone geezer bows his head as if to show how time will teach a man to fawn on whatever it is he fears. A leviathan trembler himself, even at his antemeridian age, Joe smiled at this grizzled symbol of submission, studying its pulverized pair of pants as if to ascertain the precise center where he would like most exultantly to boot. What sackcloth of a cringer had he here? What shabby warp had crossed what shoddy woof? Something of Joe's own random thread ran through a stray wisp of the past, something superior to the truckling of this declining gaffer to a switch. His mind weaved swiftly amid the tiny swoops and swirls of the arrested minikin moment until he remembered that crucial day when Mr. Colish had bustled over with a duplicate set of keys freshly made for Joe to be the first to open the factory every morning, including Saturdays, a jangling trinket of false trust and true entrapment, and kept thrusting it at Joe, but Joe shook his head, and held up his hand as if he were stopping all traffic, and absolutely refused to accept it. What spine-tingling dignity that had, what roosterlike indignation, the stammer then of that one monotonous and momentous no. It was too late. The elevator had shot up to six when it should have stopped at four. The mistake oozed frosty white spit all around the muddled operator's mouth. Life ran on with its usual stupid rush as he was advised to plunge the cage into reverse. It was much too late now to right such a wronged one all the way, to try to initiate him into the mystic rites of refusal.

As in reaching for his timecard, Joe almost poked his hand in some-body's face. Grunt as it may, it refused to budge, belonging as it did to the boss man, Mr. Colish, a real old smoothie when he wants to be, on a day when he feels least lazy, and competes with the dawn, and arrives the earliest, richly garbed in his pinpoint stripe, freshly shaved and powdered, so that he may crack down in person on anyone who dared to dash or sneak in late. Joe wondered. Which bleary-eyed boob will he catch this time? His own card punched and about to turn away, he wheeled on the watchdog with a laugh. He felt as bright as he had ever been.

"Mr. Colish, Mr. Colish."

It was a chiding singsong, but with all due respect.

Mr. Colish drew back his head.

"So you know my name. So?"

"You don't really like to do this, do you? Say. Did you see that new excuse for an elevator man? A real old rambling wreck, ain't he? You know something? I just realized why they hired him. Guess."

"Am I the boss here? Why do I let him bother me?"

"To kill us all," said Joe. "It's a plot."

"Look," said Mr. Colish. "It's okay, boy. You don't have to jump in front of my face. I don't wear glasses. I can see you're early."

"Early?" said Joe. "By some miracle, I'm absolutely the first one."

"Fine," said Mr. Colish. "Tomorrow I give you a medal of munster with a cherry in the middle."

"Very appetizing. I didn't say good morning, did I? Want me to get you some coffee?"

"No. No coffee."

"Or better yet," said Joe. "Maybe you should go down yourself. This coming to work without breakfast. Believe me, Mr. Colish, it'll do you in one of these days. You don't mind me talking to you this way, do you? Why don't you go down now and get yourself a real good feed? I'll stand guard here for you and take notes."

"Another worm," said Mr. Colish. "So that's how you're trying to creep around me."

"Pancakes and sausages and a little pot of coffee. All in silver dishes. Steaming hot. Doesn't that make your juices flow like mad?"

"Oh, sure," said Mr. Colish. "I go down and stuff myself. And you stay here and punch the cards for everybody."

"Me?" said Joe. "You don't think I'd ever do a thing like that, do you?"

"Out," said Mr. Colish. "If you want to fool me. Next time get up a little earlier."

"Oh, well," said Joe. "At least you're smiling."

"Smiling?" said Mr. Colish. "What smiling? Who's crazy around here? What are you? Are you my son or something that I have to take all this crap from you?"

"I'm just talking," said Joe. "That's all. There's no harm in that, is there? Look, Mr. Colish. I got a proposition for you."

"Talk, talk. See if I listen."

"If anybody comes in late, take it out of my pay."

"Take it out of your pay?" said Mr. Colish. "What are you trying to make out of me? When do I ever take it out of the pay?"

"Maybe you don't," said Joe. "But you do something even worse."

"Worse?" said Mr. Colish. "What worse?"

"You scare the hell out of them."

"Aie," said Big Bee.

She staggered back, clutching at her bosom where she fluttered the most.

"And what's the matter with you?" said Mr. Colish.

"Ha," said Big Bee.

"Ha, what?"

"How's my hair? I mean. I didn't expect. It's not coming down, is it? My, you should've seen the mob in the train this morning. Real animals. And here I am with my best umbrella yet. The radio had to say rain. Doesn't it make you look foolish? Oh, Mr. Colish, now that you're here, I'm so glad I caught you. You know that pattern that's been giving us all the trouble about the gore? Well, now, I think I know the way to."

Mr. Colish waved her away.

"Later," he said. "Later."

Big Bee made the time clock dance under the brutal blow she gave it.

"There's a corker for you," said Joe. "She loves you so much, she didn't even see me."

"A headache she gives me. My old reliable."

"Is she really?"

"Really," said Mr. Colish. "Tell me now. This is something I want to know. Is she your friend?"

"Big Bee?" said Joe.

"You can scratch your head later. Is she or isn't she?"

"Well," said Joe. "I'm not her enemy."

"What kind of an answer is that?"

"Hi," said Foxy Felix. "Swell day for the races, ain't it?"

"This one now," said Mr. Colish. "He comes in like a horse."

"A horse?" said Joe. "Is that why he looks so familiar?"

"Excuse me," said Felix. "I didn't know I was barging in on a conference."

"Here," said Mr. Colish. "Here's your card. Punch it and go."

"Why, sure," said Felix. "With pleasure. The top of the morning to you both, anyway."

"Now he's insulted," said Joe. "Look how he walks away."

"That worries you?" said Mr. Colish.

"Crazy," said Joe. "Why am I standing here with my hat and coat on?"

"I know," said Mr. Colish. "I know they're all your friends here but me. You don't have to prove it to me. I know, I know."

"Absolutely not true," said Joe. "Try again."

"Matches, matches. Why am I always losing my matches?"

"Here," said Joe. "Take mine. You need them more than I do."

"I do?" said Mr. Colish. "You're sure? Did you go to higher education? Where did you learn how to be so smart? You like to make me feel like a dumbhead? You get such a kick out of it?"

"Hell," said Joe. "Why don't you leave them alone? What good does it do?"

"What good does it do?" said Mr. Colish. "Can't you see? I'm not supposed to have a heart here. Didn't you know that? This is what I'm supposed to be. And this is what I am. And I like it. I'm crazy about it. You hear what I'm saying?"

"I'm sorry," said Joe. "That I'll never believe."

"So you'll never believe," said Mr. Colish. "So who cares? Go on. Get away from me. Go."

"Chasing me away won't help."

"Won't help what? Look, Joey, I'm warning you."

"Okay," said Joe. "I'll go, I'll go. I know when I'm licked. After all, what did I accomplish? All I did was make you angrier. Oh, well. See the window near the pinking machine? There is where the sun is coming in. I think I'll go and stand in it and see what develops."

But of course this democratic ray of light was denied the pure joy of mingling its motes of mischief with those floating in his frivolous eye. For really, if he had pointed at the sunbeam, and had publicized it as if it were a finger of grace in action, he had done so only for the very charming effect the mere sound of it might have, just so. Besides as he progressed from pegging his hat over the hook from which his coat and jacket hung, to giving his apron a few sanitary flips before tying himself into it, he knew that the patch of sunlight was not his to fool with, but belonged to the operators who had already begun to dribble in, mostly prattling in pairs, that it was their haunting morning hazard with which they must dally as it crackled in their hair, glanced on their cheekbones, and insinuatingly caressed their most intimate zones.

They would be happier if they had been younger. He licked the pencil to make it stick to his ear. Their powder puffs and phallic lipsticks, they peer into their perfidious hand mirrors, as sorcerers into flashy crystals, their narrowing eyes on the prowl for that which time perpetually assails, and which they can barely remember as their old true likeness. Each wail of failing to find it, what would that crimson sound be like if scented with a whiff of hartshorn or rose water? But just when he thought he could surely tell, he was blindfolded suddenly by hands with a lemon smell.

"Guess who."

"I'll be damned," said Joe. "I was just thinking of you."

"You were?" said Rosalie. "Good or bad?"

"A bird," said Joe. "Listen to what trapped me."

"I'm listening. Damn you. Why aren't you always this way?"

"What way?" said Joe. "What kind of a blouse is that? Rayon, isn't it?"

"Traveling fingers. How do you do?"

"Stand still."

"He's watching."

"He has to," said Joe. "That's what he was born for. My hand in yours, Miss Heller. We shall now dance in a circle."

200

"Sure," said Rosalie. "Why not?"

"Really?" said Joe. "You mean that? You wouldn't care?"

"Why should I?"

"You're always so afraid you look foolish."

"Who says so? I think it's a swell idea. I think we should do it every morning."

"I'm game," said Joe. "Why?"

"Because," said Rosalie. "Because if we're really happy, why shouldn't we show it?"

"No argument there. But suppose we're the only ones?"

"Then," said Rosalie. "Let's jump around anyway. Jumping around is wonderful. Maybe if they saw us do it, they'd begin to do it too."

"Dream on, old girl. You didn't see Frankie come in yet, did you?"

"Or if they wouldn't, we'd be doing it for them, wouldn't we?"

"Wouldn't we what? Goddamn that kid. He would be late today."

"What kid?" said Rosalie. "Who are you worrying about now?"

"And where, I ask you, where, if I'm looking only at you, where is the rest of the world?"

"I don't know," said Rosalie. "It all depends. Which world?"

"The crazy world of Mr. C. Look how he's watching me pat you on the head. Smiling to himself like he's swallowed the cat or something."

"Don't ask me to look. I see enough of him every day."

"My worst enemy. He thinks we look good together. You better go."

"Yes, my captain. Just point me in the right direction."

"But remember," said Joe. "This time I'm not chasing you away. Oh, I beg your pardon. I suppose you would like to take your hand with you, wouldn't you?"

"Why, yes," said Rosalie. "It would be more convenient."

"Right you are," said Joe. "I give you now a good peck in public. How's that? I don't know what it does for you, but now I feel I can switch the power on. Those gals sure love me for it. Did I ever tell you? What a job for a man. The tops. Absolutely."

Rapidly counting twenty-eight pairs of operating eyes, he began to cross himself with grave exaggeration in the name of Colish, the ghostly father of them all, but so plainly in reverse that even those who momentarily disdained him had to smile at this combination of fas-

201

cinating rat and snake. They did adore those names for him, but their hostility crumbled as he walked down the aisle like a small graceful antelope which is the gazelle. A few hands did in fact reach out to pluck at this comic underling. If Lubasch called him dearie, and Scheff and Popkin too, what harm would it do him if he made love to them as they prayed he would? None to speak of, yet it was all a fantasy as they knew. Still they would try to seize him, and pull him closer to this circumambient ache of theirs to make him understand that their hearts were in it too.

Mighty were the breasts of those who would never be mothers. For him they heaved incestuously, their quixotic son. When he had left the last of them behind, and they could no longer see his face, he let misery contort it a second, as a tribute to their ticklish situation. Turning now in full view, he whipped out his spare handkerchief and raised it by a corner, and as he set the power going for them, mockingly flagged them down. Some of the racier ladies, he was delighted to see, laughed so knowingly, he thought they would all fall down and go boom.

There was once a man and his balls, said he to himself, as he retreated to his own table, as modern a man as a man can be, a man of many voices, none of which is really his, but bubble up in his brain as springs long residing in the earth are likely to do, bepissing themselves when they see that men and women are still laboring under the same blamed sky without knowing exactly why. Which is no great shakes of a revelation. And yet who is bold enough to say that it is through sense alone that a man experiences those curious intimations of what is actually good in this world, and what is impossibly evil?

"Well," said Joe. "My little assistant. What's the good word?"

"Three minutes," said Frankie. "What the hell's three minutes to him?"

"Aha," said Joe. "So he caught you, did he?"

"Lousy nerve. He can't talk to me that way. Sonofabitch. You know what I'll do to him the next time? I'll bop him one, that's what I'll do."

"Oh, sure," said Joe. "And what if he bops you back? He can do it, you know."

"From where he'll be laying on the floor? Geh, you watch. I'll massacre the guy. You'll see. I'll pull a leg out of him. I'll break him in half. I'll make a monkey out of him, that's what I'll do."

"We're back in the zoo," said Joe. "Why in hell were you late? You had to be late this morning?"

202

"Aw," said Frankie. "It wasn't my fault. Honest, Joe. It was my old man. I had to tackle him below the knees. He would've killed her."

"Killed her?" said Joe. "Who?"

"My Ma."

"They fight?"

"You don't know. I couldn't tell that to the boss, could I? Bastard. He had no right to call me such names."

"What names?" said Joe. "Forget it. I call you names too, don't I?"

"Sure," said Frankie. "But with you it's different. What's on the fire? Got a lot of work? What do we do first? Maybe you got a package for me to deliver. Send me out, Joe. I'm ready. Anywhere."

"Ah," said Joe. "I wish I could."

But where? What rock of comfort is there on this surreal island? The sea gulls ride the tide of the confluent rivers which bind it. They seek not for fish, but for bits of offal, for the fish have fled. The bubble of ambition breaks in every basement. Spears of arrogant structures, as functional as death, are very rude to whatever clouds are sent them. God's eye is owlish. It seems the sky too is in trouble.

"Send me out," said Frankie. "I want to get out of here."

"Goddamn it," said Joe. "What have I got here? A crybaby?"

"I'm not crying," said Frankie. "Who's crying?"

"So you want to go out, do you? Okay, then, here. Here's a nickel. Go down and get me six pennies for it."

"Six?"

"Would I need you for five? Can you imagine that? He wants to get out of here. Take your finger out of your nose. How old are you?"

"Huh?" said Frankie.

"Your brain doesn't work very quick, does it? Or do you just make believe it doesn't?"

"Brains," said Frankie. "What do I need brains for? I don't need any brains around here."

"Now you're talking," said Joe. "That's the smartest thing you ever said. Come over here. We better not stand like this. Let's lean over the table like we're figuring out something. As a matter of fact, that's just what we're going to do. Jesus. When's the last time you washed your hands?"

"No hot water."

"Use cold. Look clean at least."

"Clean," said Frankie. "What's the use?"

"I'll tell you what's the use. Listen to me now. You're listening? How would you like to have my job?"

"What?" said Frankie.

"Shh. Keep it down, will you?"

"Me? Your job?"

"Sure," said Joe. "Why not? It's all yours, kiddo. Say the word and I'll fix it up for you."

"You would?" said Frankie. "You mean that, Joe? You think he'd give it to me?"

"I just told you," said Joe. "Leave it to me."

"Wow," said Frankie. "That would be swell, wouldn't it? Sure, why not? He doesn't know what I can do. He never saw me. You know how much I can lift if I want to? See this whole building? Tell him, Joe. Any time he wants me to move it down the block for him, just tell him to let me know. Hey, how about that? I'd get more money. I'd get more money, wouldn't I?"

"Naturally," said Joe. "That would come."

"Bake me a cake and call me cookie."

"Wait a second," said Joe. "Where are you hopping off to?"

"To wash my hands. I mean. You know what I'd do, Joe? I'd give more dough in the house right away. I'd take that rotten back-scratcher of my old man's and break it over his rotten head. I should respect him yet. I'd take some money, yeah, I'd take at least a couple of bucks and buy her a bunch of, what's the best kind? Just like in the movies. I'd take off my cap and bow down to the ground and kiss her hand. Whango, before I can stop him, there's blood all over her mouth."

"Look, Frankie."

"Aa," said Frankie. "What am I batting about? I must be nuts. It's no use, Joe. I can't do it."

"Can't do what?"

"I can't add," said Frankie. "You know that."

"Now, now," said Joe. "Don't be a damn fool."

"Two and two makes five. And that's about it."

"Fine," said Joe. "Exactly. For this job, what in hell else do you think you need?"

"Aw," said Frankie. "I don't want your job. I don't want it. It's better for me this way."

"I see," said Joe. "So you're a nothing but a nothing after all."

"Don't quit, Joe. You don't want to quit. Why do you want to quit for?"

"Give me back that nickel. It's mine, remember?"

"That guy Colish'll never let you go. You'll see. He never will. Never."

"Excuse me," said Angelina. "Two things."

"Angelina," said Joe. "Just in time. Tell me, sweetheart. When's the last time you heard a man scream?"

But of course she was much too discreet to say she ever had, though if the truth were known, but all at once she smiled as she did, as if he too were primarily concerned with the noise a male angel might make, but that of a mere man in trouble, never. Somehow her sweet temper was entirely his, and for an instant, he became what she was, a slender equilibrist, for what is faith but the balance this yeast-eating person achieves between the wrangling forces of light and darkness, as of love versus hate? It was incredible what sheer rot he could churn up. He felt like a flea which had crept into one of the fifty-five beads of her lesser rosary.

"Sorry," said Joe. "I bet you thought I was going to bite you."

"That's all right," said Angelina. "Any time."

"Great," said Joe. "In which chapel do we arrange it?"

"My," said Angelina. "Are you really as terrible as you like to sound?"

"Sometimes. What two things?"

"Well," said Angelina. "First of all, good morning."

"That's sweet."

"And second, can you give me your boy to help me pack?"

"My boy?" said Joe. "If he's my boy, certainly."

"Shoot," said Frankie. "Why me? I don't want to go. I don't like to work with girls."

"Quiet," said Joe. "You just became a slave. You'll do as you're told."

"He'll come," said Angelina.

"Right. Here. Take him by the ear. I make you a present of him."

"That's sweet," said Angelina.

"Very clever," said Joe. "Mocking me. Now I want you to tell me sometimes, Angie. That is, whenever you feel in the mood."

"Poor Frankie," said Angelina. "I'm sorry. But your hour has come."

"We'll exchange for a day," said Joe. "Your god for mine."

"Excuse me?" said Angelina.

"Wouldn't that be interesting?"

"But that's impossible."

"Why?"

"Because there is only one."

"Is there?" said Joe. "Then who's this one coming at us?"

Timber, when they saw what loomed ahead, Frankie and Angelina ducked out, they legged it together as if they were eloping. Old friend, old father of the boss man Mr. Colish, god in his seventy-seventh year in the guise of a crab, cyst on his eyelid, dustrag like a mace of office in his claw, he crept closer to his chief angel, Joe, munching with a lone eyetooth on a crust of menace and discontent, out for the kill against every time waster, showing in his ultimate surliness a greater solicitude for a scrap of Irish lace, or a snip of silk dyed in Delaware, than for a cuticle of a Bronx babe, or a blackhead of a Brooklyn bum. In Pinsk he married, in Manhattan he tarried. One reckless Polish night after a restive pushcart day, he grew sick of babbling in bed about a spoiled grape, and with a tremendous downbeat of his bony wings, he bore his Rebecca down with him, and sired Maxie. He still sighs over the audacity of it. Since then he haunts death, not death him. His one last cringing hope is that only his son should prosper, that all other sons are only sons of darkness, that whatever they touch should rust and wither away. Worshipful father, caresser of favorites who have mastered the proper genuflection, if your heart is where your mouth is, be truly divine, help this failing semblance of yours to spread ruin and chaos elsewhere, elsewhere stink instead of sweet smell, burning instead of beauty.

"You're on your way to heaven," said Joe. "I just prayed for you."

"Hah?" said the old man.

"Here," said Joe. "Sit down. Take a load off your feet."

"Feet," said Moses. "What feet? Aie. Please. Don't pull me."

"There," said Joe. "Isn't that better now? A real box seat. You can see everything you want right from here. See how nice? See how everybody's working?"

"Working," said Moses. "They only make believe."

"Still," said Joe. "The work does get done. Say. You sure look spiffy today. Where did you get those snazzy cuff links? Real gold, aren't they?"

"A present. He loves me sometimes."

"Sure does look like it."

"Yes, yes. My flesh without blood. They have a new word for me. Disgusting. You know what it means? If I stay home when she plays cards, she says to me, move, what smells on you? If I come here to watch, he tells me, go home, who needs you here to stink up the place? Work. You work. Don't listen to me."

"That's okay," said Joe. "I have to wait for them to finish packing anyway."

"Beautiful advice they give me. When was I ever so much under their feet? Out, they say. Go, pest, they spit in my face. Go in the park and talk to the squirrels."

"No good," said Joe. "They wouldn't listen to you either."

"An old ox. You think even a dog would eat me?"

"Well," said Joe. "Maybe a very hungry one. Hell, Mr. Colish. You know what I would do if I were you? I'd leave them flat. Sst. Just like that. Christ, you have plenty of money, haven't you? Or is it all his?"

"His."

"That's tough. Hey. You're not falling asleep on me, are you?"

"Bums, fakers, a fire on them all. God gave us laws, but who obeys them? Me now? Don't be foolish. Aie, when I think of it, when I think of it. I used to peddle fruit on Orchard Street. I told you. Better than the best show. I sat. I watched. I was happy. I was like a king. Three oranges, lady? Quick, Moe, put in a rotten one. Fool that I was. I made believe God didn't see me. Fool that I am. I still make believe. What sticks me here? Here. Right here."

"What you can't swallow, I guess."

"It rained. It snowed. How many years? A penny then was like a dollar. Halvah for my boy. Ices. Ice-cream cones. Here, watermelon man, give me a nice slice for my Maxie. Every day a present. A little pearl knife. If nobody's looking, why shouldn't I take it? A new praying shawl, silk from top to bottom. A regular crook. I take that too. Overalls. Socks. A fire-engine hat. A black water pistol. He used to run to me when he saw me come. A fine boy. A good boy. You like peppermints?"

"No, thanks. Nothing's wrong with my throat. Yet."

"You think I'm complaining? You're right. I am."

"Christ," said Joe. "I hope to hell I never grow this old."

"Yes," said Mr. Colish. "Be afraid of it. Be afraid."

"Gosh," said Joe. "I hate to think of ending up with just a pair of cuff links."

"And two tuxedos."

"Ah, yes, those two tuxedos."

"You're my size? I'll leave you one. I'll even put a penny in the pocket for luck."

"I'll take it. Shows you how desperate I am."

"Aie," said Moses. "So early. And I'm so tired already."

"Ah, well," said Joe. "Sit back then. Close your eyes. I'll give you a push if he whistles for you."

"Yes, yes," said Moses. "Goodbye, boy."

"Goodbye? You mean goodnight, don't you?"

"I'll watch you. I'll see what happens to you."

"From where? You're not going to haunt me after you're dead, are you?"

"Stay here," said Moses. "Work, work. What else is there in the world?"

"I don't know," said Joe. "Didn't you ever find out? I said. How do you like that? Dead to the world. Can you imagine? Work. He's lived so long. And that's all he can tell me."

What a shame then to have refused a peppermint, for that at least would have given him something more substantial to suck on, would have served as a cool reward for having listened so tenderly to the threnody of this old has-been. His watch chain is motionless? He seems like a stringless mandolin in a still life? More like a variable object which is always cracked than like a whole man, what has work done for him that he should croak so in praise of it? Nothing, it seems, but cause his demoralized heart to yearn more ardently for the dangerous labor of love. Sleep seemed to be strangling him.

Joe turned away to wonder. Why is it that the kid who has found love is so afraid he will die soon, while the old goat who has lost it is scared to death that he will be forced to live forever? A tall column of boxes came weaving towards him. With the innocent aid of Frankie, work came gunning for him, frightfully charming, reeling on trigger-happy legs. He had to laugh at it. It could, for all he cared, breed one contradiction after another, but he had to go and meet it more than halfway, and greet it like a long-lost brother.

Though they could have been cunning with such a small amount of work, and could have easily made it last them the morning, their anxiety to be involved in the destiny of things other than their troubled selves, as well as sheer habit, made them hop to it. Some people can be just as frisky and attractive in their virtuous moments as in their naughty, can be conveniently forgetful of the flabby guilt they will feel when once again they are idle, and certainly can, so enchanted are they at times with the pure and silent geometry of their affair with solids, arrange a series of partial shipments along their table as if they were creating a range of hills, each sharply rectangular and flat, and all in accordance with a clip board of orders so bare of items Mr. Colish called it criminal.

But then he was a very moral man. And very consistent about it lately, for when it came time for him to check, he would dig his initials into the green copies of the order sheets with a fury he hoped these colored bits of paper would neither remember nor resent, for even at their most miserly, they were still merciful to him. Bullock's, Stix, Baer & Fuller, Filene's, The Dayton Company, Strawbridge & Clothier, Carson Pirie Scott, Famous-Barr, F. & R. Lazarus, Joseph Horne, and The Tailored Woman, giant names of more than mortal, but less then godlike, import and power, names of a fearful beauty before which Mr. Colish, half-pretending to be a devoted dwarf, must daily kneel, and if necessary, caper and tremble.

As just at this very moment, Mrs. Morrison, a lusty buyer for a flat-chested chain of stores, tore out of the showroom with Mr. Colish stuck onto her fat back like a burr. What was she like, marvelously as she roared, but a red-cheeked fruit, and Mr. Colish, the most affectionate posteriority of her prickly husk? Smiling when he knew he should not, Joe tossed away the crayon he was trifling with, so impishly did he ever wish to have his hands free to applaud any pair of puffed-up characters who could humble themselves enough to play a passionate game of pickyback in public. Mrs. Morrison, she became aware of her sticky burden, and tried to slap him off. This stalled her. He leaped in front of her, and pecking away at her explosive cheeks, pawed her boldly as if her Achilles heel were lodged in her large left tit.

She began to feel what he was doing. She seized his head, not to thrust it away, but to make sure he would remain where he could continue to do it. It could be seen in her enlarged eyes what she enjoyed behind the screen of her anger. Time, she spat on time. He was a horrid man to ask her for more time. And with the shameless petulance of an overgrown child who has long dreamed of a doll which can roll its eyes coyly as it makes water, she became tearful about her poor little special order of hand-embroidered gowns. Where in god's name was it? Why was he keeping it from her? Sickness, he cried, sickness. Lovesick to soothe her, he cursed the home workers who had failed him, those lousy bastards with their change-of-weather weakness, constantly victimized by severe running colds that come so often in the spring. All this while he was shoving her back, extremely strong for a man of his size, until at last he backed her into the showroom.

The double doors were still swinging to and fro, concerned with subduing their own incidental agitation, when Mr. Colish kicked them into a fresh storm as he came flying out again alone. Enraged at the wholesale degradation he had suffered at the hands of Mrs. Morrison, he lowered his head and charged at the black pressers who were shrieking and slapping away at each other, so vastly exhilarated were they by what they had witnessed. He divided them venomously. They staggered back, great Judith and solid Octavia, holding their irons high in horror as he dived between them, and murderously made a mess of all the deeply pleated chemises they had labored so long to press. There, he flung back at them as he fled, that would learn them to laugh at him next time.

His oratorical feet planted on the craggy nape of his own Mount Sinai, and his invented beard threshed by the winds of a celestial indignation, Joe stretched out his arms as if to say, behold thy son, blind father, but that withered old root of a man who was supposed to be snoozing beside him, himself a crafty schoolmaster of the cackle, must have crept into a crater in hell, so completely had he vanished, or as Frankie would say, had taken a powder. Thus many a gesture as grandiloquent has been wasted on the factory air, or thrown away on a nearby Frankie who is sure he sees what he sees yet insists on looking dazed, as if there can be nothing more unreal to him than reality, and has to be poked and pummeled into snapping out of it, which he finally does with a single holy smokes. At which, hold the fort, Joe cries, and promptly marches off like a Marine to the rescue.

Judith of the onion sandwiches, and Octavia of the American cheese, were they doubly affronted because of their color? Their irons were still plenty hot. They looked ready to brain or brand him. But a slight tap on the arm of each was all the attention he paid them as he coolly proceeded to sort out for them the least damaged from the most. With strokes so savage that at first they were useless, they began to iron again, anger still glistening on their magnificent faces. He uncovered a hairpin, set it aside, found a box of Sunshine crackers, stuck one between his teeth, and stopped to show them. They thought he looked lovely. Their shoulders began to heave.

Called away, the cloud-clearer can only nod and wave his hand to signal that he is coming, for his mouth is busily engaged in a most pleasant conversation with a salty peacemaking biscuit. What is every hush but a bare branch which can suddenly become studded with sparrows? For wherever he walks he hears, now that the glare-eyed thing is over, a general twittering as of relief, a sound which is auxiliary to every and any language whether it be chirped in Swahili, Syriac, Lapp, Limbu, or what is known as the Malayalam. He beams at this exotic thought scooped out of the pot that will not melt, approaching as he does a Maisie Dubrow who was born on Hester Street, yet looks like a Mongolian. Chink they call her, a paper cup of water must be presented to her as if it contained spices. She twisted her ankle last week coming off a bus. She now has a curious way of limping slightly as if that were the only graceful way to walk. Once she had a tremendous nosebleed, shenanigans of her monthlies, and her blood was a memorable match for her gypsy skin. To hold a lump of ice to the back of her neck was to handle her very intimately. Nunlike was the expression of her slanted eyes, then as now, as she placed between his doctoring hands the discreet sinuosity of all she disciplined so well below her neckline. And yet, when she moves it, it moves like original sin.

What hazier configuration of her sex can there be than the contradictory figure of this floorlady who waits for him to tell him whose bottom belt is broken, serenely cradling a bundle of yokes, and a greasy box of hooks and pliers? His tact was exquisite. He hardly glanced at her as he relieved her of the box to lower himself on the concrete floor. Whose elated mouth will she finally invade with the

211

titillating snake of her tongue? Sarcasm can no longer conceal the impossible yen Mr. Colish has for her. Pitying glances daily reveal how sorry she is she is driving him crazy. A specialist in commiseration, Joe crawled under the silenced machine to sigh in private for both their sakes, and like the power bringer he longed to be, kicked at the treadle, bowed down as he was to the east, as if he were sending the current through their improbable later to change it into an electric possible now.

Where is he by this time? What is this foggy cerebration about the mean desires and agonies of the vast uncelebrated? It makes the senior gods yawn. It stops the clock. It ages oceans. It crumbles the rockiest mountains further. Her scuffed pumps see him. He smells the feet of her who has returned from doing what no one else can do for her. Who is it whose cancer-devoured breast begs him to hurry, hurry? Estelle, a quaking spinster on the black list, the more underwear she sews the more she seems to be stitching herself feverishly into a shroud.

Well, says Mr. Colish. All of a sudden, here he is too. Would Estelle like to listen to some pop tunes while she sits there like a lady of leisure? Or would she like him to show her what a door is for? She twists her legs around the rungs of her chair. She does not know how to answer this lust of his for hurting. His highly polished oxfords scrape a step nearer as if they were about to stamp out the faintly glowing coals of her eyes. Maisie leans forward on her tiny slippers to murmur to the crushed one, caressing her, calling her dear. Every shoe has a kick coming. This is no fancy fairy tale. And every prayer is a form of passing it along, and every teardrop too, so that whoever it is who reels about in heaven, cough, cough it up, is one sodden mass of bruises by this time.

Mr. Colish snorts at this touching little picture. His job is no cinch either. Hires lovebirds he does. Suddenly realizes it has become his hobby. Has no right to ask anything of anyone, of course, but how long will it take to fix that damn belt down there? And who the hell is that who is sunning herself so suavely at the window? Amelia Piccolini, another dazed one, she is looking for her mother. Looking for her what? Whose mother? Why, that particular lady has been dead for weeks. Dead, says Maisie, true, as dead as anyone that broke could ever wish to be. But then the strongest thread does break. And Amelia's eye is so fond and foolish. She peers, turns pale, runs to the

212

window. She sees someone. She is sure she does. What? said Mr. Colish. That smokestack of a girl? She is still looking and crying for her mamma? Imagine, what a sucker he has turned out to be. Must he support this grief also? Damning death for fastening itself on him like a slick and implacable extortioner, he shifts his feet one way, turns them another, then dashes away from it altogether, abruptly terminating for Joe his rat's eye view of what a terrible muddle a man can fall into.

As the boss men sink, the squirts arise out of positions no less omnifarious or peculiar, to rub the many creases out of their behinds. There is that rueful look on them of why does everything happen to me, as they publicly exaggerate a posterior act of assertion as pointless as it is elementary, which can make a whole crew of operators grin like gargoyles, their cavernous mouths distorted with all those complex and evil expressions thought to be anterior to simplicity and innocence.

He hates them now? What should Joe have done? Continue to sit on that nozzle of the oilcan without knowing it? Chew on leather and suck on grease? Construct a nest under their feet, go knee-deep into the birdlime of their lives? But if he did go in so far, so far in, would he get to know them any better? How would he be able to make use of such knowledge when he is sure it would sicken him? How miserable is his own mind, see what it does to prove it is dynamic, it dances a highland fling on one spot to the groaning hornpipes of his own thoughts which kick up a silly little storm of static dots and dashes. Yet he does get going again, as he knows he must, struggling against all those stale and arid ideas about the seeker and the sought, the victim and the victimizer, against what has begun to seem too much like the endlessly writhing confabulation of worms about worms. That which is, what is it? One last trembling glance at the superior silence of these women, what does it seem to be trying to tell him? He hears it as things are heard in the heart. They are that which is just as they are. They work. They have no words for life. They live it.

Sing hallelujah, then, he is a bum, a voluble one full of unwise sayings, a thinking bum than which there can be nothing worser. From this he can never hope to make a living. It is now very obvious to him, as a swiftly evolving self-destructionist, that in trying to uplift others, he only succeeds in degrading himself. He turns in time to

213

observe how Frankie comes to fetch him, how like a delighted butterfly he tries to alight on this blurred hunk of beef which looks like Joe, positively squirming with what he has to tell, a reek of butterscotch on his secret-divulging breath. Can see what from where? Which dressing room? Stand off with that smell and speak plainly. Impossible, the punk replies with a sensational wink, would be highly indelicate, might be overheard, would spoil it all, must come and see for himself, he simply must.

Felix, Hymie, and Georgie were already there, concealing themselves among the hats, coats and hangers. It was so lecherously dim in that dressing room for men with its one confidential window, a lust-streaked eye leering across the courtyard at the scabby butt of the Dolly Madison Hotel, patron saint of loose, discarded, and lonely women exclusively. Madame Secular, she wore no nun's veiling. Spring had sucked up her shade. A platinum blonde in the dumps, she rubbed spit on a run in her stocking, exhibiting the natural color of her weary pubic hair to random peepers. The discs around her nipples were enormous. She gazed at her rumpled bed, but sleep seemed no solution. The tinkling of wire hangers made her cock her head like a hunted animal. Silence worried her. She leaned her raw elbows on the dresser to search in the mirror for the flushed past tense of her face. The mirror failed her. Her chalky rump sagged. She poked among the toilet knickknacks, but she could not find the fig leaf of her future. Her torn lips twitched. She looked again into the glass. What impelled her to make a fist? Why did she threaten herself so sincerely? Hymie was the first to whistle. Frankie gave out with a monkey screech. Felix clapped his hands and yelled bravo. She sprang to the window, showing them her last bit of nakedness, her pocked tongue. She spat at them. She pulled so hard at the shade, she tore the whole thing-umaflop right down. Her most vociferous admirers had a fit, pushed and shoved at each other, and scrambled out. Joe and Georgie came slowly after.

It was cooler where they strolled along the corridor where it was screened. They spoke to each other quietly. They learned that neither had been amused. When they paused near the door of the men's room, it was Georgie's policy never to budge any further unless he was so ordered, Joe smiled like a priest who knew the world, and said, our women, who are white, when they begin to feel it would be heaven on earth to be gored by a lurking gorilla, change the color of their hair and curl it, while your women, who are variously colored, when they long to entice a tireless pumper for the same purpose, move heaven and earth to perfume and flatten theirs. This then is what is known as the same difference. Georgie held his broom as if it were a staff, and he a pilgrim, and humbly assured Joe that he would always cherish this fashion note of his which had been so keenly observed and so pungently expressed. Joe raised his eyebrows to an extraordinary degree, would he really? Pooh, there was nothing to it, it was all in a day's work. A repulsive word this last, though it does remind him to ask, where does Georgie expect to go from this job as long as it lasts, to more of the same dirt? But of course, said Georgie, to more and more, may it forever keep piling up mysteriously. White men are strange. They wish the world were clean. But their black brothers have faith in it only when it is as filthy as filthy can be. What is this the nigger holds? A broom, God has thrust it into his hands, and has counseled him thus, go thou with this mean instrument, and with it confound the things which are mighty. Be he high-yaller or paper-brown, he will gladly do it. This then is what is known as a sweeping fable. Neither waited for the other to laugh. Joe took hold of the broom, not to lean on it with Georgie, but to shake it gently, and bow to a better man who had said a better thing. What then, said Joe, are gnawing cares, and the itch of lust, and the furtive joy of chambering, when the merest trifle can still tickle a man? What is it the good book says? It says, be angry, and sin not. But why not laugh instead? And bust a gut. So back to work heartily, God-fearer, let us say goodbye for now. By all means, said Georgie, let us do so and part. So they separated and went each his own way. Liars, said Joe to himself, what are we but professional liars? He was hardly six steps away. We meet like sages. We bow to each other as if we knew why. We think we can perambulate together like lords of the manor in the lush meadows of the mind. We think we think. But the truth is a poor relation. The truth is apart and pale and lean. And every thought we have about it, every shade of thought, is a starving thought which licks its own shadow.

Still as inconclusive, the pockets of his brain all picked, all thumbs about thinking as he feels he has become, let him feast then on what is timed to approach him on his return to his timtom table, bearing as it does within it the very succulence of what comes next, another of

Tuesday's promising little plums. A sight which excites him so, he bites into it immediately. For here comes Mr. Colish leading a tiny woman like a changeling by her breakable china hand. How resourceful of Mr. Colish. Where had he gone to fetch that? Had he finagled his way into fairyland and bribed the elves to lend her to him? A wax image, a bloodless charm, she skimmed along beside him, swinging a satchel in which articles of prognostication clinked forebodingly. Strangely gay but soundless spells spilled incessantly over her lips. Only the delicate blade of her nose kept her eyes from merging into one large delphian eye. The sphinx too was a kitten once, a kitten which has leaped underground to claw to shreds whatever silken dreams of the future a man may sometimes have the heart to weave.

Scat, said Joe, but still she came on, eyeing him maliciously, prepared to slip him her paw. Joe, said Mr. Colish, this is Miss Cyclops. Here, he said, take her around. Joe made as if to embrace and crush her. No, no, said Mr. Colish, glaring at him. He turned a forefinger down to stir an invisible witches' brew in the air. Around, around. See that she sells something. And then out. Got it now? She had been stamping her feet. She kept stamping them after Mr. Colish had gone.

Clopchick, she squeaked, her name was Clopchick, not Cyclops. A big boob he was, like all men, like her father with his secret hernia, like her brother enlisting to be a uniformed tramp, like her brother-in-law whose only job was to grow a moustache and try nightly to rape her, so fond was he of his cock-and-bull story that it would be good for her health. She shook her satchel in the face of this gruesome member of the same lodge. What three things did he think she was selling? Ashes? Flyspecks? Pealess pods? He was warning her? If she kept this up, he would kick her out? He did in fact catch hold of her, but when she began to bore into him with her head in a very loving way, he quickly pushed her away. Afraid to play? Afraid to know then? She dropped her jaw to show him how much like a mentally deficient baby he looked. Idiot, must she tell him? Listen now. They may indeed rattle around very much like it, but it is not combs she sells, or cans of talcum powder, or tubes of toothpaste, but fear, hate, and hunger. Now how about that? Had he ever heard of such a thing before?

Damn right he had and he was sick of it. He thrust his face into hers. Now he knew who she was. She was no sibyl to him, but just a sufferer so vain that she had to make a stink about it. What surplus fear had she

216

to sell? What drooling hate? What dry and cracked hunger? From what massive volume on sour grapes had she filched that idea? She can clop as much as she wants with her tiny clopsticks here on this stone floor, but her misery was her misery, and his was his. So no sale. Got it now? She smiled unharmed. She reached up to touch his lips with her cool finger tips. Come, she said, follow me. And he followed her. He followed her wherever she went. Wherever she went to sell, until she left, he had to follow her.

Naturally then, the grammar of it would intrigue him, as he trudged back to the oft-invaded bastion of his vulnerable department, for this again was another thing he was forced to do, if only for a few more days, just a few more. Yet why was he careful not to count them? A precious superstition, if daisy yellow was the blouse Clopchick wore, and apple green her flounced skirt with the money pocket, what combination of clothes and colors would the next jinx have the insolence to flaunt? A white striped voile sundress with the briefest bolero draped into sleeves? A poplin swim suit in lemon or lilac? A dotted swiss dress for a spring morning with a sweetheart neckline and a velvet sash? All fresh and dainty would they be? Tucks at the bosom, perky bows at the neck, what would Mr. Colish, the grand designer, softly style next of each assault and piercing reminder?

Perhaps a simpleton like Frankie could tell him, but Frankie was in the silk room, matching pennies with Kitzel. Frankie waved his hand to show how fast he was raking in the dough. For once the loser was winning. Joe picked up a loose pad. He had a moment. What should he scribble? What solitary game should he play? He lost the rubber game of ticktacktoe. He tried then to draw a perfect circle. But each of his twelve tries looked like a coin which many a dead man had often fondled and defaced. Angrily switching to parallelograms, then crude squares, he vowed that never again would he ever be a flunkey to every sharer of his mortality, even if he or she be also a comrade of his witless and wobbly way. He was amazed to see he was drawing the outline of a dagger, and from its stained tip, drops of blood which, as they dripped down the page, grew larger and larger.

"See?" he said. "I just stabbed you."

"What?" said Mr. Colish. "What's this supposed to be?"

He turned the sheet every which way. He could make nothing of it. He crumpled and threw it away.

217

"Well?" said Mr. Colish. "How did she make out? Did she sell anything?"

"Not to me," said Joe. "Why did you let her in? You never let anybody in."

"I wanted you to see."

"Ah," said Joe. "I thought so."

"I wanted you to have a good look at what can happen. Do you have any idea how many of those pests I have to chase away every day?"

"Don't ask me," said Joe. "That's your hobby, not mine."

"You would need an adding machine. Hell, I said to myself, I'll take pity on this one. What did they say when you took her around?"

"They hated her."

"That pretty little thing?"

"An ugly one you would've kicked right out."

"I'm a man, no?"

"A man, yes. But what kind?"

"What kind?" said Mr. Colish. "How do you like that? I can't talk to you any more like a friend?"

"Why not?" said Joe. "You can do whatever you want, can't you?"

"No," said Mr. Colish. "Friends don't insult each other."

"Okay, then," said Joe. "I'll pay you a compliment. You know what I thought when I first came to work for you, Mr. Colish? I watched you. I said to myself, goddamn it, here at last is a guy who's not afraid to act like a real man. Look at him. Does he ever lose his head? Does he ever look scared? The hell he does. You think he's like you? Watch him, I said. He's so quick and sure in everything he does. See how he spits on the little things? He knows. He can say yes or no like a shot. He thinks big. He's going places. I said to myself, get on your horse. Try to be more like him. Get a move on. Wake up. Real young then, wasn't I?"

"You said that? You never told me."

"You could tell. You knew."

"That's funny," said Mr. Colish. "I was looking at you too."

But they could hardly look at each other now. They stretched their necks as if they were struggling with the same frog in the throat. They surveyed areas they did not see. They were delighted to discover they had more than one fingernail. They seemed fascinated by the fact that their toes were in their shoes. They hated to be caught breathing so

218

tenderly. They knew they must not think too much of what they had confessed to each other. Yet each wanted so much to hear the other say more.

"She's sick," said Mr. Colish.

"Is she?" said Joe. "Who?"

"My good news. My pride and joy."

"Oh," said Joe. "She."

"If I don't go crazy, I don't know what. Women. I'm sick of them. They're coming out of my ears."

"They usually do. So they tell me."

"Listen to this," said Mr. Colish. "I want you to listen. I should drop dead if I'm lying. Calls me up this morning. Calls me, you hear? I told her a million times never to bother me so early, so what does she do? She calls me. Got a cold. Her nose is a little bit wet. Max, she says, I can't stand it any more, I'm going right to the hospital. Hospital? I said. What hospital? You got fever? You feel worse? No, she says. What fever? Can't you talk to me without making me a hole in the head? It's my nerves. You know my nerves. Ha. Do I know her nerves. What else do I know about? Look, I said. You think I'm blind? You think I can't see you? What do you think I see when I see? I see a woman who eats and sleeps like a horse. That's right, she screams at me, insult me. Insult me when I'm sick. Why? Why did I have to marry such a miser? For months now I've been begging you. Max, let me go to Florida. I'm ashamed. I can't walk out in the street. Everybody I know is in Miami Beach. Nope, you said, can't afford it. I said to you, Max, I said to you only yesterday, please, let me run away for a few weeks to the Catskills. What's a few weeks to you? I'll be safe. I'll stay with Esther. Nope, you said, now is impossible. Later. Maybe later. You and your later. You think I'm going to wait for your later all my life? And bang, she hangs up on me."

"Nice kid. Is she always this way?"

"Oh, no," said Mr. Colish. "No, no, of course not. I didn't make her sound that terrible, did I? You think she doesn't know what's really going on? She knows. Only she's afraid to think of it. Like everybody else. When things keep getting worse and worse, it kills her too. You think I blame her for wanting to run away?"

"Then why don't you let her?"

"I'd like to run away from it myself."

"Oh, but you're a man. A man never does that, does he?"

"Wait and see."

"You didn't finish. Where did she land?"

"Who?"

"Your wife."

"Oh, Miriam. She went. Right in the hospital. What could I do with her? And the funny thing is she'll really have herself a good time there. That's what I can't understand. A strange woman. Believe me, Joe, you don't know her the way I do. You never in all your life saw anybody so generous. No old dresses for the maid we got. No, sir. She gives her new ones. And thoughtful? Don't ask. You know what she does? It amazes me. She keeps a record of everybody's birthday, anniversary, and what not. Every day she sends out at least a dozen cards. And every one of them is hand-picked. That's lovely. You think she does that because she hates people?"

"No," said Joe. "Because she's afraid they'll forget her."

"You think so? What the hell is the fire inspector doing here? He has to come here every week? Who's that talking to him? My father?"

"Don't worry," said Joe. "He'll take care of him."

"Sure," said Mr. Colish. "I can see the summons already. I ask you. How do you get rid of such a man?"

"Easy," said Joe. "You slip him a couple of bucks."

"What for?"

"To get rid of him."

"My father?"

"Oh," said Joe. "I thought you meant."

"You thought I meant. Fire inspector, hell. He can burn up too for all I care. You thought I meant. You're getting real cute, aren't you? You think you're doing me a favor by listening to me?"

"What else can I do? I'm trapped here."

"I can see," said Mr. Colish. "That dumb you are not. You're not surprised I'm ashamed of him. Why does he have to come here every day and make my life black for me?"

"Be patient. He'll kick off soon enough."

"Don't be a fool. He'll outlive us all."

"Then poison him. It's been done before."

"It's a big joke to you, isn't it?"

"I'm not exactly laughing, am I?"

"Why does he have to appear like the devil? Who wants him around here to scare the hell out of me?"

"Scare the hell out of you?"

"What a life," said Mr. Colish. "I'm telling you. The other day, I was talking to Miriam, just kibitzing around with her, when she says to me, say, is that an accent you got, or are you just trying to imitate your umdum father? I looked at her. I laughed it off. But later on, it got me thinking. And suddenly it comes to me that lately, when I count to myself, I count in Yiddish. How do you like them apples? I don't understand it. I never did that before. What is this that's coming out in me? Me becoming just like my father? How would you like that if it was happening to you? Wouldn't that make your whole insides turn over? Hah? Would you like to slobber like him? To shovel in mush like him? To piece rags together like a spider? To use your broken hands to scratch yourself every day for three hours? I know it's digusting what I'm saying. A bug. What else is he? And I'm one too if I talk about him this way. I know. You don't have to tell me."

"It's all so stupid," said Joe.

"Stupid," said Mr. Colish. "You sound like someone in my lodge. The smallest contribution will be welcome from the poorest member."

"Afraid," said Joe. "I know I made up my mind not to get excited, but sometimes. What in the hell is there to be afraid of? That some day maybe we'll be left all alone? That we're bound to die? So okay, let it come. But in the meantime, let it simmer there. And I'll go out and live. Is it pain I'm afraid of? Could be. I don't much like that. Otherwise. Why are we all running around like chickens with our heads cut off? Scared. Sure. I'm beginning to see. When you shake in your pants, I begin to shake in mine. It's catching. When I see that happen, you know what I say to myself? I say, that's torn it. Get going, boy. Start hopping. This is not the place for you."

"Get on your mark," said Mr. Colish. "Get set. Run, boy, run."

"Which reminds me," said Joe.

"Oy," said Mr. Colish. "Brilliant. Was that smart what you said."

"What do you think of Frankie? He's not such a bad kid, is he?"

"Frankie," said Mr. Colish. "What Frankie?"

"You know. The kid who helps me."

"Oh, that Frankie. So? What about him?"

221

"He can do my job. I can break him in easy."

"You can?" said Mr. Colish. "And what are you going to do when that happens? Walk around here with your hands in your pockets?"

"Ah, no," said Joe. "That's one pleasure I'll never have."

"Really?" said Mr. Colish. "Why?"

"Because by that time I'll be far far away from here."

"Ah, yes," said Mr. Colish. "Now I remember. You said something about that Saturday, didn't you? Something about, what was it now? Something about quitting your job, wasn't it?"

"Your memory amazes me."

"Look at the bastards. Look at them all watching us. They sure would like to know what we're talking about, wouldn't they? Workers, god bless them. And what've you been doing this morning? Let's have a look. What have you got here to check?"

"Just what you see."

"Only that?" said Mr. Colish. "Pack it up. I don't have to check it. I trust you."

"Thanks," said Joe. "About Frankie now. Is it okay for me to talk to him?"

"Don't be ridiculous."

"Why not? I'm sure he's got what it takes. He can manage it easily."

"He can?" said Mr. Colish. "Is that how much you like him?"

"Sure I like him. Isn't that enough?"

"Then listen to me, Joe. Stop talking to me about quitting, you hear? Or so help me god I'll fire that Frankie of yours the hell out of here."

"What?" said Joe.

"You heard me," said Mr. Colish. "When I say I'll do it, I'll do it. Come on, now, tell me. Who else do you love around here? Angelina? Kitzel? Georgie? What's the matter? Lost your tongue? Afraid to talk to me any more?"

"This is crazy," said Joe. "What in the hell have they all got to do with me?"

"Force me," said Mr. Colish. "Force me and you'll find out. I'll show you what I can do when I get hot. I'm sick and tired of taking guff from every little twerp that has a mouth to give it to me. They're all my friends here. Oh, sure. When I say no, they say yes. When I say yes, they say no. Fine, then. Let it be that way. Only I'm warning you,

Joe. Whatever happens around here, don't blame me for it."

"Wait," said Joe. "That's my pencil."

"Did you hear what I said? If it happens, it happens. Don't blame me."

"Wait a second," said Joe. "Give me a chance."

"Work," said Mr. Colish. "And that's my last word."

"Hold it now," said Joe. "Wait a minute. What hit me here? Where did he go? What's the matter with that man?"

The telephone rang. He unhooked the receiver and mumbled into the mouthpiece. He could have sworn he had said hello, but someone said, crazy? Who's crazy? And he said, excuse me, to whom have I the honor of speaking?

"The Queen of Sheba."

"Rosalie."

"A fine way to answer the phone. Suppose it was somebody important?"

"That's all right," said Joe. "I'm getting used to sounding silly."

"But I'm not," said Rosalie. "So please. Don't let it happen again."

"Okay, then," said Joe. "Very good. Let's begin all over again. You called me. Now. What's on your mind?"

"My hair."

"All of it? Say. It's a grand day for a Tuesday, isn't it?"

"Tell me quick before I brain you. What did he say to you? What happened?"

"I don't know," said Joe. "I'll have to think about it."

"Oh," said Rosalie. "So everything's still the same?"

"Shh," said Joe. "Not so loud. It's dangerous to talk to me. I hate to tell you this, but I'm a marked man."

"Just on top? Or all over?"

"I'll give you the lowdown later. We'll have to make up signals."

"Did he give you hell? He wasn't nasty to you, was he?"

"For instance," said Joe. "When you hang up, don't say goodbye, say hello. That'll confuse him."

"Joey, please, don't fool around with me. You didn't have a fight with him, did you? Why don't you be a good boy and come over and talk to me. Just for a second? Hey? Pretty please?"

"Stop worrying," said Joe. "There's nothing wrong. I was only joking. Don't you know when I'm joking yet?"

"Choking would be more like it. Forget it. I didn't mean to bother you. I'm sorry."

"Hey, now," said Joe. "That I like. Somebody is apologizing to me for a change. Me, you understand. A real specialist. Instead of helping people, all I do is make trouble for them. Hang up, kiddo. Before I string myself up. Accidentally."

"I'll see you after lunch?"

"Mean to say you still want to?"

"Of course," said Rosalie. "How can you say a thing like that?"

"Easy," said Joe. "You have no idea the things I can say once I get warmed up. I surprise myself all the time. Uh-uh. I'm getting company."

"Who?"

"Big Bee. See you later then. Bye."

"No, no," said Rosalie. "Hello. Don't you remember?"

"Ah, yes," said Joe. "Thanks for reminding me. Hello, then. Hello."

"My," said Big Bee. "That's a funny way of signing off."

"It is?" said Joe. "But then everything's a howl these days. Don't you think so?"

"Oh, no," said Big Bee. "Some things are very sad."

"Then why do you smile when you say that? You're a faker, madam. Hey, hey. What is it you use to make you smell so delightful? Could you possibly tell me?"

"Smell," said Big Bee. "That's an awful word."

"Tell me now," said Joe. "What would you do if I gave you a great big hug? Like this."

"Oo," said Big Bee. "What are you doing?"

"Can I help it if I suddenly like you? Don't tell me you're blushing?"

"He's watching. Can't you see that?"

"Of course he's watching," said Joe. "He's always watching. That's just what I want him to do. I want him to see how much I like you. Now, now. Don't struggle. Don't you want him to see what good friends we are? Maybe it'll give him an idea. Maybe he'll do something."

"Do something," said Big Bee. "If you don't let me go, I'll give you such a kick you'll never forget."

"Well, now," said Joe. "Let me see. This lady weighs in the neighborhood of. Ow."

"There," said Big Bee. "I told you to let me go, didn't I?"

"Madam," said Joe. "You pinched me."

"Pinched you?" said Big Bee. "Don't be silly. Where would I grab hold? You're so skinny, you're all bones. Ah, now, look. Aren't you ashamed of yourself? Look how you mussed me all up. Is that the way to treat an old, I mean, an older person? What was it I came here for? I know I came here for something. Ah, yes. A quarter, that's it. You must give me a quarter immediately."

"What for?" said Joe. "For damages?"

"No, no," said Big Bee. "Didn't you hear? Mrs. Colish is in the hospital."

"Yes," said Joe. "I know. I know all about it."

"The poor thing. I understand it's very serious."

"You understand right," said Joe.

"Really?" said Big Bee. "You know? What is it? Can you tell me?"

"Promise not to blab it around?"

"Yes, yes, I promise."

"The poor thing ran out of toilet paper."

"Oh, you," said Big Bee. "I didn't come here to joke with you. How can you joke about a thing like that? You're heartless like all men. You think I meant anything by it? It was merely a suggestion, that's all. I said to him, Mr. Colish, I said to him as soon as I heard about it, would it be all right with you, I said to him, if we all chipped in and send her flowers? And he said to me, I don't give a damn what you do."

"And if you ask me, I don't either."

"Imagine that? What did you say? Don't you think it's a good idea? See? I have it all here. Everybody on the floor gave me one."

"The suckers."

"Suckers?" said Big Bee. "Don't you dare say that. It's an act of mercy, that's what it is."

"Then do me one. Beat it."

"What?" said Big Bee. "You mean to say you're not going to give me?"

"I said, flit."

"Now, now," said Big Bee. "Don't be like that. Just fork it over and you'll be just like everybody else."

"That sure would please me no end."

"I see," said Big Bee. "I'm beginning to know you now. You think

225

you're just too good for us around here, don't you?"

"Why, yes," said Joe. "How did you guess?"

"You think you're smart enough to do anything you want, don't you? Well, go ahead. Throw up your job. Commit suicide. Who cares? We'll be glad to be rid of you."

"Will you scram? Or do I have to give you a good punch in the nose?"

"Oh," said Big Bee. "Don't worry. I'm going, I'm going. You think I want to stay here and have you insult me? You think anyone is going to worry about you any more? Go ahead now. Be different. Leave us and see what you'll find. But mark my words. Remember now what I'm telling you. You're going to be awfully sorry one of these days. Oh, how you'll be sorry."

9.

Now that his vagabond and hagridden day is over, and the urban sun has had its final looksee at the usual vortex of riproarious spectacles, it withdraws from his mighty Kings County with a minimal show of sorrow. The clock at home had inspired Joe to begin such cool preluding. A stray mutt trots beside him as he has but a block to go before he reaches the haven of his own kennel, the clubroom, sniffing at his pants cuff, and gazing up at him as if pleading with him to continue. He concludes it is a little lady dog. Gently then, he speaks to her, without as much as moving his lips or looking down, and tired as he is of the chasing mood, treats her as if she were an old flame with whom he could be comfortable. Surely then she must concede that, unlike him, the sun is a crackerjack at it. It can easily outstare each minikin eye which is human and giddy enough to dare to threaten it. What has it to do with the funereal or the offended? The pangs and prickings of a Brooklyn numskull affect it not. It is as pitiless as a flea. Stubby tail, though East Flatbush is landlocked, many an odd duck of a Joseph Bellinson may insist that he often capers on the outer seas of contrition, and to his eternal credit, is as often induced to plunge into the inner seas of remorse, but the sun, itself never created to be a convict in the prison house of language, is indifferent to such engarlanded phrases.

Is the sun so dumb then and so hard of heart? If its life by day seems like such a lark, what is its night life like? A growl of impatience precedes a demisemiquaver of a bark. Yet when night falls, old trot, it seems like an act of malfeasance. It allows thieves to bolt, and cowards to coalesce, and prophets to shift their untenable positions. But the moon, dear brown and white spots, is how the sun keeps its vigil over every brainsick escapist, trailing him with its misty dog's eye as if it were crucial to its existence to know what this bloke will do next, and if he will ever do it. Pausing before he goes underground, he motions to the mutt to take herself off elsewhere. It was nice while it lasted. She need not look so betrayed. He knows he must be careful not to smile, else she will stay. His pantomime about any further communion between them penetrates at last, and she mournfully turns away and trots off, leaving him with a view of an expressive tail with its own grace notes of regret, and its own faint desires of reunion.

Himself a sleek and skylarking savage with a fantastic affinity for faculative critters whose pelts are neither glossy nor clipped, he descends four stone steps in his own freedom-loving way to stand before a door he knows is locked without trying it. Ordinary creeper, boring destroyer of time, where does he keep the key to it? He keeps it where he has never kept anything else, in the most cryptic spot on his person, the watch pocket of his pants. The key means. What does it signify? What color does it have? It has the color of brass, the color of a lower mystery. Stooping a bit, he rams it home and twists to take possession of his eighth share in a third home. As debonair and easygoing as he is, what is this world within a world into which he slips sideways and softly locks himself in?

A place, a space, a simple cellar in a city by the sea, where the floor is of wood and waxed for dancing, for irrepressible exhibitions, frequently glissando, of entangled and incidental assertion. What else but praiseworthy can it be to shell out rent for such a highflying purpose? Seems puzzling though why the lights should burn so low, but then, since these were eight of the more subtle members of the younger element, insisting as they do that dimness for their groping is dazzling enough, that is as far as their love of illumination will go. If again the sofas and armchairs are stuffed after the prurient manner of the last century, they could not afford to buy anything that might be less so, so they were never heard to apologize for any scrap of furniture in their finished basement whenever they were in the process of persuading a group of pickups to park there.

Besides if at first a piece proves to be particularly hands-offish, as only too often happens, she will nevertheless adore a pink lampshade because it does do wonders for her complexion, as moth-eaten and secondhand as that may sometimes be, and she will finally allow a peck and a squeeze where she imagines it will hurt her the least, if only out of gratitude, just that. After which her partner for the evening will gradually put out the lights one by one, not that he may finally upend her in total darkness, but merely to show her how ambidextrously pacifying his hands can be, and how pleasantly to each other their cigarette ends can glow. She may then have to use her claw to encourage him to assure himself again of the veracity of her curves, and plead with him to give her a more serious kiss by hooking the heel of her hand under his chin, and fluffing her ashes all over him as a volcanic hint that she knows what it is to smoke, to come, to be on fire. Imploring, seminiferous she with her epic sigh as sensible of her need she stretches herself out, it is for her all has been so charitably arranged. It is for her sake the boys fork up their dues. It is really her clubroom, her darkness, her party.

Having thus been wise enough to avail herself of the precious edibility of the possessive case, and in turn, to yield up her yam so flashing sweet, is her memory revered? Are the fragrant traces of it retained as keepsakes? To say yes would be to bleed the truth, because in sweeping, the earring of simulated pearl torn from her lobe, the glossy button ripped from her blouse, the bent hairpins, the long hairs of her head, and the shorter and curlier ones of her bush, and whatever else she may have deposited behind her in her haste to be muzzled and finally humped, are all swept out, for when she goes, she must be gone, and all sense of shame with her. As if that were possible. But after so much mussy tunneling, a man would like to be tranquil for a while, and dust himself off, and clear the decks of his forward-looking desire for the filmy appearance of the next faceless one.

So far in, so good. But the poor flittering hearts of those other dead beats who cry out harshly at the spongy nature of the male when they feel that promiscuous tool of his approaching, and with an insulting push, lock their thighs at the last moment, why should there be so many of them? Sometimes it seems that the next willing one will

229

never come. Again and again, what is ushered in is that sad dog, that creep, that frantic growler, that unduly intimate beast known as frustration, recognized the instant it rears up, raising one foreleg above the other, ready to clout the stuffings out of the glorious compulsion the cock has to cover the hen.

Gloom of no mean violence then ensues as the spoilsports are thunderously hustled out, and sarcastically advised to put fresh elastic in their drawers, and calcify further, if they so wished, the chancrous inveteracy of their virtue, and if fruit is what they fall for, take a green banana to bed with them, and with four o'clock in the morning tears, crosshatch a thousand wrinkles on the pillow slips of their own peevishness and discontent. The tossingest lot, does it worry them that such bums should call them bitches, and mistaking their fearful innocence for frigidity, prolong the farce by promulgating choleric vows of chastity, and so deepen their isolation and loneliness? And when in haste they hop out of bed in the middle of the night to make number one, do they ask themselves why are they sitting there, is it for this they were born, is this what is called living? If so, they can always stumble back and dream. Maybe their dreams will tell them.

Peculiar kids, when their periods come, they say their sisters are here, or more forcibly, that they have fallen off the roof. Little Joe from Kokomo, a simple four is his point, will he ever make it? From now on, as he kids himself, as soon as a girl says no dice, stay away from her moistest parts. Neither consistently scourge nor entirely condemn her. Like an ideally reformed character, think a kinder last thought about her, and apply this plainer hope to her pardonable night watch, that she may dreamlessly revert to the gossamer awareness of her cradle days, and so sleep anew a satiny sleep, and be soundly comforted.

Peace, after spouting like this, why does he look so pleased? Because he has refused to budge until he could appeal, with a brilliance as indicated, to his mythical better nature? That yes, but what more conclusively excites him to feel a little too satisfied is the sense he has of having made his standing still seem so excessively eventful. Ninny so open-souled, one grasping thought in him has long been grooved, to wit, if he cares for no one, who on earth will care for him? This is the rush hour of his life. Yet he folds his wings. He scratches in his armpits. He studies the half-moon of his nails meditatively. What is the sense of all this? What precisely is he trying to prove? Ask him. Who wants to follow a man who takes so long to move?

Consequently the least clownish thing he could do, as he snuck into the back room, was to be the first to speak and welcome his own arrival.

"Stay right where you are," he said. "I love to look at you."

"Hey, hey," said Doc. "Joe. Just the man I've been waiting for. You can go now, son. Here comes a good player."

"Good player, hell," said Mel. "Finish the game. You think you're beating me?"

"There was a cop here," said Artie.

"Disaster," said Doc. "What a shrimp. See what just happened? He broke that goddamn chair."

"The cop?" said Joe.

"No," said Artie. "He means me. I did it."

"What?" said Joe. "Again?"

"I couldn't help it, Joe. It was another weak one."

"Okay, champ," said Doc. "Crown me."

"I sure in hell would like to," said Mel. "Hey. Wait a second. How did you ever get all the way down here with that piece? You know what he does, Joe? I swear to god, I've seen him do it. He pushes those goddamn checkers with his elbow."

"What elbow?" said Doc. "Look, my friend. You say that again and I'll shove your rotten face in."

"Do that," said Mel. "And I'll hand you back your bumpy head, but quick."

"You don't say?"

"But I do say," said Mel. "I'm sitting right here and saying it."

"Saying what?"

"What I said."

"You don't say?"

"Christ," said Joe. "They sure do talk to each other deep, don't they?"

"It's murder," said Artie. "You think they'll ever really fight? I've been waiting for them to sock each other for years. What in the hell's this now that's crawling on me?"

"Stop leaning back in that chair," said Joe. "What are you trying to do? Ruin us altogether? Where's Dave? Did Eddie show up yet? What's all this business about a cop?"

231

"Squat and I'll tell you."

"I'm still standing?"

"Don't you know?"

"Look," said Joe. "Do me a favor, will you? Sit on the couch here. You're giving me heart failure with that chair. Let me sit on it, okay?"

"Sure thing," said Artie. "Here. I hope you know how to ride it, cowboy."

"Still wandering around in the great panhandle of Texas. You look dusty enough, god knows."

"Every day in every way. I try, I try. Anyway, now that you're sitting there as if you were about to take off, tell me, stranger, where were you last night between one and two?"

"Me?" said Joe. "Dreaming about you."

"Ah," said Artie. "So now you owe me."

"It wasn't that kind of a dream. What happened? Somebody's been complaining about noise again?"

"Somebody's been robbing."

"Whoops."

"Bah," said Artie. "Strictly an amateur. Crept around the house like a hippo. Woke up the whole fugging Feinstein family. Didn't get away with even a single snot-rag."

"Sounds like me."

"Exactly," said Artie. "So that polecat, you know the dame, of all places, that's where it has to happen, she sends him down here to look for the crook."

"Ha," said Joe. "But he didn't find me, did he?"

"He couldn't find his head if it was handed to him on a silver platter. Hey, Doc, did you hear that one? He makes believe he didn't hear me. Anyway, there he was towering above me, twirling that stupid night stick. Quite an expert at it. I made my voice like a peanut. I sure schmeared him. Yes, officer. No, officer. You bet, officer. We'll sure be on the lookout, officer. A rookie. You should've seen the way I handled him. I said to him, excuse me if I'm too forward, sir, but the next time you're off duty, sir, won't you honor us with your presence, sir?"

"The hell you did."

"Honest," said Artie. "I said to him, and if it so happens, sir, you have no lady friend for the evening, please, sir, let it not put you out of countenance. For we, sir, we in our exquisite hospitality, only be sure to let us know in advance, we shall be awfully happy to supply you with that particular article. In short, friend, we'll fix you up."

"That's nice," said Joe. "So you finally got yourself a profession, did you?"

"Ah, well," said Artie. "I suppose it was inevitable."

"No doubt," said Joe. "That's life for you. And what, if I may be so vulgar as to ask, are you going to charge the customers? Don't go. I'm not going to hurt you. I'm just going to twist your arm off."

"Excuse me," said Artie. "I have to see a man about a dog."

"Goddamn it," said Mel. "Who the hell kicked the table?"

"I did," said Artie. "Didn't you see? That man was going to murder me."

"He was?" said Mel. "Mind if I try too?"

"Quiet," said Doc. "Leave him be. You're lucky he knocked them over."

"I was what?" said Mel. "Listen to him. The bullfrog is croaking again. Why, you slow death, you. I had you cornered. You know that."

"Dream on," said Doc. "Have fun."

"See?" said Artie. "See how nice I am, Mel? I'm picking them all up for you. What else do you want?"

"A change of air," said Mel. "A blonde with tassels. A gold clip for my folding money. You know how it is. I hate to have it lying around loose."

"Oh, sure," said Artie. "There is where I sympathize with you. As a matter of fact. Here, take your lousy checkers. Your sarcasm touches me where I really live. Another poor bastard added to the grand total. What in the hell's a blonde with tassels? I've crept around a bit in my day, but I've never crawled into a number like that."

"Oho," said Mel. "So you confess it."

"Curiosity's got me. What can I do?"

"Then come," said Mel. "Sit at my feet, sonny boy, and listen while I tell you. I'll do it like a father. I'll drill it right into your head."

"In which case," said Artie. "I have a better idea. I'll make believe I'm a man and take it standing up."

"Good," said Mel. "You do that. Now. You're ready to cooperate?"

"I'm stuck now. What else can I do?"

"Fine," said Mel. "Now think of a pair of lacy curtains."

"I'm thinking."

"Swell," said Mel. "Now get behind them."

"Ah," said Artie. "Is that where she is?"

"Don't ask questions. Do what I tell you."

"Okay," said Artie. "I'm behind them. Now what?"

"My goodness," said Mel. "What are you doing?"

"What you told me."

"Oh, you nasty boy. I knew I'd catch you."

"Catch me what?"

"Making love to yourself."

"Me?"

"Shame on you."

"What in the hell's this guy talking about?"

"God almighty," said Doc. "That's supposed to be funny?"

"On the contrary," said Mel. "I think it's very sad."

"You're telling me?" said Doc. "What are you trying to do here? Get yourself carted away?"

"How do you like that?" said Mel. "There's gratitude for you."

"That's right," said Doc. "Go on. Keep curling that lip and I'll straighten it out for you."

"What's wrong?" said Mel. "Something's bothering you? You think I've been wasting your time? What time? Where time? What else have you got to do? You're about to become a father? You're busy on a big project? You're building a monkey bridge? You're waiting for someone to come along and stick a cherry in your mouth? You're on your way to heaven? Then take a little hell first. How else do you think you'll get there?"

"Catch me, Artie, boy. I think I'm going to faint."

"Wait a second," said Artie. "Then who's going to catch me?"

"Joe," said Mel. "Joe will do it. Won't you, Joe? You see? He's quiet. Oh, sure, he may dance in here and say he loves to look at us, but don't worry, I know what he's thinking. We're all falling apart. And how. Hey, Joe? He knows. He knows why. I'll bet you any amount of money he knows. Tell them, Joe. There's no hope for any of us any more, is there? We're all absolutely sunk, aren't we?"

So begin certain little moaners, disaffected sons of certain failing fraid-cats, to bust out inelegantly into half-baked speeches of despondency in the sprintime of their staccato discontent, sore as crabs, truly alarmed by the jittery hustling and rustling of the gloomy stut-

234

terers of their own generation. What is called a depression is indeed an eye opener. The pity of it. The poor body's own poor finger seems a fiction before this fact of trouble's new name. The cold-blooded economists have sprayed the earth with quick-drying ink in order to grow such a Himalayan carrot. Sadly enough, they too have begun to nibble and gnaw at it, but it satisfies neither their thirst nor their hunger. In the meantime, charity has attracted so many needy chumps that it has become awfully afraid for the fibers of its dollars and the sinews of its cents, so keeps back a crumb here and there for itself, and ducks down behind the counter to stuff its mouth as if with a cream puff. Its health is radiant. Its lips are running over. Yet each dear day is done before it dawns.

The screw is a common mechanical device consisting in its simplest form of a continuous helical rib or thread with the cylindrical shank from which it projects. The hope is that the screw driver shall get to read this definition. It has been so long since it has turned an actual screw, it is almost convinced that to gather dust while it rusts is what it was originally made for. The welterweights of the white-collar world are deeply perplexed by the dreadful slowdown. The tint of their worry is the shade of their typewriter tan. Theirs is a coffined flesh which contends with their carking souls in daily bouts of determined thumb-sucking. Fiercer playboys in their various dim cellars are recklessly leaning back in their rickety chairs, as if behind them prowled the jeering demon of their joblessness on which they are in a fever to flop and squash by coming down on it with the superior counterpoise of their desperation and the racking weight of their despair. All other games seem dull and dippy to them. Their blood ties are uncoiled. Their blood ties are trailing. Out of the house, cry fathers and mothers everywhere.

"Sunk," said Joe. "One spit in your eye, and you'd drown, wouldn't you?"

"Hey, now," said Mel. "Why look at me that way? How about these two mugs? They're in the same boat too, aren't they?"

"Sure," said Joe. "But you don't see them rocking it, do you?"

"They're scared stiff, that's why."

"And what's so goddamn brave about you?"

"At least I open my mouth. I talk."

"Well, yes," said Joe. "That you do. It takes a real man to do that,

235

doesn't it? By the way. How's that crabby mother of yours you claim you love so much? Does she still scramble an egg for you with her dirty little finger? She uses a spoon only to jab you with it, doesn't she? Oh, the pretty little bubbles you're going to make when you go down for the last time. You watched me watch her do it, didn't you? You laughed it off. You said it made it sweeter that way. What's this? You're not getting red in the face, are you? You see that? And you thought you had no more blood left, didn't you?"

"Okay," said Mel. "That's enough. If you're going to talk to me like that, I don't want to talk to you any more."

"Why not?" said Joe. "Let's fight. Let's rock that boat. Let's rock it and rock it until we turn it right over."

"I'm surprised at you," said Mel. "I really am. What are you trying to do? Make me look like a schmuck altogether?"

"But I'm pitying you," said Joe. "Isn't that what you want?"

"Yes?" said Mel. "And what are you two guys looking at? Never saw me before?"

"Don't be a nut," said Doc. "Can't you see I'm on your side?"

"Sure," said Artie. "Me too."

"And where do you think I stand?" said Joe. "You think I like to see you guys lay down and die?"

"Horrors," said Artie. "Is that what we're doing?"

"And how," said Joe. "Right in front of my eyes."

"Then I'm really sunk," said Artie. "I'm not dressed for it."

"There," said Joe. "That's the stuff. That's more like it. The hell with this crawling into a shell and shivering every time a wrong wind blows on us. Who's got so much time to waste? Goddamn it, we're the ones who are alive. We're the world now. The hell with anyone who tries to tell us we're dead before we've even begun to live. We'll do what billions of suckers did before us. We'll live out our lives. We'll keep spinning right along until we stop. We'll make it somehow. We'll lick it yet."

"We?" said Mel.

"I must say," said Doc. "That was a jolly little bit he just tossed off there, wasn't it?"

"I wonder," said Artie. "I stand all amazed."

"Come on, Joey boy," said Doc. "Don't be bashful. Give us another humdinger. We're just dying for it."

"I have a funny feeling," said Joe. "The weather's changing very fast. If I know what's good for me, I think I'm going to build me a house with this pack of cards and crawl into it. Anybody like to join me?"

"We," said Mel. "Who the hell is we? It's easy enough for you to talk. You still have a job. Remember?"

"Ah," said Joe. "So that's it, is it?"

"Wait," said Mel. "Wait until you get the old heave ho. You'll find out then. You won't be waltzing in here, if there'll still be a here, with the old song and dance. You think you're an exception? Just wait. It'll be hearts and flowers for you too."

"Here," said Joe. "Take the cards. Tell me the rest of my fortune."

"Hold it," said Artie. "In the name of the father and the rest of that jazz. This is really getting me down, you know that? Why don't you two bums call it a draw and be done with it? How about it, Doc? Let's you and me roll out of here and round us up a couple of fillies. Tuesday's a swell night for roping strays."

"Hold it yourself," said Doc. "Keep that pecker down. Aa, so what? So what if this man's still got a job? Do we have to hate him for it?"

"You got me wrong," said Mel. "I don't hate him."

"Think," said Doc. "Who are the ones around here who pay dues? And triple when they have to?"

"I know," said Mel. "Dear Sol. Dear Irving. And dear, dear Joe."

"Listen how sarcastic yet."

"What do you want me to do?" said Mel. "Get down on my knees or something? If I had the dough, I'd pay my dues too. What in the hell's so wonderful about that? I'm sick of this dump anyway."

"Then get the hell out of here," said Doc. "What are you hanging around for?"

"For someone else to tell me. Not you."

"Then someone else will," said Doc. "By god, I'll see to that personally. Call a meeting, Joe. You're the president. You heard him. Let's boot him out of here. Let's give him what he wants."

"Now, now," said Artie. "Easy does it. He doesn't mean what he says. He'd be lost without this place, you know that. Right, Mel?"

"Sure," said Mel. "That's just what galls me."

"You see?" said Artie. "He's just proud, that's all. He'll get over it."

"Galls him," said Doc. "What in the hell galls him about it?"

"Shake," said Mel.

"What?" said Doc. "What for?"

"I'm a fool."

"Stop right where you are."

"I don't know what I'm crabbing about," said Mel. "We're lucky we still have this place. At least we're safe here. Who sees us? Who can hear us? We can still come down here and blow off some steam if we want to. The hell with them all. We don't have to be sneaking around outside. We don't have to bother with those bastards who keep looking and looking at us. What do they think they'll see? The Messiah coming?"

"Coming?" said Artie. "He's already here. You're looking right at him. Me."

"I'm beginning to wonder," said Doc. "Who is this they? Somebody's always talking about they."

"They," said Artie. "They ain't we. And we ain't they. Get it?"

"Thanks," said Doc. "Now I can write a letter home about it."

"I see," said Joe. "So that's what you guys want. A hiding place. You want to stay here and rot then, is that it?"

"I'm sorry," said Mel. "You're right. Listening to me can make anybody want to cut his throat. A guy like me can ruin everything."

"Oh," said Joe. "You're okay yet. Don't worry about it. Wait until you hear about me. Talk about ruining everything. Didn't Eddie tell you? Or Dave?"

"Dear, dear," said Artie. "You didn't go and buy Brooklyn Bridge again, did you?"

"Oh, god," said Joe. "Don't tell me I have to go through this again? No. It's no use. I can't do it. All I can tell you now is, you guys better begin looking for another president."

"See that Mel?" said Doc. "See what you've done?"

"I'm sorry," said Joe. "But that's the way it has to be."

"Shit," said Artie. "Cut it out, will you? As long as this clubroom lasts, you're it. And there's nothing you can do about it either. Jesus. I'd like to see the day when you run out on us."

"Three blind mice," said Joe. "What can I do?"

"You're stuck," said Artie. "All you can do is talk about it."

"Right," said Doc. "And play a little poker for toothpicks on the side. Real big-time stuff. How's about it, Mr. President? Want me to cut you in? Who knows? Maybe you'll win this time."

238

"Win," said Joe. "I can't win around here. I see that now. You just go ahead and play. I'll watch. If I think of anything that'll do you any good, I'll let you know. I'll even try to figure out what comes next. I'm a president. I must have a brain somewhere."

Such a must amused them. They seemed perfectly willing to leave it to him to locate the precious thing, that is, if he were so sure he had one. He shifted his royal prerogative as to tenure from the shaky folding chair to the lumpy couch. He searched each chancy corner of the back room to no avail. Another boob welcoming the difficult. The boys drew closer to the table and cut the cards to see who would deal. They looked ready to take the plunge. What made his heart do a sudden flip-flop? What caused him to remember? The toilet door was open. The water in the bowl seemed to be hissing at him.

Three had already reamed her. Bang, bang, bang. That was how they went into her, unbearably primed as they were, to put it out of sight, to pump, to explode. He knew he had to be as quick, if not quicker. The fourth and last in that short line-up of a week ago come Wednesday, a victim of a youngish kind of pimp who strutted down the clubroom with a fifty-cent lay.

Call him Bub, and his bait, Babe. Bub is to Babe as Babe is to Bub. Keel over on her mouth, pop right into his, his tongue swelled, just as her dress swished, with unctuous and wicked hints. She knew how to weed her face where the light was weakest. She was stacked. She was immensely tight. She had more curves on her than a roller coaster. Babe loved to be close by when Bub raved about her. He was her darling slob. Her periods still came. But her masturbating days were over. She was so pigeon-proud when her eloquent Bub entered into closet talk with the customers, when his throat became thick with the thrill of it as he described her as a succulent dish, with her tits as titbits, and every bit of her seasoned hide praised as a yummy pasture. Bub's Babe, he did not have to beg her, she hitched up her dress to show them her drumsticks to make their eyes pop.

Little pricks, what were they waiting for? All he had to do was give her the wink, and she would take on the four of them for a dollar. What a break that Joe had a buck on him to lay it out for all four. His own excitement was instinctive as he slipped it into Bub's horny little hand. For the thing had gone so far already that it had to go further. When it was his turn to tack into the back room to sink his shaft where

239

the others had been so delighted to insert theirs, he did not have to grope around to find her, for the ceiling light was on, and he could easily see that she was sitting on her heels on this very same couch, and grinning, and the clear hair on her upper lip was the immediate ruin of his desire, and the crook of her nose the death of his imagination.

What should he do then? Ask her to tear out his eyes? He had seventeen cents left. She might oblige him. Or should he excuse himself, and rush out to buy himself a flag, and return to fling it over her face, and like a patriot in heat, ram it into her for old glory? Babe began to wonder why he was standing there. Then she thought she knew, and with a smile that shamed him, beckoned to him, and made him sit down beside her, and placed her paw on his fly where she expected to find that his, but ye gods, what had happened to it? She kept fumbling for the business where she was sure it ought to be, suspecting black magic. She who was no slouch with swollen masses, who had such a clean hand with that cute article in a man which can swell and extend itself, refused to believe that a crafty angler such as she could have caught her hooks into nothing but cloth. Where could it have possibly slunk off to? Was it because his legs were crossed? Or had he suffered a supreme fit of folly and insanely amputated that sinful instrument of his?

Her consternation was so comic, he felt sorry for her. If only he could bring himself to kiss her and leave his humiliation on her lips. His hand shook as he offered her a smoke, trying to explain that what she thought was missing was really there, honest to god, he actually did have one, but for some miserable reason, it insisted on sitting this one out. Must have been doing what with it? Oh, no, not lately, this was the first time it had ever failed him. Failed him. She took a terrific drag. The smoke gushed out of her nostrils. So then, she must be the reason why. No, no. That was precisely what mystified and scared him, that it should remain so limp when there she was so ripe for the plucking, such a lush, such a top-notch, such a scrumptious piece. How could his thing have become so useless? Maybe she could tell him.

She said, put out the light. He said, what? She said, the light, the light. She gave him such a fierce look. He blushed as he obeyed her. He was positive it would make no difference. But why, as soon as it was dark, did she begin to whisper? What was she asking him to do? She

240

guided his head. She guided his hands. She called him cuckoo names. He could hear her. His mouth slid where? Her tongue flicked. Her fingers said, what a find. A revolving kiss is a kiss where, there now, there, and with a triumphant yelp, she turned turtle on the pillows, and she put it on for him, and she put it in for him, and goo, it was moist there where the others, it was so awfully warm there, and though she used her scissors on him and moaned, good, good, good, as soon as he had discharged the venom of his disgust and despair, she began to push him off. She knew he had never closed his eyes. She hated him.

Peace to her wilted bangs, her overpraised fat and humorless spittle, that old fustian hullabaloo about the raptures of lechery, how it endlessly elates no matter where or when or with what superb hunk of stupidity it so zestfully goes the limit, once and for all, there must be an end of twitching and cringing with senseless joy before it, of crawling up to it like a crab. Bombast as she booms in every back-scratching mind. He caught a glimpse of himself as he squatted there, so miserably stalled again. He looked for some way he could snap out of it. The toilet door was still open. He jumped up and slammed it shut.

Sol the straggler, the bushy-haired, the unaccounted-for, he moseyed in as if he had just lighted from a nag he had never ridden to a place he had never reached, and like a rumpled lay figure, had arrived at a room to which he had never dreamed of coming so soon, looking so woefully lost and ruined that it raised that kind of a goofy laugh which often greets the blood as soon as it gushes from a wound, or a leg the moment it is broken.

"He's dead," said Artie.

"Gosh," said Doc. "It sure does look like it, doesn't it?"

"Heavens above," said Artie. "When did it happen?"

"Last summer," said Mel.

"You knew?" said Artie. "And you didn't tell us?"

"I'm sorry," said Mel. "I meant to, but I forgot. Ah, I can remember it as if it was only yesterday. Double windows wide open. Moon on a visit. Delicious breeze. Bird on the fire escape with a bandaged leg. Complaining. Bandy legs here, Sol that once was, stretched out on the floor in the bottom half of his pajamas, polishing his sunglasses. And no umbrella in the house. Mother of god, I had just washed down my last bite of lobster when."

241

"What the hell," said Doc. "Who asked him to crawl in here?"

"When all of a sudden," said Mel. "I noticed a strange shape coming out of his ear. I bent down to measure it when, sit down, friend, I'm talking about you, when all of a sudden."

"Goddamn it," said Doc. "Where's that fly swatter? I'll take care of this big mouth."

"When all of a sudden."

"He and his cockeyed stories. Who the hell wants to listen to them?"

"When all of a sudden," said Mel. "I heard a knocking on the door. Door? What door? Never lived in a house with a door before. Whack. As soon as I thought of that, the tomahawk flew right where I part my hair. And stuck there. Say, that reminds me. Did I ever tell you guys about the time I got trapped in a turnstile? Real funny business. Make you pee in your pants. Rush hour. Late for the job I wasn't going to get. Cute little trick ahead of me. Drooled after her down the stairs. Fell in love with the back of her neck, if you know what I mean. Had my slug and all ready, when all of a sudden."

"You and your slugs," said Doc. "No wonder you got yourself caught there."

"What an ass. The shame of it all. I understand cough medicines are good for a cough. And when you're poor, you're pretty near being a pauper. Now there's no use your telling me I'm overdoing it. What am I overdoing? Jesus, if you ever find out how much is enough, for god's sake, don't hesitate to tell me. I'll be waiting right here with all the love I've been saving up. Built like a bull all the way through. Ever steal a bulb from a station, bub?"

"Built like a what?" said Doc. "What was that again?"

"The deaf and the dumb," said Mel. "It's their world."

"Shit," said Doc. "Why don't I murder him right now? What in hell am I waiting for?"

"Nine o'clock," said Artie. "And all's well."

"Sol," said Joe. "You look like hell. You don't mind my saying so, do you?"

"Wake up," said Artie. "The man's talking to you."

"You hear me?" said Joe. "We don't like it."

"In other words," said Artie. "It displeases us immensely."

"Absolutely," said Doc. "Come on, Solly boy, do us a favor and spill what's bothering you."

"Right," said Mel. "Uncork. We gave you enough time, didn't we?"

"Ah," said Sol. "You guys. We've sure had some swell times here together, haven't we?"

"Why, sure," said Joe. "If that's how you remember it."

"And goddamn it," said Sol. "We're still going to have them. Yes, sir. We don't need anybody else breaking up things here, do we? Who the hell do we need?"

"I don't know," said Joe. "You tell me."

"Nobody," said Sol. "That's who. I ask you. Did you ever see such a dope? Where the hell's my head? Where've I been all my life? A potsy player I've become. I swear, if I had two pair of shoes, I'd still walk around barefoot. That's how smart I am. Sock me, Joe, right here. Go ahead. Maybe you'll dirty your hand a little bit, but it'll do me good."

"Okay," said Joe. "Since you can't hate yourself without me. Hold still now."

"I'm holding."

"Wait a second," said Artie. "You didn't get yourself canned, did you?"

"Canned?" said Sol. "No, I'm still working. Don't worry about that."

"Then it's the clap," said Doc. "Be damned if the guy didn't go out and get himself a dose."

"Me?" said Sol. "How? Ever since I've been going out with her, I've laid off. I'm absolutely clean."

"Ah," said Mel. "I smell a rat. Want me to tell you her name?"

"No, thanks," said Sol. "I'm not hungry."

"No, no," said Joe. "Let me explain it to you. This is a cigarette. You don't eat it. You smoke it."

"Oh," said Sol. "I'm sorry."

"Dolores," said Mel. "Ah, there's a dear little fluffy thing for you. Did I spot her for you or didn't I? Sweet as a sugar factory. Blow me down if I didn't dance with her once. As Artie would say, what possessed me? Found she had a distinct bounce to her glide. Very peppery pusher. A real leader. Uh-huh, said I. Oh, those big Spanish eyes. They said, come to me, daddy, so you came. Delicious. I warned you about that dame, didn't I?"

"Look at him," said Doc. "He's rubbing his hands so hard they're going to fall off."

"New way of building a fire?" said Artie. "Clever chap, ain't he?"

"Christ," said Mel. "Can't you see? The poor guy looks like a team of horses trampled on him. Squashed he is. She's through with him. When a guy looks like that, it's all over. Hey, there. You big lummox you. Why do you sit there so quiet? Why don't you get angry? Get up and do something, why don't you? Bite my ear off. Pull Doc's teeth out. Smash the furniture. Use Artie here for a club. He won't mind."

"Well," said Joe. "That's one way."

"Too good for him, was she? That makes me mad. That really does."

"Her mother liked me," said Sol.

"I'm sure she did," said Joe.

"Always had a nice hello for me. Mrs. Spiegel. More eyes talking to you. I said to her once, why do you look so scared all the time? You know me. I don't know any jokes. Look, I said to her, I'm real strong. Any time you want me to beat up someone for you, just let me know. She laughed. Know what she once told me? She told me that some day, if she lived long enough, she would hang herself on the hatrack in the hall. There's an umbrella stand there too. And a big picture of lions eating people. They live kind of funny in that house. You should see."

"I'll take your word for it."

"You can't ask too many questions, can you? Still. That old man now. I always wanted to know. Why does he lug around that hot-water bottle with him all the time? He must be suffering from something real bad. But what? He never says. He keeps smiling all over the place. No one's ever going to find out anything from him if he can help it. Jesus. Where's that draft coming from? Don't you guys feel it?"

"Take a look at the window, Artie."

"Poor me," said Sol. "Damn near froze to death that night. The sea. The great big beautiful sea. I'm telling you, Joe, you have no idea what sticks in that girl. All of a sudden, like I'm sitting here with you, she gets a bug in her head she wants to go to Coney Island. Ten o'clock at night."

"The hell with it," said Artie. "It won't budge."

"So there I was," said Sol. "Stuck again. What could I do? I was afraid of her. Why was I always so afraid of her? Why? What could she do to me? I had to say to her, for crying out loud, I said to her, have a little consideration. You know I have to get up and go to work tomorrow. You do? she said. Why? Why does anybody have to do anything? What? I said. You're not asking me, are you? According to you, I said, I'm just a plain ordinary Brooklyn boy. I'm not supposed to know anything. All I'm supposed to do, I said, is run when you whistle. So what do you think happened? She whistled and I ran. Sounds great, doesn't it?"

"Absolutely," said Joe. "At least."

"Crazy," said Sol. "Right in the middle of March. If there's anything I hate, it's that kind of a wind. Keeps ripping and tearing away at you. But she, she lapped it up. Up the boardwalk, down the boardwalk, long about 28th Street, I finally got her to sit down. She was mad at the world. Didn't know where to kick it first. Fine then, I says, if you like, you can begin with me. She doesn't answer. You're shivering, I says, let me take you around and warm you up. She pushes me away. Go down and see where the sea gulls are sleeping, she says. Go on now, she says, make yourself really useful. And while you're at it, she says, talk to the waves. Ask them what they mean by making such a terrible noise only when it's dark. Whew. Did you ever hear anything like that? That's the way her brain works. It hops around like a bird."

"Some bird," said Joe. "Carry salt with you the next time."

"What next time? What in hell makes it so hot in here? Do you know she has a crooked pinky? Reached out once for a basketball with all her fingers stuck out. Wham. She knew better after that. Come back here, I yelled at her. But she kept on running down the beach to the water. Ah, I don't care what you say, Joe, there's something about her I'll always like. How do such things come into her head? I'm going to dip my finger in the ocean, she yells back at me, and if it comes out straight, then you're lucky for me, otherwise, swoosh, she's off before I can stop her. Sol and Dolores. I should've known. Such names never go together. I come to her house tonight, and where do you think she is? In bed. In bed? I say. What's she doing in bed? She's not sick, is she? Sick. How could her mother tell me she's sick when we could both hear her singing away like mad. I told every little star. Night and day. Say, I said, what's going on here? Can I go in there? Can I see her? No, no, says the old lady, you better not, let me go, I'll talk to her. I was so embarrassed. I could hear every word. Ma, what happened to my cuticle scissors? Who? I could hear her say. Sure, she says, I know he's here. I know that faithful old soul. Tell him. You tell him. Tell him

245

what I'm going to do. Tell him I'm going to Hawaii to be a nurse. Tell him I don't care if he doesn't believe me. Tell him I'll send him a pineapple to prove it. Tell him to go away, she screams, or I'll stab myself right in front of you, you hear me? Poor Mrs. Spiegel. She comes out with tears in her eyes. I swear, I was more sorry for her than I was for myself. That's all right, I said to her, I understand. Don't you worry about me. I understand. You be good, I said to her, take care of yourself. I wish we had a map here. Hawaii. That's pretty far away from here, isn't it?

"Pretty far away from here?" said Mel. "Did you hear that, Joe? Is this what he calls the end?"

"Holy mackerel," said Doc. "He really believes her, doesn't he?"

"Is this our Sol?" said Mel. "It can't be. We ought to check his dog tag."

"I'm sweating," said Doc. "Look at me."

"Sweating?" said Mel. "I'm ready to spit blood. Oh, well. Let's see now. I have a pair of queens open. Doc a big ace. And Artie here shows."

"The soiled fringe of my drawers," said Artie. "Talk about stinking cards. I'm out. Say. Did I ever tell you guys about the kid I once knew who could do the hula-hula? Including all that business with the hands. No kidding. Smart for her age. Made herself up a kind of grass skirt to wiggle around in. Had to put a mirror on the floor to see herself doing it. I peeked. I admit it. I lay on my belly on the bed and watched her with the shade up across the alleyway in all her pretty motions. Oh, my, yes. There she was practicing day and night. Pow. And what do you think finally came of it? All of a sudden she was a mother at fourteen. Shows what real concentration can do, doesn't it?"

"Nobody is laughing," said Joe. "I wonder why."

"It came out half-blue and half-green. What a production."

"No more," said Mel. "No more going steady around here. Once and for all we've got to put a stop to it."

"Really?" said Joe. "And how the hell are you going to manage that?"

"By throwing the next guy who does the hell out of here, that's how."

"In that case," said Doc. "So long, fellers, it was nice knowing you."

246

"What?" said Mel. "Who are you going steady with?"

"With you, darling, didn't you know?"

"Aw," said Mel. "Get away. You disgust me."

"Turn around then," said Artie. "Here comes somebody who never does. But never."

"I heard a noise," said Irving. "And I came in to investigate. There's always a fire burning somewhere that needs to be put out."

"Piss on it," said Mel. "Another comedian. The place is becoming lousy with them."

"As is natural," said Irving. "We were all born to scratch. Or come up to it. Or whatever else is the going phrase."

"Look," said Mel. "You're glad you're alive? You want to live yet? Then sit down before I knock you down."

"Children," said Joe. "Children."

"I brought that Debussy record," said Irving.

"Good," said Joe. "Let's go out there and play it."

"Sounds very manly," said Irving. "But suppose he did knock me down, what exactly would that prove?"

"That it hurts when you get hit. Let's go, let's go."

"Now his trouble is," said Irving. "If I may be allowed to say so. He feels superior because he believes he is suffering more than anybody else. A very common fault, I understand. The jungle and the libraries are full of such cases."

"That's my boy for you," said Joe. "Ain't he dumb?"

"Incredible," said Doc. "And the way he twists his mouth when he smiles. We ought to snap a picture of it for the record."

"And frame it," said Artie. "And bust it over his head. Take him out of here, Joe. Did you ever see such a streak of rotten cards? We'll sit here and hold hands with Sol. We're the common people. We like to be miserable because it makes us happy."

"God knows," said Irving. "I try and I try. But they choose not to understand."

"Free country," said Joe. "Watch this, men. Did you ever see how they carry out the wounded?"

Off again and staggering, how refreshing for Joe, after such an eternity of unselfish listening, to find he has a moment all to himself to squander as he may see fit, bowed down as he might be under his load, and careful as he is not to trip. What exhilarates him? Here is a mystery. After all he is also a common shuffler. He contributes his daily mess of waste products as solid as any. He licks the same bent spoon and breaks the same dry bread. He swallows whole colonies of germs of hopelessness. Yet what seems to shrink so many as they wail seems to fatten and fill him out defiantly. What is going on in him? Is it all due to the secret and inexplicable enlargement of the heart? For the more room he makes for the concerns and anxieties of others, the more does he elbow out his own selfish hell-raising self. Yet he feels less subdued than ever. He begins to sing. He stamps a few steps in a circle. He tosses Irving on the nearest couch and commands him to talk and explain himself. He is like a civilized man whose curiosity is so exacting and bold that, no sooner does he exhaust the terrors of one human snarl, he must immediately explore the freakish coagulations of another. No gun on his hip, no spear in his hand, no witch-doctor lore in his noggin, yet he is armed with a marvelous weapon. He throws back his head and laughs the human laugh while birds twitter and lions roar.

While elegant sceptics such as Irving bend an ear to it enviously, discovering in themselves a sudden distaste for shattery gumshoe sounds, for the chill hiss of irony, the brittle oscillations of sarcasm, and the mincing pitapat of charm. Only-son Irving with his fresh white starched collar yearning for the warmth of the slightly stale and soiled. What is this craze which rages in him to be other than what he is? Joe plumped himself down beside the agreeable richness of Irving's thick tweed suit. Of course Irving knows he must stumble around like a clown at the squeaky age of nineteen, yet what he also wants to know is this, if his isness is inseparable from the piano, he is toying with keys which lead to what? To kingdom come, was Joe's playful answer, to a wife who beats time with a salad spoon on a frying pan, to note-blind sons and tone-deaf daughters, to a whole slew of gut-busting grandchildren.

Perhaps it was crude of Joe to mock at him and dismiss him with the mildest sort of sympathy, but Irving had precious oils in his medicine chest with which he could soothe his luckier skin, had folding money enough to prosper the puny and pinched romanticism of his dilemma. Irving had a sweet racket. It had begun to seem too sweet to him in a world turned sour. Irving studied music at Juilliard, nobly pursuing the intricate art of it in all its exquisite assertions, lush designs, and soul-searching conflicts and aspirations. Irving made Joe feel, as Joe frankly confessed, like a choleric ignoramus who believes he is infusing his fellow men with fresh hope and insight when he stings them on the run with a shrewd curse or two. But the profane have a knowledge which is as real as spit, and may have a tremendous attraction for those who sleep on snow-white pillows, and dream of the pink life principle and not of bloody life itself.

Why then had Irving begged Joe three months ago to persuade the others to take him in as a full-fledged, paying member? The roughnecks said yes with the greatest reluctance, sensing the obvious. They refused to consider him other than a poor slob who pretended to sneer as he watched, secretly appalled at the sexlessness of his studies, asking himself, where in music is the tangibility of tits? Corrupt as they may be, they became righteous for his sake, and shrank from the evil possibility of seeing him sacrifice the culture he had so painfully acquired for the possession, no matter how brief, of any ordinary little cunt. He could come and go as he pleased. Their minds were made up. They were going to keep him as he was even if it killed him.

The elm is a stately tree. Migrating ducks form V formations. Flounders in the sea are usually wet. Oblivious mice beneath the flooring sit up to sing. What is the natural size of the chrysalis of a swallowtail butterfly? What arrow of fame is that which flies with the wind? Irving has eyes. They have begun to narrow. His mind too is made up. It is coiled like a rattler ready to strike. It suspects that it may be squashed the second after it does, but it refuses to remain limp and merely gawk at what it sees, and struggle to talk to it, and be dazed forever by the fixed tone of a tuning fork.

"Now then," said Joe. "Before you begin to practice your scales on me. I would like to tell you this. And it's only because I love you. No one here, but no one, gives a good goddamn about you. You know that, don't you? We just care about the dues you pay. And that's about it."

"So much for that," said Irving. "Do at least tell me one more thing. What's behind that smile of yours you flash at me every now and then?"

"Tears, lad. Oceans of them."

"Aie," said Irving. "And you call me a mystery. It's a pity you haven't got much of a tongue."

249

"Well," said Joe. "It takes all kinds. What in the hell do you think I'd be able to tell you if I had a tongue, as you say?"

"You look like a changed man tonight. Why?"

"Y," said Joe. "Y is a crooked letter."

"You look," said Irving. "You look like a man who's just had a short haircut. And that, as you know, is cleverly designed to make him look like he's been through hell. By him, of course, I mean you. How about that place? I've been so busy climbing ladders, I've lost all track of what's below me. This hell of yours, I mean. Have you been there recently? How often do you go there?"

"You're not afraid to know?"

"In my twentieth year? How silly."

"Well, then," said Joe. "It used to be only in the rainy season."

"And now?"

"Every day rain or shine. And twice on Sundays."

"How dreadful," said Irving. "And so very charming at the same time. You belong here even less than I do."

"I think," said Joe. "I think it's time you played that record."

"Hold it," said Irving. "Intermission. Here come your friends."

"What?" said Joe. "What friends?"

"Your very closest."

"Eddie and Dave?"

"With three of the choicest on the market, I'm sure."

"Three?" said Joe. "Why three? Oh, no. It can't be."

"That's when you usually find that it can."

"How do you like that?" said Joe. "Of all the nights to come. What in the hell am I going to do with her?"

"That's a ridiculous question."

"Quick," said Joe. "Lean over a little bit. More. That's it. I'll figure out something. Make believe I'm a pillow. Tell them I died suddenly in the night. Tell them I'm waiting to be embalmed."

"Right," said Irving. "To hear is to obey."

"Is that him?" said Eddie. "What kind of a game is this?"

"Come out from behind that post," said Dave. "We see you."

"That's no post," said Belle.

"Why, thank you," said Irving. "You have very kind eyes."

"Ah, yes," said Belle. "Now I remember you. You're the young man who plays the bugle, aren't you?"

250

"Only when I blow my nose."

"Ha," said Belle. "Cute, isn't he?"

"It's amazing," said Irving. "How easy it is to be a social success."

"Our lesson for today," said Dave. "Look, my friend, I don't mean to hurt your feelings. But do you mind getting your carcass out of the way?"

"Sorry," said Irving. "It's not part of my daily dozen."

"Then make it so. Or would you like some assistance?"

"He contemplates using force."

"Up, I said."

"He is fast losing his patience."

"What's the matter with the kid? Does he want his head broken?"

"I regret," said Irving. "I have only one head to give to my country."

"Sit right where you are," said Joe.

"Ah," said Honey. "Peekaboo. Remember me?"

"What a question," said Joe. "I devote all my nights to it."

"My favorite joke," said Honey. "And otherwise? How do you find yourself?"

"With a pick and shovel. Whatever is handy."

"Dave," said Belle. "Your friend is a bum."

"Quiet," said Dave. "Who asked you for your opinion?"

"That's right," said Belle. "Show how smart you are. Take it out on me."

"Darling," said Dave. "Let us retire to my favorite corner. I would so like to have a nice heart-to-heart talk with you."

"I may be wrong," said Irving. "But I have a feeling those two have met before."

"Oh, yes," said Joe. "And with very interesting results."

"Surprise," said Eddie. "Look what we brought you."

"Why, hello," said Joe. "Where did you come from?"

"What a lovely place you have here," said Lee. "I was just looking around."

"The girl with the flaxen hair," said Joe. "My, what big eyes you have, Irving. This is my friend Irving. He's one of your oldest admirers."

"He is?" said Lee. "That's funny. He doesn't look familiar at all."

"Oh, but he recognized you immediately."

"He did?" said Lee. "Why? What did you tell him?"

251

"Everything," said Joe. "Here. Let me have your coat. Irving?"

"Yes, master?"

"Hang this garment up for the lady."

"The husk for me," said Irving. "And the kernel for you. Ah, well. What the hell. Someday with God's help. In the meantime, I guess I should try to make myself useful."

"He's making like someone," said Lee. "Now who is he making like?"

"Hey," said Joe.

"Hay is for horses."

"What's happened to you, sweetheart? You're sure you're not standing in a hole? You look shorter tonight."

"So would you," said Honey. "That is, if you lost your head."

"Oh, you," said Lee. "You shut up."

"But I mean," said Honey. "Completely. Over a man who happens to be you."

"Oo," said Lee. "What I'll do to you when I get you alone."

"What a shame," said Joe. "We'll just have to find it and give it back to her immediately."

"Absolutely," said Honey. "Let's do that. There are enough fools in this world as it is."

"Notice," said Eddie. "She looks right at me when she says that."

"Very bitter," said Joe. "I must say. Birds in their little nests never agree."

"Still," said Eddie. "We must carry on somehow, mustn't we?"

"Eddie," said Joe. "I like your spirit. Shake. Into the valley of death rode. You will always be my idea of a hero. I'll be in touch. Until then. You take your problem away with you. And I'll take mine. This way, my dear. We haven't very far to go."

To as prim a conference as he could arrange, choosing for its site a stuffed chair the middle-aged spread of which he invited Lee to fill as amply as she could while he cautiously settled one tenth of his weight on one of its dislocated arms. Their first words politely kissed in the air in front of them. It enchanted him. It chilled her. She twisted this way and that in an effort to face him, but her neck failed her, so she crossed her legs, and showed him how much room there was for him to squeeze in beside her. He obliged and slid down to become as one with her. The first thing she told him was how much she had to tell him.

She did not know how or where to begin. She had to laugh because her head was buzzing so. Said her lips, that looks to me like a tiger sniffing at a naked lady in that picture. Said her eyes, be kind to me.

He took her hand in both of his. She had been thinking. Ever since their blind date last Saturday when he had made her so mad at him for asking her to do you know what. She had been thinking and thinking. Girls are not like boys, are they? Girls can hold less in their smaller hands, and cover less ground with their shorter legs, and can be alone less because, because their systems are different, inside and out, by the skeleton that does not show, and the skin that does. Their larger tears, their longer lashes, their thicker hair on their heads, and elsewhere their absolute hairlessness, their swellings in front, their hillocks behind, girls are sunk, they must be girls, it sticks out all over them. Even when it comes to smoking, thank you ever so much, look how they mishandle it, staining it with lipstick, sucking at it much too much, taking more of it in their mouths than they should.

Woman the redundant rib, the wicked piece of man, trained to say, yes, yes, she has but one thing to give, there are so many names for it, but mercy, she cries, even when she gives in and gives it in her wildest dreams. Look at her in her foolish awakenings, clawed her own self she has, drawn her own blood, seeing herself again, before it all fades away, sinking in his clutch in the sea, rolling with him in the dust, wiggling together amid random bones and countless immovable rocks. Masks. Would wearing masks while doing it do it? Then a girl would never know who the boy was, and not knowing, would never care, would she? And when that is settled and over with, any combination of boy and girl would meet, just like any two people, and at last be friends with their own frank and open faces. Ah, he did not have to tell her. She was awful. She knew. She ought to be boiled in oil for barging in on him to tell him what he already knew. It was the old sob story in one sentence. As different as she is, the heart of a girl is on the left side too.

"Oh," said Joe. "Absolutely. And her two eyes are on each side of her nose. And she has the same number of teeth in her mouth. And to top it all, I understand that everything she eats goes right to her stomach. What did you say your name was?"

"You must think I'm terrible."

"For talking to me this way? Don't be silly."

253

"I'm sorry," said Lee. "I was wrong. I shouldn't have bothered you. I don't know what got into me."

"Forget it," said Joe. "You don't have to apologize to me. Who do you think I am anyway? A god over you?"

"I knew I would make you angry."

"Angry?" said Joe. "What angry? The only thing that gets me is. Why me of all people? You've seen other guys. What in the hell do you think you see in me that makes you think I can change your life all of a sudden?"

"Well," said Lee. "At least you listen."

"Listen?" said Joe. "My god. Is that all?"

"You understand."

"This is incredible," said Joe. "You're getting to be real cute, aren't you? I bet you'd love it if I began to smack you around. It's a good thing no one is listening to us. Did you ever see the way she's been trying to break me down? Oops. I thought so. There go those brimming eyes. That's all I need yet. Now what does this guy want?"

"Excuse me," said Dave. "I hate to break up this huddle, but I'd like to talk to you a second. Alone. Do you mind?"

"Not at all," said Joe. "As a matter of fact, I've got something I'd like to say to you too."

"Wait," said Lee. "Can't you talk to him here? I won't listen."

"Did you ever see?" said Joe. "She's afraid I'll run away. Don't worry, Lee, I'll be back. Even if I'm headed for the boobyhatch, the door is in your direction."

"Come on," said Dave. "Right this way. It'll only take a second."

"Goddamn you," said Joe. "What in the hell was the idea of bringing her down here without asking me? You think that's all I have to do?"

"I'm sorry," said Dave. "I didn't know you were so busy."

"You rat. It's a good thing you're not smiling."

"What's the beef? A piece is a piece. I thought I was doing you a favor."

"You thought," said Joe. "Since when did you become such a thinker?"

"I don't know what you're pissing and moaning about," said Dave. "She looks mighty eager to me."

"That's the trouble," said Joe. "She's too eager. She wants to build

254

her nest here. To establish herself, but good. The next thing you know, she'll be sending me out to rassle up some groceries."

"What the hell," said Dave. "Kid her along. You can get funny with her after it's all over."

"Oh, sure," said Joe. "That's all I need to have on my head now."

"Shit," said Dave. "You think you have troubles? How about me? How do you like what that baby Belle of mine has gone and done now?"

"I could hardly be less interested."

"She's gone and missed her period."

"Beautiful," said Joe. "How did that happen?"

"She forgot to clean her navel. Don't be so goddamn dumb."

"I mean," said Joe. "What slipped up? Is she sure? How long is it?"

"Four days."

"Four days?" said Joe. "That isn't so unusual. A lot of kids are delayed that way sometimes. Unless. Unless she's trying to."

"Hook me?" said Dave. "Don't be silly. To tell you the truth, she doesn't think I'm such a bargain. Anyway. I can always crawl out of it if I want to. Imagine. A schmuck like me a Papa. In the meantime we sure do love each other. Yes, sir."

"I can imagine."

"I just thought I'd tell you. Talking to you always makes me feel better."

"Thanks a lot. And what do you think it does for me?"

"Cheer up," said Dave. "You too can be a father."

"That's what I'm afraid of."

"Pitch to her," said Dave. "She'll catch. You have to take a chance. How else are you ever going to get your nookie?"

"Oh, god," said Joe. "The same goddamn thing over and over again. What kind of a guy are you? Aren't you sick of it yet? Don't you ever think of anything else?"

"Sick of what?" said Dave. "You know something? You're beginning to worry me. Where's that old stud I used to know?"

"I buried him," said Joe. "Like a dog buries a bone. I'll be seeing you. Let me know how you make out."

"Sure," said Dave. "You'll be around. I'll tell you."

"Be around where?" said Joe. "How do you know? Maybe I'll surprise you. What makes you so damn sure you'll always find me here?"

255

"And to think," said Dave. "I used to like you."

"Now that," said Joe. "That's exactly what that broad is going to say to me. You watch. I'll bet you two to one."

"Easy, boy. You're not going to disgrace me, are you?"

"What the hell have you got to do with it?"

"You're still my friend, aren't you? You think I like to see you make a shit-ass of yourself?"

"Well," said Joe. "What can you do? To each his own. You just go and take care of yours. And I'll go and take care of mine. And some day, when it's nice and sunny, I'll come around and wheel that baby carriage for you. If we live that long. We'll both be wiser then. I hope."

Springs eternal, washed in the blood of the lamb, more sure-footed and holier than he, lecherous goats also butt their way into the buttocks of the future. Snafued rebel, he may frown at the fading color of the clubroom walls, and sigh over the sad state of the ceiling. He may murmur against what is scaly or streaked in a rumbling broken manner, but like a member of a stiff-necked people, he must come down hard, as if expressing an inherited tic, on the side of the salacious myth of sin. It seems so clearly a stupid business to be creeping back to that passerine bird with the cruel intention of offering her a poor doubtful erection. When the last button is hastily buttoned, the fingers fly to unbutton the first. Yet spring can be such a slow time. Gooseboy of all the silly cacklers who go astray, thou shalt not uncover the nakeness of a woman. That is wickedness. Thou shalt not uncover the nakedness of mankind. For that is your own nakedness. Sit you down. Say something simple. Thou shalt not unstop the fountain of her blood in the time of the first ripe grapes. There is no time to lose. This is a very poor light by which, by which to think, a very poor light indeed.

"Damn nice of you to wait up for me," said Joe. "You're sure you have nothing better to do?"

"What did he tell you?" said Lee. "Was it anything about me?"

"It's amazing what people worry about."

"Because if he did, don't you dare believe him."

"Look," said Joe. "I don't mean to crowd you, but it seems to me I had a little bit more room before. If I'm sitting, I might as well sit."

"You're still angry."

"Right," said Joe. "And what's more, I'm going to stay angry for a long long time. Let me see. Did he say anything about you? Why, yes.

As a matter of fact, he gave me some very good advice about you which I will now make up. He said I should drown you."

"Drown me?"

"You know the lake in Prospect Park? There's a lovely spot for you. Now here's what we do. It's all been done before, so it should be easy. We row out. I bat you over the head with the oar when only the ducks are looking. I tie that anchor around your neck. And ploop. Your last words are bubbles. How does that appeal to you? If it's too cold for you yet, I'll be glad to wait until it gets warmer. When does the frost come on the pumpkin? Do you still bite when you kiss?"

"You must be crazy."

"At last," said Joe. "She's beginning to understand me."

"I must say," said Lee. "I'm really disappointed in you."

"Good," said Joe. "I don't even want to know why."

"Really," said Lee. "You're not as smart as I thought you were. You can't fool me. No, sir. I can see right through you. You want me to think you're tough. But actually you wouldn't hurt a fly. You're really a sweet boy. And that's that. And don't try to tell me any different."

"Excuse me. Hey, Eddie. You mind turning that radio down a little bit? I can't hear a goddamn thing around here."

"Tell me," said Lee. "You have this place long?"

"Me?" said Joe. "A sweet boy?"

"I bet you can almost live here, can't you?"

"That's the limit, that is. That I should live to hear that. How about it, Lee? Let's cut out all this fooling around and get down to business."

"Okay," said Lee. "I'm willing."

"No, no," said Joe. "I don't mean that."

"Guess what I'm chewing. Want some?"

"Up on your feet," said Joe. "No, no, not you. I mean me. Honest, Lee, you're a good kid, and all that. And I wish you all the luck in the world. And I hope you'll be happy some day. You know what I'm talking about, don't you?"

"What did I do?" said Lee. "Did I come at the wrong time?"

"No, no," said Joe. "You just made a mistake about me, that's all. Say, did you ever meet my friend Artie? You're missing something there. You would really love him. Or maybe Doc. Maybe he would be the one for you. Now don't go away. You sit here and I'll bring them out for you one by one. And you can take your pick. How would that be?"

"All right," said Lee. "Why not? I didn't come for that, but since I'm already here, I might as well have some fun. One damn fool is as good as another. I'm beginning to see that."

"What's your phone number? Just in case."

"Sorry," said Lee. "No phone. They took it out. You'll have to come and get me if you want me."

"Maybe I'll do that some day. Who knows?"

"Oh," said Lee. "Don't rush. I have plenty of time."

"You'll love Doc. You'll see."

"Fine," said Lee. "I'm sure of it. If you're going, go ahead. You're beginning to irk me."

"I'm sorry," said Joe. "I did the best I could."

"But it wasn't good enough, was it?"

"Yes," said Joe. "As usual. Isn't this a queer thing? I know we're saying goodbye forever. Yet for a while we'll still be in the same room. All I'm going to do now is just walk across it, and it'll be like there's a tremendous ocean between us, or a great big plain or forest. Don't shout. I can't afford to hear you. And yet I'll be able to see you and you'll be able to see me. Think of such things. There are still a lot of funny games left to play."

Still chipper is he? Still fit and in fine whack? As of this most earnest now, what are these hilarious games yet to be played? After a near collision with Honey and Eddie as clinging dancers, it seems to him these ploys would be merely those of coming and going, as innocent as that, of arriving as if all is well in heaven, and departing as if all is hell on earth. The human will is like a harnessed wind. It has polarized its movements until to whistle in or to blow out, to stay or not to stay, to touch or not to touch, all trivial things in a social way, have become monstrously inflated dilemmas not worth the sad amount of spit it takes to moisten them, whether with compassion or contempt.

Not so long ago the theft of a rusty pear sent a man into a bottomless pit, and a greasy bit of string as big as his thumb slipped into his pocket was enough to hang that man, one more horrible punishment for a humpty-dumpty crime. But the enlightened days are upon us now, when such venial offences receive no more than a frown, or a slap on the wrist, or a single cuss word. But if we soothe, if not smother each other with kindlier laws, the knife still gleams, and the fist is still raised. And who is it we mercilessly butcher, for we still love to shed blood, for one step too long, or one wink too many? Why, each other massed all together as ourselves, pierced fatally by our own exclamation point. What rubber daggers and ridiculous peccadilloes. What reeling stars of this rejected night. He does sometimes amuse and amaze himself. He blinks as if he has read the answer by the moon's borrowed light.

"I don't know whether you can hear me yet," said Irving. "But have you any idea how you look?"

"Jesus," said Joe. "It sure does hurt, doesn't it?"

"What does?"

"To think."

"To think?" said Irving. "Was that what you were trying to do?"

"I don't know," said Joe. "I can't tell."

"Gosh," said Irving. "And I was about to tell you I never saw you look so stupid."

"I tell you. That sort of stuff'll kill me if I don't watch out. I don't know why I even try it."

"How about me going for some cold water to sprinkle on you? Maybe that would jolt you out of it."

"Ah," said Joe. "I sure could use a good long drink. Only I hate to go in there. She's not looking at me, is she? There's something I'm supposed to do. Now what in hell is it?"

"Take a look," said Irving. "That's a nice little conference they're holding there."

"They are?" said Joe. "Who is?"

"Your dearly beloved and Belle. Is that her name? Watch it, boy. She's coming right at you."

"Well," said Belle. "You're quite a character, aren't you?"

"Boom," said Joe. "Just like that."

"In fact," said Belle. "I think you stink."

"Well, thanks a lot. I sure do appreciate your coming all the way over here just to tell me."

"It's a pleasure, I assure you."

"That's a relief."

"Huh," said Belle. "And you call yourself a man. Believe me, if I never see you again, it'll be much too soon."

"Likewise, I'm sure."

"Well," said Irving. "That was an interesting exchange."

"A spunky kid, isn't she? She'll make a fine mother. She'll swat the bejazus out of her kids. How do you like that? One stupid little thing after another. Fooey. If that's what you call living, you can have it, brother, it's all yours."

"Now there," said Irving. "There's the inspired statement of the year."

"Now don't tell me you're disappointed in me too?"

"On the contrary," said Irving. "I always thought you had what I would call real possibilities."

"That's nice," said Joe. "Keep lying. I sure do appreciate it. Holy smoke. Now I remember. I have to get somebody for her. She can't sit there all alone. Wait here, Irv. This won't take long. I'll be back in a jiffy."

"You can go," said Irving. "But when you come back, you won't find me here."

"What?" said Joe. "You're not leaving now, are you?"

"Yes," said Irving. "I'm afraid I must. Do me a favor sometimes, will you? Give me a ring when you have a life of your own."

"Ah, now," said Joe. "That's good. That I like. I always knew you would get me. Hang around, Irv. You're the only guy around here I can really talk to. You don't want to run out on me now, do you?"

"Oh, well," said Irving. "If you put it that way."

"That's the stuff," said Joe. "Yes, sir. You were certainly right there, Irving. I liked what you said. When I have a life of my own. That was good. That was really good."

That may very well be. But who can fail to see it? They are beginning to leave him one by one. They are turning their backs on this flustered nonesuch. They are losing their patience with his retreats and retractions, with his crafty quibbling and conceited sneers. They are only people. If it is a simple yes they want, how long can he expect them to hang around and be fascinated by his thousand and one incoherent ways of saying no?

As he is now, where is he? He stands alone on the platform of choice. He licks his lumpish lips helplessly. He listens stunned to the spectacular noise of a shrieking compacted world as it recedes from him like a train roaring into a tunnel. What can he do alone? Sit by the telephone?

Stuff the petals of a synthetic rose up his nose as a substitute for the smell of human sweat? Stupidly sort out those figures in the carpet which have the shape of frisky monsters and consort with them? Open the window to the weather and wonder at the mysterious reluctance of the metaphysical mist to transform itself into tangible rain? What a pain. What is this soulful anguish resulting from a preview of mere carnal loneliness? If it can be said to speak, what can it say? It can only say, give me anything, anything but that.

"Take it?" said Mel. "Sure I'd take it. But who's going to give it to me?"

"Dope," said Doc. "Who's talking about anyone giving it to you? We're just supposing. Don't you know how to dream any more?"

"Think of it," said Mel. "Ten bucks a week for the rest of my life."

"Peanuts," said Artie. "What could you do with it?"

"What could I do with it?" said Mel. "Why, I'd live like a king on it. I have ways of knowing how. Just let somebody give it to me. I'd show you how quick I'd grab it."

"Well," said Doc. "Let's see what we can do for you. The key to the house I still have use for. But here's a pocket comb with only one tooth missing from the fine side. How would that interest you for a starter?"

"You know what?" said Mel.

"What?"

"I'm going to take it."

"Swell," said Artie. "Now things are really beginning to roll. Now me. Here's a small item of no mean value. A little golden screw I keep to weigh my pocket down. It'll break my heart to part with it, but what the hell, anything to make you happy."

"Hey," said Mel. "How about that, Joey boy? You see what's happening here. They're swamping me with favors."

"I'm glad to see it. It's a great way to go."

"Ain't it now? How about you, Uncle? Got anything you'd like to contribute to a worthy cause?"

"Why, yes," said Joe. "A real live girl. I highly recommend her. Do I see any hands raised?"

"A girl," said Mel. "I pass."

"Me too," said Doc. "I'm not in the mood. Some other time."

"What kind of a broad?" said Artie. "Say, what's all this Dave's been trying to hand us?"

"Yeah," said Mel. "Something about quitting your job. God, I thought I could make up stories, but that guy's got me beat a mile."

"What bull," said Doc. "The rotten lousy stories we have to listen to lately."

"You should've seen Sol," said Artie. "He got sore as hell. He couldn't take that. He just picked himself up and scooted out of here."

"I don't blame him," said Doc. "I could hardly listen to such shit myself."

"Well," said Joe. "That's life for you. I'm afraid you're going to have to."

"What?" said Mel. "It's not true, is it?"

"I don't know about true. But it's a real live fact."

"Wait a second," said Mel. "You mean to say you're really going to quit your job?"

"To hear is to believe. What else can I tell you?"

"This is really nice," said Doc. "This is beautiful."

"I don't understand," said Artie. "What in hell happened?"

"Oh," said Joe. "I'm just trying to show off, that's all. After all, what's the gripe here? It's my job, isn't it? I can do whatever I want with it, can't I?"

"Absolutely not," said Doc.

"Hello?" said Joe. "What's this now?"

"It's simple," said Mel. "He means. If you quit your job, we lose this place. Ftt. Just like that."

"Aw, now," said Joe. "Wait a minute, will you? What do you think I am here? Atlas holding up the world? Why does everything have to depend on me? If you guys want this place, you'll find a way to keep it somehow. If you have to, you'll do something about it. You'll see."

"Keep it," said Mel. "With what? Sneak around to a pawnshop with this comb and screw?"

"You figure it out," said Joe. "Right now, I have other things to worry about."

"Sure, sure," said Doc. "We understand. I know we sound selfish, Joe. But what's all the hurry anyway? Who knows? Maybe one of us bums here will get a break soon. How long can this goddamn depression last? I know we haven't got a right to tell you what to do. If you want to quit your job, you must have a damn good reason for it. You must be ambitious for something. But think of us. I thought we were

262

real friends here. How are we ever going to stick together if we lose this place?"

"We'll get a pot of glue," said Mel. "Stop bothering him, will you? Can't you see you're breaking his heart?"

"I just wanted him to know, that's all."

"So he knows?" said Mel. "So what?"

"Quiet," said Artie. "Will you guys hold it down a second? Why don't you give him a chance to talk?"

"What's the use?" said Doc. "He's not going to say anything."

"How in the hell can he when you jump on him like that?"

"What jump on him?" said Doc. "We had to tell him, didn't we?"

"I'll be damned," said Artie. "We're right back where we started from. I don't know why it is, but every time I talk to you, I never get anywhere."

"You know something?" said Doc. "Him I'm going to hit."

"Great," said Mel. "And I'll punch you. And Joe will step over and slap me. And then Dave will stroll in and whack Joe. And Eddie will rush in and bop Dave. And who else is there? And we'll all bleed a lot. And that, my friends, that is the way to solve everything."

"War," said Doc. "I love war. To your stations, men."

"Without me," said Artie. "There must be a better way to die than that."

"Right," said Joe. "And a better way to live. And all that sort of crap. And that takes care of that. Is there anything else you guys would like to say to me?"

"Yes," said Artie. "And I bet you'll be surprised when you hear it."

"Shoot," said Joe. "I'm willing to take my chances."

"We're grateful to you," said Artie. "And you know why? Because, goddamn it, you've given us something to talk about. You heard us when you came in. We sure hit rock bottom that time, didn't we? But now. Now we're really going to have some fun. We got something now we can talk about for years. Look at them. They can hardly wait for you to go."

"It's me who's grateful," said Joe. "I never dreamed I could be of such service to my fellow countrymen. How about that babe now? No takers then?"

"Don't be silly," said Artie. "I just told you. What's women to us now?"

263

"Then I'll be seeing you," said Joe. "Now don't you men stay up too late talking about this. You might ruin your health. It's really not worth it. Stupid subject all blown up. Phone me collect if you ever find out. How can quitting an ordinary job become so goddamn important? How?"

What can be so awesome or sinful or heroic about it? It is no more significant than the act of raising one's hand to wave goodbye. There may be some extra meaning to it at times, such as feeble implications of desertion, and faint intimations of precious skin to be lost and enormous puddles of disapproval to be crossed, but in essence it is a nothing thing to do, so meekly acted out sometimes as to be contemptible.

There was a time when God divided the Red Sea. And so Moses became a hero. Guardians of fowl clubbed foxes to death. Greener images of lust were those dragons of old which knights in shining armor clanked out to slay. They were handsome men endowed with perpetual youth. All the veiled ladyloves knew who were the true lady-killers then. Five priests secured the head and limbs of the human sacrifice, while a sixth opened his breast with a sharp razor of volcanic rock. The fanatic sixth was a brave man. He tucked his hand in the wound and tore out the palpitating heart. The ancient young knew chants and festivals. They fed the sacred fires. There seemed to be more courage in action on earth when the flipping planet was thought to be flat. Cockiness then meant sailing the astonished seven seas in leaky tubs. The old world had a new world to rape and ruin.

Flagpole sitters are the daredevils now. Potential fire-eaters show their pluck by courting the sandman in a room without a night light. Melancholy hellcats must steel themselves before they can thread a needle. Men have become remarkable for their speed in running around in circles. They have to buy tickets to tell them where they are going. They feel they have it in them to be heroes, as much as men ever were, but wherever they go, someone is always there to tell them, here is not the place, now is not the time. Meanwhile the century is flying. And the bravest thing a man can do is to go absolutely nuts and resign whatever position he has in life, and say, without having any reason for saying it, yes, this is the place, and yes, this is the time.

"But for what?" said Joe. "That is the question."

"Of course," said Irving. "I'm sure of it. I've said so myself many times."

"You don't know what I'm raving about, do you?"

"To tell you the truth," said Irving. "Less and less. What happened? I don't see any volunteers with you."

"Would you believe it?" said Joe. "They all said no."

"Really?" said Irving. "What a shame. Well, then. Perhaps. In that case, maybe I could."

"She's laughing there, isn't she? Oh, well. I guess she's trying to show me she doesn't care. Or maybe she's forgotten all about it already. Girls are the funniest things, aren't they?"

"I don't know," said Irving. "I haven't made up my mind yet. As you know, I've never had much of a chance to."

"Around and around she goes," said Joe. "And where she'll come out nobody knows. What a night. I don't think anything ever really comes to an end, do you? I'm always getting stuck in the middle. I don't know about you. But some of us ought to be shoved up and made over again. Ah, I see you agree. Carried unanimously. Now. Where did I chuck my hat and coat?"

"What?" said Irving. "You're not going to leave me flat again, are you?"

"Hell, no," said Joe. "You're coming with me. Though I'll be damned if I know where we can park ourselves where no one will bother us."

"I would suggest my house. But you always say no."

"Your house?" said Joe. "You're sure we wouldn't be bothering anyone? Then it's a deal. What are we waiting for?"

"Ah," said Irving. "That's great. I'm really glad. Wait. We musn't forget that record."

"My last hope for tonight. Good old Irving. You little mutt. Before we sneak out, tell me something, will you?"

"I hope it's an easy one this time."

"Don't help me on with my coat," said Joe. "I'm not a cripple yet. You think. How about it? You think you'll be able to give me one word, just one good word, I'll be able to take home with me and sleep on tonight?"

Irving's laugh was his loudest tonight. His utterly frank opinion was that this was the wittiest question yet. He humbly begged to be excused. Miracles were quite out of his line, though on second thought, he could append the possibility that in the course of mouthing one scintillating remark or another, he might, laying the proper

265

emphasis on the conditional, accidentally let drop that single essential word that would so operate upon the jaded vision of his friend that he would see stars for many a night to come. Whereupon Joe showed how much this had affected him by dropping his hat. This allowed Irving to comment upon the accident as an example of what can befall a man when he least expects it. Here he paused, for the sake of his own security, to revise his grip on the record. But since it appeared that his assignment was to do all the talking until they were well clear of the place, he barely drew breath to say that he had often been impressed with the fact that what will put one man to sleep will give insomnia to another. It was ridiculous not to face it. The very poorest thinkers in the world have been heard to expatiate on the morbid idea that only death can quiet the brain after it has been profoundly disturbed by what the heart has independently felt and suffered.

What then is a sentimentalist? Like the politic word–slinger that he was, Irving asked Joe to define it, and in the same breath, defined it himself. The sentimentalist is he whose manicured hands wander idly over the keys, searching for the lost chord. Which should have intrigued the man, but it was plain that Joe was already elsewhere. Closing the street door softly behind him, he held up his hand to impose silence, and with the smoothest face gazed up at the hazy night sky. He stood thus in an attitude of listening. And as he listened, he seemed to be asking.

Where is that where? It seems the ear alone has been there. How does it sense that at the early age of eleven? He must be sick in the head, said Helen. He ought to see a doctor, said Abe. He will be the death of me, said Mamma. They could not understand what was making him do it, and neither could he, but do it he did for days and days. Ribbed stockings, long and black, on the disengaged legs of a diminished body, he sat at the front window on a massive dining room chair, in the presence of prehistoric lace curtains, blue shades, tickless clocks, and tropical wallpaper blooms. The ceiling was a white field of elongated auricular bugs embossed on tin. The floor was painted red in those days. Tiles of a fool's paradise green framed the false fireplace. The mantelpiece bore three objects which augmented his audience. The first was a pitcher in the form of an elk's head with its horns in battle position and its bugling mouth for spout, the second, a busy figure in porcelain of a curly-headed churl chewing on an inaccurate

266

flute, and the third, a shepherd in soapstone with eyeballs depressed, frowning at a nonexistent flock.

Oh, wait until we tell Papa. He will hit you hard. He will take it and break it into pieces. But they never told. They were not squealers. They were afraid of scenes. When after one year of married life Cousin Gus discovered who was Sylvia, a woman who should have been his wife, he disliked her in all her flabby aspects, so decided not to live with her any more, so he deserted her with her bangles and beads, taking away with him a black case, that was all, and asked the Bellinsons to keep it for him, and that was how the captivating instrument came to be in the house.

It had a delightful shape. Its shape first, then its sound. Taboo, his first touches were furtively given. He was heard. He promised to be careful. Boy with a mandolin. It was like the title of a picture. If he went to school, he could not remember. If he had homework to do, he did not do it. What was the fascination here? Why should the world be so easily transfigured each time the double strings were idly scratched with a brown triangular celluloid pick? The blue of the sky was new. Like his exaltation, pigeons cleaved a finer air, wheeling round and round. It was a related motion. The sounds he heard, they said, beyond these walls is a world without walls. The ear perceived it, urging his boyish soul, go back where you came from, go back. He began to turn the pegs this way and that. He tried to do a little fingering. He hunted for a tune. He tried to transform sound into music, and when he failed, it broke the spell.

Before the mandolin went back into its black case to stay, he made the last day hideous for all of them by lifting his voice, as he spanked the strings, in a visceral lament for the loss of his exquisite sense of a place to which the blundering sounds he made could no longer convey him, a place which was, which was somewhere, but where? Sissy stuff, he was much too young to sigh for long over delinquent days. He scuttled down the two flights of stairs like a frightened squirrel. He could not stay in the house any more. It had become too quiet for him.

That was then. And now it is now. And his memory is so astonishingly strong and athletic that it has flung away that monolithic chunk of time, the years he has noisily lived in between, has tossed it aside as if it were a tiny blade of grass he had carelessly plucked from the sizable lawn of the universe. Seems the standing joke is that the past is

267

the hair shirt the present is forced to wear, which is the same as saying, that the present must do penance for the past, which tends to complicate the matter of what is because of what was, seems clear enough so far. Or is it?

Wiseacre at his wit's end, without fully realizing it, he has already arrived at Irving's house, and has heard Irving say, make yourself comfortable. Sight-seer at an impasse, since all chairs look alike to him, he simply sits down, and with a sigh that is yet to be heard round the world, rids himself of this one final tag end of his reflections, that time, that sunny thing, is like a balanced plank upon which the silly human animal, screeching with delight to see himself so divided, wildly teeter-totters with himself, and seesaws.

All this while Irving's hands reach out to touch each thing in turn to show that everything he touches belongs to him. Such bragging little motions are excusable, for this is his moment, and he relishes it. His piano has to be a Steinway, and his phonograph a Sonora. And there are stacks of sheet music for the one, and a huge case of record albums for the other. Stores with which to withstand a lifetime siege of silence, staples superior to words, of percussive sweetness and rage, of whirling light and bitterness, from keys to turntable, is there really room enough in one man's taut and acidulous guts to contain it all?

But the night is too far advanced to proceed so timidly. Perhaps it is wise to want one thing only, and failing that, to want only one of each kind, but if there is more than one metronome in this room, there is only one bed against the wall, and this means that Irving sleeps here, that this is his room, that he does have one thing that is truly enviable, a room of his own. For Irving it was like gaining a great big piece of health to hear Joe's whistle of wonder. He seemed to be ashamed of his shinier face as he asked to be excused for a moment. As he left, he made sure to shut the door behind him as if he wanted to give Joe a taste of how he would feel to have what Irving had.

It would feel like. Think of it. If Joe had such a room all to himself, no one would be able to see or hear him. He would boldly weep to his heart's content. That would be the very first thing he would do. He would then find a pin and prick his finger with it. He would put his tongue to his own drop of blood. He would get down on all fours and crawl under the bed and bang his head against it and howl. He would give himself over to despair as never before. He would goad God into

268

showing him how he could more effectively destroy himself. For where does a man go from here? Where is his place? Why does he do what he does without knowing why he does it? If he had a room of his own, he would allow the fluff of ignorance to collect in his mouth. He would brush himself off and sit himself down and call up visions of intolerable human agony and learn how to look at them without batting an eyelash. What happiness it would be to be free of those fake grimaces of sympathy and phony avowals of brotherhood. Let others seek their kind so that they may deceitfully lend each other a counterfeit helping hand, he would sit in his own room with his hands clasped and wait, stoically apart and away from, until that ten-armed squid of sham in him creeps out to slither away. Sincerity may then come to stay a while. And understanding with it? What apparition of an anemic dove of flightless nonsense is this? What would he understand after a monkish seclusion in a room of his own? That everyone must go on living until he dies? Only that again? With a groan that was hardly attractive, he clapped his hand to his forehead and propelled himself out of his chair.

"Just in time. I was about to fly out of here."

"Damn me," said Irving. "I don't blame you. It took me a year and six months to locate the mustard."

"Damn you is right," said Joe. "You look so happy, it makes me feel sad. What is that all about?"

"A tray," said Irving. "Ain't we fancy?"

"Food," said Joe.

"Good," said Irving. "I'm glad you recognize it."

"For me?" said Joe. "What did I do to deserve it?"

"If you deserved it, I guess you wouldn't get it."

"Swoosh," said Joe. "There goes another rocket."

"Right," said Irving. "Sometimes I'm so brilliant, I amaze myself. I'll just pull this table over. How's this? Boyoboy. You should've seen the way I slapped it all together. Glad to see you're a milk drinker. Well, then, first I thought I'd make some toast. Then I thought I wouldn't. Dig in. Don't wait for me. Then I said to myself, good heavens, you just can't feed the man a little Swiss cheese. What do you think you're doing? Entertaining a rat? So I hunted around, and lo and behold, I found me some fresh ham. Now, that of course, that tells you this is no kosher house. Five sandwiches. You think it'll be enough?"

269

"No," said Joe. "Go back in the kitchen and make five more."

"Certainly," said Irving. "If you're serious."

"Your father must be a bootlegger or something."

"Oh," said Irving. "We're pretty well off."

"Damn good half-sour pickles you have here. Slice them all yourself? Show me your nails. You wear glasses when you read? How did that wave get in your hair? Don't be bashful. Tell me more about yourself."

"Well," said Irving. "When I was born, I was so surprised, I couldn't say a word."

"Gulp."

"A little howling dummy if ever there was one. But ever since that bitter morning hour, the reaction has been such that my mouth, as my mother likes to remind me, hasn't closed for a second. That milk isn't too cold, is it? Paper napkins to your left. It's not bootlegging or something. It's real estate."

"Thanks," said Joe. "That's something I ought to know, I'm sure."

"Why not?" said Irving. "After all, a fact is a fact, isn't it? It's like the first skin off an onion. Since I seem to be definitely in a peeling mood. Seems to me if it makes you weep when you get at the core of the truth, what is the truth then but mighty like an onion? I forgot to bring some fruit. Now isn't that just like me? The funny thing is I really like my father. That is, every other day. You know what he says? He may say it a bit too often, but at least he does say it. He says, I'm a good business man. In short, he says, I'm not altogether honest."

"Lucky man. At least he knows something about himself."

"Have more," said Irving. "Don't be afraid to eat. Eat all you want, Joe. Don't wait for me. I won't bother you. I'll go over there and strum a while. Ah, I'm really glad you came. Honest. I feel. It's been a damn nice evening so far, hasn't it?"

A comical look of pained reluctance to favor such a fiction was all Joe could summon to that brutal feeding face of his. Otherwise these were perfectly endurable moments for him, for he needed his food, and in his mindless way, had none of a cat's shyness to show that he enjoyed the simple act of eating it. He did not care who could see the animal licking of his lips. Heartlessly eyeing sandwich number two coming up, he joined his hands in the praying position of palm to palm, and vigorously rubbed them clear of crumbs. When he dabbed

270

the mustard on, it was done in a blobbed and impressionistic style. When he took a bite, it was as large as he could manage. When he chewed, comma, he chewed, period. He was charming. He thought he was becoming more and more natural the more he stuffed himself, yet he did feel, no less naturally, that his face was not too pretty a sight, shining as it did with so much solid satisfaction.

The truth was he was filling up fast. And that was all it meant. He discovered he could hear better. Terrible excitement there in the left hand, as he began to listen with more attention to what Irving was playing, he measured the remainder of his sandwich with the amount of milk he had left in his glass. He was clever at it. He came out even. He rewarded himself by lighting a cigarette often called a coffin nail. A critical tyke there, that bounding and bellyaching left hand. He blew out the match with breath made visible by smoke he had already inhaled. Listen to that insulting thumper, lashing away at the right hand for failing to face it, scolding it thunderously for floating around way off there by itself like a lost snowflake. Bewildered by such a frontal attack, the right hand faltered through all its five fingers, the usual stammering of the underdog. It seemed to have numberless corners in which to shake. It took a trial run to its right. The left hand rushed after it to give it a final whack, but the right hand turned on it, and the left hand scuttled back, rather surprised, but still growling. The right hand stamped six times in a row within the space it had gained, then subsided into a broken melody of explanation which soon fell away to a whisper out of which emerged that single appeasable word it had been searching for. It was a tough baby to win over, that left hand, but at last it had to announce that it was reconciled to the inescapable truth the right hand kept hammering home so insistently. The right hand laughed. The left hand almost giggled. All at once rapid runs away from and towards each other, that was the ticket now. But this strangely trickled out as if they too had to flee with the fleeing, forced to accompany them everywhere. Joe leaned forward, straining to hear a last tonic chord at least. But that was all. It was the finish.

"Oh, well," said Joe. "I'll applaud anyway."

"That's the spirit," said Irving. "A tremendous thing, isn't it? Ah, what we need here is someone who can really play it."

"You did all right."

271

"Rot. Don't let me fool you, Joe. If you knew what was what, you'd know I pretty near killed it. What's all this? You didn't go and leave all that food for me, did you?"

"Don't worry about it. I did all right too."

"I thought you were a bigger eater than that. God. So you think I did all right, do you? Of course I would certainly do otherwise if I had an ounce of real talent in me. As it is. Say. This stuff isn't so bad after all, is it?"

"Sometimes I think. What good does it do to be so goddamn modest?"

"The truth is the truth."

"So I've heard," said Joe. "By the way. I'm sorry to be so ignorant. But who wrote that jazzy little piece you just played?"

"Oh," said Irving. "Some chap by the name of Beethoven."

"Beethoven?" said Joe. "Why, sure, I've heard of him before. A promising kid, wasn't he?"

"Sonofagun. What a thing to say."

"So help me," said Joe. "That's the first natural smile out of you since we stepped into this house."

"Really?" said Irving. "That's awful."

"Well," said Joe. "Cheer up. Once you do a thing, the chances are you can do it again. Hold what you have there. Let's have a bit more of that milk. Oops, don't drown me. Here's to you, Irving. No matter what you decide to do with yourself. I have a feeling I'm on your side."

"Thanks for saying that."

"It didn't cost me a cent."

"I wish," said Irving. "You know what I wish, Joe. I wish I could change places with you. Don't laugh now. Just for a year. For six months even."

"Hey, now," said Joe. "What's the matter with you, man? Don't you know when you're well off?"

"Yes," said Irving. "Well off. It sure does look like it, doesn't it? I see I'll have to explain that."

"I'm your guest. Pile it on, son."

"There you are," said Irving. "That's another thing that amazes me about you. I would be bored stiff if I had to listen to a semieducated snot like me. But you look at me as if I'm the first person you've ever had the chance to see close up, as if I were the only one alive, or

272

half-alive, it doesn't seem to make any difference to you. The hell with you, Joe. You're so damn human in everything you do, it's easy to hate you. You know that, don't you?"

"A light, mister, a light. Let's be calm whatever we do."

"How can you afford to smoke so much?"

"As I say," said Joe. "Let's be calm. Let's behave like men. A smoke is a smoke, but a real act. Forget it. Why should we listen to anyone who tells us it's impossible? Wherever you go, they jump on you. Boy, are they glad to give you the needle. Damn me. How do you like the way I'm off and running again? It's as bad as having shingles, isn't it? Why should we always have to look around first and see how everybody else is doing it before we can even spit the way we feel is right for us? Who are these jokers who keep telling us, get back to the end of the line? If these are what we call men, then I'd rather be a worm. Even if I'm only a Joe-worm. Which lately means a real troublemaker. Boom, boom. Almost as good as that guy Beethoven. You don't happen to have a nice juicy apple here I can crawl into?"

"You haven't been talking to my father, have you? You know what he says to me?"

"Shut your goddamn mouth or I'll kick you in the ass."

"On the contrary," said Irving. "He says, you can keep it open as long as you want. You're absolutely free to do it. You're free to do whatever you want."

"Great," said Joe. "Sounds wonderful."

"Is it?" said Irving. "Why? Because of the mere sound of it? Hooray. Say free and everyone's face lights up like the Great White Way. Hearts beat faster. Hats are tossed in the air. Free. It's like a rally in the ninth inning. It's like watching Babe Ruth hit a home run with the bases loaded. It's like ice cream on a hot day. It's so refreshing. It melts in your mouth. Free. There's the biggest lie yet."

"A peanut. There are bigger ones, I'm sure."

"My father," said Irving. "A great big picture of a man. You wouldn't think so looking at me, would you? Maybe I'll suddenly shoot up yet. Who knows? A real rock. He takes up space. But I mean. With a spine on him that makes him sure about certain things in a way I'll never be. One night when he was having supper, I sneaked up on him and slammed the hammer down on his eating hand. He stuck it in his mouth, picked up the fork with his other hand, and went right on

273

eating. You see all these things here? If I said to him, take it all away, he would take it away. If I said to him, put it back, he would put it back. No give. I'm like a first mortgage he loves with a love that will never end. He's some kind of a miracle that should've happened to you. I mean that, Joe. I can't use him. I'm not the son for that kind of a father. He laughs when I tell him that."

"Hell," said Joe. "I would too."

"Naturally," said Irving. "And so does my mother. A mother, as I'm sure you were about to say, usually comes with a father. Well, yes, in this case, it's true. She's a nice, quiet, gentle mirror. Of my father. If she has a life of her own, I haven't found it yet."

"Incredible," said Joe. "How did you ever get stuck like that?"

"I had pull," said Irving. "I got myself born into it."

"Next time don't mix in."

"Isn't that chair comfortable? You're not worrying it's getting late, are you?"

"No, no," said Joe. "I'm just squirming around trying to figure this thing out. Not that I really think I can. Or even that I should. Just the same. Maybe they should take the strap to you. Like a friend of mine likes to say. It seems to me they should really stand in front of you and block your way. Then you'd have something you could knock down and kick aside. Am I making myself clear? You need resistance. They should make you feel there are certain things you just have to do in this world."

"Like you, for instance?"

"Like me what?"

"Like going to work. Like making a living. You have to. But I don't."

"I do?" said Joe. "Who says so?"

"But you do," said Irving. "And that's all there is to that."

"Something tells me I liked you much better when you played the piano."

"Don't get sore," said Irving. "Look at it this way. I can quit school any time I want. Tomorrow if I feel like it. But you now. Suppose somebody came up to you and said, my god, Joe, what are you doing there making believe you were born to be a shipping clerk? Why don't you quit? Why don't you give yourself a chance? Why don't you go out into the world and see what you can do with yourself? Why, you would say to him, you're crazy, pal, you know why I can't quit. I need money. I have to live. And he would have to say, yes, I'm sorry, I understand, I forgot all about that. But what do you think would happen if I said to someone, I can't quit school because I can? I don't have to go any further, do I? That's what takes the heart out of me. There's no excuse for me. Absolutely none."

"But for me there is. Is that it?"

"Obviously."

"Oh, boy," said Joe. "There's a pip for you. That's a new one on me, all right. I can't because I can't."

"You're a quick study. That's for sure."

"Then how is it," said Joe. "What's the use of telling you when you won't believe me?"

"Try me and see."

"I've got news for you," said Joe. "I'm quitting my job."

"You're doing what?" said Irving.

"I'm quitting my job. And it seems to me that if I'm actually doing it, then it must mean I can, even though I can't. Wouldn't you say so?"

"Holy cow," said Irving.

"Now look," said Joe. "Don't just go and overwhelm me with words."

"I never thought. I don't know what to say."

"Then let me say it for you," said Joe. "I know all the questions and answers. No. I'm afraid my mother doesn't like the idea. Yes. The boys know all about it, and they don't like it much either. No. There's no other job. Yes. I know these are awful times. No. I don't know why I'm doing it. Yes. I do know. No. I don't know. Is everything clear now? Does that do it for you?"

"I feel like a fool."

"Now that," said Joe. "That's another whole new subject."

"The things I said. Why did you let me go on talking that way?"

"Relax," said Joe. "You still get a passing mark."

"Thanks anyway. Thanks for telling me."

"It wasn't easy."

"Ha," said Irving. "Remember? You asked me to give you one good word. But look what's happening now. You've given me one."

"That's interesting. What word?"

"Do," said Irving. "And damn all else."

275

"Whatever that means."

"Thanks, Joe. I'm very grateful to you. No more thinking. No more. The only way to do a thing is to do it. School? The hell with it. It's going to be a cinch now. What's today? By the end of the week, I bow out. I'm going to say, excuse me, but I quit."

"Quit?" said Joe. "Are you crazy? Who told you you can do that?"

"Whoa, now," said Irving. "I don't understand. Isn't that just what they're saying to you?"

"Sure it is," said Joe. "But this is different."

"How? We're both human beings, aren't we?"

"The difference," said Joe. "The difference is that you're not me and I'm not you. Quit. How do you like the way he grabbed at that word? Did you ever sweat and break your neck for it? Who ever gave you permission to do anything like that?"

"I don't mean to nag you," said Irving. "But you're a little bit mixed up there, aren't you?"

"Imagine," said Joe. "Trying to turn the tables on me. All right. I wouldn't mind. If you heard about what I'm doing after I really did it, and then went out and did something like it yourself, okay then, that would be your funeral, not mine. But not now, kiddo. No, sir. You're not going to pull anything like that on me now."

"I'm sorry," said Irving. "What's the use of kidding myself any more? Look at the way I live. It's getting me down. I just can't sit here forever and watch the rest of the world go by. I don't know what. Or how. But I just have to do something."

"Oh, sure," said Joe. "Go ahead. And when you do, they'll blame me."

"You?" said Irving. "Why? Why should they do that?"

"Because I say," said Joe. "And when I say, I say. The mouth goes. And it goes and goes. And whango, before I know it, I've put my foot in it. And I'm gagging. Why did I have to tell you? What good did it do? What in hell did it prove? That I was thinking only of myself? All it did was make you jump after me like a monkey. Quit. Sounds simple, doesn't it? Damn it, Irving. Don't turn your face away. Listen to me. Why don't you listen to me? Just listen to me a second, will you?"

Listen to what? What more could this caustic agitator add that could unsay what he has already said? The damage is done. His own remark-

276

able inside blush tells him. Secret of a death-defying trick, how to be a lifetime hero in one easy flipping jump. Soon there will be a trillion million frantic roosters with their surplus feathers flying, clawing him aside to flit ahead to do it before he could, crowing the cheapened little tune of quit, quit, quit. All will seem like the real doers. All but this man here. What a miserable strain to add to his song cycle. How well he knows it. It is the classic whine of one who feels he is about to be squeezed out and superseded. Turn away from such a dry and squeaky conclusion he must, for it is abundantly clear now that he has tried to charm the sense out of anyone listening not like a man at all, but like a fidgety mockingbird. There is no need to wonder why. This has been his musical evening.

10.

Out of his Wednesday dimout he comes now, the outcast ghost of himself sustaining yet his taciturnity, while the late convolving daylight, as well as the curlicue voice of Rosalie, twines around him, a redeemable mute who still broods over the unsingable hours of his working day. Declining assistance from others, through self-respect, he tries to disembarrass his mind of that Colish haunted time by opening his eyes to the island haze, and his heart to the human shuffled dust of the street on which he walks with Rosalie, the intrusive and frisky earthling he is so fond of.

Construe it as singular that the soul should rejoice when the body rots, that part of the orotund silliness of what it believes should be that its residence in the flesh is its forty winks, its famished era, its passover time. For it knows there is honey in the body as well as bitter herbs, that there can hardly be a more festive symbol of its existence than a Rosalie face. In whom does she live and move? She is everyone's sweet-lipped sister in her sprightly lover's pace. Her smile is such that if he would dare to meet it, it would stagger him. Pity now his reverie, by peeking at what he should not, he has artlessly reminded it of that nowhereness into which it must soon bleatingly sink. The wind can tickle. The cloth of a spring coat may be green where no grass is allowed to grow. There is no fresh gathering of clouds in the west. He is plainly coming to. To abide within is not to abide with her. He knows he can no longer examine the poetry of her presence with a skeleton's tedious stare. Wayfarer, awake. She laughs from her step-ins up. Hers is a noble way of wooing. She intends to punish him with the pleasure of listening to her.

Here are flowers on the sidewalk. They look good enough to eat. They have names, of that she is sure, and she has seen a rose, and remembers she made a meal of lilies once when she was dreaming, and does know what orange blossoms mean, not that she is hinting, but suppose now she has to turn around and go into that florist shop to get some of those they had outside, she would have to point at the ones she wanted like a baby, which would be funny, though no funnier, in her estimation, than actually having to pay for what can be picked for nothing, which is what she did once upon a time at a camp in the Catskills where they grew wild, those were the days. The camp site was pretty high up, and it had an Indian name, and she cut her foot on a shell in the water, and a branch gave her a black eye when she climbed into an apple tree, and the counselor she had a crush on tried to grow a beard, and she kept rubbing sticks together to make a fire without matches, which she never did because she had only two weeks in which to do it, which was the limit that year for each poor kid to spend in the country for free, but she was never pushed into poison ivy, and there at least she was lucky. Sang all the old songs they did, round the campfire gleaming, sweet afton among thy green braes, a onetime thing, two little three little Indians, cricket on her cot, half of her lifetime ago. Scratching her mosquito bites in her sleep, bluer milk at the break of day, a bird can die before it can fly, she held it in her hand. How about cats? Do they eat only live ones?

One night there was such a terrible clap of thunder, she had to dive under the blanket. God, if he wants to, can destroy a whole mountain, yet he will take the trouble sometimes to flash out at her that way, which is kind of thrilling, he being a he. But to pull up a bunch of carrots by the roots for the first time, that was her top sensation, for her it really was, for a flower on a stalk is not like a vegetable in the earth, one is further away and the other is closer to, which means that one is what the other can never be, which is not saying much, anyway, it was true, the older boys kissed the older girls, and sometimes the younger. The plash and hiss of it on the leaves, when in the woods they had to go, this of course was for his ears only, the girls could see what it was the boys had to take out. She screamed too and ran away, but honestly she could not understand why they should be running away from a familiar thing like that. Once a boy fell on her. She was curious, so she let him try, but he did not know how. And once she almost ran right over a couple just when they were doing it. She had to go into the country. She had to live until she was nine before she could get such a full view. Of what? Was this it then? Was this what she would have to do some day? She had a wild flower stuck in her hair. She took it and threw it at them.

That was how she was at her adorable age. Passion then, as he could see, was no fierce wild beast before which her child's cheeks burned or her grass-stained hands trembled, but was more like a blot on the landscape to which, to say it majestically, she had to show her proud little fanny. Of course it was a cute part of her anatomy when she was a tomboy, but all at once it gets to be sizes bigger, which at first it must, and then a girl, that suddenly, does begin to have second thoughts about it in relation to what she once saw, and then the fun begins, did he see how that man looked at her? All sorts of cuckoo men constantly do that, even that potbelly past his prime who just ambled by, the poor thing, how can she have anything against him for looking her over like that when she must admit that she, especially, has never been afraid to show what so fascinates them when she walks and weaves her way through the most crowded streets?

The subject she is on is so tricky. Fourth Avenue is wider than 28th Street. What is the proper thing to do? What is the natural? Pigeons let fall their droppings the moment they must. The sparrow is never suspicious of the shape of its wings. Monkeys and bears, and other amusing animals, wear what they have outside. Uncaged men clown when they exchange the milkman's handshake. Corseted women in high society who remove the panties from their baby lamb chops before they sink their teeth into them have that red devil in them too. Some of those who serve them, in their kitchen way, hack at chicken legs for fricassee, flushed with the old knowledge of what warms the blood where slippery babies come from. Perfect stunners, turning a cold shoulder to the reek of men, will skip into the woods to wrap their arms around the trunk of a tree. Ah, nature. Where has she been rushing off to? This is surely her silliest April. Permission granted, he

281

can kick her right now, if he is so inclined, into next November for talking so much about what she hardly has words for. Or would he rather grab her and kiss some sense into her? Is that what that smile means?

"Oh, at least," said Joe. "What else am I living for?"

"Well, then?"

"It's not enough," said Joe. "After what I heard, I want something more, much more than that."

"Why, Mr. Bellinson."

"All right to ask you?"

"Of course," said Rosalie. "I thought you never would."

"Okay then," said Joe. "Got any pennies?"

"Pennies?"

"Right," said Joe. "You know. For a newspaper."

"Shoot," said Rosalie. "Did I bite on that one."

"Like to give me a good punch?"

"Pennies," said Rosalie. "Oh, well. Let me see what I have."

"Bless you, my child. You're a good sport."

"Now he touches me."

"What's wrong? You're fully dressed, aren't you?"

"And what if I wasn't?"

"Ye gods," said Joe. "How do you get all that junk in one bag?"

"That's right," said Rosalie. "All I need is your hand in it."

"What's all the squirming for?"

"Easy," said Rosalie. "What do you think you're doing there?"

"Um," said Joe. "That's a nice back you have there, you know that?"

"For your information," said Rosalie. "It's a little higher up."

"I'm just feeling around. Which reminds me. I always meant to ask you. How do you look when you're naked?"

"Wonderful. Here. Go buy yourself some reading matter."

"You think I never think about you, don't you?"

"I think," said Rosalie. "I think we better move. We're blocking traffic."

"Hell," said Joe. "I know. Maybe I do kid around with you too much. But you know how I feel, Rosalie. I'm really a very serious guy."

"Like today, for instance?"

"Oh," said Joe. "That. I don't know what made me bark at you that way like a mad dog. It must be such fun for you to be with me lately."

"The funny thing is," said Rosalie. "Yes. Somehow it always is."

"Love," said Joe. "She comes romping in."

"Disgusting, ain't it?"

"Well, no," said Joe. "As a matter of fact, sometimes I rather like it. Like right now, for instance."

"My god," said Rosalie. "I must be hearing things."

"What's wrong? Can't I like you sometimes?"

"I'm flabbergasted. Who is this friendly cuss?"

"It's me," said Joe. "Joe. The guy with the full heart. And empty pockets."

"Help," said Rosalie. "Hold me up. This is too much for me."

"Hey," said Joe. "Did that guy bump you?"

"Gosh," said Rosalie. "A big fat one, wasn't he?"

"That's funny. It seems to me I know him."

"He's right," said Rosalie. "We shouldn't be standing here in the middle of the street."

"Then let's get a move on. How about it? Isn't this a real pisser of a day? You're not in a hurry, are you? How about walking down a station?"

"You think we should?"

"Why not?"

"I hate to remind you," said Rosalie. "But they're waiting for us."

"They are?" said Joe. "Who is?"

"Don't you know?"

"No," said Joe. "So I forgot. So what's so terrible about that?"

"Nothing," said Rosalie. "Let's walk."

"Aren't you going to tell me where we're supposed to be going?"

"And go through all that again?" said Rosalie. "No, thank you. I don't think I have the strength for that."

"Arf," said Joe. "In the doghouse again."

"Well, well," said Rosalie. "So this is fresh air."

"Careful now. Leave me a little."

"Look," said Rosalie. "Look. Look how fast it's going."

"What is?"

"The day."

He looked. He also sighed. So here it is again, the twilight. And the sky, as usual, is full of pity for itself. It seems to be engaged in such a

283

boneless kind of bitching. Its violet blood rushes to its head. It keels over so smoothly. Somehow it makes her feel so sad. Day, day, go away. Come again some other day.

He laughed as he hooked his arm around her. How, he asked, could she be so mean as to deprive him of her eyes which seemed to be on a dreary pilgrimage to Mecca? What real reason was there for feeling so low-down? A day is a day. She could, if she was bright, simply be brave and wave byebye to it. Or if she truly yearned to keep it ever in sight, he was quite willing, to show how free and easy he was, to turn west with her, and chase like a mad bull after it.

She barely smiled at this breezy idea of a baby. What is this that has come over her? Lost to him as she was, her profile of the marble stillness of a skygazer, so all in all gently disdainful of this frivolous human object beside her. It seemed brutal to ask her to tell him what had bewitched her, but his jealousy demanded that she do so. She was ashamed to say. She was afraid it would sound so sentimental. But something had made her see it, and see it with terrible clearness, that death, that death is a kind of failure of light. Was she right? When it will be she does not know, but one day soon, she too will have to close her eyes. It will be darker than dark. And in that darkness, which is waiting for her, she will see nothing, she will be absolutely dead. She laughed so shyly at the thought. That is what death means, she said. There will be no more light for her. No more.

"How true," said Joe. "How terribly true. And so, as the sun sinks below the horizon, we take leave of this isle of paradise, land of the palm trees, and assorted nuts. Am I traveling too fast for you? What did you eat today?"

"Do I sound so sick?"

"Oh," said Joe. "Just a little."

"Whew," said Rosalie. "A little is more than enough. I'm sorry. I guess I shouldn't be thinking about such things."

"Quit it," said Joe. "The hell with all this apologizing. Look, kiddo. As far as I'm concerned, you have a perfect right to think about anything you damn please. You're with me now. Remember?"

"My," said Rosalie. "You're such a gentleman."

"Me?" said Joe. "How dare you."

"You wouldn't mind too much, would you?"

"Mind what?"

"If I died before you. It would be terrible for me if you went first."

"It would?" said Joe. "Wait a second. It doesn't have to be right now, does it?"

"No, no," said Rosalie. "I was only talking about when the time comes."

"Oh," said Joe. "That's a relief."

"You know what I mean now?"

"Oh, sure," said Joe. "You have to struggle through Wednesday before you can get to Thursday. And then where are you? What I mean to say is, you're sure you want to hear this?"

"I'll die if you stop now."

"Die," said Joe. "That's a good one. I get it. We'll come back to that later. What I was trying to say is. The way the damn thing is arranged now, you live first, and then you die. Now isn't that stupid? Did you ever meet anyone who's in love with the idea? Of course not. Now the way I figure it, it should be just the other way around. We should be dead first for a thousand years. And know it. And then get born and live. How could we make any mistakes then? We'd have all that time to plan exactly what we would do in those sixty or so years we'd be alive. Hey? How's that for an idea? Ain't it a corker?"

"Absolutely not," said Rosalie.

"Then I guess I better begin all over again."

"How can you be dead and know it?"

"Wait a minute," said Joe. "I just thought of something. We have the same thing now. We already know how people lived before us. A fat lot of good that's done us. We still make the same mistakes they did. Every damn single one of them."

"Yes," said Rosalie. "Even to die."

"How is that again?"

"I said, even to die."

"That's what I thought you said. Why, sure. Even there we feel we're making a mistake, don't we? I like that. That was real smart, Rosalie."

"Don't worry," said Rosalie. "Tomorrow it'll sound stupid."

"Smarter yet. Listen to the kid, will you? Hold still. Let me see if I can knock you over."

"Another slap like that and you will."

"There," said Joe. "That's what I like. Get a little fire in your eyes.

285

Say the hell with it. Whatever it is. It can't be all that bad, can it?"

"Why?" said Rosalie. "Why did it have to happen? What did she do? She didn't do anything."

"Who didn't? Who are you talking about?"

"Pauline."

"Pauline?" said Joe. "Who's Pauline?"

"What's the difference who she is?"

"What do you mean what's the difference?"

"It's all over now, isn't it?"

"What is?" said Joe. "Goddamn it, Rosalie. Don't make me angry. Talk."

Into the breach, old boy, once again the world is cracked. Girlish cleft of it, fresh teen-age sinkhole of sighs, of what is it made that it should be so fickle and brittle? God's discarded hope, of all the loony laws it dumbly obeys, this seems to be the looniest, that as soon as it begins to fall apart for someone else, it must also begin to fall apart for him. Say bitch, say bastard, but no sooner does he feel a bit more credulous and expansive, when another hard luck story must come busting in to cramp him by pouring out its soul, and fouling up his time.

All this while Rosalie was talking, she was telling him. Her bad news from a far country, so sharply did she sense his hostility to it that she could not as yet spill it without misplacing her dots, and hurrying her dashes. Whose blonde moustache above what painted lip? What curls hid whose cauliflower ear? Not a single ounce of blood ran? Pauline with her tiers of the waviest straw hair, her long placid nose, her popeyes a total flop, when the mother instinct is drawn to the diaper smell, she had to go and drag her boy friend Manny along with her, to kiss and cuddle a two-weeks old squawker born to a vague third cousin in the mortified borough of Brooklyn. There was another young Manhattan couple there, two butterballs who had been recently hitched, which made six of them round the kitchen table for tea and crumb cake, all of whom, as they learned from each other, were unanimously in favor of feeding by formula, though each proudly claimed to have been breast-fed. Came time to go home, as come it must. Tomorrow's tiresome work impends while idle babykim's face grows fat and flushed in sleep. Sweet is the breath of its know-nothing which is so mysteriously in collusion with the know-

286

all of the stars. Mr. & Mrs. Rolypoly had an old Franklin knock-mobile. When Pauline and her Manny learned it was going their way, they said, swell, how nice. For it was exciting to think they would have the whole back seat all to themselves where they could take the fences side by side after that cunning fox of their complete future entwinement for as long as the ride would last. Manny, the grease monkey, he hardly had a mouth, but he did have his muscles. He had an eye for the inner works of Pauline's machinery. They clicked. There was a good reason for their going steady. Five long wet kisses later the car blew a tire right where the downgrade began on the Williamsburg Bridge. So they had to stop and climb out to fix it. The men, that is, Manny mostly, for it was he who took charge. It was he who was jimmying that rear tire off its rim with his massive behind jutting out in the roadway when all of a sudden a roadster made contact with him, and there he was, flying through the air with the greatest of ease, a dead man.

"The stupid sonofagun."

"You see that?" said Rosalie. " You see what can happen?"

"What in the hell was the matter with him? Didn't he know enough to watch it? What was the other guy doing? Picking daisies or something?"

"Can you imagine now how Pauline feels?"

"People," said Joe. "They're a pain in the neck. Who cares how she feels? Why the hell do you have to tell me all this? What am I supposed to do about it?"

"You can feel sorry for her, can't you?"

"All right," said Joe. "I'm sorry for her. Okay? Does that do it? Can we talk about something else now? Who is she anyway? How did she get into the act?"

"What a louse you are. She lost him. Can't you understand what that means?"

"Sure I do," said Joe. "It means that before you know it, you'll be seeing her flopping all over some other guy. That's what it means."

"Oh, no," said Rosalie. "How can you say that? She'll never get over it, never."

"Hooey."

"Don't say hooey," said Rosalie. "Suppose you died? What do you think would happen then?"

287

"Wonderful hand," said Joe. "Always so nice and cool."

"You think I'd get over it so quick?"

"How's your back teeth? Do they know what your front are doing?"

"I'll say," said Rosalie. "After all. There's nothing I like better than strolling along with you while I talk to myself. You're really such a darling to let me do it."

"Ain't I though? It's amazing. I don't understand it. How do I come to be so sweet? You think I get it from my grandfather on my mother's side? Or is it from my grandmother on my father's side? It's a puzzle, I know. But it must mean something. What do you think it means?"

"It means," said Rosalie. "It means that you hate people. That's what it means. You really hate them all. Except me, of course."

"Really?" said Joe. "Why? What makes you an exception?"

"Because," said Rosalie. "That's the way you're going to get to heaven. It's hell trying to talk to you, you know that?"

"That's a funny coincidence. I have the same trouble."

"Then why don't you do something about it?"

"Don't worry," said Joe. "I will. One of these days, you won't hear a peep out of me. It'll be tough. But I'll learn how to be quiet. I'll learn."

"Funny fellow," said Rosalie. "He's always busy about something, isn't he?"

"Such as," said Joe. "Now my stomach is beginning to growl. At least I got you all the way to 23rd. You were going to remind me. Where do we go from here?"

"Brace yourself."

"I'm braced."

"Then I'll tell you," said Rosalie. "We're going to the garden spot of America. As you call it."

"Oh, no," said Joe.

"Oh, yes," said Rosalie. "Ain't it awful?"

"Oh, god, no. You mean to say we're going to eat at your house?"

"It's all right," said Rosalie. "You don't have to go."

"How could it be? When did I ever say yes?"

"Please," said Rosalie. "I just told you. You don't have to yell. If you don't want to go, don't go, that's all."

"Don't go," said Joe. "That's a joke, all right. The best yet. I don't understand it. How did I ever get stuck like that?"

"Because," said Rosalie. "You're absolutely crazy about me. Didn't you know that?"

288

"What crap."

"Thank you," said Rosalie. "Now I've heard everything."

"What are we stopping for? Walk, walk."

"What?" said Rosalie. "More?"

"Yes," said Joe. "For me this time. Do you mind?"

Not at all. Why should she? With a mere shrug of her shoulders, she confirmed this one more piece of utter transparency, that as always it could be oodles of fun to arrive with him at the heyday of the blood in the evening time, that further, it could indeed ravish her soul to be so indiscreet a cookie as to become engulfed in his snapping mouth, that in addition it could be such a frightful pleasure to see that he considers her to be the very symbol of a snap fastener, or of a gripper zipper, so that it was finally such an unspeakable joy for her to have that sturdy heart of hers feel like a ruined city suddenly, broken in and without walls. So why should she?

"That's right, said Joe. "Go ahead. Act as if I'm killing you."

Said with such a public wave of his street-side hand that a yellow cab thought he was flagging it. The cruising driver slowed down to a walk and stuck out his capped head. Joe shook him off. The blue beard on that man, to whose tortured cheek does he apply that bristle? Puffing within the tent of her lavish flower print, an old married with dragging feet brushed against him. He smelled his share of the liberal sweat of her scorched exertions. Arrived at the year of his pimples, decked out in a porkpie hat, and two off-key eyes, a young hopeful revealed his vulgar longing for the Vienna woods as he whistled a path between them. Most grateful for all so far, where are more of these offscourings of dippyness and desire? Should he come close again to his Rosalie and ask her if she sees what he sees? No, not yet. For incensed as he is with love, and all witless seekers of it, a little birdie tells him that silence is still his best bet.

Sound what alarm in whose holy mountains? Who will ever be fool enough to listen to his three belligerent words a day as with the edge of his voice he slashes away at the spherical body of sense? Not even he will, not even he. Ah, in sleep alone does the voice rest, yet in dreams there is much talking. Who talks? What is it they say? Blabbermouths all, even there fear gives to their familiar faces a fast shuffle, and prankishly deranges their dreary pictures of the lower moiety of a man engaged in simulated warfare, of the quaint seed pods of his soul ripe

289

for a speedy corruption. So many words smack the air, but nothing is ever heard as in say, saying, said.

Say that when Rosalie kisses, she kisses as if she were sucking nectar. Say that often her teeth come into play as if to eat into the very winking of his eyelids, into the truthful and witty articulation of his bones. So much of life is built around the mouth. What are these baffling sounds in the shape of words which issue from it? No wren, crow, or robin need ever ask such a question. Cats of the same family are content to lick each other. One beetle easily grasps the full significance of another. But if a superior being like Rosalie collides with a higher animal like Joe, she begins at once to plead with him, tell me all about you, tell me, tell me.

But what is there to tell? She soon discovers that he can be dumber than the dumbest beast when it comes to confiding in her. One day out of the goodness of his heart he put his lips close to her nearest ear and offered to show her his navel. He was fairly sure she would make big eyes at that. She made a fist instead, a funny girl's fist with the thumb sticking out, and hit him squarely on the chest with the heel of it, and cried out at him, go to hell and stay there, do you hear me? Such a manly little fellow as she was, of course it was obvious she had completely forgotten she hardly knew him well enough to take such liberties with him, but he kept his head, and did not retaliate, as he was sorely tempted to do, by parting her hair in the middle or by caving in her nose, but waited until she had returned to her switchboard, and then he laced it into her over the phone, forcing her to listen as once again he asserted his unalienable right to be a closed book to any person, especially when she begins to make such improper use of her mitts and her mouth. Yet that very same night, he sat himself down to write her that famous letter.

What exactly did he write? As he turned himself inside out at the kitchen table with his sister's best note paper and her dappled fountain pen. To get within reach of what by going where? What was the burden of his noise? He thought that when he scribbled 'with an alacrity born of boldness' that he had 'no fear of being incriminated' if she knew that he too was waiting recklessly for 'the dawn of a brighter day' as on he ploughed like a stupid ox through 'the mire of life' that he was actually saying, here, this is what I am. He honestly thought so. Like a lunatic on a ladder, terribly younger than his years, he imagined he was scaling heaven as he proceeded to retch out his entire headful of purloined phrases, scrambling sincerity with sin, mixing guilt with heartiness, positive that the bite and sting of a wisdom hitherto unexpressed was clearly visible in the very ripples and undulations of his carefree handwriting. Frisk him further, what sort of a fool is he? If life, as he says, is for him but 'a lick and a sniff,' why is it he does not feel cheated? He is here for a moment, he will be gone the next. How can he say 'so be it' to that? Thus he entered into the simplest phase of his letter where meaning did seem to thicken in him, where he felt he was translating for her his proud no to what was, and his ironic yes to what was yet to be. In the meantime, what? Should he continue to womanize? Should he too build fantastic bridges of spit and blood between reality and desire? Should he bark freely in the more populated streets? Should he do his high-school suffering at home? Dear affliction, sweet little sister in distress, enough said, what more can he bombard her with except, perhaps, with this one last shell, be slow, he warned her mysteriously, in burying the dead.

Good grief, for such a letter, surely she will flop when next she sees him, and embrace his knees, and weep, and thank him to a delightful excess. Gape of a fish, shaky candle in a skull, this odd duck has his own way of quacking. As a matter of fact, as she was quick to tell him, she was very excited when she came home and found the letter in the box, and snatched it out, and ran immediately into the toilet in the hall where she could read it in private, not only once, but twice all the way through, which made her stay in there so long that her brother came out to pound on the door and ask her if she had fallen in or something, so naturally she had to flush the water and come out, and maybe it was because she was kind of tired after a hard day's work, but she had to confess that at least half of what she read was way over her head, so that maybe sometimes, it did not have to be right now, they could read it together, and he could explain it to her, and then she would know, especially that part where he said, what was he laughing about? And to think that he had hoped she would be able to decipher it for him. He asked her for the letter, and when she gave it to him like one hypnotized, he tore it into four pieces and put them in his pocket. He patted her cheek. Let her love as she loves. Let us, he said, forget that I ever wrote it, shall we?

And turn with the ease of those who are light of heart from the petty

291

and annoying sins of a man who is making progress to a cooler consideration of other subjects, as pure objects, of heaven and its hymns, of groves and twilights, of delicate maidenhair ferns, of brown buckwheat groats, namely grits, of suntan toilet seats, and Sacramento yellow cling peaches. For which of these, for a purifying second or two, can he show the least degree of desire? He never dreamed she had such thighs. The wide crack between the door and the floor gave him enough light to see by. He tried to remember. Did he breathe at all? Please, she begged him, come to this party, come and see me for the first time outside the place. Would that be safe? Would that be less sneaky? Should he do more than merely finger her at the factory?

He traveled across the bridge to that queer land in which she lived, and when he entered the railroad flat where it was exploding, there was a scream like a rebel yell, and the floor had a decided slope to it, and the Dixieland record ran down while everyone stared at this aristocratic boy she had given such a terrific build-up, and the bugeyed hostess handed him a blue paper hat in the shape of a cone, and a horn which he raised at once and blew, not knowing what else to do, and the whole gang laughed, and Rosalie took his hand and led him through a big long kitchen where barley soup was cooking and into a toy bedroom where he tossed his hat and coat on the heap piled up on the single bed, and he reached out for her like a sleepwalker, and she fell on him and tried to crush his mouth once and for all, and moaned, and pushed so hard against him that he staggered, and his nails caught in the scratchy material of her party dress, and was this love, or was it murder, what in the holy hell was it? Who was this most marvelous devourer?

He tried to keep his eyes in his head. He tried his best to keep from laughing as he fell against the door and closed it with a crash. He clutched her by her buttocks as there in the dark she pinned him. Would that every muzzler could thus save himself from a bad fall, and find such solid and delicious things to hold onto, but it was frankly a clumsy position to sustain, for her much too earnest arms had got themselves caught under when they should have been over, and one of her eager beaver feet had the peculiar idea that the first level of heaven was his instep, and her belly had slipped deplorably, and she was near to putting him out of commission with her seven blind knees, and maybe it was because he was wearing his old maize ones, but somehow his shorts had become crucially twisted in him, so he took away his hands from where they would soon return for a dividend and used them to help him arrange a more functional embrace, and slowly made her aware of her lips and steadied her into a simpler kiss so that the result at last was that for him too time did what it did for her, it stood still.

She to his gum of spearmint and he to hers of juicy fruit, no doubt there was a sleek little house mouse crouched at the cold iron leg of the bed who wondered what these usurping animals in their clothes would do to each other next. For what man intent on entrance is there who does not feel there is always some joker watching to see if he does or does not bungle it? So he must be nimble, he must be quick, he must, if it comes right down to it, shake her out of her useless swoon, and by suggestively plucking at what she wore, make her understand that the thing to do now, in all innocent haste, was to bunch her dress at the waist, and unhook her sheeny brassiere until it dangled, for did she not say to him, come and see me, come and see?

She flung back her head and gasped. What inflaming vision of what wet dream was this? She could have held a penny between her thighs without letting it slip. Certainly there is no question about it, panties should fit this snug else they would never shoot down to make such a cunning angle just where her hair must be that much lighter. The ringtailed roarer, he decided then that it would be wise to go back on his tracks before proceeding further, to blanket the fire a spell, to rest his lips on her shoulder and sniff her baby skin, but before he could do that, their tremendous eyes met, and suddenly the serious part of what went down in history as a nice evening's enjoyment was all over.

She tottered away from him and plumped down on the edge of the bed. You looked so funny, she giggled. You looked even funnier, he exploded. He did a lot of laughing, but she laughed much louder and longer. It seemed to be such a satisfying finish for her. As she stood up to piece herself together, she made believe she did not see what still stuck way out in him, what still fascinated her. She borrowed his comb to fix her hair. She wiped his lips for him. She tugged at his tie. She kissed him on the tip of his nose. She found his own hat and coat for him. She sentenced him to come back for more of the same in the same country. She walked out before him, shielding his spear. He left as he came, without saying a word to anyone.

Sceptic in trouble, if the northeast wind is the sky-clearing, and the northwest the sky-clouding, in the teeth of which whimsical sail clapper did he blunder back from his common voyage of discovery? Complicated airs did frolic round his pea-sized brain which had been blown upon by her fiery elemental breath. Lust is a haze in which, in spite of his suspenders, his pants must soon fall. What precisely was his for the asking in this opportunistic virgin who appeared to be more desirable than the most predatory daughter of joy? Cupcakes on Wednesday, newspaper kisses on Sunday, cumulative weekday dust, grinds of cigarette ends, sly fluff under the bed, frank phlegm, ferocious sessions according to her rhythm, resulting squawkers to circumcise, sameness, drearihood, and oblivion, to die a death in life so that she may live as she must, as the world wills it, all that and more can he have for the privilege of burying his nose in her cisatlantic armpits, of daily stomping up the stairs after her tenement butt.

Very tenderly expressed. Very. So her pink and possessive body will block his view, will it? Her insolent shadow will ever be in the way of his seeing. Of his seeing what? Rosalie as she is and will become? But who is Rosalie? What is she? A king crab? A barnyard fowl? A basking shark? A pillar of fire? A tiger of the sea? She is only a girl, sonny, only a girl. What can be so fantastic about that? Her simple human face is sharp with ordinary hunger. It seems to be listening for its kind of happiness as a bird seems to listen for its brand of worm.

Will it ever come to her through a wriggler such as he? Without him the world would still turn over, yet it is around him, and him alone, she feels she must move. So says the foolish knock-knock of her monogamous heart. And constantly assails him with the gush of its conventional cries. Bone of my bone, tie with me the true-lover's knot. Flesh of my flesh, fear not the twin temptation of my polygamous nipples, or my fever sore, or the perfect occlusion of my teeth. Honey child, do creep in and come in between me with the full sanction of the law. And that is the sum total of what is known as the catch to it, what Rosalie yearns for as she lowers her nubile lashes, and shyly exhibits the precocious jut of her marriageable behind. She is nobody's fool. Yet her blood has so tricked her that she is positive that the pleasure she promises her Joe-ship will easily last him his entire lifetime.

What then is marriage but the triumph of matter over mind? Four miscellaneous clowns can always be found to hold the four poles of the portable canopy beneath which such a union would be religiously consummated. The kids who squirm will be dragged out to do their duty. Those relatives who rarely drink will become ridiculously drunk. The mother of the bride will honk in her soaked hanky. A spiteful grammarian, she will further punctuate the untidy ceremony with her theatrical hiccups. The bearded joiner of hands will be the biggest attention grabber. The rich black sound of his Hebrew will stupefy these two pale English-speaking participants. For once the supercilious bridegroom will sing small. He will mumble what he has to repeat with a dreamer's mouth. He will meekly make his ring around Rosalie. He will somehow manage to crack down on the wineglass wrapped in a napkin with the terrifying force of either of God's own superstitious feet.

His will be done. The sheep are in the meadow. The cows are in the corn. She will tuck a doubled cushion under the small of her back. She will have no messy cherry for him to crack. Are these his drowsy days? Where on earth is he walking? Flashy silk weaver of his falsifying sex, he simply does not know how to wave his flag properly. He has yet to learn that the deepest graves are often dug in mid-air when, with too much picky thinking of the connubial, the bachelor mind finally blacks out.

"Save the pieces, sister. I sure got somewheres that time. Oh, my, yes. So are you listening? So what do you think I did right after that? Hook onto me and I'll tell you. I just took the million bucks and slapped it down for a new pair of eyes. Don't look so surprised. I'd do it again if I had to. Though I'll be damned if I feel I can see any better. Maybe you're the kiddo who can tell me. Why does a chicken cross the road? Halt. Who goes there? Look me right in the eyes now. When exactly does white become black? You're concentrating? You think it's true? Is tomorrow really another day?"

"You smoke too much."

"Only that?"

"I'm hungry."

"Please," said Joe. "Give it to me slow. Or you'll knock me over altogether."

"We just passed the station, did you know that?"

"So what?" said Joe. "So it'll be 14th Street. You always said you wanted to travel, didn't you? By the way. What were you humming there so nicely?"

"The last rose of summer. By the first Rosalie of spring. I felt so happy. Remember? Talk, talk, talk. I'm getting to be like you. I'm beginning to hate it."

"What should we do then? Make with our fingers?"

"We can go home and eat. That's what we can do."

"Home," said Joe. "There's a big deal for you."

"Sorry," said Rosalie. "That's the best I can do."

"Look, Rosalie. I must talk to you."

"Oy," said Rosalie. "Where does he get the strength for it?"

"Are you going to listen to me or not?"

"Did I tell you?" said Rosalie. "I went to the movies last night."

"Rosalie," said Joe.

"No, no," said Rosalie. "Wait. Don't get mad. I'm not trying to give you a run-around. I'm just trying to save you the trouble, that's all."

"What trouble? Where trouble?"

"You're such a bad boy, aren't you? You're really poison for me. That's right, isn't it?"

"Now, look, kiddo."

"Really," said Rosalie. "I was so glad my mother dragged me along."

"The hell with this girl. I can't talk to her."

"Movies again," said Rosalie. "You know how it is. I was just sitting there looking up at it, trying to forget my troubles when zowie, that big scene came. That was a swashbuckling hero? How could a twerp like that ever give me goose-pimples? Say, you know something? I don't feel so pooped any more. This is going to be fun."

"A ball of fire all of a sudden. When you take off, you really go zooming, don't you?"

"He loves me," said Rosalie. "He loves me not. I ought to kiss his hand. He makes life so interesting for me."

"Is that from the movie? Where the hell did that come from?"

"From deep inside of me."

"Goo."

"There," said Rosalie. "I guess that'll hold you for a while. So like I was saying. There they were up on the roof on a hot summer's night, stuck in the melted tar, a girl you could whistle at, and I wouldn't blame you if you did, and a boy who was a little bit too pretty for me. Where does a man get himself such a perfect Roman nose, and a widow's peak on a wavy head of hair? It can't possibly be the real stuff. Ah, well. I was just sitting there, watching them drool over those big, fake stars, when all of a sudden, what does the guy do but whack himself on the side of his head and bawl out at her, Mary, says he, we just can't go on this way any more. Well, now, I thought he meant you know what, but no, as it turned out, the poor sucker was all wrapped up in himself. Do you happen to have a Life Saver on you? Swell. I'll take a whole one this time. Don't worry. I can talk with it in my mouth. I happen to be what is called ambidextrous. Many thanks, my dear. So this Mary now, the adoring little woman, the typical wet rag, so sleek in her Hollywood permanent, with her rosebud lips, and large rouge spots, all she could do was look like she just swallowed the wrong way, and say to him, but why, darling, why? Came the flood. She had to ask? Ask me now. What exactly ailed him? She wasn't nuts about him? He had one foot in the grave? He had to have his teeth capped all over again? Look, he says, look at this world. He almost pushed her off the roof. It stinks, he says. Now that was brilliant. He suddenly discovered he had a nose. So she says to him, but sweetheart, I don't like it either. Oh, sure, says he, but not like me, you don't understand. I, says he, I'm a man, it's different. Ach, said my mother. What's this with you? You got ants? You can't sit still? Sit still. I said to myself, what is this anyway? Where did that idea ever come from that a man is more than a woman, that he needs more and has to go out and get more? A man. Did you ever notice it? As soon as he begins to shave once a week, he thinks he has to carry the whole world around on his padded shoulders. Honestly. I didn't know I was going to do it. But I clapped out loud, the couple smooching in front of me bust out laughing, when that rooster told his chicken up there on the silver screen that she would be better off without him, that he wasn't good enough for her. I got to get out of here, says he, I'll just die if I stay here. But where will you go? she says. What will you do? I don't know, he says, I don't care, all I know is I just got to get out of this dump and out into the world. Whoops, she grabs him around the neck. Then take me with you, she bawls. She almost dived right down into his tonsils. You must, please, you must. No, he says. Yes, she says. No, he says. They were pretty good wrestlers. I must say that for them. It got so damn

297

silly, I couldn't look any more. I said to my mother, you can stay here if you want, but I'm going home, I've had it. Go, she said, you make so much noise, I'll be glad to be rid of you. So I went home. Wow, was my bowels in an uproar. Isn't it terrible how we throw away our hard-earned money sometimes?"

"Aha," said Joe. "I see. So you thought that stupid ass was me, did you?"

"Excuse me," said Rosalie. "But I'm afraid I'll have to spit this out."

"Go ahead," said Joe. "The street is all yours."

"Foo," said Rosalie. "It always makes me so thirsty."

"Then don't ask me for it the next time."

"Don't worry," said Rosalie. "I probably will. It's your fault. You're always so sweet about it. You're not such a bad guy after all, are you? You know what? I think I'll hang on to you for another week or so and see what happens."

"That's right," said Joe. "Go on. Bore me. Give me some more of that junk."

"You," said Rosalie. "I'm surprised at you lately. So damn serious all the time. Why don't you relax? Why do you have to give yourself such a hard time? You'll get rid of me finally. If that's what you want."

"Hey, hey," said Joe. "It was a tough fight, Ma, but I won."

"Stop it," said Rosalie. "What are you grabbing me for?"

"Oh," said Joe. "Just to be sure I hear everything you say."

"Then listen," said Rosalie. "And stop trying to squeeze the life out of me."

"Another tender soul."

"I'm sorry," said Rosalie. "I know how you feel about it, Joe, but what can I do? The truth is the truth, isn't it? I can't hide it from you. How can I lie? Even if you hate to hear it, I must say to you, I'm sorry, Joe, but this is where I live, and these are my people. And so help me, there's nothing I can do about it. Even for you."

"Damn right," said Joe. "Even if you could, who the hell am I that you should?"

"I'm sorry," said Rosalie. "I'm a dope. I don't know how to say it any better."

"I always forget," said Joe. "How old are you?"

"Old enough to know better."

"It's a dirty trick. That's what it is."

"What is?"

"You change too fast," said Joe. "You're shooting way ahead of me."

"Me?" said Rosalie. "I'm a dope. I just told you."

"Okay," said Joe. "I know when I'm licked. I'll go with you to your house."

"Oh, no," said Rosalie. "Not that way."

"Quiet," said Joe. "I know what I'm doing."

"No, sir," said Rosalie. "I'm through giving you bitter medicine."

"Don't be such a sap."

"You keep my middle name out of it."

"How do you like that?" said Joe. "There's a woman for you. When I finally say yes, she begins to say no."

"I don't care," said Rosalie. "I don't trust you all of a sudden."

"Don't trust me?" said Joe. "What do you think I'm going to do?"

"The way you've been acting lately, who knows?"

"My dear Rosalie."

"Yes, darling?"

"Ah," said Joe. "How sweet. You answered me when I called. You're going to listen to me for a second. No wonder I can't tear myself away from you. Now don't misunderstand me, sweetheart. I like games. I like the way you've been playing this one, bouncing along so beautifully with right always on your side. You see? I admit that. Just to show you what a peculiar guy I am, I'm even rooting for you to win. Otherwise. You know what they say. All of life is still before us, kiddo. So let's step on it. Let's dive down. As for me, you don't have to worry. You'll have plenty of chances yet to fool around with that idea you love so much of you and me together. You don't have to worry. This is not the end yet. It never is until it is. There is always more to come."

11.

For as long as it takes him to do what? Joy of whose realer life is he that he should promise the sole object of his love's excess that his flaming quips and penetrating cackles will inevitably invade and illumine this darksome world of worriment and mirth? Spiraling away from the set orbit of assorted sidewalk bores and stray guttered losers, by what rude instinct does he stand so opposed to the superior swish and avowal of a flowering Rosalie he can hardly claim as wholly his? If this is not the end yet of his hopes of more happy accidents of topping himself, what is there to add to the marvels already mentioned? That he is an exceptional clod who can still pop his lips and click his tongue at casual tears and sneaky temptations? That in his high and proper earnestness he can be sentimental enough to believe that the silly body is the principal calamity of the sillier soul? That he can be a pompous grave lover and eater of unroasted peanuts on occasion? That in bold contradiction to this he is as often possessed by a vice more formidable than the greed for virtue itself, namely, the simple fondness for life as is?

Sorry companion of her own uncertain ways, tailing her like a dumb animal down the subway stairs, no doubt pacific oceans of space and sierra mountains of breath must first be invoked and expended before this prodigious nobody of nowhere can surface to a more believable level of his multimuddled life and become aware of what is actually happening to him. Which is simply that he has acquired a limp, blessed as he is with ankles so slim that sharp bits of stone and gravel, looking for a home, are likely to pop into the gaps devised by his beat-up oxfords, especially the less alert left one. As close as he can be to what he is fast becoming, he can hardly plop down on a splintered bench on the downtown East Side IRT 14th Street station without observing that all the tinier misfortunes will befall just that man who, in doubt as to his ability to take it, is ever anxious to have the most challenging disasters come crowding in on him even as he counsels himself to watch his step. Though the spectacular continues to elude him, as up on his feet again he grinds his heedless heel in some kind of fresh man-made muck, it is clear that here is one plain rusty sparrow who still suffers these lapses of viewing himself as a preening eagle perched on the topmost twig of an evergreen aspiration.

A precious high-flown image of himself which was pretty well shattered by the violent lurching of the train as the sullen silence between him and the rest of the world as represented by Rosalie was so riotously sustained. He was sure his seat was lumpier than hers. A double page inner spread of picture news came tumbling and flapping through the car to wrap itself around his right leg. Like his mind it said, I can go this far and no further. What a bore to be always kicking against bits of action, action everywhere, but not a single flitter or smidgen of sense. He turned his naked face upward to study the insulting ads. The diabolical cigarettes had never been whiter. The comic union suits clung as of old. Weary of being so critical, he proposed the same inane smile to a jar of slick cold cream as to a can of insipid baby food. What a comfort to know he would soon depart the stupid blip of this underground in the exact blundering way he had arrived.

What right has anyone who is such a belittler to be asking? Who cares who loves who around here in this vile stench and stretch of screeching hostility? How soon will every circumscribed arc of his lopsided rattling existence be smudged and swept away? He was ordinary enough to know. Every man carries with him his own safety curtain. He became as one totally blind on the bus they caught at Spring Street. His signs of life were reduced to the evenly spaced shooting pains in his lower jaw. It was still Rosalie no less who had to nudge him to hop off at her rotten overpowering Avenue D. While her spunky spirit was working itself free, his had to remain a tight little knot because of where he was and where he was going to be. She behaved like an unbreakable chain as she linked her arm with his. She began to radiate her own ideas. She strongly suggested she would always be grateful for the privilege of clinging to him. Hers was such a sacred idiocy. She seemed perfectly willing to be as patient with him in some impossible heaven as she had been for so long on this equally impossible earth.

Even as he sighed so wrapt was he in that sinful rip-off of wishing himself elsewhere that he had to encourage some ancestral elitist in him to emerge full-blown and stroll beside Rosalie like slowness in a toga personified, his purer noseholes pinched against this vulgar tree-less Lower East Side inelegance, suavely retreating behind such weary heavy lids to a more Latin country of the cypress and the coliseum, content to listen to the clashing of imaginary quoits, and rest where he can in the sexless shadows of sundials. Sensing which a loyal citizen of the neighborhood in the shape of a tricky male child snuck up at him from behind and powdered him precisely where he normally sat with the ample blue chalk on his trusty flat stick.

Bull's-eye. While the rank outsider stood there thunderstruck, wondering if what hit him was real, Rosalie yelled out, why, you little bastard, and took off like a hound on the scent after that wire-haired runt who did not exactly hoof it as kine unto their pastures move. But where he twisted she easily turned, zigzagging after him so cunningly that by the time they reached the corner mailbox, she had her foe in her hands, ready to be licked, stamped, and posted. One good smack would do it. Instead Joe was amazed to see that first Rosalie gave the kid a good bear hug, and after a quick game of butch-kepeleh with her hot head against his, requested and received the chalked stick with a sweet smile, and swinging out at the air with it like the wild thing she really was, began to giggle, delighted with this chance to pay tribute to the mongrel image of her own childhood.

To each his own. A brown paper bag of potato peels crashed at his feet and spilled out its guts. Death said, let me have a body. Prize view of such trash in its purest manifestation, as the plot against a man thickens, pride may forbid him to poke it aside with any of his available toes or be so easily sucked in to get the ball, mister. Before he knew it, he had already scooped up the battered red bouncer, and wheeling without looking where, uncorked such a wild throw that it was the candid opinion of a first-floor female with a rag of hair and an inflamed eye that he ought to be shipped right back to the minors. He could hardly agree more. He doffed his chapeau and bowed to her with a flourish, acknowledging how natural it was that she should become such an intimate part of his life, belonging as they both did to a race which believed it should continue to live, if only out of curiosity. As if to reward him for this something borrowed, something old, Rosalie and her crony came skipping back to whirl him around and flail away at his soiled seat with their bare hands, sharing the same delighted laugh each time he staggered.

Thus was he brought these so many steps nearer a destination he seemed to overdread. The squatters on the stoop shifted to each side to provide a lane through which Rosalie could proudly escort him. Other fascinated onlookers moiled about, contributing inaudible profundities. As the shy couple invaded the musty hall and began to climb the invisible stairs, a gasper of indefinite sex clattered past them on ghostly roller skates, nicking him on his prominent shinbone. He clutched his seeing eye, crunching on eggshells. His reluctant palm squeaked on the greasy banister. He could plainly hear the mysterious hum of twitchety animals, chewing the fat and creating smells in their airless hidey-holes. He balked. He called for lights. But Rosalie had already landed him safely on her floor. Pushing aside the baby buggy that blocked her door, she laid hands on the spook and pulled him into the glaring light of her aimless and perishable world.

"Aie," said Rosalie. "Tell me somebody. Is he worth all this trouble? Golly Moses, look at that face. What are you looking at in that way? You've been here before. Oh, my god. What smells here? Mamma? Where's Mamma? Ouch. Who in the hell put that there? Hangers, rubbers, what's all this junk doing on the floor? Where's Mamma? Damn it. I'm going to kill somebody around here. Hey, you, Jackie. I'm talking to you."

Her kid brother sat at the table with one shoe and sock off, picking at an infected toenail.

"You idiot," said Rosalie. "What are you doing there? Is this the place for it?"

"It hurts," he said.

304

He had wonderful fifteen-year-old eyes.

"Hurts?" said Rosalie. "I'll give you it hurts. You little slob. Can't you see who's here? Come on, now, beat it. Get out of here."

He limped out of the kitchen.

"You see that?" said Rosalie. "I always have to talk to him like a dog. God certainly gave me a brother, didn't he?"

"Yes," said Joe. "And him a sister."

"Oh, sure, sure," said Rosalie. "If you only knew what goes on around here. Where is everybody? They didn't eat yet, did they? Sit down. Take your coat off. Take mine too. Golly Moses. What's burning here?"

"You, I think."

"Do you blame me? Do you see what I find when I come home?"

"Well," said Joe. "The door is still open."

"Oh, no," said Rosalie. "No flying away for me. Close it like a good boy, will you? Gosh, I better shut off the gas here, but quick. The lazy dogs. Can you imagine that? They didn't even set the table. Drop that and come here a second. You know anything about cooking? What do you think this is?"

"Um," said Joe.

"What's um?"

"Looks like leather to me."

"Liver," said Rosalie. "Imagine. Leaving it flat that way. Oh, boy. Wait till they come back. Will I give it to them."

"That's okay," said Joe. "I like it well-done."

"Good for you," said Rosalie. "I hope you like your soup that way too. And what are these, pray tell me? Speak to me while I can still hear you. They can't be potatoes, can they?"

"I wonder," said Joe. "Are you sure you live here?"

"Oof, the steam."

"Who knows?" said Joe. "Maybe you landed me in the wrong place."

"Oh," said Rosalie. "Sit down. Didn't I tell you to sit down?"

"You mean like a guest?"

"Guest, hell. You see what kind of a guest you are?"

"Poor old Rosalie."

"You said it. What do you think I should do now? Should I put on the light again? Aw, let it all get cold. Who cares?"

"Excuse me," said Joe. "I think I see something."

"You do?" said Rosalie. "Where?"

"Is that a little leg or isn't it?"

"Why, it's Millie," said Rosalie. "Oo the little dreamboat. Look at her."

Millie the dilly the great big silly, she sits plump in the puddle she herself has made. Black are her snappers, the pristine coals of her eyes, her humorous hair honey-colored, prison is what she is playing, deliciously smearing her amorous snot all over her ladykin, her captive, her boobie doll. Make ah-ah-ah on the tussie because she is a meanie, Millie is, to be so young that her age can still be figured in months, a few days short of nineteen, dimmie a tiss. Aunt Rosalie, she is absolutely dippy about her.

"Oh," said Rosalie. "I'll kill her. That's what I'll do. You hear how she makes me talk to her? Gosh, what's happening to my knees? Excuse me while I squat. Where's my sweet face? Oh, no, you don't. Stop or I'll shoot. Run away from me, will you? Ah, that's a pussy. Come on, now, out you go. Watch the head now. Whoops. I got you. Monkey. Listen to her. Is that a laugh? Who ever laughs that way any more? Tickle, tickle. Let me see. You fat here? You very fat? Look at her, will you? Did you ever see such a delicious thing? I could eat her right up. Oh, yes, I could. Let me take a bite right here. A big big one. Oo-whah. What do you do with a kid like this?"

"You change her diaper."

"Ho," said Rosalie. "What the funny man say. Ha, ha. You no wear diaper. You wear panties. You a big girl. Isn't it a shame? She lets her soak this way for hours and hours. It's no use talking to her about it either. Off with the damn thing. Golly. They ought to put this in a museum. Look at that rash. You poor pussy. You come to me. You smell so awful, but I love you. Ah, that's it. Around the neck. You give your Aunt Rosalie a big hug and a kiss now. Oo, that's so good. Tighter. She loves her Aunt Rosalie, doesn't she? Look. See how she loves me? Say you love me, sweetheart. You love me? Say it, dear. You know how. Say it. Say you love me, honeybunch. Say it. You love me? Say you love me, darling. Say it."

"Otherwise," said Joe. "All you need is a tin cup."

"How do you like that?" said Rosalie. "She won't say it."

"Be proud," said Joe. "Beg her some more."

"Shucks," said Rosalie. "No luck with her either."

"If I may," said Joe. "Let me help you out of this."

"Oh, brother, do I need it. Wise little bird, isn't she?"

"They all are."

"Thanks," said Rosalie. "I know she can live without me. Am I all creased up?"

"Don't worry," said Joe. "I'll smooth you."

"Well, well," said Rosalie. "Come in, come in. I understand you all live here."

Hilda was ordained to be her sister, and Mack her brother-in-law, and her mother her Ma.

"You call this living?" said Mack. "Hey, boy. There's a puss I can love. Come on, Miss America, try again. Maybe you'll come out with something real cute this time. Ha. I got that one in quick, didn't I?"

"The man," said Rosalie. "He comes in first."

"Sure," said Mack. "Didn't you know? I push. That's how I get places. See me later and I'll show you just where. Beg pardon. And who can this gentleman be? Is that the bum we've been waiting for?"

"Bum," said Rosalie. "Look who's talking."

"What's he doing there? Playing hide-and-seek?"

"He was brushing me off."

"Really?" said Mack. "No kidding? Is that what you call it? Say. That I like. Step aside, brother, and let a man do it who knows how."

"One more step," said Rosalie. "And I'll bop you right on the beezer."

"Mack," said Hilda.

"Okay," said Mack. "Okay."

"I hope you'll excuse us," said Hilda. "We were right here all the time, but we were called upstairs to say goodbye to an old friend."

"Excuse us?" said Mack. "Upsie-pupsie. Ain't she the polite one?"

"Please," said Hilda. "I'm deaf enough as it is."

"With those enormous ears? Excuse us, hell. Who's been waiting for who around here?"

"Watch it, you nut. You're stepping on the kid."

"I see her, I see her."

"That's right," said Hilda. "Go ahead. Pick her up that crazy way. Break her arm or something. That's all we need yet. Trouble, I'm

307

telling you, it's got us surrounded. What's this cancer of the blood? What kind of a thing is that? How can that be?"

"Cancer of the what?" said Rosalie.

"I got a bellyache, Ma," said Hilda. "You think I should eat?"

"Bellyache," said Mrs. Heller. "My heart is ripped out."

"What heart?" said Rosalie. "Who are you talking about? Wait a minute now. Who's been sick in this building? Oh, my god. You don't mean Goldie, do you?"

"Yep," said Mack. "The chicken's cooked. You can mark her off."

"Oh, no," said Rosalie. "It can't be."

"Run upstairs," said Mack. "She'll be glad to hear that."

"Goldie?" said Rosalie. "That big husky one? I don't believe it."

"That's funny," said Mack. "That's just what the man said when they pulled the switch on him. He didn't believe it, but he sure in hell fried. Which reminds me. Hey, bud, come here a second. You look like a regular guy. Did you ever hear the one about the gazook who was sick in bed and his old lady trots up to him and says to him."

"Mack," said Hilda.

"Or the one about the, let me tell this one, this is really a pip."

"Gee whiz," said Rosalie. "What is this lately? A contest or something? One after the other. Everybody dropping off like flies. Who's the boss around here? Who's in charge of this show anyway? Where is that guy you call God? What's he trying to do to us here?"

"Brilliant," said Mack. "Now me. So you hear? Listen to this one. Five little girls are playing hospital in the basement when the janitor sneaks up to them with a hot-water bottle and bending over the smallest one."

"Mack," said Hilda.

"Goddamn it," said Mack. "What in the hell is this? Did you ever see such a nag? Always on top of me."

"Mack," said Hilda. "I'm talking to you."

"Okay," said Mack. "I hear you, I hear you."

"Wasn't it just a gorgeous day?" said Hilda. "Did you people get a chance to enjoy it? Aren't men the devil? Funny animals. What kind of pleasure do they get out of telling such nutty stories? I'm sorry. I don't know why I'm coughing. That's all right, Joe, you can smoke. Only the next time, please, don't give Mack. He'll scrounge all you got if you'll let him. Ah, you look fine, Joe. Real nice. You really do. I've been looking at you. Why don't you sit down? There are plenty of seats here for everybody. Don't stand there like a stranger. Here. Take this one. Aie, what's this object doing here?"

"Oh," said Rosalie. "Just settling down for a long rest. Your lovely daughter's. A dainty article, ain't it?"

"Well, now," said Hilda. "Aren't you a fine one? You didn't have to leave it on a chair, did you? He'll think this is the way it always is. Here, Mack, throw it in the washtub. Take it, I said. Nasty little kid. Does it just to spite me, that's all. How's the job, Joe? They keep you busy these days? Oh, guess what, Rosalie?"

"I'd rather not."

"I weighed myself today."

"Good," said Rosalie. "Have fun. I don't mind."

"I mean," said Hilda. "On the same scale outside the drugstore. And would you believe it? I gained a whole pound since yesterday."

"On what?" said Mack. "On three Indian nuts?"

"Ah," said Hilda. "Don't worry. I know what I'm doing. I'm really after it now. I'll get back what I lost or bust. Or bosom. Or whatever. Move that ashtray over. More. He has to use it too, doesn't he? That's my Mack for you. How do you like him so far? He's the one I had to go and marry. Did this ever happen to you, Joe? I mean, all of a sudden, you don't know why, but you take a good look at yourself in the mirror, and golly Moses, like Rosalie says, you say to yourself, who the hell is this who looks just like a pointy old pencil? Did it happen over night? I still can't figure it out."

"Keep trying," said Mack. "It'll come to you. Here's your chance, Joe. If you want to leave the room, just raise your hand."

"Please," said Rosalie. "Let her talk."

"Are you kidding?" said Mack. "Can you ever stop her?"

"Do I hear right?" said Hilda. "Is that his sweet voice again? Did I ever tell you, Joe. I dream about him. I wake up in a sweat, my eyelashes sticky. Can't stay on his side. Pushes me. Pokes me. Blows in my ear. I have to get off the bed six times a night to shove my head out the window. Otherwise I'd suffocate. And then the light comes. And I thank god. And I look at him, and I say to myself, who is this man? Where did he come from? What does he want from my poor life? What?"

"Jesus," said Mack. "I keep thinking about it. Did I draw me a royal

309

flush the other night. Once in a lifetime. All I had to do was lay down the cards and rake in the pot. Only we had to be playing for toothpicks. That's what killed me."

"Here," said Hilda. "You see this, Joe? You see this place right here on my finger? Absolutely nothing there, but it's been itching me for days. I feel like taking a knife and cutting that spot right out. I'm bothered. Why do I let myself be so bothered? Maybe Mack's right. What else am I good for? Okay. I think I'll say yes. I think I'll have me another baby."

"Another what?" said Rosalie.

"Why not?" said Hilda. "Let's make it real crowded around here."

"Mamma?" said Rosalie. "Where's Mamma?"

"Let's pile up the misery while we can. Let's get really good at it. Champs, like Mack says."

"Oh, shut up," said Rosalie. "That's enough already. Really, Hilda. What goes on with you anyway? What do you do all day that you can't find time to comb your hair?"

"It isn't combed?"

"Disgusting," said Rosalie. "Look at it. Hanging down the sides like a witch."

"It is?" said Hilda. "But I just combed it."

"You worry me," said Rosalie. "Have you been doing anything to your eyebrows? Who are you when you're you? What's happening to you lately?"

"Well," said Mack. "It's this way."

"It is?" said Rosalie. "I had an idea you would be the only one who could tell me."

"Who else?" said Mack. "Wait until you hear. There once was. You're sure you want me to talk? You better tell me now if I have your permission. I've been so damn busy lately with nothing, I hate to waste my time."

"I'm all ears," said Rosalie. "Can't you see?"

"That's your problem," said Mack. "So all right. So there once was what is called a woman. And then there was another one. And another one. Until by cracky the whole world was crawling with them. And that's when the world went phtt, just like that. And you know why? Because men had to go and live with them. That little whangdoodle there that lives below the belt told them it would be a terrific thing to

310

do. So the jerks, they went and did it. What is this? You're not squashing me yet? Thanks, Joe. You're making them act like ladies for a change. So what is it I'm really asking you, my friends? I'm not asking you to flood me with money. I, personally, hate the stuff. All I want you to give me is just one rag, one little rag to wipe this kid's nose with. If you're wondering. I once tried to sell nutcrackers, Joe. Do you get the picture now? Does that explain it?"

"You dope," said Rosalie. "Why are you putting the baby on the table? Don't you know we're going to eat there in a second?"

"Look," said Mack. "You see? That's my wife right there. If she wants to call me a dope, that's okay with me. But not you, understand?"

"Oh, dear," said Rosalie. "I insulted him."

"Another goddamn woman on my head. I'm beginning to feel like one myself."

"God forbid," said Rosalie. "That would be awful. Where would we get the clothes for you? Don't just sit there like a dummy. Get up there and do something about it before it happens."

"I will," said Mack. "I'm going to separate your head from your body."

"Mack," said Hilda.

"Look at him," said Rosalie. "His hands are shaking."

"That's okay," said Mack. "Keep talking. Just give me a chance to roll up my sleeves. It'll only take a second. A real wiseguy. She thinks just because this guy's here, she can, ow."

"Boom," said Mrs. Heller.

"Jesus," said Mack. "What in hell hit me?"

"You," said Mrs. Heller. "You don't get soup."

"The hell I don't," said Mack. "I got it all over my head."

"Oh," said Rosalie. "What a clunk. Can she handle a spoon or can't she? Oh, I'll die laughing. Take him away from here. I can't look at him. Did you see that, Joe? Did you see how she did it? Oh, Ma, you're a real pip. You're absolutely wonderful."

His unrelated and crueler eyes looked but could not agree. Mrs. Heller, then, who is she actually? What does she look like? She is a cat-and-doggish character with canalboats for feet. She confronts a body. She scratches out of her scalp the scurf of a flaky self-distrust. She has scads of hair on her bulky forearms. She has a strawberry

311

patch on her left cheek. She constantly doctors herself. She is shingles. She is varicose veins. She is fluid in the inner ear. She has turbaned her aching head with a stolen hotel towel. She is fearful of losing her lumpy identity in the neglected spaces in her skull. She has no apparent neck she can scrub. She is thick in her leaning forward. She sees through people. She sours the air with her ancient mother smell. She howls when she catches herself in the act of loving for the fun of it. She has buried one inept husband, two spinster sisters, and three male misshapen babies. She often dreams she is riding the waves. The next morning she hides a herring behind the sink. Is she so far-gone then? What common disgust is her saving grace? Her heart, her mammoth heart, regularly dislodged, lashed, ripped out and trampled upon, yet it ticks, it twitches, it carries on, a permanent stay-at-home, sneering at that which comes to it without human design or forethought, defying the powers that be and those yet to come. She crunches on random crusts of bread so that the fires of her wrath may be continually fed. So that she may be humbled, the sun and the moon, and all the host of heaven are spread out before her, but she has made her face harder than a rock. Wizards in high places are arrayed against her so that nothing of her shall be left, but she laughs at their cellophane, scotch tape and tiebacks. All hail to Mrs. Heller, she is one dame who is mad enough to believe that when she dies she will not be dead.

"Foo," said Mrs. Heller. "This is the good one who loves me? Murderer. Look at the present she brings me. He comes. He sits. He looks and he looks. A new golem. He'll change the world for me? Hoo-hah. Such a gentleman. You hear what he says? He's says he's glad to see I'm looking so fine and healthy. Rosalie's Mr. Joe. Another liar. Maybe you want to kiss me too? Come. Don't be bashful. So you'll smell from me a little, so? What now? Am I sitting on the floor? Where is he looking? A pisher yet. God should give him my troubles. Then he'll know."

"Mamma," said Rosalie. "Please."

"Please," said Mrs. Heller. "All I hear here is please, please."

"I must say," said Rosalie. "You sure do have a beautiful way of saying hello to company."

"Wow, yes," said Mack. "Why don't you treat him like you did me? Why don't you just haul off and conk him on the head?"

"Sorry," said Mrs. Heller. "He's not mine yet."

312

"Thank god," said Rosalie. "I'm beginning to be sorry I am."

"Who needs him?" said Mrs. Heller. "Such eyes I should have here yet?"

"My fault," said Rosalie. "My fault. I should've called the whole thing off."

"What's the matter, darling? Something is hurting you?"

"I take it all back," said Rosalie. "Today you're worse than a rabbi. Today you are absolutely not wonderful."

"So?" said Mrs. Heller. "So wait until tomorrow."

"Gosh," said Rosalie. "You think I'll still be alive by then?"

"My healthy one," said Mrs. Heller. "She's dying already."

"Help," said Rosalie. "Who will help me? Run for the hills, men. The dam has busted."

"What damn," said Mrs. Heller. "Who damn? Fresh. No respect for your Mamma? You want me to klop you?"

"That's the stuff," said Mack. "Get hot, kid. Pour it on, the both of you. Make it real goofy now. Give us the whole works. See what I mean, Joe? I used to love to go to the circus. Now I don't have to. I get it all for free right here."

"Mack," said Hilda. "The baby is eating a hairpin."

"Boing," said Mack. "Right on time."

"Mack," said Hilda. "I'm talking to you."

"Maack, Maack. What did I hook up with here? A nanny goat?"

"Oh," said Hilda. "What's the matter with you? Can't you keep quiet? What are you always butting in for?"

"The guy has to know, doesn't he?"

"Know what?" said Hilda. "Oh, this is terrible. Really. I'm so ashamed. I bet he thinks we're this way all the time."

"So he thinks," said Mrs. Heller. "So?"

"Ah, Mamma."

"Ah," said Mrs. Heller. "You three fools."

"Three?" said Mack.

"You think I was sleeping?" said Mrs. Heller. "You think I didn't see how you begged him with your eyes to listen to you? It's the end already if this happens. A boy. A snotnose yet. And they fight like dogs in the street to talk to him. All of a sudden he's a chocolate soda. He's a month's rent. They can't go to the toilet without him. They'll jump from the roof if he doesn't lick them and say I love you. Why?

What is he? A god? He'll give happiness? He'll support you? He'll make you a millionaire? No, no, Rosalie. Let him talk. He's got a mouth. Let him tell me. Who is he here? What does he want from us? What?"

Only death could be ruder. Clucks and excited females, heedless and high-heeled gap jumpers, ill-devised and looser assemblages of furious atoms, hairy cranks with broken nails, tumorous and feral queen bees, raging sows, monstrous spring-a-leakers, they certainly can make a mere pipsqueak sweat in his second-day collar as he gulps down his pride and girds himself to asnwer as lightly as he can such thrilling and Hellerish damnifications. Why lightly? Is he the kind who does not care if he is caught delicately pissing away the time, while others cast off all restraint and spit on every written and oral law? If it is her rule to rise at six o'clock and shatter the morning hush with her rapid collisions with whatever scarred table or broken chair blocks her balmy way, is it his habit then to milk the evening of the same day of its gigantic toomle by squeezing out of it a quick succession of twilight sounds such as those made by swishing silk or shaking leaves? Perhaps it is he who is really the creepy and fearsome one. Perhaps she has to hurl her inexhaustible stock of sticks and stones at him because she senses that he wants so much more than she will ever know, and so much less than she can ever imagine.

"My dear Mrs. Heller," said Joe.

"Yes? Yes?"

"It seems to me the least I can do."

"Yes?"

"Is to tell you that the reason why I've been so quiet."

"Go find a stamp, Rosalie. He's writing me a letter."

"Is that I've been sitting here and wondering."

"Aha? So?"

"Tell me," said Joe. "I'm really anxious to know. What do you call it here? Dinner or supper?"

Hog of the world's wit. He held his breath as she tried to stare him down. The swollen muscles of her face slowly subsided as she tore the turkish towel from her head. Supreme contempt for his slippery ways silenced her. So that was the sum and substance of what he wanted to know. So now, of course, she would have to break her neck to bring on the bellycheer. She would have to hitch up her apron and scrape around and serve him. Her eyes wished him war in all its ways.

So that as of now he knew that simple hunger was not to be the principal cause of his eventual death. Still snarled in all the follicles of her flesh, weary of the incessant double shuffle of his mind and the hula-hula of his heart, he made a great effort like a gallant warrior to steady and sustain his failing separateness by concentrating on the clitterclatter of the tarnished cutlery as Rosalie fetched it out in handfuls as if for an army waiting to be fed. Mack swept Millie off the table. Hilda yelled for Jackie with each plate she planted. When he failed to appear, Mack went to locate him and brought him back by the scruff of the neck, firmly guiding the mutt of the family to the smell of near meat.

Peeping into the kennel of Jackie's world, how comforting it was for Joe to see again a boy's magnificent disgust with the miserable fluster and fuss of older people. Clumsy bellyachers, let them, if they so wish, be agitated by illogical ideas and peculiar emotions. They are the clawing ambitious ones here. Let them gather figs where thistles grow, or thrash around to try to teach the fishes how to swim. Jackie in his fearful purity would sit there where they so arbitrarily sat him down. He would eat absolutely for his own sake. When he saw the soup coming, he grabbed a spoon in one hand and a slice of rye bread with the other. He scowled. They were serving that man first. But that man knew at once what to do. He passed his plate to him immediately.

"Oh, no, you don't," said Rosalie. "You give that right back."

"That's all right," said Joe. "I can wait."

"Please," said Rosalie. "This is for you, not him. Look at that. He's gobbling it up already. You little pig. Didn't you hear me? Okay. You like this ear of yours? Hah? You want me to hand it to you? Ah, that's a good boy. You hear me now, don't you? Next time don't be so quick to take, understand?"

"Hey," said Mack. "Did you see him give her that evil eye? You're sunk now, beautiful. He'll cut off all your buttons again."

"Oh, yeah?" said Rosalie. "I'll sew them right on to his pretty little head if he does."

"Ha," said Mack. "See how quiet he sits there? Jack, my boy, show the man there your baby-blue eyes. Like looking way down a shaft. A lot of people think he's an ignorant little bastard. But don't kid yourself. That kid there knows the score. No dame's going to cross him up

315

and get away with it. No, sir. He knows a million ways how to get even."

"Oh, sure," said Rosalie. "And who shows him how?"

"Me?" said Mack.

"You," said Rosalie. "Partners in crime. A new thing we got here."

"You said it, judge."

"Silence in the court."

"I should say," said Mack. "What else? By the way, your honor, when you bring me my soup, and I do hope it's before midnight, just try to keep your dainty little finger out of it, will you?"

"Toothpicks," said Rosalie. "Look what she's carrying in. Will you please come over here and sit down, Hilda, and keep an eye on this so-called man of yours? Squat, I said. I'll do the rest. Please, Joe. You eat. I'll be with you in a minute. Start. Don't listen to this new pal of yours. Eat, eat."

"Yes, ma'am," said Joe.

"Oh, boy," said Mack. "What did I tell you? A riot, ain't she? I'm absolutely nuts about her. Imagine me living in the same house with a fairy princess like that. Oh, so lovely to look at, that's for sure, but to listen to sometimes? Whew, don't ask. You better watch out, bub. One more yes ma'am out of you like that, and she'll have you eating right out of her hand. I'm changing chairs and moving over next to this guy. Any objections here? Well, I'll be damned. Shake, pal. Today I am suddenly a man."

"It must be terrible not to be sure."

"You can say that again."

"It must be terrible not to be sure."

"How about that?" said Mack. "Ain't he lucky? I think I'm beginning to like him. Hold the phone a second. Is that a piece of meat you got floating there?"

"Yes," said Joe. "And it looks to me like it's yours."

"Arf," said Mack. "Say. I didn't know I was so hungry."

"I can eat a little myself."

"So?" said Mack. "What do you hear from the mob?"

"The usual."

"They tell me you're from Brooklyn."

"It's no secret."

"Got a cousin in Bensonhurst," said Mack. "Used to be a bookie."

"Good for him."

"Sells barber supplies now."

"Not so good."

"Say," said Mack. "Maybe I should look him up. Naa. Not that mug. He'll never do anything for me. Not too bad a tie for a knitted one. Ever play baseball?"

"Just about every day for years."

"Let me see," said Mack. "I'd say right field."

"No," said Joe. "More like shortstop."

"Could be," said Mack. "Take a gander at this. See this thumb? Broke it twice behind the bat."

"Hell, that's a tough position."

"You said it," said Mack. "But that's me. You wouldn't believe it looking at me now, but I used to be a pretty husky boy in the old days. And busy like a cockroach. Had me a flock of pigeons once before this gal here came into my life. Know anything about them?"

"No," said Joe. "Except they can let fall and fly."

"That they do," said Mack. "Around and around like my head the morning after. Wow. You must be kidding. All this for me? Well, thank you kindly, my pet. I know I don't deserve it, but. Throw us a hunk of bread there, Jack. Attaboy. Hears well, don't he? My pal. I really get a kick out of him. You know what he did last Sunday? Mind if I tell him, Jack? He pasted up his eyes. With what was it, Jack? And kept it on all day. Hell, I guess the kid's got a right to do it if he wants to, but finally I had to say to him, what the hell, Jack, what's up, what's the idea anyway? So he said to me, this is the idea, I want to know how it feels to be blind. How about that? Ain't that something now? And they go around saying I'm the one with the cuckoo ideas around here. What's the market on characters? You think we can rent him out?"

"All set now?" said Rosalie. "Is everything on the table?"

"Yes," said Hilda. "We're eating. It's okay now. Get Mamma."

"I'll try," said Rosalie. "Mamma. Mamma, dear. Whew. I'm so hot I could die. Mamma, please, don't make believe you don't hear me. Come and sit down. May I show you where, madam? Fine. You naughty girl you. You look so worn out, I hate you. Napkins. Shoot. I knew there was something I forgot."

"Sit," said Hilda. "I'll get them."

"You know which ones?"

"I know," said Hilda. "You told me."

"Told you," said Rosalie. "Fat lot of good it did me."

"I'm sorry," said Hilda.

"Don't be silly," said Rosalie. "You think my whole life depends on it? I should always have such troubles. My, but that bread's disappearing fast. Good. I like to see that. Some more bread here, Hilda. Give these men here some more bread. Use that butter too. Use it all up. Heigh-ho. What's tomorrow to us? If we're eating, let's eat, that's what I say. Excuse me, sir. Do you happen to have anything on you to fan me with? Or should I go and put my head out the window permanently? Ah, look at him. Poor Joe. Ain't it incredible? How did I manage to get you here? Did I twist your arm? I seem to remember. Was that me down on my knees, begging you to come?"

The very shape of the jest danced in her eyes. His poor old plight, it had two heads now, his and hers. It was such a delightful situation. She laughed like a spendthrift, sending him a generous spray of her sweet vegetable breath. Every frail should grow as plump in her perplexity, and her lips as swollen in the pouting position, and her cheeks as proud of the telltale suffusion of their positive blood, and the breast with which she tips his arm as nigh to bursting in its skintight pod, and her formidable thigh as shapely and encouraging to the hand which fondles it as a man's healthy hand should after it has snaked itself under the table.

"And what," said Rosalie. "If I may so ask. **What** strikes you there as being so funny?"

"Are you undressing me?" said Mack.

"Yes, you," said Rosalie. "Sitting there and looking at me as if."

"As if what?" said Mack. "You see why I'm dotty about her? All I have to do is give out with just one little smile and she jumps right into my arms. Feet first."

"What's the matter?" said Rosalie. "Didn't you ever see me before?"

"Not this way, kiddo."

"Really?" said Rosalie. "And what does that mean?"

"You don't have to worry," said Mack. "He knows what he's got there."

"Oh, god," said Rosalie. "That's exactly what I'm afraid of."

"I should be so afraid," said Hilda. "Which reminds me. I saw the funniest thing the other day. I say funny. It really wasn't. You know

318

how these things are. I was standing on the stoop, burping the baby, when all of a sudden they came charging out right past me. What's the good of a fight in the house? It has to be out in the street. They love to give a show. They want everybody to enjoy it. What does Mr. Eklowitz do, Ma? I mean when he's working. Is he the pants presser? Or is that Mr. Hyman on the fourth floor to the back? Anyway, Lillian, Lillian Elkowitz, there's something nice about that name. And boy, what a name she's got. I don't have to spell it out for you, do I? I wonder what she charges? More for the old and less for the young? I once had a girl friend in school. She was so ugly you could hardly tell her from a rhino. Yet all the boys were after her with their tongues hanging out. Sure, I know. You can build up quite a bank account with men that way. But I know Lillian. I'm sure she doesn't do it only for pin money. She likes doing it, damn it. Go do her something. At least she brings what she makes into the house. What else would the two of them live on? Excuse me. What's this supposed to be? I thought we were having chops."

"Chops," said Mack. "Wait a minute. Don't tell me. That's something you eat, isn't it? Or is it part of your face? Explain yourself, woman. Let's have no fiddle-faddle around here."

"I don't understand it," said Hilda. "Wasn't there enough money for chops?"

"Money," said Mack. "There's another one. Seems to me I've heard that word before."

"That," said Hilda. "That is what you used to make."

"Sonofabitch," said Mack. "This is how. As you can see. This is how with one word she always makes hash out of me."

"Of course," said Hilda. "That's the first thing I must do when I wake up. Naturally. So as I was saying. They got right out in the middle of the sidewalk and there they squared off. They sure do look like each other. He's a nice looking man, isn't he, Ma? Ha. I can remember when he used to come home from work. He'd catch hold of me and give me little slaps here and there. Only they weren't really slaps. I was only a kid then. Seven or eight at the most. But I already knew what I was made for. You learn fast in this stinking neighborhood. Only I never could understand why a big hulk of a man like that would want to fool around with a little pimple like me. What could he actually do? I mean, how was it possible? Ma was the watchdog. She

319

used to yell to me from the window every time she saw him coming, didn't you, Ma? They say that right after the mother died, he and his daughter. Of course I have no way of knowing how true it is, but everybody on the block tells me that's how she got started. Anyway. There's one thing you can say about Lillian. No matter what the time is, she always comes home to sleep. That I approve of. What puzzles me though is why he waits up for her. Could it be he's jealous? Boy, did he stand there and give her the works. He has to tell. If everybody knows about it, right away he feels better. I ask you. Aren't people something? Aren't they now?"

"Okay," said Mack. "He says yes. You can continue."

"Thank you," said Hilda. "That was exactly my intention."

"Talking and chewing at the same time. How the hell do you do it?"

"I'm a woman," said Hilda. "I know how."

"Hey, hey," said Mack.

"And Farmer Grey to you," said Hilda.

"Mercy," said Mack. "You sure are a sizzler tonight, ain't you?"

"God, yes," said Hilda. "But what's the use? Tomorrow I turn back into a pumpkin. Control yourself, mister. What you got on your mind, I'm not in the mood for. Are you the animal of the week? You and Mr. Elkowitz. I was talking about him, wasn't I? Now let me see. In what position did I leave him? Oh, yes, the usual. He was bulging out there in his pants, making with the thunder. And Lillian was standing there with her legs very tight like a model, with one knee stuck out like come and get me. And with such a smile. You know. Ye gods. He was just a man to her. No wonder. Anyway. Every time he would come out with a new name, he would haul off and spit at her. Down, I mean. Right at her feet. He was a pretty good shot. He would hit her shoes two out of three times. The only thing was that after a while he began to run out of spit. He kept on making the same motions, you know, with his head and his mouth, but nothing came out. Well, that finished me. I knew it was silly, but I couldn't help myself. I had to explode. I laughed so hard that he began to laugh too, looking at me. I said to myself, what a thing, isn't this wonderful? I mean. Here was a man who was over the river already with his life, in a real fix, and yet he could see himself as I saw him. I ask you. What's the matter with people today? How can they still take themselves so seriously? When things get this tough, it all becomes ridiculous, doesn't it? What does it mean today when you cry? Or sleep? Or go to the toilet? Who's kicking me? Or work? Or don't work? Can anyone tell me? Why do we go on living like this? What does anything mean any more?"

"The salt is here," said Mack. "But I don't see the pepper. I'm in kind of a whirl. Do I talk in my sleep? How did this woman here know what I was thinking?"

"You hear that?" said Rosalie. "She's stealing from him again."

"It's really aggravating," said Mack. "Here I was waiting for a chance to come out with something like that, and she goes and beats me to it."

"What a shame," said Rosalie. "My heart bleeds for you."

"Excuse me," said Mack. "Is that your natural color? Or do you always get this purple when night falls?"

"If you're asking me if I'm angry," said Rosalie. "You're goddamn right I am."

"What in hell for?" said Mack. "Who said anything to you?"

"Of all the dopey speeches I ever heard," said Rosalie. "You mean to sit there and tell me you agree with her?"

"Except for that work stuff, absolutely."

"Then you're just as crazy as she is."

"Jesus," said Mack. "Is this girl young."

"And how old are you, if I may ask?"

"You don't know a goddamn thing yet, do you?"

"No, Papa," said Rosalie. "You can wave a stick at me. I'm just a poor little ignorant pigeon. Can you imagine the nerve of the guy? Sits there and eats like a horse. And then he tries to tell me he doesn't want to live. Nothing means anything any more. Ho, ho. All together now. We might as well laugh it all off."

"From one mouth to the other," said Mack. "I sure got luck tonight."

"Luck, hell," said Rosalie. "It would be a lot better if you had a little more gumption."

"Right," said Mack. "I can see. You're beginning to get the idea, pal. That little girl there feeds me. She lets me sleep here. She brings the money into the house. She can talk to me any way she wants."

"Aw, now," said Rosalie. "Don't be so sensitive. What did I say? I didn't say anything like that, did I?"

321

"Of course not," said Hilda. "He's just a little tired, that's all."

"Tired?" said Mack. "What in hell have I got to be so tired about?"

"Here," said Hilda. "Let me have your plate."

"What for?" said Mack. "I'm finished. Anybody can see that."

"I said," said Hilda. "Let me have your plate. That's better. Anybody here for more mashed? Mustn't leave anything over, you know. You, Joe? Are you all right? Can I help you with anything?"

"No, no," said Joe. "Thanks. I have enough."

"You're sure?" said Hilda.

"Oh, yes," said Joe. "Plenty. Don't worry about me. I'm fine. I'm all right."

So all right it seemed to him shameful. Ghost of a guest. He charmed his mouth with a slice of charred liver. Fear suggests flight. Fear of what? How incredibly kind of them to let him listen as they nitpick and wrangle until their permanent sores for his benefit are laid bare. This is a fork. This is a hair. This is a home where each sits by each in his or her inflexible eachness, living together. Or so they say. This is where this man will soon be like that man. Sheness all pervasive and dominant. A woman's hair is much too long to be swallowed. The more desperate kitchen highfliers are inclined to be mostly men. They do believe that when a woman gives before she takes, whether she be referred to as low bridge or high-pockets, when she revels in her role of dynamic receiver, she is sure she alone is the kissable one. Once again it seems that position is everything. Curious that when straddlers of the subnovice kind, such as he knew he was, first attempt a similar joy ride, they will often land at the nearest stop light which glows as red as their realization that they have been cherishing the wrong thing between their legs.

"Bless you," said Rosalie.

"Wow," said Joe. "That one sure caught me."

"It happens."

"Sneezing is good sometimes. It wakes you up."

"I'm glad to know you were sleeping."

"I mean," said Joe. "It clears the head."

"Not me," said Hilda. "Me it makes dizzy."

"It does?" said Joe. "I guess it depends on how many times you do it."

"Do what?" said Mack.

322

"Sneeze," said Hilda.

"Oh," said Mack. "For a second there I thought you were talking about."

"Never mind," said Hilda. "We know, we know."

"I like the way men grin," said Rosalie. "Don't you?"

"Love it," said Hilda. "So Joe? Tell me. How's the old job? They keep you busy?"

"You already asked him that," said Rosalie.

"I did?" said Hilda. "When?"

"For crying out loud," said Rosalie. "Why do you keep harping on his job? Job. His job's all right. Can't you find anything else to talk about?"

"Okay, then," said Mack. "I'll take a chance. Watch me go. And where I'll land I'll never know. Did anyone here ever play chess by mail? Or fix a flat tire with spit? Or run scared with your ass glued to your chair? Do I hear anyone ready to take over? Or try to have a good heart to heart talk with a woman's foot down your throat? Who knows dummy talk around here? Please. If you'll all keep your seats, I will now do an imitation of a man who's just lost his dearest lady friend. And is damn glad he has. I see I can't climb the next fence. So I'll have to call the whole thing off. Well, that all flopped, didn't it? A funny thing. Now that I've licked every inch of my plate, I'm not so hungry any more. What a business. You chuck something in your belly and you get all puffed up. You begin to spread out in all directions. You think you can lick the whole world again. Lick. Get it? You give me enough room and I can spill over this way every day. And deep into the night. For instance. I beg your pardon. You were about to say?"

"I've been thinking," said Joe.

"Oh," said Mack. "So you're that kind, are you?"

"What are you like when you're working?"

"When I'm what?" said Mack.

"You can hardly remember, can you?"

"No," said Mack. "But I sure in hell keep trying."

"Job," said Joe. "It's a rotten business any way you look at it."

"It is?" said Mack. "How so?"

"Because," said Joe. "Believe me, with so many people out of work these days, it's just as tough to have a job as to be without one. Did you ever think of that? Think about it. Maybe it'll make you feel better."

323

"Applesauce?" said Rosalie.

"Feel better," said Mack. "Okay. I'll do you a favor. I'll let it work on me. If you mean it's rough on everybody, I agree. But I can tell you this, pal. I'd rather be in the spot you're in any time."

"Who knows?" said Joe. "Maybe I can swing it for you somehow."

"Applesauce?" said Rosalie. "I'll keep saying it until somebody hears me."

"What?" said Mack. "I'm sorry, Joe. But with all this racket around here, I didn't get what you said."

"Why not?" said Joe. "Somebody has to get it."

"Get what?" said Mack.

"For the last time," said Rosalie. "Applesauce. Yes or no?"

"Goddamn it," said Mack. "Put it down, will you? We'll eat it, we'll eat it. Can't you see this guy's trying to tell me something?"

"After all," said Joe. "A job's a job. You wouldn't care what it was, would you?"

"Jesus Christ, no," said Mack. "I'll take one of those if you don't mind. I don't smoke much, but sometimes. Talk about jobs. I mean about working. Listen. Maybe I can tell you. You know what kind of a guy I am? I'm a nothing. That's what I am."

"You and me both. You'll never be lonely there, boy."

"No, no," said Mack. "I didn't mean that. Give me a chance. I know I'm bothering the hell out of you. But listen. Maybe I can explain it to you."

In a strain endurable, he hopes, just a bit more than merely Mack, boldly mimicking the voice in the burning bush. All rumpled as he is in his charged up hair and rolled up shirt sleeves, seems he is about to confess he has as yet all of his original teeth in his vivid head. As slapdash as, consider him as he sits there, a recent smear, trumping his own ace, stringing his lopsided pearls of wisdom, growing his own ash. If Mack then is a man who shines his pair of all-purpose shoes more often than he shaves, if he has his sideburns clipped higher than most, if his ears collect wax as a bank collects money, if his mouth is generally free of those pesky sores of acidity, if he has a diabolical fondness for baked beans and walnuts, if he is built to soak up sunlessness like a sponge, and has never had the clap but once, and has tried, but failed to be a hustler at pool, he is to be pitied, perhaps, but never to be spoken down to, for he is happy in a way that, for instance. What

324

is there to be so ashamed of? If work is not work, what in hell else is it? Hilda screamed when he told her, when he came running to her and said, I can be the janitor of this building.

You a janitor? Disgrace, cover up the face, with what sort of philosophy of what is right for a man is this flop of a woman here so pie-eyed? When sewer-wise he shoveled and pushed his daily acre of snow for two winters, the men would lean on their tools and laugh and kid the ass off him because he thought it fun to be death on the stuff, or when he rode the ice wagon with a seventh cousin who stank, or when down Wall Street like a mule he lugged his sack of new phone books to exchange, she was not there to see it, so his sweat and strain were highly respectable.

Dainty, dainty me. She droops. She makes like a dying swan because her delicate nose has discovered that the man she is tied to is no mere prime stinker, that he is not as full of piss and vinegar as she hoped and prayed he would be. Yet that one memorable day not so long ago, on a park bench freshly painted, before the final kiss that kills, he gazed into her brimming eyes like stars, and said to her, with this nature, darling, I thee wed. Catch me quick. I am floating free. Breathe if you must, but close that murmuring mouth of yours. For what love loves, love should love. Curtain. Can it be the raw morning already? Why so thoughtful in these idle seasons and dry spells? What is he now that he was not before? A dog is not a cat. An eagle is not a bat. Paper pickers in the park may envy generals in the army, but the power is not for them, and neither is the glory. Dungaree man, the humble itch is on him, any kind of work is his meat. If you can give it to him, give. Otherwise leave him alone. If in this life his luck is running out, it makes him dream all the more of what small jobs might be his for the asking in the next, even if it be only to scatter brimstone over hell, or restring the harps of whatever stony hearts remain in heaven.

"Oo," said Rosalie. "The sweet air here. Rustles of spring. Are those church bells I hear? Am I still a living lump? What can it be that's tugging at my heart?"

"Or bringing home the sheep," said Mack. "I was born for it. I'm just the kiddo who can do it."

"Aie," said Rosalie. "That piercing voice again. How it runs right through me."

"Or," said Mack. "Polishing up the gold on that gate with a silk rag. Can't you just see my two fat lips dripping with honey? Or pocketing a little bribe now and then, nothing over a dime, there I draw the line, to let only the delicious babes sneak in to find out just who is screwing who around there. Or while I'm changing my silver laces to talk to you the way I'm talking to you now. See how I see it? Busy, busy. What difference does it make with what?"

"The flying of the flies," said Rosalie. "And the buzzing of the bees. Listen. He's got me doing it."

"I once read a book," said Joe. "Where a man."

"Out," said Hilda. "Out from under there."

"Where a man without hands strangled his mother. And the foreman of the jury said to the judge."

"Can you imagine the snot?" said Hilda. "Tearing my last pair of good stockings. You little sack of potatoes. Look at that red button in the middle of her face. Drip, drip, Millie. Here, now, blow on this. Blow real hard now. Why, it's music. Did you all hear that? She makes a noise just like her father."

"Whee," said Rosalie. "That's what I call a dig."

"I wanted to say something," said Mack. "What was it I wanted to say?"

"Ah," said Rosalie. "Sweet mystery of life. Methinks the hour has struck. You hear those kids upstairs? Comes this time of night, and for no particular reason, they begin to dance. Whoops. Clap your hands. Who can kick the highest? Come, Josephine, in my flying machine, and up we'll go, up we'll go. Hey. Was that me singing like a canary? Did you bring an extra strait jacket with you, Joe? I think I'm slowly going mad."

"And how," said Joe. "It's a real ball here, isn't it? How can people be so different? Here's a guy who's just dying to work. And me. I was born to be a bum. All I want to do is just sit and think. For ten, twenty, thirty years."

"You're all witnesses," said Rosalie. "I tried my absolute best."

"For example," said Joe. "If I too can sew on a button, what does that make me?"

"Come again?" said Rosalie.

"I'm saying," said Joe. 'If I can do what a woman does, does that make me more of a man?"

"I must say," said Rosalie. "He does speak a beautiful French."

"It makes me mad," said Joe. "It really does. The bosses we have in this world. They wouldn't do to a horse what they do to a man. What is work anyway? Why should a man ever have to beg for it? That's what I can't get into my head. Though there's plenty of room in it. If this guy here can't get that little thing he wants, then as far as I am concerned, the whole world stinks."

"There," said Rosalie. "What did I tell you, people? You see now what I mean? Ain't he a darling? Isn't he sweet?"

"Rosalie," said Mrs. Heller. "Get the tea."

"What?" said Rosalie. "What tea? Why, Mamma. You're talking."

"Yes," said Mrs. Heller. "The bear again. She is here."

"Oo," said Rosalie. "I'm so afraid of her."

"Such a face," said Mrs. Heller. "Come here and let me look at you."

"Ah, Mamma, Mamma."

"What is it? I said a dirty word?"

"Why are we all so foolish?" said Rosalie. "Why? Why do we keep plaguing ourselves? Why can't we ever relax a second and be happy?"

"Happy," said Mrs. Heller. "For that we need an appointment."

"You were the one," said Rosalie. "You used to slap my hand. Weren't you always after me not to keep picking on a scab?"

"I'm sick too," said Mrs. Heller. "You think I'm not sick?"

"I know," said Rosalie. "I understand. You said tea. Right. Now what do I have to do? Pick the leaves? Go to the well for the water?"

"Why," said Mrs. Heller. "Why am I breaking my head? I have to fight with him? It helps me if I say no? If he wants you, let him take you. Let him take you already and let me live. You hear me? You, Mr. Joe, I'm talking to you."

"Terrific," said Joe. "There's no other word for it."

"He speaks," said Mrs. Heller. "But him I don't understand."

"And here," said Joe. "Here I've been thinking. Let her talk. Leave her alone. Why tangle with someone like that? What does she mean to you anyway? She's just a plain, simple woman. Not your speed at all. Just leave her alone."

"He says," said Mrs. Heller. "But here he is. Bothering me like a boil."

"Shows you what I am," said Joe. "Now you don't have to answer this, Mrs. Heller. But is it true what Rosalie tells me? She tells me that you have only one kidney left. And even that one is. And yet. There you are. You get along. Somehow you live. To me that's terrific. She also tells me you once had a tumor on your lung. And that you had that taken out and a couple of ribs along with it. And what else? There was something else she told me."

"You mean my skin?" said Mrs. Heller.

"Ah, yes," said Joe. "That mysterious rash. That was lovely. That was a real break for you, wasn't it?"

"Oh, sure," said Mrs. Heller. "It cost me a little. But I enjoyed it."

"And now," said Joe. "All of a sudden I come barging in. A new disease. Ain't that funny? That's a real howl, isn't it?"

"I'll soon die laughing."

"You should, Mrs. Heller, you really should. There's no better way to go. After all, you're the lucky one around here. Who knows what's going to happen to you next? Maybe soon you'll be losing your left ear, or your good right arm will drop off, or your honorable double nose. Who or what will do that for you, I just don't know. But you can be sure of one thing. It won't be your Mr. Joe. No, ma'am. Not if I can help it. I'm just like a cockroach that runs across your floor. I'm going to leave you just the way I found you."

"Then," said Mrs. Heller. "Then why did you come?"

"Just to say hello, Mrs. Heller. And then like a good little boy to say goodbye."

"Goodbye?" said Mrs. Heller. "What goodbye?"

"Just goodbye," said Joe. "And fond farewell. That's all."

"But I said to you, take her. I said, take her. Didn't you hear me?"

His answer pervaded his whole entire mouth. What if he should disgorge it now upon this pitiful table where each yes and no, like each cup and saucer, had been so imperfectly paired? Incomprehensible mammal with her belated yen to suckle him, he wanted to say to her, tell me not to take her, consider me not in such a light, for my soul, the sniffer, is still contained in the seed, and crouched therein, immovably torn between love and loathing for the seminal smell. Behold how the child in me is still the official spokesman for myself. Its mere hoppity of a heart is yet to be enticed into that stall where it can be coupled with its own convict mind which already nibbles at the hay of human devotion with a greying, penitentiary mouth. Few man-made words as yet complicate its cognition which is but a curl of smoke. What has

328

it to unfold? What to surrender? What need has it to consult the flight, appetite, and song of birds in order to ascertain what time of day plus night would be happiest for it to crash dive into some lamentable lovelife? It is no more than a monkey, madam, and as such, a ridiculous leaping shape which constantly cries uncle as it wraps its tail around the nearest flagpole, which is the only way it knows how to link itself with whatever else is living.

To which astonishing clump and cluster of what has agglomerated in his insides, the April fool, he appends his amen, and tickled pink with the way he has crawled out of what he has crept into, proceeds to magnify his happy daze by shifting the twinkle in his eyes to her time-discolored hair just so he could wonder what species of irrelevant lice have lately slept there, answerable only to her. Just so he could wonder, and know he is wondering, with that pure vitality in him which is related to the energy which collects in a cloud, and agitates the sea, and causes so many patched and lonely underdrawers to flutter on the clothesline.

What rot this is really. If flight was impossible, sitting still could hardly be endured. He tried as always to see the serious and rosy side of the situation so that he himself would look big and loom large, capable at last of lifting the unliftable, of raising that imponderable veil which so imperfectly conceals the savage and startling image of his destiny. Mrs. Heller thinks it is one thing. He is positive it is another. And this is when the comic comes in, when conceptions clash, when eyes dissimilar in size and color are slantwise arranged in the common head of existence, when a real bum of a boy and a completely unrelated gone woman are forced to become partners by some footman to fate, and must puff their way through the paces of a waltz to polka music.

"Great day in the morning," said Joe. "How the rafters rang. And the angels sang. It's a whirl. It's a mess, isn't it? It's kind of interesting if nothing else. There I was as usual hung up, leaning against the lamppost, waiting for a cross-town bus. Making out I was invisible. Trying to save myself some trouble. Who can blame me? So what do you think happens? All of a sudden the eyes of America are on me. Are we all tea with lemon drinkers here? I must know before I give myself a good scratch all around."

"That's an answer?" said Mrs. Heller. "That's the way a man talks?"

"Damn right," said Rosalie. "That sure is the way. It's not only the latest, it's the living end. Even dumb little bunnies like me can do it. Like you think we should exchange big toes before we say no to this crummy marble cake and the weak tea that's supposed to go with it? Lemon, says he. What can a twist of lemon do for me now? What I need is a dash of blood. His, of course. That'll put a real charge in me. I'll be my little old perky self again."

"And to think," said Mack. "Only a second ago she used to be the light of his eyes. Poor kid, I sure do feel for you. Turn on the waterworks if you must. As for me, since he was kind enough to ask me, I'll be brave. I'll take mine straight and see how I make out."

"What a lovely new game," said Hilda. "May I play too?"

"Why, sure," said Mack. "Skip right in. It wouldn't be complete without you."

"All right, then," said Hilda. "I'll be the coward this time. I'll sneak away to put a little mother's milk in mine."

"A little what?" said Mack.

"What a bore," said Hilda. "Must I repeat everything?"

"Mother's milk," said Mack. "How the hell did you come up with that?"

"If you must know," said Hilda. "I sent away a coupon."

"Another deep one," said Mack. "What are you so damn bitter about?"

"Because all we give each other here is love, love, love."

"And where the hell do you think you're going?"

"I told you," said Hilda. "To steal away to do that little thing."

"With your curly little tail between your legs, of course."

"Dear, dear," said Hilda. "The stupid thing does show, doesn't it? Well, what I can't help, I can't help. Especially when I have to drag this dirty bundle with me wherever I go. Or don't go. Which is usually the case. Daddy's normal child. Ain't she the clever one with her clothes? Ripped again. Wide open for inspection. I guess I'll have to take a tuck in this article too the first thing in the morning. See how we divide the labor here? I keep her decent. And he keeps her poor. How is that for quoting from the good book? I never read it much, but I did love to smell those old pages. Feet, do your duty. Easy now. Gosh, I hate to say this, but my tookie sure does pain me from sitting so much for nothing, waiting for something real to pop. Which it rarely ever does, does it? What a shame we're such ordinary people. We never do any-

330

thing worth a damn. The only thing we know how to do is not to let each other live. Take me, for instance. If I really had the nerve, I'd go into the bedroom closet right now with a scissors and a nail file and scrape and snip away above the knee until my leg dropped off. I haven't decided which. So it would take me all night. So what? At least the next morning, life, as she is called, would suddenly become a lot more interesting for the rest of you people here, wouldn't it? The only question is. Is your friend Hilda big enough to do just that one simple thing for you? Absolutely not. And that's my whole story up to date. And I'm afraid you're all stuck with it."

"Sit down, damn it," said Mack.

"I thought you would say that."

"Then why the hell did you start it in the first place?"

"Because," said Hilda. "I knew you would let me finish. You're always so considerate. Aren't you, dear?"

"Imagine," said Mack. "Woman on her way to take a pee. Did you ever notice it?"

"Now, Mack."

"Has to do it in style. Will say anything to get a big send-off."

"She will?" said Hilda. "Is that why I went to town that way?"

"For crying out loud," said Mack. "You have to make a federal case out of it? If you have to go, go. No one's stopping you."

"Oh," said Hilda. "It's okay. I'm no baby. I can hold it in."

"Correct," said Mack. "Now you know what you're here for. To suffer. Like a human being. And not like a hunk of cheese. Where did you get all that stuff about nobody ever doing anything? How about this guy Joe here? Didn't he just do something? He had guts enough to say no, didn't he? And if that's not doing something in the spot he's in, then you sit here, and I'll go to the toilet. I'll really have to."

"Sorry," said Hilda. "As much as I dislike to go against you, my pet, I'm afraid I can't agree with you there."

"You're not trying, girl. Try. Think a little and you'll see what I mean. You great big lovely dope."

"Now, now," said Hilda. "I would like to inform you. To insult my intelligence now would be very foolish of you because tonight is my night to be as smart as the whip you think you hold over me. And to prove it to you. I have only to say this in the alley voice you always listen to with such devotion. You can snap your fingers at me and clap

331

your hands for attention all you want, but I know it as I know that this is a five buck wedding ring you gave me. Just saying no, she's not for me, the hell with her, is not exactly what I would call doing something. Doing what? Rattle it off to me, why don't you? Give it to me straight."

"You hear that?" said Mack. "If I yelled Mamma now, the wrong woman would jump up. Was there ever a man so all alone? Me, Mack, the friendliest father a kid ever had. And more to come. Ain't it positively hell sometimes? Notice how she carries her ears on each side of her head as if only she was tuned into the truth. Who knows? Maybe the little lady is right. If a man can't keep his pecker up, how's a woman ever going to get any action? And action is just what any woman gets all the time, only she never knows when she's getting it. Even when all it amounts to is getting pushed around. Up goes the eyebrows. How I do love that. Look. Her face is filling out. My darling Hilda. You are so beautiful when you listen. Why the hell do you ever have to open up your mouth?"

"I hear you," said Hilda. "Even when my head is bowed. How I love it when you give me the Indian love call. It thrills me so. I hardly know where I am. I can feel the sea coming nearer. I am buried up to my neck in sand. But God is good to me yet, sending me just enough air from his Brighton Beach so I can take a good long breath and ask you, how can it be that a man like you, you big ape, you used to go after bigger game in your younger days, didn't you? How well I remember. Like slapping together a tin box your dear little bunnies soon outgrew. That was doing something, that was. And messing around with that shoelace guy, your old lady's boarder, who cut out the you-know-what from Mrs. Dumchick's poodle because, as you told me, the female animal had a certain kind of fascination for him. You helped him. You saw the blood. Big things, big things. Like matching six flies against one spider in an old peroxide bottle. Or pounding out slugs on a special stone in your backyard for important phone calls to fluffy spaniels like me, tearing up the grass around my feet as a lesson to me when we were hiding the shame of it in a semiprivate bush in Van Cortlandt Park, showing me so gently how to paddle in Luna Park Pool so you could feel what belonged to me, and only to me, even when it had the willies under water. My god, can it be that a man like you is still concerned, gosh, I was no higher than 6A the last time that

332

fancy word came popping out of me, with the same old household problem of how to shut me up? What is this awful comedown? Where is that dear old sweet patootie of mine? Where could he have gone to?"

"Where, she says," said Mack. "Keeps saying where. There's a hatchet deep in my head. There's a real foul blow for you. And here I was going to ask her to give me an alcohol rub before I slipped my flab and various aches between last week's sheets. I wonder. Is this the same strange doll who creeps up on me in the dead of night and buries her two fat sticky lips just where the hair is still thick on me? Pigsticker. Get lost, stupid. Said the crippled rabbit while he was out hunting for lettuce and met that skunk. I swear. If my stomach wouldn't rumble so much, I would know how to rest my case. What are snacks? Are they something you sail in? How about it, cutie? The beauty of Israel is slain upon thy high places. Do you know where that comes from? Or where you do? Your whole garden last April was a window box full of weeds. And you were the biggest that sprouted out of that. How did you manage to land here? Was it a slow grind on a turtle's back? Was it a merry trip by covered wagon? What's come over me? If I know you from way way back, why should I be drawn to you now so suddenly?"

"Puzzles," said Hilda. "Why ask an amateur like me? What a pair we are. Empty spools and dented tomato cans. Don't lay it all on my back. You're my yesterday's headache. Why should I bother with you now? How should I know what holds me together? I must be the final way the worm turned. Why do I see those awful shapes when I close my eyes? Why should I be afraid to look at such wonderful colors? Ah, you were so sweet there, Mack, when you heard me call, to open your pouch to me again. You cad. You call that security? Ha. Always remember. When a female person with the rag on says no, she don't mean, yea, man. Now don't you beg to differ with me. You can laugh at me all you want if you think it'll help me put on a little weight, or buy you the haircut you can't afford, but I'm warning you now. Don't you dare try to tell me I can't speak up for my sister who needs me to do that. I'm sticking with her no matter what. And don't you forget that either."

"Cried the little lame duck," said Mack. "As she came charging out of the right tunnel. Just to spite me. I'm amazed. I know now why I went haywire. Ain't she a gorgeous creature when she pins my ears back? She's got an extra wing somewhere. And me with my flat feet. I

333

sure was with her there for a split second, flying so high I nearly reached the sky. And of course those outside flips I was perfecting made me forget that after all this brilliant sunshine, there was bound to be a change in the weather, which as we all know always travels from west to east, and is as dependable as a baby's behind. But trouble. Ah, trouble. That can come from any direction. Right? I am now about to recite. A man and his job is soon parted. And it always leaves him brokenhearted. I'm so damn double-jointed, I can bow to the ground sitting down. Like my old man used to say when things went blooey with him, shit, piss, and corruption, and he was a very educated man for his time, he really was. The end was near. So he cried in his beer. Ho, what men are these who wear their legs in parentheses? Gives us a paw there, fella. That's the ticket. I'm telling you, man, it sure does my heart good to see you. How's the family? Always keep so cool where it counts? Is there anything I can do for you? I mean. Like you did for us tonight. Like the way you kept your eyes and ears wide open, and quiet as a mouse, made this whole sappy world turn and turn all around you. That's all you did. A fluke. A mere nothing. Hey, look at him. He has to smile yet. He has to make like he's happy about it. Can you imagine that?"

"I made a mistake," said Joe. "I moved."

"Don't let it get you," said Mack. "We all have to do that sometimes."

"But now," said Joe. "Now that I've been brought back alive. What now?"

"Sneak out, pal. We won't look."

"And leave you all like this? After all that?"

"Look," said Mack. "We're all very kind people here. And when we see that someone's been sitting here too long for the good of his soul, and wants to go where he can stretch and breathe regular for a while, why, we don't stop him. We're kind people here. We let him go."

"You make it sound so easy."

"Goddamn it," said Mack. "I'm trying my best."

"I'm sure you are," said Joe. "Only you know something? I never dreamed it would happen so soon. You're all beginning to hate me now, aren't you?"

"Shit, man. What in hell else did you think would happen?"

"And all because I was such a damn fool and let you all spill the beans in front of me. Is that it?"

"That's it, my boy."

"Yes, yes," said Joe. "I hear you and wonder. What would happen to me if I came and lived here?"

"Oh, now, man. Watch what you're saying there."

"I would sleep on the floor."

"What floor?" said Mack. "You mean here? In this house?"

"And use my friend here for a mattress."

"You would?" said Mack. "No fooling?"

"No fooling," said Joe. "And live by licking her chops. Without her I couldn't move a muscle, could I? And train my lily-white hands to keep her plumped up like a pillow. And size her up every night, fixing in my mind every one of her creases and knotholes so I could chew on her softer parts first. Strawberry ice cream for everybody if I make it. And as this lovely construction job, Miss Golly Moses here, begins to fall apart before my eyes, I would hide my face in what's left of her hair. Our bobbed existence. The shame of it all. And while she's lolling there, the terribly happy one, smiling at scenes from her childhood, and tearing off her extra toenails, in this our daily bed, I would do the usual. I would be her coal fire. I would be a man, my friends. I would send my garlic breath into her mouth until I paralyzed her into becoming me. A must for us all. Christ, you didn't think I was going to stroll through life without finding out how that feels, did you? Of course I do realize I'll have you all giggling like mad, listening to me through the walls while I go right at it. But I kind of like the idea of that, don't you? And I would unstick myself and grunt and roll over. And fall asleep like a rat after a heavy meal. And dream away while I haunt the premises. And hang around. And stay here. And dream my way back to where we say we were all so happy in the delicious blood stream, in that satin-lined little nest, in that safe warm sac of all our beautiful beginnings."

"Man the lifeboat, Rosalie," said Mack. "Your ship is going down."

"I assure you," said Joe. "I would learn how to do that perfectly."

"My dear, sweet Joe," said Rosalie.

"Yes, Miss?"

"My howling voice in the wilderness. My own pick and shovel man."

"Why so I am," said Joe. "And a very good morning to you too."

"How did you know?" said Rosalie. "Who told you?"

"Told me what?" said Joe. "That you would want to murder me?"

335

"No," said Rosalie. "That I would be the happy one."

"Oh, dear," said Joe. "That was a miserable thing to say, wasn't it?"

"Why, yes," said Rosalie. "That's why I'm pinching you."

"Ouch," said Joe. "So that's the important message. You'll excuse us, folks. This is the kind of stuff that goes on all the time."

"Yes, indeed," said Rosalie. "Come rain or shine. He likes it fine. It brightens up his every hour. As you can see."

"The moon is up," said Joe. "The wind is rising."

"And here you still sit," said Rosalie. "Sucking on your last peppermint. Absolutely disgusted with yourself. You poor thing. You look so footsore and weary. What have you been doing to yourself behind all that smoke? Did your nose grow? Did your head shrink? Are your clothes all in place? Are your ears reamed out? Would you like me to pick your nose for you before you go? Ha. I made you look, I made you look, I made you buy me a penny a book. You see what he's doing now? He's looking at me. He's really looking at me."

"I made it, friends," said Joe. "It worked. It's all over."

"You're crazy," said Rosalie. "When it's just beginning?"

"Ah," said Joe. "This goddamn bastard thing. I just can't squirm out of it."

"Gosh," said Rosalie. "It's a good thing this is a solid table."

"I have to take it out on something, don't I?"

"Love," said Rosalie. "It comes and goes so quietly."

"What love?" said Joe. "Where love? What are you babbling about? I'm not talking about you and me. I'm talking about myself. I'm talking about quitting my job. I'm talking about having to tell everybody in sight wherever I go."

"Oh," said Rosalie. "That silly thing."

"Now I love you," said Joe. "Now I really do."

"Wait a minute," said Rosalie. "Let me get this straight. You mean to sit there and tell me you think nobody here knows?"

"They do?" said Joe. "You told them?"

"Of course I did," said Rosalie. "Why shouldn't I? Is it such a great big secret? What's so terribly wrong about it?"

"Then why," said Joe. "Why in hell did you bring me here?"

"Joey, darling."

"What Joey? What is this Joey darling all of a sudden?"

"All they said to me was. Will you listen to me a second? All they said was, okay, if he feels he has to do it, let him go and do it. That's all they said. What in the world did you think they would say?"

"Well, now," said Joe. "That was mighty decent of them. I'm so glad I'm here to thank them all in person."

"All they said to me was," said Rosalie. "Okay, they said, so he'll leave his job. So what? Will it make you any different? Will it make him? Why eat yourself up alive about it? If it's not this, then he'll have to find something else to do, won't he? So what's all the fuss about? What does it change? It doesn't change anything at all. Really."

"What will I have to do?"

"Something," said Rosalie. "Anything. How should I know?"

"Watch your mother look for nits?"

"Nits?" said Rosalie. "Who's got nits? Jackie again?"

"Can't you see?" said Joe. "She's ticking them off one by one. She's a corker, all right. She couldn't care less. She's not even listening to us."

"She loves his hair," said Rosalie. "She always did."

"I love," said Joe. "She loves. You love. What a disease. I'm so wild about the idea. I'm so nuts about it, I tell you what I'm going to do after I quit my job. I'm going to make it my business to do nothing. Just for the love of it. Absolutely nothing. In that way, our beautiful friendship will be kaput. It'll have to. I'll be out of your hair. And you'll be out of mine."

"There," said Rosalie. "That's exactly what happened to me in my sleep last night. I can't imagine what caused it. My whole left leg was frozen dead when I woke up. I had to shake it a whole hour. Was it that loose button in the mattress that's always bothering me? I never felt such a draft. Was it a ghost? Did some dirty rat, like someone once did, sneak over and spritz cold water on me?"

"You'll be free," said Joe.

"I can still remember," said Rosalie. "I had this walking stick with a dog's head for a knob. I had to keep moving great big barrels of beer around."

"You'll say, that guy?" said Joe. "You'll say, sure, sure. I used to know him. He was that joker who just melted away."

"And all the time," said Rosalie. "All the broken-down faces on the block came floating down on top of me. Slices of fruit, bobbins, hair nets and keys, tremendous pieces of plain, ordinary rain. I felt I was right in the middle of things. Rumble, tumble, there I was in my next

337

best dream this week, slaving away, flopping around in a mountain of peels in pumps with six-inch high heels. Hilda crying in her magic cream. Millie in Mack's brushless. Mamma in Mrs. Colish's mascara. I said, who? I said, what? I had to take two dishes out and put three fishes in. I was bent so far over, I just couldn't see who it was who had the gall to keep sticking me. I slipped on my gloves. I kicked my shoes off. I said to myself, oh, you stupid little thing, if you don't start laughing at your boy friend now, when do you think you'll be able to tear yourself out of this? Ho, I swear to god. Hearing you talk this way reminds me. It does. It surely does."

"And here," said Joe. "I always thought you were so simple."

"I said to myself," said Rosalie. "I said to myself, laugh, I said. And oh what a relief it was when I woke up. But now. I'm so tight inside. I'm all so mixed up again. I feel I can weep. I don't know what's the matter with me."

"And your one and only heart ran back to Mamma. And the band played on."

"If only you wouldn't touch me."

"And that," said Joe. "That was only a dream. And of course this isn't, is it? People always go from blood to fire this way, don't they? Why, it's the commonest thing. And then of course, when they simmer down a bit, like your Mack and your Hilda, they always play cat's cradle with a piece of cake string, don't they? My eyes, my eyes. I don't believe it. I see a circle of light. I see the blue of heaven. Now that's a bridge. And that's a scissors she's making. And there's what looks to me like a cradle. They're going so fast. And those are knitting needles. And that's a spider's web he's flashing at us, isn't it? I should be saying good night. But here I am. Spilling my ashes all over the place. Ah, happy, happy days. Making my ring around Rosalie. Look up, look up. If you keep hanging your head, how can you see that I'm only human after all, that I'll never be able to hate you now, never, that you can't lose even if I have to kill you some day? You little worm. You know my hand is warm. I don't know why you're shivering."

338

12.

This noise will have to stop. This trembling especially. Old sock, old kid, prosper and rise, tick and go on to fresher courtesies, to games less chill and demanding. Many a chocolate in silver foil is called a kiss. He does hate thee, soft shot word, as he hates the sweetest part of himself. How often is it said that in the dwellings of the good is where the wicked one flips his lid, his unholy feet running to destruction. Tick again. Be hell on wheels. No doubt when morning comes, night once was, that flumed and arable, that sable multiplicity with its changeable silk and thicket snatch, with its spotted snakes and patronizing stars, its paw imbued with blood, its tail, its nostril, clawing him under with the more silent and deeper accidents of sleep. His loin cloth became legal tender. His negotiable brain seemed to have a nougat center, the sticky tissues sprinkled with pistachio nuts. His heart was found alive after searching the river. He was the last arrow in the quiver to be discharged into the sea. He resisted the elements. He fled from the rattled sharks of desolation. He rose.

Indeed it takes a topsy-turvy man to come out on top, to bull his way through the immovable articulation of his more than fuzzy words, fouled as he may be and tangled in the scabby trains and classes of his thought, until he unites the parts of each of the wounds it pleased him to suffer yesterday, and cheered by the spine-breaking reflection that every beginning is fatuously designed to befuddle the world, finally succeeds in piecing himself together brilliantly. As to his second home he was tending, gently inclined to doubt the strength and duration of this aura in which he walked along Madison of his newfound, but feebly created separateness. Last night's mouse was mother's little helper too when it left its calling card in a likely corner, plainly showing, by means of such assignable phenomena, its contempt for this resolve of Joe's to ward off, for one whole day if possible, that constantly grasping cloud of loiterers and witnesses who must first merge their breath with his, otherwise they cannot breathe. Indeed, indeed. So much of what seems to be so ingloriously human will continue to explode into fragments for him, but it remains to be seen what sort of luck can ride with a man when he wants to do anything natural if he does not work within view of where birds are nesting, and rabbits rub noses, and the grass grows wild, and the red squirrel emasculates the young of the grey.

In the absence of tapers or spills, ideational flickers of the idler in the place of his legendary shipping table identity, his limpid eyes imagine they can see all living things together at a glance. Strange. He speaks to no one, yet mum is definitely not his word. Incredible the amount of mystic muddlement of what can shimmer in a man when in his doodling he submits to the lush imbecility of his April. He buckled on a third crumbling chimney to his one-dimensional house. He allowed the door a knocker, but refused to give it a knob. He made rain to fall on the rising land-line. It drove most heavily on a bell without a clapper, and a washtub without a bottom, and a sandglass without sand. A superfluous mote came to rest beyond the edge of the paper. A glass oddly blown leaned against a tree, an elderly pine seemingly, partially restraining the head of a fish which resembled the great barracuda. Puzzle. Why should a single question mark be fixed in the contemporary bubble issuing from its cold-blooded mouth? Answer. If his father's father, unlike his father's son, could discuss with God all the familiar mysteries in a skullcap and earlocks, this must mean that everything is always more than a little alien and ungodly. He added to the shingles and slats he had piled near his main structure, and careless of the law of stresses and strains, attached a gigantic ear to the side which sloped the most. The imp of inspiration urged him to set the whole affair on fire. Where today should the first snarl of smoke in him show itself? In his upper storey or in his lower? His pencil dallied in the vicinity of the tree. The very foliage of his brain was as yet a comfortable blur. What believable flame could he draw that would strike terror into the glassy heart of that greedy fish? He had a book of real matches on him, but before he could locate it and bring it out, Little Bee screamed and ran full tilt at him and tried to climb up his back, and he had to chuck everything to espouse her cause, and deprive himself, because of the fright and frailty of a mere person, of the uncommon pleasure of bringing ruin down upon his house.

Watch it there, you screwy little bugger, and stow away that gat before you get your fat little head bashed in. You monkey, you heard what I said me? And with that, Joe brought down his open hand and took a mighty swipe at him, but Frankie ducked, and the blow landed plump on Joe's own hat which the pup had pulled down at such a mobster's angle that it clung to its moorings somehow though seriously shaken and crushed. Staggered as he plainly was, and with no time to lose if he still hoped to claim his victim, Frankie the Flopperoo, he squeezed the trigger blindly and discharged a jet out of his water pistol that arched its way right merrily into the wrong eye. Joe's eye, of course.

It was therefore very generous of him to support Little Bee while her giggles subsided, but she began to gasp and cough, and when he bent down to see, an awful color had crept into her face. She did not die of it this time, but oh, that asthma, there were times in the past when she daily thought she would, weeping bitter tears into the can of stove polish, slapped kind of hard for diluting it, missing so many precious classes in school in her ninth and tenth years, time of her daintiest figure. It was so unfair. One time the funniest kind of doctor came, and he cracked her bones, and he said to her, stay away from that old cat's hair. But the one she loved best of all simply gave her a powder to burn, the incense of which did relieve her. And she would catch and kiss her mother's worn hands, and joyfully snuff in again the stale smell of onions so deeply grated into them. What so much choking does to a body's heart is nobody's business. Little Bee sighed and rolled her bulging eyes, humble in her inability to tell her favorite fellow worker, with whom it was such an honor to share the same air, what it means to have to huff and puff. What happiness? Who happiness? Sometimes just to be able to breathe is enough.

341

Such is the marrow of her experience, simple bull terrier stuff. Such is its very mucous, as in her life the kindly light of her noon dims and the glitter of her afternoon cruelly betrays her as a complete washout. What she nipped out of the cuff of her chartreuse smock was a slimsy nose rag speckled, as he was pleased to see as she fluffed it out and pegged it to her shapely nose, with the June time blue of a robin's egg. Those pastel smiles of poor observers, those with which he tried to brace her made her blush, more with exasperation than with embarrassment, because she knew that what lurked behind each and every one of them was only that cute teddy bear of kindness again, and not that fiery ram or stallion of lubricating love. More than slightly tolerant of the coarse honesty of her sweat, he placed his hand on her fat round shoulder, the better to indicate what ran so mockingly in his head. What a shame that even on a Thursday the simplest desires should be just those blimps which go bloop. Oh, look on me, said Little Bee, how wet I am, how red. She flinched at the funny way he laughed. She was afraid to understand what it meant. She began to barrel herself backwards in a flustered pantomime of fond farewell to you, you crazy boy, and as she did so, keeled herself right over on Kitzel who flung his arms around her fiercely to keep them both from hitting the deck.

Hold it, said Kitzel, shoving Little Bee away from him with the heel of his hand, your silly giggling makes me sick. In this, in this alone is the source of real suffering, to yearn for a tooth or two to crop up for the third time, and get clipped instead where last night two of his final molars had been mauled out of him most amazingly. For a moment he was all lopsided with tenderness for the tremendous swelling of his cheek. The collision had jarred a streak of sluggish blood into the valley of his tongue. He swallowed it back to begin again, his lips barely moving. Imagine, when it was all over, that damn dentist challenged him to play a fast game of chess. That old dumb trick of changing his name, the Doc calls himself Dimmer now, but he still looks like a Dimmovitz, blabs too much, that five by five with a fist like a club, wires of hair springing out all over his bulky body, got that twist to his beak by banging it against his own baby buggy, to his wife he bows now, but had to ship her off after the honeymoon to have her business stretched, hoped for a boy, but Bubbles is what came out. Like those frightful original teeth of Kitzel's, they had been patiently leaning against each other and rotting away side by side for years, so that what remained for the pliers to clamp on came away with a sickening crack at the first good clench. First one, then the other. Dimmer, he came out with his best chuckle, and calmly advised Kitzel to can that noise as he held him fast with his knee, and jacked the chair down to lay the little coward out decently. No use shaking like that, fella, have to hack away at the gums here, and then the book calls for the hook. Say, did I ever tell you the one about the, naturally your blood is red, if it ever came out green, that would be the time to drop dead, about the, open wide now and relax, the shepherd who was counting his sheep? Seven, eight, hello, honey, nine, ten, get it? What a screamer. His clownish tool further lacerated what had already been slashed until at last, by digging as far as the belly button, he obtained a tolerable purchase, and gritting his own gold inlays, pried out the roots of the smaller baby, together with a magnificent chunk of bone that big. Whew. With what a soft and professional whistle did Dimmer stare at the frightful mess, then slowly brought it closer to his nose to smell the swatches of angry flesh that clung to it, to see if, but the cluck in the chair groaned, so he had to prop him up again, and pep him up a bit by pulling on his hair, plastered down as it was with a pint of sweat. The suction pipe gurgled. The swabs were absolutely soaked. The hook kept slipping, so it became vicious. No matter how or where it tore, it did not even begin to budge that big bastard of the interlocked root. Shit, said Dimmer, and yanked down the drill to bore out holes way below the gum, but the wriggling shrimp, who shelled out a buck a week when he could, received such a flash of pain that he flapped like a fish, and the burr caught his lip, and made him bleed in a new place, and plead for another shot of novocain. That decided Dimmer to take the mallet and chisel to him. You think I have no heart? Whack. You think I like doing this? Whang. The chips flew. Dimmer was about to split. His hands trembled as he groped with the tweezers to see what he had shattered, and when he discovered that he had bungled that operation too, he lost his dignity, he cut loose, he began to slap away at that boy, he really began to beat me. Me, Kitzel. I said to myself, why? I said to myself, what is this? Every time he ripped something out of me, he would shove and slap me. I felt so sorry for him, I thought I would die. I became like a stone. I said to myself, you, it's you again, you, you were rotten right from the start, and you're rotten now, and you will always be. Why? Why do I always have to give everybody so much trouble? Why?

Die then, says the dust. In every puff of me you kick up, there is peace. Fusty material, butcher's meat, despise yourself as you are, the hash of today, and the aspic of tomorrow, and learn to love me, as you love your fluid glimmerings, your sly decays, your moist sores and sorrows. Fat chance, to such a crooked and bitter speech, Kitzel's reply is only a cough. His eyelid twitches. From a source vastly more improbable, some hearkening angel orders its silliest fly to scout his head and report on its structural ability to support the invisible machinery of a halo. The warm air, as it rises, tenders him a lazy kiss. An immense perplexity as to where he should hide himself in his insignificance freezes him in the military position of at rest. He stares motionless. He waits for whatever else will be gracious enough to snake itself into the interfacial silence. An airship of cost sheet paper dove lightly at his old mangled shoes.

Missed you that time, said Hymie, launching a hearty laugh with superior aim and effect. He bent his bull neck to gaze with satisfaction at Kitzel's melancholy whiskers. He distinguished him further by means of smart little love taps on his overgrown nape. By gum, said Hymie, I like this boy. When it comes to worrying, he sure has got me beat. How exquisite of Hymie to come busting in with the outrageous good nature, the incomparable tenderness of the elemental man. Such beaming figures often bulk large in optimistic dreams. With grey eyes the size of little elephant eyes? Hardly ever, though never did there more plainly gleam in any pair such a plump affection for a skinnier brother in Moses. From picking his nose a second, he flung out his hands. Hymie being Hymie, he became entirely his basic gripe. He frankly sneered as he held up the mirror to them. The race which creeps into factories will never creep out again. To make more graphic the disgraceful condition of city people, he turned himself into a crocodile, a sponge, a snail, a creature of lint and fog. He looked but failed to find for them their wide open spaces. There were walls to their east, and walls to their west, and from their south they were elevated by four floors, and their only north was a ceiling of spider webs and sprinklers. He shaped an igloo for them which, he explained, was a house of snow. It came to him that there were polar bears in the Arctic Circle. He slid a bit from the top of the world to

344

alight on his own delirious idea of how the day there is divided from the night.

The deers ran in Saskatchewan. Poetry is there somewhere in the tracks of glaciers, and forest fires. Each season flames with reason. How smooth is the penguin breast of time, of white and flightless hours, beaded with brilliant gauds of blue icicles. British Columbia, happy land. Sheep couple with goats. Herds of swine and flocks of quail float log flotillas down the rivers of Manitoba. Heap excited and heap confused, Hymie found himself in a blizzard. He roared out his challenge to it. He cracked his whip and mushed his dog sled of furs and blubber through the howling province of God's own heart's desire. The mooseheads, it would put lead in their pencils just to see all those folders from Canada with all them color photos snapped from the air. With all of his northern lights nicely aglow, he rocked on his heels like a redwood about to topple. He smashed his fist down on the metal table. He caused the whole indoor world to quake. Now, he roared, now is the time to break out into the open, to be a big thing, to make a big crash. To clear himself sufficient space, he swept them away from either side of him as if they were dolls. The shorter one who was Kitzel squeaked. The taller one who was Joe smiled.

Once again he was the wise man who had to give ear to the song of fools and the fierce wailing of those who know they are whipped, and turn tail all too soon, and cringing before the pissing grubs who straddle them, join house to house, and lay field to field, until there is no place where a squelched and humble croaker can be positioned alone in the midst of the earth. Alas, it is a foul end to a foul beginning. Though life's eternal whisper is, I will come again, that which is far off and exceeding deep, who can find it when all at last have to sizzle and seethe in the same old fire in the same old place? Their restlessness trickling into the rosiest clouds, even in the honeyed spaces of heaven, they will say, this is not it, this is not it either.

Patty cake, patty cake, baker's man. The bay leaf is a spice. And so is the black pepper. The spectacled pelican swallows its marshy things without thyme or sage. Pray do tell us now about pemmican which is what if it is not a preparation of dried meat and fruit, and suet and sugar, compressed into small cakes so as to afford much nourishment to a cramped and wayworn clerk of silken and circumnavigable undergarments as he expounds as he explores the image of himself groping, helplessly coiled round the deep root of his I. To tumble into the swamp of involvement is to reach the peak of attrition. Space was mentioned. Mere elbow room was meant. Even that has become eminently desirable. As the mingling increases, the going gets tougher. A man gets sick of acting too cold and cuddling a spirit so flat and stale.

He had to whistle sharply through his teeth before he could sensibly arouse the saddest dogs he had ever seen. Kitzel and Hymie obeyed when he signaled them to draw closer. They warmed to his lively face. They seemed to expect wonders of him, so sure enough, he put it to them straight. What has two eyes in the back of its head and can see everything in front of its face? Colish, said Kitzel. Naa, said Hymie, a pineapple. God, said Joe, paining them with the smiling manner in which he produced such an unpopular bird. After all, God is God. So let us not be too bitter about it. The dear soul is still best known by that moniker. Actually he is a sweet old character who is often amazed to learn that the conception of him as a holy terror has not entirely fallen on evil days. For example, he was enormously interested in that news item lately of a middle-aged couple in Winnipeg, speaking of Canada, who sort of pushed around their pigtails, their only five-year-old daughter, because she mocked them, and refused to pray. The Doodads were lipping away at a furious rate when the kid skipped into the room. Since they knew her quite well, they were not ashamed to ask her to join them. She smiled and paid no attention. Mrs. Doodad slapped the child and struck her with a cleaning fluid bottle. She then handed the weapon to her husband because he was a former hockey player. Mr. Doodad struck the baby several times as powerfully as he could. A hard nut to crack, when such fond caresses failed to knock her out, Mrs. Doodad placed her knee on the sinner's chest and strangled her. This accomplished, the parents carefully bundled themselves up, and marched hand in hand to a vacant lot, and prayed all night in sub-zero weather.

Well, so much for that. So one fine day, oh, my brethren, let us beg of God that he enlarge our hearts in such a way that we may be forever collapsing with love for the boundless expansiveness and infinite flexibility of all his curious designs and ways, God was hunched over his roll-top desk, in a wrinkled palm beach suit, encouraging cancer of the lungs with his chain smoking, stacking his mash notes, stamping WHY BOTHER ME? on the sad scrawls of the usual squawkers. He had not slept well last night for some strange reason. Even now there was a round red speck on his forehead, the stigma of some obscene human dream. He had the peculiar feeling that he was not alone. He seemed to feel the hot puff of man breathing down his neck. He jumped a little. His freckled hands trembled. He pinked himself with his Eversharp. He pushed over the paste pot. The outrageous unfairness of it all so impressed him that for the first time in centuries he unstoppered his ears to listen. He made a nice tableau as he sat there with the massive balls of camphorized cotton pinched between his fingers, smiling childishly at the soothing sound of the absolute silence which disclosed what the living discover as soon as they die and ascend, that heaven is reserved for God along. Here in this hexagonal room where the perspiring walls had not been papered since creation knows when, he could select his herring and fry it without being told where or when. He had thought of marrying once. But that was eons ago when that devil, the first she, had proposed that he come into her in a fork of a walnut tree. There were no saints as yet to preserve him from temptation, so he had to call on his own inspiration. He improvised preliminary words. He plucked out the Adam in him. What was left was a snake. The humiliating memory of how he had been obliged to crawl out of that one filled him with such rage and shame that he dashed out upon the balcony, and leaning far over the balustrade, flipped his smoking butt right down upon all the living citizens of the world.

Jumping Jehoshaphat, what an ungodly way of showering them with such feeble sparks of the famous punishment of his fire, they shrieked wth glee to see how they had flushed him out and forced him to pay such a glowing tribute to the hateful fact of their godawful existence. What was his faith if he could not believe in them? From millions they had become billions. His grandpappy eyes became like saucers at what he heard and saw. Babies in their bassinets employed their pink little hands to enjoy the sleep-inducing pollution of a spermless pleasure. The rich were half-famished for takers of their inexpensive love. They composed odes to childbearing, shivering in their furs. Schoolgirls gasped as they fingered their purpling nipples. The poor petitioned for a reduction of their dismal numbers. They ate oleo instead of butter. They were the fattest of flag wavers. Tried and true lads played pocket pool with their testicles. Brilliant Jews longed

347

to be goyim. The blind kissed the bald. Greying mashers explored adolescent twots with their heavily veined hands. The crookbacked and the consumptive purged a great deal of what otherwise ailed them by sleeping head to foot. Barmaids were for barflies their only swigs, their double shots of thinnest honey. Beautiful black boys cried because they failed to be as cruel as the white. Hordes of weary shufflers carried picket signs which read, down with the menopause for women, and the climacteric for men. Jeweled dowagers implored burly men in spotted jeans to try their luck. Drugstore cowboys had nothing to say but fuck, fuck. The lonely blubbered. The queerer cases winked and grinned. Those who could held up their crutches.

God help them. To think that the musty curse he had laid upon them should be the source of their miserable fun. Caution. God breathing very strangely here. The ground beneath the citizens began to shake and sway with the violence of his self-disgust. They trembled and screamed and clutched each other. They were sore afraid that the shock of his passion would scramble their brains. But God staggered back a step and unclenched his fists and covered up his face. And he wept. And they said, look, look. And they cried out, O God our God, we are prepared to rot when the time comes, but please, do something to relieve our present and particular troubles. And by god, he heard. And he looked up. And he said to them, yes, I will try, for it seems such a little thing. And they cried out, yes, he is our dread Lord, he is our one and only God. And they gave him thanks. And he smiled and cleared a space. And he said to them, come now, place your troubles on this spot as quickly as you can. And they said, yes, yes, we will. And they did. And when they had done so, he said to them, now, just plunge your nippers in the pile, take potluck, see what fresh trouble you can pick out. And they looked at him. And they greatly wondered. And they said, must we? And he said to them, yes, you must. And they bowed down their heads. And they said, to hear is to obey. And they did pick. And when they had done so, they felt of the new tribulation they had fought for to graft unto themselves, and strange to say, they found it different, and very bitter. And they raised high their arms like dry branches, and they cried out to him, O Father, our Father, you can spank us later if you must, but help us now to get rid of what you have made us take in exchange, for it binds and frets us, it makes us feel so blue inasmuch as it is not at all what we are used to.

And they fouled their garments. And they wept. And God sighed. And he shook his head. And suddenly he snapped his fingers and yelled out, look. And by gum, when they looked, their old troubles had been restored to them. And they touched them, and they hugged them, and they rubbed them with spit, and they licked them all over, and they found them good. And they were seized with a gladness that was all-fired maximum. And they hollered, and they shouted, and they beat the drum. And they praised the Lord. But he had to turn away and bite his lips to keep from laughing, for he was afraid they would see how easily their aging friend had outsmarted them again.

And so, my sparrows, until the next time. That old war horse, his wisdom hath wings and wheels, hath it not? Ye gods, said Kitzel, that was a whopper, that was. More, cried Hymie, tell us more. When you hear the next signal, said Joe, it will be exactly a week and a half past the witching hour, so let us be up and at it, men. And suiting his action to his words, he cracked the stiffness out of his knees, and clapped himself over the heart to get the blood to flowing, and challenged them both to broad jump against him from a standing start. A lark, a lark. He toyed with them. He leaped a foot beyond Hymie's finest effort. Most decidedly an injured bird, the best Kitzel could do was to finish a bang-up third.

"He's such a little fellow," said Miss Golschman, the one authentic blonde in the place, afflicted with the roundest arms of palest gold, and the frail oval of a madonna face, who ran the office, as she seemed to control her life, with the haziest eyes, and a smile as soft and cynical as history when it lazily looks back on itself, as if to compare the bloodstained canticles and siren songs of its past with the sleeveless vamps and hot licks of the popular ditties of its present, with the result that, once again, it decides it is full weary of both because it fails to find in either the faintest trace of virginal arrangements in its soul, or fresh arrogancies in its body. "Maybe that's the trouble."

"Oh, yeah?" said Kitzel. "I'm big enough for you any time."

"Only your face, darling. I suppose you fell on it, didn't you?"

"Oh, sure," said Kitzel. "I always fall on my right side when I'm playing gitchy. Next time I'll do better. I'll fall right on top of you."

"That'll be nice."

"Oo," said Hymie. "What she said."

"Now this," said Miss Golschman. "This is altogether a man."

349

"Right," said Hymie. "You bet your big um–um I am."

"Charming," said Miss Golschman. "He even speaks a kind of English."

"That's it, baby. Talk to me, talk to me."

"Well," said Miss Golschman. "I can say this. You do smell divinely."

"Oh, yeah?" said Hymie. "What happens to you when you sweat?"

"I perspire."

"Haw, haw."

"And when that happens, I do just one thing, darling."

"And what is that, my dear?"

"I stay away from people."

"Hee, hee," said Hymie. "What a cold fish."

"Yes," said Miss Golschman. "And so like a flower. Buy me some posies, do. I was so thrilled when he breathed into my ear. I was a lily of the valley. I was a slightly pink rose. Or was it like golden ripe wheat you said I was?"

"Aw," said Hymie. "Lay off."

"The donkey blushes."

"You lousy squealer."

"He does speak right out, doesn't he? Tell me, darling, I'm so anxious to know. How is your three-year-old Doodie, the boy wonder with the three blue teeth? And how does your little Linda grow? She fine? She go all by herself on the potty? She no got chicken pox?"

"What chicken pox?" said Hymie. "What's a matter with the dame? She nuts or something?"

"And the missis with the tiny waist, keeping it slim over the slimy washtub. I like what you told me about her. Is she old enough to vote yet? I can't remember. Does she take the pills before the tonic, or the tonic before the pills? What a life, really. She tries to be strong and lovely for you, and you dearly love the child, don't you? Of course he does. What a question. But something terrible happened to him that changed his whole life. He caught me fixing my stockings once."

"Caught you?" said Hymie. "You stood there. You let me look."

"Poor man," said Miss Golschman. "I do feel I owe him something."

She slowly hitched up her clinging dress on the side nearest to him.

"Behold," she said. "The world is suddenly interesting. Don't you think so?"

"Sure, sure," said Hymie. "You got spiffy legs, all right. Anybody can see that. But what in the hell's the good? What do you ever do with them?"

"What you should do with yours. Walk yourself right away from here."

"You're goddamn right I will," said Hymie. "Sonofabitch. Can you imagine that? I was feeling good for a change and she had to come sneaking in. Come on, Kitzel. We can't stay here. We smell. We're not good enough."

"Did they go?" said Miss Golschman. "Are they really gone? Well, that's good."

"Ha," said Joe. "If looks could kill."

"And they can," said Miss Golschman. "And they do. Tell me, Joe. Are you such a damn fool too?"

"God, yes," said Joe. "I like women."

"Even bitches like me?"

"Well," said Joe. "Things are rough all over."

"Please," said Miss Golschman. "Don't make me crack this lovely made-up face of mine. You'll spoil a whole morning's work."

"Alice Golschman."

"It's a name. It'll have to do."

"Age, 25."

"Well, now, aren't you the little gentleman?"

"College, Barnard. Favorite river, the Bronx. Author, God. Composer, the wind. Hobby, riding in the middle of hired nags in Central Park. Attitude, see her educated posture. What goes on behind those blueberry eyes, mighty mysterious like the two Siamese cats she keeps. Ambition, to be the second wife of an orphan who's an only child. Occupation, office hack. Term of office, forty years. That, if I'm not mistaken, makes it about thirty-seven to go, doesn't it?"

"Damn you," said Miss Golschman. "I hate people who guess right."

"You used to think I was stupid, didn't you?"

"Well," said Miss Golschman. "If I remember right, you used to think so too."

"Naturally," said Joe. "But now. I'm telling you, girl. My eyes are wide open. And what, I ask you, do you think I see?"

"Me, for one thing."

351

"Yes," said Joe. "I think I do."

"And you're so very sorry for me, aren't you?"

"What can I do?" said Joe. "You know my weakness."

"Ah, yes," said Miss Golschman. "You're the idiot who loves everybody, aren't you?"

"Please," said Joe. "Let's talk about happier things."

"All right," said Miss Golschman. "Let me see now. I do know a little bit about baseball. Will that do?"

"I'll be damned. You know who you remind me of?"

"Babe Ruth when he strikes out."

"No," said Joe. "My sister."

"Really?" said Miss Golschman. "That's frightening. I had no idea you were brave enough to have a sister."

"Why, sure," said Joe. "And a brother. And a mother too."

"Bully for you. I understand that rarely happens."

"There you are," said Joe. "You see? We're really gassing now, aren't we? Aren't you glad things are so slow in this dump?"

"Decidedly," said Miss Golschman. "It does get to be amusing after a while. Which reminds me. Mr. Colish called."

"Oof."

"I'm sorry. Were you about to say something?"

"I don't understand it," said Joe. "I feel sick all of a sudden."

"Our father who art in hell, why must we mention thy name?"

"What in the hell happened to him? Why didn't he come in this morning? What's eating him now? What does he want from me?"

"Oh," said Miss Golschman. "Nothing much. Just to look after things, that's all."

"Oh, he does, does he? Well, now ain't that just fine?"

"You know?" said Miss Golschman. "Sometimes you really surprise me."

"My god," said Joe. "Suppose I never did?"

"I guess it's a trick, isn't it?"

"What is?"

"How can you be so old and so young? And both at the same time?"

"I touch my toes," said Joe. "I eat my porridge. I sing in the elevator. I cry in my sleep. I kiss myself in the mirror. I always try to do something for my country. I make all the sad people wave their goddamn little flags."

"It's not much," said Miss Golschman. "But it's something."

"My dear Alice," said Joe. "You're mighty like what a real woman should be. So let me ask you something. If the nicest words keep coming to my mouth lately, what do you think it means? You think I have a chance? You think I'll be able to make it?"

"Poor kid. You have become the one, haven't you?"

"Jesus Christ, yes. Did you ever see anything like it?"

"They flock around you like flies. I keep looking through the glass. I've been watching it."

"What gets me is. What did I do? What's so special about it?"

"Well," said Miss Golschman. "You are quitting your stupid job in what they call these terrible hard times, aren't you?"

"You're goddamn right I am."

"Well, then?"

"Yes," said Joe. "I know. They can't understand it. It kills them."

"They do seem to be mighty excited about it."

"They're crazy. They think I know something they don't."

"Ah, but that's not true, is it?"

"Of course not," said Joe. "Who in the hell do they think I am?"

"Thank you," said Miss Golschman. "That's all I wanted to know."

"What a smile," said Joe. "This is absolutely incredible. Where are all the men? Why aren't you married yet?"

"I have delivered my message. You may now kiss my hand."

"By god," said Joe. "I think I will."

"Dear boy."

"Sweet lady."

"Bless you, my child."

"May all your troubles be little ones."

"And may all yours," said Miss Golschman. "Always be big ones."

"Terrific," said Joe. "One does amuse oneself here, doesn't one?"

"Oh," said Miss Golschman. "That night when I chucked that blazing ring of his out the window. Talk about fun. There was a game of catch for you. We were greased lightning together, we were. Ten minutes after we met, we were already legging it for second base, in a tropical heat wave. I was mighty anxious to hand-pick him, all right. And he turned around and stripped me of my feathers. We locked wings on the lam, two city jungle birds. Oh, my gin and tonic sparkle. I used to throw such lovely parties for us to lose ourselves in. But when he got to be a little too light on his feet, and a little bit too loose around the mouth, and I thought I was getting big with child, I sure did wind up and give that stupendous gem of his the old heave ho. My last chance for happiness. Whee."

"Excuse me," said Joe. "But is this love you're speaking of?"

"Goodness me," said Miss Golschman. "Where did all that come from? Surprising little eruption, wasn't it?"

"It did rock me."

"It knocked me for a loop too."

"Alice Golschman. Engaged. I must say. Things are sure popping here today. Who the devil was the guy? What happened?"

"He was the son of a lot of cash around the house. Oodles and oodles of it. I do hereby confess. After seven long sleepy years, I still paper my dreams with the stuff. He was also, of course, a real bone in the throat to his dear old Mom. His feelings about her were nothing to brag about. He hated the woman because she was only thirty-eight with a very nicely perfumed and striking figure. I saw her only once. She warmed my hands and made such big eyes at me. What slips in through the nose does sink itself in the mind, doesn't it? O Barney, Barney, wherefore art thou? As far as I can remember, since I do refuse to forget, he did have himself a very busy time that year. He slipped on the ice on his twenty-first birthday. He made hay with a needle called Hazel. He drew a bye in a tennis tournament. He broke his own world's record for holding his nose under sweet water in the shallow end of the pool. He puked when he opened a book that had no pictures in it. He failed to finish his third sophomore year at his fourth college. His father retired from woolens to meet his sudden death with the two younger kids when the family Buick tangled with a tree a stone's throw from their summer castle near Saratoga Springs. He was a whiz at describing things, Barney was, including that triple funeral. He was throwing his share of the dirt on the coffins when it came to him in a flash that the only way he could possibly show his gratitude for this business of three down and two to go was to become a forester. Or a tree surgeon first. He couldn't make up his mind which. His Mom just hauled off and smacked his face when he told her, for according to her, he was already a brilliant chemist. He could take any amount of her money and always make crap out of it. Well, now, it's easy enough to laugh, but what would you do if someone with a name like Barney tossed a great big diamond ring in your lap?"

354

"Ha, I would say thanks a lot, I guess."

"Of course," said Miss Golschman. "But I, you understand, I had to do much more than that."

"Something tells me," said Joe. "This is not going to be a very nice story."

"My dear boy," said Miss Golschman. "It's a thousand times worse than that. It's an absolutely stupid one. I shall now take this tasteless green thread off your shoulder and flavor it with my sen-sen tongue. Fight, team, fight. What makes me do it, I wonder? Why am I standing here making you such a hole in your honest little head? Why don't I just mosey off and powder my nose instead? Or go right back and try to find out once and for all who's been robbing the petty cash of the larger coins? It must be me. Who else could it be if I took that ring to a jeweler, and the jeweler said, lady, my dear, you leave it here and I give you five thousand for it spot cash. Merciful heavens, when I heard that, I grabbed the article and ran out of that store in nothing flat. I sort of floated on the sunny side of the street. I sang a song my mother taught me. I said to myself, now look here, this is final, as soon as that gallant knight pops his head in tonight, you take that awful thing from your bosom where you've been hiding it, and give it right back, you hear? It was like my own father talking. But naturally, I didn't listen. Shame on Alice. She was a nosy lass. She was a greedy gut. She lost her innocence on the other side of the looking glass. Pish-tish. Slap me in the face with a wet fish. When the lights go out, I have trouble holding back my body. When the sun is out as it is today, I do list where the melting west wind plays. Mother of mine, when the liquid human heart leans towards me, I can hardly wait to give my soul away."

"Hey, hey. Sing to me, sister, sing."

"You rat. You made me wag my little tail, didn't you?"

"Finish, finish."

"What else is there to say? He had to cross the ocean in a sailboat. So I had to part with it."

"In a sailboat?"

"Or let me see," said Miss Golschman. "Or was it plastic surgery he wanted done on that slight hint of a hook on his gorgeous Roman nose? What I do remember is that I took that bone of contention, by which I mean the ring, and aimed it right where he said he wanted to be fixed, but it was dark, and I missed by a mile. Did I ever tell you I once had hopes of studying medicine? This is really true. I mean it. It

355

all began when I ran for water to wake up a drunken sailor with a broken back. I found him behind the old slaughter house in the tiny yard where Klein the tailor was raising chickens and growing corn. Oh, those summer childhood days. I'll never forget those terrible stains on his shore-leave uniform. And the sweet way he smiled up at me. He knew which little girl had saved him. You can imagine what peroxide dreams I had after that. I was a real dumb bunny I was. I was barely ten. But I had a sneaking suspicion even then that something very plain was behind it all, merely and clearly sex, so I was always kind of proud of the vision I had of myself as a lady sawbones, queen of her own charity ward, white like a dove in her mercy, shaking her kind but stern finger at the fakers, fondling, and of course, curing the incurables. A louse with ideas about lice. A silver bullet fired from my female brain. Somehow I feel the time has come for me to raise my skirt, and disappear from view in a cloud of dust. Ah, me. I suppose if we aren't completely paralyzed today, we're merely crippled, aren't we?"

"You must be right. But I just don't follow you."

"Just say you'll take it, that's all."

"Take what?" said Joe.

"Buy yourself some time. At least that."

"With your soul?"

"No, no," said Miss Golschman. "I'm talking about my savings."

"Oh, for crying out loud."

"Seven hundred and ninety-nine dollars exactly. That's the great big bundle I offer you. The dollar I'll leave just to keep the account alive. You don't mind if I do that, do you?"

"Mind?" said Joe. "What money? Who needs money? How did you ever get mixed up in this? What I'm doing, I'm doing only for myself. Don't you understand that?"

"I'd spit in your eye if you told me anything else."

"Forget it," said Joe. "What a woman. I can't take your money. You know that."

"Fine," said Miss Golschman. "If that's what you feel you have to say to prove to me you're really a man. But I'm telling you now, Joe. I'm absolutely set on this. I'll kill you if you weaken and don't quit. You hear me?"

"I'll try," said Joe. "What else can I do?"

356

"Of course," said Miss Golschman. "I'm sorry. It's not easy. I know."
"Oh, you goddamn people. Where do you all come from anyway?"
"Ha," said Miss Golschman. "It's a joke, isn't it? Even I didn't help.
And I'm supposed to be one of the good ones."

"Oh, but you are," said Joe. "Goddamn that phone, it would ring
now. What a thing to spring on me. Ah, I'm really sorry, Alice, but I
simply must tear myself away. You crept into my heart. Your memory
will ever be dear to me. Give us a good old shake. Swell. Though part
we must. Listen to the way that damn bell rings. I'm sure you will be
kind enough to understand me when I say that I must carry on. In the
apron of my country, like a Yankee-Doodle boy. I must answer. I
really must see who's next."

Rings on her fingers, bells on her toes, when boyish mockery steals
the show, it makes of gentle intelligence an extra, a mute with its
pinkish make-up flaking, a sadly tumbled stand-in stashed among the
drops, a submissive droopy pants, eating crow. He rudely extin-
guished the intended brightness of his fixed star of the first magnitude
with his harsh questioning hello. No answer. He listened awhile to the
stammer and hum of older silences recoiling into icier distances into
which the fiction of a voice had shrunk, until at last it gathered actual-
ity enough to whisper most pitifully, remember me?

Rosalie. Mistaken for a dog as he was sure he had been, he imagined
it would only be polite to growl like a very mean one. He did elicit a
Rosalie titter. Pleased by his quick success, he softened his imitation to
whine and yip like a pup whose paw had been stepped on. What a
lovable character. She prized it too much, so he crossed her up, and
began to moo like a cow whose milking had long been delayed. With
such deep sympathy did she cluck, he instantly became a high-
stepping hen, to whose red wattles most fleshy and naked, he introduced a lordly rooster, chased by a common pig, mixing it with a fresh
little lamb. He began to gurgle joyously like Seder wine out of a gallon
bottle. Owls do hoot for perfect mice. Rainy nights are not ideal for
the courtship of cats. When she really began to laugh, he made like
morning came, and the cage cover was lifted, and Rosalie, the charming Polly, she did want her seeds, and she did want her crackers. She
begged him to stop or she would wet herself.

A mere growing child. She could make no crude distinction as yet
between what truly communicates and what hardly speaks. Funny

357

how age does tell what age will tell at any age. Though her brightest suspicion was that love, in spite of her latest dream scene of a stony bush replete with snarling birds, very disquieting, expanding into flame-throwing beasts whose ponderous intention was to couch themselves one upon the other, that love simply made its passes, was a silent thing, yet she could not imagine how the rest of life as such could be sane or fruitful, or a speck of clarity in it achieved, without the miserable blur of human words. His skin bracer, his live wire, he must accept her vibrations as she sends them. A Siamese twin of inseparable self-affection. That was how she felt, since he was kind enough to ask her, just about fair to middlin this morning, monstrously rolled about, too impactly infolded.

Fiddlesticks. See how it is only now her dawn with him does begin to break, as she listens to their destiny like a dickybird calling them together, how one by one her sluice gates are beginning to open, as a consequence of his seriocomical presence, to spill out some of her nicest scale steps, her shyest gathers, her most private accordion pleats. The last she knew she was a servant in a great family. She was the one who was in charge of the bread. Her huge platter fell with such a clatter that she sat up in bed and said, no, thank you, quite prepared to snap off that sill-pecking sparrow's head. I dreamt I had me a reception hall. What does a queen do when her common lashes are flecked with coronation tears? Basta. So this then is my court. And this my mansion. And here I am, so finely squeezed and shattered this morning, scratching myself all over my sainted body, eager to make the choicer oranges bleed, charmed by, yet suspicious of my own she-girl aroma which wows the hee-hee, the he-men. She who worships the self alone as dear, the object of her love will never perish. Her breasts do astound her. She has a sort of hands-off admiration for her hair. What she has to stuff her stockings with are but two in number, and what is more, are both so amazingly alike. Her dun-white navel is most like a mantic eye. The gospel of her clitoris is grand, namely, that it is not to be used for striking children on the hand.

You tumble me? How dare you say less and less? If words will not do it, what will? Fighting off the screaming meamies because of last night and his spectacular visit, killing care and grief of heart, what other way is there of flying down to Rio where she can roll and sideslip and set down her sunlit innocence smack-dab in the middle of what? What

358

is this knot of wonder in her that seems so unknippable? Separateness is said to be a tragic condition. Sense of multiplicity brings on panic. She had to unriddle the presence of a fiery blood clot within the filmed half-moon of her forefinger nail. She had to unpick the appearance of a brother blood speck in the runny yolk of her bimonthly breakfast egg. The coffee grounds contained her fortune, whirling before her eyes counterclockwise. Muffled in their funk holes and corner, preschool outriders of the sun, wild-eyed with street cunning, did contrive to dazzle and ambush her. The bus driver grinned as he greased her lifeline with a squashed nickel. This man was once dust. In the train she found herself a seat between two actual people. One was a fat boy in a blazer who had one foot in a bucket. The other was an absolute scream who stippled the beak of her multicolored nozzle with a mummer's cream. As she who is Rosalie ascended, her right foot sliched on a gnaw of spit on an exit step. How far is it up this inclining street? Where is Abyssinia in relation to Brazil? She crossed over. She hopped to it. She came closer and closer to him.

Oh, my heart, she said in a little speech to it, why are you so suddenly fit to bust? Where are you going in this human gitchy-goo? Why are you knocking the pedestrians over? Where are you rushing off to? To my partitioned off place where in my haste I will again fail to drag him through my gate. To circulate round him the fuming botheration of my love. To ring in my sting. To cling as close as I can to my constant prince, jealously forgiving him as I must for swamping the sense of me entirely in his treacherous solicitude for flusher eligibilities such as Miss Golschman, and sick my ravishing gimme on him until he is fairly gobbled up. My pants chasing arf-arf to his skirt shy woof-woof. My sparkling map is his helpless trap. My soil is where he is buried. My sea is what he swims in. Breasting my froth. Dog paddling through my spray. Ah, if I sing, I sing me no song of sixpence as I go me to slop me over, like the booboo Mr. Sackman made when he gumshoed in for my blue-black ink, and tipped the whole bottle over, leaving it for me to sop it up somehow. So of course his mess had to be mine. And I was a fool to think I could ever avoid it. Like you think you can when I make my own puddle of feeling for you to step into. My lunch money is doled out. My duty calls me, whooee. What is this useless labor? What is all this endless toil and trouble? Two still means two. Two will never mean one. But never. Loosen my hidden pins and fan my brow. Are you ready for the kill? Have I been rough on you enough? Can you say you know me now? And without giving him a chance to give her the works in the form of a crushing answer, she laid him low with the kindest laugh she knew, and clicked down the receiver.

"Wow," said Frankie. "Who the hell was that?"

"Jesus," said Joe. "I must say."

"I bet you that was the boss. Was that the boss, Joe?"

"There's a pip for you. Beautiful stuff. Absolutely."

"Sonofabitch," said Frankie.

"I'm kind of cuckoo too. I just stand here and take it."

"Yeah," said Frankie. "Sure. I knew I was right. I bet you I know what happened. You want to bet me, Joe? I bet you he went down his cellar with a candle to get himself some of that old lettuce. I bet you he fell over a barrel of money and broke his ass. So he calls you up to bawl you out for it. Hah, Joe? I bet you I'm right. I bet you he's croaking. I bet you he's dead already."

"Jump, jump," said Joe. "Who cares?"

"Ah, boy," said Frankie. "Wait. You'll see, Joe. Wait until he comes in. Wait until I get a hold of him. I'll grab him like this, see? I'll pick him up and bounce him up and down for you. I'll kick him in the nuts. I'll knock his eye out. I'll burn his hair. I'll take him like this and tear his ears off. I'll break his nose. I'll stretch his big rotten mouth for him. I'll make him yell for giving you hell. You watch me, Joe. You'll see."

"Frankie the killer. My friend and your friend. The punching bag."

"Wham," said Frankie. "I'm warming up already."

"So you like my hat, do you?"

"Me?" said Frankie. "What hat?"

"Come over here," said Joe. "I said come over here. That's right. That's a good kid. Joe won't hurt you. He just wants to take a good look at you. I thought so. How come you got all that dirt on your lip?"

"Dirt?" said Frankie. "That ain't dirt. That's crayon. That's a moustache."

"Aha," said Joe. "And what do you think this is?"

"Aa," said Frankie. "Go ahead. Hit me all you want. That don't hurt me there."

"Sorry," said Joe. "I'll try to do better next time."

"That's okay," said Frankie. "Say, you know our Georgie? You know what he just did? Guy in the freight elevator says to him, who're you shoving, you black bastard?"

"Who said that to him?"

"Some jerk with a truckload of stuff. What a schmuck. You know the kind of guy. Picks on me. Bumps me hard with his shoulder. So Georgie bends down, and powie, right in the old breadbasket with his head. Boom. Boy, you should've seen that guy go down with his hangers. Flatter than a pancake. Right on his mush. The winner. Yea. I picked up Georgie's hand. I said, thanks, pal. Got me a coke out of it."

"Always make a profit. That's what I say."

"Hey, boy," said Frankie. "What a beautiful day outside. Just a little wind, that's all. Wish I had me a bat and a ball. Smacko. Right over the fence. You want to bet? I bet you if you went out to Coney Island, you'd find a lot of people in the water there. I got a friend, I could kill him, he holds on to the ropes and pees. Yow. Watch me go into my old bellywhop. You like them big waves? Say. Did you ever hear how Georgie blows in an empty bottle? Sonofagun. He knows how to do a lot of things, don't he? He was showing me how to make a rabbit with his hands, you know, right on the sidewalk where the sun was, when a funny old geezer with a rope around his neck comes over and says to me, excuse me, sir, is your name Rudolph Hassenfeffer? I look at Georgie. He looks at me. Should we tell him? Phew. You know dead pigeons? They sure do stink, don't they?"

"I don't know," said Joe. "I haven't smelled them lately."

"I bet you he eats them raw. You want to bet me, Joe?"

"Who does?"

"That old guy I was telling you about. He had two little skinny ones in a paper bag."

"That's right," said Joe. "Go on. Tell me more. Maybe I'll believe you."

"Honest to god, Joe. Ask Georgie. He'll tell you. He saw them too."

"Crazy people."

"Bugs, I swear. You know what he said to me? I don't know why he picked on me. He said to me his feet were falling off. He said to me he didn't look it, but he had another kid coming. He said he was ashamed. He said he'd give me a thousand bucks if I stood in line for him. Honest. Ask Georgie if I'm lying. He'll tell you."

"What line?"

361

"You know," said Frankie. "For bread. Hey. I just got a terrific idea. Listen. How's this for an idea? I think I'll go down to the police station and tell them I want to be a dick. Special squad. How about that, Joe? You think that's a good idea?"

"One more minute," said Joe. "That's all I'm going to give you. I'll be damned if I'm going to listen to you any more."

"Aw," said Frankie. "Gee whiz. Why can't I do it? Why not? All I need is a badge, that's all. You think I'm afraid of them? I'm not afraid of them. I'd walk right over to them and flash it right in their goddamn faces. Bastards. I'd say to them, hey, you mugs, what's going on around here? What's the idea anyway? I'd say to them, hey, you know my friend, Joe? Yeah, Joe, that's right. Well, he don't like it. Yeah, you heard me. You stupid idiots. Stand back or I'll bop you one. So how about it now? Let's get started there. Let's fix up things. For chrissakes. Let's get going there."

"Twelve o'clock," said Joe. "And all's not well."

"How about that, Joe? You think that's a good idea?"

"A dilly if I ever heard one."

"Goddamn it," said Frankie. "I like talking to you. You know that?"

Owdacious puppy with gobs of gaflooie in him, the cute pavement rat, the perfect city hillbilly, he rises above his own frankier dilemmas and shelves them as solved, stifling with his sincerest flattery the darker sophisticated cries, such as, my heart with yours refuses to interlock, will you please tell me why? Which is the way great blunders from little ninnies grow. Bored stiff with so much fiddle-faddle, the tired wavering optics begin to see this as that. A rabbit on the loose seems to loom larger than a lion in a crouch. The imagination is an oarless skiff which bobs on the scum of the ocean as if it were a fussy battleship. Flames shoot forth from the cool and patient life of the elbow. To think of red cabbage is to blink at the whiter emotions. Nonthinkers find that brains are also good to eat.

As soon as Frankie hears it is lunch time, his feet in their partial socks begin to burn. When he breathes in, he whistles. Caught by the hair and held upright, he freezes his shadow behind him, sneezes hard, forcing himself to listen with terrible attention as to where he must next venture forth to run down quick for Joe who today must eat in so that he can look after things that hardly exist, as Mr. Colish has ordered. How slowly does Frankie's memory absorb what bubbles on his lips. A carton of creamed coffee for his sugar-loving master, an immense club sandwich of warm corned beef, refuse the pickle unless they have the half-sour kind, and a cinnamon bun without raisins if possible, or a wedge, if such there be, of cheese and pineapple pie. Umpteen times did he repeat it with his second wind and nonstop style until its delicious order was hopelessly scrambled, yet he was positive he had it straight, standing there so erect, thumbing his nose at the shufflers and snufflers who passed by to get their feed, the flat faced and hollow eyed who no longer knew what aim or purpose meant, while in his jumping jack of a mind the safest errand suffered a great glory change into the most reckless mission.

So off like a flash with the cash he goes, fabulously plural in his motion in his excessive shorts, while Joe still clings so avidly to his one spot that it soon degenerates into a disgusting, scalelike form in which most of the external organs twitch, leer once or twice, and passively disappear. Moving all, he is himself immovable, until the pestilential air is infused with a purer rage. He smiles as he lingers. He scans the space between his fingers to find the place where his woolgathering began, and when he feels the faint breeze Frankie left behind him come creeping in again, he quickly closes his fist on this initial bloom of his afternoon. Mummies of kings in their conceited dust may have the luck to see the sun and sand again so long as the pyramids stand beneath which they lie entombed, but the first boy, that tease, that stem, that endless paragraph of a promise of joyous immortality, will always nullify the last man.

Though the sprockets in Joe are sharp and sound as yet, and the inside of his Thursday mouth a moist velvety red, and his east coast ears do respect, since they feel they can fathom, the knee-deep things the waves keep saying, something about skippers coming, and the great central pulse in his men's-room head, bent lower than it need be over the washbowl, he is still intent on his single healthy wish to power himself ever nearer to his eventual finish with his stinging paper cuts and lavish suds of yellow soap against the rush of icy cold waters of revival running on his wrists. Yet something still sticks in his craw. Still bleeding space white for his own delight, he shuts the faucet tight as if to see he can floor himself with the attenuated thought that as much as his vanity may insist on touting him as a real smart cookie, the fact remains that the more he shapes his course full south of the border of sense to reach the dulcet cove of savvy and intelligence, the quicker does he run his keel aground on the irascible reef of his northern oafdom, his sensibility lashed and whipped into shards of bitter spray, the last bit of his mother wit nailed fast to the mast of his everlasting ignorance.

Thoroughly thoughtsick at last, he unreeled the roller towel none too gently as if to take in all the blustering sail he could, and wiped his hands in its coarse fibers until their drab individuality became a bright universal pink, counting the while the multitudinous specks on the mirror as if numbering his morning mistakes, viewing with a wonderful hostility that old standing joke of his, his self-annulling, his barometrical, his debatable, his hilariously wimpled phiz, otherwise known as his face.

A jolly cockroach, exceedingly proud of its perfect sense of direction, marched straight through the arch of his right shoe without his knowing it. Without his meaning to he trod upon and squashed with a crack this rival critter, this superexcellent dead game bug, recoiling from what he had reduced it to, to goo like his brownish guilt, to a stain like his shame, to a pitiful smear of his mind's own mop material. If this too be food for thought, then this is the limit, he is desperately in need of help.

He hurried back to his tin-plated packing table to get his alfresco eating over with, showing a courage rarely recorded, for he knew now what he had known before, that everything which moves must take its chances. Beginning again when he should be ending. Young men will think. Young men will think what men have already thought. Like his carton of coffee which had slopped over. With hands as sticky as his curiosity, he parted the slices of bread of his sandwich as if he were laying open his own thick skull, and saw what did not surprise him, that the meat inside was overrun with fat. The Danish was not what he had ordered. It was highly varnished to resemble cake. It had a pool in its center of puslike custard. More to gag on, more to regurgitate. While time, while time. Glorious dispenser of such largesse. Great banisher of such swill. Will it ever mingle for him the proper oils, salts and condiments? Will it slacken at last the coils of his smaller intestines so that the all too solid cyst of his self-concern may detach itself and slide through? For his spits are turning in him much too fast. And his tumbled soul is in torture as it testily dissolves in its own black and acid liquors.

Cast ye up, cast ye up. Such a vigorous interior action is no longer child's play. Good lord, I saw as it were the appearance of Satan, the old southpaw, with his many arms of fire, and strewn about the parochial divisions of his hell, the prismatic bits of prehistoric lies and visions. And a spirit passed before my face. And the hair of my flesh stood up. And as a partridge sitteth on eggs, and hatcheth them not, I felt again the failure of all my efforts to deliver myself of myself. And I became as one who striveth with his maker, and saith unto him, take away my life, for I am not better than my fathers.

He bundled up his garbage. He flipped out his apron. He tore apart the clots in his morning hanky to increase the blowable space. He checked to see if he had cigarettes enough to last him for at least six or seven smokes. He disentangled his keys from his pocket comb, readying the equipments of his exile. As a figure, he begins to recede. Simple poorling, bereft and fleeced, when he regained the snug retrogressive toilet, he picked the darkest of two stalls to latch himself in, and banging down the cover of the seat, eased himself down upon it with a sigh that had as much power to it as the failing light of the unshaded bulb of twenty watts. Only his shoes could be seen. He puffed. He sucked in the smell of CN mixed with piss. He sighed again. He bowed down his head as quietly as he could, and blew out a world he knew would never be his. He rested.

And wee-wee with him, perched as we are like pixies on the gurgling water box, climbers in our childish spite, determined to haunt him rather than he should continue to haunt us, appraising as a possible weapon the floating brass ball which is the principal organ of the works. How positively distasteful to see him so pulped and pegged out. Strange that matter in such a condition should sometimes be called radiant matter. Which shows how dimly we ourselves twinkle as he sends up his bluish haze in the midst of which it is clear that he does not squat there trembling, his eyes all blubbered over with tears, fearful of every ray of light, lest it should discover him. Or that, tugging at the chain of the flush with such a wildness as if to make sure that the last of his bile and bitterness should whelm up and engulf and muffle him, he fell into immediate convulsions, and died away in his own arms.

A scene too tender to be conceived by many. The intolerable truth is that there has been such a progressive enfeeblement of what is dramatic in him that what he is at present is simply a silent cuss who flicks off his ashes, and in so doing, completely fails to amuse us. After all. What are we in relation to an orange or a star that we should be so quick to sneer at what we imagine to be, as we finger with pride our own raised welts and reddish scars, but the palest of minor pricks, and the thinnest of leaner pickings? Is what issues from our mouths more capacious and aromatic? Do we seminate what we breathe or spit upon? Do livid little lice appear at our merest touch? Are we ourselves of the substance that feeds fire?

A trolley car conductor once said to us, hey, small change, push back to the rear, and when we did so, furious as hell that we should be spoken to that way by a greying boar with chipped tusks and a wilderness of hairs up his nose, we saw coming into our heads a giant sunflower from far-off Kansas, the Sunflower State, and we were afraid to grow with it, and we scrunched down, but the less room we took up, the more we felt we were in the way, a stopper, a plug, a squelched interpolation, while flaking sickle shapes of inglorious names in gold leaf flashed by, made nebulous by neon people, and we stretched our throats and we howled we did and bared our teeth like wolves, for the distress of the way edges all men's spirits, and we bayed, because once again six or seven seconds had passed without producing anything that could make dense again for us what is truly strange or remarkable, that would assemble about us the vapors of that rare antiseptic called common sense.

What does it matter where we are? We never seem to have any luck that way. Thus we sheepishly languish while our rusts and smuts and mildews collect on us. And like Joe himself we get to thinking. The paleozoic designates a grand division of geological history. The clinkstone gives off a ringing sound when struck. The funnel is shaped like a hollow cone, tapering into a tube, through which the softest of liquid complaints may be run into another vessel. How gently does Joe abide it, the good man. His pitying smile plays upon the scummy water as we, who are his woolly artifacts rolled up into one, go under, sinking heavily to the bottom, his lopsided bale of worm's meat. The awry bulb glows less like a weakling in celebration of. The usual naked woman forcefully scrawled on the wall, flung down without abutments or supports, her plunging figure embrangled in the cracks and currents of a viscous emotion, her grainy rump crosshatched with crude male humours, yawns, scratches herself where her hair is most poisonous, muscles shut her cavernous slit, and sits up to rub the merry kohl of make-believe out of her eyes and into his.

Joy to the world. The old ark, he do seem to be amovering. Whatever sleep-swollen weeds may or may not straw his way, he does often incite himself awake with his own ardent manhattan imaginings until he believes he is God's own ghost writer of genesis, the creator of terror and tears, the prime weaver of wit and address, the jerkin of horsehide, the original cosmic snot, both forge and furnace out of which came limping the very first germ that laughed, an inflamed world-self fleeringly stepping itself up and up. In many a rise, many as comical a fall. So that the swaggering parabolics of himself as a divinity like a grizzly bear must be periodically burlesqued. His fur must always be flying. The same old clown is still the same old sap. He had failed again to endear himself to himself, which is the usual human failure in the clutch. He has falsely enriched himself with his toilet trappings and barbaric substitutes for clarity and sense. His rumorous imagination is like a rattletrap of an old-fashioned flivver in which he shimmies in endless ground loops and u-turns through the muck of his ideas like a hen pees, in twangled arabesques of apocryphal and chicken-shit excitement. He prevails upon his spread-eagled mind to straddle the lanes so that it may enjoy the red fictitious thrill of flirting with the raven onrushings of life, missing its death by inches. But no regal or real or literal sideswiping of the truth as yet. Not yet, not yet. While his demure self-seeking partially emerges, as a flower peeps through the grass. And this is what he calls resting.

Time. Give him a bit more time to see. Does he smile now as he should? Does he cough like a crow as if signaling to himself to swoop down where he may defecate on a dryer leaf? Is his beak immersed in fake lakes of fume and fire? Is he still bent double in that unamusing rut of his of piling the bones of human errors on the peelings of human mistakes? But of course. For he is still thinking. Thinking. Though every form of thinking so far has fouled him up.

What is this strange and difficult exercise? The wise say, out of nothing, nothing can come. Thinking itself is amazed to discover that in the forepart of each and every brain there are mossy places, and in brain the same, rear areas of considerable patchery. Thinking about thinking. It becomes so real, thinking does. It walks and talks with me

367

in my funny old greenhouse. We link arms. We exchange looks. We pass and repass where lies the shattered glass of universal modes of behaviour, in and out of books. Our fingers fuse as we toy with the texture of those accidental continents formed by the mold of ancient meditation. We gather straws to show us where next the wind will blow us. But thinking is my closest and most compulsive relative. By its very nature it must finally turn and tear itself away from me. It is only then that I see that from its stern is hung a tailpiece of tattered streamers which is all that remains of the twisted ways in which the nestlings and newcomers of other days, which were more like one whole night now returned to haunt the next batch, did seek so unsuccessfully to sit straight and fly right.

Ghosts illiquid, impartible hemoglobin, incursive biological of the past which is the inexpugnable infusion, the very coloring matter of whatever blood at present is mine and thine. No one ever knows whom to blame for such a stain. The touchiest are constantly bellering, out, damned spot, and stay out. Or wondering whence cometh that being between worlds, that interrogative bitch which catfoots in to claw and crimp us until we no longer know whether it is for ourselves or others that we are bleating, and bleeding, simply that. Or whither goeth what bringeth and taketh. Or which what is which. Or who is exactly where. Or why not quit, quit for shame, for this is tops for comedy and confusion.

He shook his head so furiously it was a wonder it stayed on. He tried to bat the blankety-blank spots out of his eyes. He wibble-wobbled a bit where it was mostly ill-lit. His two cold feet in their crinkled shoes were crazy, man, so frantic were they to wriggle out of standing as he made them do in his own skull. What now? What final fantastic vision of himself was this? What could these tremors of that far-off future be which snaked along the opalescent spine of his joy stick?

What there is to feel has to be felt. How ridiculous he looked in it, wearing again what his memory had lashed around him, a small square leathern box on his forehead, and a similar one on his left arm. The hooks and crooks of Hebrew words on cringing slips of paper. Spittle in snuff and wails and feverish rocking. And time, it did pass. And a whisper ran around that it was the year twelve million in the month of the crapulous pig and the changeless cuckoo. Ah, god. It is so terrible to be merely human. What availeth these amulets and charms and phylacteries when there will always be a creep who will never know and who will always be asking? Always this, always. Where in my core lies my answer? Where in my substratum is my pith? What kind of an animal am I?

Incontestably a flop and a bore, a most villainous unutterable, a blundering, whining, hair-losing, wetting, squealing one. Which is how the ponderous toilet door opened its rusty yap and just as mockingly closed it. Charmed to be sure. Which is the same as saying that Joe was once again a cool and alert customer, capable of replying in kind and exchanging with reciprocal grace a series of satirical bows with a stub of a broom squired by Georgie, porgie, lemonade, pie.

He sure gwine pick up his sword and shield to study war some more in the old army shoes he wore. That stubborn and subversive nigra, intoning his pacifistic spiritual turned killer, rendered, with such a cunning suggestion of strangle holds and razor slashings, entirely on his insurrectionary breath. Yet so seriously determined withal that when the last of those hellish quavers of his had subsided, he began to hum and then to whistle it as if by such slow grass-growing means the pearly gates to his brambled tongue would have time enough to open, and the sprays and sprigs of his longing for a white and whiter life would further stretch and articulate their blasphemous little buds.

Stands revealed again as sold american, a microcosmic coon, moving none too freely in this limited space, he grounded his arms, and brushed away his sighs and scuffles and his tongue clicks. What a load of crap. What a crippling sin is this earnestness. He brought his hand down with a slap. Reporting for duty, sir. Of course, he inferred, to be destined to be a segregated soldier does seem a crime and disgrace, but is it any more so than to be a white jew making like a sniper, allowing himself to be so poorly placed and hidden by god knows what smoky impulse right here in this languid stink when he could be outside, floating around, as irresponsible as a feather, getting himself lost in princely ways paved and heroic, in that great sweet enfolder of a world, blessed as it is today with such clear and sparkling weather?

"Just like a nigger," said Joe.

"Yeah, man," said George. "Ain't I though?"

"Always trying to make believe he can forget his troubles."

"Troubles like in bubbles."

"There he is," said Joe. "Everybody's black bastard. Who doesn't

369

know him? He's that lover of wicked filth and mouse turds, ain't he? Why, sure. We all know his fascinating history, don't we? It stares us in the face. He's Georgie with the great big beautiful teeth that's never had beef enough. Funny situation. They glisten. He boils. He licks his lucky penny. He buys dream books to pad the crutches of his third sister. He drums on his head. He blinds his father for a week with one punch. He crashes through the jungle with his broomstick."

"Yea," said Georgie. "The sap's running. I knew it would."

"He shines," said Joe. "He's a shine. He's not for me. And he's not for you. Because why? Because he smells like a river in Africa. Because he stands there like the pure white lamb he's not, looking over Jordan, gazing out to sea, shading his worried eyes. Ah, says he. So this is what the birds have crapped on. Bullshit. When he sees Jesus, he changes color. The sky for him is full of rosy shrimps. The crabs, especially, are attracted to him. He near busts a gut. He wades in where he's not wanted. He sings."

"Oh, I'm a regular pisser. That's what I am."

"It's no use," said Joe. "You haven't got a chance."

"Not a ghost of a glimmer," said George. "Open that door, man. I just got to take a look at your face."

"George," said Joe. "I'm warning you. I feel mean today."

"Oh, my brother."

"Oh, my god," said Joe. "Here we go again."

"How can I praise him sufficiently? His words are as a lamp unto my feet and a light unto my path. Can you see my hands? They're pale and trembling. When did you start blazing like that? How come you're so goddamn inspired?"

"Simple," said Joe. "Because I just can't tear my eyes away from what's happening to you. It's all pretty damn disgusting. I know that. Maybe you're the one who can tell me. What in hell do you think it means?"

"Why," said George. "It means you're the all-around perfect jew, man, that's what it means. Revenge. It sure is sweet. Like ham bones, brother. Like watermelon hanging on the vine. Quoth the raven. Rapping at your chamber door. Son, I do hereby nail you to the cross. And there I'll be very happy to leave you. Do I get my cigarette now? Or do I have to come back at you with some other brilliant thing?"

"You get your cigarette now."

"Ah," said George. "Good shot. Glad to see the old wing is still working. For these small favors, I do thank thee, God. And thy humble servant, Joe. In whose tender presence I shall now drop me pants and squat a while. Shit. Sure is tough to ditch this lingo once it gets a grip on you. Well, now, here's a pleasant surprise. There's absolutely nothing floating in this here bowl. That's what I like. So long as everybody remembers to pull the chain, there's plenty hope for all of us yet. Even if this seat is kind of cold and discouraging. The trouble with me is I don't smoke enough. Any flies where you are? You feel bushed like me? God knows what I've done today in the way of work except dream a while and scheme a while. Though I did spill my seed last night with a little bit of a woman I was very careful not to. Now here's something I would certainly like to have your opinion of. Put the case this way. If the best your father can do is to dig graves out in Queens, and your mother to pluck chickens in Brooklyn, would you say that what sticks to their clothes is just the food you need when taken by way of the mouth to produce in you a single nodding purple flower? Or if you follow me, that great green urge to get going and rape and piss on this wonderful white man's life before your pistils get all covered with dust? Mother of God. I sure do hate a guy who's always telling me he's tired. I crush lilies. What do you vent your spleen on? You got an idea how your bones are connected? How's your tubes of understanding? They clogged too? Bastard spark. It just burned me. I tell you, sweetheart. I still feel it in my heart. All we have to do is keep the mouth flapping long enough and we're bound to suck in something. You understand what I mean now? If you do, knock twice. If you don't, don't bother. After all, I'm letting it all hang out for your sake, not mine."

"Fantastic," said Joe.

"You like how I look inside out? Did I give you the business or didn't I?"

"So help me," said Joe. "I never knew so much struggle and suffering could have so much zing to it."

"Rip into me, boy. That's what I'm here for."

"Good old George. He's a real big brother to me. He's so sorry to see me go."

"And he hopes to hell you never come back. You better watch it, son. It's a funny, funny world outside."

371

"It is?" said Joe. "Which world?"

"Why, goddamn it, the one you're going to make yours."

"Oh," said Joe. "That one."

"I tell you. We sure in hell need someone like you out there."

"We do?" said Joe. "What for?"

"Holy cow," said George. "You mean to say you don't know?"

"George," said Joe. "I never lied to you. And I'm not going to start now."

"Well, I'll be a suck-egg mule."

"God, I hope it's only temporary."

"I swear," said George. "The things you bump into sometimes. It's got me so woozy I can't tell my ass from my elbow. Maybe if I cut my toenails tonight, I'll find out which end is up. Whew. I charged right in here and what did I find? There he was, locked in for the duration, with no sign of his pants showing, so no one had to tell me, bunched up in there like a million people rolled up into one, funny how you feel those things, sitting there and studying how to tackle the world like it's never been tackled before."

"Me?" said Joe. "That monster? You must have a screw loose somewhere. Didn't I ever tell you? I'm a coward, George. What're you trying to do? Frighten the piss out of me?"

"Ah, well," said George. "A kid's a kid after all."

"It's incredible," said Joe. "Really."

"You lighting up again? Remember, boy. I'm your best customer."

"Once they get a thing in their heads, it's no use, it's impossible to knock it out. A hero all of a sudden. Stick out your hand. You want it or don't you? Don't be proud. The whole country's coughing. You might as well be stupid too and join the crowd."

"Well," said George. "If you put it that way."

"Thanks for leaving me my finger."

"Ah," said George. "I don't give a damn what you say. There's something big about you."

"Big," said Joe. "That's exactly what I was waiting to hear. You got a thousand years or so? You're in no particular hurry, are you? What would you say if I told you she had seventeen legs at least? And four red eyebrows? And a pearly dot in the middle of her puss like a pin stuck in? And a kind of juicy fuzz all over her boyish body? And horns? And tiny wings the color of your nails? And the size of her eyes when she first flew in, god, I hate to think of it even now."

372

"That damn butt. Stuck to my lips again. Sometimes my mouth gets so dry."

"It's funny," said Joe. "I can never believe anyone ever wants to listen to me."

"Why, you poor little mamma's boy."

"Ah," said Joe. "Wait. Wait until you hear what I really am. You'll say that again. And more."

For what he is, he is at any given moment, regardless of the sum of its essential conditions and attendant facts, much too much the spectacular wrestler with the trivial and the ridiculous, the very symbol of a punk who roughs in his limited imagination with his purple passions like a strictly emotional cocker. For which reason his telling must be queer and fumid at first, with the shadow of his hand materializing on the wall as a rabbit crouched in despair of imminent dispersion, earless, cocoa-colored and monocular, feebly nibbling at its own dumb preliminary tricks.

He began again. He tried to tell how he came creeping home last night, his hat-size universe many sizes smaller, his gloom-encircled eyes decidedly weak in phosphorescence of faith, his cuffs rimmed with the grey dust of powder-puff recollection, his guilt-sharp nails carting home a whole acre of most black and immoral dirt. Still nothing with nothing. True, the foyer light flared up and blew as soon as he flicked on the switch. But that of course was just his luck lately with all manner and means of illumination. Whereas other snide buckos are veritable bulls whose bumptious roars constantly rock the earth wherever they may decide to be ringed in the nose and tethered, a shrinking calf like himself can hardly bear it when a few simple wire hangers take it upon themselves to tinkle him in. He shushed them and listened. As feathery as he can be and exquisitely modest on his feet, he will like his kin become progressively more lumpish and unsteady, and as meek as the meekest when he too stretches himself out in bed. It seemed to him that those who were already flat on their backs were much too quiet to be asleep.

If the soul was once a sigh, it is now made flesh of their flesh, operating in it peculiarly, numbering without hope a thousand tender ideas of itself in an agony of juxtaposition to others. Theirs is that nightly horror story of thinking out things. Sleep is an enormous meadow, the bigger the image, the bigger the lie, where dreams come with their boots on to complete the process of trampling down their

373

three-leaf clover lives. Hissing stream, flowoff of fancy conjecture, splattering down the sides of the toilet bowl, discreetly easing itself. So long held in. The flush mechanism unleashed its ten hysterical gallons with all the roil and moil of a mammoth uproar at sea. The faucet yipped like a demon dog. The sceptical cake of soap cackled between his hands. His personal crusty towel was streaked with the gorgeous spots of blood of his last close shave. What a tosspot of moral sensibility, every sting of which is dramatically doubled. What a charming nightcap view of the unduly wicked dangle, big as you please, and you be damned, of rinsed slip and stockings from the shower ring, plunderers and despoilers of space. What a frightful effort a man has to make to think in order to maintain himself among things. While the spunkless acid in him churns, turning chicken before the looming shadow of a lamp on his way to the kitchen where the homely light did rout that terrifying sense of otherness in every thing contained therein, and made it stick, so that his stomach, really disgusted with all this blithering guff and gas, could sensibly growl at last, shovel me down something quick.

Rats on that contemplative body which is inclined to give the light-foot spirit sport whilst poking around the refrigerator for a hard-boiled egg, a dish of junket, and the rosiest apple, pilfering from nowhere and joyously exuding as he does so many more of his superior thoughts, such as, what a mild shock it is to discover that too much of one thing is not enough of another. Or when solids are in a subjunctive mood, they wish they were pluperfect fluids. Or though Hamlet's stars are out tonight, and what do they do when the window is flung open but cast their splashy optics back at the earth as if it were the blinking miracle, what was once so dark for him when he was just a boy is now so much darker for today's green sap whose sillier grop-ing sends him spinning round the squishy axis in him endlessly until he resorts to blind eating as the only gimmick that can put a stop to it, saying in effect, with that touching brutality of gesture and tone usually reserved for those loved the most, back in your breadbox, crumb.

He read while he ate, propping up the book on the sugar bowl. The perceptive city man, how strange that he should have such a pitiful desire to swop spit for light, yet live so little under the sun. Does seem like a dirty mean slinking fellow, yet he is famous for not leaving food

374

stains on the pages of the filthiest-looking book, so grateful is he for this most innocent means of pacifying his natural parts, of anticipating his eventual dissolution, of slowly dying to himself. We follow his eye as it runs down the bottom of the page to read. What is a cowslip in Great Britain is a marsh marigold in America. If we finish that footnote with him, and support with our smile those drooping umbels of yellow fragrance, we will surely grow soft in the head along with him in this small Brooklyn kitchen whose size is of such a funny influence that for once we feel that we have become more than mere stolid producers of dung, or dreary fillers-up of privies, or sightless bait for fleas.

Where hokum lives is the land of bosh. We hope we feel we imagine. The crap artist is he who hoohoos at his own owlish attempt to give scope and dimension to an itch or a sneeze. The stupidity of us does keep superabounding, floundering on a treadmill of print which we furiously skim so as to travel away from where we usually coast, and when we do, how it does puzzle us, for if the so-called east in us remains a place of intricate passageways where our visceral blindness still worms, how can we praise our far west as the clearest external eye we can ever hope to possess when the first thing it sees, like a pioneer staggered by his reckless affair with space, is a false pond on the prairie?

The answer to that is simple. When your buckskin clothes begin to smoke with bullet holes, the time has come to clear the table and take unto yourself a cool slug of milk. If the wall is to the sink as the stove is to the clock, how deeply is experience colored when there is just as much whiteness without as there is within? Barely scratching the surface, he sat down again to read in that same borrowed book where his age of anxiety is immediately dwarfed by its vast simplified past, terribly pleased that all should seem so pleasant in this earliest morning hour of his continuous present.

Item. When their grain or grass eating gets scarce, one mule will not hesitate to ingest the tail of another. Children everywhere do see their charming resemblance to us as donkeys. The mystic treks of men and beasts of the last century were rarely made around a kitchen chair. Snow is also in the category of the cruel and the insensible. Sure is a howling mystery why the wind should blow where no human being can hear it. The ever green finger of a fir tree points out where upwards is. Only a fatherless child would dare to make his faint tracks on the motherly hills and dales of such an eerie landscape of minds anonymous. How perfectly does the prairie dog dread the penultimate fury and despair of the starving wolf in winter as he lopes in to assault with tooth and claw the frost-bound roof of the house, tearing up the passages, snorting into them, plunging his earth-stuffed nose further and further in until he consummates, which is as God wills it, his horizontal relationship with his marvelous fellow creature. If the heart erects its warm little crosses in memory of the numberless fleas which also went west, the cooler mania of the mind is to rook itself of its real nature.

Charging his lungs with the Merlin smoke of transfiguration, he moistened a powerful finger and turned the page. Indifferent to the more familiar geography, he followed the bend of the Wind River and cheerfully skirted Rattlesnake Ridge with the giant steps of the first white man to impinge on the Big Horn Basin, and the boiling mud springs and spouting geysers of Yellowstone, striding towards that fresh phenomenon of hell breaking loose with all the confidence and elan of John Colter, the original mountain man.

Look on me. Look how high up I am. Look on me splurging it, playing the giddy goat, apartment-house fool, no crock of riches can now comfoozle me, no want can make me kowtow to any spectral materialization of my decline through the cruel offices of disease or hunger. Far more manlier now is my daydream of refusing to pay tribute to how I appear to others by prematurely squeezing a headless pimple. As I squat on my sturdy legs, the fine powder of my pettiness falls from me. I need no longer stoop to read my fate in the color of my stool. It is natural for me to shiver, for I feel in me the incredible stamina of a star. My fear of death is in a deep freeze in these Rockies where the fearsome Blackfeet winter. I am an amazing cuss. I wrap myself in my single blanket and send up a smoke signal of success, for when I sleep I know that I shall rest in sweet and full possession of me, and of me only, and of no one but myself. As for the rest of me, I can only say that it went thataway.

He had already traveled so far elsewhere that when that bug angrily swooped down on him in superb fashion to buzz his nose, he pretty near jumped out of his skin. His very own eyes were recovered to him. His throat felt cut. How short-lived is our courage in the presence of eternity, especially when it is not our own. The day will come when the small stock of our sensations will become shockingly smaller. When people say comes the awakening, they mean the comedy is finished. The rest is soon told. So fabulously ugly and enormous was that insect, so monstrous a deviation was she, and such a jealous product of the parenthetical night life of the truth inescapable in its interplanetary ubiquity, that she caused him instantly to suffer from cold feet, scaring him spitless, exposing him beautifully. She fractured him. She laid him low. She sure did stop the show. The horrified coward, his only hope now was to make like a piece of wood and play dead, but the insatiable prima donna, she kept hovering before him in her helicopter way, fluffing out her cloud-woven fuzz, archly display-ing the obscene length of her swab and stinger, boldly holding up to view her prime grasshopper parts, defying him to guess where in her dropsical organs of vision shone good and where evil, curling her innumerable legs more and more round the gratifyingly thick aroma of his flowering disgust and fear.

Had she departed when she should, she would have lived to tell it. What flaw in her made her so susceptible to the contagion of his own fallibility? It seemed at first that she was merely mocking him when she flew into a panic as he raised his paw to take a swipe at her. Crashing into the thirty-second day, and the first phase of the moon on the calendar, pinging wild flight music off the light globe, she proceeded to butt her head into three similar white walls successively until she hit the ceiling, bringing him to his feet with the realization that she was seriously distressed and crazy and lost. If the devil were not the devil, he would never scheme to desert his own. That hideous little beast without the foggiest notion of where the open window was, each of her harrowing leaps and collisions seemed so spitefully to foreshadow the neurotic trick of the century of remaining up in the air forever. He waved his hands in an effort to show her how she could go out as she had come in. But she was past help. And he looked ridicu-lous. He rolled up half a newspaper and waited for her to settle within reach.

Snarl of a spectator cat, cough and quiver of crueler latitudes of space, sleepless conscience spying, supercurious clip-clop of a super-natural horse, prickle of window-framed illusions and backyard effu-sions, incredulous gathering of the clan, calling all creepers, daze of

377

infant cooties in their inflamed and congested lairs, pismire conspiring with a dumb wood louse, silverfish sporting in bathtub scum, pale wash, shimmering roaches in heat, congregations of dreamers weighed down by their rusty iron wills, scrofulous are the grassplots where goblins fornicate with infidelic and lush disasters, the color black fenced off and murmuring, this is how death, the muzzler, tromps on her tail in his left-handed honeymoon with life, the big mitt man, the grifter, tear-assing around with his cheating devices while the drugged city sleeps.

Her circles grew shorter and shorter. She spiraled out her last appeal, and flumped down heavily, affixing herself with a final plop of surrender midway on the wall, turning every bit of her back to him. He leaned across the table and smashed her flat. He stood there stunned. He smiled as he drew back to study what he had so signally achieved, softly saying to himself, my god, how it does my heart good to see myself employ my incomparable endowments, and burn my immense forces far into the night like Edison's electricity, to assure myself that mine are indeed the limbs of vertebrates above fishes. He flicked off the miserable flinderation with the utmost grace.

With this blood smear for my copestone, for what fine deed have I laid my foundation? I have crowned my edifice with a common flag. I have set a snare for myself, and I am also taken. Ah, I pray thee, leave me, love me no more, for I am destined to be the author of much evil, and the father of many white lies and minor killings. So quick to acquire dishonor, majestically powered by the madcap bubbles in my think tank, compelling myself to duel with the distilled phantoms of my own creation, so selfishly pleasure-bent, I shall gather knowledge of myself all of my life, and then die like an utter fool.

"And the word," said George. "The word was made flesh and dwelt among us."

"Yes," said Joe. "And it was such a nice clean little thing until I touched it and fouled it up, but good."

"So you say. So you say."

"It was too much, too much. It makes me sick to think of it."

"Okay," said George. "That's enough of that crap."

"Right," said Joe. "That's what I say."

"Sonofabitch," said George. "The kid's ruined me. He's left me all the cheap words. I must say. It sure burns my ass every time I hear

378

somebody say what he has to say, and then see him try to crawl out of it. After all. Who in the hell do you think I am? You think I'm one of those dumb lazy bastards who never want to listen or try to understand? You think I don't know why I'm huffing and puffing so much? Why, it's a joke, man. I'm just trying to be very clever here. I figure if I make all this noise, I'll make you believe I didn't miss a thing, that I was really in there pitching with you all the time, terribly moved by everything you were kind enough to throw at me, and what's more, knowing why. You ready to bust your sides laughing? How's that for a fakeroo?"

"Sorry I made it so tough for you."

"What God said to Jesus."

"Really?" said Joe. "What an amazing coincidence."

"The hell with this kid. No matter what he says, he kills me. He makes me crazy about him every time."

"I think," said Joe. "The time has come to bless this toilet, my new home. For never have I been so happy anywhere. Or so successful."

"That's the stuff," said George. "Now you're doing it. Hang in there, boy. Chin up. White tie and tails. Top hat. Pip, pip. Courage, lad. Everything feels so droopy on me. Hate to leave you little stall. But duty calls."

"What a shame," said Joe. "Really. The better man, he bows out."

"How do you like that?" said George. "Can't get my pants up. Clumsy all of a sudden. Poop. There goes another button, I could've been twice around the world in the time it's taking me to get out of here. And to think that all I ever asked of life, as I said, was to give me enough room to run around in circles. I'm in. I'm out. I'm on my way. In dreamland I must've been. My bullet head wrapt in the clouds. My red corpuscles floating free. Having such a gay time. Camping out with the angels. Thought I was God's own voice speaking to you through me. It's like I'm telling you, man. All you have to do is press the little valve down and the music goes round and round. Here's your hat. What's your hurry? You warm enough in there? You want me to bring you some clean socks and underwear in case I come back? No answer. Joey, my pal. You have nothing to worry. It's a cinch. All you have to do is step out into the cold cruel world and you'll come out frozen stiff. Because you were born for it, brother. It's your fate. It's your destiny. It's a crock of shit."

"Well, well," said Felix. "Who is that there sounding off so big here?"

"Felix, my old friend."

"Okay," said Felix. "What've I got to lose?"

"My pal. My long lost buddy."

"Drink," said Felix. "The curse of the nation."

"Hey, hey," said George. "I feel those old pains again. I hear a trumpet blown in the city. I am changing back into myself. Hold your lip there a second and listen to me. You one-eyed chipmunk. You broken cue stick. You sad six ball in the side pocket. You got your fly all checked? Is your face set forward to the east? Are you ready now to azzle back a bit? Watch me now. I have but to touch you with my rod, and all, all your iniquities and abominations, they shall be stripped from you like the pussies from a pussy willow. Like so. And so. Until, by god, I don't give a damn if you never smile again, but please, whatever you do, throw us a butt before you conk out, and save the last waltz for me."

"Poor fella," said Felix. "What's that guy in there been saying to you?"

"Why, you stupid piece of humanity."

"What in the hell is all this with the compliments?"

"You blind or something? Can't you see it's my own love I'm spreading?"

"I'll be damned," said Felix. "And here I've been thinking it was only manure."

"Hey," said George. "What's the matter with your hand?"

"This?" said Felix. "It's okay. Just nicked it a little. Getting nervous in my old age."

"Real blood," said George. "Uh-uh. Something tells me the fun is over."

"Goddamn nuisance," said Felix. "I thought I stopped it."

"Hold it up now. Hold it straight."

"Oops," said Felix. "There goes your clean floor."

"What a bandage," said George. "What did you use? Your old drawers?"

"Hey, Joe," said Felix. "You want to come out and take a look at this?"

"Ho, ho," said George. "So that's it, is it?"

"What is? Isn't that Joe in there?"

"Shh," said George. "What are you trying to do? Wake up the dead?"

"I would if I could. What in the hell would be wrong with that?"

"Ah, now," said George. "That's the way we want it. Just oozing away nicely. Funny looking cut. Is that a J? Or isn't it?"

"Sure does look like it, doesn't it?"

"Another mystery."

"Just tie it up tight. And the hell with it."

"You skinny old jerk," said George. "Why did you let me stand there and talk to you that way? I could've saved you some blood."

"That's just it," said Felix.

"What is?"

"You were talking to me."

"I was?"

"Who talks to me these days? All I get is these goddamn dirty looks."

"Me and my kind heart. How did I get trapped this way?"

"Ah," said Felix. "I'm telling you now. You can kid all you want. But there comes a time. There comes a time."

For even a poor patient plug like himself, browned off unto the very knobs of his knees and the fixed limit of the cysts on his elbows to get tearing mad and foam at the mouth, precisely as would any other gaffed and afflicted soul who is frankly fed up to the gills with their disgusting accumulated snot. The conies are but a feeble folk, yet they make their houses in the rocks. But these insidious termites here are infinitely feebler. Influenced by, and sharing as they do, the same spectacular blindness, the beast they have in view when they look at what they know as Felix is a perfect goat, a pip of an animal with its long weathered line of notorious hair attached and alertly resting on his landsliding upper lip. Home is where it really hit him. Bone soft and blood weakened by a solid week's cruel focus of their divining rods on him alone as the devil, he found himself fogging the reflection of his face in the bathroom mirror, hating that hoodoo of a moustache with so much of their own unreasonable venom that he lathered it for the kill three times, but each time his trusty straight razor failed him.

He turned to see what sudden puff of wind had rattled that tiny toilet screen he had painted white two years ago come May, and saw

381

that the starfish on the glazed glass were all ablaze, amazed that such a common design could become such a classy sparkler, clearly feeling himself impelled to think like a child in the face of it, that of all things it is the sun which can be the freest and freshest with every dull and opaque fact, that if there was a little bit of gold left in him it had not become dim, that if the shadow is often the symbol for the soul, we are all to be congratulated, but this, this is what happiness looks like.

What a scourge of sweet sentimental rot, he was glad to discover that the free sample of after-shave lotion could burn like fire. The hereditary evil of his face could easily be muffled in a towel. But where his heart was, there was still a good deal of unusual activity. And the powerful aroma of his good woman's black coffee seeped in. And just as he was about to emerge after slicking back his hair, love approached on padded feet, scratching on the door, proclaiming an emergency. If she had taken her salts last night, she ought to have told him, he who was her pestilence and her plaster, her gall and her leech.

Vexation and viper, worm in the heart of her once upon a rose, stop a second and consider, what is clear by now? That when she makes her death, she will be doing the dipsy-doodle? That she will be removing her blindfold and unlocking her handcuffs so as to scatter abroad her withered buds? That he has failed to sour her mouth permanently? That he has run out of ways of inaugurating a reign of terror in her eyes? That there has never been enough sun in him to drive off the miseries of her morning mists and her evening fogs? That her monthly flow has subsided to a trickle? That her immemorial years of yielding to his mongrel entwinement have strangled her fictions and reestablished her facts? That when she feels the constriction on her chest, she will eat her chicken cold?

Her oatmeal has thickened. Her toast has curled. Her coffee perks when it should not. Her asbestos pad is turning black. So purely now a washout in her snowy drawers and honest bra, and faint bouquet of common grasses, she will have to drip the rest of her water when she comes back, comes rushing back to me, with her spit curls flat, and her slippers slapping, and her knickers ruined, and her posterior rumpled, and her pulses out of whack, and her weepers wild, and awfully complicated, with all the terrible fluctuations of what must be love, what else can it be? And who will she be then? And how will I know her?

Ah, up shit creek are we all, we smell each other in passing, and we think we know. Blunt buzz saws of surface penetration, awful staggerers, sensational disciples of the school of panic where flit collides with flitter, we humble and humiliate, we pull down and raze to our own disgraceful level every fat chance we have of ever really knowing just who and what we are with a glance and a goose, with a single backflip of the brain. Excessive rage reduces the flayed body of sense to a perfect shambles. Fabulous effort to frig them all has fouled the few strings of his thought. Makes him laugh as if most of his marbles are missing.

Is this the room then where the mind of man can be at rest? Bugs is sad is the pressure of events is the cruel hard times is cuckoo. What does it matter now if the old kidneys are on the bum, hardly sagaciating as they used to? Narrow are the tubes through which the occasional quicksilver in a person must come balling the jack. Funny how the whole of life develops a sympathetic limp when industry lags. Sometimes the good ideas come so swiftly leaping, so overspread with the salmon flush of inspiration that they raise upon the skin innumerable prickles. Surely the king of all parasites is he who has acquired the knack of sponging off the future, so rich in doubt, of his two little kids, the boy at seven has Chinese eyes, the girl at eleven is positively Swedish looking, his two solid pippins in whom he has invested a whole slew of bites and kisses, his ping-pong partners, his piano and violin team, his two lambent flames whose burgeoning souls he frequently brightens by sliding across to each a newly minted dime at breakfast time. They are nuts about food for squirrels. They also cry for tuna which is the chicken of the sea. Ralph and Ruth, hallowed be their names.

Old jabberwocky, be quick now and sprinkle a blessing upon them, for the minutes are flying like arrows before the wind. Hear a father's fervent prayer. By their pearly links which are still continuous, by the blazing future tense of their flickering and their shadowing forth, by the prime historic fact of their fresh imprints and dimples, by their fruity essences, by their keen and spiny fundamentals which are still intact, may their bread when it falls always fall butter side up, may forbidden fruit merely make their fingers sticky, may they come to know, much sooner than their father, that without the wicked man, the world cannot move.

Why, sure, I know. I know I am struggling to run me up a bankroll, and parlay my bets in this clip joint of universal greed and unrest. And there is no one here who can help me hit a real lucky streak down the homestretch. But please, as a last favor to me, do observe now how this magnificent escapist here, this right good square-dealer, otherwise known as Joe, how this perfectly virtuous adventurer delays at stool, reddening the tender skin of his tookie on the cold oval seat of inaction, dreaming grey and desiring brittle, unlearning entirely the use of his legs as he makes his hopelessly smoky trips to the half-baked deserts of his Middle East and the partially charred jungles of his South Africa, wonderful examples all of his charming asphalt accomplishments, while this vile factory sneak, yours truly no less, is constantly on the move from morn till night, operating realistically within a small practical area, tagtailing the sleek corpus of security like a jackal, fawning on freedom from want, testing his trick knee before the exigencies of simple existence, a fuckup after his own fashion, snaffling some money of the folding kind, which is death of the color green, a pushover for the supernatural pleasures of competition, shrewdly absorbing his daily snootful of compliance and subservience so as better to refill the lamp of his oily responsibility to his light ones and bright ones, and trim the wick of his awful duty to himself, and sigh and laugh a little, quite often strangely, all shivery cold at the idea that he might be the one to falter and sink, while others, all the others kick their heels high and swim, and shove him down and drown him in their spray.

See how afraid? The truth is he is so afraid. He has lost a whole glassful of blood and he has spilled over. And yet. See also how by some magic somehow he has managed to thread the maze of the thorniest of his thoughts, in the territory of his thinking, there are no tulips, with such gigantic and enraged, such playful and precise footsteps. While the minutes collapse like a clumsy pyramid of clowns, and the seconds fall apart like all the toys of fake aspiration. And the hazy logical in its loosening tights hangs by an eyelash. And fact and fancy do obviously grin like twins at each twist in the elegant braid of time. And the question still remains whether on the one hand to laugh at that somber faintheart Joe, nursing his purse and his pecker behind his swinging door, and polluting the air with his shrill sea gull cries of make voyages and pass water, or whether on the other to sneer at this craven simp Felix who resembles most a crab on crutches in his one-man crusade to recover the holy land of higher dying for his fellow workers who adore the pain of subsisting on pins, whose proudest wish is simply to submit to the plot which life itself spins.

Squiffed, seeing two moons, more than slightly shicker, what a long yarn this has been, during the course of which we have all been whirling like conical spools of white thread, each seeking to be wiser, stitching the flares of our sins to the common bodice of our crimes. If such has been the case, what does it matter? If there has been a little understanding of each other along the way, who can say we are any the less for it? We all feel so plural sometimes. And so gaily irreducible and lost. Dizzy people, these are dizzy times.

"Yes," said George. "And so bright and beautiful too for anyone to come into this house of piss and flog his dummy for us. What a puzzle. I don't understand it. If I am the only helpless monkey around here, as I thought, how did that bozo get in the same cage with me? I must've skipped a month and gone gathering nuts in May. I sure do love this spell of fair weather we've been having, don't you? Something tells me there's a strange new nation outside we ought to investigate. I'm sure if we had the proper tools, we could easily break through this south wall here. Tomorrow I must bring some curtains. And rugs to scatter. And plush for the seats. And a couple of sketches I have at home, which I myself once dashed off, one showing the moon through a smear of clouds, and the other featuring three feathers, and the simple nude figure of a person sticking her tongue out. It's really crazy how every time my upright little broom wants to take up the slack it goes slish-slush. All of a sudden it's quiet again on the Potomac. Really astonishing how our man Felix here opened his backflap and his wonder grew. And his jockstrap fell from him and the baby linen of his brain. Whatever the hell that means. And his shame like a diaper rash. And he kept asking himself, who is this black sympathetic ape who sends me back my own awful faces? You call these men? These are my brothers? And he raised his battered trombone with his damaged hand and blew out a terrible blast. And of course, as usually happens in such a case, the walls came tumbling down. And when the dust settled, the rains came. And the rivers entered the sea. And they found us all floating belly-up. And the mother fairy said to the father fairy, did you see that bird fly past?"

385

"Bird?" said Hymie. "What bird?"

"Quiet while I finish. Goddamn it, Hymie. If you want to come in, come in like a man."

"Gosh," said Hymie. "How did I know you were standing there?"

"A hole in my back. That's what you made."

"Jesus," said Hymie. "Here. Let me rub it."

"Easy now," said George. "Higher. A little to the left. Ah, that's it. Hold it right there. And the father fairy said to the mother fairy, yes, I did. And she looked at him and she said, but what was it? And he smiled at her and he said, why, that was hope, my dear, for those funny human creatures made of flesh. And blood, she said, yes, I sometimes see them, and I hardly know why, but I do so pity them. And he had to smile again before he said, are these really your eyes? How lovely, my milk and honey, how perfect you are in everything, you are so right to do so, for of them it is truly said that hope comes to them only when they see the possibility of death, which there is, there always is for them. Oh, dear, dear, dear, she said. If that is their true, their one and only consolation, does it come to them often? Do they see it as you do? My precious, my heart's own, she said, tell me. Why, when you were fast asleep, did you scream last night? And he smiled, and he said to her, I screamed because I thought it would help. And he smoothed down her golden hair, and he straightened her red sash, and he kissed her smack on the lips."

"He did?" said Hymie. "Hey, I like that. That sure was pretty."

"Lovely," said Felix. "Sounds like a nice couple of kids."

"Fairies," said Hymie. "I never knew they were like that."

"Funny," said George. "How the whole world loves a story. No matter how goddamn silly it is."

"Ha," said Felix. "If that was silly, then we're all in the soup, I can tell you that."

"Say," said Hymie. "You know something?"

"I know I'm making a mistake," said Felix. "I'm letting him talk to me."

"I used to see one all the time."

"You did?" said Felix.

"Sure," said Hymie. "One time I saw it all winter."

"A fairy?"

"No, no," said Hymie. "A bird."

"Oh," said Felix. "A bird."

"That's what I said, didn't I? It was a real cuckoo one too. I remember it was a long time ago when I was a little jerk this high. How's that feel now, Georgie? You like that treatment? Some pair of hands, eh? I remember. I used to wipe the frost off the window to see if it was there. A bird. Can you imagine that? Boy, we sure did freeze our balls off in the old days, didn't we? Remember those longies that used to get you in the crotch? So we slept with our stockings on. So I ask you, did it help? Remember those terrific dreams you used to have when you fell asleep way down under in the middle of those big heavy puffs? Oh, those Russian goose feathers. Shit how the time flies. I remember. It always used to come flapping on our clothesline in the backyard. It could be snowing or not. It made no difference. It always came right on the dot for weeks right after school. A real black looking thing, kind of green and rusty around the neck, with a beak on it like a little piece of dried-up lemon peel. And what a sore red eye. Must've had lice in it or something. Every time it opened its mouth, it coughed like it had a cold. I said to myself, what the hell, how can you stand there like a schmuck and eat up all of it yourself? So I opened the window, tore off a hunk of my bread and schmaltz, and threw it. The first time it didn't see me do it. But the second time, wow, what a catch, right in the middle of the air. I used to call it Butch. We had lunch together this way for a whole week. Until one day, wham, did I catch it from my old lady. Boy, when she socked you, you stayed socked. So I had to keep the goddamn window closed and eat what was mine or I was a dead one. The only thing was, how was I going to tell Butch? It kept coming back and looking and looking at me. Inching up that old clothesline more and more every day. And me chomping away right in front of it, and shaking my head, I'm sorry, until I thought it would fall off. I could see it was shrinking fast. I just couldn't make it understand. And that eye getting worse and worse. I was some friend, wasn't I? The funny thing is, I still can't whistle worth a damn. What a stubborn bird. It had a kind of what do you call it on its head. A crest, that's right. It was about three times or more the size of a sparrow. Any of you guys know what it is?"

"Why, sure," said Felix. "It sounds just like my grandmother's ashtray."

"Excuse me," said George. "But don't you think it sounds more like mine?"

"No kidding now," said Hymie. "I really would like to know."

"Ah," said Felix. "Poor old Hymie."

"Me?" said Hymie. "Why?"

"I don't know," said Felix. "I just thought I'd say it."

"Well, thanks a lot," said Hymie. "I sure do appreciate it."

"So tell me, kid. How's the old sex life? Been shooting any pool lately?"

"Oh," said Hymie. "Just enough to keep me in shape. You know how it is."

"Hold straight now," said Felix. "Did you always have that thing there?"

"What thing?"

"That scar there over your eyebrow."

"This one?" said Hymie. "Sure. That's the one the bird made me."

"The who?" said Felix.

"The bird," said Hymie. "I just told you, didn't I? Sure I did. Like I told you. That was the winter I had me chicken fats on my bread instead of butter. With a little salt on it, man, is that delicious. So I said to myself, watching old Butch there, jesus christ, how can you have the heart not to give it, at least a taste? So I looked around to see if Ma was looking. Ma with those big green combs and that real red hair. Eighteen years dead. I can't believe it. A wonder of a person. What funny thing could have killed her? What good does she do me holding up that headstone? Ah, well. There she was near the old coal stove, with her head in the steam, a stick in her hand, busy boiling the wash. So I sneaked open the window and stuck my head out to stretch out a piece, and whango, this is what I got, right over the eye with the beak. Boy, was I flabbergasted. What I mean to say, my blood, it sure did jump out like it was going on a holiday. Go know what a bird is thinking. How long does a thing like that live? You think it's still alive? The way it flapped around me. Swoosh. And then it flew away. And that was the end of that."

"Well, now," said George. "Let me see. I think I'll start right here and sweep in that direction."

"Right," said Felix. "It's like I always say. Give a man his head and he's bound to make his little pile."

"So help me god," said Hymie. "Six stitches. Right here."

"Really?" said Felix. "Where? I don't see anything."

"I know I'm a sucker," said Hymie. "But hell. I just feel sorry for everybody. What can I do?"

388

"For one thing," said Felix. "Get off my feet, goddamn it."

"Feet?" said Hymie. "What feet? I don't see anything."

"That's right," said Felix. "Go on. Blow on me."

"Skinny old bastard," said Hymie. "You still like that crazy succotash? How's the hand? You want to listen to me a second? Listen. I got a real good proposition for you. You get me a raise."

"I get you a what?" said Felix.

"You get me a raise," said Hymie. "And I tell you what I'll do for you. I'll do a plastic job on your nose there you keep sharpening. Pow. One shot. Just like that."

"Back up, boy. I'm warning you."

"How can you help it? You can't help it if you look like a rat."

"Now all of a sudden this thing is beginning to hurt."

"You think I didn't see you?" said Hymie. "Don't worry. I saw you. I was there. I saw you slash yourself. I said to myself, aw, fuck him, the bastard. The guy's so miserable, the biggest favor you can do is let him bleed to death."

"If I have him," said Felix. "Who needs Minerva to watch over me?"

"It's just one of those things," said Hymie. "So what if you're my boss around here? I don't have to kiss your ass every time I see you, do I? You know what I wish? I wish this whole place would suddenly catch on fire. You know what I would do then? I'd jump right up and start throwing everybody right out the window. And you know why? Because we all stink on ice, that's why."

"Well," said Felix. "I could go in there and sit down and not have to look at him. I could do that."

"Sure," said Hymie. "That's the way. Show me the shape of your behind and I'll tell you who's who. What did I tell you? Here comes another one. Kitzel. Old droopy drawers with the banged-up mouth. Careful, kid. That's a full fire pail you're stepping into. What a gang. Everybody keeps creeping in here, squeezing in, looking out for number one, trying to save his own hide. Listen to old dark meat here. The Wabash Cannonball. Some day he's going to die laughing. And that quiet one in there is going to do it by smoking his head off. And you, you little jerk, by gargling too much. Boy. Talk about being scared. I can smell you all a mile away."

"Then smell your share, you fathead," said Kitzel. "And get the hell out of the way. I would like to get over to that sink there. Do you mind?"

389

"Sure thing, buster, but first. Let me loosen up a little bit here. One, two, button your shoe. Three, four, spit on the floor. Pass, friend. Holy mackerel. What did I rip? Did I rip something? Jesus. Did you hear them old bones of mine creak? Whew. I'm telling you. It's going to be a cinch for me to croak. Four bends. And I'm half dead already."

"Droopy drawers," said Kitzel. "Creeping in here. What are you anyway? A wiseguy or something?"

"Hiya, kid. How's my little ray of sunshine?"

"Suffering," said Kitzel. "What else?"

"Attaboy," said Hymie. "That's what I like. Let's keep pitching in there."

"Oh, sure," said Kitzel. "Sure. If you had what I have, you wouldn't feel so goddamn chipper, I can tell you that."

"You lousy little coward. Why didn't you break his hands for him?"

"I got to rinse," said Kitzel. "I got no time to talk to you. I'm all shot to pieces as it is. How do you like that? I really got my pants wet."

"Clumsy yak," said Hymie. "I tried to warn you, didn't I?"

"I tell you," said Kitzel. "It's a good thing I got only one mouth. My sweet old Mamma, for years and years, she used to keep pushing cotton with camphor up my ears. Even when I bumped my toe or had the shits. I knew it was silly. But I didn't have the heart to tell her. My brother that I slept with, a whiz of a kid, when he was hardly six, he was already chasing after the horses in Prospect Park, training for the Olympics. What a shiner he once gave me in the toilet with his knife when I accidentally on purpose pushed him in the tub where he was drowning a big fat rat in a trap. We used to use an extra throw pillow in bed so our asses wouldn't touch. Jumpy, don't ask. He just died falling out of a chestnut tree in Yonkers, believe it or not. He used to say to me, you little prick, if you want to know about pushing, ask Papa, he'll tell you why Mamma's always in the goddamn fix she's in. He used to get so excited he would begin to slap me around. Look, he used to say to me. Look how they're pouring out all over the world. They're coming out in billions. And unless we begin to use them for cement or build bridges with them, we're in for a lot of trouble in this house. And he would spit right between his teeth, missing my eye by inches. Crazy guy. Always had brown around his mouth from tootsie rolls. One trick he had. He could name you all the Vice Presidents. But he was wrong about Mamma, and the babies he could see coming.

Because after me, I don't know why, but nobody ever made it."

"Praise the lord," said Hymie. "And a damn good thing too."

"Goddamn glasses," said Kitzel. "Always steaming up on me. Wandering around. Lost in a fog. All of a sudden I begin to sweat like a pig. Ashamed to wipe myself with such a hanky. She pressed me three. I don't know what I did with the other two. Ow. You know where that bastard really made me a cripple? Where he scratched my tongue. Right here. And I keep beating my gums like somebody's paying me for it. What a goof. Really disgusted with myself. Did I ever tell you guys, I guess I never did, that we're still sleeping on only a mattress? A living doll. Want to see real blue eyes? I'll show you sometimes. Me and her two flower pots, I don't even know what kind, and that's her whole frigging life. So polite. Always scrunching away from me after the ball is over, giving me more room than I need. Talk about positions. That's where I'm king, fellas. But very careful, like I say to her, please, let's not have one of them snotty little kids popping up in here. So what if I can still wiggle my ears? You can't get a bank to pay any interest on that. Jesus. If I could only hock something, and pay that murderer, and never have to see him again. Ah, well. What I say is, whatever it is that comes out at night, let it crawl all over me. It has to live too, doesn't it? Honestly. It was the queerest feeling. I suddenly looked up from my cage behind the wire, and I said to myself, either I'm off my nut, or everybody's dead or something. Where you guys been all this time?"

"Out on the lone prairie," said Hymie.

"I felt so blue," said Kitzel. "It was awful."

"Flubbing our dubs, boy, bunking out under the stars."

"I still have my first collar button," said Kitzel. "Did I ever tell you?"

"Fantastic," said Hymie. "What a perfect day for the bluefish to run. Did you ever see a better day for fishing?"

"As for me," said Kitzel. "I once got smacked in the tunnel of love. All the rest has been downhill all the way."

"And," said Hymie. "Let me see. What else? And if I had what I had yesterday, I would be chomping away on a whole Hershey bar with almonds right now."

"Ah," said Kitzel. "But Mary Pickford. There was the sweetest one of all."

"Pickford? What about Theda Bara?"

391

"And Clara Bow," said Kitzel. "And Esther Ralston. And Barbara La Marr. That lovely flower I never could believe in. But you know who I really used to love? Agnes Ayres."

"Blondes for the little guys. Brunettes for the big."

"People," said Kitzel.

"I swear," said Hymie. "Talking to you is like swimming under water."

"I smell people in here. Am I right?"

"Sure," said Hymie. "You see smoke, don't you?"

"Then I'm saved," said Kitzel. "I'm back in the world. I'm still alive. The hell with the boss. Who cares? It's terrible. You should see those women out there."

"Quiet," said Hymie. "You want me to bounce you around?"

"Not a stitch of work. You should see their eyes. Terrible, terrible."

"That's right," said Hymie. "Come a little closer, son, and I'll tear you apart like a herring."

"Always with the hands," said Kitzel. "It's a good thing you're my favorite animal."

"A can opener," said Hymie. "It can't be."

"Excuse me," said Kitzel. "But that was your hand you had in my pocket."

"I'm groggy," said Hymie. "Who carries around with him a can opener?"

"A man who opens cans," said Kitzel. "So goddamn slow in the head. Don't you know the facts of life yet?"

"I'll be damned," said Hymie. "And I suppose if I stuck my hand in this pocket here, I'd find me a can of sardines or something."

"No," said Kitzel. "Just a plain old beat-up mouse."

"A mouse?" said Hymie. "You got to be kidding."

"It's rubber, you bum. Can't you see?"

"A mouse," said Hymie. "Let me out of here."

"Why not?" said Kitzel. "When a guy works in a joint like this, he's got to know what certain kinds of animals look like, don't he? Here now. Feel this. What do you think I got in here?"

"If it bites me, I'll kill you."

"It never did before. Go on, now. Stick your filthy paw in here. See what happens."

"No, sir," said Hymie. "I pass. I'm really afraid to look."

"Silly ass," said Kitzel. "Hairs from a horse's tail. See? And in my left here, a cuff link I found wrapped in a dog's license. And in this back pocket, just an ordinary ping-pong ball. And here in my vest. Makes me look like a real big shot, the way it's stuffed. Hold the phone now. What can this be among my many precious papers? Of course. A piece of tissue paper from a box of cologne. And what else? A tiny magnifying glass. My picture on a pony. And two tickets for a short beer. Here. Is this what you're looking for?"

"Chocolate," said Hymie.

"Ha," said Kitzel. "Look at them little eyes pop."

"Whee," said Hymie. "I'm a kid again. I knew he had it on him. A whole Hershey bar. Um, boy. Does this hit the spot."

"Easy, now," said Kitzel. "This is for everybody."

"Well, now," said George. "I know it's not morning yet, but I'm suddenly waking up."

"Sure," said Kitzel. "Step right over, boy."

"My," said George. "What a big piece."

"That's okay," said Kitzel. "I got another one."

"Another one?" said Hymie.

"Joe?" said Kitzel. "Yell out in there if you want some. I guess he doesn't. Felix?"

"Thanks," said Felix. "Might as well while I'm resting."

"Good," said Kitzel. "I had an idea you guys could use it."

"Excuse me," said Hymie. "Did you say you had another one?"

"Sonofabitching thing. It's beginning to burn me again. I wonder why."

"Hand it over," said Hymie. "You're breaking my heart."

"Maybe if I sucked a little piece."

"What?" said Hymie. "What are you trying to do? Kill yourself altogether?"

"Hold it now," said Kitzel. "Who's that coming around the bend? Frankie. That's good."

"Goddamn it," said Hymie. "Did you ever see such luck? Just when the last piece is about to drop into my mouth, that bum has to come in here."

"Hiya, fellas," said Frankie.

"So like I was telling you," said George. "That scary old aunt of mine with the big loopy earrings like a gypsy, and the flashy bandana

393

wrapped around her nut like a mammy down on the old plantation, man, there was a lot of voodoo behind that hoodoo face, and I ain't just feeding you the bull, the result was, it got to be so, it was me who finally had to be the bad one, and give her the bum's rush right out of there."

"Extra," said Frankie. "Terrible accident outside. Read all about it. Extra."

"It was real sticky," said George. "It was the first time I ever had to touch her."

"Gloop," said Frankie. "I think I'm breathing. Is this the old treasure house? Said the goldfish to the guppies. Say. Who's got a tired old dollar bill on him he's ready to rip up and throw away?"

"She had an arm on her like a stick."

"Honest," said Frankie. "I'll take anything up to a penny. Or less. Or whatever you got. Come on, fellas. Throw it. I can catch. Ha, boy. You ought to see how those guys pick up them dames on Eastern Parkway. Strunz the Bagel, I keep hanging around, so he says to me, hey, kid, you want to go hunting with us tonight? How much dough you got? So you see? What's wrong with you guys? This is your poor old Frankie that's talking to you here. Can't you see how nice I'm begging?"

"It's no use," said George. "You can take it from me. It's no use any of us looking for a place where we can be all alone. Because there just ain't no such animal, my honeychild. Colder than a witch's tit, like they used to say. Great jumping grasshoppers. I can still hear her howling like a Louisiana wind. Pass me the makings there, master. After that little bit of sweetness, I got a craving in me for a smoke way down to my bones."

"The makings," said Felix. "Arms like a bum's rush. Bones."

"Thanks for the butt," said George. "You're a real sport, man."

"That may be," said Felix. "But honestly. As God is my witness. All I'm trying to do is to play catch up with you here, that's all."

"Chow," said Frankie. "Holy Moses. It sure is a foggy day here in London, ain't she?"

"Did you ever notice?" said Hymie. "He's got a real good sprayer on him once he lets loose with a sneeze."

"That he does," said Kitzel. "I never had such a good wash."

"Not that you need it," said Hymie.

"Well, thanks," said Kitzel. "I could say the same for you."

"Whoops," said Frankie. "Ain't they just dears? Look at me. I'm a piggy-wiggy. I'm a sugar bun. Slap me on the wrist, me darlings. I'm a booful blossom."

"Stinkweed," said Hymie. "You still pull your taffy much?"

"Me?" said Frankie. "I'm the merry widow. How can that be? Come. Don't be bashful. Put your arm around my teeny waist, sweetie, and we'll give the dogs a workout, and seal it with a kiss, yahoo."

"I wonder now," said Hymie. "You think he'll be able to eat that piece of chocolate with a broken neck?"

"I know you'll kill me if I ask," said Frankie. "But when you said I had a good sprayer there, was that supposed to be a joke?"

"No," said Hymie. "It was only a mashed potato."

"Peeyoo," said Frankie. "Pardon me while I hold my nose."

"She must've worn a thousand skirts," said George.

"I'd say at least," said Felix. "How about you, lunkhead? Do you happen to have an opinion on the subject?"

"Well, now," said Hymie. "It's funny you should ask. You know the big hole I got in the middle of me when they ripped me right out of me mudder? Well, I hope to hell you'll keep this to yourself, but that's what my smallest boy calls my poopick."

"Toot-toot," said Frankie. "You hear that? There it goes again."

"And if that's not clear," said Hymie. "Let me put it another way. It's easy enough to say, give a man a horse he can ride, but what I'd like to know is, where in god's country is he going to get the saddle?"

"Toot," said Frankie. "I bet you there's a boat lost somewhere."

"So help me," said George. "The whole thing was like a dream you think you're dreaming."

"Shoot," said Frankie. "If I had a canoe, I'd sure go see. I got time. I'm not busy. Maybe I'd put a red sail on it. And take along a whole barrel of beer. And roasted peanuts in all my pockets. And down the old river, the old Hudson I'd go. Merrily, merrily. Gently down the stream, I mean. Say. Ain't that a song or something? The old oaken bucket, she ain't what she used to be. Funny how it all comes back. Eight's good. Snake eyes. Shoot. Little Joe again. Hey. You know something? I'm not scratching it any more. I bet you that rash is getting better. I bet you there's a million lakes in this country. And

395

trees you never saw before. And birds with big long tails. And grapes in the sun. And apples on the ground. And all them other little fruits. Yow. Here's a nice little six again. Okay, you suckers? Who's got me faded? Make believe I just rolled. I bet you I'm getting lucky. I bet you if I eat up all my grape-nuts tomorrow, I'll find the bunny in the bottom of the bowl."

"You see that?" said Hymie. "You see how happy he is? He doesn't need it. Why spoil everything by giving him any chocolate now?"

"Would you believe it?" said Frankie. "They all laughed when I sat down at the piano."

"Quick," said Hymie. "Hand it over before it melts away in your hand."

"Gee, dad," said Frankie. "It's a Wurlitzer. How was I to know it was only a squeezebox?"

"All right, you little bugger, off."

"Charge," said Frankie. "Lay down boy, you're dead. I stuck you when you wasn't looking. Gee. I sure wish we had some real swords here. We'd go out and wipe out some of them lousy sharks that's eating us up. You and me together. Hey, Kitzel kid?"

"I've been standing here and thinking."

"Yeah," said Frankie. "Me too."

"What breaks us down," said Kitzel. "Well, anybody can see that. But what winds us up and keeps us going no matter what, that, now that's a real old-fashioned mystery, ain't it?"

"Listen," said Frankie. "Suppose now. Suppose it never rains no more. Like it looks like now. That means, let me see, that means all the ducks'll be sunk, don't it? Ha? How's that for using the old bean?"

"You said accident," said Kitzel. "What accident?"

"Two guys kissed. As if they liked it. I saw it with me own eyes."

"Ah, well," said Kitzel. "Here. Take it anyway. Have yourself a ball."

"Gee," said Frankie. "For me? Oh, boy."

"So, you hear?" said George. "So like I was telling you. Every time I'd come home, yipes, there she'd be, high up on the bar stool I can't remember who it was asked me to snitch from the corner saloon, with her stuffing like little crab apples sticking out, trying to evening meal herself a trifle here and there, and mooch some cold chitlins maybe, or a dry chomp of celery, or some mustard greens, or, as we keep climbing downstairs, cadge herself the crumbs what's left in the pleats in the paper from a cupcake, or the old brown skin from last week's banana, the patience my mother has with the sick and the wounded is something to see, believe me, with me old Aunty there, clicking her beads round her witch's neck, slowly twisting us all up in her wrinkles and her words like a born storyteller from the old days, keeping us tied down to what danced in her eyes until we were ready to drop off, there was such a peculiar flower smell on her, dead set on sticking it into us, how Uncle Bulben, her old yapheaded hod carrier with the grin, blew up in his sleep, and with his eyes wide open, did the bagpipe trick until he conked out, that is to say, he just up and died."

"Which all means," said Felix. "You're not exactly whistling Dixie, are you?"

"I swear," said George. "By my sister's ratty crutch, I'm giving it to you absolutely straight. That is, I was going to, until I suddenly remembered that just the other day, I first noticed it on Tuesday, I think, Sis went and painted a long beautiful snake on her stick with two heads, with my old water colors, so that's out, because if I get too close, it's liable to bite and poison me altogether, you follow me? Gosh, I hope you understand. I hate to raise my voice in this palace of ours brimming over with goodies because I know it'll be disturbing my friend in there real bad, but anybody who thinks there's a hiding place in this world is just plain cuckoo. Or like you guys say, meshuggeh in the noggin. The truth is, you don't have to go out looking for such things, they come to you. We must be men here. We must understand that."

"So your sister's a crazy old cripple," said Felix.

"Yes," said George. "It's nothing new. Now what do you think was the first thing that aunt of mine did after she made sure with the mirror test that her poor old stay-at-home had really copped a sneak, going west, as we all figured it, by way of Poughkeepsie?"

"I'm almost afraid to ask."

"She put his eye back."

"Good," said Felix. "Now we're getting somewhere. Would you care for another smoke to help you make it?"

"I would," said George. "And scooped out both his ears. And pounded on the wave in his nose, which she never did like, until she got it running due north and south."

"Damn matches are getting damp."

"And the wind in the dumbwaiter blew. And the plaster fell in the tub where she kept her brooms. And she rattled off something in her babbo language. And when she looked up, five mice were wrapping a fox in a window shade, and where the cat's face once was she heard a funny tinkle, and the floor buckled where the ghost of her Holy Roller grandmother sat, and she cried oo-ee, and when the sun shone in she saw there were fresh cowdrops all over the place."

"Another sonofabitch in trouble."

"I mean to say," said George. "She sure did raise the hackles on me every time she took off that way. Though I guess I should be used to it, because it kind of runs in the family. This queer habit we have of getting ourselves glued to a window, trying to get a peek at what's what in the world through the waves and cracks in the glass, especially when the rain's pouring down like mad all over it. After some fifteen nights of it, I don't know what kept me back from choking her. I said to myself, tired as I was, what's this silly little life of ours getting to be? Like a record by Galli-Curci when the needle gets stuck. Like a carousel going round without music. And we-uns riding them six white horses just as wild as dead. And all that sort of crap. Until all of a sudden, boom, it all finally came out. What did the worms do when God wept? Is the whale of feeling in me a mammal or a fish? Who likes to bring home a tiny surprise of caraway seeds like I do? Sometimes I feel like saying, go fuck yourself, all of you. Who was the hyena? Who was the louse who laughed when he saw her face break up, and heard her say that what hurt her the most about the whole deal when her hubby died was the simple little fact that my old man went to the funeral in a sweater and pants that didn't match, and to top it all off yet, wearing a polka dot bow tie? It was me, of course. It was me who had to move in and be the murderer. It was while she was weeping bitter tears that I pushed her out."

"I keep saying it's spring," said Felix. "What else can it be?"

"Five gets you ten the Yanks win the pennant."

"Talk about tearing up the peapatch."

"As usual," said George. "Doing what all weak people do. Plunking myself down the road of guilt, me and my little banjo."

"Yes," said Felix. "Reminds me of the puppy I saw yesterday, a real bright-looking Dalmatian, riding up the escalator backwards with his little dickey showing, knitting himself some red wool socks."

"Green, as I remember it."

"Well," said Felix. "I would leave all that up to God, wouldn't you?"

"I certainly would," said George. "It's tough when those hangers refuse to drop. Don't I know. And that damn tenpin keeps wobbling but won't fall. And the smallest runt in the class, with only one lousy leg and half a brain, breaks the tape ahead of you. God. How I used to love that fifty-yard dash."

"Unbelievable," said Felix. "Just think. Think of all those souped up people before us who lived like they were always racing their motors and stalling, making a million detours for us, rushing to the slaughter for a bit of bread and water, bitching and bawling."

"God, what a Barnum and Bailey that must've been."

"And here," said Felix. "And here we still are, trying to push ourselves into the picture, the very latest style of men that is, you may be a better specimen than most of your type but just the same, packing ourselves into the same old can of confusion and stink, you can call me pisher if I don't get drunk tonight, waiting like lambs for the big chief in the sky to put the lid on us."

"And put the lid on us he will."

"And the hell of it is," said Felix. "Every man jack of us here can read and write. Do me a favor now and check for me. Is my back really up against the wall?"

"I can hardly tell which is which."

"Then I'm in heaven," said Felix. "And I'll never know how I got there."

"I'm standing on a dime too," said George. "It's no novelty to me."

"I don't mean to butt in," said Hymie.

"Hi," said George. "You look good, kid. Been sunning yourself?"

"I don't mean to butt in," said Hymie. "But what's all this about a horse?"

"What horse?" said George.

"The one you were talking about."

"We were talking about a horse?"

"Sure, you were," said Hymie. "Don't you remember? Which one did you mean? Did you mean the one the farmer had trouble with?"

"Well," said George. "Let me see now. You're one, two. You're the third from the left, aren't you?"

399

"You know the one I mean?" said Hymie. "The one the galoot was training so hard to live without eating, and just when he thought the old nag was getting the hang of it, boom, she went and dropped dead. Ha, I love that old story, don't you?"

"The rain," said George. "It droppeth as the gentle dew from heaven. Kitzel, my boy, you're splashing again."

"What can I do?" said Kitzel. "I have to rinse my lousy mouth, don't I? Aa. You know what I'm going to ask you to do for me one of these days?"

"Mop up after you," said George. "That's about all I can see."

"Tear a leg out of my ass. Then I'll really know what pain is."

"Sorry," said George. "I'm afraid that's a little bit out of my line."

"Come on," said Kitzel. "Put me out of business, boy. I'm all shot. See what a kvetch? I can't even hold this glass straight."

"Aw," said George. "What the hell. Pity yourself. You're entitled. Rinse. Splash all you want. Try to be happy."

"Hello?" said Frankie. "No, no, goddamn it. How many times I have to tell you? I got five men in here. Five. Right. And I'll need at least six bucks apiece to spring them loose. I said, loose. Right. And ship me a special pair of earplugs for me here without fur. Earplugs, you blubberhead. Yeah. That's right. And don't forget the gloves to go with the gats. No. Not cats, gats. Yeah. That's right. And tell Sylvester, all right, then, then tell Maxie, okay, then tell Hershie the hotshot to get the hideout ready. The one under the boardwalk. Yeah. Near the old drinking fountain they used to use for horses. That's right. And get me one with some real meat on her this time, will you? Like Sophie B. who lives with the butcher. You know. The one my father eyes all the time. Yeah. That's right. And tell Buggsie if he's going to trim the window in that drugstore tonight, in case I need, to get me some. Hello? Hello? What? Where the hell did you go that time? Jesus, man. Dunk your doughnut later, will you? I said your doughnut, you little prick. Who's a hophead? Yeah. That's right. And break in my slippers for me. We just got to give old man trouble here the slip. The slip. The step-in. The tight little panties. Oo, mamma, how I would love to. You can laugh. But I'm telling you. Yeah. That's right. The weather's perfect. The clock's cuckoo if it's telling me. You better wear your muffler. And park your gum before you. Drop dead. Goodbye. Hey. How about that, fellas? I said all that pretty good, didn't I? It's all set, Georgie. Right after the day after Yom Kippur, we all break out of here."

"The friends I'm making lately. Did you ever see?"

"In case you didn't know it," said Frankie. "That was my cousin Sookie I was calling."

"If I had a white uniform," said George. "I'd come for you myself."

"Hey?" said Frankie. "It's all a lot of crap, ain't it? Here's the way I figure it. You want to listen to me a second?"

"It's no use your climbing up on me, ivy. I'm not your wall."

"Here's the way I figure it," said Frankie. "When we're all together like this, goddamn it, that's the time we have the most fun. Hah, Georgie? Don't we have the most fun? It makes no difference what we say, does it? Smoking, spitting, laughing, pissing. What's the difference? So long we're all together here. Just a bunch of guys. Who cares what's happening outside? You know what I mean?"

"Oh, sure," said Georgie. "You're all finished now?"

"I don't know," said Frankie. "I think so."

"Fine," said George. "Then go wipe yourself."

"Not me," said Frankie. "I never do that before dinner."

"Okay, bub, let me see your working papers."

"Papers?" said Frankie. "What for?"

"The time has come for you to lay down your life for your country."

"Me?" said Frankie. "What country?"

"X2. I'm depending on you."

"Aw," said Frankie. "I quit the secret service yesterday. You know that."

"Once in, you're in. No one can quit. You all set, boy? Now here's what I want you to do."

"No, sir," said Frankie. "I'm sorry. I'll have to ask Joe first. I don't do anything without asking Joe."

"Quiet," said George. "All I want you to do is to go out there and see if the flood is over. Or whatever the hell else it is everyone here is so goddamn afraid of. Now don't look so stupid. You know what I mean. Fly out there. Be my little dove."

"What dove?" said Frankie. "I swear. I don't know what you're talking about."

"Goddamn it," said George. "Look at you. When's the last time you shined your shoes?"

"I don't know," said Frankie. "Why?"

"And all that scratching you do in public."

"Oh," said Frankie. "That's okay. It's really getting better."

"Better?" said George. "My god. The way it's been moving around, it'll soon be right on your pecker. And before you know it, ping, that thing'll break and fall right off."

"I can see," said Frankie. "You smell trouble."

"How about that strong black salve we used to use for boils? Or mashed flies and melted butter? That might do it. Or fats from the chicken or grease from the goose. Or just a plain paste made from baking soda. Slap it on. Spread it around. Let's be doing something. Let's get moving here. Or if that doesn't help. Get your rabbi to write down something against it on a slip of paper and swallow it. Some people even use their own pee water. You may not know it yet, but some people are really nuts about staying alive. Even when they know there's no hope for them. Absolutely no hope."

"Look at him," said Frankie. "He's like a rooster. He's swelling."

"It's this," said George. "It's this hanging around and letting everything happen to us without lifting a finger to stop it, that's what gets me."

"Ow," said Frankie. "Let go. You're breaking my arm."

"The sun," said George. "The fiery orb. The celestial body. The fresh crushed look of blood on the faces of real people. The wind soft before setting for the ram and the bull. And more bull. The funny long shadows. The vistas down side streets. The sacred pigeons waddling on the ledges. The big insurance clock. The immense sycamores in Madison Square Park. And bull again. The late gold of the walks. The pale crescent of the increasing moon. The fleecy clouds unfastened and undone. The cool of the evening. The sweet stars to come. You little bum. The very ceiling of your heaven is out there."

"Hooey," said Frankie. "I never could believe in that stuff. What can I do?"

"You can skip in and out the heavy rumbling traffic."

"I hate Peter Pan. What's Peter Pan to me?"

"You're a boy," said George. "No one will bother you. Spread cheer. Have the time of your life. If a woman's cross, chalk up her number on her bottom. If a man's wearing a beard, look behind the alfalfa. If you meet six stiffs like us, call up the boneyard. If you see two Fords with

402

their bumpers locked, separate them. If you find an olive branch, bring it back in your beak. Play the game fair and square, pardner. Go out there, and come back, and tell us all is safe. And like a flash, everybody will fly right out of here. And I'll be able to clean up, and call it a day, and get back to normal, and drop down on my knees and thank god I'm still what I always was, and always will be, a nothing. And nothing is good enough for me. Including my flip side. You little tramp. You get the gist of it now? Are you ready? Will you go out there? Will you do it?"

"Oh, no," said Frankie. "I just told you. I'm sorry. I'll have to ask Joe first. I never do anything without asking Joe. No, sir."

"Ye gods," said George. "I've been playing with a dead mouse."

"Gosh," said Frankie. "I better be careful. He doesn't like it when I talk about him too much. Say. Did I ever tell you the time he was making believe he was choking me, and Mr. Colish came over and said to him, my dear fellow, when you're through with him, do you mind taking care of me next? Boy, I bet you he remembers that. I bet you he's so warm in there he's ready to melt away. Say. You know that funny old fan Miss Golschman keeps in her middle drawer? Maybe I could snitch it for him. Or get him a cool malted milk. Or a cone. Or a popsicle maybe. Who's got a dime here to keep him going? Oranges he never eats. He just likes to smell and look at them. You think he's all right in there, Georgie? I bet he'll be good and dead before I do anything. Maybe I should just slip him a glass of water. How about that, Georgie? He gets sore as hell if I bother him for nothing. You think maybe I should?"

"Pitiful," said George. "What else can I say?"

"He's so quiet in there. I don't like it when he gets so quiet, do you?"

"Poor Frankie."

"Maybe he's sick in there. You think he's sick in there, Georgie?"

"Poor little fella."

"Excuse me," said Felix. "This is no little fella. This is a little mutt."

"Says you," said Hymie. "Listen to the man."

"Look, bub, I'm warning you."

"Great," said Hymie. "One word and I'm getting his goat already."

"I'm warning you now," said Felix. "You may think you're safe, sticking so close to him in there, having such a swell time lapping up all his love. But don't kid yourself so fast. You're not in heaven yet. I'm

403

warning you. If it's ever a question between you and me, if ever our dear boss gives me the sign to put the skids under you, I'm telling you now, bub, out on your ass you'll go."

"Really?" said Hymie. "And what do you think I'll do when that happens?"

"You'll disappear into the distance with your big ears flapping in the breeze."

"I'll separate your fucking little head from your fucking little body. How do you like them apples, bub?"

"I like them," said Felix. "How shall I say I like them? I like them. I like them like I like myself. I like them like I like you. That's how I like them."

"Arf-arf," said Kitzel. "Look at me up on my hind legs again. I'll take one of them weeds, if you don't mind."

"Sure," said Felix. "Why not? You're quite a little shit yourself, aren't you?"

"Absolutely," said Kitzel. "In that respect, I'm right on top of the heap."

"Honestly," said Felix. "What in the hell's the matter with us? What makes us all such goddamn suckers here? What is this Joe to us all of a sudden? Our new father? Why are we hanging around his neck? Is this an order? Who is he to us anyway? Why do we have to stay here and sit shivah with him until we all rot away and die?"

"Ah," said Kitzel. "What's the use of crabbing? He's the man in there, all right. And you might as well admit it."

"Holy mackerel," said Felix. "How can anyone so young be so blind?"

"Practice, I guess."

"Smiling again," said Felix. "What are you smiling about? You think if you keep twisting your mouth like that, you'll begin to look like him? Look at that. It's getting to be a real disease."

"Listen," said Kitzel. "You want to listen to me a second? You know what he says about you?"

"It's peculiar," said Felix. "I've noticed it lately. Every time I start talking about him, I begin to sound like a real cluck."

"He says," said Kitzel. "You're sure you want to hear this?"

"Could I stop you if I didn't?"

"He says you're the only one here who's got it in him to be a real success."

"Aw, now," said Felix. "What shit. You can do better than that, can't you?"

"So help me god," said Kitzel. "Ask Hymie here. He'll tell you."

"Yep," said Hymie. "Qualities he said the guy has. Can you imagine that?"

"Qualities?" said Frankie. "That guy?"

"Yes, sir," said Kitzel. "And a thousand virtues on top of that."

"Go on," said Frankie. "I don't believe you."

"Don't believe what?" said Kitzel. "Hey, now, look. What are you butting in for? Did anyone ask you? All right, wiseguy. What's a virtue? You know what a virtue is? I bet you don't even know what it is, do you?"

"Maybe not," said Frankie. "But qualities. My god."

"Ah," said Kitzel. "Remember, Hymie? Remember how he used to talk to us?"

"Used to?" said Frankie. "What do you mean used to?"

"Them were the days," said Kitzel. "We'd be standing by his table, just shooting the breeze like we always did, when he'd say to us. Remember that time when he said to us?"

"I don't understand it," said Frankie. "Why do you keep talking about him like he's dead?"

"He said to us, maybe I shouldn't talk because I haven't lived long enough yet, but something came to me in the middle of the night in a silly dream I had, and when I woke up, I thought, gee, it sure is sad how the world leans one way, and all the people in it the other. And he'd go into his shot-putting stance and make believe he was throwing an elephant a thousand feet. How about it? he'd say to us. Sure is time we began to find the good more interesting than the bad. Got any ideas how to swing it, boys? You remember that, Hymie? Did I get it straight? Remember what he said to us?"

"Hell, yes," said Hymie. "I sure do."

"He always said a lot of things to us, didn't he?"

"And how," said Hymie. "Ha. Remember the time we were schmoozing around in the entrance and a guy walked by and coughed. And Joe looked at him, and he said to us, that's all we'll ever know about that bum as long as we live. Hey? He was always coming out with something like that, wasn't he? Like the time we were all looking out the window. Remember that? Three cars piled up, what a crash, but nobody hurt, not even scratched which was a goddamn miracle,

405

when all of a sudden he takes all the change out of his pocket and chucks it out the window. And we looked at him, and we said to him, hey, what in hell are you doing? And he said to us, sorry, boys, I just saw the piper out there. I got to start paying him."

"Boy," said Kitzel. "That was a real lulu, that was."

"I ran down," said Frankie. "I picked it all up and brought it back to him."

"Right," said Hymie. "And he got real mad at you, didn't he?"

"Mad?" said Frankie. "He almost killed me."

"I tell you," said Hymie. "When that bozo got serious, it wasn't so funny, was it?"

"I'll say," said Frankie.

"That's okay, fellas," said Hymie. "You can lean on me. I'll hold you both up. I feel kind of relaxed myself, thinking about all those things. Say. Remember when he asked the boss for the afternoon off to go out and plant himself a peach tree? He sure had his nerve talking to the boss that way. Always got away with it too, didn't he? One time he said to me, now hear this, when you show someone you really want something, watch how his eye gets cold like a dead man his head. He always gave me his bread. Remember the first time I asked him for it? He reached over and gave me a good stiff pat on the head. He wasn't heavy. But he sure could hurt you more with one finger than a lot of guys with a whole hand. Hymie, he said to me, I will gladly help feed your face, for no matter how hungry a man is, he should always be ready to say, even when he knows he doesn't mean it, my dear cafeteria brother, I will wipe out my life for you as a man wipeth out a dish, wiping it, and turning it upside down. Yea. And when he said that, we all clapped. Even Felix here. And everybody turned around to look. Remember that?"

"It's what I've been saying," said Kitzel. "He was the man, all right."

"He sure was," said Hymie. "The heart, he'd say to me, that old ticker there, that's your heating system. And he'd poke me with his finger to show me where it was located. Once you let the fire go out in there, he'd say to me, you're sunk, you're a goner, you're extinct. Don't be afraid if they think you're crazy. If you got coal stored up in you, throw it in, burn it all up. Let's keep those feelings going, boy. You hear me? And I'd say to him, sure, I hear you. And he'd say to me, oho, so you like this slop, do you? And he'd toss me a slice of gum.

And he'd put his arm around my shoulder. And he'd say to me, Hymie, you thick thing, leave us be patient. Let's you and me just stand here like two cows for a hundred years. About giving milk, who knows? But gee whiz, there must be an intelligent moo left in us somewhere, don't you think?"

"A monster," said Kitzel. "I'm telling you."

"A real cuckoo," said Hymie. "Absolutely."

"But at least he knew we were alive, didn't he?"

"Right. And he wasn't afraid to show it either, was he?"

"Ah, no," said Kitzel. "Not that man. No, sir. And that's the guy Felix has nerve enough yet to call a faker."

"What faker?" said Felix. "When did I ever say that?"

"You said he'd never quit, didn't you?"

"Sure, I said that. So what?"

"So you're wrong," said Kitzel. "That's what."

"I am?" said Felix. "That's funny. Gosh. I know I get very tired sometimes, and my eyes ain't all they used to be, but every time I take a look, like now, I find the boy is still here. Now how do you account for that?"

"Well," said Kitzel. "I'd say, because instead of a head, you got a cabbage there, that's how."

"Swell," said Felix. "At least you can see that much. Why can't you try now to see a little bit more? What quitting? Who quitting? The guy's still right here, isn't he? When that door swings open, who do you think is going to walk out? A monkey? A bottle of beer? A can of tomatoes? What?"

"Don't worry," said Kitzel. "He knows what he's doing. He knows."

"I give up," said Felix. "I tell you. If I were sitting in there and heard you say that, so help me, I'd blow my top. I'd say to myself, it can't be. Me doing it for such boobs? I'd say to myself, nope, that settles it. I got my own life to live. And until I can figure out what I really want to do with it, I'm going to stay right here."

"But you don't understand," said Kitzel. "He's got to quit now. He's got to do it."

"You hear that?" said Felix. "Smug little bastard, aren't you?"

"Now what in the hell does that mean?"

"It means," said Felix. "I'm a pretty good bloodsucker myself. So I know. Let's face it, men. He's cherry pie to us. A lumpy matzoh ball. He's our meat, all right. And we've been having ourselves a swell time feeding on him."

"Flip," said Kitzel. "Watch this butt go right in the pail."

"Hold everything," said Felix. "Hold it now. It just came to me. I knew it would. Why didn't I think of it before? Suppose now. Sure. Here's what we do. It's really very simple. Suppose now he just kind of disappears. You know what I mean?"

"Disappears?" said Kitzel. "Where?"

"Here," said Felix. "Right here. You get what I'm driving at? This is the only way we can help him."

"How?" said Kitzel. "Explain yourself."

"Okay," said Felix. "So I gashed my hand today and lost a little blood. That doesn't mean I can't think straight, does it? Look. You guys are always talking about doing something for him. Well, now, here's your chance. Let's stop saying he's crazy. How the hell do we know if it's true? Right or wrong, my foot. Who cares if he's right or wrong? Let's give the kid a chance like none of us ever got. If he says to us, like he certainly will when we ask him, if he says to us, look, I need at least six months to a year to think this thing out. Then okay, we say to him, you stay right here, boy, and we'll take care of you until you do. Hey? How's that for an idea? Is that tremendous or not?"

"Here?" said Kitzel. "In this toilet?"

"Sure," said Felix. "Why not? Can you think of a better place? Who ever comes in here but us? Who will ever know he's here?"

"By god," said Hymie. "I think the man's got something there."

"Take care of him," said Kitzel. "Say. I kind of like that. And no one will ever know about it. No one. I bet you it's never been done before."

"Never," said Hymie. "Who would ever think of it? To stick by him. To show him we're really his friends."

"Are we game?" said Kitzel. "Are we all set?"

"Sure," said Hymie. "The hell with everything. Let's do it."

"Yea," said Frankie. "I knew something like this would happen."

From a trickle into a stream into a decided torrent, in a ridiculous exchange of all the bubbles which burst from their spittle works, the good Samaritans, forgetful of self to an unusual degree, they made with their arms as if they were flying, their vision peculiarly retracted, looking most like intense sea gulls on a hazy day who turn their backs on the sea, and oar themselves so mysteriously away from shore, and further inland, soaring deeper and deeper into the maze.

They would all chip in. They would get him his meals easy. So happy were they for once to feel they were more than merely a quorum of coexistent zombies, with such a poor history of never having enough of any one single thing, they vowed they would be unsparing of the flapjack and the muffin. They pitchforked him bales of shredded wheat for his forage grass. They linked him pork sausages lavishly for his hearty meat breakfast. They steamed him clams. And backtracked to make the butter flow. And poured him numberless cups of coffee as served at the Waldorf-Astoria. And tore time apart like long links of hot dogs. They joined forces to devil him a dozen eggs for a salad lunch, with blobs of miracle whip, with olive for green, and radish for red, all set up grandly on a tray. They exceeded excess. They bore him hot to his lips a bowl of clam chowder from Childs, or a weekday tomato and rice, plus a plate of dainty chicken croquettes with tiny peas and mashed, and a decent wedge of warm apple pie, topped off with a slab of pungent cheddar cheese.

What plentitude of crust and crackling fat and crunch of bones and catering to the belly, from which piggishness in its entirety the picky outer man flees, but the mindless inner man, he abideth, a food bag and furnace, to line his insatiable insides, to sweeten his strong Salada tea himself, and freight the brimming passageways of his brain with Biblical honey. May our belches erupt when needed. May god spare us any further shock, but it is already supper time. So they said to each other, no, we will not have fish for him unless it is fillet, and whatever kind of meat we get, with it we must have freshly grated horse-radish colored by the beet. Yet in spite of this resolution, whole pyramids of cans of King Oscar sardines kept sashaying in, so strongly was their taste for cheap food conditioned, flanked on the left by a regiment of Columbia River salmon, and on the right by close gold ranks of smoked butterfish, close by them shores of cockles and shells. They scooped him out mounds of watermelon balls. They shelled him walnuts for his wine. Malaga. They unveiled the entire spectrum of ices in his mouth. They conjured him a flash of brandy which he drank.

Warm grows the cosier. Turkish carpet flows the reddened bark. His memory in ashes, fine flakes of it rising, riding a Bermuda high. What were once moles are still sightless stigmata. Pink spots are where the petals of the rose of pale aim and ambition are adrift in the finger bowl. Special pet of his toilet intimates, congealing goons and body snatchers, they slowly drew tighter the drawstrings of the distance which would soon separate them again, making nice to him, nice, by the light of dinner candles. Heavy hangs the head, rushing to complete the picture, they laid him out in coarse khaki underwear on a rickety army cot, with the sides of the urinal for bed posts, and a roll of red silk page markers ripped from a cathedral of prayer books for his pillow, as an amulet against the cruel dream swellings of what is evil in the mind when it is imagined to be in a safe condition of sleep. Alas, my days are long, but my nights last forever. They couched him with a coalsack for cover, borrowed from the spaces in the Milky Way which are vastly black, beneath a canopy of heavily woven smoke, his longing for real light checked by a clumsy nightshade of blue crepe paper wrapped around the weak bulb of twenty watts which was always kept burning.

It is considered to be a part of the coma. This comfortable daze of being in a state of betwixt and between. Like so. While one limp leg dangles over the smoky lip of hell, the peak of the unruly head pokes itself into the related blur of heaven. Though the best sort of life is one of profound insensibility to either. If only because further reflection seems to confirm the fact that time in a man tends to fall into a sort of wild-eyed trance as a result of constantly turning its back on those ticking things which cannot be faced. A ravishing thought sired by noddins out of drowse. So that all told, what is known as life still rides death just as every woman on a horse used to ride sidesaddle.

But how about his evenings? How will he ever be able to live through them? Still so unselfishly intent, they blared forth their inverted thirds and imperfect triads, in a sort of last fling and flare-up of ragtime service and rhapsodic sacrifice, lurching and laughing so much alike, all of their feet stamping on the concrete floor in anticipation of endless copulation, their itchy fingers massing to turn up the trump card, and undrape the final dragon which is lust pure and simple.

For a man like Joe who has always been so frank and free about his natural need for nookie. What solid pleasure it would be for them to haunt the back alleys and beat the bushes to supply the stag with some hand-picked peach after a world-wide search, such as the naughtiest farmer's daughter from the French, a jerk-off, the old man, his pants stiff with sweat and manure, standing there in silhouette, as if to symbolize the peculiar intrusion of the incidental. Or to begin again, to bed him down with a cool blinder from Greece, or a soft and dreamy bombshell from the Black Forest, or smuggle in whole a trousered Turkish belly dancer, or a quick spread of jail bait from Buda and Pest, or a bit of jam from Japan, or a real smasher from down Piccadilly way, or a fiery little twerp from Trinidad, or vary his flutters with a slim wild thing from the Great Barrier Reef, or a wondrous scarlet woman from Bialystock, or a pickup with a prodigious bust and bottom from the Pillars of Hercules, or a furacious giggler from the Philippines, or a classic avalanche from the Swiss Alps, or a slow lesson in curves from Mesopotamia, or if worse comes to worser, simply kidnap a whole float of living dolls from the tournament of roses in the bestest land there is for the tightest sweaters and the longest stems, each babe trained from birth to tease a man with the uniformity of her summer tan, her hygienic private parts, her pagan American teeth, each in herself a solid erector set, cunningly built to represent in composite his cunt under canvas, his squiff under glass, his little bit of blonde fluff, his fat little pussy to dig in, to scratch, to go meow for him for his Manhattan nights' entertainment.

How all-fired warm and moist in the crotch inevitably. How like tinder the condition of the combustibles when a man has thrust upon him such an impossible diversity of rich and rioting possibilities. The wonder to Felix was that they could still breathe. He bowed down to them. He sneered. Of course, he said, he should have known better. Like all superior failures, so accustomed were they to sport with and sponge on creatures like gods only, it was certainly asking much too much of them to descend so low as to help a simple human creature. He said all that with the hope that if it did fail somehow to wither them, it would at least hold them for a while. But his only reward for trying to flag them down and put the clamps on them was to divert their attention to him, to his everlasting regret, for what they actually tried to do now was to lift him up on their shoulders as their pale and holy clown, their reagent with the overlong nails, their bony rattler with the numbered hairs on his lip whose marvelous idea had released them for a few precious moments from that oppressive feeling of ever

411

being so dismally useless, though the drama of it was only too brief, playing itself out like a shooting star in the imagination where the truth is belled, but the lie goes freely everywhere. It was while they were perpetrating this final piece of folly that the door was pushed in by Mr. Colish who sent them all scattering and running for their lives.

The ancient buzzards had to imbed their beaks, the patriarchal bosses had to tame the sorry apes with their bare knuckles, the slave drivers of old were utterly dependent on their whips, the olden wardens and worriers had to inject their managerial poisons to make an impression, as gain is like the foxglove, and greed is like the jimson weed. All the amazing graven images before Christ had to hurl their awfulest thunderbolts before they could make the weakest bench warmer hop to it, but today's simple boss, watchdog astonishingly clean shaven, his teeth meeting hard so as not to chatter, his twinsights trained on the touching idea of making every bit of his capital bulletproof, always blustering because vaguely terrified, whenever he has to deal directly with any of his apparent sheep, he has only to show his face to scare them almost to death.

Just as Joe must face forward if he wishes to be seated correctly in his stall, so has he no other choice but to observe further that when a person enters, the whole of him arrives. The dung of thinking animals, for such penny dreadful droppings, many a hopeless deadhead has been drummed out of life. And how. This perpetual rushing through every second, which is like a wink of blood to begin with, is what ruins us all. It is time Joe showed enough spirit to concede that every man, be he master or slave, has an inward spiral motion with a central upward current always moiling in him. He is therefore his own whirlwind, entire and complete, indifferent to what has sped before him, and what will come lagging after. Old twitch and tug is tentative statement, is like the secondary quill of a sparrow's feather, is like the pappus of a dandelion, the frail plumage of thought.

Bright boyish filmy character, what a funny wind machine turning in two-reel time, still in his early flickers, when such ghostly thoughts surge up from the vasty deep of his mind like starfish to intervene, like whales to delay the action, the grim floor-gazer, studying from underneath the restless loafers of a magnificent shipwreck of a manufacturer, soon sees that his own second-class vision has become blurred. Though he can still observe that Mr. Colish has come as the last straw

412

to break his back, having already said enough to this last true listener left on earth to make it only too clear that if God is in his heaven, this man is well established in his own hell, his days swifter than a weaver's shuttle and spent without hope, his soul as usual choosing suffocation and death rather than continue to drag on in its worn and weary way, a perpetual reject with a sissy propensity for crying wolf, his every experience lately like a caustic alkali, causing the very fibers of his life to shrink and become stronger for one reason only, that they grow more receptive to lies which can then assume a more saleable and silky luster.

What is it Mr. Colish is saying that has not been said before? He has to pace even where there is hardly enough room to do so properly, so has to wheel where he talks. Dreamt of scent bags and sparks flying upward. The corner of his gayest confusion is the point where the most whimsical of his nerves meet and intersect. When he woke up, as he thought, he found the discarded chrysalis of a butterfly in his twin bed this dim-lit morning. How was that possible? His heart left him in the lurch with a cruel independent leap. The cliff and cave dwelling part of him made him sit up in a strawish rabbinical beard and gossamer nightcap of batiste, the gorgeous lace of which tickled his long inclasping girlboyishness. It was a good thing nobody knew. He was such a softie. He was once a picked man. He could easily become wishbone for the whole world. He was perfectly toilet trained. His daffodil modesty made him look down to see where he was still undressed. His love was like a wax candle which he could never light because his wick was missing. What a thrill it was to see his Miriam drinking in her own arterial blood, but when he cradled her cheeks and asked to share the cup, she turned turtle on him, and it could be anybody's bare behind, and it was sad how their waters barely touched as they violently receded, and he reeled in his line, all limp and mucked up, for he knew that this too was only part of his cheap mustard dream of mingled hate and desire.

As Miriam keeps saying, my stars. The squeamish will protest, but the day must begin somehow. It is really strange how the ordinary little quirks will often engender the most mystifying forms of behavior, including the crying jag, which is guaranteed to cool off the warmest possible child-giver. Uses her brain so very little, yet seems to suffer so very much. It does not always follow, but it does seem that

413

squawking does come more easily to those who prefer the quickie to the long slow pull. Used to be such a comfort to have a man around if only to scratch the unreachable area between her shoulder blades. Her hair gets blacker every seventh day. She is quick to paste sharp false nails on her blunted ticklers. She has earned her fine crow's-feet by years of senseless peering into her own mirror-enchanted eyes. Hers is the scent from afar, the scent without a sequel. What she offers is the most consequential, the most farseeing bush anywhere. She is still so sensitive to the man touch, her crazy bone is everywhere. Lush grows her daily necessary lie in the swampland of her twilit interior. She has been known to say, dwelling with great effect on what occasionally transpires beneath the solid externality of her smooth unbridled bum and sculptured bosom, there is hardly an animal alive we do not eat, but no one knows as yet what to do with people.

As the whole of life is under fire, rolling inward as a leaf at the margin, ready to curl up and die, so it is impossible to tell from what graspingly bitter memory such a charming involution of the brain is derived. But it does prove she can oscillate a little, her thinking largely menstrual, her body the princess again, the primrose, its glad curves resuming its joyous skin game in the sweet high grasses, snaking itself along all the old bypaths of prick me and tingle, touch me and palpate, right on the border of red rag coupling, seeking traction for all that is so terribly blind and slippery in her. In the ancient well of the heart, the primeval ooze is at its usual level. On the creaking pulley is caked a sample for matching with last century's blood. The green scum is dumb. The cilia, without a doubt, the hairlike fuzz of the strange turbellarian worm of the dream causes tiny currents in the dim pool of the unconscious, mercilessly stirring up its lees and sediment.

Always so busy, busy. I, me, Mr. Colish. Midst a murk so over-blown comes my mumbling self to mock me and kiss me sad adieu. I am still dreaming, dreaming when I should be. Dog my cats, what a botheration. So upset am I by all this helpless taking to the air that I feel I am about to invade the dense foliage of complete and final disintegration just as a little warbler bird flings itself into a tree. My life so far amounts to this. I hustle to come in here. I find this Joe of mine. I pull the chain. I spill the works. I find he is fresh even when he is quiet. Every time I use one word, he thinks up a million more for me. It drives me crazy this constant talking that goes on inside of me. I am beginning to wish. How wonderful it would be if I could dry up like a leaf and be blown away.

Funny I should remember. There used to be a park in Pinsk in my day where I saw a bear slip on a watermelon seed. When I first saw red, it leaped at me like the lion of Judah. I touched a pigeon. I chased a peacock. In my little man's suit of light summer wool, I was like a picture out of a public school book. In this my third or fourth layer of dream, I am amazed to discover that much of my ground is still green. In spite of all the minus in my life, I find I am still a man with plus overflowing in him. I must also confess that as of now the order of things is thus. I say blood. I keep saying I see blood. But before I can ever hope to wear my Papa's high choke collar, I know I must take into account the curvature of his enormous occiput and the natural cameo of the crosshatchings on his pushcart neck. When I was seven he gilded the eagle of America on the buttons of my overalls. He broke my chatterbox. He kicked me where my crotch begins and ends. He made my soul dissolve in his yellow acid kvass. As I lay fainting before his eyes, he dictated my buster brown until I was nine, saying all ladies love fruit.

So I keep remembering. So many unspeakable pits and stems. I had to sleep with him under two quilts and a canvas cover the night my baby brother was extracted from my mother and instantly died. The slimy thing grinned once. He willed me his Siberia. I see his afterbirth in the shape of the Star of David. I see it as the peculiar cross I bear. As I was horrified as a boy just beginning to have slept with my Pop in the wintry white of his helpless wet dream seed. I remember well the mess a caterpillar makes when crushed against the trunk of a rotting Powell Street maple. I was still such a foreigner. I made a fire of his pith of wood. I also threw into it his lonely back teeth and the soft interior of his bones. The next thing I knew, I had stabbed the dog at the point where the bullfighter kills his bull. And I was wet again with blood. And I cried like a baby.

Ah, god, my god. I am so loaded down with the kale and the heavy sugar, I feel that something in my head is about to bust. I can only take so much and no more. I know. I can see myself. I know when I am licked. In Lithuania I was a herring. In Poland I was considered a bug. My universal lice traveled with me in the seams of my cap across the ocean blue. When I went to the toilet, they went too. My piss is the urine of Africa. My spit can belong to San Francisco. My sewer extends from Roumania to Revere to Rivington Street. My wastes and infections would just as soon appear in Babylon. My rash in hell is my reward in heaven. I am so glad the Irish have their lace and the Chinese their pongee. My wind and my wise men come to me out of the east.

Oh, people, people. The old heart's cry. The sightless goat that is all horn and hair. The beast that is all back. If all I ever do is crawl on its hairy surface like a fly, how would I know what it is to relish the full open face or delight in the whole eye? If part of me is here, and part of me is there, who will ever know me as I hide my screws and my stitches? Who will pity my special smell? Who will tolerate my real seasoning and my spice? If there is never any place for me to put myself, why should I care in which land I live or in which country I shall finally die?

As so fond and cold. So stupid and personal. You pitiful bastard. Wake up, wake up. Your royal flush is beaten. Your crooked deal with time is dead. Your last good head is crushed in your troubled sleep. You dug your divots too deep in your dreams. You really goofed. The time has come to become. Wake up, wake up. Wrapt in a foolish pajama tangle, his wrists to his elbows ingeniously trussed, his armpits inflated and pinched, his connective link in his collar a strangled chicken's neck, his parallel legs stretched out into long prison stripes, his drawstring to his groin a clever hangman's noose, his spine of stone an astonishing spiral, his shallow navel bare, he tried his very best to break loose, making himself a million wild promises, trying to do it with hate, trying it with love, reaching out and clutching for it, finding life so good and wanting more of it, he did what a child would do in the same extremity, blindly crying out, save me, save me, and God was good to him, and he woke up.

The light drew beads on him. The breeze struck him queerly. It was such a tiny morning as yet, quaint and secondary like a backhouse, harsh and dark with the relentless cawing of the crows of aftersleep. Their news is delightful. They are terrible if they say, if everything in life has a meaning, then all the cells of the mind must be filled with the sting and the honey. More and more will the rarely empty interim spaces seem hateful. The life story of any common Colish creature will hardly tend ever to end. When a man is a long time coming up, he distends the corpus of his career, he skins and he furs, he modulates

416

and shades, he appends a whole new index of shadows and blurs. His burning night eye will see no evil until it is bathed in boric acid. The corn plaster of his philosophy is a dirty old thing, torn and crumpled, dangling for days. He sports with his massive conscience like a great antarctic whale, churning the ocean white with his tremendous flukes, intensifying the blue with his mysterious spout, gaily harpooning himself with the keen and splashy cry of there she blows. There she goes, the hooded figure of his new-found sense of shame and guilt at how his stir crazy brain has busted out, gliding down her right of way with a toot-toot, nudged and nosed into the very heart of her enormous bay by those furiously symbolical little tugboats of poodle wrack and bulldog ruin. There goes dear little sister sin dropping her drawers while skipping rope.

Such a vision did actually come to him, immersed as he was in silly incidentals. He said he saw what he thought he saw, as if he knew he had to see it funny, or see it not at all. At what he ought to look he was afraid to see. He tried again. He took the long way around to ascertain his name and his honor. Across the gap between the beds, the keys to the factory lay untouched. Though it was barely seven, hardly normal talking time, the receiver was already glued to Miriam's ear. He began freshly to macerate the round toothpick he had kept in his mouth all night. His mind felt chipper and independent. It imagined it was a stallion so it could snort and rear. Quite unlike its usual gait of canter and trot, it became the essence of gallop when it sneered. And yet if it were suddenly able to fly, it would cringe, afraid to try.

Certainly there is world enough and time to say this much. It sure does make a simple man squirrel alert and rat tense if he is legally forced to coexist beside, if he has to coil and cockle, to rummy and casino with the weed stained, the sperm steeped, the flower grained, the toilet water mentality of a female in constant flux, as the stars go to bed undraped, so goes she, with a dame who has long exchanged the original bright mortality of her witty pupils and healthy whites for the duller slate, the more durable marble of grey-veined sameness and conformity, as a good percentage of her hair was piled up so, she was inclined to shape what seemed both snail and shuttlecock, with a squaw whose bill in rage runs from scarlet to purple, with a frail whose one-track mind veers from thoughts like sticklebacks to ideas like cockleburs, with a sullen cow whose hefty balancers are hung just

417

a shade too correctly on her, who sweats as rarely as she sleeps, with a fuming human who proposes her six equal square faces to God's huge and incalculable indifference, furious at the careless way he keeps listing her among the dumb clucks and also-rans, superlatively opposing his many other brutal dispositions of the partly alive and the almost dead with sincere murder in her heart and bitter chocolate on her tongue.

Who is she if she is? What is this mystery? Is the clock the face the fool the wall? Has the rose the heart to bloom to paper? Is it compelled to do? Has the piggy bank the snout to oink the money to snuffled space? Is the pink the hollow the luminous of the conch the vertical scope of the sea it sighs? Do the canary little chickens of china still cluck in the muck of time what passes as it stands still time after time?

What do the fat old mother mind say? She say, whereas, she say. She a feathered. She a fat old hen, precisely as these two toilet comedians and mates do so vividly see her, high-stepping everywhere with her queer pedagogical slangish pecker, clearing her crop for the word whereas, very upper-class, from the imperfect assimilation of which she intend with great to-do to lay beside the strangely active pellets of her feces her array of small misshapen eggs, the color of corn splotched with crimson, of puny contrasts and shaky comparisons between what is merely human and what is massively and serenely savage, making with her first cackle something like this. Praise the stinking polecat cause his purr is as clean of manlike love as his claw of divine compassion, cause he hath no need of applause when, in strutting about with most beautiful hostility and malice, he accidentally paws the tigereye and lips the tiger lily, whereas man, mister big himself, mines the one and plucks the other as if it purifies him instantly to have pleasure and profit make pee-pee on his soul.

Very nicely piddled, old gush, old faultfind and vituperate. As it ought to be terribly obvious it is only when the stale gumchewing thoughts of these two helplessly impacted people are torn apart and turbulently intermingled that fresh parallels and universals will sometimes rush in, delivered at last of prop of place and crutch of name, rot removed and restored to rose. As old mother mind, she say, impatient to expound further, letting fly from her in her haste such superfluous feathers as her supercilious belief in the absolute superiority of siskin noises to our harsh raving voices everywhere, in the turtledove excellence of the stormy petrel swoop, in the incomprehensible presence of the yellow-nosed albatross at the state fair, the provincial lark at heaven's gate, very fussily demanding of Colish, before she deign to continue, that his lonely name be lined with live slave ants, that his very fishy mind-speaking be writ out in the juice of flying beetles. Imagine, speeding up, she squawk something awful, to wit, see the cankerworm, the aspirin ignorant, the happy imbecile, without the slightest notion of what am gobble guilt, see how with wonderful insect intensity, how with its whole being it feeds on leaves of trees of fruit and shade, so perfectly at one with what it eats and what will eat it, see the jay, the swamp frog, the thicket of canes, the monk, the pouched rat, the Atlantic snail, the oily candlefish allied to the smelt in the North Pacific, see the fundamental tick, the tit, the fallow deer, the grinning fox, see how he gets wind of the Rhode Island Red he will rip into shreds for his missis and the cubs with a single sufficient sense, whereas that mess called man, that real gone goofy guy, he with all his fabulous equipment fails to seize and devour with any real deep down satisfaction the tiniest grain the grit the gravel the merest fleck of what first things mean, growls at, sheers off, shrinks back from the sober manner in which life schemes to keep so freshly green the idea of his supremely commonplace death to come, the perennial croaker, sponge and soak, he swills his nightcap of malodor of lees of deeds undone, seeker of the soft and languid forgetfulness in violins and seaweed, tosses off with desperate joy his daily stirrup cup of filth, his hair of the dog of double reeling, his quick snifter of stale aphrodisia, getting much dizzier as he does, flatly fails to catch the drift of the immense and inarguable meaning of his own bodily fear of his own bodily substance, scaly old stumblebum, hesitates before a fiber, runs from the simplest woof, his faith in the reality of other people like wax in the noonday sun, his trust impalpable dust, old wane, stoically grinding down his soul to the size of a pebble with the help of the devil, entertaining himself with his marvelous conception of God as with a hyperactive Yo-yo.

The old blind bat, Colish the krazy kat, his glow is not his glimmer, his aurora is not his aura, his looking is not his glass, his fleece is not his first blush, poor old peter prick, he says his, he sighs his darling, he moans his sweetheart, involving himself with his desire more and more, with its object less and less, reduced to a groan with much to atone for, he has come full circle round all his Miriams, hardly grateful for the exercise, his breath gone, his heart pounding in him, deeply ashamed to be staring at what has merged again into a mystery mothering a phone, crying out to someone who was obviously other than himself, ah, god, how can I live with her all my life when I know nothing, absolutely nothing about her?

How, says he. The nerve of the man. Since he more than suspects that not to know is also a way of knowing. The way today is neither short nor gay. The way to stay is not to go away. The way not to fall is not to fly. How dare you talk to me in this childish way? The cry is always for the individual to be original. It is really wonderful to see how sooner or later every brain, no matter how often it imagines it still does intercommunicate with the superior bees and the grander butterflies, will get to buzzing with the same express and local flies.

He must say. Even now he does not have the foggiest notion of how to contract the distance between himself and this other person, who happens to be his morning miriam wife, after so many attempts to catch her on the wing, she whose certain something smell is the come-hither of a solid sender, trying as he does to remember when last she snapped her garter at his enormous hard-on, gathering her lip rouge, while her glad hand toyed with what was supremely his, her red comb to his hot pepper, both so bridle-wise, so murderously socking it in. With all so much a blurred mummy in her all white bedroom where he lies panting, easy pickins, a greaseball, a glass jaw, a low-down fuzzdutty ready to blow a fuse as for the last time he rolls his eye over his statuesque lemon, his cruel sickener, his big cow come undone, as her merest accidental glance, her slightest making of a mouth magnifies his blue funk, enlarges his rabbit heart in a cheap chicken-wire hutch of haunt and fright, a peeved juiceless minus quantity with whom she has never seemed more disconnected, though she is on the phone at all hours of the day and night, very frankly spacing his bowel movements for him more and more, this professional witch of scare and constipation, this insomniac jewel of a flutterbump, this flushed bed bunny, this fruit and gash with the diving deep V neck and approachable danglers of firm slick amphibian fame, this quack at love and folding-money wangler, this fag hag, this seemingly immortal lounge lizard whose long white umbilical telephone cord seems to wind down and around to vast and improbable distances.

Where was he now? He kept groping, as he felt he must, through those vague candlelit regions of holy deadlock where the sheer impossibility of two living at peace with each other becomes even more impossible. By placing himself in her place, he could clearly hear the roar of those terribly reliable winds of Mosaic indignation, at a point where his roving spirit was so unhappily alienated from hers, where she was obviously in communication with planets and persons unknown, with incomprehensible milky excrescences of astral cunning and atavistic cognition, lying there and listening, not talking a blue streak as she usually did, but entirely listening to god knows who and god knows what, leaving him in total ignorance of what was being said to her, constantly sensing a conspiracy and vainly calling for help, until his fright and fury worked in him so much it would finally end, as the calculation was, by shortening his life and quickening hers.

Hers is whose? What is hers? If he was this kind of a fool, what kind was she? With his head thrown back and his eyes raised, he surely expected the nearest angel to hand him down the golden answer, but as so often happens, it was the alarm he had set in his own head to go off at seven that suddenly rang to tell him bang off. It was such a happy coincidence, it made him laugh like a crazy one, which made her eyes meet his as they had never met before. Horrors. You think me off my rocker, dear wife? You no like what you see? Be patient, my silly one. Though you spruce up your precious hope of outlasting me with real pearl and diamond flash, which is the most brilliant corollary of your all-out endeavor of your black satin desire to live forever. Though your Ma fed you malt beer and Fleischmann's yeast and fought with you the excessive flow of your first outspoken monthlies. You were no pale snip or dusty butt or sickly skinnymalink even then, my big lovely hefty jazzy piece. Though your Pa wrapped your cold feet in his frail Yiddish paper, his raw thin face as wrong side out and socialistic, which was his own queer way of trying to keep you in the fold. Though your prim little sister with the chiseling eyes dreamed only of acquiring real estate, she lost her life in a fight with her first goy husband, a shrimpy Polack seaman with tartar blood, because she tried to parry his unlawful pocket blade with an ordinary soup ladle. It makes you boil the way some people go. Though your one and only kid brother was always so sweet to you, he just about managed to reach his sixteenth year when he had his brains scrambled, chess and

421

science were his other joy rides, when thrown down upon the cobblestones of West Street from the dashboard of a bucking Ford. You saved half your life to buy a stone for him. Though your mother died poorly of a mild infection of the little toe, and your father followed with a tremendous thrombosis, leaving you his rusty old turnip of a silver watch, which you hammered flat immediately because you always felt that the principle of time passing was strictly the invention of a male. It is reasonable to suppose that age is a rat which is even now building its nest in the crafty double-dyed roots of your hair. Though your experience so far has some fine depth to it and real drawing power, you have yet to learn, my dear, that no matter how much you twist and turn, lie and burn, thrive and connive, life is still such, it is impossible to get out of it alive.

Oh, his aching belly. That he should have dared go looking to find such a conclusion like a flower in the wilderness. It sure was a dilly. Laughing freely at her, he had to crow. It was a real fantastic one, that was. It was a truth with such grave sweetness and grandeur to it that, in order to impress it upon her fully, he jumped out of bed to do something very simple.

"Yes," said Joe. "I know. And you came back and killed her. And the funeral's tomorrow. And now, thank god, we can all go home happy."

"What killed her?" said Mr. Colish. "Where did you get killed her?"

"Well, well," said Joe. "Was that me really speaking? And how have you been, my dear fellow? And where have you been vegetating today?"

"Kill," said Mr. Colish. "I don't kill. Do you kill? Why should I kill?"

"Okay, now," said Joe. "Let's get moving there, mister. You let yourself get trapped this way again, and I'm through with you, you understand?"

"I say, let her suffer first," said Mr. Colish. "She'll suffer plenty yet. Don't worry."

"Damn bastard," said Joe. "Haven't you got any brains any more? The next time think a little bit, will you?"

"Ah," said Mr. Colish. "God knows I try."

"Whoa, now, wait a minute."

"It's not so easy any more. But I try."

"No, no," said Joe. "I wasn't talking about you. I was talking about me."

"You, me," said Mr. Colish. "A mess is a mess. What's the difference?"

"Excuse me," said Joe. "I'm a little puzzled here. I thought she was in the hospital."

"Hospital," said Mr. Colish. "That's a hot one."

"It always is, isn't it?"

"Did she give them a hospital. Don't ask."

"Hate to interrupt you, boss, but you're sure wearing out that shoe leather."

"Wait until you hear," said Mr. Colish. "Again you'll say, I don't believe it. She's not there ten minutes, that woman, and she's already fighting with the nurse, knocking off her cap, tearing down the blinds. I say more light, Mrs. Reilly. When I say more light, I mean more light, Mrs. Reilly. Aie, the way she tells it, it's enough to make you dance with tears in your eyes, or if you're not too healthy, to drop down dead. Is this plaster falling? If it has to fall, it falls on my head. Oo, she tells me, what a funny feeling. Oo I'm such a nervous creature today, she says. Way way up in me where I never knew it could go is where the wind blew to tell me. In her nightgown from the terrace in her bare feet she comes back. I saw a rainbow, she says. I saw a few quick drops fall miles away. I saw a fat old pigeon fly through smoke. I saw a new aerial shining. Like twelve o'clock forever, I saw myself standing in the sun. You silly old goat, she says to me. You never see me when I look real good, do you? I wait for you to see, but you never look. Ah, you should see what I saw, she says. I saw a naked cat in a flower. I saw a sore like a spider. I saw a rat in the tar. I saw pimple people. I saw a baby tree waving at me way down below. I threw my comb at a little boy blue dot. I felt so light and free. I saw that what was far to God was near to me. I saw your Joe, my Max. I saw him come down to me, screaming like an eagle. I saw my world, my husband, and I can tell you now, it is not ended yet. What ended? What did she mean? What was she talking about?"

"She said she saw me do what?"

"Don't say crazy. Everybody says crazy."

"Holy cow," said Joe.

"Crazy," said Mr. Colish. "I'm sick and tired of hearing them say crazy. What does crazy mean any more? What?"

"Don't ask me," said Joe. "I'm just a stranger around here."

"No one knows. No one cares. It's terrible, terrible."

"All I know is," said Joe. "If I can still walk, I'm getting the hell out of here."

"Dirty glasses," said Mr. Colish. "And piss on the floor. That's all I see here. So you hear? So she says, sorry to spit and spoil your day, Mrs. Reilly. Cheery, beery. Boom, boom. You are music to my ears, Mrs. Reilly. When you sing like that, I know you love me like I love you, what did I touch? Come see where my scalp is red where your hairpin scratched it. What is this black stuff doing on my hands? On my where too? I asked for a phone. So where is it? Of course I know why I came here, but why should I tell you? Ah, come here, darling. You come here and crank up my bed while I fix myself up for my big fine handsome doctor. Fix herself up. Something smells here like a baby made. Flush, flush the water. See if it helps. So she puffs more white where her white is a little too green. She makes her lips look like next year's blood. She makes merry with the bracelets. She switches the earrings. She changes her bed jacket from a gold one to a blue. She breaks the string from her pearls. Her heart she leaves exactly the same. Ah, Mrs. Reilly, sweetheart. The way you keep looking at this old lazuli stone of mine, I can see, it's yours already. Take it, take it. So what does poor dear Mrs. Reilly do? She takes it. She screams, she pushes it away, she says no, I can't, I mustn't, but she takes it. So hah. So right away the sun goes down. She is getting old, my wife, she is falling apart. The sheet is creased. The mattress is too lumpy. The hands are sweaty. The enema is too cold. Ah, Mrs. Reilly, what a stinking business. What can I do if my brain shrinks and my bunion grows? You ugly thing. You can wipe your own nose. I am not paying you to pity me. I can do a much better job on myself than you any time. So there. So put that in your bedpan and swish it. So you see? So what's the use of telling you any more? You can bust, and that's all."

"Ah, well," said Joe. "Here I go sitting down again."

"If it's too much, it's too much. No one has to tell me."

"Maybe if I keep quiet, he'll go away."

"But what can you do?"

"A few more puffs," said Joe. "That ought to do it."

"It's like," said Mr. Colish. "I swear. It's like I think I'm not listening to her. I'm just like you. I say to her, please, don't tell me any more, I don't want to know. But I keep listening. And every word she says sticks in my head. So there. So go know what's happening. So you hear? So when the doctor comes in, she says, who is this? You are not the doctor who sent me here. Where is my doctor with the red hair? A snotnose yet, poor kid. Does he know what he's getting himself into? So he smiles and he says to her, sorry, beautiful, but the only doctor we got left today comes with black. The compact she throws misses his ear, but not by much. So he laughs and picks it up and he says to her, here you are, Walter Johnson, try again. So she looks at him and she says to him, you sound very familiar to me, do I know your mother? Oh, he says, you are much too young for that. Now, he says, what seems to be the trouble here? Oh, she says, it's really very simple, I'm sick of being a Jane, I think it's time I became a Joe. A Joe, he says. Well, now, Jane, let me see. Your tongue is clear. Your pulse is normal. Your eyes are a little wild. You will soon be scraping your carrot again. That is my honest opinion. But if you will take off your smock and turn yourself over, I think I can show you how to tell when company is coming. Ah, she says, of course. You are certainly very sweet when you begin to play this way with your little packages and do with it all your shipping. But as for me, she says, I'm sorry to say, but I smell a rat. You do? he says. I don't see why you should. Look at me, for example. I go to bed every night, he says, I put myself on, I pull myself off, I pick a lot of cherries, I look for the fat behind my eyes, I see that life is a fight between yes I say and no I go, I see the world is still dancing in a circle, I am no fool, I am not altogether blind. Foo, she says. All you know is what I know, which is to run away when things get tough. Excuse me, he says. But I am afraid you are in a very dangerous condition. You have two great big bumps on your chest. Well, she says, you know what a show-off I am. I always carry them with me wherever I go. I am hardly here an hour, but I already see that what is really mine I can never give away. As for you, you troublemaker, you may now take a giant step. Back, she says, who said you could touch? Now, now, he says. When you make fists like that, you are only telling me your hands are empty. You funny duck. You ought to know when you steal my ideas, you steal trash cans. Your eyes are becoming so small. I can see you are losing your switch. Isn't this nice? Your high color is coming back. The farmers need rain. There are various people here who are actually dying. This shrunken head looks like Max. Did you bring all this candy here by yourself? Did your special flowers come? No, my hollyhocks, she

425

says, they didn't come. Why should I have such a big sore here on my lip? Oh, it was like pins stuck in, those terrible looks you used to give me when I came to the shop. What could I do? So I picked myself up when I heard you were quitting your job, and I said to myself, move, do something like it, you bitch. A yap without a muzzle, a real girl dog. Did your uncle ever sell cheese? Is your mother a tall thin woman? Tell me the truth now. That is her smile you are smiling, is it not? Well, says he. Your lower belly has the bends and your armpit is definitely a little cloudy. Why beat around the bush? The more we feel we are like somebody else, the less we have to be what we are. Today you have my brains. Tomorrow I will suck a lemon with your mouth. And next week, if it should happen to snow, it will be just my luck to see it come down the wrong color. I am so glad there is a nurse here to carry out your slops. Damn your hooks and eyes. I am always getting myself caught. I can tell you now. If you come any closer, something you may not like will have to happen. You mean? she says. Yes, he says, I mean. Oh, she says, you should only go to hell. Will you please be a good boy and go to hell? You are so cute, I could eat you up. What makes you so nice to me? Your very high position in society, he says. You may now button youself up. I have seen enough. I should say you have, she says. Kiss me. Tell him to kiss me. If I had my scissors, I would trim my toenails. If I had a hanky, I would blow up a storm. Oh, thank you. I do so love a man's. It is always so big and white. It's funny how this pain travels. I think I will order me a dish of rice and cinnamon. I know I am only a tomato, but what gets me is, why should I fail algebra twice? Will you please stop sticking me with that leaky pen? Oh, he says, I am so sorry. It was only a little experiment. I was trying to see if I could change your spots. Silly boy, she says. You know me. What's the use? I turn up the fire, down the fire. It makes no difference what I do, I always boil his eggs too hard and his mush too thick. Can I interest you in a nougat? Or are you partial to nuts? Well, he says, I used to be. But lately, I don't know why it is, but the longer I live, the more I like the plain ones. Clock me now while I run twice around your bed. Your maid will wear your spangles. She will dance a two-step with the exterminator man. If I am not mistaken, you left some lima beans to soak. And a little birdie tells me that most of your potatoes are still in their jackets. And that you have a bad habit of neglecting your short hairs. The way you keep turning your back on

426

things, I can already see the lily on your chest. I must say I am one sly dog who knows that the cats have only one way of doing it. Open wide now. Open wide, I say. If you behave yourself this spring, you may well live into the summer. Yes, she says, I know, I know. I must give in. I must do the hard thing. I must go back. I never knew hands could be so gentle. I wanted to jump off the roof. I kept thinking about you and thinking until you came. I just had to talk to someone. What harm do I do if I dream this way? Dear sir, we are smaller and more cowardly than wolves. I very much appreciate your exposing me to the cold of this world. Just you give me enough troubles and I will become a real philosopher yet. Yours very truly, Miriam Colish the latest monster, who will go home now and try her best to live the only life she has to live. For a day or two anyway. And then, of course, I will go back to my old tricks. Oh, how nice. He likes me, he likes me. While we are still together this way, let's you and me play. Let's you and me have a tickle fight. Oh, he says, with pleasure. I am entirely at your command. But first, he says, you must show me how generous you really can be. You must do me the kindness to give some blood. Blood, she says. Of course. Blood. Yes, blood. Blood for my enemies. Blood for the dead. Blood for the world I hate. They will never expect it, will they? Oh, how I will laugh. I will laugh so. Mrs. Reilly, you will do me the honor now to tie up my hands and prepare me for the slaughter. Mrs. Reilly, rub me with my ring. Mrs. Reilly, scratch my back. Mrs. Reilly, kiss my foot. Mrs. Reilly, pack me up. Mrs. Reilly, open my veins. The excitement. The yells. I come home. She jumps on me from behind the door. Surprise. I fall down. I pick myself up. She throws confetti in my face. She makes me kiss a new kind of dog. I look around. The house is full of packages. I say to her, my god, Miriam, what is all this? So she says to me, these, she says, these are all ties. So I say to her, all ties? I say to her, what do you mean all ties? So she says to me, oh, wait until you hear. You will never believe this, never. So I say to her, I wonder if my mother is wandering out tonight. I have a feeling I should go now and give my father some bread and milk. If you will excuse me now, I think it would be best if I made an appointment with you for later. So she says to me, oh, no, please. How can you leave me now when I came back with a fat Jewish chicken? The pinfeathers almost killed me to clean. I made you a shrimp cocktail. I even mopped under the bed. I will broil you my heart if you want me to, but you must listen to me, you must. So you see? Just like you had to listen to me, I had to listen to her. So. Otherwise. Tell me. How long you been lost in there? Heard any good Pat and Mike jokes lately?"

"Ye gods," said Joe. "He expects me to answer him yet."

"It's funny," said Mr. Colish. "When I pee at home, I am absolutely quiet. But when I have to go elsewhere, I always stand there and whistle."

"Lucky me," said Joe. "I sure will have something to tell my children."

"Sometimes I even hum a little. For god sakes, my dentist said to me, brush your gums or something or your teeth will come popping out of you in no time. What I don't understand is. How is it I still have so much hair?"

"How is it you still think anybody gives a damn? That's what gets me."

"I don't think," said Mr. Colish. "From you I expect."

"Jesus," said Joe. 'I tell you. I'm blown up. I'm full way up to here."

"In that case," said Mr. Colish. "Why don't you do what I do? I just stick my finger down my throat and make room for more. I think. I think my nose is bleeding."

"Your nose is what?"

"Otherwise," said Mr. Colish. "I feel great. I tell you, Joe, I could do a little fox trot right now."

"Did you say your nose is bleeding? When the hell did that happen?"

"What a color. I'll use it on my nightgowns next season. You think I should use toilet paper? What do you think it means?"

"Wait," said Joe. "Wait for me. I'm coming out."

"What's happening to me? I think I'm going to faint."

"Oops," said Joe. "I got you. Easy now. That's right. Everything is going to be all right now. Now. Here we go. Let's sit down. That's a kid. Now you're doing it. Now put your head back. Way back now. Good. Now where's your feet? Your feet, man. They have to be higher than your head."

"What higher? I've been living this way for years. Where are you pulling me? There's no place."

"Wait," said Joe. "Hold it now. Suppose I close the door this way and

428

pull you over. No, that's no good. Gosh. You're a pretty heavy guy, you know that? Hey. There goes my best shirt. Stop kicking me, will you? That's it. Up you go. Watch your head. You okay now? Christ. What kind of a hanky is that? Take your hand away. Let me take a look. For crying out loud. Is that all it is? Whew. You sure had me worried there for a while, I can tell you that."

"And to the bargain," said Mr. Colish. "I even peel potatoes sometimes."

"Forget it," said Joe. "It can happen to anyone."

"How am I sitting here? Did you put the board down?"

"I put the board down."

"My perfect inside man. Did I say a two dollar raise if you stay? Make it four."

"Excuse me," said Joe. "I think it would be better if I stepped out. It's getting awfully crowded in here."

"Seventy dozens more," said Mr. Colish. "With that new gore. Should dye more silk and stock it. If the New England territory is so lousy, I should switch him to the Midwest. I was so smart. I saw it all coming. So I stopped selling to the little stores. I see them splashing gasoline. I see the flames shoot up. I see the walls fall. I leave it to God to give credit to all those cripples. Is Brockton the world? Is Rapid City on the map? Why should I creep to South Norwalk? My father says his father used to say, you can't climb a mountain by sliding down on your ass. In my next life, if I'm still alive, I will manufacture red snot only. And on the side, a batch of my mother's applesauce. When the truck comes tomorrow, I want you should be there and watch. Whoever cleans up this place should clean it up good. What am I paying that schwartze for? If I could be that big and black, I'd mop up the whole world."

"Why, sure," said, Joe. "Now I know you. You sound just like the Mr. Colish I used to know."

"Look at me," said Mr. Colish. "The way I am sitting here, I know I am going to live to be a hundred. I feel I could lift two pencils the way my back hurts. If you ever get a minute, drop in on me in fifty years. I'll be in the stable with all the other broken-down horses. I'll be buried in the third pile from the left, wearing my work gloves and clippers, chasing a duck. Throwing my gray hairs to the fish. Squelching mud on my workers. Wiping my poor old ass with wet grass. I

429

wonder what's the matter with me I can't shut up. Did what's his name spray the place? What am I breathing in here that's catching? They say in the old country they still walk on wood. I hear you are the champion folder of step-ins. I used to be so warm in my red mittens and poopkie hat. For women who want their breasts developed, they send a hand. They send. Don't laugh. Somebody is always turning the tables on me. I don't know where it doesn't stick me lately. When I made the final arrangements this morning, I had terrible cramps every two seconds. A crook giving himself the hook. Down by the water where men wet themselves. I once saw in the movies a whole boat made of glass. Every time I dream, I can never get my feet dry without drowning. You little piece of dreck. Are you taking a drink? What are you doing out there? All of a sudden I walk into the closet in the middle of the night. I go. I walk. Somebody sent me? What did I expect to find there? Their kind permission to live? Their rotten eyes rolling on the floor with the old shoes? The bread I am taking out of their mouths? Crack. I step on a ball of camphor. I pull down the dresses. I feel fur. I am sure I hear something behind me flying. I push myself back behind the coats. I put my head back. I open my mouth like a cat. I hear myself saying, help me, somebody, help me, please. But New York is so packed and deaf with dirty money. And in Florida they are busy adding color to the green oranges. I have a feeling if I think too much with my bladder, I must be passing stones. Shivering old cocker. I never did like socks with clocks. And until I get used to the dark, I will always push away from me white on white shirts. I sound like those insects in the wood, making their little clicks. Twice I had sickness with spots. When we came to the new country, we all had to make the jump quick from typhus to tumors. You not only have to live the same, but you don't even have the guts to die a different death. What is that tap-tapping to me from upstairs? From where I sit, I sure do hear the craziest rumors. Half the world is bats and the rest are pulling bloomers. On this day of days, my eyes are so good, I can see a mountain through a hole a pin makes. But how, I ask you, will I ever make anything fit when my whole life is like a size in between? The cabbie I picked up sang an old Hebrew song. The sun came in for six whole blocks. I felt so hot, I dropped off to see my old lawyer Lipsky, originally from Lodz. I said to him, I never did like your lower Broadway. I said to him, who is your tenth partner this time you are outliving? Hey, you old shitface? A real smart old schmuck, in a goatee

430

yet, and vest with white piping, smoking my lies out with his Italian twists, wising me up in his pearl tiepin and carpet slippers. When I bowed low and asked him if I could still back out from moving the factory, he held the match so long, he almost burned his hand. I understand the white workers get cheaper the deeper you move down south in Dixie. I had the funny idea of shipping the heads by sea and the rest by land. Who is really on top any more? If I am his bottom belt, then he is my treadle. I can still hear that shyster sucking his rock candy for his cough. He gave the same name to seven sons. In some ways he has no luck. His daughter became a dressmaker in prison. All the flies try to fill up the little holes in his face. Why do I keep looking behind me? I lose a lot of life that way. I wish I had his strong cold eye. The things a man has to do to save himself. You think you know? You think you know anything yet? What are you counting and jumping up and down for? When I was young I had to use my ears to hold up my first straw hat. Now my head feels like a balloon. I see I don't have to go to California to catch crabs. I know you're trying to show me what the score is by bending your knees and breathing in deep. But god-damn it. How many of them lousy pushups do you have to do until you can say you hear and understand me?"

"Eight," said Joe. "Nine. Ten thousand or bust. Just like Hymie. I'm puffing like I'm dying. I'm sure in good shape, ain't I?"

"I gave it to you good, didn't I?"

"You said it. You sure gave me the works. You took me like Grant took Richmond."

"Look," said Mr. Colish. "I'm standing. I can move my feet. I'm lighter. I'm ready to fight again. You next? Who's next?"

"Mr. Colish," said Joe. "I'm sure your dog has fleas. But I would be very proud to shake your hand."

"What's the matter?" said Mr. Colish. "There's no more pressing cloth? You have to go around like a slob? Tomorrow you start clean. I want to see you in a new apron."

"What a man," said Joe. "You never give up, do you?"

"Look at you," said Mr. Colish. "Where's the good color you used to have? What makes you so skinny? Do you eat? When do you sleep? What do you do when you're not making love with such big eyes? Dancing with your hotsy-totsy Rosalie day and night. Where do you take her? You have money enough?"

"I listen to you and I wonder. It's funny how you get used to people,

431

isn't it? A man like you fooling around with a nothing like me. It's a shame. Really."

"Everybody needs somebody. What can you do?"

"Mr. Colish," said Joe. "I'm going to save you from a fate worse than death. For your sake and mine, I'm going to step it up. I'm going to beat it while the beating is still good. I'm going to pass out of the picture faster than a bunny and quicker than a fox. Honest. I'm suddenly afraid. I see now. If I hang around another week I'll never make it. It has to be this Saturday."

"I wonder," said Mr. Colish. "Maybe I shouldn't take the train. The doctor said, if you want to live another year, walk, walk. Excuse me while I fix my tie and clean my nails. If you want to face the world, you must look nice."

"I know," said Joe. "I know I have my nerve, asking you to let me go this way, leaving you in a hole, with no one here yet to take my place, but jesus christ, what can I do? If nobody else is going to help me, then I'll just have to come to my own rescue. Saturday. This Saturday is going to be the great day."

"Please," said Mr. Colish. "You will kindly step aside now. And when I say step aside, I mean quick."

"Ah, now," said Joe. "Wait. This is wrong. Why should we end this way? Why are you suddenly so cold? What's there to be so sad about? I'm young yet and healthy. I'm really fine and raring to go. After all, what am I? I'm just a plain ordinary guy who's trying to do something very simple. Did I come screaming to you that I was right? I came to you very quietly. I said to you, I have lived this life here with you all I can. It's finished. Now I must go out and find me another. It was just an idea that came to me. Is it such a crime to have an idea like that? Look how it's changed me. Why should everybody hate it when it's done such wonders for me? It was like I was blind before. Now I see everything by it. For me it lights up the whole world. And everything I see is so wonderful. And so terrible. Terrible. Who wants to see so much? Why should I try to do what nobody else does? Why should I keep pushing myself where I am so afraid to go? Yet here I am, a complete mystery to myself, and still at it so strong. Isn't that something to celebrate? Hey, Mr. Colish? How about that? Why should we be such sad dogs? If a man doesn't weaken, we don't sit down and cry, do we? We yell. We laugh. We say hooray. We cheer. We cheer, don't we?"

Alas, no, not here. Age before beauty, said Mr. Colish, without softening in the least as he stepped out first, glaringly cold, weary and immovable. For no one, not even he could abide any longer that slick smiling chiseler known as faith, or that crafty egg-sucking animal which men, hiding in the bush, still call aspiration. No, not here, not in this peculiar joint where daily effort wanders about in one vast dust cloud of doubt in a man-made light wholly fringed with fear, and the shrinking future is viewed through the vacuous eye of a needle, and the flaws in the white silk of space are the fast increasing shadows of signals and signs of decline and disinclination, and the women behind the counters are visibly preparing some fresh kitten fits for the delectation of Joe who returns now to his table, in strange high spirits, like a wild man scattering his mess of fine clauses in one last long breath, as if seeking relief from relief, from that criminal feeling of his of endless third-degree exhilaration.

As the burglar thrills when the tumblers of the safe of his future fall into place and the door clicks open, his heart leaping in its crib in anticipation of accruing to itself untold cash and valuables, his bootleg eyes buggered out in the glare of his torch, his reckless desire to be a lone wolf, an entire separate nation unto himself, about to be appeased, so did Joe now tremble with joy and terror, amazed that he should have placed himself in such a position of great peril, suffering quite a bit, in his own quaint way, from the vicious pleasure of taking the law into his own hands, shocked as any tame goat would be which suddenly breaks its tether, though it loves to be in the flock, and without quite knowing why it does so, consults its pride and impulsively decides that the time has come to act the desperado, and forever after live dangerously among the rocks.

But now. What the mischief can this possibly be? The first to come from a long way off to pay him some tribute, as he was surprised to see, was Little Bee, approaching him at a portly herald's pace, bearing before her on an empty card of lace, as if it were a jewel upon a cushion, the fine husky comma of a single cashew nut. He said to himself, what the blazes. His sudden smile was something to see. For one who had lately been practicing to be a social leper, he did well. He bowed, pinched her playful gift between thumb and forefinger, and popped it into his mouth. When Angelina came next with a hairpin bent to suggest spectacles, he was easily persuaded to do the old grand-

433

father act. Big Bee shrieked at the ignatz who thought her corset string was a piece of spaghetti, and as such, something slick and juicy to slurp down. When Octavia, the presser, brought him the rusty core of her afternoon apple, he stored it in a vest pocket with such care and dignity, it broke her up right where she stood. Maisie Dubrow was sure that if he scaled it he would further break the ice with a round polished stone she had fished out of a brook in the heart of her Catskills. From Rosalie dear came one sharp little ring, and the beautiful gift of silence when he answered it. With the slowest of slow smiles, Miss Golschman then came to present him with a frightening mask she had made by scissoring out slits for his eyes and a diamond shape for his nose in a fresh sheet of black carbon paper. It charmed him very much. It was so powerfully simple. It brought everything to a fitting close. It was then he decided to bring home a gift of his own.

13.

Where the bird just was, the branch trembles. The sound of scuttling reveals the late presence of a rat. The quick invisible fish will show
by their sportive bubbles that they are long gone from where they have
once been. What grass is not absolutely smashed still quivers where
the elephants have recently passed in all their vast immensity, traveling trunk to tail. The bones of old upstarts litter many a rocky ledge,
reviving memories of blood ooze and vultures. Take heed, my lord
and master. In the translucent wake of the evening mind comes the
critical thunder of trotters and trumpeting cranes. The camera shutter
clicks, but the shifting image sneers. When things are ordered differently, at first nothing is clear. The sun what sets is not the sun what
dawns. The shadow is caught, but the substance escapes. For the black
creature unconscious, flitterbat forever night-clad, it is always
cockcrow. Subway rails tell senseless tales of a screeching rush and
crush. If the city man had a soul, it would lag far behind his body. His
confused ideas of which came first, and what comes next, are like
clouds of mites and midges, backbiting pests which hover irritatingly
about all the fashionable classic beasts which are themselves despots of
space and satraps of time, fantastically multiplied, of his impossibly
crowded world of aviary shrieks and jungle roars, of moiling ocean
mixed with earth.

Ponderous slow coach, bumping along strictly by the book, past master of delay and dillydally, made spiritually thin by constant surface motion, bogged down in a fearful muddle of hush my heart and tush my senses, where does he ever finish where he begins to look? Everlastingly mired in mere traces and trails, he sees the glow but fails to catch the worm, sees the strong claw marks but not the coatimundi, the quiet sane freckles but not the common crazy clay, the regional tan but not the universal rot, the high flying trapeze but not the daring young man, not the snail but only its cold wet spot.

The mind, the mind, that marvelous basic creeper. Dread lord. It drives a man crazy, it does. Cry you mercy, kind sir. Have pity on us. Mow us down and weed us out. Why do we need to press so close one upon the other? If the breath I breathe is yours, whose death will I be dying? The tighter the world gets, the more the sense of my own importance is squeezed out of me. My stars, what sort of age is this we have fallen into? When was the old world ever so rich and full? Is the illusion so perfect? Or is it really true? Are we monsters of a different order? Are we merely boasting and ever so slightly hysterical? Yet it does seem to us that with the same old eyes, we have more to see. With the same caustic mouth, more to stuff in and suck up. With the same foolish heart, so much more to be fond of and to follow. The swallow back home. With a cry for forgiveness and a sudden clumsy swoop, to restore to him his fool's cap and bells of a budding intellectual. Most nervous and modern kind of hopalong, while so many still cough and creep about in the dust he raised, he has already taken for himself another smart step forward, dragging them along with him, helplessly attached as they are to his flying anchor and tripping line.

Feeling fit and chipper and in fine whack, the mighty hero stands plunk in the middle of the train midst a massive underground miasma of mental motes, trapped in an optimum dose of dangerous contact with improbable people, pressing his precious bundle to him with both hands so that no real suspicion of his doing funny business can fall on him, showing by the demure expression of his hide-in-the-corner face that when there is less movement outside, through a natural reaction, there is bound to be much more inside, trying to prove that if man is always assaulted in his own time by a relative swarm and superabundance, today it is the thought-life of the brain which is not quite the same. It is like a trip in a jointless dream which has no journey's end.

With his head so lifted up, what do the silly ads say to his sales-resisting soul? They have the nerve to reiterate that muchness is still everything, and bigness just about all. With a smile that dazzles no one he dares to oppose it. Profounder idiot, a stray at heart and natural mute, among these incidental passengers who are to him as so many midgets, he has wit enough to see himself as a cool giraffe, fabulously stationed, ruminating high above, nibbling on the choicest leaves of lofty matter, so serenely foreseeing, under the aegis of gods whose legendary names no longer have the power to make us tremble, the eventual triumph of people over things. For him who can so conclude, death is far off.

Or so he hopes. Talk about a brain teeming with tentative ideas. Most certainly it is painful to get so involved in a passage so bare of some juicy piece of mayhem or killing, but somehow it does serve as an interlude while the stage is being set for the next sustained scene. The hero must fade in as the villain fades out. While we splice our broken reel, his silent screen flickers and jumps. For the space he lost, there is no time to spare. The key is in the lock. The knob is in his hand. The best things in life are free. The world, she belongs to everyone. After all, what is this elaborate quibble? Whether this be a dream or not, the die is cast. Let it be his America or bust. Surely it does take guts to build roadblocks such as these to keep the timid and lazy on the run. He may be flung down from all the ancient high places in his fearfully fantastic efforts to get at the whole blasted truth. Nature does have a way of taking vengeance on those who would work miracles. But such a sublime experience would make his modest star to shine and his simple name to ring forever and ever. It would hardly hurt him in the least. As Mamma says her father used to say, it is good for a man to bear the yoke in his youth.

So lightly as yet in this case that there was more than enough snap and ginger in him to slam the door behind him as to make the whole house shake. The baby giant, he strode through the short stretch of the foyer as if it were one of the grand divisions of land on the globe. No doubt the original serpent himself is happy to see with what high proud passion this gullible hothead can still believe in and obey the sly dictates and deceitful promptings of his most treacherous innermost self. The very symbol of naive contravention and stormy delinquency, he burst into the kitchen like a preview of a sudden summer shower. Trust him to put on a good show.

"There she is," he said. "What did I tell you, men? There's the dearest, the sweetest, the dreamiest, the loveliest gal I know. What ho? Are all my subjects here? Where are all the banners? What's the good word, bird? Confound them court musicians. Why ain't the band playing?"

"Quiet, you crazy fool."

"Ah," said Joe. "So. So this is the way the master is greeted?"

"I'll give you a master right away."

"What?" said Joe. "No sweet smile? No carpet laid? No special kisses?"

"Goddamn you," said Helen. "I told you to keep quiet, didn't I?"

"Ho," said Joe. "Look who's saying quiet."

"Honestly," said Helen. "I don't understand you. What's the matter with you anyway? What kind of habits have you got? Were you born in Borneo or somewhere? Every time you come in here, you have to come in like a wild man."

"Black death. I learned a new way to kill a person today."

"That's right," said Helen. "Go ahead. Touch me. That's all I need now."

"Here," said Joe. "Catch."

"Don't you dare."

"It's for you," said Joe. "Don't you want it?"

"Oh, sure," said Helen. "I know you. Something silly wrapped up again. Another joke."

"I'll be damned," said Joe. "How do you like that? You see what I mean? Go be nice to people."

"My goodness," said Helen. "I can't even push him any more. What is this? Are you getting bigger? Or am I getting weaker?"

"Well, now," said Joe. "Let me see. When's the last time I beat me up a woman?"

"Please," said Helen. "Don't be such a pest. Can't you see I'm busy? How the devil do you do this? Do you boil the milk first or later? What a head. I can never remember. Darn it, when I want a spoon, I find a knife. Do me a favor. If you see me shaking, hold me back. I'm a fiend when it comes to pepper. Now where did I put that cup of rice? Holy smoke. Did you wipe your feet outside? I hope to heaven you didn't step in you know what. Soup I have to make yet. Did you ever see anything like it? What do I know about making soup?"

"If you don't mind my asking. You're my favorite sister and all that. And I do want to be nice to you if I can. But what the hell's going on here?"

"I'm sorry for you all," said Helen. "But I'm afraid I've been elected. I'm your cook tonight."

"Cook?" said Joe. "Why? What happened? Where's Mamma?"

"She's lying down."

"Lying down?" said Joe. "What for?"

"So you can yell and wake her up. That's what for."

"Now don't get fresh," said Joe. "I'm only asking you a question."

"And I'm giving you an answer."

"What answer? Is it her head again? What's wrong? Where is she?"

"Shh," said Helen. "I just told you. She's all right. Stop making such a fuss, will you? All she needs is a little rest, that's all. If you want the whole story, I'll tell you. I just didn't like the way she looked when I got home. My boss had a sudden call his house was on fire, so I snuck out early. So I said to her, quick, march, out of here, go and lie down. I said to her, what are you trying to prove, that you can kill yourself? I said to myself, I don't care what happens, I'm going to win over that woman if it's the last thing I ever do. I said to her, if you're worrying about your poor dear sons and what they will have to eat, pooh, you leave that to me, I'll cook them up a supper they'll never forget. Of course I had to slap her around a bit and give her a bloody nose and all that, but I finally convinced her. You know me. I get shaky in the knees when I pick up a carrot, and I let every potato I meet push me around, but when it comes to people, by gum, I can be just as tough as anybody."

"Mamma sick. I don't like that."

"Well, baby, neither does she."

"Goddamn it," said Joe. "It's really beginning to get me down. Every time I think I can relax, boom, something else happens."

"Hey, now," said Helen. "Let's be watching it there. What are you trying to do? Break all my eggs?"

"Hold still," said Joe. "Let me choke you a little. It would make me feel so much better."

"Sorry," said Helen. "I'm through playing patsy for this week."

"What's wrong with you? A woman is supposed to give, give, give."

"Back, I say. Or I'll clout you one sufficient to make you see stars."

"Can't I even cry on your shoulder?"

"I told you. I'm full up this week."

"Mamma sick. It's ridiculous. Why all of a sudden should she be sick?"

"She had one son too many."

"The lousy cowards," said Joe. "What else are they?"

"Oh," said Helen. "I'm so sorry. Did I just cave in your ribs? I know I have a very sharp elbow."

"The bastards," said Joe. "Who's in charge anyway? If they're really up there, why the hell don't they come down? I'll fix them. I'll learn them to come picking on the people. Who needs them? I don't need them. They don't know it yet, but they have a rough customer here. I'm no baby. If it's we who made them, then it's we who can break them. Out. Finished. Scram out of here, you broken-down characters. Can you imagine the nerve? They think they've got you licked before you start. According to them, you're already dead, but you haven't got enough sense to lay down. You watch. I'll give them a real battle yet. You'll see. If they push me, I won't budge. If they won't open the door, I'll keep banging on it anyway. I'll overpower the bums. I'll slap them down yet. You'll see."

"I'm such a silly goose," said Helen. "So what if the pot's boiling over? Or if I forget to salt? The thing to remember here is that a great hero and philosopher is sounding off."

"Ain't he though?" said Joe. "And so handsome too. God. Sometimes it gets to me too. Do you keep a kosher house here, lady? May I park my bundle on your busy little head? You'll thank me yet when you see what's inside. Now I ask you. If you can't hide at home, then you're really in a jam, aren't you? And I don't care what kind of stale bread you eat. You just stand there and I'll wear you down like a stone. How about this? I know I've been much too reckless lately, but I hereby challenge you and Abe to a tournament of checkers right after supper. That is, as soon as you wash the dishes and Abe dries. Unless you think there's already too much static in the air. If your heart's too full to speak, just nod. As you know, I'm always ready to defer to you, my dear."

"It's not fair," said Helen. "I must talk to Mamma about this."

"I hear her," said Joe. "But so far. Nothing."

"He there," said Helen. "He's getting younger by the minute. But me. What's the use? I'm just about ready to drop."

"That's it," said Joe. "That's exactly it. You see what I mean now? That's exactly what I'm here for. To catch you, girl. To hold you up."

"No," said Helen. "It can't be. Is my brother Atlas? Am I really his sister? Why didn't somebody tell me? Is this the mighty arm? Where's all that muscle that used to be? Look. The air is clear again. The sun is streaming through the window. You blind me, man. Pull down the shade. You're melting all my butter."

"Wait," said Joe. "Holy mackerel. What are you doing there? You're not really going to do that, are you?"

"Stand aside, mister. This is a very delicate operation."

"Stop," said Joe. "What are you trying to do? Blow us all up?"

"What?" said Helen. "With a little rice?"

"A little?" said Joe. "Ye gods, Helen. Have you any idea what would happen if you put all that in? You'd absolutely flood the place."

"With one cup of rice?"

"Helen, my dear. You must pull yourself together. You're home now. You're all right. You're safe. You're in Brooklyn with millions of other people. This is no dream you're living. This is reality, dear. You must wake up."

"My goodness," said Helen. "And I was going to put in three."

"I knew it," said Joe. "I don't know what it was, but something told me I had to get home fast."

"Some brain," said Helen. "You may now take the key and lock me up. I suppose if I keep standing here in my high heels, my feet would begin to kill me, wouldn't they? If I have the ammonia out, there must be a reason. You suppose it's that old dutch cleanser in me? I'm such a superior woman when I'm chasing dirt. You sonofagun. What's there to laugh when you see me with a jar of prune juice? Apples should fall on your head. Why did you come home so early to catch me? Do you like French toast? Borax and brown sugar. There's a combination for you. I remember I once made some good French toast. I'll tell you the truth. I'm mad and I'm sad because I expect a phone call, and I don't know what to say, but I may as well be honest with you. I don't see a darn thing here that's fit for a man to eat. Not yet anyway."

"I had a dream last night I was feasting on graham crackers and grasshoppers. God knows. It may come true yet."

"Right," said Helen. "Talk about snails and puppy dogs. Did you ever tell a person to go to hell straight off? It's the only sure way to do it, isn't it? If you ask me. Love is mostly in the eye. Love is a great big

441

fat lie. Or something so very similar, it doesn't even pay to go into it. Here you are talking to a lady and your hat is still on your head. You don't have to give me such black looks. I went into at least a hundred stores last Saturday, but I couldn't find a single garment that would fit. I've been a perfect twelve so long, I'm beginning to feel like a freak. It must be like Mamma is always trying to tell me, those who can think only about themselves, and if you ever find any other kind, you just cable me quick, are those who are absitively and posilutely the most mixed up. The awful thing is I have another birthday coming up next week."

"Excuse me," said Joe. "But how is that again?"

"Bananas," said Helen.

"Well, yes," said Joe. "That much I do understand."

"There must be some bananas around. If there's sour cream in the house, we're saved."

"I don't know why it is," said Joe. "But I feel like I've been hit on the head like chicken little."

"That's right," said Helen. "Go ahead and mumble. It always helps."

"All right, now," said Joe. "That's all, sister. I'm sorry to tell you, but this is it, kid. Put up your hands and defend yourself. You're not going to kid around with me any more. No, sir. I don't care how you scream, my lady. I'm going to knock all that private little world stuff right out of you."

"Watch it, clumsy. You'll poke your own eyes out."

"Out. Out, I say. Damn gloomy business. I'll fix it yet."

"I may be crazy," said Helen. "But I smell geraniums. If I don't water those plants, Mamma'll kill me."

"Stop," said Joe. "Stay right where you are. Helen, my dear. It's all over. It's settled. You have nothing to worry about. After tonight, Mamma never gets sick any more. No, sir. Not while I'm around. When I settle a thing, it stays settled. All I have to do is snap my fingers and it's done. Magic. Just like that."

"It's incredible," said Helen. "And he hasn't had a bite to eat yet."

"And what's more," said Joe. "I'll tell you another thing. I'm going to go out now and put away my outer wearing apparel. And then I'm going to be rash and wash me my hands and face all over. And spruce myself up generally. And when I return all stripped and ready for action, what do you think is the next thing that's going to happen?"

442

"You're going to pitch in and help."

"Right," said Joe. "Abracadabra. And jumping shoelaces. I'll show you what I mean yet. Wait and see. Drop them tools and face me. I will now pass my hands over your eyes, and you will completely relax. I said, relax, not flop. You're too heavy to hold up. You will relax and forget. You will fall into a deep sleep. You will not snore, however. No matter which way the wind blows, it is always sensible to keep the mouth shut. As in closed. And when I say to you, come into my garden, Maud, you will wake up. And presto chango, you will remember again how wonderful it is just to be alive. You got it all straight now? Right. You can open your eyes now. I said you can open your eyes now. Aw, come on, Helen, be a good sport. I never ask you for a favor, do I? Come on, now. Don't make me do all this work for nothing. Open up them eyes. Open I say."

Meanwhile back on the ranch. The sun burned down on the bunkhouse. The blue jay screamed at the peacock and the bull. The cat carried its two mangled kittens to the safety of the shade trees. The road runner ran the rattlesnake into the cactus. The little basset hound had a large curly dream in the chuck wagon. The rooster wiped his bloody pecker on the hog through the wire mesh. The robber baron lay dead with a bullet in his head. The cattle grazed. The villain was climbing the windmill. Time in the shape of wind and dust came rushing on in all its cruel possible posses. Most secretly intent on corralling her wild movie horses behind closed lids, Helen, the true sagebrush gal and Rocky Mountain lover, she stretched out a rigid arm due west. They went thataway, she said in such a basso profundo ghostly tone of voice, Joe almost did believe he had her in a trance, until she smiled and gave herself away.

Giving him to understand, her bright buckaroo, sharing as he did her booted and spurred, wholly sunlit enthusiasm for highly contrasting westerns, that she thought it was only fair he should leave to each his own wagon ruts in life, his own peculiar grass roots and bumps in the ground, his own bone orchards and badlands to roam in, his own individual brand design. Hers, of course, would be something on the lazy order, preferring as she does to have her letter lie on its side, soo bossy, while his on the other hand always tended to be a variation of the more complicated whangdoodle, a hybrid collection of interlocking wings with a wild flying central figure.

443

Surely it was her backwards bucking, stiff-legged jumping, extremely justified woman's duty to point out to him that only a sore tenderfoot like him would ask an old sourdough like her to droop mid her pans and allow the shotgun of her mouth to rust while bitter antigodly sounds of trigger talk and wrangling could be heard everywhere, and the striking fox fire, like the very phosphorescence of fright, could be seen playing about the horns of every poor devil, threatening to shock dead that very tension in life which makes the kettle to steam, and the cow's tail to twitch.

After a long day's ride without the necessary chaps and gloves of the common will to survive what has to be endured, even the toughest Brooklyn dude will learn that it is always cheaper to grow new skin than to buy it. If he were indeed her brother, and as such a real loyal hand, it was surely time he stopped being so plumb loco about coiling up his rope and dismounting just when those low-down rustlers of disease and death were foully lifting every straggler from the herd, and instead buckle on a fresh gun belt, hurl himself into the saddle, and take up the chase with the sole aim of shooting those shady meddling rats full of daylight. So git along little dogie. It is good when a man is so quick to understand. It does save time.

So he git. They say that he who flies well, flies quick. Old mortified balled up. Old used to love to tumble in mid-air. Old butcher's boy of hustle and moxie whose international brainwork seemed to be so interesting because it was as bent and crooked as a dog's hind leg. What profit is there in digging fence holes forever? What fool does not know that the shimmy is either a chemise or a dance? What good is a fact without its ragged edges? Actually as things go, polished apples are not to be eaten, and waxed floors are not to be walked on. The darker your own way gets, the more must you send out the emissary of your hand before you. Thinking on the run has always been warming work.

He had hardly reached the clothes closet when he was already asking himself, what the devil is happening? It had to be. It must be old man trouble, his very oldest buddy, who has so deranged his compass that the needle of his affections keeps flying off in all directions at once. It must have been the same old tramp who said, if every road we take in this one and only life of ours is tricky, is inclined to slope straight downwards to death, then it hardly matters which way we face, does it? The question still remains, as it so often does in the course of human events, how many howling little hims can one humble little he handle?

Precisely as many as would make clear again that no matter which crow is croaking, it always turns out to be Joe. Peculiar thing about him, what plump sparrow of spite was it that had pecked its way into his head, and with the spastic insolence of any former free thing, keeps constantly chirping and chattering to itself? What sort of straying critter had he become that he could no longer control how much each separate moment of his dumdum bullet of life should be shrunk or distended? Surely the time has come to stop rattling around long enough to confess that ever since last Saturday when he had so fearfully announced he was going to bolt from this ninny world and burn all his britches behind him, he had never felt less like his own boss. Of his interims and interludings especially.

Pippin-hearted, smelling coal gas, breeding petty unhappiness in this horribly limited semidarkness of his, he refused to switch on the foyer light lest it reveal him even more as a grumbling bore and forlorn gazook who, if he moves at all, moves mostly in blind descending fashion to the very lowest pitch and dungeon of himself where no light, as we commonly know it, is ever allowed to enter so that it seems to him he is standing up in his own tomb, a cranky and bewildered paralytic whose punishment for setting out to make progress in reverse is reduced to a ridiculous expansion and glorification of the shorter steps and the smaller rooms. When he disunites himself from other surf ducks, this is what his delving does. Freedom such as this to wonder where one lists is for the stronger men. For the simple basic kid it is such a complicated thing to have a life away from life. If his character was his fate, he had to conclude he was particularly cursed. He felt his back was already completely broken from bowing down so much to the inevitable.

Quickly relieving himself and as quickly washing his hands, he paused a mere second or two to rake his hair with a comb but slightly wet before he went swoosh right out of the bathroom as if he were a ruffed grouse which rises straight up and swiftly when flushed. When the romantic rebel is alone, he rarely acts, he merely moves. Thick all around him go slithering his scragulous words, hisses and hints, innocence wet and by experience bleached.

445

Assault with intent to kill, with his feeble mental flickers, was he happier as a crocodile when he first emerged from the symbolical mist? But of course in time the slime and the curious warts dried and faded, and he was all hair and instinct for a good long while, a red-eyed spook scowling alike at fire and ashes, rain and blood, a casual eater of liver of kith and kidney of kin, until one fine day he heard the queerest rumbling upstairs, and he scratched his skull with his five thumbs, for believe it or not, it was in his very own head it was happening, the most unique sensation yet felt by any animal, for all at once he saw himself as something separate and distinct, and he staggered, and he let loose with such a bellow, so terrified was he by this monstrous notion of himself as an individual, and he began to run uphill, the wrong way, and if the truth be told, he has not stopped running yet.

When nature thus betrayed itself, people all over the world began to kill themselves. Wild to get lost and end it quick. One man said he did it because his penis burned him and he had to bear it all himself. Another said, my brother hates me. Yet the loosest word in the language is love. Only yesterday a woman said, my seams are not straight. She willed her suede gloves to the next crop of strawberries. A much deeper and darker one said, I was always alone, I never knew what I was here for. Her hair got caught and her scalp torn off in a papermaking machine. And this happened in the old lush days. How common and whimpering, when the old universal cry goes up of blur me with the world, blow me fine into others, every living soul is warmly concerned with higher mathematics. Yet way within the cold and heartless metaphor of millions, one is still one. How strange that only humans should suffer from this sort of supreme unasked for condition. It must be as Mamma says, the only thing that holds God together in his heaven, as the one grand concept of what is single, is the fact that he has the power somehow to keep us apart here on earth. She says that if she ever had the chance, she would walk right up to him and pull his beard. Sometimes even she is driven to say that.

To have her so relatively bubbling and defiant in these terribly disenchanting, grossly uncouth and intimidating days was such a rare satisfaction, gave him such an awful boot every time, because then it seemed she was quite as young and frisky as he was, mostly leg and wing, perfect frying size, as if she were a deciduous plant freshly risen up, a honey stick and leafy vegetable, a crawly root, a kind of all too human malcontent and brawler with his rant in her and his raving, or a gay and reckless strain of herring, defying the shoals with its tiny fins doubled, the dippy dapperling, cheerfully flashing through those ever narrowing inlets of risk and reprisal, as if gasping and flapping were all, as if boyish insurgence was the only living breathing way to a life without death, and a death which bore no resemblance or had any relation to human life at all.

Strange how some bodies of people are so embrangled with and devoted to each other that any door that is really closed between them is absolutely an unbearable thing. Sharply braking himself as he neared Mamma's bedroom, he crossed his fingers and peeked in. In his indecent haste lately, it seemed he was always trying to perform the trick of the week. He hoped he would see her in a position he could more easily understand. This wholly obscure and imported woman with her useless fine nose and slender aristocratic ankles, this towering indoor sufferer, this ineffable phenomenon of simplicity and patience, he prayed she would be relaxed for the time being from the usual cruel throbs and fool pulsations of what she insisted was her own harrowing stupidity, a classic example of how fond she was of honest embroidery, her sincerely greying head slightly propped up on her own two pillows in their more lighthearted pink cases, fearful for others, and as steadily forgetful of self, a figure so absolute in its assumption of silence that it shames the sea which heaves and the earth which quakes, with every bone and shadow in her so whittled down and turned by time that it had a Biblical glow and edge to it, her heart a remarkable jumper, her teeth still sound, a truly alive and living mother, facing him squarely, merely at rest.

How cruel that the smallest disasters should have such amazing sticking power, while the simplest hope gets itself torn away like a loose hair caught in the teeth of a comb. What is this terror of what is hooded? Mamma was so turned away, lying on her side as she did, that not even the tip of her head showed, so perfectly had she shrouded herself in her thin plaid blanket. They say that death gets truer the longer we live. Reality is a rat built into the floor, furry and enormous, sneaking after us everywhere, snarling and squeaking underfoot. Seeing what he saw, his became the saddest monkey's face. Picture of his Pa standing on the bureau, poorly enlarged from a blurred nickel

447

photo snapped in the street, fixing so scantily the faint brief life that once was, like himself, standing there, partially absorbed into the body of death, roughneck disarmed, smart aleck subdued, struggling to parse invisibility again, and conjugate nothing.

Heavenly father, distant cousin, shady dweller with family and companion train, compassionate enormity stretching out the earth even as a bed, should she shrivel some more as she must, spare her these bouts of meeching sickness, which she regards as such shameful idleness, for she is a lady who has never worn a gown deeply voided at the breast, or has ever mistaken dancing dolls for human beings. It was so mysterious. It could be anyone who was lying there. So bitterly withdrawn, yet somehow still so gentle. The shades were only half drawn. The world might feel insulted otherwise.

As for the former Princess Helen, that family famous living doll with her skin of royal white and her lips of royal ruby, whose fantastic bloodline, by the meekest imagination, could be traced so far back that it made old King Solomon seem like a fresh pleasure-loving pup, and the grim death-defying Sphinx the most recent dead-end kid with a broken nose, it figures she would be more than mildly disturbed, she who had been so suddenly reduced from her pristine high estate to third-rate cook and bottle washer, degraded to haunt and police the kitchen like some inferior brand of pig, feeling of her nose to ascertain if it were actually thickening into a snout, she who felt herself to be a marvelous formation, a priceless construction, an irritable rose, a blooming idiot skidding on a grain of rice, allowing her pots to boil over with her own irrepressible bitters, receiving all in all such a sour foretaste of her future as a mere woman, that it was plain she would be highly combustible by the time he rejoined her, as indeed she was.

Yet she could endure an immaculate house. She has lately been saying damn you a lot. The story is so awful because it is so ancient. These runty plagues and pint-sized inflictions, what finally happens is that it gets us all. Her daily life, of which she now had no other, was becoming a bitch. It used to be how much she could span of ease, how far she could stretch with pleasure. As it once was, let life propose to her the most exacting game or tournament it pleased, she was sure she would reach the finals. Torrid vascular bundle, with every reasonable housekeeping vein in place, never too mincy about ornamental pieces of iron or linen, or ever caring very much how her toilet waters were arranged on her old chest of drawers with its wobbly knobs and vaguely bothersome nicks and scratches, or if the muslin curtains were improperly dyed or too profusely dotted, or which way the clock or radiator leans, or how any damn silly tassel hangs, there once was in the vast intimate vault, in the far reaches of her brain and in the amplitude of her heart, a constant swelling and rising, glow and blaze, diastole and incandescence, giant's stride, great guns booming, wonderful flurries only, stately posture, the highest jumping-off-place. The tiniest shift of attention towards what is more immediately available to the eye, and other associated senses, is by the very devil himself considered to be a truly shocking fall from grace. The deeply fond and fanatical, as they fuss and fume, will often shuttle between the fag end of exultation and the grandeur of extremes.

You unspeakable rip. You prick-eared rabbit. You foppish roller of balls of dung of beetle contemplation. You dull uneatable eye of a dead boar's head. You move so ponderously in your pretended calm, you positively slay me, showing off how kind and considerate you can be, how sickly clear you can see into this cluster and mixed coherent mass of what is known as a sister, second-class citizen, eligible sob stuff, filmy incongruous creature. With her cleanest rag in hand, she was kneeling on the table now, hopelessly enlarging what was already an enormous smudge on the wall.

It is terrible to think of it, but will she always have to retch before she rallies? Will she go to smash in a flash? Will the sheeny stack of her hair slowly lose its light? Will the skin of her heels grow horny? With her terrific potential dragging, will she take to deathbed watching with a fixed grin? Will she pinprick to flay herself alive? Will she lay off the lip? Will God go soft and spare her the pain of watching his own raging and distracted thoughts invade her brain like a swarm of maggots and mice, of feeling his own green-eyed ideas crowd into her soul like a batch of bloated toads so hopping mad at the tyranny of things in general they will forever remain frozen and convulsed? Will time turn? Will men change? Will she herself bear a brilliant child who will babble at birth of more splendiferous inhumanities to come amid strange illuminations?

Many thoughts like tiddlywinks, though they may do a lot of snapping, do flip around in the air a very long time. Fully ashamed of having already committed so many raw and revolting atrocities of

449

pity and compassion, Joe reached out and tapped Helen on the shoulder as gently as he could, cautioning himself to take what was coming like a man. Almost before she felt his touch, she whipped around with her arm upraised, most sanely and splendidly ablaze, coiling herself to give this dumb cluck such a smack, but when she saw that awful understanding smile of his, it confused her so, the only thing she could think of that would be less than fratricidal was to hurl at him that soft and inoffensive rag, making sure to miss his face.

When a trillion years ago they were both as yet very fair and young and like quicksilver together, they used to suck in turn at the same skinny little striped peppermint candy cane. They never used the same hanky, if they used any at all, but they did touch noses. Blowing bubbles is also a common intramural sport. The male mind sees itself alternately as bear and bull. But when it ranges too far, it turns cow where it falters, becomes a mere tail switcher, lowers its tame head grasswards to graze. The desire to coalesce marches abreast, but we are all born to travel through life in tandem, kicking each other and pinching. Men in their cool metaphysics still dream of releasing and enlarging themselves by entering in force and cleaving to the close essential warmth of the blood stream of similar animals. The seraphim are fiery and purifying ministers who know a thousand ways of keeping a man locked for his lifetime in the cradle of his own deep. The bars are down. The tigers are trickier. These are such sad bad sea-gull days for scorpioid and simian thinkers. Midst the archaic clamor of crashing symbols and long braying horns, of clanging phobes and blundering spears, and the lovely scream of horses whose hocks are broken and whose lungs are pierced, every hero is slain in such a vain battle as faintly limned above, spouting flame and fluid rock, worm of the world, which way are you inching?

To market, to market, in the cool of the evening, almost gay for such a sarcastic creeping thing, pink involuted slug, poised up so high on his tippy toes, tiny and unseen, gummed to that inner idiom, so drifting and drawn out, of a timid stationary idiot, there with the restless cockatoos and the fetid monkeys of the human soul, a bribable underling of the flesh so smart it required a million or so years of such careful and tender cultivation to reach its present wild state, so oddly composed of hazy recognitions, smoky bafflements, queer fish problems, crumbly little specks of pimento ideas, and partially nibbled imaginings.

450

Whose fruit is that which lies rotting upon the ground? Why, mine, says time, rolling over on its side to show how spotlessly its belly has been ripped open. The measurable aspect of duration, it speaks. Through a ghastly clodhopper like Joe, everything becomes possible. Sulking filibuster, as wedge between worlds, so glory be and ghetto inclasped, he imagined he could still escape from the suffocating constriction of his own boobyhatch, and surface to a more plausible and bracing level of sense, by means of his usual nip-ups and horseplay, so to begin with, what he had received full on the chest, he very gallantly returned.

My, but she was a snippy one. She snatched the airy bit of cheesecloth from him, a thick glossy strand of her hair swinging wildly before her cold blazing eyes. Of course it then followed that she would spurn the offer of his hand as she came bouncing off the table, as nimble and graceful as a boy, to jar and elbow him aside. Recovering as quickly as he could, he elevated his fists, and adopting that square stance so beloved of bare-knuckle days, sternly informed her that, as chief pride and mainstay of his sex, though as such he was quite unknown as yet to the world at large, as he was always so fond of saying, he was ready to fight a woman any time. Her reply to that familiar bit of his windmill boxing, wild footwork, and spit spraying, and such like feeble-minded stuff, was to turn on both faucets full force. This great rush of sound meant to drown him out did just that so nicely that he decided to dispense forthwith with all intermediary steps, and to his own shame be it said, actually began to tickle her. Naturally he was quite willing to admit that he was the lowest thing on earth to resort to such dastardly tactics, but it did seem that the best way to cut her most royal highness down to size was to force her to laugh, as one might fondle a goose before passing a black shiny knife across its soft slippery neck.

Like any good book says, we all dream big, but live small. She laughed as she tickled him back, slowly relaxing her low boiling point from such constant active duty. She realized she should be more like an older cat which still slyly observes every little hop and twitter, but knows from bitter experience that it will never catch the bird. He tried to cooperate by setting the table for her, while she sluiced the lettuce and practically scraped the carrots away. Boom, did she hear that? If that sad thistledown, otherwise known as Thelma from next door, is pounding the common wall between them with that snazzy high

451

bouncer he bought her, and though mamma spank, and mamma make red the toosie, at four pretty near five still pulls out her own hair and eats it, why should it seem so wrong if this most devoted fan of his is trying so hard to break through this last flaking barrier between them and join his mark with hers?

The nerve of some people's children. The monster I killed last night, the size of it, you should have seen. If that boy friend of yours calls you tonight, please, let me talk to him. If you will copy me and put two spoons together like this back to back, we will both be able to go clickety-click and clockety-clack. Ping go the strings of my heart. Leave us now hoof a fandango, you old dance hound. She was that dream I saw in a five and ten cent store. Luck comes sometimes when you are sleeping. I learned that song at my mother's knee, and other joints. Grin, grin. But there is a reason for everything.

Oh, but indubitably, if she may be allowed to interrupt him a split-pea second to check her failing pulse which has landed in the cellar after suffering such a terrible losing streak. As Mamma's famous Reb Ben Yudel would advise in his lofty rabbinical language certain of his more semiblind and superstitious ones, when they became too far sunk in the slough of sustained hunger and hallucinations, to apply the thin bereaved essence of worried heads of fish, spoor of cat tracks, ancient chicken quills which children well within the pale once used to scratch out the mystic configurations of born to live in sorrow in imitation of their elder berries, dried-up tissues of threats, mummies of lies, vague rainbow promises, streamers of stray maidenhair chewed by goats, cold straw warmed by the cow, water lilies in season, or any old clump of dusty crab grass found growing between the cracks at a point where their lower ribs had been previously torn and punctured, without their knowing it, by their own neglected nails, and thus take a sort of holier-than-thou blood count while still in a slow-burn.

You absolute foof. Never mind asking me, how is that again? That is how again. And that is all you need to know. Looking down on me in that snippety way of yours will change nothing. This is still my promised land as much as it has ever been yours. Long may she wave in this tiny steamy kitchen to which hand over heart we must pledge our allegiance, if only because we can still live here so freely and have us such loads of fun, two can play this game as well as one. The table is on the other foot. The shoes are turned. In the United States of Joe is

452

where the rush-rush confusion trees grow. One person alone is always a dead end, but in this house it takes two, which makes it even cozier. I have a very strange feeling this present you say you brought me is a little thinking cap. A dream in hush, night is falling, in tender black velvet, if I may be so nosy as to guess, with a contrasting pompon of tight rose-red crash or swirls of blushing organza for be gay my heart, or else be damned to you. I hope it is light so I can wear it tilted.

This game is called, one fool encouraging another. What I am afraid to call my ideas always come to me like grapes in bunches. Item six million and one of my tremendous scattering, to wit, if this should be our last supper, who will turn this water into wine? Give us a loan a second of your ratty pocket comb. My hair is in Dutch. My poor head lives in that pepper mill near my rumpus still and rhubarb patch in the seaside city of drifting pity where a lot of saltless surplus thrashers like me, who can only paddle like dogs, are thrown back where they belong with their water wings on the black blurred beach, which is literally crawling with the usual soggy bawlbabies and sandy snots, by the huge breakers of their own tears and fears.

As I fink I think. Every thought I have lately is worth as much as the precious prize they bury in each and every box of crackerjacks. Every man of jelly has a clock in his belly. If my Joey is already here, can my Abie be far behind? Has my girlie act been spotted and signed? Will I get my tips when I pass the toothpicks? Should I go on the warpath, like an honest Injun should, against my own paleface lies and evasions? Should a plain everyday lady lioness like me spruce up the overly licked much too sharply tailored inunderstandable cubs of her jew imagination with tufts of the male wildebeest, the stale, tallow-tasting, spittle-wet chenille of death caught between her teeth in her own privately endowed, happy, happy Africa, with clusters of love apples of shiny artificial red, few of us know how bitterly greed contends with envy for the color green, with the palmetto leaves of fan-shaped compassion, or with the running fat of related hens who fly over fences, or the congealed memory of our yellow kissing cousins and their wiggly mascara streaks of having wept at the decline and fall of our father just to be social, or sprigs of our coming babies'-breath, or the simple daisy chain design on this sorry shred of a dishrag? Should it all or which? If we are all but mere flecks of crumbling humus, as Mamma indicates when she gently rubs between her fingers her bit of indoor cactus earth, why is it the world is so full of

453

my kind of vegetable, and very little of what seems to be yours?

Luftmensch of the week, come down to my level, and tell me if you can. Do the Laplanders leave what they love? Do lively young girls dress only to kill? Are the real men mostly under cover? What are these stories going around about a bunch of quitters, a whole gang of freshly packaged bull throwers, each of whom is made up to look exactly like that loudest ringer in yet of what is new of all the dingdang Bellinsons, namely Joe, being such terrific big shots, such extra special heroes, just because they have the gall to shove off in their leaky rafts from the shores of gripe and gitchy-gloomy for the sole purpose of shooting up and revolutionizing their own scraggy little half acres of isles, like those cuckoo bolsheviks in the old slapsticks with their great big bushy beards, unbelievable hammy acting, and their coal-black orbicular bombs that turned out to be duds, while certain other shabby and bewildered schleppers, who seem most to resemble us, are made to feel like such awful cowards and cruds, just because they have the good sense, derived from that guardian angel instinct which rarely lies sleeping in the shrewd ancestral blood, to throw their aprons over their heads while the economic thunder growls and the fiscal lightning flashes, and with their very ordinary hands clutch to them and shield in their warm and eerie insides what little of human baggage they still possess and hold most dear until this nasty storm called the depression blows itself out?

Out and over. Will the Messiah come first to niggers and jews with a chin chopper chin? Will thinning love having wept crept get a whole lot worse before it gets spread with rancid butter? Before my unmanageable speaking apparatus conks out on me completely, speak, splain it to me. Why is the sky so high? Why did you let a dizzy dame like me get started? You who are the one and only star of this show. When I take my blue skirt down to the tailor to shorten, shall I take him your shiny pants to steam, dreamy tin soldier, indrawn son of your mother, tell me before I drive you batty altogether with my gab, when can we ever hope to have some peace of mind again, when?

He does not know. He cannot tell. The time a woman has to waste on a man. A man. Which naturally means the usual bluffer and ingrate, sweetie-pie so darn conveniently deaf, though he rests now mainly on one long slim leg like a flamingo, so swank, so Florida grand as if his entire clothing were rosy-white, his shoulder blades tipped with scarlet, poised there so ipsy-pipsy by the table, as if he were indeed a question mark in the form of a bird so exquisitely joined together and turned it was impossible to see into or understand, though he poses himself there kind of precariously, as said, with the frail and false composure of the average permanent boy, and tries to show her how easily he can withstand her now constant bitter snapping at him, how impervious he can be to these trifling female tempests of criticism and attack, by folding the plain paper napkins in such fancy triangular fashion.

Think of it. How refreshing it would be if he could only come right out and say, I am wrong, what a terrible mistake I made, I see now, I thought I was a real bonebreaker, a natural born buzz saw, a boss of me every tiny mother-loving blood cell, a delightfully whacky Boston Blacky, a bravely droning bagpiper of mystic beeps, and what not, but I see now I am no different from my own darling sister, to the dot, bless us both if not. Just like me, as you can see, such an awful fool and always so afraid, just to turn around on my heel, to peel a grape, to care for some him, to cream my face, to expose my hair to air, to open or shut an eye, to look directly at blue, to whisper I love you, if I fly I die, who knows where to go and what to do, if I follow my nature so innocently it is sure to kill me, if I ruin the lives of others I will never have a life of my own, I will fall apart if I start, I will crack if I don't turn back, I will never get away with living for myself alone, never. If only he could say something like that. Her head whirled with the mere possibility. She grabbed him and made him face her. She actually begged him with her whole body to tell her he understood what she meant, to say it just once like a good boy, to change his mind about leaving his job, and stop scaring them so, with sickness already in the house, and more trouble coming, with all of its input and no output of sorrow and grief. But when she saw him go pale right before her eyes like a man and not like a boy, her heart dropped, she bit her lips, she wanted to tear out her tongue, she could have eaten herself up alive.

Which was not so brooklyn-bright of her, was it? A great mob of supperless children came screeching around the corner with huge staring eyes, as if they were chasing a cloud by night even more wild and threatening, traveling so fast that in a twinkling the whole brutal affair resolved itself into a single street cry which echoed in the most spooky way, kill you, kill you, kill you. A rish of soft violet thinking sucked in the kitchen curtains. They sure were busters all right, those kids, rudely stamping out for her two short flights down the thin

455

shrinkings and scratchings of her snarled mental play to the tinkle of a pink and penny silly merry-go-round hitched to a serious iron-grey horse with sweaty blinkers on him and a tattered straw hat. Forced to stick way out, his fearfully big stiff ears looked pathetic and ridiculous, twitching and revolving, still as anxious and alert as the day they first made contact with the air which always seemed to belong to somebody else. A delicious little miss some eleven months old, with her soiled shift showing and her sporting money already spent, was standing in the gutter, weaving like a drunk, staring at this great strange beast with a frown so pure and enchanting that time itself became terribly jealous and said, enjoy it while you can, this too will not last. In the meantime Mrs. Lourie's identical twins, who were as famous for swopping impeccable shiners as for peeing crisscross in the street, had climbed onto the front axle, and while one bold scientist held up the shamed animal's tail, the other kept peering way up underneath. The carousel man just cranked. A few paces away from his feathery profile, four flat broke members of the junior Mohawks were nursing a sickly fire in an empty milk can to melt out its valuable lead. The smoke had blackened their lids and lashes. Their eyes looked beautiful. Two were squabbling a bit. For the sake of his higher education, the chief had his pinky firmly hooked in a little brave's nostril. Any dog has this advantage, it is already down on all fours.

Children, children, as Mamma says. Conceived so blindly in such green grimy despair in their muddled rickety beds in an indescribable panic of lust by lower middle-class crabs, these bruised and doubtful offspring, they swing from miserably sustained sitstills in armless chairs in cold dark corners to explosive flurries of shocking action and shrieking delight in flight towards light and passion no matter how intense or cruel. They come in many moods and colors. A writhing and menace to the blighted peace and balance of whole nations, ardently soiling themselves as if in revenge, piercing every tottery playing-card partition erected against their democratic stares and smells, they often fret all day and wail all night. They will lie there looking plucked, their thin blotched hides stretched over brittle sparrow bones. Or gull the general public with flesh extremely flushed and glad with thyroid glandular fatness. They keep the queerest hours. They will eat dirt and get hives. They will report on their digestion from both ends. They will coo like doves for full-time love only. They will see things upside down for the first six or eight weeks, and as

456

often as not, for the rest of their lives. The sound their hearts make slowly changes, going from bloop to blip. Where they lose skin, they form scabs. For them there is no such place as that dear Longfellow forest primeval where every poor greasy redskin, dolt easily crocked on firewater, unmannerly eater of broken meats, is a fierce noble savage who is extravagantly fond of fire in all its sweet domestic and high religious uses, where the dainty squaw would never dream of crucifying and roasting entire enemy tribes, where the animal is to the insect as the snarly honey bear is to the cruel single-minded bee, where the stinker skunk, the gluttonous porker, the vicious mink, and the cowardly antelope abound in gentle cleavable masses. Whose shy blood then have these hungering riflemen of the gutter and stunted glare-eyed tigers of the sidewalk to sip? The sidekicks, they have no one to slay but themselves. They sure do know a thing or two of what to do when the time comes.

But not Helen, heaven forfend, not she. Just when she had her brother fairly hooked, it makes one wonder, she hardly seems to have the common ordinary manners of a woman, does she? Others like her, who are not meant for this world, are flung out into it nevertheless. Once long ago in class when she was reciting her loveliest composition yet, I Wish I Had A Cat, her second-grade teacher, Mrs. Merkles, slammed down her ruler and sharply informed her once and for all that it was quite impossible to love a thing, only a person. You must learn that lesson, said the fiery redheaded Amanda Merkles, flushing and flinging herself about in the most adorable and tempestuous way, and even then, she challenged, you just try it sometimes and see. Helen, the blooming little idiot, with her tender virtue still sheathed in long black stockings, and her shapely rectitude as evenly starched, and her simple local innocence as spick-and-span as her white middy blouse with the red anchors of adventure on the high seas of life hand embroidered on the peaks of the navy-blue collar, she was so thrilled and flattered by this terribly bitter challenge hurled at her that she decided right then and there to switch the whole entire, rosy, wide-eyed, tingling body of her affections permanently to people.

As if anybody gave a damn. With the way the world was even then, it would have expired at her feet with admiration if she had vowed instead to deal exclusively with hairy worms and spiders. Where love by itself goes leaping, as it must and will, what fresh shattering glimmer of illumination will it find on the other side of the worn

457

crackling blind? Nothing else but this again, that there is one lovable thing we all learn how to do quite well, and that is, to fail each other.

She snapped down the shade as far as it would go. She would not have it. She gathered herself together. Her cheeks became round again. Her ambits or orbs seemed easily as large as fluffy cupcakes, all suffused with the soft lemon glow of a porous desire to be nibbled at and eaten until she could travel again the narrow alimentary dominions of pity and shady principalities of rue and sacrifice, so that through some such stark blind kind of alchemy, this stray particle of humanity that she was might finally become a fixed star, with her own beneficent wink and blink, beaming upon all, a kindly captain of her district in charitable lifts and apron strings, beacon and guide to the eternally lost and wandering.

Such as this animal in the field who hardly cared if anyone was watching as he rested on his bony haunches smack up against the table which he himself had set, chomping down on something he had to confess was very crunchy, and in between, doing a very masterful job of licking clean the jam-sticky fingers of his left hand. She was so amused to see how, tired of waiting for her submerged outer self to break through to the surface again, he was bobbing along all by himself with annoying ease, coolly feeding his face. She had to push him more than once to make him aware of her. She knew how risky it would be to ruffle up his hair affectionately just to show him how sorry she was for having been such a pill, so she took up the package he had brought and tore it open. Two white satin nightgowns, slyly tailor-made, actually came spilling out. She caught and clasped to her whole stupefied body these shamefully expensive gifts, goggling at him, and turning her head slowly from side to side, her jaw twisted and fallen more than far enough to show him how much it pained her to be on the receiving end of such a screamy and treacherous surprise.

Steady, gal, said Abe, stumbling in, are you a frozen statue, or have you turned into milk altogether? Ba, ba, black sheep, said the exalted silk man, any hole in the wall is a port in a storm, and laughed in the loosest fashion as he fell from a fearful height into his usual seat, which was a heavy oak chair on the short end of the table. You must forgive me, he said, bowing reverently in the direction from whence he came, while his rakish hat dropped dead right at his feet, I am a little high on a few free shots of that old red-eye, bought for me in a blasted speakeasy by Boris Bolnick who buys from me the scraps, you understand,

458

may it rot my guts, as I hope it will, for I feel a chill, though these are the warm smiling faces that I love so dearly.

He grinned. He rolled his eyes like happy dice. He speared his hat with his toe and swung it high into the air, clapping his hands together at least twice before he caught it. He was the first, the only one to cheer. Though they had yet to make a sound, he shushed them violently. He had real sensational news for them. He was leaving as soon as the night became pink for the great canal in Panama on a bleary-eyed banana boat which even the flies have brushed off, to pick those treemenjous whingding locks for a particular friend of his, a wispy Hasidic, who only last week had begun to walk on water for the first time.

And once again it was lilac time. And so bock to beer. Lower the boom, comrades, on this old pro of the self-perpetuating leer and sneer. For what last in the dooryard bloomed for him was this very dark and acid unfolding, that when he died and they split his belly open, they found in it a passel of the strangest things, such as, pearly-grey eggs of petty gangsterisms which failed to hatch, stains and stoppages of hope deferred, vast cleavages of sin, the sludge of fear and the muck of helplessness, magnificent blood-streaked corkscrews of the creeping flesh of dusty promises and dirty tricks, immense hollows where the blows of fate made their lasting impressions, startling post-mortem burbles and gurgles of the soap-bubble opinions of himself held by others, hideous echoes of his dog's tongue lapping the stagnant puddles of his worst globe-encircling gaffs and howlers, crumbled mountain ranges of terrible memories, foolish moves, and heartbreaking mistakes, the sparks and tittles of a senseless terror still issuing from the tissues, areas of pale blue blots where his blubbering kept concentrating, stray globules of his animal fat, oily and obnoxious with guilt, soiled sugarplum fairies, and several stray nubbins of dried snot.

You used to love me once, but now look at you. The truly disgusting thing is to be forced to make a living when all a decent man ever wants to do is find a way of life. But who understands that? And even if he does, when has he ever learned how to help? Take this latest for instance. That old crone in her beltless black sack and rusty fanatical wig and seamed tree-trunk face, shambling back no doubt from her part-time job of locking up the Garden of Eden each night, as soon as he saw this wandering rock blocking the best part of the street, he saw

459

red, it is hard to tell why, and he made up his mind to walk right at her to test her guts to see who would give way first, right on Rutland Street where the squashed cat once lay for three days, when all of a sudden she loses her grip on the string bag she is lugging, and watch it, out come bouncing and rolling everywhere a whole flock of eating apples, big navel oranges, rosy apricots and a honeydew melon, elegant pears, a coconut in its native dress, two knobby sticks of horseradish and a single beet. Ah, she wails viewing the wreckage, how long and bitter is my life. Now, now, little mother, he says, you must not weep and talk that way, or bend and break your poor old back, I am really a great prince in disguise, and before you know it, I will have all that lovely loot of yours back in your old bag. Allez oop. And it turns out precisely as he had promised. And she scrapes and bows a thousand times and kisses his hand before he can stop her, and hauls off and gives him such a punch in the side that it still hurts.

You never know what will hit you next, do you? Of course I had to kill her. I tell you, I laughed myself to 'sleep last night. Or was it slept myself to laugh? As any snickering idealist of a kid brother or sister can easily see, his loosenings are only partial as yet, but his cracks are seriously widening. Children, as Mamma would never dream of saying, whoever tries to uplift another, soon discovers he is merely degrading himself. The greatest pleasure in this world is to take a neck and twist it. By the same token, if you happen to have one, the most eminently successful man is he who robs Peter, and then proceeds to rob Paul. The way the cards fall, they simply fall. So tired of living on radical street in all that thick smoke talk, and sick of his own blue stubble and hacking cough, Papa once said, bad times mutilate the body, good times soften the soul.

Pass the animal crackers. Hold up on what looks like soup. You may, if you like, place a bit of candied sweet potato on my tongue, and I will still say to you, who is so clever as to catch his own eyes in the act of moving when he examines the puzzled loathsome endlessly charming totally unacceptable image of himself in any spotted mirror? Proud and shifty as we are, life is terribly like that, much too cute and quick for any of us. While death. But where are you going? Where are you all rushing off to? While death, my dears, death is like that dingy dismal suffocating dumbwaiter, scented with the sour slop of cats, into which screechy enclosure each of us must at last be stuffed, for

460

death has supremely that squeegee underground mentality which insists that there is always room for one more, bundled up to be drawn down and down into that shivery luscious darkness which the soft-bodied naked limbless worm loves.

Do I freeze your blood? I see people in their rumpled beds puking to the right and left of me. And to my countless friends across the sea, joyous plucking and pleasant dreams. Saying which, he smiled as his eyelids drooped. He sagged alarmingly. He hauled himself up long enough to scatter the boundless seeds of his weariness and despair with a hand so pure it had never felt the weight or clasp of a ring. It began to infuriate him that he should fail to anchor his elbow on a table he thought he knew so well. Woozily disturbed and riled up as he was, he managed to flip out his hanky and fumble at his nose. Where the lint was invisible, there he picked it. Scornful of logical transition, he stretched out a commanding hand with a great orator's cunning.

You desperate cracker-crunchers and bitching mental cripples, with the way the world is wobbling on what always looks like its last legs, with so many mean and unchosen ways of being done in lurking in the murky shrinking air around us, what utter fools we would be if we failed to snatch with alacrity, as they say, at this last solid fact and sensible solution life has left us, which would be such a proud act, which would be such a tremendous slap in the face to all the lip-worn sanctimonious yea sayers, which would be such a fierce bursting asunder of the rusty outrageous chains which bind us to this dreary irredeemable underdog's life, which would be nothing less than the whole family signing this simple and subtle thing known in these fancy-delancy, dismally enlightened, pen and paper days as a suicide pact.

He grabbed his sister's arm and squeezed it. He winked elaborately with the entire side of his face. He sat up straight with the remarkable dignity of his mother. He beamed all over his brother. He hugged himself with his own full consent, quite content to be threatened with the very theatrical mishap of loving himself to death. It was at this very gaudy moment that Helen and Joe, without having to exchange a single glance, agreed that the time had come for them to show that they were intensely delighted at last with something which was beyond criticism or envy. A grand idea, said Joe. Helen said it was immense. Inspired common sense is what she called it, as ready as any

461

to seal the deal as she joined in a round of jolly handshaking which at Abe's insistence had to be repeated twenty-eleven times.

Malatesta. With his remaining wits set on fire by his intolerably delayed and perfectly selfish hunger, Joe seized a knife and fork in either hand and proposed they begin at once by eating each other. When Helen declared that such a thing would hardly be kosher, and that they would be much better off if they decided to gorge themselves first on this spectacular last supper of hers which she had prepared for them with such loving care and thought that it ought to do the trick entirely by itself, Joe was quick to reply that he was inexpressibly willing to risk even that, for as even the most inspired poisoner in the world could see, his condition was such, and here he chose to dramatize the situation by spearing unto himself the thickest slice of tomato and the crispiest seed roll, it positively screamed for the most prompt and immediate action. Gay and greedy as it may seem, whatever there was to eat, he ate.

"Gosh," he said. "What hit me here? Was I hungry or wasn't I?"

"Ah, me," said Helen. "His mouth is free again. I don't like that."

"Once again, dear heart. I ate too fast. I ate too much."

"Quitter," said Helen. "Not before you finish this, I hope."

"Oh, no," said Joe. "I couldn't. No more of that rabbit food. Please."

"I do so love the way you throw your crumpled napkin in my cup. You simply must show me how you do it some day."

"Sorry, sister. This is strictly man stuff. I don't know why you women are always mixing in."

"You must be very sure of what you're doing."

"I hear you and I will speak."

"I suppose you know. Papa was such a great smoker too."

"It's the way you wax floors," said Joe. "That's what's going to do it."

"A real desperate character, aren't you?"

"God, yes. I'm so afraid of everything, I have to be."

"Too bad," said Helen. "Of course. I'm really very sorry for you. But this time there's no getting away with it. You'll just have to help me with the dishes."

"It's funny," said Joe. "Are you sure the window is open? I'm absolutely dying from the heat. Hey, boss, wake up there. Abie boy. Can you hear me? Am I coming in clear? I need help fast. I have a big fight on my hands. It looks like there's another mountain to climb. And one more river to cross."

"Shh," said Helen. "Leave him alone."

"He sure does eat fine with his hat and coat on, doesn't he?"

"Oh," said Helen. "He's very religious. We must honor him for that."

"And so we do," said Joe. "Another cup of tea, my good man? He's sucking lump sugar, I think. How's about this last bagel like a rock? Believe me, it would give me the greatest pleasure to be able to serve you."

"Foo," said Abe.

"By golly," said Joe. "That's exactly what I've been saying."

"Lousy little show-off."

"Dear old Abe," said Helen. "Now there's a man for you. How are you anyway? Are you comfy where you are? Would you like to stop dunking your sleeve? May I take your hat and coat? What can I do for you?"

"Crazy little bastard," said Abe.

"Uh-uh," said Joe. "Something tells me I'm in for it."

"What?" said Abe. "Who's pulling me here?"

"That's right," said Helen. "Stand up a little. Now you're doing it. I'll have you stripped in a second."

"Goddamn it," said Abe. "Can you imagine such a thing? Night and day. Day and night. Setting there and squawking. Without a rest. Ploop. It raises the hackles on me head. It's the living limit. That's what it is."

"Yes," said Helen. "You are so right. That's the way it usually goes in this family. As soon as one bozo stops, the other one begins."

"Disgusting animal," said Abe. "How long can it go on this way?"

"Excuse me," said Helen. "Do you mind if I just lay your stuff right down here? Things are going so good, I just hate to be absent even for a second."

"Hey?" said Abe. "What do you think it means?"

"It means," said Joe. "It means I'm sunk. That's what it means."

"I tell you, kid. This tops them all. Absolutely."

"You know," said Joe. "I wonder about this. I do get a little pale around the gills. But I never throw up. It must be my nature, I guess."

"Honest to god," said Abe. "It's enough to scare you spitless. There's a hen out in Jersey that's laid nineteen eggs in six days."

"Woof," said Joe. "And I thought he was talking about me."

"Look at him," said Helen. "He's breathing again."

"Stupid bird," said Abe. "What in the hell is it so excited about? What's it trying to say? Can anyone tell me? What's got into it anyway?"

"It's heard," said Helen.

"Why, hello, there," said Abe.

"I tell you," said Helen. "That poor old chicken knows. Somebody must've told it about your brilliant highflying brother there. Some damn rooster, I suppose. All fat and fluffed up with the news from the local market. It gathers. It rolls."

"I'll be damned," said Abe. "So there you are. I've been looking all over for you."

"The question is," said Helen. "How are we ever going to bear it when the whole world gets wind of it?"

"Pity you don't smoke."

"A girl hasn't got much of a chance here, has she?"

"Girl?" said Abe. "What girl? You're no girl. You're Helen. You're my sister."

"Why, that's wonderful," said Helen. "How did you ever guess?"

"Easy," said Abe. "I just closed my eyes and listened."

"Ah," said Helen. "So you're really not as far-gone as you look, are you? Of course not. That's never happened before, has it? Look at me now. Can you see what I'm doing? How many fingers am I holding up?"

"Three."

"No, dear. Try again."

"Two?"

"Right," said Helen. "That's the way. Don't be afraid. Speak right up. Only don't lean your hot little head on me. Otherwise I'll never be able to help you."

"Help me," said Abe. "That's a pretty melody. A tune that really haunts me. How does the rest of it go? Help me. In a pig's ear, says the world."

"Your eyes are red like poppies. Flecked with foam are your lips."

"Sorry," said Abe. "You ought to know me by this time. When I mean what I say, I always speak floodingly."

"Yes," said Helen. "And when you weep, you weep alone. I know."

"Off my back, kiddo. I'm warning you very quietly."

"But I'm appealing to you," said Helen. "Don't you understand? We have a real problem here."

"Bring out the bit, boys. She's a nag again."

"Now don't make believe," said Helen. "You know what I mean. If you're the oldest here, you should take charge. Really. It's up to you, son."

"Shame on you," said Abe. "Trying to sell me such a cracked record."

"You dog. It's getting to be impossible trying to talk to you."

"Huh," said Abe. "If you think that's bad, try this on your old stapling machine. Right down here in the sewer, right underneath your feet, there are real live alligators splashing around. Brr. And big black snakes."

"Rats," said Helen. "I should climb right back on my pedestal. Where I understand I belong. Instead of fooling around with a peasant like you."

"Yes," said Abe. "And rats big as cats."

"And in this clean little stable of a house, as anybody can see, there is just a plain old horse. I don't mean to be a killjoy, mister. But what's this craze for sugar all of a sudden?"

"Well," said Abe. "Scratching myself in public this way is surely a disgusting spectacle for such a pure character like you. But like Caesar said. My sister is whole. But my gall is divided into three parts. Pending a more serious disturbance in my lower gut and upper respiratory tract. And for why, my wiseguy? Because while you are chewing your nails and gazing with delight at my gleaming front teeth which slightly overlap, I will tell you why. Because there are people, people everywhere, but not a single person who thinks. But here in this tender family, how are you ever going to stop the gush? As for example. Me now. The bastards. They went and shifted the stars on me just when I was sewing my left eyelid to my upper lip. Stop me if you've heard this one. And I gave such a yelp my heart stretched itself out straight. And I hit the ceiling, supporting myself on the tip of the flame of the candle some joker was holding with perfect aim of hate to the rear end of my nightshirt. But you know me. I kept my head and hung out the moon to dry in the daytime. And quick as a flash, I found my mask again where Mamma keeps her odd ribbons. And I felt like a sack of nuts and bolts. And I rubbed the tips of my shaky, safecracking fingers of my right hand in the palm of my left.

465

And I began to scale and hop the fences. And I prowled around in the dark and damp of other people's minds, stealing every stupid idea the dummies forgot to nail down. And when I climbed up the steps tonight, I felt I was creeping down. I was in a real fine fix. Now I remember. Sourballs are those hard candies we used to suck. I said to myself, no matter how bitter your luck has been lately, you must spank your Yiddish mandolin, and stay as sweet as you are. I am afraid I will have to talk to my lawyer first before I can tell you any more. But I do hope and pray you will have the grace to say that this brief little speech of mine does answer your question."

"Oh, but it does," said Helen. "Like nothing has ever before."

"That's what I love. To have such a pair of eyes boring right into me."

"I do my best," said Helen. "And I swear to you right now. I'll continue to do so."

"Nuts," said Abe. "What's this developing here? It looks like I'm getting a boil on the back of my neck again."

"Believe me," said Helen.

"It must be something bad simmering in my blood."

"I'll always remember this as the night I got to know the first thing about you."

"What?" said Abe. "I can't hear you. Who the hell's that banging on the wall?"

"Oh," said Helen. "That. The little dear. She's human, I think. Your brother here. He had to go and buy her a ball."

"Sonofagun," said Abe. "It can't be. What's this bump behind my ear? Have you got one too? Let me see."

"Stupid," said Helen. "That's only your bone."

"Hands, you bums, get away from me."

"Slap," said Helen. "There. Maybe that'll fix them."

"Thanks," said Abe. "Doggone it, man, what's got into you? You can stop a hot grounder with your chest. Or walk across the third rail. Or let a woman get under your skin. But there's one thing you should never do. And that is, begin to feel yourself. You never know what you'll find. Ow. Now what in the hell is this? I must've sprained my thumb when I socked that big fat schlub for throwing that loaded pair. And me trying to play it cool, betting against the dice. Four whole bucks ahead. But where my winnings went, I'll never know. If you look in my hat you will find a note which says, if I don't take a bath tonight, I'll rot away. Listen. Can you hear it? Ever since I had the pink eye, when I rub my eye, it squeaks. My ditty about the great big city. I once said to Mom, gosh, how many crazy people do we need? And she said, one is enough. Would you like to bet? I bet you if I go to Pocatello by foot, I will immediately stop picking my nose. Not to speak of never sneezing in Stillwater. Or stubbing my toe in Tuckahoe. Would you believe it? The only time I ever crossed the border was when I went to Atlantic City once? I guess. I suppose I never travel because I am still too stupid and proud to stick out my particular kind of neck. But who knows? I may change for the worse. Somebody may light a fire under me. I too may try to see if I really belong somewhere. If not in Daytona Beach, then in Elkhart or Steubenville. Some day I may stop making these safe little circles around the nearest fire hydrant and break out to Tupper Lake. Or hie me down to Haverstraw. Are you high on Helena? Have you had many Little Falls? Where else in this Lake Superior land of ours do the mighty gentiles laugh themselves sick when they contemplate us? O Pawtucket, you pup. O Pasadena, you flaming rose. Why am I making sounds like I am beating my breast? Where is the helping hand I expect from a brother? Who will hand me my trusty stick? I must run down to Jerusalem within the next few thousand years. Or I fear me I know who is going to get himself nailed up next."

"There you are," said Helen. "You see? What can I do for you if you won't take aspirin? I keep begging and begging you."

"You look like a decent sort of person. I wonder if you could do me a favor."

"You poor little Jewish fella."

"Next time when you're at it throw me out with the rest of the garbage."

"It's hard to believe. But you still don't know whether you're coming or going, do you?"

"Well," said Abe. "It's like I said. I have a pretty good idea where I am. And I do seem to remember the faces."

"Splendid," said Helen. "I knew you'd snap out of it eventually. We sure can use some real lively looking people around here. Though there's nothing new at the poolroom, I do know who's on second. Before I kind of slide back to my own troubles, which would only be natural, is there anything else you would like to know?"

"Everything," said Abe. "Tell me everything."

"All right, then," said Helen. "I will. If you're dying to know where Mamma's been keeping herself, which I see you're not, she's in bed resting. If you really want to know what's cooking, then I'm very happy to inform you, you've already had it."

"You said it, kid. In more ways than one."

"Oh, please," said Helen. "Go away. Don't talk to me."

"My dear Miss," said Abe. "We love you dearly. And we value your opinion very much. But."

"Oh, sure," said Helen. "You don't have to drag me around by the hair. I understand. Tip your hat. Bow down to her in the street. But once you get her alone in the house, bop her on the beezer, beat the lovely bitch black and blue. Blow the woman down, bullies, blow the woman down. Only men can be rabbis. And great speakers. It's wonderful how it came about. And noisy ringmasters. And smiling philosophers. And wise old creeps. Who was it always had to run down to the store for Mamma? I did. In the Bible it's only the men who go down to the sea in ships. Who heal the sick. Who shear the sheep. Who tumble down walls. Who unroll the scrolls. And dig the graves. My stars. What is this wonder that I behold? What is this thing called man that he should be so marvelous in all his parts? I get dizzy. I faint every time I think of it."

"Run down to the store for what?"

"Don't be such a wiseguy."

"I see you've been reading a good book lately."

"Yes," said Helen. "I admit. I do peek sometimes."

"Well," said Abe. "No sense crabbing about it."

"What will the men folks do when they hear about this? Will they send me to Siberia? What will happen to me?"

"What happened to you when you washed my shirt with my fountain pen in it?"

"Nothing," said Helen. "You just turned a little blue, that's all."

"Or when you branded me with that flatiron?"

"You nut. You kept trying to spit on it to make it sizzle."

"Or the time when I came home from school that day and my eyes were crossed?"

"They were?" said Helen. "When was that?"

"I never told you why, did I?"

"You must be very rich, destroying bread like that."

"It was," said Abe. "Let me see. It was the year I parted my hair in the middle. So all right. So I knew I was on the spot. So I had this crazy urge all of a sudden to look like I really had a brain. How many bags of water did I throw out of the window? Old Flanagan the cop came to see Mamma because I chucked horse manure into Goldfarb's hardware store and hit his Heckie over the eye with a piece of ice and knocked him cold. You said to me, run, go hide under the bed. I was such a dumb nasty little animal. Oh, sure, I had real fine parents same as you, but I suppose I was always a little bit too hungry and cold to appreciate it. You know why I hated you so much? You used to hum when you did your homework. A simple thing like that. I guess sitting in the last seat in the last row for two terms does something to a guy. Clumsy ass Miss Pratt, she had to go and break her knee when I tripped her up to remind her I was still alive. I said I was sorry. What more did they want? But they just wouldn't listen. They went and shipped me off to that ratty school for the worst kids with only men teachers in it. And that, my children, was how they saved America."

"Columbia, the germ of the ocean. I'm hearing things for the first time."

"You sonofagun. You were always on my side."

"So?" said Helen. "So every chance you got, you slapped me around. You idiot. What was the sense of that? What were you trying to accomplish?"

"Look," said Abe. "I'm talking. Don't rile me up. Don't jump me with such damn questions when you know the answers as well as I do. Even now. Look at that expression. You goddamn freak. You not only loved your father. You had to go and love your mother too. Angel on your dimpled knees, always scrubbing them red painted floors. You charming child. You fought back plenty. You were born to make me look lousy."

"I must say," said Helen. "It's getting easier and easier."

"Look," said Abe. "Let me put it this way. If you grabbed hold of me now and said to me, Abe, my dear fellow, what is the price of potatoes by the peck in Peru, I would have to say, I am very sorry, my pet, but I do not know. I bet things are so rough in India somewhere that if I sent them my ashes mixed with these olive pits and fish bones, they would kiss my feet. By return mail, of course. Go ahead. Just for the fun of it. Ask me now who buried George Washington's horse, and watch me sweat. I guess the best brain is like a piece of blotting paper. All they had to do was shift the decimal point on me, and my mind, it went

469

ploop. But trouble. That I could spell out every time. So I brushed my shoes and fiddled with my hair, trying to get over the disgrace. So what happened? I kept waving my hand like a maniac, begging them teachers to let me take a crack at every question. I said France was colored pink. I said Greece imported pencils. I said if you want six to go into nine like a knife goes into butter, and still carry one, then surely you must take into account the human element. Surely, I say. The stupid idiots. So what if I answered wrong? I was in there trying, wasn't I? They sure did make a sucker out of me, making me break my neck for nothing. I was transferred forever and I didn't know it. I hardly knew how to wipe my nose yet, and I was already out of this world."

"Damn you," said Helen. "You never said a word. You never told us anything. How could we know how you felt?"

"I said to that gym teacher, shut up whose mouth, I said. I was fed up with that muscle-bound bastard way up to here. He said to me, quiet, or I'll send you up that rope to stay. I said to him, do me a favor and take a jolly trip for yourself on those flying rings, it just so happens you are interrupting a very serious conversation with my gimpy pal here on the happy and prosperous state of the nation. Is that so? he said to me. I said to him, you know, I said, you have a grand way of speaking, let me congratulate you. He said to me, I'll give you a shot in the head right away. As you can see. He was a real scholar and a gentleman. A tremendous bull with cold grey marbles in his head instead of eyes. Hated the way I parted and plastered down my hair. Began to sneer and flick at my ear. I backed away from him and said, you're too dumb to know it, but you're a rat in a trap yourself. I said to him, I'll give you a real good tip, I said, if you ever get lost in the belly of this whale of a world like me, you'll find the best way to get out is to build a fire. Hey, Mr. Meyer? How do you treat your own kids? Biff, boom. I sure reached him that time. He whipped the medicine ball into my middle and knocked me right off my pins. I jumped up and charged. Lousy bastard. He caught me full in the face with that great big paw of his and held me off. He was a very witty guy. I struggled like crazy. I kept swinging and kicking, but he just crossed his legs and yawned. I didn't know how I got home that day. I was so mad, I couldn't see straight. No one else was home yet, so Mamma said to me, please, you must go, this is our last five dollars, who else can I trust? If that's boiling water on the fire, I sure would appreciate a nice hot cup of tea."

"I don't understand it," said Helen. "Where was I when all this happened? Was I alive too?"

"Pour," said Abe. "But don't slop."

"I don't suppose you would want lemon."

"Boy," said Abe. "Were those the good old days. Look at me rubbing my hands like just before the feast, mother. Did you put the butter away? Where's the black bread? Woo. The wicked wind howled. And the slashing snow flew upward. Whirl, whirl, little girl. Funny how things pop into your head. What great leader was it I followed then when I scrambled over the chicken-wire fence and tore my hand open on the rusty barbed wire, leaving a rich trail of blood on the pure white drifts of my brief but exciting childhood? I'm a top A-1 nobody. And in spite of the odds, I intend to maintain that position. Silly of me to become so conspicuous. Oops. Sprayed you a little then, didn't I? If I'm in such a hurry to spill it, I shouldn't be stuffing my mouth so much. As for you, you aggravating mystery, it hardly mattered what you ate when you had it. You were always the plump and rosy one. You played like a queen. You had your own rabbitskin muff. You toppled off that tower of egg crates I built and split your tongue right down the middle. You were the happiest little tike when the windows frosted over. Where I saw daggers and silver dollars, you saw volcanoes and stars. You never tried to scratch my eyes out. And so we lived and loved. Hey, old gal? If we really had dough, would we ever know winter? Your bed was behind the door, so maybe you heard, but you never saw. But there was Pop every dawn, a cuckoo socialist, a real fine millinery man, all tricked out in his religious getup, rocking and shaking, his sharp face pushed in the corner, trying to get through to God, the bitter cold creeping into his clothes. Say, remember old Fanny Baum, our first boarder? She bawled me out because she sat down in the dark on the toilet seat I splashed when I aimed bad. A skylight in the toilet yet, what riches we had. God, how dumb we were. How we moaned and groaned because all we had for supper that night was some hard stale bread and water laced with something colored like coffee. Pop was singing and making weird faces. But nobody laughed. I said to him, hit me, hit me, do something I can understand."

471

"Hit you?" said Helen. "You're crazy. Why should Papa hit you?"

"Because," said Abe. "As it happened. I had just robbed the First National and was laying the loot right down at his feet."

"Moan and groan," said Helen. "Go on. When did I ever do that? When did I ever complain?"

"Look," said Abe. "I'm making a fist. What do you think I've got in it now? Guess."

"My whole insides," said Helen. "And I don't have to guess either."

"Why, it's Mister God himself, of course. Don't look so surprised. If I say I have him, I have him. All of him, right here. Except for failing to make sense, easiest trick known to man or beast. Splendid personality. Very active bugger. Sure does the cockles of me heart good to have him so near and yet so far. If I could only hold him to me like this for the rest of my life. But who can be that strong? Who can keep his hand closed forever?"

"I can't," said Helen. "I'm not listening any more."

"Right," said Abe. "Don't blame you. As a family, we do manage to meet once a spring at least, don't we? Is this what they call food today? Remember when I used to be the garbage pail of the family? That's the way. Wipe up the crumbs. Clear away the mess I made. But stay out of my reach, I warn you. Because sometimes, believe me, I just don't give a damn for anybody. But anybody, you understand? Imagine Mamma bothering me with such a silly little thing. I kept saying to myself over and over again so I wouldn't forget what I had to buy, I want a bottle of milk a loaf of rye a large can of salmon a quarter of a pound of butter and a pound of onions and a small bottle of white vinegar and a box of fig newtons, please. Man, how I used to love that cheap sweet stuff. Me, Nick Carter, the great detective, me, one of the Liberty Boys of '76, gripping that lousy piece of green paper in my homemade mitten, battling the nasty wind and snow, looking like over the hill to the poorhouse in my groggy shoes and crappy Mackinaw. Am I tearing you all to pieces? I hope your eyes are filling up properly. At least you're sticking with me. And for that I do thank you. Boy, I was so het up inside, I actually crashed into a parked horse. The animal was steaming. Fancy meeting you here. It sure was a white and whirling world. I checked to see if I still had all my marbles, and on I went, gaily on my way. Damn fool. What could I feel through my mitten? By the time I got to the grocery, that five dollar bill was gone.

472

I looked and looked. But I never found it. The wind had ripped it right out of my hand."

"Oh, no," said Helen.

"Oh, but yes," said Abe. "It sure was a perfect day for my boyish heart to be out a flitting and a flying, wasn't it?"

"Oh, you poor thing."

"Well," said Abe. "At least."

"God," said Helen. "What did Mamma say when you got back? Was Papa there? Did he say anything?"

"Say," said Abe. "What say? Are you kidding or something? Don't talk to me about them, please. What characters. Really. One was too good to live. The other now, she's just too damn good to die. Did you ever see anything like it? It had to be my luck to get myself mixed up with such people. I ask you. Who wanted it? Did I ever ask for it? Why did it have to happen to me?"

"You're forgetting," said Helen. "It happened to us too."

"Sure it did," said Abe. "But I was the first."

"The first," said Helen. "What does that mean?"

"It means," said Abe. "I wish you would scratch my head too while you're at it. I'm desperately dirty. I must make an appointment with you for a shampoo."

"Boy," said Helen. "Maybe we don't live in Brazil, but we sure have a lot of nuts in this family."

"Why am I a nut? Because I'm trying to tell you the truth?"

"No mail today," said Helen. "Not even a bill."

"Oh, sure," said Abe. "I understand. You don't have to answer. You're lucky. You're different. You're still a woman, aren't you?"

"I am?" said Helen. "I'm not so sure any more. I'll have to check first and let you know later."

"But you are," said Abe. "You lucky stiff. You're excused. You have your own private little business. You don't have to go out and make your way in the world. Who expects anything of you?"

"Bang," said Helen. "Here we go again. I'm a rag. And he's wiping up the floor with me."

"I'm not saying we're better, you understand. I'm just saying we're different, that's all."

"Keep it up. See where it'll get you."

"And a hell of a lot better. In many ways."

473

"My," said Helen. "We sure love ourselves a little bit today, don't we?"

"One good push," said Abe. "Like this. And what are you going to do about it?"

"That does it," said Helen. "I knew I'd have to slap someone today."

"Watch it," said Abe. "You keep swinging away in that silly way and you'll knock yourself out. Hooray. Today a terrible roaring tiger. And tomorrow just a tame little cat. You'll change all right, you shining light of the world. Boy, how you'll change. You'll skid. You'll grow every which way. You'll soak your dirty wash daily. You'll cook your delicious little casseroles of leftovers. You'll have your darling little brats. You'll spank. You'll dust and dampen. You'll dry your old mop. You'll pinch pennies and squash bugs. You'll spray your closets and light the Sabbath candles. You'll always be trying to slap some sense into your husband like you're trying to do with me now. I tell you, woman, you got it made. You have a terrific career ahead of you."

"Damn you," said Helen. "All you're good for is to give me cramps."

"At least that's something real. What more do you want?"

"Ah," said Helen. "What the hell. Dear old Abe."

"Who?" said Abe. "Does she mean me?"

"I'm sorry," said Helen. "I didn't mean all that. Why should I ever jump on you? You've always been so good to me."

"Ho, now," said Abe. "Let's not get too hysterical about this, please."

"But you have," said Helen. "Who else is there? You've always been the one I could depend on. You know that. But sometimes. I don't know what's the matter with you. Don't you realize yet what's happening here? Why do you think I'm carrying on like a maniac? Why do you think Mamma's so sick?"

"Sick?" said Abe. "I thought you said she was resting."

"Sick," said Helen. "And she won't lift a finger. She won't say a word."

"Aw, now," said Abe. "What are you trying to hand me here? You mean to say it's all because of our friend here?"

"Of course," said Helen. "Who else?"

"Go on," said Abe. "I don't believe it."

"But it's true," said Helen. "Think what it means if he quits his job. Did you ever stop to think of it? It's enough to make anybody sick."

"Ridiculous."

"Ridiculous, nothing. It's the beginning of the end, that's what it is."

"Relax," said Abe. "What has to come has to come. How can you stop it?"

"Beautiful," said Helen. "I love the way you said that. Incidentally. My boss is talking about a cut again. How's yours behaving lately?"

"Oh," said Abe. "He's sniffing around. He's getting ready to clip us again."

"Job, job, job. You're so right. The lousy thing. I'm beginning to hate it."

"Then hate your share," said Abe. "Be a man. Go on to something else. Stop shaking so much. The bastards. Let them do what they want. They're not going to have me sucking and crawling around them."

"What a family," said Helen. "Everybody such a big shot but me."

"Stick with me, kid. I'll show you how to go under."

"Think," said Helen. "Think what it means. We're all working yet. We're still so lucky here. Why should we go out looking for trouble?"

"Because," said Abe. "Because we all need the exercise. And I'm sick of sitting here and saying because."

"Who knows?" said Helen. "Maybe if we just sit tight and hold our hands over our eyes, maybe it'll pass us by. Maybe it'll just fly over us this time."

"Dream on, baby. Dream on while you can."

"Is that our phone ringing?" said Helen. "No. I guess not. The other day I was trying to remember. What are some of the early spring flowers? I'm sure our little green shoot here could tell us. Am I crazy here or is it really getting cooler? I could scream my head is splitting so. If we had a shady tree, I'd sleep out under it tonight. Who was that uncle we had who once slapped Papa? Remember? They were arguing about why in America people have to live so up and down when it seems so much more natural to live sideways. Broken Nails, Idaho, that's me. Is there an emery board there on the closet? I'm mad as a wet hen, but I'm too tired to reach out. Well, thank you, dear Joey. There's a brother for you. After all I've done to him, he can still be nice to me."

"Ah," said Joe. "If I only had your guts."

"Please," said Helen. "Go away. I can't look at you lately."

"I don't care what you say. I'll always love you just the same."

475

"Well, well," said Helen. "Will you listen to that? What brought all that on?"

"Patience," said Joe. "Since you're dying to know what's what with me. Keep in touch. Maybe I'll be able to tell you some day."

"What some day? Now. Tell me now."

"Sorry," said Joe. "It's no use. I can't. Hey, hey. How about that? We sure had us a wonderful talk tonight, didn't we?"

"We did?" said Helen. "When?"

"Gosh," said Joe. "It's just like war, isn't it? I mean, all of a sudden, there you are. I mean, you're kind of relaxed and just bumbling along, when boom, they've got you up against the wall, and they're taking pot shots at you. And you begin to duck. And you scream bloody murder. And you try to escape. You're pretty damn clear in the head what you're trying to save. You have to do something quick or else. You sure do know what you're fighting for. You know what I mean? Somehow it peps you up. It really gets you up on your toes, doesn't it?"

"Should I pinch him where he sits?" said Helen. "Or should I just throw water on him?"

"Hard times, hard times. What a precious lesson you are teaching me."

"Water will do. There."

"Good," said Joe. "Thanks a lot. I'm glad to be baptized. That sure does put the finishing touch on me. Say. I just had a wonderful idea. If Mamma's feeling better, let's celebrate. Let's all go to the movies tonight."

"Movies?" said Helen.

"Sure," said Joe. "Why not? It's not the end of the world yet, is it?"

"Shh," said Helen. "I think I hear something."

"Excuse me," said Abe. "How's the hot water situation? I'm so stinky, if I don't take a bath tonight, I never will."

"I knew I heard something. It's Mamma. She's calling me."

"Good," said Joe. "There's a person I can talk to. You watch."

"Be quiet a second, will you? Let me think. What can I give her to eat? I must get her to eat something."

"Stop worrying," said Joe. "She'll eat. You just leave her to me. I'll take care of her."

"Oh, sure," said Helen. "Of course. We know now we can trust you. You're just the one for it, aren't you? Another week or so and you'll be in a real swell position to take care of just about everybody, won't you? It's such a wonderful feeling to know we can really depend on you. Can you imagine? Everything has to fall on my head. What's so wrong with warm milk? Would it kill her to have a boiled egg? Or some cream of wheat maybe? If I say tea and toast, you back me up, hear me? Gosh. Who knows? Maybe we can still swing it. Maybe we can still ship her off to Lakewood for a week or so before it's too late. I hate to sound selfish, but I had such lovely plans to run off to the Cape by myself this summer. I'm coming, I'm coming. Don't you dare go before me. I'm not through fighting you yet. You're not going to get ahead of me. You're not going to win over me every time. No, sir."

Lunging into action like the mean and bristling wildcat she felt she had to be, groping and clawing at him as if he were the galling and pigheaded image of fate itself, she clutched at his suspenders, and when he twisted free, grabbed him by the seat of his pants. It was such a novel sensation, his voice instantly became that of the other sex. Much too plainly fearful of sounds of tearing and being torn, he dragged her through the foyer, shrieking and slapping her hand. She quickly changed her grip to a handful of cloth and flesh at the ribs and whirled him around. They began to giggle as they grappled. They pushed and pulled each other the length of the living room, now nip having the edge, and now tuck. She was certainly a shade ahead of that timeless flying shirttail of his when he tripped and caught her just as she plunged into the bedroom. Helplessly meshed together now, they stumbled and swayed, and fell right across the foot of the bed.

Poor Mamma, she had to be quicker than she thought she could ever be, or they would have broken her legs. They bounced her so high, she felt they had launched her to drag the stars from the sky. Her wise eyes became as wide-open and childlike as April. It seemed such a pity that the long endlessly twisting line of her life which she had been so patiently unraveling had become brutally snarled again in a fresh and impossible way. What space could still be called hers squealed on its casters, grinding itself into splinters. Whatever time she had left creaked and cracked. The faintly green walls seemed amazed that the cow in the landscape should keel over. The window shade sprang up all by itself with a terrifying rattle. A looming presence, very much like Abe, took shape in the doorway, dangling a woman's slipper by the heel. Joe raised himself up on his elbow from where he was sprawled across the foot of the bed to see what heights of delight and

477

rapture he had managed to rouse up in his one and only mother. She was pressed so far back, his heart sank.

What a terrible way to be looking at him. He had lived with her all his life. He had never seen her this way before. Queerly hunched against the headboard, she met his gaze as if she were staring fearfully at him through a thin network of leaves and branches. Fear and coldness together, an absolutely new animal thing. Without being able to put it into words, he decided this had happened, while they had been lolling around here, trifling with the minor emotions with their soft tropic-loving bodies, she has been ranging far and wide into the tundra of the mind, its furthest north, where love and pity, like the earth, are everlastingly in the grip of permafrost.

Every human head in its most solemn and pitiful ignorance bears its own cap and fine cover of ashes. As of now Mamma's chances are very excellent that her children will be able to afford to bury her with her shoes on. Those gadgets shaped like the heart, such as her golden locket, they might have to sell to cover the cost. The white worm of belated sympathy wriggles with insufferable glibness through the black empty sockets of her nameless skull. Once again that old blowhard of extremes sends us these huge dry-eyed winds of bleak inner confabulation to swirl round about and chill us. And yet facts are facts. Even that which is said to be larger than life is hardly as large. Her mouth twitched to show him how far he had driven her. As if he were the devil himself, he marked the change. Her strange woman hands fumbled underneath the covers, rabbits of despair, wrangling snakes of abdominal pain, the very wolves of whitening blood. If he were really looking, he knew as always that it would hurt to look.

What is this which haunts him more than most? How come it is usually he who is chosen to have such true adventures? Terrified by his luck, he sat up abruptly and vaulted off the bed. In that refreshing instant in which as yet neither foot touched the ground, it could be said that his heart did wholly experience the supreme airy pleasure of knowing that he had become now and forever a powerful dynamic part and substance of what would eventually kill her.

Certainly the sign of a real thinker is when he can rearrange his clothes and pick his nose at the one and the same time. It is amazing what a zest and flair he still had for family life. Like the natural he was, he played it mostly by ear. So that whenever Mamma examined him so sadly, as she did now, as if he were some kind of a hopeless idiot, he

478

knew somehow that it was perfectly safe for him to grin and scratch his armpit like an ape. It must have been the incalculable force of inspiration itself that felled him as he came down on one knee in a manner he hoped would draw the eyes out of her head. Clapping a wild left hand over his heart, and stretching forth the right to the extremest limit of its appeal, he burst into song, shaping each over-sweet vowel with an amazingly elastic, operatic mouth, suing for her love and mercy with a wonderful discharge of words and music entirely soundless.

Abe reached out to clonk him over the head with the floppy shoe, jealous enough to try to nail him to the floor. Helen began to pat Mamma on the cheek and shoulder, as if competing for her attention, while commiserating with her on the diabolical fact that sons are invariably male, and as such, clowns from birth, entire, intact, and inextinguishable. This is where Mamma crossed her up. For what were her first words but, have the boys already eaten? Like horses, said Helen very stiffly, flinging herself off the bed, stung by this obvious show of partiality, this cruel reminder of her status in life as a mere female person, woman ever the servant of man, the one job she would never be able to quit.

Everyone was so touchy tonight. Suppose we fail? We feel so weak sometimes. Suppose we suddenly lose each other? We have been together this way so long. We are ready to poop out every time we think of it. What will we do when those clopping human-hating Cossacks of change and division come charging in with their heartless knouts and their sabers to flog and cleave us apart? What will we do? How will we be able to go on?

Numbered among the maudlin scenes not to be relished. It passed as shadows are pleased to pass. Profoundly weary as Joe already was of incurring all the risks and suffering all the penalties of recklessly flapping across the last frontier of full-time feeling, he was mighty glad to be joined by the others as they hovered about their mother, still disposed to be right merry by teasing her, calling her a deserter, telling her she was a lazy Mary, will you get up, but actually very much distressed that their one tower of strength should presume to topple so before their very eyes at such a ticklish moment in their lives, propos-ing a string of firecrackers, a brace of clawing cats, a powerful magnet, a smoking pot, a system of pulleys, anything to get her out of that bed. All this while, as if unconscious of what they were doing, Abe was

479

feeling for her pulse and Helen her forehead for fever, as gently and slyly as they could, for they both knew only too well how much she hated to be touched.

Let go, said Joe, tearing at their impertinent hands. Get away from her, he said, bumping them aside and interposing his own more illustrious and saintlike body. He did so as the result of the latest. The timid implorer can be a bold explorer as well. He has lately discovered his very own mother.

He turned to pull up a chair and swung it around, nicking his competitors cleanly on their vulnerable shins. His brother and sister howled, but they gave way. Coming into his own, a power in the land, he sat down and leaned forward, resting his elbows on the edge of the bed and clasping his hands as if praying to God that one day it would be his proud boast to be able to say to anyone who would listen, I knew this woman who was my mother, I actually spoke to her, I saw her for what she was when she was still alive. It is always so aggravating. Just when we are about to come a little bit too close to each other, the clouds quicken and the heavens part, and the dread interloping arm of the Lord shoots out to bar the way. And why? Because he is so afraid that if we ever really met, we would never speak to him again or have any use for him at all. Thus in one insulting way or another he is always saying, no, not yet. At this moment the grand and mighty hypothesis was meaner than ever. He said to the doorbell, ring. And the doorbell rang.

Sure is a grim reaping time when in comes Sam and Yetta Grushkin, of all people. And this is what is called company. Joe just sat where he sat. He simply refused to budge for such vaguely related creeps and chronic wrecks of distant relatives, scowling at them so fiercely that Helen intensified her insincere gay cries of solicitude and welcome as she shooed them in and settled them somehow on the other side of the bed. As for Abe, he knew his time had come. The last smiling man, he hailed them with his least impolite hello and goodbye, and bowed himself out.

Queer shattered schnooks, graceless visitors blundering mid the gainlier Bellinsons, ganglion burdened and killjoy green, even when they swear they have dropped in only for a second, what good are these sad and scabby tailwaggers who simply come in between? Ragpickers of whatever pity is left in other people's sore and troubled hearts, they blotch time and debase space with their drooping organs

480

and decaying eyes. So difficult is it to believe in them, they cause the tear in the eye to dry before it grows large enough to drop. Only too often the subordinary are not the salt of the earth. They would fascinate more were they fattened ducks killed by suffocation to keep their blood. It must be very exhilarating to be rotting away at such a fast clip. What affliction brings among other things is the lovesick tapeworm of God's closest attention. Who else but him is always going further? If a droop like Sam is dumb to begin with, God decrees that the sky-ignorant stack of bones become an upholsterer, silencing him with the hammer and filling his mouth full of tacks. Still sporting with this riffraff he created, he inflames his kidney and collapses his lung. Then tenderly afraid that Sam may still have some fearsome word in him which might somehow slip out, he gives him cancer and carves out his voice box. If Sam's shriveled hand is stretched out across the bed, who shall turn it back?

My brother and tenth cousin, if thou too are brought down to hell, to the very sides of the pit, speak to me only with thine eyes, and I shall spurn you with mine, for as God has rendered you, you are disgusting to touch. Sam's final lock of hair hangs limp. It is useless for him to be listening. While his Yetta screams and pounds her trick knee, further unhinging her loose nerve knots, Sam turns his pockets inside out, idiotically scrounging in the seams. Jittery rejects and tearful scrappers, succulent examples of what to part with and leave behind if life is to be lived without this jugular catch, this diphtheria-death in the throat, they seem to encounter windy days only, undergoing daily some spectacular cloud-speed change, drifting fast way off into the outskirts of existence where the seething wreckage of their violent Jewish hopes is piled high on a tiny clump of grey, swampy, theological grass. They have the leap and squat of frogs. They croak. They tell things.

As Yetta does, spewing forth every fuming word as if direct from under her armpits. Her hectic clockwork is governed by stem-winding bugs. She will not loosen in water. She gathers fluids to excess. She glistens. Blimp which never rises, bunged up barrel, gasping man-eater with stoppered gills, she has interspersed the charming roar and splutter of her internal combustion with multicolored switches of hair, flaring styes, carnal-minded stays, and blood-chilling miscarriages. She has been with child, she has been in pain, she has as it were brought forth wind. All but once. Since then she

481

seems continually to be tossing in the senseless labor of a woman who has had her ovaries removed. She can mash down leather with her gums. Fantastic how sharp little slivers of impossible pride keep working up through her charity prickled and highly principled skin. May the hospital people drop down dead, may their tongues be slit slantwise, and their eyes fail from looking upward, imagine them mixing money with death, they absolutely refuse to take her calcified father into their crummy section for incurables unless she first agrees that when the time comes she will scratch up enough cash to bury him herself.

Ah, my darling, my precious Mrs. Bellinson. I have my hand in his mouth every day. I wash out his woolies every night. I am a lake of suffering. He has so much hair left. If he were just a little bird in a cage, I would open the door and set him free, and say to him, go and tell God. Go, my dear, and say to him, God, thou great busy bee, I will exalt thee, I will praise thy name to the skies, for thou hast done wonderful things, thou hast made of this woman a heap which shall never be rebuilt. Death and transfiguration, she laughed so scornfully at her own massive heretical self that she began to cough, fetching up a huge gob of phlegm which she swished around in her mouth and swallowed back.

All so cynical and excitable as she is, she is ignorant of what? How is she so inferior? And how is she low-minded? Obviously it is not every such mutilated cow in whom affective change works swifter than thought, who can go so childishly grinning into the grave, and spin out to be so charged again and proud-glancing, the queen is in her faded cotton, counting the house, refusing round ripe fruit, a renascent bulge, a rowdy blaze, shedding her fiery hair, bursting at the seams with shameless love, where are you, my darling Sam, are you all right, my sweet, that face of yours, those eyes, they will kill me, kiss me, does it stick and tear you so much, what is in your hand, little father, is your shoe on, boopsie, are you all buttoned up? She dried his palms. She dusted off his lap. She raked back his hair. From out of nowhere she popped a red pill into his mouth.

And Sam said, where am I? If I unveil you, I unmask myself. Woe unto my crown of pride, what is this fresh bitterness? He stretches forth his neck. He hisses like a snake. Everything goes straight to his face. If he lives long enough, he will stop feeling. If he scratches himself, the last bit of his blood oozes out. If I am his Yetta, should I lick it up? I go toopeh, toopeh all day. Do I have to eat soap to get sick? I run even while I sit. Do I know? Where should I look first? Lately I smell only wet feathers. The moon sees. I use too much bluing. I am very lucky yet. Mrs. Simkin from next door, the purple card player, is watching Papa for me when she is dummy. And I broke the ladder. And I burned the beans. And bedbugs came to ask me. But the stars said not to listen.

And God said. Habit-haunted crows, embroiled crabs, kickers against the pricks. Did I speak to you in secret from the beginning? Did I not make you so that I could break you? A blabbermouth from the word go. Did I not tell you so? As your duly elected Maker of Jam and Preserver of Pickles. Did I not clothe the heavens with blackness, decree sackcloth your covering, make you drink the dregs of the cup of trembling before parting and death? I do declare. Whose moody skull swarms more with ghosts? Whose frisky old pump is more surrounded by phantoms? Yea, I, even I, have revealed it to you. Yet you roar all like bulls and mourn sore like doves.

Bummers all. You give me such a stitch in my side, you tear me all to pieces, cries the Lord, himself half-blind with tears, and like Yetta, wringing his hands at this wickedness which is not wisdom. Desecrated by gastric pain, aflame with unholy heartburn, not built to take it, he is forced to feed upon such movable and immovable human feasts. He falls off the swing once a week. He used to have the face of a great big beautiful doll with sticky lashes.

One coolish night he sent Yetta a burglar to chloroform them as they lay sleeping with the limp baby between them in their one sagging bed. Her lipstick was smeared as part of what was stolen. Her muff was moist. Her pins were loused up. The bunny had eased itself profusely. Its hives were cured. Its colorless eyes were closed. What turns entirely blue is likely to be dead, picking its parents clean of its crumpled ears, its satin smackers, its seasick shoes which gleamed, which weaved and pattered so whitely through the exalted ground floor of their lives.

See the joyous pounce and pulsation of what once was. How it raises its jagged and frothy waves everywhere. Dear Mrs. Bellinson, you listen like an angel. You are so sick yourself, how could I do this to you? Where is my bag to blow my nose? I hid my carfare somewhere. What ice is left in me will melt by summer. The poles are dusky. The seas are restless. Now war is all the world about. The earth is all one

483

great eye, all drowned in one great tear. Hallucinations and henfruit, flax and flippancies of fire, swing out wide, crab the wind, chase hence this ugly night. She who lives by the clock will die by her own ticker. If only, if only, she tapped her forehead hopelessly, if only she would stop thinking, she would be all smiles again. She tried to show Mamma how it would be, but her lips would barely quiver and stretch.

And this is a mess, a real prime stinker. The nerve of the marginal and illiterate, who was she to become so pale and rattled, fascinated by the window, yearning after the door, dying to escape from what awful necessity of tearing clutch and outrageous backfire, what thick bluish haze of mixed emotions? Like a truckload of lumber, all the lies of a lifetime rumbled by. Counterfeit coal chinkered down the chute. A duo of dishonest cats sobbed beneath the window. When a body tries to hold faking to a minimum, for the moment no words will come. The paper appeared in her hand like a rabbit from out a magician's bottomless high hat. Look, look. I have no shame. This is why I have come. She flipped the dastardly thing free of its folds, artlessly frank of her own distaste, dangling its evil printed form over the bed, appealing solely to Joe to save her from it as if it were a vicious rattler which he alone could safely toy with, impervious to its fangs, slick skin and all.

In the name of Mamma, the son, and the ark of the covenant, he took it from Yetta and held it open like a scroll. How black and utterly abominable, when shall the rage of these petty humiliations subside until it is merely anger? She was applying for a loan of a measly fifty bucks. You is become a maniac for money, Mr. United Big. So it has come to this, my country. Darling bud of America, sprouting into rich excess of consumables laid end to end to remain uneaten, into uncounted frozen hummocks of hard goods clogging your arteries, for you I pine, your greening soul scaling the glinting mountain of dime, rounding the cape of good quarter after bad, mongrel securities, brain-washed collateral, negotiable and tax-free bonds, spare us the pain of soft selling us down the river of debt, lay off our fiscal-ignorant, mail-order eyes with your leeching gold and discoloring pennies, go frig yourself with your dollar sign.

With exquisite continental manners, freshly roused to be at his fictitious best, he smiled and shrugged his shoulders at this ancient foolery of fear of and respect for what is known as mere money, at this

perpetual hand-kissing and heel-clicking of the cringing soul before
the stupid stuff, showing class and the proper spirit, like every super-
sensitive purist who is still a jobholder should, if only because
Mamma was such an interested witness, he waved aside Yetta's warning that she might to her great sorrow be forced to default, motioning
to her in the kindest way to supply him with a pen with which to do
the deed. What a cagey kid. What a relief it was to be able to say yes to
someone in this cruel spectacular time of his of always having to say
no. Propping the paper on his knee, he rapidly inked in the required
information. He cosigned with a flourish, forging this tiny link, very
gallantly joining his life with hers.

"And now," said Joe, the moment he heard the front door close
behind Yetta and Sam, inclining his compound head to a vast audience
of one. "If I may, I would like to introduce myself. I am a poor lamb
who has lost his way. My sister is moping. My brother is soaking. The
last time I looked, I still had me a mother. I know you never accept a
tip, but if you would kindly direct me to her, I would greatly
appreciate it."

Mrs. Bellinson gazed light years beyond him, still silent, still
absorbing.

"What say?" said Joe. "Wasn't that a pip? Hey, kid? How did you like
that one? That sure was a lulu, wasn't it?"

"Yes," said Mrs. Bellinson. "A lulu."

"That's all right," said Joe. "You don't have to climb out of bed now.
You can kiss me later."

"A good boy fixes the pillows."

"I'm fixing, I'm fixing."

"She used to be like a flower."

"I'm sure she was," said Joe. "Who wasn't?"

"Please," said Mrs. Bellinson. "Don't punch so hard."

"Sorry," said Joe. "You know me. When I do a thing, I damn well
overdo it."

"I remember," said Mrs. Bellinson. "I can still see him. Lazar
Cohen, the father. If people are like animals, he was a horse. Black
with great big bones. The whole day, like you say, it was whoa and
giddyap. A lucky little Yidel, he ran away to America to carry coal for
Rubel Bros. To eat the dust. To sleep with sacks and barrels. Only Papa
could make him laugh. The bad ones fly high. The good ones drop
down quick. With rags and old iron. Cases of seltzer broke his back. In

485

this small world there is always a place for creepers to sell salted pretzels on a stick. Everybody said the mother was the weak one. But when Lazar sat down, Rifkeh carried him. She had at least five who died the first year. The doctor said, eat, for god's sake, you are getting so thin, soon you will be all nose. She laughed. She kissed Lazar on the tip of his nose. She packed a suitcase with a pair of blue pot holders I once knitted for her. She ate glass and drank shoe polish. A very foolish woman. But smart too."

"I'll be damned," said Joe. "She did save some money that way, didn't she? You sure you got enough air in here? How's this now? You in a good position to eat?"

"Yes," said Mrs. Bellinson. "I am in a very good position."

"Yump, Fritz, I gif you liver. Rouse mit the sadness from the bed. Rouse, I say."

"If it has to be, it has to be. In every family there has to be a crazy one."

"Look," said Joe. "The champ of all time. With one wave of this here mighty hand of mine, I can make anybody miserable. Ha. You thought I was going to say something else, didn't you? Boy, are you easy to fool. Damn this rug. Like some people I know, I can tiptoe through the tulips, but a toe dancer I'll never be. You're such a brilliant woman, I must ask you. What makes me break out this way? All of a sudden I am sixteen other guys. Is it all because I am still what they call young? I start out with gimel and end up with aleph. This is the way I've been pounding away all day. I can jump all I want, but the grass is already growing under my feet. My life is really here, but I feel I'm half way out there somewhere. If I ever go out like a light, the sun will still rise and shine, won't it? The nerve. If I keep this up, there ain't much hope for me, is there?"

"Yes," said Mrs. Bellinson. "You will drop. But do it you must."

"Didn't I say this was a woman? Didn't I say so?"

"Only pray it shouldn't last too long, that's all."

"Oh," said Joe. "Don't worry. It can't. It won't."

"Good," said Mrs. Bellinson. "I am so glad. Only I think you should know. Before you almost put my eyes out. Now you are trying to break my hand."

"Ah," said Joe. "I'm sorry. Was I doing that? What's the matter with me anyway? I can't make a move lately without murdering someone."

"It's all right," said Mrs. Bellinson. "I used to be a wild one myself. I understand."

"You were?" said Joe. "When was that?"

"When I was with Moses in the wilderness."

"Ho, I bet you were."

"But today, you see, I am here with you. It's like a dream. A thing like this I did not expect. I am already a different person. I'm beginning to feel so much better."

"Great," said Joe. "I really hope you do. You know what Helen has nerve enough to say? She says you're sick because of me. How do you like that? Isn't that something now?"

"Talk, talk. All the trouble comes from talking."

"I know I'm bothering you," said Joe. "But gee whiz. What can I do? A man has to take a chance sometimes, doesn't he?"

"Yes," said Mrs. Bellinson. "A man."

"Absolutely," said Joe. "Look. Let me try to explain."

"Please," said Mrs. Bellinson. "Don't try. I don't want to hear."

"Just tell me," said Joe. "Just say I'm right to quit my lousy job. There must be something better somewhere. Tell me I'm right. That's all I want to hear."

"I can't," said Mrs. Bellinson. "Please. Don't ask me."

"Why not?" said Joe. "Who else can I ask around here? Is there anybody else who can tell me?"

"I told you," said Mrs. Bellinson. "How many times do I have to tell you? It's your life, not mine. Do what you want with it. Only please, leave me alone."

"How do you like that?" said Joe. "Did you ever see anything like it? Here I've been depending on her to help me out. And I can't get a decent word out of her."

"Aha," said Helen. "I thought so. I knew you'd be bothering her."

"Fine," said Joe. "Then you're not surprised."

"By you?" said Helen. "Foo. How is that possible?"

"Look," said Joe. "You poke me one more time with that blasted thing and so help me I'll."

"You'll what?" said Helen. "That's right. Just ease yourself down and cross your legs again. Amazing fella. Always underfoot. Isn't he, Ma? Say. How do you like this for a lovely tray? If the ding-dong tea is cold, just sing out. When did you make so much blueberry? I made

487

such a mess looking. Where in the world do you keep everything? No, no. That's not for eating. That's for decoration. That's the last good pussy willow. You there. Tomorrow you bring Mamma a yellow rose, you hear me? Darn it. I spilled the sugar, so I had to sweep twice. There, now. Doesn't she look nice? Just like some rich lady in the movies."

"Excuse me," said Joe. "Is that supposed to be toast?"

"Of course it is," said Helen. "I burned it myself."

"How clever. You must have some other talent. Let me see. Now what can it be?"

"I can see right through you."

"Yes, yes," said Joe. "As Mamma says, what can you do? Every day must have its low moment. And this one is mine, all mine."

"Oh, sure," said Helen. "Of course. It would kill you to relax."

"Relax," said Joe. "That's for dead people."

"Well?" said Helen.

"Fantastic," said Joe. "Do you see what I see, Ma? She's opening up like a hibiscus. She's fresh and gay again. It's a positive miracle."

"Nonsense," said Helen. "I always do that when I'm not too busy."

"Not too busy?" said Joe. "Don't tell me. I heard you on that phone."

"God, yes. Did I get myself an earful."

"Let me guess. It was the wrong number."

"Watch those sparks, will you? How is it you never burn up?"

"Ah," said Joe. "So it is love again. L-o-u-i-e. Is that how you spell it?"

"Oh, yes," said Helen. "Louie. You know what the man says? He says you've got to be everyone before you can really be anyone. He said he saw the moving hand. It was written across the sky. And was it luck? Certainly not. He was just trying to do what comes natural to him. He says. He says it came to him when he was practicing on his ram's horn before the tiger's cage in the zoo in good old Prospect Park."

"Das strumpets blow. Hey. Remember that one?"

"And you think you're a cuckoo one, don't you?"

"That was when he was Peter Vassilevitch Kutchyurheadoff, the great Russian basso with his boots on when the moon was full."

"Ah, but when he was only John Smith. Then I really loved him."

"Louie that crazy dope. I tell you, kid, he's the one."

"He does amuse me, yes."

"Is he coming over? What's the latest with him? What's he up to now?"

"Excuse me," said Helen. "Is this a private party? Or can anyone sit down?"

"Sit down, you say? Why, my dear. Have you forgotten again? This is still your home. You must try to enjoy it while you can."

"So give me some room. Why do you have to crowd me so?"

"Because it purifies you when I breathe on you."

"I ask you," said Helen. "Isn't this plain awful? I can hardly lift my arms to show you. What did we do when the time came? Why, we went right out. We didn't say a word. For years we worked and slaved away like dogs. And so far all the space we can afford is from here to there. My goodness. What a hollow sound you make. I didn't bust anything, did I?"

"Wait," said Joe. "Wait until you die. You'll get even less space when they bury you."

"I swear," said Helen. "It's really got me puzzled. What do you do in such a case? What do you say? I pick up the phone, and he says to me, hello, is this the Red Cross? Such a high trembly voice. So touching. Such big tears in it. He must have acting in his blood. Of course I knew who it was right away. So I says to him, yes, my poor fellow, what can I do for you? So he says to me, please, ma'am, I would like to report a natural disaster, myself. Well, sure, I laughed. But it gave me such a twinge. I don't know why, but it hit me so funny. So I says to him, sorry, lad, we're all out of bandages, try me again tomorrow. Help, he says, what is this tomorrow? Tomorrow is out of a book. Tomorrow is the day after when it is always too late. Help me now, he says, now. It is now or never. God, I thought to myself, what kind of a silly joke is this? Sir, I says to him, you are forgetting who I am. I am not God who has all the little babies in his hand. When you hear the tone, it will be exactly driving me crazy time. You hear me? Hello? Hello, there, I says, where are you? Hello, he says, is this the Red Cross?"

"Funny," said Joe. "Very funny. I must say."

"Honest," said Helen. "I'm not exaggerating. Why do you men always have to talk as if it's do or die? Why can't you be reasonable? My

489

god, after all, if you want to live with other people, you have to give and take a little, don't you? Of course you do. Don't shake your head. What else can you do? You have to live like other people live. What other way of living is there?"

"Ah," said Joe. "But that's just it. If you never get the chance, how will you ever find out?"

"But he's had his chance already. Can't you see that?"

"What chance?" said Joe. "For a few measly months? Don't be ridiculous. You really think that's something? I'll tell you what a chance is. A chance is for a whole lifetime. That's what a chance is. And nothing else but."

"What?" said Helen. "A whole lifetime? Damn you. What are you trying to spring on me now?"

"Oh," said Joe. "Just a little ace I had up my sleeve, that's all."

"Holy smoke," said Helen. "It can't be. What do you mean for a whole lifetime? For what I'd like to know? For sucking your thumb in public? For winding yourself around a lamppost? For smelling paper flowers? For crashing parties? For picking lint out of your navel? For undressing every woman with your eyes? For what I'd like to know? I mean, after all. Don't be afraid to shock me. Explain yourself. Give it to me straight."

"If I told you, you would know everything."

"Fool that I am. Why do I let him aggravate me?"

"Because you love to live dangerously. I suppose."

"I did flip over another rock, didn't I? Serves me right. Butt me, as they say in France. I'll imitate the master. I'll try smoking my head off."

"Won't take much doing, will it?"

"Look, Ma," said Helen. "I'm living it up. Hic. The next thing you know I'll be hitting the bottle. Well, thank you, Joseph. You're awfully clever to hold the light so far away, but thanks anyway. Hoo. Excuse it please if I blow in your face. Rather you than Mamma any time. Mercy. It's a darn good thing we don't talk this way every day. I'd be dead inside of a week."

"Don't be silly," said Joe. "You're stronger than you think. Everybody is."

"And to think," said Helen. "I was so afraid I would die all alone. I hate it when Christmas comes out on a Wednesday, don't you? What a fake everything is. You turn away for a second and the paint peels and the ceiling cracks. Yes, I know. I was always a little weak in the head, but darn it, I used to sit up so straight. In the cowslips and the heather, in fair or foul weather. I can hear you jingle the loose change in your pocket. I can hear you say, she is not an old crow yet, but she is already croaking. This is what happens to the rest of me when the body takes over. Hoo. Believe me, if I were an Indian now, my name would be Burning Mouth. I didn't tell you, did I? I had such a pleasant experience today. I bumped into Ceil Caplan in the subway on Franklin waiting for the New Lots train, and she was wearing bangs and bows all over. Boy, I can tell you, was she glad to see I couldn't believe my eyes, this real flashy individual out of nowhere, her monkey jacket swinging open, shooting out her knees, and snapping her chewing gum right in my face. Oh, you little hammers in my head. What goes on around here? Isn't it time we cut out the fooling? Where's the profit? What's the good of all this crazy paper work? We file away the originals and flood the world with copies. She looked like a clown with fever spots. We see people every day we will never see again. I remember she had the first wrist watch on the block. She used to be such a tender blushing thing. Now her tough eyes tell me she knows how to walk on live coals. Her tongue is what keeps her tail from dragging. Her little tom-tom never rests, calling all men. The filthy old trackwalker raised his lamp to look her over. Talk about your disgusting creatures. I turned up my eyes like an old frump. I looked around for a place to spit. When she saw the face I made, she laughed. She said, you see? She said, I used to play the field, but now I go steady. I said, how nice, there's nothing like being particular, is there? Dear me, she said, isn't this awful? I know that people are getting colder and colder, but I never dreamed I'd see an icicle hanging from your nose. Well, I said, we're none of us exactly broiling in the sun down here, are we? I said, I think it's lovely we're both going home to mother. Are you made up to look Japanese? Or are you just pretending to be Sarah Bernhardt sleeping in her coffin? Darn, she said. There I go again. I always make the same mistake. I always think I'm the only bitch in the world who's out for blood. Goodness, I said, I had no idea I was reporting for duty. It's a gorgeous looking crowd here on the platform, isn't it? I would say if you throw your hip out that way once more you will surely cripple yourself. Do you always stand so near the edge? Gent there with a jeweler's glass in his eye reminds me. How's your fat little brother the Buddha? Does he still shave his head? Did he ever go to the synagogue in that monk's robe he wore around the house? No, said Ceil, he never had the guts. People who stick out in front think they have the right to criticize. What luck that I should meet you in the rush hour of my life. I was always so afraid you would take more than a lady bite out of my apple. You had such black sparkling eyes. And I seem to remember tinted stockings. But you never had the long-division blues, did you? I see, said Ceil, you need more than a shape to hook a millionaire. How do you get to believe you're the only one in the city who's white all over? Are you still in the thick of things? I've just been to the moon and back. Where have you been flying around on your broom lately? Oh, I said, nowhere in particular. A real clod. I don't get off the ground much these days. I just make sure the door is locked, and sit around and hold hands. And fool with the lights. And try to sneak through the usual message, which is help. And when that fails me, as it usually does, I try a little table rapping and talking to the spirits. I have a silly habit of speaking to anyone. Dead or alive. You do? said Ceil. Why, that's wonderful. Think of my luck now. Since you're so psychic, maybe you can tell me. I have a terrific lump on my breast. You think I should have it removed? I said, what? I said, oh, my god, don't tell me. Look, she said, the train is coming. Look at the fools. They are already tearing us apart. I said, no. I said, wait. I said, Ceil, darling, what are you saying? She said, whee, she said, you see? What's there to worry about? When I get in a jam like this, it's impossible for me to fall. Is that your hand I'm touching? Who are these angels who are trying to lift me up? Bye, now. You be good, you hear? Oh, you musn't look at me that way, please. I know it's rotten, but what can you do? We can't all get off at the same station at the same time, can we? I tried to get out a word but couldn't. Everybody was looking and listening to her. I said to myself, oh, you stupid, I said. I tried to grab hold of her before it was too late, but they pushed her in before me. Before I knew it, I was pinned up against the pole. I was crazy to fight. My ears began to ring. I felt I was going up in smoke. I was so afraid my bag would fly open and all my precious things would go spilling right out. I said to myself, good, good for you. This is what happens when you get careless and lose control of yourself. This is how a fool like you gets caught."

"Jesus," said Joe. "You couldn't know. How could you know?"

"Is that a ball of yarn under the bed?"

"Don't bend," said Joe. "I'll get it."

"I should dust," said Helen. "I should get up and do something."

"What ball?" said Joe. "It's only a shadow."

"Oh, my. I guess I'm seeing things."

"People," said Joe. "I tell you, they can drive you crazy. Once you let them get a grip on you, you're sunk, they never let go."

"She didn't pick on me. I picked on her."

"Hell," said Joe. "Sometimes it's best to be selfish. You just have to learn how."

"Like Lou's aunt," said Helen. "She's made up her mind. She says she's going to be buried in her ratty racoon."

"Why not? Anything to be comfortable."

"I ask you," said Helen. "How many mistakes can a person make in one day? Gracious. What a kick I gave Mamma last night. It drives me crazy to get a seed caught between my teeth. The sign said, this door is open to everyone. I felt my insides melt with happiness. Even in my dream, I knew I was dreaming, and drooling on my pillow. I was giggling because there was actually a sand pail on my head. I felt my nose and it was shaped like a key. I stretched out on the third rail and sizzled in the blue flashes. All the stupid letters I ever typed came floating down like autumn leaves. I picked one up and it said, the jig is up, you can hang up your spikes, and fold up your hootchy-cootchy show, we know now there are bones in a rat's tail, and cooties in your shrubbery and that, woe is me, life is but a sleeper jump, we found traces of it in your sink wash. Oo was I mad when I saw what was stamped on the back. Return to sender, it said, address unknown. What was I racking my brains for? What was the great big joke? All of a sudden I was trapped in a screeching world of chalk and dripping candles. I tried to wake up for the first time. I bashed my head against a filing cabinet. I went slipping and sliding through a whole field of pearly buttons. I said to myself, are you off your nut, or is that a monkey in your hair? The next thing I knew I was fighting to shut off the alarm while the tiger held me in his mouth. Sideways as I was, I saw there was no flesh on my hands, so I unbuckled my shoes and began to kick the door down. I felt such a pain shoot up my knee. I was about to break through when I woke up. What a fix. Why should we

493

care? What's on the other side of anything? How do you separate the leeches from the crabs? It was really. It was the strangest dream I ever had. There were absolutely no people."

"And not only that," said Joe. "Absolutely no sense."

"Wait," said Helen. "If you think that was silly, wait until you hear what Louie said when I told him. Your royal highness, he said, I hate to tell you this, but that door is death. Death? I said. Don't be ridiculous. What have I got to do with a thing like that? Only this, he said. I can see it all from way out here, your black petticoat is showing, I want to thank you for this peep into the nature of things. Excuse me, I said. Can this be mister four-eyes speaking? The same, he said. But I'm supposed to be in love, I said. Why should I want to die? Because, he said, it's like they say, love makes cowards of us all. The things I pick up in books. It would curl your hair. Aha, I said, so that's it, is it? So that's what's happened to my dreamless nights, and the lilt in my voice, and the roses in my cheeks? Oh, bosh, he said. What does it all matter so long as our hearts still beat as one? Thank you, I said, you cheer me up tremendously. Why, you lovely little bundle of joy, he said. You ought to know by this time. We're young. So we're the walking wounded. And that's it in a nutshell. To me, he said, it explains everything. Well, hooray for you, I said. Is that the operator clicking the phone? Where are you calling from? From the tavern on the green, he said. I've been swilling beer and soaking up experience. Splendid, I said. Bon voyage. You'll soon be floating out to sea. But before I forget, please, do me a favor, and don't keep phoning me with those slugs of yours from the same place all the time, they'll be laying for you. It's too late, he said. I was clumsy and got caught. I begin serving my life sentence Monday. I said, what? I said, what are you talking about? He said, I only mean to say I found myself a job. My very first on earth. I said, really? I said, why, that's wonderful. How did you do it? What kind is it? What does it pay? Tell me. He said, I'm going to carry a sandwich sign on stilts for a famous restaurant downtown. I said, no. He said, what do you mean no? I was lucky. I just barely qualified. For god's sake, woman, I'm going to work my way up in the world. Isn't that what you want? I said, you're crazy. When did I ever say anything like that? He said, sorry, I no hear good. You make with the joke, no? Oh, I said, I can't. I just can't stand the idea of your being a sandwich man, you hear me? Oh, he said. Well, in that case, there's only one thing left for me to do. I must quit before I start and spend the rest of my life lying at your feet. I said, yes. I said, fine. I jumped on him then. I said, now you're talking. I said, don't you worry so much about being a man. I said, I don't care. I said, no matter how much it hurts, you must wait until you can use your education. Did you ever see anything like it? I was so glad he called. I saved him just in time."

"Why, you sonofagun," said Joe.

"What do you mean? Didn't I do right?"

"Sure you did right. But how about me?"

"You?" said Helen. "Where do you come in all of a sudden?"

"Boy," said Joe. "I tell you. This sure cops the cake. Can you imagine that, Ma? Did you hear what she said? Him she tells one thing. Me she tells another."

"I can tell you one thing," said Helen. "You are making yourself extremely popular by yelling."

"But I'm asking you," said Joe. "If it's not good enough for him, why is it good enough for me? Since you're chopping away there so fine, why don't you tell me? Why do I have to do work I hate and he doesn't? Why? What am I here? The scum of the earth?"

"Roses are red, violets are blue, I have a bulldog at home just like you."

"Oh, sure," said Joe. "I know. I'm only a lousy mutt in your eyes. What else?"

"If you can't see the difference, there's no use talking to you."

"What difference?" said Joe. "You want me to strangle you or something?"

"Go on, Ma," said Helen. "Have another cup of tea. There's all the time in the world. We've hardly begun to warm up yet."

"Hoo," said Joe. "I swear. I haven't felt so peeved in years."

"I know it's awful to say this," said Helen. "But every time he gets excited, he makes me laugh. I wonder why that is?"

"Look at them," said Joe. "It's disgusting."

"You used to smoke a pipe. Whatever happened to it?"

"This one gets sick. The other one can't even cook. What good are they to me anyway?"

"I beg your pardon," said Helen. "I had no idea we were living only for you."

"Jesus," said Abe. "What a bath I had. I never knew it could feel so good. I must do it more often."

"Well, blow me down," said Helen. "I hardly recognize the man."

"Of course," said Abe. "I had to scrub real hard. But as you can see. It was well worth it."

"For you," said Helen. "But not for me. I don't have to look. I know. There are pools on the floor. There's a big fat ring around the tub tonight."

"Well," said Abe. "Something had to give. How's it going, kiddo? Still flying high?"

"Oh, I do pity you if I have to go in there and clean up after you."

"Balderdash," said Abe. "I tell you, people, that pink soap is a fake. The lather comes out white. Hot diggety. How's this for an outfit, Ma? It pretty near killed me. But I broke out some new pajamas and socks. The robe is a little tattered. But what the hell."

"You're not fixing to stay home tonight, are you?"

"Why certainly," said Abe. "I understand it can be a lovely experience."

"I don't get it," said Helen. "Is this ground-hog day? What's today's date?"

"I don't know," said Abe. "It's a real problem here. You think I should sit down between two such dirty people?"

"Why not?" said Joe. "It's much warmer this way. You've been using my comb and brush lately. Why?"

"Sorry about that," said Abe. "But what can we do? We all have our little crosses to bear. You take me for instance. There I was laying in all that steam and thinking. It's bad enough to be a flop all your life. But suppose my hair doesn't grow after I die? Can you imagine the shame of it?"

"I'll try," said Joe. "I feel I owe you something."

"Of course my toes will curl up. But will that be enough?"

"Well," said Joe. "Maybe your nails will take up the slack."

"Dang my buttons," said Abe. "I knew you would say something to comfort me."

"And here I thought my spit was turning sour."

"That could be," said Abe. "But let me ask you something. If money doesn't rule your life, what does? He can't answer. Is your ears pinned back? Is your nose on straight? Does your blood ever run cold? What do I hear tell, boy? I understand you have muscles you haven't used yet."

"Lies," said Joe. "All lies."

"But you're the talk of the town," said Abe.

"I know," said Joe. "It burns me up. Take it from me. It doesn't mean a thing. Today it's me. Tomorrow it'll be some other guy. It'll pass. You'll see. It'll all go away.

"But where does he get the nerve to do it? That's what they want to know. How can he just go and quit his job? He must be doing it with something."

"Yes," said Joe. "With my heart in my mouth. If that's what you mean."

"How do you like that?" said Abe. "Did you ever see anyone so slippery? I'll sock him in the eye right away. Looks like I'm staying home for nothing."

"What nothing?" said Joe. "What are all these eyes on me? What do you all expect to hear?"

"You dope," said Abe. "You're lucky people still want to listen to you."

"Okay," said Joe. "All right. If you really want to know, I'll tell you. I really can't do what I'm doing, but I make believe I can, so I do it. You understand?"

"Perfectly," said Abe. "You mind saying that again?"

"I told you," said Joe. "It sounds silly, doesn't it? But it's true. Who's ever brave or strong enough to do anything in this cockeyed world? Who? Did you ever stop to think of it? It's terrible what happens to us as soon as we grow up. One second we're afraid to live, the next we're afraid to die. We're always shivering in our boots. We're so damn paralyzed. We don't know what to do. I know I make it sound too simple. But there it is. How will we ever do anything worth a damn unless we make believe we can, and just go right ahead and do it?"

"So," said Abe. "So that's the great secret, is it?"

"I tell you," said Joe. "I don't know how. But it works."

"Yes," said Helen. "Sure. But suppose what you make yourself do is wrong? What then?"

"I'm only talking about doing what's right. That's all I'm talking about."

"But darn it," said Helen. "How do you know that? What tells you? How can you be so sure?"

"All ashore that's going ashore. Listen to my joints cracking."

"There he goes again," said Helen. "It's the same old story."

"I have to be so careful how I stretch. The sky is much too low for me lately."

"He flares up like a match. He goes out like a dying quail."

"Ah," said Joe. "But remember. I'm the guy who had the measles twice. Leaping lizards. Who sprung me here? How did I get loose? With one flick of my nail, I can rip things apart. I feel so strong tonight, I could swim across the ocean and back. Where I keep my hat is my home, I suppose. What gives with you all here anyway? Why do you want to get a boob like me going? Don't you know yet when you're well off?"

"Hate to come between enemies," said Abe. "But I think he has a point there."

"He sure has," said Helen. "And I hope it's sharp. And that he sits right down on it."

"Honored lady," said Abe. "Yours is most certainly a losing cause. But you sure said a mouthful that time."

"How does it happen?" said Helen. "What is it with this man? You mean to say he's going to escape us again?"

"Well, hell," said Abe. "I can take him by the throat, like so. But damn it, if he resists me not, I have no choice. I must let the villain go."

"Aw, now," said Joe. "It's okay, Ma. Don't look so worried. It never lasts long. They always get over it."

"Do I live here too?" said Mrs. Bellinson. "I'm afraid to say anything. With the hands yet too. That I don't like."

"Children," said Joe. "What can you do? Let them play."

"Play," said Mrs. Bellinson. "From so much playing, somebody will cry yet."

"Ah, but it won't be us, will it, Ma? Are you finished with that? Let me take it away."

"Here," said Abe. "I'll handle that."

"Pass it along the line, boy."

"And of course," said Helen. "I have to get stuck with it. Don't you dare start anything new without me. Wait till I get back."

"Beep," said Joe. "Come in, Brest Litovsk."

"Oh, no," said Mrs. Bellinson. "Don't look at me, please. Tonight is not the night to fall into anybody's mouth."

"You ready now?"

"For what?" said Mrs. Bellinson.

"Raise your right hand and repeat after me. I, Mrs. Bellinson the first, hereby swear that I will smile once a week. I further promise that god willing I will rise up out of my sickbed in one day's time, and make you all blintzes."

"With pleasure," said Mrs. Bellinson. "Only tomorrow is Friday."

"Ah," said Joe. "Better yet. Make me a pot roast. Make me that lovely old chicken soup with the noodles and lima beans."

"Not for me," said Abe. "I like it pure with a few oysterettes."

"It's sad," said Joe. "Does the world know your chopped liver? Or your gefilteh fish? No wonder it's hardly ever merry any more."

"Yes," said Abe. "The poor suckers. I do pity them. Or that cold beet borscht. Or those thin crispy little potato pancakes. Or that stuffed cabbage. Or those prunes and sweet potatoes."

"I ask you," said Joe. "Must there always be a special time for kreplach?"

"I know I'm a fool," said Helen. "But I brought pretzels."

"Shoo," said Abe. "I wouldn't dream of eating such trash."

"Don't grab," said Helen. "There's plenty for everyone."

"Ah, well," said Joe. "It's like they say. Life needs a little salt now and then. So I guess I'll try a handful. What have you got in the way of drinkables? Any of that malt beer left in the house?"

"I would like to know," said Helen. "When did you become a cripple?"

"But my dear Helen," said Joe. "You make such a lovely servant. You don't want to lose your job so soon, do you?"

"Oh," said Helen. "I understand it all now. Poor Mamma. I feel so sorry for her. If you want to know more about waiting on someone hand and foot, you can ask your mother. She happens to be a woman too."

"She does?" said Abe. "Since when?"

"It's true," said Joe. "No sense arguing with her. I've noticed it myself."

"You did?" said Abe. "Then why didn't you tell me?"

"Well," said Joe. "You know how it is. You keep saying to yourself, today I must tell him. But the day goes by. And you always forget."

"My mother a woman," said Abe. "Can you imagine that? Not that it makes any difference, you understand. After all I always kind of liked her. And I must say, she can be very useful."

"That settles it then," said Joe. "She stays."

499

"Yes," said Mrs. Bellinson. "I will say. But you. You will all go."

"We will?" said Joe. "Where?"

"You will all go," said Mrs. Bellinson. "Who can stop you? Can anyone stop you?"

"Stop who?" said Joe. "Who's going anywhere? I'm not going anywhere. Are you going anywhere, Abe?"

"Don't ask him," said Helen. "You ought to know. You're the one with one foot out the door already."

"Which foot?" said Joe. "Right or left?"

"Aw," said Helen. "Let him go, Ma. Who needs him around here? He doesn't even draw interest."

"Well, now," said Joe. "That's a fine thing to say."

"I thought so too. Isn't that a coincidence? The only thing is, I know I'm lowering myself when I talk to you. That 's what worries me."

"Why, you stinker."

"Children, please," said Mrs. Bellinson.

"I'm sorry, Ma," said Joe. "But I can't help it. She gets my goat."

"So," said Mrs. Bellinson. "So ask her nice. She'll give it back to you."

"Ho," said Joe. "That's me old mother. That's the way to talk. Who would want to leave a person like that? Hey, Abe? What do you say?"

"I say," said Abe. "Get your pretzel-sticky hands off her. If that woman is going to live with anyone, she's going to live with me."

"Really?" said Helen. "And where do I come in around here?"

"Okay," said Abe. "I'll let you have her every other weekend. How's that?"

"What weekend?" said Helen. "Are you cuckoo or something? A mother always lives with her only daughter. Everybody knows that."

"Ha," said Joe. "You see that, Ma? I told you. You can relax. I got them fighting over you."

"Yes," said Mrs. Bellinson. "A fine toomle. Very good for my head. Like my mother used to say. Watch yourself now. This is the time to be afraid. When everybody is too good to you."

"You know something?" said Abe. "For a person who believes, she can be very suspicious."

"Yes," said Helen. "Shame on you, Ma. You're not being very nice. Really."

"Nice," said Mrs. Bellinson. "Not nice. What could I do that was

500

more terrible? Good, you say. So I was good too. I talked and talked like you. So ask me. What did I do? I kissed my father and my mother. I picked up my skirts. I took my pots and feathers. And I went into the boat. And I left them standing there. Two sweet little people. Holding hands. Getting smaller and smaller. I cried. I died but I moved. I went. I left them. And I never saw them again, never. And tomorrow I light a candle for my mother."

"Oh," said Helen. "I will never light a candle for you. Don't ask me. I will never do it. I will die first."

"Whew," said Joe. "It's very warm for April, isn't it?"

"Yes," said Abe. "It is kind of close in here."

"Imagine," said Joe. "Living on a farm. It gives me a kick thinking about it. It must've been really something."

"I'll bet," said Abe. "How was it, Ma? Did you commune with nature? Were you a creature of the woods? Is there something about the birds and the bees you can tell us that we don't know?"

"Brr," said Joe. "How about them Russian winters? Did you go to some kind of regular school? Were you far from town? Why is it you never talk about it? Tell us, Ma."

"He came in all bloody from the barn."

"He did?" said Joe. "Who did?"

"I screamed when I saw his face," said Mrs. Bellinson. "How my heart jumps even now. I still dream the red light is falling on me. If I was four, I was a lot. I remember. I see myself so plain. I am on the floor again. The stick is my river. I am knitting a boat. My fingers skip like little goats. A child, what else? I push the gold thimble over the paper bridge. I hate cats. Cats are murderers."

"They sure are," said Joe. "Their eyes. That's what gets me. Are you listening to this, Helen? Mamma's talking."

"Listen," said Mrs. Bellinson. "You hear? The whole house is shaking. She is banging her head against the wall. A new thing in America. This is the way she talks to the world. Poor Mrs. Mittleman. Her winter is over. She is big in the belly again. Her heart is like a stone. She catches me on the stairs. She pulls me to pieces. I made a mistake once. I gave her an onion. I listen. It is like we are tied together with a rope. Her Essie doesn't talk yet. Her Itzik will never grow. I say to her, let me kill them for you. I make her laugh. My Papa, God rest his soul, was a very wise man. He used to say to me, the walls of the poor are thin so we should always be able to hear them and never forget. For what does God himself say? Forget me not. Don't break my heart. Be with me always. Yes, yes, I know. I can see by your face what you are thinking. You mean he's asking this from us? How can that be?"

"What did I say?" said Joe. "I didn't say anything."

"The usual fool," said Mrs Bellinson. "I sit in this bed and make believe I know. The ceiling is not the floor. The door is not the window. That is how much I know. I used to scream and run. I used to understand that flowers and mud are better than the best words. But a head I still have. So I remember. I talk because I remember. There are some things I still remember."

"It's such an exciting life you lead here, isn't it?"

"I live, I live," said Mrs. Bellinson. "Sometimes. I don't know how to say it. Sometimes what is happening to all people is happening to me. And that is more life than I can live. I am not my Papa. For me it is too much, too much."

"Oh, god, yes," said Joe. "It's hell, isn't it? I know just what you mean."

"Too much, too much."

"Welcome," said Joe. "Welcome to my society."

"People," said Mrs. Bellinson. "They are so funny. They do two things I don't like. They can't live without bread or a roof. And they get older. And then what do they do? Without asking anyone, they all just go and die anyway. It's a very funny habit they have. I watch. I see. I once said to my Papa, I don't like this, Papa. Why should this be? I'm afraid. And he took me by the neck. And he pushed back my hair. And he said to me, you are a devil, you play too much with ducks. People were dying before you were born. Is this such a new thing? And I said very quick, yes, for me it is, yes. And he looked at me. And he said, I am sorry. I spoke without thinking. Tell me again. Which part of you is afraid? And I said, all of me, Papa, all of me. And he smiled. And he said to my Mamma, come here, Fanny, listen to the child. There were dates and honey on the table. And grapes and wine. And a cake baking on the coals. Why do I shiver when I remember? I can hear the wind and the rain now. I saw the dog kill the rat. I saw the dog fall under the wheels. I came late. I was their last. And my Mamma came over and said, let me see your hands, you are as black as a gypsy, what is this up your nose? Fear, my Papa said, she is terribly afraid. And my Mamma said, ah, good, we must tie her hands. I am afraid too. Today she gave away my best candlestick to Mendel the beggar. What will it be tomorrow? And my Papa laughed and clapped his hands. And he said, tomorrow it will be me. I am next. And I said, oh, no. And he said, oh, yes, you must give all your life. You must never be afraid to give. Some day you will give me back to God. And I said, oh, no, Papa, never, never. And my Mamma said, look, she is banging her foot. I think she is getting ready to dance. And my Papa said, she is like a storm already. What will she be in years to come? And I said, I will hit God. I will hide you in a tree. I will give him a goat instead. He will never find you, never. And my Papa smiled and he said, when he comes to look for me, I will tell him myself where I am. And I said, oh, Papa. And I began to cry. And he kissed me. And he put his hand over my head. And he picked up his eyes and he said, O Lord, my God, the soul which Thou gavest her is pure. Thou didst create it. Thou didst form it. Thou didst breathe it into her. Thou keepest it within her. And Thou wilt take it from her, but wilt restore it unto her hereafter. O Lord, my God, as long as the soul remains within her, I wilt give thanks to Thee, God of my fathers, Sovereign of the universe, Lord of all souls. And I listened to him with great big eyes. The Hebrew was beautiful. And my Papa kissed me again and he said, blessed art Thou, O Lord our God, who hast sanctified us by giving us this child. And my Mamma said, Amen. And I hiccuped. And my Papa wiped away my tears. And he poured the wine."

"And he gave you to sip," said Joe. "And you felt warm all over."

"Yes, yes."

"And you weren't afraid any more."

"No," said Mrs. Bellinson. "Only a little. I was always a little."

"No wonder you miss them. I sure can understand it now."

"Miss them," said Mrs Bellinson. "Understand. These are only words. Wonderful people. Was there ever anyone so good? I can talk and talk. But who would believe it? Would anybody ever believe it?"

"Times change. This is already another country, isn't it?"

"I remember," said Abe. "I used to know so many of those prayers. But ask me. What do I know now?"

"You were awful," said Helen. "You never wanted to learn."

"I sure in hell didn't. Papa loved me for that, didn't he?"

"It's a shame," said Joe. "I wasn't much better myself."

"Oh, fine," said Helen. "It's always nice to be so sorry. When it's too late."

"Ah, well," said Joe. "Let's not get too downhearted, men. We're still a bunch of lucky stiffs. We have Mamma here to pray for us."

"Brilliant," said Helen. "Give that man here a kewpie doll."

"Hey?" said Joe. "How about that, Ma? Am I right?"

"My Mamma used to say," said Mrs. Bellinson. "If a fool is happy, why tell him?"

"Tell me what?" said Joe. "I don't understand."

"He is holding my hand. He is lost again. A baby yet. Why do you make yourself so foolish? One touch and you should understand. A god I am not. Today I hold you up. Tomorrow I will drop you. You are a hot potato. You don't believe. It's a pity. For you today it is not easy. I know. I understand. Who are you in this country? Your father is dead. Who will ever tell you? Do we have to go to Jerusalem? What do we need to make us believe? I remember. I once threw a wild stone. My hand was not the hand of God. I am sure he was looking and laughing. But when the policeman came into the house and my Papa saw his face, he said, this is a person too, I must welcome him with all my heart. But my Mamma said, no, I will never shake his hand. But she made the policeman a cold compress and gave him spring water to drink. What my Mamma knew, she knew by heart. She could count so beautifully in her head. She did not need a pogrom to make her believe. She did not have to ask like we ask, why not fifty fingers? Why only two eyes in the head? Which Jew will be the last to die? How can we live without clocks? How do the fishes know where to swim when it is dark? You laugh. I think it is very fine that you can still laugh. But my Mamma did not have to do anything. She did not have to ask. She believed. To me that is always wonderful."

"So that's how you saved your country," said Joe. "You threw a stone."

"Yes," said Mrs. Bellinson. "The devil always finds a way."

"Oho," said Joe. "Don't tell me you know that old rascal too?"

"Have respect. He's a very old friend."

"I'll say. He's always hanging around, isn't he?"

"Yes," said Mrs. Bellnson. "You see? He too believes in something. He believes in us."

"Sonofagun," said Joe. "You must be twins. How did you get to be so smart?"

"You must believe," said Mrs. Bellinson. "I know I am a pest. But some day you will feel it too. You will. You'll see. It's like my Papa used to say, when God says you must, you should. Was there ever anyone so wise and gentle? He understood why people must dance. Or play with cards. I remember now. One day he had to go to market with his wonderful beets and cabbages, but the peasant who drove the wagon was sick with a swollen leg. So my Papa said to the poor man, give me your eldest son, I know he likes to use the whip too much, but he knows the horses well, and I will sit beside him, and I will watch him. And the man said, yes, take him, Reb Chaim, show him, may he always travel in your light. And my Papa smiled and he said, then pray for us both, we may easily stumble. But they laughed and would not believe it. And the boy hitched up the horses. And he and my Papa mounted the wagon, and they drove off. And because the sun was already high, they took the road that went through the forest. Now this was a very dark place. Here the singing birds never came. The air was a little too cool. Children who crept near the edge saw witches in there and the ghosts of men. But the foxes knew where to run. And the grey wolves loved it. And my Papa said to this boy who was so beautiful, you are shivering, give me the reins. And the words were hardly out of his mouth when a gang of gypsies jumped out of the trees with long knives and pulled my Papa and the boy off the wagon. Just think. This was in the old world. This really happened. But just when they were about to cut their throats, one gypsy threw up his hands and cried out, stop, I know this man, this is Reb Chaim, he is a good man, he is our friend, he lets us use all the wood and grass and water we need, never does he drive our people away, let him go in peace, this is Reb Chaim. And so thank God, this was how their lives were saved. And when they came out of the forest, my Papa laughed and said to the boy who was still white, crack your whip, be happy, surely you can see now, it is sometimes better to be good once than to be right every day of your life. And my Papa began to sing. He had a fine clear voice. He loved to sing. But the boy said nothing. And my Papa thought to himself, this is a deep one, when we get to town, I will

505

buy him new boots. And so he did. And he gave him figs and Turkish delights too. This is how happy my Papa was to be alive. And the boy took and the boy ate. But he never smiled or said thank you. He had such smooth pink skin and the clearest blue eyes. His thick hair was so blonde it was almost white. And my Papa noticed how the boy looked at him from the sides of his eyes and he wondered. And he said to himself, who knows, maybe you smell different, a boy is a boy, do you always have to creep so far into a person? But his heart felt heavy. And he thought of home. And he motioned to the boy to drive faster down the road that was so empty. And so they traveled together this way, sharing the same seat. And between them was this great strange silence. The sun slipped down. The wind moved away. The sleepy horses barely raised the dust. My Papa sat there and dreamed. A hundred years later when he shook himself and looked up, his heart turned over. The whole sky had become a terrible green. He saw it on his hands. He saw it on the boy's face. His hair was wild. His blouse was blown up by the wind. The boy began to curse. He stood up so big in his new boots and lashed out at the horses with all his might. My Papa cried, no, and tried to stop him, but the boy was too strong for my Papa and pushed him down. And my Papa was so afraid and tried to hold on tight. And he said to himself, ah, dear God, is it now, is this the way I am going to die, thrown from my seat, weak and helpless and hating him? Oh, yes. He told us. This is what my Papa said. He was afraid and full of hate. But when the rain came down, my Papa could not help himself, he covered the boy with his own coat. And the boy took what was given to him. And again he said nothing. And my Papa said to himself, old fool, it is enough, his soul like the forest is still a dark and dangerous place, watch your step, you think you are bringing him light, but you are only burning yourself on your own little candle. For one man this is more than enough for one day. The storm ended. The stars came out. The horses stumbled, bringing my Papa home, sad and wet and cold, a great failure. Oh, how happy we were to see him. We flocked around him like birds. We hung onto him and we kissed him. What did we know? We followed him into the house, thinking only of the gifts he had brought us. But when he came into the light, we saw at once that he was very sad. And we began to pull at him and beg him to tell us why. And he sat down and told us. And when he was finished, he lifted up his eyes and he said, as God is my witness, that boy will never ride with me again, I swear it. And we all cried out, yes, you are right, Papa, never, never. But my Mamma was quiet. She stood back with her hands in her apron and shook her head. And she said to my Papa, why should he want your life, is this your whole story, you believe so in giving, why should you be so unhappy now that you gave? And my Papa said, no, no, it is not the giving, it is not that, you must understand me, I say this boy will never ride with me again because he does not believe, I saw him, I know. And my Mamma said, what did you see? And my Papa said, I watched him, I saw, when we came to the image of his God on the road, he did not cross himself, he does not believe, do you understand now? And my Mamma said, ah, yes, I understand now, poor boy, what will become of him? And my Papa said, what poor boy, what can we do, we must believe, what are we if we don't believe? And my Mamma said, we are still what God made us, we have to go through this life together just the same. And my Papa looked at her and he said, my own words, you make me feel ashamed. And he sighed. And he pulled his beard. And he thought. And his face became very bright. And he looked around him and he said, I love it here, this is a good house, I am very hungry, are all my children here, what a wonderful looking table this is, which dish shall we give to the boy, who will take it to him? And I jumped up and said, I will. And I took the dish and ran. And when the boy saw what I had brought him, his eyes opened and his face became very red. And he said to me, wait. He went for the whip and broke it on his knee. He gave me the pieces and said, here, take this to your father, he will understand. And I took it. And I went flying back. And when my Papa saw what the boy had sent him, he laughed and clapped his hands and tears came into his eyes and he said, I saw soldiers in town, they marched up and down, boom, boom, I can still hear the big drum, was anything killed here, who will dance for me, the world is safe for one more day, I have kept you waiting long enough, let us eat. And he washed his hands before eating bread. And he said the blessing. And all that we touched and ate with him was good. And the next day the cat scratched him. I can see him now. I remember every word."

"And that," said Joe. "That was in the old country."

"Yes," said Abe. "The man with the smile and the beard. I think I'll remember him now."

507

"What a woman," said Helen. "I never heard her tell that story before. Did you?"

"No," said Abe. "Never."

"You hear that?" said Joe. "We're all wondering about you, Ma."

"Yes, yes," said Mrs. Bellinson.

"I tell you," said Abe. "You have to take that extra step. You have to try to help the lousy people no matter what. That's the way to show you can be big. To be really free like Grandpa. Right, Ma?"

"Yes," said Mrs. Bellinson. "Sure. Help. Another beautiful word. Day and night, that's all you hear. How can you ever rest? Where can you run? Is there ever a stop to it? In this world, if you want to be good, you will always be in trouble. You will always get it from all sides. Like my Papa. He knew. He had to say to himself, please, don't disgrace me, try to remember, be good, try to help. This is true. Every day he had to fight with himself. And if not with himself, then with somebody else. You say he was free. How was he free? He was not his own boss. Was it his to give away? But he gave. What could he do? One time the owner of the farm came to him and said, you are a wonderful manager, Reb Chaim, and I respect you very much, but tell me, are the cows dying, what is happening to all the milk? And my Papa sighed and said, the cows are well, Reb Fishel, but the people here, that is the great trouble, if milk is cheap, they are cheaper, you think that is right? And the owner said, you hear, I say to him one word and he gives me a whole history, I am talking about the milk, the milk, Reb Chaim, where is it disappearing? And my Papa said, about the milk, I would like to say to you something very simple, the milk is for the babies, Reb Fishel, the corn is growing, the barley is ripe, come have a glass of tea with me, you look tired, I forget, do you like it with milk or with lemon? And the owner said, what babies, what are you talking to me babies, do you mean the goyim here, what money do they have, where, how much do they pay you? And my Papa said, you ask me but you know already. Aie, said the owner, I knew it, he gives it away, every time I turn around he is giving something away. Yes, said my Papa, and when I do, I do it in your name. Ah, said the owner, thank you, thank you with all my heart, Reb Chaim, you will not only ruin me, you will drive me crazy, God help me, what is this with you, look at you, did the devil come to you in the night, what is this with your face? And my Papa said, ah, yes, this, it was a little thing, but I have learned my lesson. What lesson? said the owner. I forgot myself, said my Papa, I was a fool, yesterday when I went into the barn, I saw the cat drinking right from the cow, and without thinking, I chased it, and it jumped up and scratched me, it cost me blood, you see what a fool? And the owner said, why do you keep saying fool, I don't understand, you were right, if it was me, I would have chased it too. Yes, said my Papa, but you it would not have scratched. And the owner said, you hear, what is this now, why you yes and me no, you are making me dizzy, Reb Chaim, what are you trying to say? And my Papa said, behold, Reb Fishel, see what God has made me, where is my skin, I am also formed out of the clay, can I walk on hot coals and not get my feet burned, this is my portion, babies, cats, boys who do not believe, they come around me daily like water, this is the gift of God and my curse, love tortures me, what does it do to you? And the owner said, it used to make me sick, but now I have this bag of money, I think I will need more than tea, it is very warm today, but you make me shiver, if you are working so much for God, why should I be the one to pay you? And my Papa laughed and said, ah, but that, Reb Fishel, that is your portion. I laugh, said my Papa, but I know, his hand is laid on you too, your eyes are red, your children are scattered all over the world, my little one here listens as if she understands. Come, said my Papa, let us walk through this field and go down to the river, and talk a little bit together about who pays and who keeps, remembering death, and what we still dream about, the world is rushing away, the grass is growing without us, take my arm, listen how that bird sings, come, my dear friend, now is our time, let us walk and talk. Yes. So they walked and talked. Yes. And that, my children. That was my Papa. That was how he lived. That was how he passed his days."

"Impossible," said Joe. "How can it be? How can such a man be dead?"

"Poor Mamma," said Helen. "Now you'll be up all night thinking."

"I thought it was a mistake," said Abe. "But now I'm glad I hung around."

"Just think," said Joe. "It's enough to make you roll on the floor and howl. We may never be together again like this. And what can we do about it? Nothing. Absolutely nothing."

"It's the truth," said Abe. "What kind of a system is this anyway? You can't be happy for a second lately without having to pay for it."

"What is this?" said Helen. "A convention of cats? Did you both stay up all night practicing? How did you all get to be such a mess?"

"By living frankly and fearlessly," said Joe. "How else?"

"You ungrateful cuss," said Helen. "I washed all the dishes myself. I brought you pretzels. What else do you want me to do for you?"

"Kill time."

"But you're doing that already."

"And this," said Joe. "This is only Thursday."

"His tongue is hanging out," said Helen. "He'll never make it."

"I wonder," said Joe. "Will it be such a disgrace if I can't finish what I start? I can still see my hand before me, but nothing is clear. And no one here will tell me. What a pity. No one is asking for an encore. And here I am in such fine voice tonight."

"It's remarkable," said Abe. "The things a man can do sitting down."

"Right," said Joe. "As for example. He can easily fall apart."

"Pull in your head," said Abe. "Pack it up for tonight. Like they keep telling us. The end of one thing is merely the beginning of another. You ask old Uncle Abe here. He knows."

"Isn't this hell?" said Joe. "I honestly thought I would know by this time. I thought I would be absolutely sure."

"Boy, were you dreaming."

"What was I doing then? What hit me? Was I really all that miserable? What made me say I would quit that goddamn job?"

"Who knows?" said Abe. "Maybe you stepped on a crack. Or swallowed an orange pit. Or forgot to change your socks. It could be anything."

"It's awful," said Joe. "I just can't figure it out. If I quit, the whole world will hate me. If I don't, I will hate myself."

"Hell," said Abe. "Why give yourself such a hard time? At least you had the idea. And damn it, you did go right out and do something about it. Who the hell ever gets as far as that?"

"It's really touching about you two," said Helen. "I must say."

"Goddamn it," said Abe. "There are no two ways about it. Either we're for each other or we ain't. The rest is crap. If you'll excuse me."

"I don't see why I should," said Helen. "But I'll try."

"What's the sense of kidding ourselves? This is an awful tricky business we're in. We're none of us going to make it."

"Sounds great," said Helen. "The day is done. The race is run. And wonderful stuff like that."

510

"I guess," said Joe. "This is certainly not the time for me to be saving my spit. Because all of a sudden I understand. What I don't say today, I may never say tomorrow. And that would be such a calamity. I mean to say. Put the lid on me, mother, I am all ajar. Was it you, Ma? I see you understand. Was it you who said, the hell with all the rest, there are just two commandments we should follow in what we call this vale of tears, and that is, do good, and be merry?"

"Oh, yes," said Mrs. Bellinson. "Who else could it be? I am always saying."

"What a fierce face. How did you ever get to look like that?"

"Always," said Mrs. Bellinson. "It's my greatest pleasure. If they don't come to me, I go to them. I fly around. Every time they ask me, why do you rejoice, I say to them, I rejoice because this is my son. I was like a tree without fruit until he came. Behold. Truly God has been good to me."

"Why complain?" said Joe. "At least I make you sing."

"My dear friend," said Mrs. Bellinson. "If you knew all there is to know in this world, it would still not be enough."

"There," said Joe. "That ought to hold me for a while."

"You must believe me. If I knew where you were going, I would gladly follow you. But my hair is tumbling down. And I am not wearing my glasses."

"Or your golden slippers," said Joe. "Or the crown I promised you. It's rough. I know."

"Oh," said Mrs. Bellinson. "Maybe it's not so bad yet. Who knows? When I looked yesterday, I found. We still have some old clothes to give away."

"If you mean with me in them, I do thank you for telling me."

"We live in the same house. We don't have to shake hands. Who kicked away my shoes? Why do you look at me so funny?"

"Because I just love to see you run out on me. Because everyone in this house has fluffy little wings but me. That's why."

"I forgot to look," said Mrs. Bellinson. "Let me see. Starch I know I have. And sour cream. And cornflakes. I must remember carrots. And juice oranges. If I don't get too tired, I will mop under your bed. I will turn the mattress. I will shine the silver. I will rip off the lace and lower the hem. I can hardly wait until tomorrow. I must take the knives down to the butcher to sharpen them."

"I envy you," said Joe. "It must be wonderful to be so full of plans."

"At least," said Mrs. Bellinson. "He can keep himself clean now without me. That's something."

"Peculiar person. She thinks she has to have a life of her own."

"No one has to tell me," said Mrs. Bellinson. "It is a very dangerous thing to become too familiar with your children."

˙ "Amazing," said Joe. "It must've been an accident. What made me bring her a present tonight?"

"I warn you," said Mrs. Bellinson.

"Listen how she cracks her knuckles."

"If you try to stop me now, I will fight."

"Ah, Mamma."

"I can scratch. Watch out."

"What did I usually do before I got to know you? Did I hop right through you? Or did I just step over you?"

"You saw me. You looked."

"Poor old kid. How did you ever get stuck with a punk like me?"

"You see?" said Mrs. Bellinson. "I get sick one day. And this is what happens."

"Jesus," said Joe. "It just came to me. Am I right, Ma? These are the good old days. We are living them right now."

"Good," said Mrs. Bellinson. "So that's settled."

"Aw," said Joe. "Go on. Beat it. Get away from me, you selfish thing."

"So? So let go."

"Let go, hell. You know I need you here."

"So where am I going? Am I going so far away?"

"Dear Mamma."

"What now? What?"

"Promise me one thing."

"Anything. Anything."

"Whatever you do, please, don't go and die on me."

Mrs. Bellinson laughed for the first time.

"Oh, no," she said. "Don't worry. I won't. I must live long enough. Especially after tonight. I am so nervous. I can hardly wait. I am dying to know what you will do. I must see what happens to you. You don't have to worry. I'll be here. I would die if I didn't find out."

14.

So you came to me and you said, with your phantom flesh agog and
your rococo mind aglow, rapt as you are in the lusty beauty sleep of
your early spring, you amiable public apple, you may be partly green,
but someone has to eat the wormy ones, hugging unto yourself with
huge wet kisses your old lost self, as if being separate again were a joy
rather than a disaster, sly by night, what are these dark ocellated spots
all over your body, you most sumptuous peacock of the peripheral,
you sure do look mighty naked to me when you strut around without
your parentheses, in an uphill dream, streaming towards me out of the
rich teeming center of your ripe and rhetorical shut-eye, in which you
double to trouble the stub of my life, heart of my heart, I am so rarely
all alone, am I such a shark that you should be such a pilot fish, you
skinny comedian of the comma, making whoopee in advance, of
what, planting your choicest obscurities in the rear locker of my
brain, in a splendid war of nerves, in a scheming, twisting jumble of
tea leaves, spaniels, and sunspots, your aspiring pompadour electrified
by these slick ponderosities of the intricate and the difficult, your
premonition pooped, your whole lower lip ubangi, your immense
corpus of suspense tumbling down upon me like an avalanche, alp,
fast snowing me under, stumping me with your skyscraping transi-
tional fences, straining to shake loose of what is lazy and low-down in

me by means of such swollen empurpled barriers, bringing out the scramble in me and slipback, you whelp, I was not born to hold your horses for you, for to tell the truth, what are you but a green hand, an infant rustler of ideas, a primitive of the imagination, piping up to me out of the gay ultrasimplicity of your best spree yet of posturing as pure spirit, to burn my tail, to put the finger on me, to tromp on my last legs, loose upon the world with illegal eagerness, walking your beat with your differing little billy at a dangle, as self-seeking as any rookie lunatic, when all of a sudden you slugged me, you stood over me and you said, while you dream only of blundering into outer space without asking to what end, I must remain on the spot, and be renewed inwardly.

Then do so, robinson crusoe. While I, wildeye, while I who, loving as I do to hug the shore line of logic, willing enough to be your friday morning footprint, your shape of things to come grooved in the cool elemental sand of, master jellyfish the jew, his mark, surely there must be a bit of such bellinsonian anti-journalistic japery in all of us, I see I must sidle up to you like a crab if I really want to level with you, I for who, for whom what is not instantly plain is ever a pain, for whose leachy sail limp comprehension the simple is never simple enough, who dast not show it, when assailed by your savagely complex indoor cyclonics, that I may not come up to snuff, can only, I repeat, can only bobble around clumsily in the cloying, crying evil, wholly incriminating suck and swirl of your suprahuman yap, can only, what can I cling to, I have always been so afraid that my death would have a circular motion, coefficient of your chills, costar of your spillways, the poorest possible stopper to your pitilessly brainy pouring upon me your bursting all bounds, a crock of trickles in comparison, a dull scintilla of ordinary spit, a faceless rambling wreck, a pale shrinking inutility, a prize old pisser myself, fazed and amazed.

Whale of a fellow. Whopper of a bottleneck. Ye old splurging windjammer. With your hide so slithery, and your spout so spirituel. Am I merely the bubbles in the giggle water of my sleep in your deep? What fribbling, what fratricidal, what fleeting immateriality of my raw and ridiculed flesh do you imagine you embody? You cant across me like a ghostship. You capsize my bearings. You give me the shakes. Land sakes, man, what is you where you is at? Is you the grim wave of the future? Is you the bitter spray of the mounting chaos of the corporate inmost mind? Is you to its endlessly raging scuttlebutt sternly conditioned? Is you tiding me over until you can trample me down as the new white terror of excess and extreme? Is you out to swamp me, sucker? Is you billowing to leave me beached?

Fluke of the ages. I see now, I see. So this is how sense is so often washed away, you typical snotty, self-infatuated idealist, whose crooked rudimentary hairs of wild unmanageable ambition to be adored are so illusively doctored with imitation star dust, your entire blood embroiled with black market meaning, no wonder your baby syntax is inclined to get all balled up, when your intellectually gamy, dream-torn dialogues, and intimate bedridden speeches, which, since all movement of the physical kind has the darling tendency to become more and more superficial, may get to be one day the latest craze, are so cunningly dredged out of what may be called your unduly vulnerable bosom, and clotted blind gut.

Cheers. Sure is awfully decent of you to fuddle me for your own recreation. Like the big word said to the little word, why am I less sincere than you? The worst snaggers are usually snippets. If this be the breeding season for happy-go-lucky virginal leapers, then the torpid inflated toad, he must hop to it and get wet. He who like you despises the interlinear as the refuge of simpletons will gladly sustain these oversubtle crises of interpolation. Just to see if I crack. Or shiver my timbers. How it doth frazzle me to play follow the leader with you. As one second you burlesque the big-time bounding main, and the next the little petty eddy. Your whole head must be sick. You are made of mud of the original flood. Your mania for glittering alluvia, your salted gorge of screaming detail, positively exposes you as one of the most peculiarly unamerican noodnicks. As all your flashier forefathers did likewise fume and fizzle out as they fled from the crafty magnetic fangs of massacre and martyrdom, curses on your similar flair for comfoozling the current weary masses with your fierce for revenge, your fightinest unorthodox messes of scratchy vowels and clashing consonants.

What I know of as words have always failed me. I will not feel blue if you kiss me sad adieu. So wickedly do you crowd me, I barely have room to throw my own fits. My nights are hell when I have to damn you. Your close work is the sticky matter which is ruining my eyes. You make me feel so thick in the middle. You are as brutal with my

515

feeble balancing act as the cranky atlantic which never runs out of breakers. You keep saying there is time, time. What a relief it must be not to feel rushed. The glossier this becomes, the easier it will be to skim. I seem to be reeling upward in my flight. Please, sir. If I am all at sea again, are we all alone at last?

What an honor it has been, your reverence, that you should even dream of diving for your most lustrous pearly ideas with me glued to your back, which is how the solid little smitch of firm ground we have abstracted from the improbable swamp of history is flash-flooded again when both skull and shell go plunging headfirst into the scarcely visible, the rashly overpraised pool of the future, and all our pretty hopes of pulling through in one piece upended by the backwash, and you so jumpy, guarding your jugular against me, my gosh, it sure is handsome of your holiness that you should still choose to sound the depths of the many little ripples which roil the surface of your slap up mind with me, who am just about the shallowest configuration yet of your oodles of higgledy-piggledy, prickly, sickly, far too chummy, gangling, wrangling selve‑ ₁which is what a bellywhop to take, whang-dang it, how I do love to make a splash, but then you see, what goofy thrasher could possibly be more slangish, for the stormier the scud of words, the more I imagine it means, sharing as I do the same damn pitiful, punched in pillow with you in this truly gorgeous pushy country of pile it on and squeeze it in, so that we rarely see daylight, and our thinking is rushed, soon degenerates into that sort of forced labor which is mainly devoted to the tooling of some gleaming thing until it is triggered to deflate and displode us more instantly yet, blast it, what else but fright makes me fly blind, surely the luckiest bird about to be is he who is pecked to death through the shell, what is my whole life if it consists of one such single shrill peep, you keep breathing on me, clouding my glass, my eyes burn as they reflect the saucy whitecaps of your much saltier assertion of your seething yeas and nays, while I can only pitter-patter, what does it matter if my brain waves zig when they should zag, my offensive nails are pity brittle, my private parts are patent pending, the black dog is on my back, my gullible heart is up for grabs, in this slushy day and age where every growling, scowling bastard, otherwise known as me, is soon faced with the exquisite choice of becoming either a blot or a blur, runty beefing bleeder, as already I dwindle as I tend to indwell more and more, drooling my dreary bibful of why should I be the one to fail so early in life, and who in these dissolving nightly shots of a fancy city bloke slickering with his innards ever stops to give my loutish daily rushes a tumble, and woe is me in general until I finally flip, my god, you can imagine then, your worship, how your flaring itch to ditch me thrills me, how doubled up I am in admiration for your rapturous quickie squalls of spiritualizing, for your ravishing high color of a romantic in heat, for your heavenly urge and surge to be so purely for once the speaking shadow of what is more hushed and holy, more sugarsweet and evergreen, in the profane, the bitter slanderous, the simpering, whimpering totality of us, talk about trouble, you can bust, what goop of a droop, gob, what a string of queer fish, my farfetched tribute to you for the funny awful way you try to enhance the frightful giantism of these days, so trial balloon abounding is our top of the morning time, to jolly it, to inflame it further with your own towering flashy uproar of insurrection, your scorcher to torture, your one spark too many, hold on hard now, this may be my last whack of giving you what for, for the uncanny ancient mariner skill with which you mock and rack my raft of wobbling doubts and double-takes with your single circling wave of faith and revelation, until I feel ready to throw up, ulcerating in my own acids, licking my own spittle, whereas in the beginning of my getting up all I dreamed of doing was to, was to, I knew I would forget, and now I hardly know how to stop, toadying to you while you jump ship, why should I walk the plank for you, why must my drag direction be at the mercy of your cross-wind force, where in the blind, the unlit, the search-me circulation of my blood will I find the sticky wicking, the one tarry cotton twist of thought that would calk the crazy split between us, what can I say on the subject to leave you laughing, how in hell can I throw fresh light on what is older than the hills, heaven help me, let me sleep on it, for god sakes, leave me alone.

For this is way too much. But way, but way. Much too much of unmanly killself crammings of those jumbo jawbreakers of them there slickery eye-bulging underworlds of speech, of spitty brooklyn broils of read them and weeps, of endless cold creeps slashed from the strangulated white gut of the plotless, of unlicked puffed up pasties of the plush and poetical, of dreamy creamy junkets jammed in a jackpot wonderland where jew boys once so full of schmaltz are fast becoming insipid assimilating schmucks, of winesap juices wild of wishful-thinking, of heaping umpteen helpings of harum-scarum adultera-tions of the truth, of the stupid deep fat of sluggish bull sessions of the brain, of that swirly mystifying stuff in which so many drag-ass infra dig pigs and icky sheet-white pissabeds love to laze, in such animal satisfaction to wallow, with a wahoo each time they root up a wee glim of the dim inside dope of a thing, which is what if it is not a rum scatological rumor, a fool cock-teasing fiction which naive horn-rimmed sperm spillers, primed as they are each night by the sappy prehistoric short-arm practice of self-love, celebrate as the frigging life force, which is the usual swill, which is far, which is much too much for even a swinish grumbler like me to gorble down me already sadly glutted, vastly wrongish throat.

Blear eyes if all seems dark. Queer dear bum steer. If you are that part of me that takes the heart out of me. Backlash inseparable from the body at birth. Atrabilious flutter kick. Fluvial conscience cul-de-sac. Velly snaky psyche. Abashed squeegee abyssal. Shim sham shimmy of shame. Quasi little quibbling where quails the quack. If quidnunc a punk. If now and if. If with white pinks and prick songs, you twinkled out to scull through much life's much and immin-gling scum-de-dum. And scallop the slug. And cowry every baby winkle and trivial wrinkle of the brain. Oblongata suffixing polyp so ganglion gay. Surely the muchness of too much is such. If you did then dive into that red display sting ray dream sea to bring me some quaint coral notion of your spiny teething ring quiddity. So mighty like the walleyed pike. To pick a bone. To break a straw. To sin eat the stale unfinny infusoria of our frail planktonic trance of no advance, of our pretty darn plural insignificance. Until even you feel stuffed to the gills. And supremely sick of the whole setup.

Ach, du kleine schmeck, what a schrechlich crock du ist of ulterior dreck und das immer bitter piddle-dee-dee. Gee. And all on account of me. As there you squat in the chilly privy of your subaqueous silly ass subconscious, for shivery shakes, squarely roosting there on that reek-ing one-holer, joost to fatisfy someping yumping yeesus how crud-dled and griping in you, the sapless lees strained from the most crapul-ous minds of so many staling centuries, as it seemeth, as it pileth up even here in this grand potluck land of the utterly stringulated and shit out of luck, of blah strikebreaking nonblushers, of mucho fanatical

518

epicures, of farty milk-fed heart failures, of pushy gringos prissy of their piss, clobbering coloreds and faking success, suffering such flushes that.

O thou great rich bitchy gratuitous. What offal dung dis is. When stung by you to digadigadoo. To snap right back at you. With what yapping suctorial jawless maw is mine. With such wholly smackerel. With such esurient lamprey rapture to smelt you out until you is every bit unperched, and if possible, completely pickereled. In a rising world of waters of. Where the sulphuric springs of my stupidity doth spurtle out of me like winking. Bed-born into this big drink of pissy wicked pickings. So dully mulling in this world annulling lull. Finking bassackwards. What a pithy. What am I wading for? When will I begin to reel myself in?

Criss my cross my center of toss my crowded with crisis. You can betcha my heart. I aint a spoofing now. For snagged as I am in your sadly deterrent, self-snarling current, though I seem to stand amazed at this phase, I do tumble to this much, though a big flux like you may feel you have all of forever to spin on your flip side until you spill out your hilarious ad libs and hot licks and id lies bleedings into that real gone groovy gulf of meaningless ultimate meaning, but me now, I see now, as I set this sedimental off-key slinker of mine to climb at half past kissing time, what a smacking lift I get when my love myself alarm goes off, mere damn whats the diff, weak lack logic what not that I am, I know now, I have only a lifetime to catch your drift.

With my gang slang fug. With my back fling of a thing. With my entailed body english. With my freak lips afire. So afraid of closing cold. Trading treble ifs and turning clang color. O basta boogie mio. When will you woogie me out of here? I fear I am nowhere near. If sol-fa. If what this means is not at all what you meant. If I toot so far oot until I laughing break. If I flub my dub when I beat my skins to gravel your astral grinds and bumps, to give you what the first rebel gave the drum. You try it sometimes. See how far you get. If like the square I am, I simply fail to dig you, then hell, I might as well debag my slow drag, disassemble my temple tremble, reed out my split and stunned from your brainy ever black, and turning my back on all other such handsome dives and retreats, quietly retire up my own fundament.

Where else can I slink to hear myself think? I would wind up just

519

about where I began. I would be such an ass if I refused to do so. And yet, my ineluctable, polyphonic pet. As in the meanest thing a god is hidden. As certain entrails are numbles. And no one is much obliged for the oblique. As you turn on me turtle. As you butt me, kiddo, to bubble me all about. As you continuo to henticipate me where I also cackle be. As ever so slowly you thumb-suck me down into your woolly otherwordly, more and more about you seems to be sinking in.

Conjure man, with your capriccio witch stick, your topple time will come when you impale your old joe blow effigy with your own odium, wizard of the blat and the bleat, with your raise cain repeat marks and your back to the bush oscillations, not forgetting the rests, am I beginning to read you right? If I twit you like a twerp, will I finally twig you? Is you the pappy lineal sap? Is you motherkin to me? Is the spindle side of your seem the spirit rousing spin, the eternal feminine twist what schists and spools me? Are you insooth the ever living truth that youth is literally a scream? Are you like death in one breath? Are you all one creature? Are you like a knife between my teeth? Are you dummer as well as deef? Are you partially ape-crested? Are you excessively poisonous in your wild state? Where do you go at alpenglow? Are you furious because I am curious? Are you fagged from the awful drag of double-teaming on me in our daggers drawn world of either slash or? Are you aghast at last that the cutting questions should be coming so thick and fast? Are the self-winding parts of your two-timing speech past parsing? With what snare too sweet for words did you sucker me into swallowing a whole batch of the withered little bodies which a short way back were some plums, yahoo pioneer fruit, brute yield of memory's wild west, from which the real rough sense of what is passion red and seed stone swollen has been flitched and pitted, which is hard on me, gulping as I go, aspiring to know, with what soulful come-on, to hark back a bit to them aforesaid shrinkled little bodies, did you con me into consuming such a splendid pile of the prunes and prisms, the prudish vocabular schisms of the babblative boring, hymnal cloying, teetotal time destroying sterility of your white protestant present tense?

Insolence. You almost had me there. You spotlight hound of my shaky ground. You stony phony. You grandiloquent dumb show for gallery gods only. You bitter mime of the sweet springtime. You

520

liminal late bloomer. You mum old inman of this most grievous monologue you encouraged me to gouge out of my own green head. You only tear yourself apart when you try to cut me dead. You stupid dread to go to bed. You after dark fake of the silent take. You would-be cock of the walk-on. You pst pst pisspirer. You bluer scenery chewer. You part-time stunt man of the present slump. You volunteer drool of O my god the pain of it school. You soliloquy crocked interlinguistic page crasher. You awful suddenly. You me-tooing burst of booing. You O you O you. You soul-sick clipped dick. You bit-playing dybbuk on a joey sleeper jump.

Hambone of the high appeal to heaven against me. Tell me now before you take a bow. Were you basking in my asking? Did you laugh with anything like love at what I last asked you above? Are you the congestion which results from such a question? Are you as tipsy tired as you can be from carrying the torch a cappella with me? Are you the whole reeling world's morning after mouth? Are you all ears as it appears? Are you in medias res without a face? Are you like a feather altogether? Are you destined to be friendless because you deal with the endless? Are you ringing wet from being so beset? Are you the rattled here hating moocher who is frantic to frogleap over me into the funk hole of the future? Are you already alas too anciently frightened to be deeper into life enlightened? Are you running afoul of your own howl? Are you the wrong dog barking up the wrong tree? What makes you chime so much of the time? Could you turn around a bit so I could see?

Holy jumping jinnee. What did I rub? Was that my heart flaming out? How did you get so high above me again? Man, how this burns me up. That a grub like me should have a mind's eye so all the time awry. Glory be. Are you the same bloke I always invoke? Is that thee I see, lording it over me, so pasha silken aslant on thy sacred white elephant? On which. A likely beast. On which you ride herd on my every humpbacked word, piling crimp upon comeuppance, until it seems to be a perfect incarnation of poor little ole me, a ruinated head what went to bed to re-experience red, simply paling again before the all-powerful, and pitifully crying out unto thee. Great rich shucks. Night wrangler of rant of starry-eyed strays and sheepish sleepers. Bridle-wise maharajah of heavenly blues and infinite views. Tell me before you bell me. Are you the dumb bunny who thinks this is funny? Are you like some wild idea too long held in? Are you fringe

521

fat of merely this or that? Are you fricative of faulty chemistry? Are you as inwrought with the wind and water of disunion as I am fraught? If as we ferret with our weasel words into the warrens and wambles, the fewtrils and fusts, and of all the most equivocal, soups and suckholes of our quaking penetralia, I am the clown who is likely to drown in his own juices, will it always be you who comes up smiling?

Wahoo, as the feller says. If by cracky, if not by krishna. If life, if life. If life is a quickness which none of us can express, how can I make it hindoo clear who needs who around here? And here I thought. With all the precious fluctuations of a feeblish word-pecker and finking paper-rat. As I traced and effaced myself apace in every inch of space. As my witless wonderment went white. As my boll weevil boring into our soft central mentals and tongue-red reiterations went round and round till round went the ground. I thought I was about to know vertigo. I thought I was getting closer and warmer. A local festering worm. A real beggarly little nit. I thought I would simply go to bed. And that would be it. And now. I am in so deep I could actually weep. I feel I will soon pass out unless I make water.

O chaos and cold night. Who will give light to a babbling wight who is none too bright? Down, bowzer. One at a time, please. Who was that last ghastly? Who was the ghostly I had so to gird myself to greet? By all the rattled gods. If only I could become a little karma. So become. So who is stopping you who? Who was that autocratic little crassitude who cribbed from me my sexless seamarks, my cool unwinking thinklessness, my all my urchin beginnings, my clutch of singulars and clears, my sighless preoral silences, my pure and simples, as it once were, and created in me such a coo, such a kismet confusion of colored kisses and castes?

Lovely rant this. Who now who? Who was the drab? Who was the bheestie who watered down and bewrayed my bronze age rage, my pigman paganisms, my bratty new world snores, my bedsore nigglings and nevermores, my beastly ratting on myself, with his saintly sticky second comings, his infernal wakes like internal bleedings, his priestly spills and pours for chrisakes? Who? Are you asking me or telling me? Who was that whisht now? Who was that deeper creeper? Who was that vile kid who rudely undid the icky vials of my id? Who was that carve guts? Who was that lower silurian? Who was that cat's

522

paw cloaked in sleep's clothing who caught me unawarés and grabbed me by the short hairs of my growing pains and greening coalitional guilt?

Gently, gently, for god sakes. Do you want to cripple me altogether? Who was that bloke who should only choke? Who was that bhang and bindweed of such bitter screed and holy smoke? Who was that bonze who threw the book at me? Who was that pale retch who sent me up the river for such a stretch? Who was it who? Who chained me here in this echo chamber? Who? Who? And so on and slow on. And further far into the night. And the boohoo sum total of what it blats to mean, as the cry still goes out, is simply deliver me, deliver me from this absolute tops of a tumescent, of a multiple what in hell is it, from what, even in this self-centered, know-it-all century, I can only call myself. Ah, bah. If only I could find a word for it what still has the bark on it.

Peeling fictive. Shiver of leaf. Lowly notional flower. In its daffydil ovule hath it hid me. Within its recessed buds, it lets my roses sleep. My fuchsia of nodding minutia. My loving meed of locoweed. My daisy chain of chirm. My fools parsley of chitchat. My slipshoes of nightshade are falling from me. My turfy toesies are becoming webbed. My draggletail as filthy as a comb. My bunch grass of good grief. My furfur this far and no further. As one would say, no, no. I know, I know I must. No one has to tell me. I must rise and go now and say bye now before I go blotto. For all my gaffs are blown. My sub rosa objectives snafued. As crossed as I am lost. My sickness is my failure to unthink myself link by link as thought itself would if only it could. Mere wishing will never make me well. The day I come clean, I will say what I mean. What is this colder cold I feel is coming? Was the air made blue for your sake too? Are you as drowsy as I am with disbelief?

They say sleep is a candling. No doubt, no doubt. The onus is on us. The real dumb dodo is he who carries on this way until he is carried out. The best of us are born to be a lifelong yawn. Somebody has to skirt these skreaks. You were always the cool one, you were. You who came straight to me from chasing rainbows, smickering with such a dazzling inconsistency at the black bent and aching intent of every darkling aspiring to be a finical fireball. And a constant drag too, as witness you, and devil to pay.

523

Smackerel what a shocking show of teeth. I feel like two other guys, falling between a rock and a hard place. I do try not to, but I must say. When you can smile at me at dawn as you smile at me at dusk, that, old shake, that will surely be the day. As your immense wild faith in your own farseeings and futurals takes another crotchety turn in my own tense and divided skull. Tis hardly strange your chiefest charm should be the chilly way you change. From dragoman to darkmans to dragon's blood. In floods of and scuds of supplemental feigns and fourflushings. Shifts and shufflings so much sleeker in sleep. Chicken little switcheroos past understanding.

A candling, as they say, to spot with stifled cries the whited staleness of our false fronts and the ruddy clots of all our sodden fibs and sticky lies. As rank as rude. As still you brood on how to freeze me out. As you egg me on in sooth to say. In this land of the livid liar, I shall build me a smallish fire. With the bitter truth as faggot. And crackling good sense as instant kindling. Which once again is all pretty obviously balls and more bull. More fag time in ragtime. More cold slag of a conceptual glitter like fool's gold which in fancy you fondled like a maniac until you fanned the flame. More thick ash and smoke of a smutty ponderation long gone phut than a mere punk like me can easily insufflate, or give a flying fuck for. As more and more it keeps coming to me, it comes. A boor of the bootless with bum days only. A traumatized gimp tending to grey out. A grounded for good whose one great dream is hardly any more to limp in ahead of the pack, but simply to go the distance. As you yelp for help. As your hand is still stretched out, fearful as you are.

Feeblest fool of a noctambule. What have you come to? What sort of rat caper is this? Every supine time you realize you are only human, you start fussing and fuming, as the hell of your mortality enlarges itself, you quail, trembling lest you fail to tick out your every given tock, you begin to shrink into yourself, squiffed, if not snotted, by that miserable moonshine, that mickey finn of mere living, of anything, anything to stop yourself from thinking, a voiding blunder, a one night's wonder, your life, she begins to run out, as your spunk goes kerplunk, alas, you begin to drag your ass, and stupendously freighted as you are with all this pluralistic crap, ponderously fall into a pissing funk. Crying out, I am wasted, wasted. A hissing all a time with an unhappiness so filthy ancient and common. In this your

524

prime. In this your first flush of your mad rush to fling yourself into the slip stream of every other man jack's towering flameouts and joy stick thinking. You so highly unstrung, so criminally young, so young enough yet for black to be your favorite choler, to loathe your future coexistence with the same shallowness as you did your former, to stay so stupid so long after birth that you really think that all that has ever been thought you have already thunk. You of all creeples. The worst rattler yet to rest eternal. The very most at giving up the ghost.

Silliest swain, go to, go to. If you have lambed enough of this sheepish stuff. So whitely scratching where the wool is short. Flinging your woo in all sorts of whether. If you spake already your strongest word and it will not stand, coo, you might as well address yourself to sucking cowslips for all the good it will do. As you go wide again when you should be going withinwards. As you refuse to rub your smackers with secondary shits. As god himself gets his wind up. As even the sminking twerps say in passing, a pox on your old fandanglements. When will you break your maiden? When will you wake and sing? When will you begin to do what others only talk about?

For this is it, retarded chit, this is now or never. For every potential poo-bah. For wah-wah passives everywhere. For your brother butterfingers and upchucking pups. For coeval colics anonymous. For collateral ballocks and limp concurrent cocks. For all the little fellers and flowery fuckups. For the welshers of the world, the time has come to tremble. The possum players once had a dance they called the second chance. The selfsame feebs who fail to face the future now can only fail to face it once. The dipso wishing wells are drying up. The shaggy death-desirers shamble into their pads and remain in their places. The rising gorge of gulls imbrues the eerie shadow play on the bat-haunted screen of the brain of our most animistic and religious scuffles to survive beyond the grave with its quaint anti-christian stink. The fingerlings of self-hate flip and proliferate in clear and ambling floods. The mainland fox munches on little mummy apples. The seepages of self-love are saltier. The fit to be tied, be they fledglings or fossils, feebly dream of clambring up the shaky beanstalk of chance and risk just to cock snoots at the giant roots of the fee-faw-fums of their fears. The sorrowing apes, like toyless children, count the sighs and count the tears. The fierce dog star is a howl even when most sirius. It tee-hees at us homeless fleas. It jeereth at us with the high thin laughter of the hereafter. It twinkleth among the trumpets, ha, ha.

They say the race of birds was created out of innocent light-minded men. The reflective state is like a mirror on a swivel. The impulse to bare all bids us open an issue in the heart and hinder part of the head. The imp intuition pulls us by the ear to make us wild guess at what has grounded itself in the blood. My own little finger tells me. This is not the crawly root or the fattening grass. Or the pith or myth of any appreciable matter. This is the blind spot, the embolic bubble, the embryo sac of any inkling, the primal spiracle or breathing hole, the one undying and indivisible cell where the truth is said to reside but the sun never reaches.

Why should God aspire to ride a cockhorse with such a cunning little cove? Is this a ploy the soul too can enjoy? Can it so pleasure the body to play rings only around itself? Tell me, brother, how do I go from one part of you to another? Will I ever contrive to slip you five while I am still alive? Are you so fraught with naught you can never be caught? Are you just too cute for words? O what an O springs up in me O. A million. What am I saying? A trillion times have I tried and tried to tag you, but I am the flit who is still it.

O juggernaut of crushing thought. O baby, baby. O past master of vaster imperceptibilities. Are you really for real? Where have you left me a leg to stand on? If you shared with me your howdah seat, would that orient me a little better? Shall I sift for my spitting images in the cosmic samplings of your spoor? Shall I sit with you shiva under your shittah tree until you shush your shivaree cries of whereat lost again lies that lone funny stone under which we both of us hide at the top of the tide, and softly groping for its suffixing itness in the greenest adverbial area of your migratory mind, as if to redeem the real theme of your dream in midstream, entirely imbue me, as you slyly lichen unto me, with the seepy time bliss of symbiosis?

Till we, till we. Till we minish to a spanking finish. Till how you say the livelong day? Kiss me, my fool. You flaming swish. You can make anything sound simply heavenly. As first you snarly-snarl. And then you lick my hand. With the whole improbable length of your fiery narcissistic tongue, to torchlight me, flambeau, through the deepening gloomth of the many, to blow bellows on me and kindle, with your whole mixed bag of tricks, this vasty flaring up in me to become one, and only one, as me myself alone, sonofagun.

As again and evermore. Is it too brash of me even to ash? Is faking all? Is fire of desire? If I dispense with all sense, will I glow when I know? Will it all finally be just happy, happy me? Will it always be me who says wowee? Am I about to choke as I go for broke? Was that yoohoo who giggled then? Oh, but of course, of course. Laugh and make light of it. Let it run thick, let it run. With this your last great passion, gross martyr of us all, of your everymans sleepers sweatspirations and floptime inceptives and buzz-buzzings.

The air itself is not so full of flies in summer. As with shoo, as with absolutely no face color, you begin to feel what a fish feels when sucked whole into the mouth of another. As you grasp at straws to grow new everything. As your palms is to sand as your hair is to coconuts. As you grapple to recall when once you was a springtail resting on a rush, bending and extending your cunning caudal stylets for that one final tremendous jump into becoming a dominant land animal with a villainous thumb for gouging out the weak little sister eye of the truth, and scabbing over, if not bedizening, the raw empty socket with a diabolical gift for gab. As the disease of debagging yourself is a mind malady. As with that special sweet scent of yours, you pervade the prevailing bush to seminal more such pretty please fantasies with spent asexual spores. As the she-pussy lay spirit when she loses her lapper can give us none of her lip. As any male-man who fats himself with the reddest genital heats and richest marbled meats and ripest jubilations of real reeky love is every apt inch a frigging wonder. As what the hell. As you know so well. As all else is foul smell and blood in a bag. As suffering sassafras, surely sdrivel, sdeath for sure, sreally smashing how I keep feeling for and seeing you as.

Inbeing as nipper veiled by night, bobbing for your own throat apple with the craziest maloccluded cusps for that one most ultimate incandescent bite. Pricky crackjaw. Crashing aboriginal bore. Scrunching interstitial invective. Swamp rat of the subjective, with your priggish ears laid back, snarling rife with antilife, skulking near the pelvic arch and adjoining bones, grasping as it were a gelding knife. Wattled seaweed was your swaddling clothes. A slimsy straw your swagger stick. Weeping willows no longer shade the place where first you slipped and did the split. They say that chance fertilizes many

527

things. From the bitter centrality of syncarps to the sweet froth of syllabubs. From africas of marrow bones to amulets of spider lapped in silk. From whales to emperors, from coots to cats. From silent butlers to parrots of the past. From salacious seminars of double stars to after-dark dickies to yellow dingo dogs. From dry grins to danger's voice.

Ah, if life again. If life. Like I told you. I warned you to watch out. If this here life of yours can get awfully iffy in a jiffy. If this clash and convulsion of spirit is like tearing your own face. If such vain merriment tends to looseness of life. If who can blame you if father time is out to frame you. If God the farther and farther. If he hisself is strangely built to be more afraid of lying than of dying. If soon he must egress to greet you at sunrise at the summit of yes. If such happiness is nervousness of a terrible kind. If the whelming tide of thought did thunder at you to purge and disperse. It must be these cuckoo hours you keep. As you fudge the clock to shock what time is left to kill to a lingering standstill. As you say they say just to keep saying.

They say the fleetest beast to bear us to perfection is suffering. You can trust such a horsy to keep its tail up. They say that such a revelatory sight renders many of them naive roughriders so melancholy that they dismount in one huge knot to drench themselves with such basic simples like sow thistle and succory until body and breeches, they become so soiled they often see two suns. They say we have much to rescind if the blasts and buggeries of our sexciting conceptuals are ripped out of us by reason of wind. They say a naked man, to a modest woman, is no otherwise than a picture. They say we should look at life through the purple veil of the grape. They say as the fool thinketh, so his third glass clinketh. Before the rich can tick, they have to hic. The pale poor are puky barflies who keep buzzing the only begotten, the barkeep of their suckerdom, for the price of another stiff one. The conglomerate louse prays for one on the house. The spit cotton are best forgotten. The stumblebum goes rum-te-dum.

Look, ma, no hands. My lands. See how long my laughing jag has lasted. They say that God himself hates a gloomy bastard. My barmy pose has grown a blossom nose. My bandy legs are bibble-babble things. My proud babel is fallen. Good lord, deliver me. God knows, I have never been a lush greatly loaded with superlative gush, but I never

528

have trouble seeing double. As taps I go tippling with my ardent spirits where the shed light upon is powerful poor. With my winkers streaming with strabismical meaning. Queering my whither away by never saying when. Quenching my sense of shame which is my oldest fun game. Quaffing my daily magnum of my cheap domestic bubbly, of my belchy lethal likenesses until they burke me down to the dimming down of me dregs. Until the air I suck like a dying duck. As you would too if it happened to you. Until I feels I swear. I thinks I see a certain solemn shape. Quirking its inky pinky. Death, let me smell your breath. Before I drink my crock of the customary blood, let me deliberate on it. You look so dead beat. Let me calla your lily for you. Let me not gloat and play the giddy goat because some fellow shit of mine is even now crapping out before me, yet he wept and prayed and I never did, because it thrills me every time I realize I am already one up on so many, so many. And so many yet to come.

Why should you look at me with such disgust? I often blow my nose this way. Like they say. What begins with hilarity must be expelled with sorrow. As going uphill I play it for belly laughs. As going downhill I weepers creepers. You never knew I could run you ragged with such a ringading of a gamut, did you? If I may fill you in above the din. As combine I must with your chemic climaxes to combust. If my shameless tending is to catch you bending. And kick you babbit as if you were my worst habit. Before I cry you mercy, kind sir. Have at me not with your lippy sword, my liege lord. I mean you no ill. I am a crowing child still. A real irrelevant rat who loves to say scat to all your clawed and purring logicals. As I rumble so loud to eliminate the mortified farts and shambles of my shames. I can fling you no filth any funnier than my own feces. I am far fonder of my balls than my brains. I am the cagiest beast who knows the least. I am the latest black-tongued bleeder. I am the jew agitator of my day. I am diddle-diddle dumpling, as I hope to swan, I went to bed with my smutty ducks and sockings on. I am my younger self arrogantly saying to my older, you may now go and fug yourself.

As if that were all. As if that settled that. As they say unto this very day. If you show wonder, you are likely to whistle. Whew. My word. Fancy meeting you in this flophouse. Where oh, no, please, not you again. Where really what rotten luck to remain so skin-deep stuck. Where surely you realize your chocolaty running matter to dare all and bare all is scarcely the yum-yum stuff for a dry old stick like me whose cool and classical sex, a cloaked figure of speech carved like marble out of the grave morbidity of my own proud flesh, is much too refined to be your valentine at its most vulgar, freely to inmix with your obscene halloween tricks, and bend way over backwards to cuddle to meet your cocksy and romantical challenge to trick or treat. Where honestly, if the truth is the best swindle, it slyly constrains me to confess that the inalienable prig is still the most perdurable and pastest part of me. Where naturally it follows that my forced howdy-do to the more fashionable likes of you is as buttery as my fluttery heart is blue. Where gosh yes I am ever fearful you will give me another earful. Where what in hell can be worst where after you I come first. Where jesus, just so you can shoot your works, you goes and jerks open your whole flyful of fatuous amorality smack in my easily appalled of what is laughingly called my chaste and noble kisser. Where awright aweready, since you must show me that you too can be one of the boys. How is your every little thing?

Where so help me. I never saw anything so excitable. Where certainly even the most soulful old stud will say it is no sin to be sizable. Where as your cheeks grow red as cherries as you plays with your twig and berries, your paling reason goes to grass on the senatorial side of your ass. Where this ancient jazz of jacking off is simply to pull the usual rock. Where eek the once shrinking and secretive life of cock is stiffening, is beginning to stick out all over every open bit of space. Where christ you feel so stupid if you still show shock. Where thunderation who knows what can be afoot when the phutzing fovea of our eyes are joined at precisely this fixation. Where foo. Where whole new ages of wilder action are warmly in motion only for you. Where more tumbly than humbly you try to queer my prat falls of my faith in fear, if not in actual trembling, and crab all my cloud swings of contemplation for me without ever liberating my lips, or what pains me much more, without even once begging my parsnips.

In such gay dog glee at getting a rise out of me. With your famous first words which are strictly for the birds. With your bolder way of navigating your ballsier body through the sperm-shooting rapids, and yet another spurt, and what is it but sheer rhetoric to sea change from showboat to sedimental squirt, and the raven and voluptuous rivers of the night, with what masturbating quiverations of fun in flight from syn to tax, it is always milking time when the mind and the hand are one, to reach this steeper acclivity of an insight with its sunny oncoming commas, as in the slip-slap waters of your swing-swang odyssey you snooze, that the young soul, if it resembles anything, is showy much like a shallop on a shakedown cruise. With your smile damn you smile. You sure said it that time, kid. With your additional plumper plum to be of good cheer, you scum, the worst is yet to come. With your come to think of it, your blacker plodding knowledge of how great day of reckoning is your need to deep squeeze your bigger selfisher butt of nothing but self, self, self, into the perilous, the wind-blown perch with me, until like I was your last heave offering, you shove me off the continental shelf.

Until two falls out of three will make the weakest one the winner. The loser where he lies in his clock calm can hear his bed ticking. His killing time is still his best blood sport. I see I must prevail on my own mother to pin me to her star-spangled cushion. I already hate the prick pain it brings. Why should dreams alone be sure things? It is singular how often the crud in me craves after a good bodily image. In the sense of being clear, it is becoming very plain. If I can smell my own dog sweat, I must be arf mad and arf insane. The beauty part of it is, I am beginning to feel sure, since I am a fool already, I can certainly afford to be positive, that my destined direction is simply the one I take. So why should I worry then, why should I care at which infernal fork of the future I shall crack up and be stripped bare, since the sheepish live only to be shorn, when it was in some vast bloody angle of the past that I first blundered and allowed myself to be born? If my crazy conjugations are as old as grammar, then perish the thought, but I often wonder how many other migrant pickers of unripe conjunctions and hollow parts of speech have had to hark, hark, to such a question mark.

I suspect that if to lapse is to sink, then to mill is to move in a circle. I suddenly see that woe is me can never be more than three little words. I have a very strong feeling that false knowledge is what a man calls himself. I suppose there was a time when my toes too were right down there at the end of my feet. I hate to guess how silly I can get. I keep dreaming of the day when I too will become a body snatcher of sense and make time with plumper numbers. I pray I shall always be able to find my way into the vagina easily. And ejaculate with pleasure the full

531

load of my singleness as I come together. And love myself all to pieces just the same.

I deplore it too. But what more can lip work do? Where for a faint heart as fine and a babble mind as broad as mine, where midst the current erections and inflections of the carnal word in this gritty ass-to-ass city, will I ever scare up by sumptuous sunup the most rousing and proper housing? Catch me asking who. You must be clowning. You who are always so quick to fulminate. The people, no. The people, never. With their sniveling nit-scratching philosophy of shrug and search me. With their chanting cant of poor me, poor everybody. With their volatile ribs as beaded as their vociferous bones are bent. With their wetter dreams and unrealer lays until the pukes and blueballs of complete frustration come to stay. With their groveling gratitude for the super-duper boon of mere elbowroom. With their pigheaded trust in the mass mind principle of my pet and petty opinion of first or bust. With their god alone is the only answer. With their lust for education to level the nation. With their quite contrary strut of their but and but. As they rush in to say in their underhanded way. There will always be womb for one more.

Where thy will to live or die be done. Where once you evolved as a man, you must crawl back again if you can. Where from beating around the bush too much, the sorriest of your puns are pinkened by your own particular gore. Where notice it the next time. When the madrigal whiteness of mother wit sight reads what sang in the blood before the flood, the aborning boy smiles with joy in the matriarchal keep of his mockingbird sleep. No doubt when more light appears, this too will vanish. And with your most piercing eye you will see that all truth is shadow except the last truth. And you will sit tight and listen. And when the imponderable silence harrows the inarticulate heart, you will actually hear it happen. And your skeletal thinking spells will be vastly amended and invested with flesh. And from the vantage point of your sessile position, which means not free to move about, your flagging brain will rally to whoop it up, and you will again be seized with ideas like quick little winks of blood.

What other hope or delight remains? What great bounding hound of heavenly sense will chase hence this heathen foxy grandpa night? What chick-chick wit will sway the hawk-headed god of day? What is this creature man anyway with his potential divinity and charm when he consents merely to be the bearer of the copulating arm? What scarlet sunday sins can illumine a woman when she inserts the plain weekday prick of mundane pins into her mouth? What hush-hush nudities of hale titty and tail do blind men fail to see that they are never known to blush? Who in his own gangland of sex is the last to be a seizer? Why is why the word of wonder? Who commands the quailing to challenge their own matchless dream images while being mirrored and misled?

Surely it is they, they who say, if you dread naught, you will fear nothing. The cluck clucks. They say, if you had your life to live over again, you would simply turn chicken. They say, if at first you only see what they can see, then you must look, look again. Though at what they wot not. They say there are just as many fools among the insane as among the sane. Since the worldly-wise are all eyes, having been to bedlam and back. They say that soon some mere mortal man will be the next skipper of the big dipper. They say, they are ready to match your ha-ha with their hee-haw any time. They say when a seed of thought is beaten this small, it will inevitably bug us. If they lie, call them horse, spit in their eye. They say we must cup and leech the disease of dying as if it were a simple fever, or some form of disorderly conduct.

How odd that I should love to use the word like a switch. The more serious I get, the sooner I sicken. I pale when I realize that immortality is a conception loaned to me for my lifetime only. Through my portal veins I fear the bubble of my I is bobbing along with the rest of my red stuff until brimming with spleen it lights into my liver and bursts just to play host to the abstract capillaries of who knows whose ghost. My breath must come quickly, quickly, while me and my beloved body can still do the bunny hug. My first legs transfers to my last that faint weak pleasure to be free. My rump is ruminating the rudiments of wrinkling. My heart's alarm is exquisitely set to dingdong, red rover, red rover, the witching second my worries are over. My primary piss hisses to be subsumed with my prostate pains. My longiloquent crush on life afflicts my lingual musckles. My fickles of flickers are flying south without me. Whose butcher's dog will lick up my blood and brains? I say, if God is death, then I bow down to him, I believe in him.

Tears, idle tears, who knows what they mean? My head feels so sore from butting up against. Am I too young as yet to say we have really met? Did I come to grief after forcing belief? As what natal mirage did God last loom large? Was his kingdom long gone before I gaming for it came? Did his luck entirely depend on me being always the joker? What real chance did I ever have to top his hand when the one he dealt me was so sick and without a single stopper? What great heap of faith in his own heaven have I laid up to raise him until he is forced to say, I pass, this is higher than I can go? What the deuce is my jewish denomination anyway that he should draw me to him to make of us the only pair? Can I even hope he will finger me and hesitate before he shuffles my rotten poker face right back into the pack? If the rest is howling darkness, would sharing his singing silence be best? Questions, the queerest questions, it fairly staggers me to think how often I have tried to play for keeps for his forever and ended up with mine. Why is it so humiliating to be ranked with the merely human? Do green little figs dwell more reasonably within his digs? Has he always had a special feeling for knaves and kibitzers? Since when is it a sin to go leaping from him to hymn? I can hear him calling, time, gentlemen, time.

If I say I am feeneeshed, I must mean I am bafoofked. My trumped up future lies face up. My brainy bid for the fat kitty of afterlife had to be a bluff. My home away from home is empty of high honors. My funny country is full of piteous cards. My native land is a nightmare of little numbers. Like my fellow cockeyes like to say, if only I could get my panic-struck eyes unstuck, I would surely count myself among the missing. Sometimes I catch myself wondering. What has no ears but it listens? What is that farfetched sense of fatness in me more familiarly known as my soul? Will it ultimately wane so thin as to make me jump out of my own skin?

Clairvoyant sheeny shitface, if it smells assimilation on me, let it smell its share. Temper, temper. I feel its blain is where my bulla should be. How long now has its bow-wow, or seeing-eye head been buried in the childish blindfold of my catty, my own bristling escapist arms? How I hate them when they say, if once I lose this much of my light, it will be with me perpetual night. Why me? What do they expect me to see? In such a contagious daze themselves from so raptly worshipping the very ground they walk on, bent double like the funniest static birds over their broken basic blendwords, striving with their faint shrill sounds to arrive at god by spelling dog backwards, cheep-cheeping for that one sucker to come who sees so straight that he must shoulder the whole burden for them and theirs, spiritually speaking, they seem to be begging me to throw my gaze in a great arc upwards. Yet they say I must live as if by the side of the grave and looking in. Horrors. The view from their end of it must really be something.

They say. What do they say? Let them say it. They say that as a breaker of imaginary cherries, I must leave no virginals intact. I can go blow, they know. They say if I am in a fool phase as I am now, then for shame, I shall be a fool in everything. They say, a fat lot they care, if hap-happiness is hardly job, mimitating me as if I were a horse with the staggers, or any kid with the gid, that if I hang on as I do to the higher things through hearsay only, which continually do tickle me as they slip in one ear and out the other, that if like a stiff my boundless scanning of the storied uses of suspended animation has me bushed, that if like a jerk I can barely remember in this oddball befuddlement of mine when it was I first receded and became so quaintly divided from what solider citizens call real work, then rats, like they say, it definitely behooves me to get a move on.

As it certainly doth, as to prank up my baser, my bummer body somehow, with the lavish truth to tell, with the usual muck, with tut-tut, with caftans of softer grace engirdling, with extrasolar calicos, with shore clothes of whitest dazzling hopes, with scarfskins of a silkier consolation, with the rosiest risibles, among other impossibles, with chrisms of a more consecrated thick of things, with zut alors, with mixed blessings on its rarefied pst, until it ist as thistly and lumpen as once it wast, let it become a monster to too many, not to speak of the rest of youse guys, and circumnavigate, like they rarely ever sigh, the coxcomical self-sufficient cutie-pie with a corresponding slobber of my own kisses, since I am not up to snuff, and staking my all on the grand mystique that it is always greener elsewhere, if not otherwise, flip for its final resting place in the unpeopled roves and reaches of my lands, here we go again, of way out there in outer space. But one little room can be an anywhere. Anywhere, anywhere at all, just so I can. Say as they say.

O knock it off. Knock it off already. Softly, softly now, while I stretch. While you kvetch, why should the pleasure be all yours, it must be epochs since I felt your qualm little fingerer questing mine,

how many great frosts and fizzles ago was it when you first came to me
and you said, while you remain the selfsame where my spitty hex on
you hawks the spot, I the richer I must do the camel bit, being free,
white and fumpty-one, and try to pass through the purblind eye of
your O to be by my own blithering passion transcended. Or was it
merely upended? Surely there was a snare in there somewhere. Ah, so.
If again we are stumped, let us now enquire what I mean when I
invoke.

O my soul at large. So daft named and oft blamed. Blasted out of
your wits by your own depth charge. Be careful I beg you. Be careful
especially at night. For as I still love you the most, next to myself, I
must here and now tell you. Your crux of morning cometh, the crowing watchman said. Your vast retch of rage to upstage me is abating
fast. Your floodmark is becoming faint. Your sour grape she is ripen-
ing. The darling worm of doubt is dossing under thee. The orphaned
stink of your inorganic single-think shall never come to papa, come to
papa, do. For this is the sickener and the gall. This is what will slay
you by slowest ifs and inches. If you continue to flout the fertile
exfoliations and famishments, the ebullient affrontage, which bees
only to abut, the mightier earshots and misses, the red errings, the
posh gosh, the whole swelegant flagrance and froward march of my
surface factuality, though you never knew it had so fierce and fash a
foofer, if in your finking and fibstering you would continue to, then
your much more flamboyant paraph with which, as spencerian soul,
you first signed youself in, as idioblast it, you simply had to try to cell
yourself dear, your still more crybabyish, so to shriek, your superior,
your fata morgana of a forbidding interior, so fathomless in great
straits, shall alleluia, shall go snail pale and poop out.

Whilst blandly stuffocating in thine own bare ugh. Whilst leave us
face it. If in your blackest hold on me, which is always where your
bum steerage is likely to brig me, you still dare to deem yourself my
sole and dearest shipmate on this torrid wanderweek of mine through
the tropical sargassum of warm and warmer guesses, if in my clausal
mania for symbol seeding you can weed me right, on this telltale,
tear-ass trip to the shilly-shally shores of more's the pity and woe
betide me land, on this plunderous voyage through the sobbing and
pellmell seas of sublunary pain, if one can take such shallow slop for
true sounding, through hoo the hithermost moral reefs of concres-

cence with the stony sufferings of those long bone dead, a real bitch of a jaunt which only my jocular balls and oracular blood can make, so belay me, if you bewail me still, wisp of my will, bosun of my heaving bosom, I shall lower the boom on you, and declare you to be a stowaway.

With socko with what sky-high kicks. With right away renascent and rompish and once more rapture rent with heys and rays for me first. As really rot me if not. As snotwithstanding your constant weeps of snide and self-conscious schnorring, my fairly soothfast daily round of whirling world is still a shindig, my pure as pitiless second hand sweeps. As swishful thinking seems summarily to be scything mine early grasping grasses from thine ancient silty bottoms of land sakes in such great in groundlessness in last-gasp gleams from suicidal dreams. As alas and alack, as one of us sooner sighs, one of us may never come back. As say. As in sudden revelation I realize that iffen I wishes to see myself as something indubitably separate and distinct from this whole droll foo on you, what a surmise, I have only to appear upon this here mini-stage in the converging spotlight of me own two eyes. Een and just as one lighted lamp does not require another lamp in order to be see, saw, seeing, seen.

Gee, what a break for me. See how the second vertebra of my own neck serves as a pivot for my own head to turn upon. As apart from being cracked one more crap artist comes full circle. As your every little movement is becoming more and more my own. Thou whitest lie which ever whopped. What in the world am I swaying? Can you still say I am, I am, there is none besides me? How come you came so fast to froth? Did you ever know such a joe glow? I can see in your cavernous holes for eyes, it is highly unlikely. As the fitting end you fear is near. Who cares if you sleeve me now? I always knew I had the brighter face. As when I think, what heartsbalm, what throatease, what a world-wide mitzvah it will be. When I sink down into my one and only death, I shall drag you right along with mi, mi, whilst misericording with one last lyric in me lifting, rifting, to give you alone the mercy stroke. As wuxtra. As only I shall rise to my own surprise. As get ready, get set, go I. As rouse mit de body from de bed. Out of my way, boychickul. Here comes nothing.

As hare, hare, now. You said it, bub. As thus with what similar signs of nonplus which are as parlously punning in us hart we so

537

hoppy to go hippety with the hugeous rabbit of hubris in him into this breath-taking bonanza of another bright and stunny day, as if hey, this very house itself had said, have one on us, after what to our glowing horror, had begun to loom more and more like the world's last night. For plainly it is only by impitating him like so can it be shown how intimately he has implicated some immoral minority in the subjectivism of his cyclical impulsions and magnifique impediments.

Seems such a sorry sop now that his doubtful betters are invariably the quicker giggle getters. If he has finally merged into himself, he can only ask, where have you been all your life? Whether it be your weakest momentary worry how unwonted and unwanted his will he or wont he might be. Or your own faintest fiat fifing. Or your simplest yea-saying or neigh. Or your meanest fain to fling and funk the whole thing. Or your slightest moue at his always dafter morning after. Or your slowest burn at this wiseguy way he makes his turn. And yet everything, but everything. Even the tiniest prick of coloring, tattoo takes time. Why bust a blood vessel staring so when you damn well know it does? Even your byplay to boff me one with the back of your brain, that too is an elapse, as christian a way as any of committing history together in this hear, hear, in this jesuitic and vengeful diaspora of darksome jew ideas in the newly whorled of blue-eyed america.

Where low, as joe. If that be possible. Where in toto if the truth till now be told, even that buddy boy, that latest hallucinated original, that incorrigible incrassated incubus, that do tell swell, that lexical lecher illogicaling with every illiterate nodding noodle, that most mazing minute man of ever more revolutionary alarums and radiations has, exactly like us, as often heard a much simpler and earlier bird, which is to say himself, say at least as much. So all right. So tell me. So where is progress where? So what the heck then is man at his very highest when the more dashing he comes, the sooner is he dashed?

Esk, esk. How else will you learn you already know everything? So ow. So what then, sez he, and gives me a good zets, could be crueler or more self-defeating than this, that precisely where he would feel a private itch to philosophize, whether at half-asleep with such a mammoth of a word or soundly at stool, he would find himself scratching a perfect mock-up of a public fool? You may go humph if you like. But

538

really. It was just as if. Between you and me and baby makes three. How blushing kid? How bloody behind? How baa-baa backward can you get? It was as if as yet he could feel he had only made wet.

As clocked at a smile a minute, and how would you like my fist in your face for breakfast, the exploring pit man, old pro joe, super at summary while sunk in resumption, the wildest harker barker yet, he yawned abyssal more, with tongue of tantivy, tantara, his throttle thranged with as many eftsoons of solecisms as egads, proliferating vernal booboos from a single lame brain as branch, and stretched out his entire remaining life on earth even as a bet, since his biz as a born gambler being to go, man, go where the action is, you were there schmecking around, you saw it, as milksop as any for blood money, as all out for a flutter, at this most chancy chime of his strife, he favored heads over tails, flipping for fringe benefits, and tallis all, all as yet, regardless of how religiously he reran his one-reeler, with that awful sinking feeling, hey, mister, your flyday is open, which jeered him no end, because it meant as he saw that he still had a future to face this whole livelong, singsong night, movering so unduly with his filthy pelf of self from flashy shadow shows of indecent exposure to splashier ones yet of the nakedest immersion, as all your moralizing innards take a similar churn, until so saying, he simply aspersed, he sicked his own soul, he shuffled out of his solomon's seal, and became the world, as poles apart, as perfectly pitched, with parallel orotundity, turning on the waterworks, inter alia, christening his miracle-minded ex-body, rub-a-dubbing his aladdin, frogkicking himself in his own ass, as he strove to breast his tempest thinkalings and smatterings of with cold conjunctive ands, as gauche with sturm as with drang, struguggling to cross his rubicon, or any other allegorical shiver by the same name, as anomalous in his snagtime as any swirlfool afore him, to shoot himself at least some such rapids, to take at last, like a triumphant infant, his first, his one irrevocable and decisive step, before what, what was too late, only to find himself bolt awake, as bogged down and bereft, as eh-eh on the brink, as bare and beached as ever seemingly.

While you are still so far off aloft. You are so brave sitting idle. So righteously unable to see what all this has tortoise. As if you never knew that it is mental cowardice to chase rabbits, meaning ideas, unless you are prepared to shed blood. Your false pride as thick as your feudal hide. As if living it up a little has little to do with looking a tittle

539

or two inward. As if in shrinking your attention span you were out to prove you were the perfect putz. As if you merrily subscribed to the lie there was nothing more to you than meets the I. As if all the heart you had was something slimy you wore on your sleeve. As if in its deepest plot your own penis had never been tied into a fancy knot. As if, my god, ever since we got pigged in together here, you have done all you can to queer the pitch, and blink at this bigger thing in the offing, just as anything with an eyelid can easily eclipse the sun with a wink, as if with your whole being you were pledged to deny the crowning, the consummate drama your own caramba and incredulous head contains.

For the lowlier characters clobbering time does come oftener. O what lust for ingloria in excess of excelsis. Tim-tom. Are you still as timid as I am to go all out? Are you always this puzzled as when to scab and when to strike? Are you as loth to be as lachrymal as our lugubrious lies when they lapse? How about them bastards with their better luck next time? I thinks I hears a rather bitter titter there. Is this still your so-so phase when the simplest truth has such touching trouble sinking in? Are you aching all over to give it a good scratch? Are you simply looking for to cool it? With what other slight delights do you shorten your nights? You most solemnly swear? Are there really as many fools as there are people? Imagine how long the world has been waiting for such a whopper. And then there was the ocean. That too was once between us.

So that you must still ask. Was there ever such sly circularity of dog in the whole of this animal kingdumb? As from was to is there, bubba? Is there hope for us after all? After all, after all is said and done, whether insensibly short shrifted or shot through with fun, we did do what we did, fending off the passage of time with paper spears, sorcering our sumless space fears with stuttering feets, coercing our cataracting eyes until the very lenses fogged and failed us, because rue it or not, if we want to make it big these days, we must show no pity in this stuck-up city, according to the law on the availability of victims, as you retched to void me in vain, we snuck in some beefier revelatory bits, we tried to touch bottom to betray less bull, so as not to louse it up, we searched only in the seams of intimation where we could always start from scratch, and bloody well know it, we joshed joiners, we jumped the tracks of mob movements, we kept doodling with damnation, we took us a flyer, squirreling with a will after the slightest fulguration of the truth wherever it did flit in the forbidden branches of the brain where seeing is not always believing.

How about you? Is the story of your life a rushed job too? Is your late-blooming breath, as mine, much too short as yet to laud the long essential swing of things, too impotent to insufflate the main chance instead of its subsidiary happenstance? Was that you mumbling that peg? You mind sneezing that again? As upon your own word, are you as peculiarly crippled by precisely the similar syndrome of half-saying? If the less said the better, shit, man, why bother saying anything? Schooled so soon and strangled as we are by the cocksy strictures and stink-lists of the stupid ass, why guess who if you already feel blue? If these are other days, listen to who says, where then are the other ways of breaking through the bombast of older blood groups with the business end of the mind, to congenial cries of keep that pecker up, of irradiating the surface of the black unlettered lie with the most burning words until the less illiterate truth underneath looms a bit more luminous?

Ah, the passion with which. The pity of it is. Must the voice at the end always go so high up? Oh, but that it must. As if the great new noise now is simply to sound sick. Whereas once it was laughing last. How inevitable that the asker in his asking should indelicately ask. If we dared to take the time, what on earth did you take? If we really pulled it off, should we put it there, kid? Certainly, said we to us. A word like a hand reaches out, followed by a word again. See, see what a long, long sentence we have just served. Was it only for us the world was waiting? Woe unto us. Where are all the glad hands? What will it avail us if we exult too much? If such colossal conceit is hard to beat. Leave us then begin to let us. Lest no one will be left to listen. Let us pray that we may. Let us conclude in the proper mood. Let us make our peace in the lowest places. Like the higher animals. Let us walk the last mile with a smile. Let us only say, it was a weak, it was only a wobbly little wand we had, but we gave it a whirl anyway. In the name of Joe the father, and of Joe the son, and of Joe the holy most, amen.

"I tried," said Mrs. Bellinson. "I was so worried. I came in five times to see if you were still breathing."

"Wow," said Joe. "You don't happen to have an extra head on you, do you?"

541

"But I didn't have the heart to push. Careful. You'll knock the milk over."

"I tell you," said Joe. "It's dangerous. The next time you catch me going to bed, slap me, you just give me a kick where it'll do the most good."

"I was surprised. Abe was like a mouse. Even Helen said, quiet, please."

"Quiet," said Joe. "Is there really such a country somewhere? I thought I was such a hotshot. I thought I was going places, but all I did, I guess, was flop down in one spot, and let myself be carried away until I overslept. I'm still rubbing my eyes. Nice to be such a night animal, isn't it? On which side of me is my one and only right hand? Is my broken back where I left it? Do I need a tool for this? You look kind of real. Tell me."

"No, no, the juice first."

"Ah, yes," said Joe. "Of course. The juice first. A wandering rock all over again. Okay, now. Drink up you old sleepyhead."

"Slowly, slowly."

"Hooray," said Joe. "I didn't swallow the wrong way."

"No," said Mrs. Bellinson. "But your hair is standing up."

"It figures. It always does when I forget to sprinkle it a little. Well, now. So this is the land of the living. And you I suppose are the queen of the day."

"Funny. I am always smelling smoke lately. Eat, eat. You are late enough already."

"Why, it's Mrs. Bellinson, as I live and breathe. Is that really my Mamma there?"

"Ah," said Mrs. Bellinson. "If you had another one, believe me, I would quick, I would run and call her."

"Absolutely," said Joe. "I would too. If you still have legs, use them, I say. Run."

"If there were two of us, maybe you would listen."

"Oh, there's no maybe about it. It would be a cinch. I understand that two can say as little as one. Make it two eggs this time. And two pieces of toast. You mind if I hang around awhile? Somebody here is very clever this morning."

"All night I was thinking."

"Oh, boy. It's getting to be a real disease, isn't it?"

"Farina one day, oatmeal the next. That I should have such a brain that I never get mixed up. I shake every time I think of it. All my life I prayed I should become so perfect and good."

"And me," said Joe. "I always have to taste first to see if I put in sugar."

"I've been thinking. If I clean the bathroom tile today too, and tear up your old pajamas for rags, you think I should ask for a raise?"

"Of course," said Joe. "What have you got to lose? Is it too late to make it scrambled? Christ, I bet I was a million times happier when I played with pots and pans. Sweet pickles. Now how did that pop into my head? Bring out the green peppers, Ma, I must be pregnant. Is there any of that old pumpernickel left in the house? Did you happen to bake anything with poppy seeds? How about parting with some of that precious plum jam? How would you know it was me if I didn't make you nervous? No kidding. I must begin to stuff myself. I must get fat as quick as I can. Otherwise. Just think. If I already feel so guilty, what will I be able to put in my mouth next week?"

"My dear son."

"Speaking."

"If you want to live by bread alone, I will do all I can to help you."

"Why, you sonofagun."

"You know my sickness. I am always looking for something to do."

"It's no use," said Joe. "There are some people you have to kill right off. They're just too damn smart to live."

"I can't remember. When is the last time I slapped you?"

"But my dear woman," said Joe. "You must understand. I'm just not used to a servant speaking to me this way."

"In America?" said Mrs. Bellinson. "Wake up, Joseph. I am afraid you missed the revolution."

"God, yes. Among many other things."

"Believe me," said Mrs. Bellinson. "If I were young again, I would say. Today the kitchen. Tomorrow the world."

"You would what?" said Joe.

"Not my hand, please. It is too early for me to dance."

"Whoa, now. Wait a second. I've got to figure out this new development."

"That's all right," said Mrs. Bellinson. "Take your time. Passover is late this year too."

"Passover," said Joe. "Ah, so that's it. Now I'm beginning to get the idea. Ah, macushla, macushla. Maybe I'll reach Manhattan again. But I know now. I'll never set foot in the promised land."

"Yes," said Mrs. Bellinson. "I can see. It's going to be a long hard winter."

"And the pity of it is I have such beautiful straight toes."

"I wonder what it is," said Mrs. Bellinson. "Do I like headaches so much? Why do I fix my hair so tight? What's the use? I know my old pins are falling out of me. But when I'm with you, I can never hear them drop."

"There you are," said Joe. "That's life for you. Break. Let's have a smoke. I always forget. You don't smoke yet, do you?"

"No," said Mrs. Bellinson. "I'm afraid."

"Really?" said Joe. "Why?"

"Well," said Mrs. Bellinson. "I know if I smoked, the next thing I would begin to drink beer."

"Right," said Joe. "Of course. And that would lead to painting your lips. And before you know it, you'd be playing poker with the girls. And then, god knows. I understand. You don't have to say any more."

"I wasn't going to."

"Ah, Mamma, Mamma. You think you'll ever amount to anything? What's going to happen to you?"

"If you'll look, you'll see. It already has. Here. Wipe your mouth. Remember. You have to go out in the world."

"Where were you when I was born? Didn't you have any pull? How did you get to be my mother anyway?"

"It was dark. I had the wrong ticket. My hands were like ice."

"Fumbled the ball again, didn't you?"

"And my lips cracked. And my nose running. And such knots in my hair. I was surprised. You know how afraid I am of cats. The doctor said, quick, clean him out like a herring, cut him in half like a candle, kill him, kill him. I was so disgusted with myself. I dropped another stitch. They say for a boy it must be blue. I wanted to scratch your eyes out, but I couldn't even give you a good pinch. I tried. But I didn't know how to get rid of you."

"And damn me. I suppose. I was just too damn weak to help, wasn't I?"

" No, " said Mrs. Bellinson. "Not weak. Stupid. You hardly had your eyes open and you were already smiling like an idiot."

"Yep," said Joe. "That's me all over, all right. Hey. If that clock is telling the truth, then I'm really in trouble."

"I woke up feeling sorry for myself," said Mrs. Bellinson. "Now I know why."

"Ah," said Joe. "Just the person I've been looking for. How's the old pocketbook today? You think maybe you can spare me a nickel for fare?"

"And I thought he was going to pay me for overtime. I can see I have to look. But I hope I don't find."

"Jesus," said Joe. "What riches. Give, my dear. And be happy you can give."

"Take, take. Five, ten. I feel lighter already."

"That's the stuff. Go for broke. Make it fifteen."

"Maybe it's my glasses," said Mrs. Bellinson. "But lately. Believe me. It really hurts me to look at you."

"Yow," said Joe. "That's the blackest one yet."

"Yes," said Mrs. Bellinson. "I know. But what can I do? I see so few people. I have to hate someone."

"Oh, absolutely. How could you live otherwise?"

"Usually it's me. But today you have the honor."

"Ah," said Joe. "Thank god. A success at last."

"I know I don't look it. But don't worry. I can be very useful sometimes."

"Madam," said Joe. "You just said a mouthful."

"So all right. So I said. So if you want, I'll even shake hands with you."

"That's the stuff," said Joe. "I knew you were a good sport."

"Flypaper. I can't get rid of him."

"Okay, now?" said Joe. "Are you all set? Would you like me to buy you a plot of ground in Herald Square? Should I give your regards to Broadway?"

"Give, give. Only go. Do me a favor and go already."

"Aw," said Joe. "I bet you say that to all your children."

"Please," said Mrs. Bellinson. "Go in good health. And come in good health. Only please. Don't bother me."

"Wonderful," said Joe. "I knew you'd come through. Now that I have your blessing, that's all I've been waiting for. I must say. My stiff upper lip seems to be working fine these days. The things that bother me. Ah, well. Another day, another inch. I don't know why, but I have a feeling I finished second. What is it between you and these same four walls? It really shakes me up. When are you going to break down and smash up everything? Ah, believe me, Ma, I would kiss your hand. But I guess my nerves are shot. I just can't judge distance lately. Otherwise, my dear. Remember now. If there's anything else I can do to make your life a real hell for you, for godsakes, give me a ring, you have my number. And I'll be back in a flash, without the cash. Oh, boy. Did you hear that one? I sure do slay myself, don't I? So there's absolutely no hope for you. So what? I'm still your boy. So why worry? If I keep saying it, I must mean it. I'll always be good for a few laughs."

Such as, since it is invariably darkest before the yawn, sure sign of the elemental mind in a state of lapse as it sallies forth to size itself up with its first lisping letters, as sensing it is time to cut the crap, it starts with running scared, the subject of its own sarcasm, as taking the smallest view of himself, he breaks out into the open air, boldly flying from the truth, as one who lives back to back with himself can never hope to see his own face, as a fact, with no sense as yet of zooming in on anything, as assailed by sun and emblazoned by light, he begins to sing, bye bye blackbird, have you any wool, as classically as he could in his cracking voice, always happiest when highest pitched, as if he were raising his own siege, as if he were resuming his own particular lifetime, his syncopating eke at an all-time peak, his pristine arms swinging by his sides, playing it cool.

15.

How is that for stuff and things? Did you ever really think that he? Who in this flip, this far-out, fun city could have so figured? What other hophead in the highest could have thus? Until he kind of out-fussed us? As the planet-stricken in their puppyhood are inclined to become overly pituitous. What are you hiding on your hip there? Who in his implausible entirety could possibly enjoin us from an interjection as clearly abirritant as it is anonymous? Since you seem to be drawn up so stiffly. What are his haps without the addition of our hazards? Who among the angelic orders would hear us if we cried? Beat it, brother, you bother me. To rough and rack him up as we romp a bit here to close up our ranks. To beat him to the light. To take him by his by and large. To perish some such gruesome thought as with a visible wibble we try to re-enter a world which wails as it wobbles. How strange it seems how soon the best of us becomes a facinorous worry-wart, or worse, a great stone face. The funny thing was the sky could not be bluer.

How is that for rooting in the old belly button? Whatever else. This you must believe us. You will never get with it if you keep griping. If one day you are jumpy and the next jaded, you will always be wondering what on earth gives here anyway unless you can grasp the clear sunny necessity for one human being to relate, and then equate, his absolute helplessness with the utter hopelessness of another. Yes, yes, we know. There are times when it gets so tough. And blowing your reddened nose is your last resource. And so often you feel just like you were about to be put to bed with a shovel. What then do you have to lose if you relax and take this tiny little breather with us? Until your mystical why matches our multiple wherefore. Speaking in terms of blood. For how else can we baby ourselves along until we balance him out? With look. With this heir apparent ad-lib bib on us. For in the fewest possible words.

Who cares which birds are flying in thirds? Such paleface hung-ups, such tuckered out trumbiniks like us rarely give a hoot in our own ripe world of rot what, subjacent in his borough, a freshly subverted feeb of a heeb may see fit to wonder. Since it is redskin plain that any rhapsodic punk may be in the pink as far as his few unisons and universals go. As what contingent milky way can that common white cat be lapping? Or what precisely is that with a whole rosebush for a hat?

Seems like we are swinging in that area where the simpering vision slights the many as it slanders the more. As the king is just as alack in his county of sassing back. Are you looking where you should? What can those twelve satirical sea gulls be so eloquently skywriting? Since you seem to be asking, let us put you wise for once. For a coastal spew of a sly sophisticated jew, he sure is turning out to be a real feeble kind of ecumenical cluck. Of course. You would never say unless you were shocked. What an insulting in-joke to be sent so free franking. But look at it this way.

Maybe it was that old serpent in us which made us feel so mean, if not murderous in the morning. But imagine. Just when we thought, well, now, here is another fairly insignificant first generation who gives every indication, as he should, of being a complete all-american bust, since he is so schwartz in his scattered and stigmatized numbers that we would hardly expect him to punch his way out of that crumpled paper bag commonly known as history, with its constant ho-hum, and occasional ha, and so timeworn and minority-minded in his shiny traditionals that we are quickly irked, if not considerably pissed off, any time he fails to subscribe to every single crooked letter of that same old megillah of grampus gloom as god-imbedded as its grief is man-made gitchy, we are frankly appalled to find instead that he can barely cover the five short blocks on Winthrop to Sutter in his bilingual Brooklyn by the sea, speaking semi-ghetto-wise, without switching himself on until he is largely aglow with a sort of quasi-gentile elation, without, you guessed it, committing joy just like a goy.

To which we must say. Guessed it, my foot. Who among the most sub and jective of us is so situated above this world that he can circle it with such a fine un and sympatico flourish? We at least. We do know, we are like the barber pole turns, as its peppermint stripes, like our pet second-best thoughts, gaily whirl away, and just where they will snake up again, nobody knows. Surely you can see how lightly he steps over this uncurbed dog grunt.

If the truth is indeed the radiance of reality. Is your own failure to follow in his footsteeps as fire-new funny? Is your polar position in relation to his prime meridian as politesse as it is pointful? If we can believe you are still listening to us in your great rush. If in your vast impatience to shake the him out of us, you can only come out with something like suffering cats, or even shitcakes, we must ask you, where then is thine own ravishing self to which you refuse to be true? Somehow we can all sense that, when we are young, we can afford to do anything, even to grow wise and old. Seems like we can always hear the universal rumble of the elevated train coming on. As quickly now. As he began to sprint to make it. If speed after him we must, what can we possibly say, since to play it altogether dumb is to play a coward's part, that would place him in a better light? Perhaps only this. Since he was not a dog, which he almost was not, he did not expect to have his day.

Or what in the whole of his going to work in x number of wanderyears of his geocentrical lifetime he had never been able to grab on that slovenly mobbed rattlebox, that abusive dim-bulbed stinkpot, that rollicking reptile of a train on the New Lots Avenue line, in fine, though not very, that holy grail tripe of thing which the least refined and asinine riders, as worldly-wise as they may be in their shoving and their elbowing, still so simply refer to as a seat. So that if there he is again smiling in the most unlikely places, it is only because he is so pleased to see that from the beginning of time, and for this trip only, that one strap left was destined to be his.

Somehow as always it was the shyest seeing time for his compunctious and commiserating christ-alikes. His distinctive germinating ears grew unto this side of gruesome in this decided gehenna. At each station of his cross, he was forced into a state of bumpery with so many backs and fronts. At times he felt he was drinking in the dregs of his own head. He could see his heart work was already cut out for him. And god knows what else to boot until his bobtailed butt was buried with all the other fagged and bitter ends.

Wiseguy of the world, what are you saying? Is this then the way to take root, eyeball to bloodshot eyeball, confronting your own future flaws as reflected in the schizophrenic glass, coagulating with this whole diddled row of defunct fearers, combusting with their luciferous orbs and browned-off coalitional bubs, swaying ever nearer mouth to mouth to resuscitate of them sub people their miffed flab and mooning fluts, immissing on their stalest bogs and illucid uplifteries, stiffening in the stand-up socks of seldom bathers, cobotching their basic job of bitching, remarking sadly the characteristic way each cringing shoe creases, singling out the least luckless unbelievers to alight upon, scratching with mythical valor in the nearest mortal crotch?

It seemed as if the oversoul, stripped down to its synthetic underpants, were sotto saying, you unilateral ass, and softer yet, what the fuck is the matter with you anyway, getting yourself sucked into such a tight spot of shadowy rot, if you are already absolute reality itself, what possessed you to poke your perfectly realized nose into this roiled human mess, as peace unto yourself personified, why should you go so red to your roots as if you were suffering from a suppression of irresistible run-ins with these pale recessed punks, try to remember, when were you last asked to move over for the nonce if not for evermore, my dear, why are you hollering in my horrendous here, how can you hail me only to fail me by thinking only of sinking right through the floor?

As all the while the fastidious rubberneck was feinting himself into all sorts of gorgeous subliminal knots, his sleeper exterior ears could clearly hear one cheap scent say with a giggle to a cheaper, gee, it was so damn dark in that movie there, I sat me right down on a boogie. Only too bloody often, in some coomb of cozier correlated light, like a child's piece of place, where the toy cosmical mind can hopscotch with the whole spectrum of shades to come and clowns to be, a preposterous little pink and party poop of a pussycat comes slinking in to prove how patently she can preempt precious space without possessing a single democratic bone in her body. Of course it is always sad when you can scat only while you scan. But then again, if a boogie is merely another name for a black, it has long been common knowledge that if you want to bring yourself back alive with a bang, you have to begin somewhere.

At which point this suppressed fetch-thing of a train, shrieking as if it had never before enjoyed the excruciating experience of a curve, lurched him right into the receiving end of a stiff positive posterior which definitely said, no parking, please. This of course gave her friend, the other bitter kissing improbability, the terrific chance first, to take her own timely umbrage, and second, to misread his smile which actually said, you are making a great mistake, lady, I wouldn't dream of it even if I could, so that third, she could be witty to the extent of, hey, is he looking for a smack in the mouth, climaxing with a bit less audibly, who does he think he is, your bed-partner or something? Naturally any woman's once dewy mouth would be so devastated if it were as fresh from chewing her mother's widowed arm clear up to the elbow, with strings of the tough matriarchal tendon sticking between her teeth, her twisted lips longing for that one nice clean wipe, the question being, according to this touchy piece of tattletale, whose guilt-stained eyes would survive her mother's disappearing color, what with all those high words about such low things as useless vaginal ointments and infusible suppositories, and clocking the old trout's charming diabetic comas, and compulsive vomiting, and each other's red revenge of interminable sadistic retreats in the theatrical toilet, with their skimmed milks boiling over, and slimy rubber sheets, and chipped bedpans, and thunderous falls in the dead of night.

Otherwise the cool eavesdropper is doing real well. That is to say. How is it he seems to know, as he continues to limp in late with his intermittent comments that people, as they are called, are composed mostly of passion, and that somehow it is just this passion in people which is always taking a turn for the worse? So you hear? So I suddenly developed this great big floater before my eyes. Just like a sea horse. No kidding. Light kills me lately. Rose fever. What a shame. So he said to me, Aunt Fay, look, the fishes are all naked. Similarly if any realist were to hew closer to the scatological truth rather than the

551

spiritual, as he is inclined to do so anyway, he would soon find that the most clockwork kind of chemistry can suffer such a sundering subway change that the mixture becomes so blasted rich it backfires. Who me? You must be off your nut. And such a smell rises.

As the perfectly innocent swain keeps trying not to bump knees with the generally zoftik, the baby grand girl of his dreams. She is bent over swaying, seeming unaware of his many sly glances of a sexy rhythm all his own. Her far-gone eyes are fixed on her goal. She knows she is on a journey. What has her solo life been as yet but a series of dry runs and soft fluffs? Yet her chordal pillars are as firm as round, as umpah as her paps, her supertonic itch at absolute pitch, her golden chromatic hair in good account, her unpainted fore of finger following all the frisky ups and downs of the open score before her, as if treeing the capital animals of all three clefs, as if shaking out a whole tone poem of bare bodkins, finny trebles, mooty points, pastoral lays, embracing dicta, and original keys, as if tracing back in her blood the one symphonic moment when the world was born, as it will die, in the funniest fission of splitting adams, and a final laughing crescendo of eve, and a fiery shower of wildly running figures.

Like I say, the whole thing was insane. Don't tell me about sugar in the blood. The next thing I knew they were painting my lips and tying my two big toes together. No sense kidding myself. In this old pull-over of mine, no one is going to take me for a snappy dresser. Boy, when they grab you by the balls, that's it. How about it, Bobby Boy? Been getting any lately? Look at all those pricks reading Popeye and little Orphan Annie. Man, you can see for yourself. The shit is flying everywhere. But why, Daddy, why? Christ almighty, what can I say? The old malarkey it ain't what it used to be. Sometimes the truth seems to me to be dead only from the neck up. And sometimes both ways. Maybe it is because, as I duck and shift my weight, you have many souls, my lambkin, but only one body. So that you as you must always be prepared to shut your goddamn face. So that, gently, gently now, let us pray. If thine left flank mortally offend thee, pluck it out, and turn ye to thy right.

Where once again it takes all kinds. Old stretch here with his sniffle, Count Cold Contracting, seedy aristocrat with scotched noseholes, skinny slumming slur without an ounce of schmaltz on him, his brown brush moustache a perfect match for his heavy beaver hom-

552

burg, his lofty clamper encroaching on his nearest inferior's creaking strap, he kept the elongated bump of his unfinished face coldly averted from the fixed gaze of the grim companion of his episcopalian bath, as disloyal a contester of his intestate as he had ever had, a clinging hennaed mite mostly spit curl, her miscible mummer's name apparently mud because her ample lips kept moving, with her dogs barking so she felt she was going to drop unless he wangled her a seat somehow, working on him, and working on him, and wearing him down until he suddenly unbent by leaning over what seemed to be a man just long enough to say with all the force and elegance of the managerial class, why don't you get up, you black cocksucker, and go back to Georgia where you came from?

With such a whine, whine, nigger baby. Do you remember how we used to play, twirling our gay little hands that way? As in this deathly silence which ensued, this huge male ape, or something as sincerely simian, you could actually see his whole heart sag with the rending weight of so many red centuries of white hope infinitely deferred, as with his preglacial eyes the poor bastard stared off into space as deep and as dark as his own long acquaintance with grief, with that utterly hopeless, more than human expression of a caged gorilla which his old massa here, stationed on the other side of the bars in his unconscious role of captive audience, was still studying with such wicked joy and guilt, you could hear God say, if you were listening, if this is what I have done, then I deserve to die.

If it is possible to conceive of any creature, risen or otherwise, calling it quits with such a rush of bloody logic to the brain. On the contrary, as Joe himself would say, you say you love life, and you still want to live. Even though you realize soon enough that being born is merely the first frustration. And if the next stop did not happen to be yours, you would never budge an inch, but simply stand by and do nothing. But the joke is on you when the best you can do is to save your own neck. Forgive me, father. I am such a base interim type, yet I had this sweet little flowering in my insides. It is certainly strange how self-hate engenders hatred of others. Until so much for now. Naturally. But you may do well to remember, as you look back on this brutal subway blitz, if ever you are balmy enough to do so, that it is likely to be such little things like this, that, and the other, which can make or break your day.

Even though, like this doll of a Friday one, it was already such a dazzler that by the time he had bucked his way out at Fourth and 28th, the common ordinary sun came as a complete surprise. It was just as if he had staggered out of a movie in the middle of the day. For a split second he imagined that if he batted his eyes in a certain way he could stop the minute hand of the two-faced factors timepiece from slipping further south of nine o'clock while he gallantly headed north to continue to play that game which he had begun to call, hoping for the best. He had barely settled into his stride when he was grabbed from behind in a bear hug.

"Jesus Christ," said Joe. "What now?"

"Guess who."

"Who? You're a goddamn nuisance, that's who."

"Oh, boy. I sure caught me a live one, didn't I?"

"Okay," said Joe. "Okay. I give up. Let go."

"Joe, you old sonofabitch."

"Well," said Joe. "That sounds familiar."

"Shake. Make like your cockeyed. Remember?"

"Why, it's little Marty."

"Marty? Marty who?"

"How should I know? You tell me."

"Sam. Sammy Peterfriend. Don't you recognize me?"

"Peterfriend. Um. That's a nice name. What was it originally?"

"Aa," said Sam. "So I banged up your hat a little, so what?"

"I hope to hell you're getting paid for this."

"Paid," said Sam. "That's a pretty good one. Now me. You know what I just heard? You won't believe this. But they're hanging Danny Deever in the morning. Honest. It's the truth."

"Happy little fella, aren't you?"

"Well," said Sam. "I ain't handsome, but I don't have fits."

"That's good news."

"Good old Sam from Alabam. That's me. With a one, and a two, and a three. Roses are blooming in Picardy. Rose of Washington Square."

"Sorry, kid. I'm late as it is."

"Say, remember the time we cracked that old safe on Powell Street and all we found was a bag of pennies?"

"Ah, no," said Joe. "You're not going my way, are you?"

"A boy soprano," said Sam. "Wow. Talk about luck."

554

"Hey, now. What's wrong, son?"

"Sorry," said Sam. "Didn't mean to push you in the gutter."

"That's funny," said Joe. "Marty used to do that, not Sam."

"Climb upon my knee, sonny boy. Ah, I tell you, there'll be a hot time in the old town tonight. Wah-wah. You get the picture? Me on the old washboard. And you plunking away on the uke. How about it, Joey boy? Can you still juggle them balls? How are you as a straight man?"

"Perfect," said Joe. "Can't you see?"

"What a putz. And here I was thinking of building up a dog act."

"Now look," said Joe. "I don't mean to be too pushy. Or anything like that. But if you can't make it, just tell me, and I'll carry you."

"It's these goddamn garters," said Sam. "They just won't stay up."

"Then nail them down or something, can't you? What else is wrong with you?"

"Well," said Sam. "Since you're asking."

"Wait," said Joe. "Don't tell me. I don't want to know."

"There's this funny squeaking in my ears. Listen. Can you hear it? I just don't understand it. Sometimes I think it's my left. And then I'm sure it's my right. Maybe there's a little bird trapped in there and it's trying to tell me. To stop jerking off, I guess. Okay. I don't mind so much having time on my hands. But what the hell am I supposed to do with this thing I call myself? No kidding. It's bad enough to be low man sometimes. But right now, I swear. I'm not even on that totem pole. Now you take yesterday for instance."

"No, thanks," said Joe. "Honest. I wouldn't know what to do with it."

"Take it, take it. What have you got to lose?"

"That's right," said Joe. "Rip off all my buttons. See if I care."

"Say," said Sam. "That sure was a loose one, wasn't it? I'll keep it for a souvenir. So you hear? So I spent the whole damn morning wandering around on Sixth Avenue, reading them chalked up job open signs. You know where that slave market is? Well, anyway, the trouble with me was I had on a fresh white shirt. With them floozy french cuffs yet. I knew I didn't look the part. And I just couldn't get up my nerve. But I finally said to myself, what the hell, who are they that I ain't? So I kind of loosened my tie and rumpled up my hair and put my head down and scrambled up one of those dives and pushed my way through and said to the man there, I see you're looking for a lot of dishwashers up the

Catskills. So this baldy bastard, he doesn't even look up, and he says to me, sorry, bud, but it's not for you. Hey. What dog crapped here? How did he know? Did I give off some kind of smell? Anyway. The next time I thought I'd be cute. So I tried talking like my Italian neighbor. Would you believe it? I'm damn good at it, but it didn't work. So I thought to myself, be smart, let's try that Chinese laundry bit. But it was absolutely no go. The bastard knew me without looking at me. So I hiked over to the Paramount and just squeezed in before the prices changed. And boy, by the time I came out, was I fogged up. I put out my hands in front of me like so. But that crazy sidewalk, it kept coming up to meet me. So when I got home, I said to my mother, I hope and pray you have something special for me to eat. So this very bright woman, she says to me, well, now, there's sugar, salt, bread, pepper, chicken fats. You know, the whole works. So I said to her, you better save that for dear old Dad. As for me, I said, I think I'll have a bowl of cornflakes without milk for a change. And just when I picked up my spoon, the table began to walk away. Is this where you turn? Or is it next block?"

"Next."

"Ah, that's what I thought."

"Wait," said Joe. "Let's cross first. How did you know I turned?"

"Oh," said Sam. "I've been watching you."

"Watching me?" said Joe. "What in the hell for?"

"My, my," said Sam. "We're a little bit stuck-up there, aren't we?"

"Watch it, will you? You almost tripped me up there."

"Look at that string bean. She thinks her ass weighs a ton."

"Whew," said Joe. "I know I made a mistake. But I just saved your life. Did you know that?"

"What?" said Sam. "That old rambling truck? Go on. I saw it coming a mile away."

"Okay, okay. So you can hop around on one foot. You don't have to prove it to me. I knew you were a genius the second I saw you."

"So help me," said Sam. "I'm not clowning. It's just that lately, you know, I've been noticing this right leg of mine is trying to get away with murder. So every time I catch it, I say, okay, you sonofabitch, I'll fix you. So you see? I make it do all the work."

"Yes," said Joe. "So tell me. What does the doctor say?"

"What doctor?"

556

"Any doctor. And the sooner the better, man."

"Ha," said Sam. "Thinking about that broad reminds me."

"Sam," said Joe. "Sammy Peterpickle. That's funny. It just doesn't ring a bell."

"How about it, boy? Would you like to feel a real muscle? No, wiseguy, not on my dome. On my arm, right here. Just like a rock, hey?"

"It must be the material."

"Material, hell. I tell you, I had faith. I moved mountains."

"Great. That's always nice work if you can get it."

"Pah," said Sam. "Pit."

"Be damned," said Joe. "Right between the teeth. I never could do that."

"Big deal," said Sam. "You file a little space there and you got it made. If you have to spit, spit straight ahead, that's what I say. Who cares which way the wind blows? Yow. I got such an itch between my toes now, you wouldn't believe it. I feel like Horatio at the bridge. You know what I mean? It's like you know a certain big word. But you're afraid to use it. Because if you do, right away they say, listen to the fucking little show-off."

"They sure do," said Joe. "There you're absolutely right."

"Did you see that? There's a guy who's looking for a good swift boot in the behind."

"Easy, boy. So he bumped you. How else would you know you're alive?"

"The fat bastard. He still eats meat. I can smell it on him."

"Come on, pooch. You're pointing the wrong way."

"Hey," said Sam. "I must say. You've got a pretty good grip there yourself."

"Look, Marty."

"Sam."

"You're aggravating me, boy. I told you I was late, didn't I?"

"Sure, sure," said Sam. "I'm with you. I'm moving. So okay then. So where were we? Right. So what do you think I did right after you people moved away?"

"Let me guess," said Joe. "Looking at you, I would say you grew."

"You sonofagun. You're warm."

"You shot up to your present enormous height of five foot flat."

"Absolutely. Right on the button."

"Great," said Joe. "I'm so glad I got this far. I guess that finishes me for today."

"Man," said Sam. "I tell you. It got so. We didn't talk to each other for gosh, sometimes six, eight months. I can feel it. What a balloon for a head. It's murder once you get started, ain't it? Way down that lonesome road. Some of us nitwits go on foot. And some of us roll on wheels. I remember a gypsy in a store once told me if you have a pot to piss in, you have a good chance of outliving your only son. Now that's cute. What the hell's that guy doing with earphones on? That kind of walk reminds me when you make in your pants. Can you imagine the schlub? I was hardly eating solid food yet, and he was already telling me to exclude myself. Gosh, would he hop around and holler. I had a habit of puking in his direction. A real fine type, my old man. One time we were having bupkes for supper, which means practically nothing, when all of a sudden he says to my mother, Essie, he says, tell the little shit there. And he stops and starts laughing. Mazeltov. He had hit the jack pot. He had found the right name for me."

"I wonder what it is," said Joe. "What makes me such a sucker lately?"

"So naturally," said Sam. "So like now. You see what I mean? Every time I think of it, my head gets so low, I pretty near kiss the ground. My mouth sure makes up for the rest of me, doesn't it? I just said the hell with it. I stepped right on a crack. Now if I could read lips, I would know what you're trying to say. Hey? How about it, boy? You still carrying that torch on high? Remember how we used to run relays from sewer to sewer? You could always count on me to drop that stick. Christ. After awhile. It sure is a howl. You begin to develop a kind of feeling for yourself. You know what I mean? For years you stand there like a prick in the toilet in front of the mirror, looking at yourself, saying to yourself, holy mackerel, it can't be, is this pitiful looking little jerk really me? You get to feel so sorry for the poor bastard, it's enough to break your heart. You finally have to say to yourself, jesus christ, stop futzing around and do something already, will you? So I tore out that ad from an old Scientific American and sent away to Atlas for a body beautiful."

"But that goddamn old head. You couldn't do much with that, could you?"

"Well," said Sam. "You know what the bible says. The prick is all."

"Shoot," said Joe. "And I always thought it was just the opposite."

"I don't know," said Sam. "Maybe it's the way you look under your hat. How about giving me a little piggyback? That ought to get your blood to flowing."

"So help me," said Joe. "This guy's worse than a monkey."

"Or better yet," said Sam. "Alley-oop. Just put your foot in my hands and I'll flip you over like an acrobat."

"Incredible," said Joe. "You're sure you're human? I never saw such wild hair."

"Wild?" said Sam. "Man, you should see me when I get up in the morning."

"What's going on here? Somebody must've moved that corner. I never knew it was so far away."

"Oops," said Sam. "There's a head sticking out of that manhole. Maybe that's the gink who did it."

"What gets me is," said Joe.

"Ha," said Sam. "That reminds me. Tell me now. I always wanted to know."

"Why the hell didn't it rain today?"

"Did you lay those broads?"

"I would've had so much fun missing you."

"Or did you just muzzle?"

"Marty," said Joe.

"Sam, goddamn it."

"Sam," said Joe. "Let's stop right here and now."

"Talk about being mixed up. Wow."

"I'm sorry, kiddo. I'm afraid you've hit me at the wrong time. I just don't know what the hell you're talking about."

"Stan," said Sam. "Stanley Simkovich. What are you shaking your head for? You remember. And that, that big schlang. What in the hell was his name? You know. The guy who looked like Andy Gump. Marv. No, no, Morrie. Morrie the moocher. My stinking pal from way way back. I must be going batty. How could I forget his name? The louse. He still has my old jackknife with the corkscrew and other stuff in it. I remember when the whole damn bunch of us. Wait a second. Don't rush me now. We were all marching down to that crappy old movie house on Snediker Avenue to see the Son of the Sheik when all of a

559

sudden one of those dogs in front of us slips on a piece of watermelon, and whango, goes right down on her tuchus and busts her frigging beads. Yeah, man. And who do you think catches the little bitch on the first bounce? Yeah, you, you dumbbell. The big hatchet man. God's own mad lover. Putting your arm around me like a real pal. Milking me of my last penny after that stupid pot put the finger on me. Sorry, says she right out loud, you'll have to send that schmendrick home, we ain't used to robbing the cradle. So naturally. Since it was such a lovely summer's day. I said to myself, wake up, fella, this is America. So I went right home and had me a movement so big, well, what can I tell you? You can see for yourself. I'm still red in the face."

"Snediker?" said Joe. "When was there ever a movie house on Snediker?"

"Take your time," said Sam. "It's still early. It'll come to you."

"You're nuts," said Joe. "Why should I ever do a thing like that to you?"

"Well," said Sam. "What can I say? That's what life was in the old country."

"I think," said Joe. "I think I better look in my hat. Maybe I'm not really me."

"It's standing around in the sun this way. That'll do it every time."

"Wait a minute," said Joe. "Now I remember. Wasn't he the coal man with the hard hat and the moustache cup?"

"Who was?"

"Your father."

"Hell, no. That was your old man, wasn't it?"

"You know something," said Joe.

"I know I jumped you," said Sam. "But gee whiz."

"In another second," said Joe. "I'm going to pick you up and shake you just like a rat."

"That's okay," said Sam. "I'm in no hurry. You're the guy with the job. Not me."

"Hell," said Joe. "What's all the fuss about anyway? You were all kind of small in your family. All you peterpeckers. As I remember it. All exactly the same size. Like little birds in a row on a branch. Now what's so goddamn terrible about that?"

"Small, says he. Giants, giants. All except me."

"Some exception. I must say."

"And if you want to know why, I'll tell you."

560

"Come to think of it. So my coffin will be bigger than yours. So what?"

"He said to her, four's enough, get rid of it. So she took her biggest hatpin and shoved it way up in her. She must've been scared stiff. Maybe a wire hanger would've been better. Who knows? But I was stupid. I thought I was absolutely perfect. So I came oozing out anyway. Flapping my ears. Look at me."

"My god," said Joe. "Of all the crazy stupid things."

"Yeah, man. The going gets real tough sometimes, doesn't it?"

"I'll say. I'm so glad you're getting a kick out of it."

"Why sure," said Sam. "Why not? Why else would I climb down out of them trees?"

"Only the next time," said Joe. "Do me a favor. Don't save the next dance for me. Know what I mean?"

"Do I know what you mean?" said Sam. "Listen to the man. You think I'm a dope altogether? Is there something behind me? What are you looking at? Ah, now, wait. Wait till I scoop up this newspaper here and I'll show you something you never saw before. Looks like blood smeared. Man, didn't you know? You're talking to a guy who's been there and back. By way of Poughkeepsie too. No shit. Nobody has to tell this baby the score. Like right now. I don't know what it is, but something in the air here tells me I better make up my mind quick. Either I hie me home and count my chickens before they hatch. Or. Get this. I shut my fool mouth and amble over to Bryant Park and take a leak."

"Smart little cookie, aren't you?"

"Hooray," said Sam. "He's beginning to remember me."

"As for me," said Joe. "Gosh. I must be awfully dumb. I can see myself going only one way."

"That was a real kick in the ass I gave you, wasn't it?"

"And the funny thing is," said Joe. "Look at that crazy gal waving at me. I'm always bunking into some pest who keeps dragging me in the other direction."

"Yeah," said Sam. "It's a rotten shame. I know. But christ. I had to suck somebody's blood. And you just happened to be available, that's all."

"Right," said Joe. "You're a real pro, kid. And I think you're just grand."

"Gee, dad. You ain't a woofing me, are you?"

"Cross my heart and hope to die."

"Shit," said Sam. "I know I'll always be a little schmuck. But at least for today. After this powwow with you. Crap on the world. I don't know why. But something tells me I'll make it yet. You'll see."

"Sure," said Joe. "What the hell. Hang in there, boy. We're all flukes."

"My god," said Sam. "What did I tell you? This man here is a prince. A prince, I tell you."

"Shake," said Joe. "For god and country."

"Oh," said Sam. "At least. And likewise I'm sure. And if you never see me again, it'll be too soon. I get it."

"Then let go already."

"Hey, hey," said Sam. "Look at what's ambling over here. Mamma mia. Just the kind of dish I'd love to leck all over."

"Fine," said Joe. "I'll ask her for you."

"Wait," said Sam. "Hold it a second, will you? Let me show you that little trick I promised you. I'll do it quick like a rabbit. You take this old newspaper. You're watching? And you fold it in half like this. Watch me closely now. This'll slay you. And then you set it right on the ground here just like it was a little tent. See? It looks real nice there, doesn't it? Wait. That's not it yet. Goddamn me. If I can't leave you laughing, what's the use? All set? Here it comes. Stand back now. You're watching?"

From alas to a lass, as only Joe could, in his going such great guns in his gamut of reaching for the highs and lows in people, while his flickering vision of freedom flashed like a sword in the fierce light of day, as happy to relate, right then and there he decided to wind up this particular vigil as colossal and humble swineherd to humanity, by simply backing off and sneaking away. As old peterpuss there, obeying the simplest concept of divine order which suggests that some of the grandest stunts in or out of nature can only be done strictly by the numbers, and serving his separate sentence as he was, began his own count off to end all.

"My god," said Rosalie. "Is the whole world crazy today? What's that little man doing there?"

"I'll tell you. Don't turn around. Don't look."

"You're not related to that whatever, I hope."

"The sonofagun," said Joe. "And I thought I was the only one who

562

knew how to do that trick. You see. The whole idea is. Whoa, now. What's going on here anyway? You're practicing to be your own grandmother? Let's be pulling in that old stomach there."

"You're never late," said Rosalie. "What happened?"

"Please," said Joe. "Don't ask. I'm ashamed to tell you."

"Ha," said Rosalie. "That would be the first time."

"Be damned," said Joe. "Wait a second. I just have to take a peek. Oh, boy. This is really a howl. There's already a whole ring around him. Uh-uh. Did you hear them groan? That's the stuff. He's trying it again. Watch. Let me show you. This is what he has to do. First you understand he has this newpaper propped up there on the ground. Fine. Now. He stands on his left leg and puts his right behind him and grabs hold of it with his left hand like this. Ah, you're real sweet. I love the way you pay attention. Very good. Now he takes hold of his left ear with his right hand and in this position, watch me now, he begins to squat down to try to pick up that newspaper with his teeth and stand up without falling down. Watch it. I almost broke my neck that time, didn't I? Hey. Listen to them cheer. The lousy little shrimp. He's done it."

"And now," said Rosalie. "Anyone for wolf are you ready?"

"Well," said Joe. "I think I better not. I never like to play with people who are so pale. They're sure to beat me every time."

"Ah, Yusseleh, Yusseleh."

"Um," said Joe. "In Yiddish yet too. I guess that means we're still friendly enemies. In any language."

"Talk about tricks," said Rosalie. "Wait. Wait until you see the one Mr. Colish is pulling."

"Colish," said Joe. "Now there's a familiar name."

"Oh, boy. I sure would like to hear what funny little saying will come popping out of your mouth then."

"Oh, you would, would you? Hell. What's the difference now or later? I always intended to choke her anyway."

"Hooray," said Rosalie. "Some real attention at last. I've been waiting and waiting for it. Aw, now, come on. Squeeze, squeeze. You can't hurt me. I'm a fountain. I love to go whee."

"It's okay, mister," said Joe. "We're only playing. You can go about your business now."

"That's right," said Rosalie. "You heard the man. Scat."

"Did you see that? He was already making with his fists."

"Gosh," said Rosalie. "Do my eyes deceive me? Or is that really a cape he's wearing?"

"And how," said Joe. "And a beret. And spats too. Why, the old goat. He must be eighty-five at least. Look at him. He's still standing there. He's listening."

"I'm almost afraid to ask. That's not your grandfather, is it?"

"Yes?" said Joe. "You were about to say? What's up, old boy? Are you having a dress rehearsal today? What's the message, little father?"

"Uh-uh," said Rosalie. "Watch out. Before you know it, he'll be selling you something."

"In that monocle? Not in a million years."

"What a nose. I don't like the way his hands are twitching."

"Fantastic. Everyone is getting to be so nosy lately. What's that in your hand?"

"This?" said Rosalie. "I don't know. He just slipped it to me."

"Who did? He? Let me see. Why, it's a whole goddamn letter. And all so nicely typed up too. Well, well. I can see he's not your grandfather either. Listen to this. 'Dear Miss. You are very sweet. I have been following you for days. Your shining eyes tell me you are a rising star. But that guy with you is definitely a sinking ship. If you allow him to embrace you again, I shall be forced to take legal remedy. Kind lady, will you give me your hand one day soon to kiss to show me what a woman is really made of besides? My own dear wife took the gas pipe in the city while I was cutting the grass from under her feet on my estate in Orange County. Just because I happen to keep an animal, certain people call me the cat's mother. I keep hoping you will come to wash my windows. Until then, since I know that only money can bring you happiness, I have decided to deposit a silver dollar for you every week for a month under my own name. All I ask of you is to pass on this favor, and I will make you rich beyond your fondest dreams. With the sincere hope that your seams will always be straight. Your friend in need indeed. Moe Moskowitz. The glue king. P.S. If you think this is a joke, just ask your mother whose name I forget to tell you how I swindled your father out of his life savings on that little millinery deal. (Please turn.) What do you think of me, son? Pretty good for a man of my age, eh?' "

"Oh, my god," said Rosalie. "Was that him? Where is he? Where did he go?"

"What?" said Joe. "You mean to say you know the man?"

"Oh," said Rosalie. "Oh, what a dope. Oh, I'll never forgive myself, never. You saw him. He was right there. I could've smacked him right in the face. Oh, it would've been so easy. I could've scratched his eyes out at least. Oh, wait until my mother hears about this. She'll murder me. Oh, I could kick myself. How could I be so stupid? How could I let him get away?"

"I'll be damned," said Joe. "I knew there was something fishy about that guy."

"Can you imagine?" said Rosalie. "You were ready to wipe up the floor with him and like a fool I had to go and interfere."

"Where were your eyes?" said Joe. "Didn't you recognize him?"

"No," said Rosalie. "How could I? It all happened way back there before I was born. I never saw the man before in my whole life. You have no idea how hard it is to get my mother to talk about it. I still don't know what really happened. Just bits here and there. How they were such great pals and worked in the same place where they made feathers or plumes or something. And how this louse would never bring his wife or kids with him, but would come alone every Sunday night, and they'd play pinochle for pennies, at first, and my mother, she never did like him and kept warning my father, she'd be slaving away making potato pancakes, and that clown would get behind a sheet with a candle and make like horses and rabbits with his hands, you know, and my poor father, what a soft touch he was, he would laugh until he cried. Until the next thing you know, there he was chasing after that guy all over the factory with a pair of shears in his hand. Now I ask you. Why can't they have benches here? Would it cost them all that much? What a stinking city this is. There's nowhere to sit down. You can drop dead for all it cares."

"And nowhere to take a pee either."

"Now look at that," said Rosalie. "Did you ever in all your life see anything so affectionate? This damn rayon slip. It's always twisting itself up where it knows it shouldn't. Imagine. Even it. It too has to have its way. Excuse me a second while I. Yes, I know. My rabbi says, never adjust yourself in public. But if you have to, you might as well, is what I say. Now you take last night for instance. Get back in there, you stupid thing. With hems this high, imagine if I had knobby knees, like some people I know. And I just happened to say, you know, I said,

I've always been so fond of this forest-green dress. And my sister looked at me and sniffed in that aggravating way she has, and she said, I'm sorry to have to say this, but from where I sit, it sure looks bottle green to me. Oh, I said, I wouldn't be surprised. Oh, yeah? she said. Why? Because, I said, from where you sit, with those eyes of yours, you couldn't tell a bee from a baseball bat, so what does that prove? It proves, she said, that I can still very easily see that you are beginning to fill out like a balloon. What? I said. Me fat? Where? There, she said. You see what I mean? That's the trouble with you young people today. You refuse to face anything. Well, hell, I said. I'm facing you. Isn't that enough? Oh, yes, she said. It surely would be, smarty pants, if you had enough brains to see yourself in me. God forbid, I said. By the way. Since you're holding the baby, which I don't think you should with your running nose, I think you should know. There's a roach about to crawl up your leg. Where? she said. You think I should take an enema? You lousy rat, I said. Why do you keep trying to tell me my life is going to be exactly like yours? I do? she said. Imagine the loony guy. He comes up and tells Mamma he's willing to change his name from Bussa to Bernstein all for your sake. But get himself circumcised, absolutely not, no, sir. You're crazy, I said. What are you trying to tell me? Ah, she said, I tell you, kid, if that big lunk was chasing after me like he's chasing after you, I'd let him catch me all right, and poison him afterwards. Hilda dear, I said, we all know you're a little cracked, but lying this way won't put you together again, so why do it, why? Because, she said, in the first place, this happens to be true. And in the second, I can't understand why you ever have to use a needle when you have such a sharp tongue. And wait a second. And in the third, I'd rather be crazy than cruel any time. Cruel? I said. All right, I said. I'll bite. Why am I cruel? Because, she said, every time I ask you if I can wear that dress, you say to me, what for, you never go anywhere. But Hilda, I said. It's one of the few decent things I have left. What else would I wear to work? Besides, I said, you would look dead in this color, you know that. In bottle green? she said. Go on. It lights up those flecks in my eyes something terrific. Flecks, I said. Circumcised. Where do you get all those nutty ideas anyway? But it's my favorite color, she said. Bottle green always was. Well, I said, it could be for all I know. But it so happens that this rag here is forest, not bottle green. Bottle green, she said. Look, I said.

You have two noses to wipe there. So do us all a favor and get busy. But I tell you, it's bottle green, she began to scream. Bottle green, bottle green, bottle green. So I said, okay, okay, I said, have it your own way. What's all the yelling about? We'll all be dead in a hundred years. What the hell difference does it make?"

"You sure do lead a full life, don't you?"

"Can you imagine getting into such a hassle about anything as petty as that?"

"Who's Bussa?"

"Really," said Rosalie. "I must say. It's a lucky thing our bell is busted. Otherwise. You know what that crazy nut's been doing lately? He's been stuffing messages in our mailbox."

"Oh," said Joe. "So that's how he keeps asking for your fat little hand."

"Who does?"

"Bussa."

"No, no," said Rosalie. "What's the matter with you? If I didn't know you were smart, I'd think you were an idiot. I'm talking about Abramowitz. Or is it Moscowitz? Or whatever his name is now. Would you believe it? My father actually had him right there by the throat but that sly rat talked his way out of it. I guess my father figured, hell, why should he get the chair for killing such a worm? So what was the result? He handed him down to us. Forever and a day. Hey. How do you like the way English she is spoken here? I bet you I know what you're thinking. You're thinking, the way this gal's been gabbing here, she's sure to wind up with her tongue in a sling. Just the same. What? It sure feels great to cut loose sometimes, doesn't it?"

"You're so damn charming either way. Don't mind me. Go right ahead."

"Now don't punch me in the eye for saying this," said Rosalie. "But you can be sweet if you really try. Every other week, that is. I'm so glad we're not rushing. This is just like playing hooky, isn't it? I love to be with you in the street this way. Some people's idea of fun. I walk half a block with you, and I talk as if I'm taking a pleasure trip around the world. Oh, my. Now look at that, will you? Why do people want to show each other things like that? If there's anything I hate to look at, it's a goiter. Next to my own shining face, of course. I fooled you that time, didn't I? I mean. It says novelties, but I wonder what they really sell behind that dirty window there. Say. Remember all that stuff about tong wars and opium dens? Like I was reading the other day about someone who had a green thumb. I bet you if we had one tree here, we'd think we were moving through a whole forest. Sometimes. I know it's mean of me, but when we're together this way I keep wishing the sky would fall right down on top of us. Anything to bring us a little closer, I suppose. Like that Moscowitz man who's been haunting us. Why else would he do what he does? At first. You know. Since we don't get much mail worth a damn, we thought it was kind of funny. With his grand opening note, telling us, 'It may smell bad for a while. The pest is here.' He rules his own paper, as I'm sure you noticed. Right after which, he didn't waste much time with another roman candle, 'Now if you want to cry in company because you're already talking about me and nothing else, just put pepper under your nails and kind of pass your hand over your face. For this tip worth a million, I expect payment in advance.' What a mentality. Or trying to break our hearts with, 'Folks, I see I'm in this world like a sailing ship in a bottle. How I got in I'll never know. And now I'm beginning to wonder. Can you help me? How do I get out of here? Without losing my pants?' Or just sending us a smashed chocolate cherry with the message, 'Okay to eat. Been washed.' Damn cute and all that. But whoever answers anything like that? So I guess he got a little sore, because the next thing we got was, 'Like the mouse said to the elephant, am I boring you, dear?' Gosh, you should have been there when Mack tried to explain that one to my mother. We kept asking her, who is this maniac, do you know him, why doesn't he sign his name, what does he want from you anyway? Because it was always Dear Madam this, and Dear Madam that, but it was like she was superstitious about it, she knew, but she was afraid to say. Until that poor thing, really, he became pathetic altogether. Telling us, 'Listen to the nerve of my youngest boy. Gee, pop, he says to me, you're such an awful gonif, how do you expect me to bow down to the ground to anyone like you? So I say to him, who are you to talk? Did I ever spend my nights six times in the hoosegow? Was I ever caught with my bare hands looking for pleasure in the pants of bums and boys in the toilets in the subway?' How about that? said our own dear Mack. That sure does sound like a real fairy tale, doesn't it? Get it, get it? That Mack. He thinks all his brains are in his elbow, so he keeps poking and poking you. Honestly. It was getting real stupid to let ourselves get

568

sucked in deeper and deeper that way. So the next time. Can you imagine anyone begging you to tell him, 'I couldn't pass water all night. What do you think it means?' So I said, that's it, that does it, finished, we don't even open them up any more, we just rip them right up and throw them away."

"Goddamn it," said Joe.

"Now we're both mad."

"What is this between me and the wind? Every time I want to light up a cigarette, it springs up like mad."

"Wait," said Rosalie. "I'll stand like this. Maybe that'll help. Like my mother's always saying when you have a gumboil or something, just don't pay any attention to it, and it'll go away. Yeah, yeah. A real Jewish scientist. I hope you have enough matches there. Like the other day, you hear? She had just come up. Puff, puff, that's the way. She had just come up from bringing down the garbage when she happened to look out the window, leaning her hands on the pillow, and would you believe it, there he was, that disgusting creature, actually tearing open her bag to make a list of what was in it. Yow, I tell you. I can see you can hardly wait to hear. She let out such a scream that sixteen people were stumped to death trying to get there first to pull the fire alarm."

"Really?" said Joe. "Anyone we know?"

"Oh, loads," said Rosalie. "I'm sure you've read all about it in the papers."

"You're darn tootin I did. How could I miss it?"

"Charge," said Rosalie. "Into the valley of death rode the six hundred. Now, now. Don't be a damn fool and try to lift me."

"But damn it, you're not cooperating."

"I warn you. You're going to hurt yourself."

"What a lump. I might as well try to lift a whole building."

"You're a nut, you know that? What's the point anyway?"

"Lady of Spain, I adore thee."

"I should say," said Rosalie. "That's the least you can do."

"Zop. Zing went the strings of my heart. Oh, tell me, pretty maiden, do. When's the last time you made whoopee?"

"Ah, well," said Rosalie. "I guess that's just your way of relaxing."

"Forgive me," said Joe. "I must've been mad. I don't know what came over me. All I know is that all of a sudden all I wanted to do was to pick you right up and take you out of all this."

"My hero. Out of all this where? Sounds very familiar."

"You know something?" said Joe. "You really look scrubbed today. Or is it just that you're beginning to lose your baby fat? You're never afraid to stop and look me right in the eye, are you? Don't quote me, kiddo, but you're becoming a witch. As a matter of fact. I hate to say this. But I'm beginning to appreciate you more and more every day. Especially when you jump me with your whole body. And push out your lips that way. Goo or no goo."

"Ah, now," said Rosalie. "Aren't you nice? It means. You love me just the same, don't you?"

"Whoosh," said Joe. "I knew we'd come out at this end of the tunnel. Tell me better. What are all those folks doing there at the freight side?"

"Aw, come on, now," said Rosalie. "For once in your life. Before you jump in there and get your head knocked off altogether. Break your heart and say it. Say you love me a little. Say it, you fool. Say it."

"What the hell," said Joe. "What is this anyway? What am I here today? A mountain? Everybody's monkey's uncle is trying to climb me."

"Or would you rather tango?"

"Oh, my," said Miss Golschman. "Look at them. Ain't they just too sweet for words?"

"Don't ask me," said the man. "I don't know from nothing."

"Shame on you," said Miss Golschman. "Don't you just adore lovebirds?"

"I just told you, lady. I don't know from nothing. I'm just here to do a job."

"Hi," said Joe. "Who's your jolly friend here?"

"Here," said Miss Golschman. "He's your friend now."

"Sounds lovely," said Joe. "What's all this?"

"Is that the fella?" said the man.

"Yep," said Miss Golschman. "That's the fella, all right."

"Okay, then," said the man. "Here's the sheet. Let's get going, mac. I ain't got all day."

"See you later," said Rosalie. "I've got to run."

"Right," said Joe. "Singers. Wilcoxes. What are all these? New machines coming in?"

"Nope," said Miss Golschman. "All the old ones going out."

"Ah," said Sally Scheff. "There he is. There's the rotten traitor."

"Yeah," said Mae Popkin. "Look at him there. The faker. Making believe he doesn't know what we're talking about."

"Darling," said Lil Lubasch. "Sweetheart. How could you do this to me? I was crazy for you. I loved you like my own son."

"Aie," said Scheff. "Play, gypsy, play. I knew we'd have trouble with this Hungarian."

"What son?" said Popkin. "You never even had a male animal in the house."

"You see?" said Lubasch. "I ask you. What else can I learn from life? For years, for long, bitter years with piecework I sit next to this particular woman. The stains on her blue sweater there I know, how should I say, like I know the swollen veins on my own hands. Every day she never shuts up with her Ginger the crazy cat. How many times a day does she look at me and say, where smells the gas? I try my best. I try not to watch when she cleans out her ears with a hairpin. Boom, like a bell. Right after she eats, she belches. Do I have to look down to know all the places she cuts out from her shoes for the bunions? Sometimes I can't sleep from the same song she sings to herself. It's true. Why shouldn't you believe me? I know exactly the time she has to go to the toilet. And what do I find out now? I find out she's got a big black hole in the middle of her face. And that's her mouth. And that, my friends, that's the whole person."

"You hear that?" said Popkin.

"I hear," said Scheff. "I'm still in this world."

"You dummy," said Lubasch. "When was the last time you looked?"

"Gee," said Scheff. "Ain't I lucky? Now she's on me."

"You know," said Lubasch. "You have plenty. You save them. You roll them up fifty in a piece of paper."

"So help me," said Scheff. "Why do I have to knock her on the head? I know the pot is cracked."

"It says there on the penny, it says, in the people you got to trust."

"There you are," said Popkin. "You see what it means to be a college graduate?"

"Wonderful," said Scheff. "I was always so jealous of her."

"Liars," said Lubasch. "Bags of bullshit."

"Present," said Popkin.

"Here," said Scheff. "Attention, everybody. Teacher here is calling the roll."

"I'll call," said Lubasch. "I'll keep yelling. Who takes from me my living, takes from me my heart's blood. From this you want to make fun? You want I should play ring-around-the-rosy? An old fats like me? Look. I am already out in the street. I ask you. From here, where do I go? To the bank where I got no money? To pay the rent for my room with two cans of beets I got left? To creep under the Brooklyn Bridge to sleep a little before I die? Yes, to hell, quick. To the graveyard I will go. And you will all go with me. Like hungry dogs. Making in the street. Crying for a bone. Howl, people, howl."

"Oh, my god," said Scheff. "What's the matter with you anyway? What are you trying to do to yourself here? You're only making it worse."

"Yeah," said Popkin. "For chrissakes, Lubasch. This ain't the end of the world yet. Get a hold of yourself. Be a man."

"Away from me," said Lubasch. "It's too late. I'm all fire inside. I'm cooked. I got such a stitch in my side, I can't breathe. Gevald. Can't you see? I'm already dying. I'm dying, I tell you."

"Help," said Popkin. "Quick. Grab her there. She'll flatten me like a pancake."

"I'm here," said Scheff. "I'm helping."

"Damn it," said Popkin. "What a sack. Did you ever see? Why does she want to go and die now for? Can't she wait until lunch time?"

"Oy," said Scheff. "I'm falling over myself. We got to find a place to put her down."

"Stupid head," said Lubasch. "What's a matter? You need practice? You can't hold me without pinching? Wait a second. Please. Let me finish my business first. Here. Take it, sonny. I want you should have it. Take it, take it. Don't be bashful. Use it in good health. Remember me when you drink. I love you just the same."

"Lubasch," said Popkin. "Your new thermos. What are you doing?"

"He doesn't want," said Lubasch. "He won't take. He's afraid he'll smell from me. He makes me look sick. Look at him. He's got more blood in his face than I got left in my whole system. Aie, there was a time, I tell you. I could sing a spring from Mendelssohn. High, high. I could jump to the roof like a cat. I had a tail right here I could move up and down. I was a real flashy kid. Go believe it. And now. Do I have to tell him? He knows. He can see. I am like a spool without thread. Like a needle without a point. A cold iron I am. I am all, all squeezed out. I

572

could bust when I think of it. I come to work today in my new shoes and what do I get? A ticket to my own funeral. A matinee yet, too. I am already late. I got to rush. I can't wait, darling. If you don't take, I break. Like this. Watch. I break it in front of you like it was your own wedding. Smash. Crash. Mazeltov. Goodbye and good luck. Mazeltov to you all. Big and small."

"Holy mackerel," said Popkin. "Am I seeing things? Is that Lubasch running a sprint?"

"After her," said Scheff. "Quick. She'll break her neck there on those crazy high heels."

"Wait," said Popkin. "Don't go away, folks. We'll be right back and pass the hat around. How about that old Loobie there? She sure put on a real good show, didn't she?"

"Well, now," said Miss Golschman. "There you are. You never know when things are going to break for you. It was a long dry spell, but it finally came down in buckets."

"I ought to be shot," said Joe. "What the hell was the matter with me? Where were my eyes and ears? I could've warned them. They could've stopped him. This would have never happened."

"I thought you knew," said Miss Golschman. "He was always talking to you about everything."

"I don't know," said Joe. "Maybe he did. I don't remember. I must've been asleep or something. I guess I was only thinking of myself."

"Ha," said Miss Golschman. "You and the rest of the world."

"Where is that guy? How can he skip out with the whole factory this way? Why didn't he wait until tomorrow when nobody would see him? Is he trying to take revenge or something? What the hell kind of business is this? Where is he? Let me talk to him."

"It's no use," said Miss Golschman. "He's not coming in today."

"Ah," said Joe. "Of course. He's no fool, that man."

"Look, fella," said the man.

"Yes?" said Joe. "And what's eating you, old boy?"

"I know it's tough on you all and all that sort of crap. But christ, I got me a whole truck and helper waiting there. You don't want me to lose my whole business, do you?"

"Don't ask him," said Miss Golschman. "You can see. He don't know from nothing."

"Boy," said Joe. "You can say that again. Only before I go, just let me ask you. Just once."

"Fire away."

"Why me?" said Joe. "Why does it have to be me?"

"Because," said Miss Golschman. "Some stupid clown a billion or so years ago just happened to point and say, hey, you."

"And that was it?"

"Pow."

"I couldn't avoid it, could I?"

"Silly boy," said Miss Golschman. "You should thank your lucky stars you're still right in the very thick of things."

"Thick of things," said Joe. "It chokes me all up. That's me all over. A good sport, as always. Hike. Just follow me, sir. Since I don't know your exact name."

"Bert."

"Okay, Bert," said Joe. "This is it. What can we do? It's you and me then. I'm sure they couldn't have picked two better men. What the hell. Let's face it. Fun is fun. But somebody has to get in there and help hang the goddamn people. Right?"

To which sarcastic mode of speech, begging your pardon for this slight delay, with the simultaneous promise to make it snappy, of all that is so singularly comfy and cruel in any raw beginner's concept of complicity, what could Bert me no buts there, that grim droopy collage of grimy city grey, that great neutral nothing knower, corny as all getout, what could he possibly say? Say, you say. You mean to say something in the actual shape of utterance? From say, the slapdash amelican shamble from the ah of bah to the sah of dah? Hah? Or way wah from separating the sheepish surs from the stiffest sups, colliding, cocker, with the sharp abutments of every crux east of contra, lid flipping all bind and lashings of tion, till freer fast to fly to the far west of the mind where the most lovely maximums of mals tend to multi? Jeepers, just as any illiterate ass can be as flippen with his own two lippen, the lowmost likes of you are rarely at a limitable loss in all your fros and fromings, are you? Who says? With mayhaps those few fetishic fetters of your own lazy lean-to letters? Or the whole alpha and you betical range of the closures and crankshafts of curlicuing consonants to the doozy plosions and howls of dot and dashing vowels? Or any or all of them red net alerts of those unpredictable flits and flirts, of the flashier finds at the far corner of thought, of all that is so palpi and pita in the peewee passions, the singswings and the surds, of all them chickadee and cardinal word birds? If such is so, then forget it, mac. You are absolutely on the wrong track.

Oh, but there was a time. Is that you trembling all over, trying to express yourself? A time when sound was all you knew of sense. As when the cradle creaked and a great nose was blown. When you could be listed as a pair of googoo eyes and that was about it. Even today the best you can say is tut-tut like a tiger. Go on, boy. Tell it. Tell it like it was. That really. That sneer came pretty near ripping off my hair shirt. That truly. That terribly touching time when you were first lanced by a ray of light and lapped around by rippling color. Smacking the mouth at that simul to taneous. With that real gone feel of feeling to felt. Being as yet all smiles this side of dada. Yet you were never bolder when you blew your spit bubbles which seemed to be saying. Since every begun must have its beginning. Until your soft malleable skull was grassed over with sufficient silky hair to reflect some of the suave and tara-boom-dee-ay rhetoric of the sun. Surely you remember. Most of us drowsy bottle babies were never more than a mere dimple away from being that dippy. So inevitably, ups-a-daisy it had to be, as by tremendous split personalities you were tossed into the air to shake and show you how high was up, to give you, you pinhead, that cheap thrill which is the pull of gravity, until you arrived at such a carnal knowledge of the scream that you actually soiled thyself.

Dollink boy. As who was it just said. Even when in kicking against the pricks, you were always so highly aboriginal. As in still eschewing words, you were quicker to sneeze than to say please. As in once upon a tip of the tongue, there where as in a trance the truest tales remain untold, you dummy, you managed at last with the help of the scarred leg of a table to struggle to your feet, and you were so stunned by what you saw way out there beyond you that you were rendered speechless. Rendered as in being literally torn apart by a railroad flat tempest of terror and joy. As if perpetual June had pervaded your jaw. Imagine being that cracked already. As if dear old December seemed to be saying with some heat, damn you, if you see life as one insuperable season, you will always have reason to get cold feet. Dumbfounded as you were by the himalayan scale of doorways. By the tropic wonder of window and the alpine warning of wall. But since you had no labials

575

as yet to lay such lively ghosts with such a lickety string of ells and doubleyous, the next thing you knew, there you were, standing in a corner of the universe with your blamed arm over your eyes, blubbering as if your dear little heart would break. The classic agony of what is separate but equal. The usual poor little red-eyed make in the pants.

As if already you were a lone lusty lost soul on the loose lamenting, oh, it is great to be alive but. Do you have a second? Can you imagine what a ball your life would be if not for that baffling bastard backlash of a but? How can the blood bear it? Try to tell us what. What was it with you anyway? Was it the wind chill factor? Was it that you were already rubbing others the wrong way with the wobbly nonconformity of your woeful knock-knees? Were you suddenly in receipt, like it was a singing telegram, of your first cuckoo call that you had a final birthday coming to you? Was it that as far as heart went you had heaped up a lot of lyrical loose change anent your precious self, but none of that real groovy greenstuff to spring a single other captive spirit as yet? Were you wondering who was pippa and why it passes? Had old madame material success, so freudian-fat with ill-fame defied all time differentials to give you a preview of how like a stripper she would slyly expose only suddenly to close for aye the grand canyon of her glacial wicket right smack in your face? Or jesus. You may well ask, but who can say? No wonder that for a time there you were inclined to flame up even when asked such a simple question as, did you make eh-eh today, and if pressed for an answer, proceed to blow your stack.

For which fine solemn fit, your impolitic eyes were made to pop, and your fallible mouth to fly open, as your constitutional due from out the blue, by the very father and mother of a tremendous smack. That stopper supreme for swingers who have yet to swang. The shocking tenor of which no single spoken word could possibly impart. So that, as your ears rang with it, you were so implausible as yet that the best you could do was to wallow in sickening whelms of self-pity, set to your own whimper without words. Oh, like so, if war is all the world about, where shall I betake me? And where on this earth shall I subsist? And so on so passionately until pow stood for you can plotz, and wow for watch it now, and gee for plain old ecstasy. By which rock em and sock em means you could at last compete with the current rat-shy cat which could claw at the knob of the toilet door as compellingly as you could. Your own mouth was never much of a mighty machine to move mountains, was it? Such a mini violet could only turn itself into a complete mum. You were like figure five in your first reader, showing a boy without a caption, holding out an empty bowl, making his wants known. To face such music then meant to do so silently. It was like in the street when choosing up sides. You knew at once what it meant when no one pointed a finger at you. You felt like the heel of a loaf. You made vegetable sounds inside of you as if you were an onion thrips or a cotton flea hopper. You began to think. You thought. You began to blush where once you blubbered. Your highest of jinks became the dangerous journey you took every morning in your bare feet from the darkest africa of your bed to the eerie drinking hole of the front window to see by whatever light there was which way the day would jump.

Though you dang well knew there by the very hang of your droopy drawers that you would just about drop down dead if it ever decided to do so in your direction. So that, naturally, since you were just like any other schmo from the word go, the whole of your eloquence then consisted of clearing the throat and swallowing hard. With absolutely no hem to your haw, as seeing what you saw, such sporting views upon vistas of swinging strikeouts and scratch hits, of your future as full of unsuccessful blisters and embarrassing muffs, of desperate slides to steal home, upending in broken neck. Thou sardonic snot of extreme funk and dast not. Seems you were already shrewd enough to conclude that if you were the sun, you would bypass this punk planet, and rise up more hopefully someplace else.

Ask, ask. You might as well. What makes fear come first to last as always? Why should your every crooked path to break out be a straight inroad to ruin? Is it you who is about to retie your laces and crack your knuckles again? Are you the worst of all the universal jittery jokers? What is this daily dread of yours of being done in? Is it pus? Is it what the eye itself exudes? Is it as faint and impalpable as the very surprint of the unsaid? Is it the great pinch as well as the rub of that constant predicament which is particularly hard on people and pants? You rarely hesitate to speculate, do you? You latest absolute inability to give us the lowdown. What can your involuntary giggle evolving into a dirty laugh tell us? Or that humid and hopeless language of your heart which is so much like rain mixed with snow?

Only that suddenly it has come around again to sock it to me time with some more of the old saws and truisms.

To whit and to whoo. It is only the onrush of too much reality that brings on that rash. It is not too surprising to discover that diarrhea is so closely linked with the thought of death. Against which this Bert will brace as that Joe will jingle. Many a crick in the neck comes from turning the back on the other guy being butchered. Those sinking spells in the pit of the stomach are designed to distract you from the shame of not being able to cope. There is no doubt you are inclined to crack and blow a gale when your faith in others is like a candle in the night wind. As of now you can avow that the best way to call on god is to grind your teeth. Shit, man. As the word is made fluid from flesh. You get funny with me and you will find yourself flat on your back, looking up at the sky and asking why. Just as you can suffer the throes of asthma only where the real action is. How extremely possible that stuttering all told is a cruel satire on that stupid yearning in us for one simple speaking self.

Oh, god, talk about being bushed. Look at all you heavy breathers there, so skittish within the skull, whether to left or right of nerve center, lacking a suitable sleeve to laugh up into, as your right white skin goes rotten in recoil from the much riper red riot and presently superior saga of black, with your running gag of a pose to follow your own nose and fuck all the rest, your secondary eyes even now shining upon that which is not, trying to appear so perfectly poised and unflappable. As always. The fool keeps fooling himself first. It does really get to you. No one is that much of an avoid boid. You always manage to show that you have heard what you have heard, and seen what you have seen. You may honestly believe you have not betrayed yourself, but there is something you do, as Bert does, with one or more parts of your queered body which is a dead giveaway. As standing in for us all, he finally does favor us with the whole lovely lyric of his tic by twitching his higher right shoulder, running his finer forefinger under his nose as he sniffed, and with one quick lick of her lips, went white in a wonderful quiet facial phase, quite done, until the next time.

"Yazoo City," said Frankie. "Here we come."

A sappy slave of all he surveyed, he was swinging himself on and off the tail gate of the truck by dangling from the knotted end of what

578

was surely the sorriest history ever recorded by a single twist of hairy rope.

"Ah," said Joe. "Good. I can always take it out on him."

"How about it?" yelled sap the same, smiling all over as if he were already enjoying the highest and wildest flight he would ever attain in that stunted and heckled struggle of his to rise up in the world. "You want to bet me?"

"There you are," said Joe. "You see what I mean? That's life for you. For today only. He Tarzan. Me Jane."

"Well," said Bert. "Just try to live with it. If you're the type, you're the type. The crap a man has to listen to. He okay there to give me a hand?"

"Who?"

"He."

"My chief cook and bottle washer there? I thought you said you had a helper waiting for you here?"

"That's the ape. He said to me, a buck for the whole business. So I said to him, I'll tell you what I'll do for you, kid, since I see you're clever with your mitts, shadowboxing so fancy there, I'll make it an even ninety, spot cash, right after, absolutely, so help me whoever. That's me. I don't like to crap around too much. So he said to me, aw, man, be a sport and split the difference with me, I'm the last poor nut left on my family tree, which is what it sounded like, and I'm working my way through kindergarten to learn how to fuck a duck. Check. So I said to him, my boy, that story of yours grabs me right here, you got yourself a deal. But I'm telling you right now, I said to him. You'll have to move your ass fast if you want to work for a big-shot capitalist like me."

"Good old Bert. It is Bert, isn't it?"

"Okay," said Bert. "Okay. You can stop feeling me up. You think I'm a momzer altogether? He can have his lousy buck. All I want is some action here. Will you tell that little schmuck to stop screwing around already?"

"I sure will," said Joe. "The man says, stop screwing around already, Frankie. You'll have to excuse the lad. He just about goes nuts every time he hears what he thinks are real men talking. You own this bus yourself? What do you use for power? Is there a team of horses up front?"

579

"You hear that?" said Bert. "This sure is my lucky day. Another mug with a mouth."

"At least it has four wheels. I think. What's that flapping on top?"

"My heavy underwear," said Bert. "I always rinse it and hang it up to dry on Good Friday."

"You should, you should. It's the bounden duty of every good citizen in this fair country of ours to air his drawers if he has it in his heart to show the world his true colors."

"And my old lady keeps telling me I get pissed off too quick."

"What makes you so pale? Do you eat enough?"

"Fuck my eating enough."

"Ah," said Joe. "There you are. That's exactly what I mean. I tell you, Bert, you're so ripe for a change of scene, a blind man can see, your whole body is begging for it. Even that fluky cap you're wearing looks so fagged out, I'm surprised it's still sitting there on top of your head. As for your mouth, if you'll excuse my saying so, it sure is getting to be a mess. But you still have real sharp eyes there. Look around you. Can't you see? It's springtime, Bert. Take my word for it. Somewhere. I don't know where. But somewhere there's a whole new green world waiting for you."

"Fuck what's waiting for me."

"Sure," said Joe. "I would say that too if I were you. But did you ever stop a second and listen to yourself? When did you begin to slip so fast? Where's your gumption? What's happened to all your pioneer blood? Are you strictly in the junk business or something? What's the use of collecting all that lead in your pants? Look. Maybe if I try, I can light a fire under you. Why don't you get up there right now, and I mean now, right up there like a king behind that wheel and take yourself a little spin out into the country? Why not? Who else is ever going to back you up this way? I swear to you, before you know it, you'll be breathing deep again. You'll be free of those pesty things called people. You'll wash that awful bloodshot right out of your batty eyes. You'll find lake water so clear, you'll be able to look in and see yourself like you were a new man. And chances are there'll be a duck. You'll see sumac. I'm positive about this. You'll see them bees pushing their little things into the latest flowers. You'll see sunshine on stone walls. And chipmunks chasing each other like mad. Somehow I have a feeling. You'll see pine trees making carpets for you with their needles that

580

smell so glorious. And gangs of frogs galumping. And lilacs in bloom. Let me finish. And green grasshoppers galore. I think. And if you're lucky. So help me, Bert. You'll find hickory nuts. And wild phlox."

"Fuck your phlox."

"Yazoo City," said Joe. "It can't be. Sounds wild."

"And fuck your fucking story. And fuck that fucking shyster for suckassing me into taking on this fucking job. And fuck all these fucking women here throwing me such fucking dirty looks. And fuck my fucking truck here for breaking down every fucking mile. And fuck this fucking lousy sidewalk I'm spitting on. And fuck God for fucking me up every time I think I see a little fucking light ahead. And fuck you too. You know what I mean?"

"I'm sorry to say," said Joe. "But I'm afraid I do."

"Fuck what you say. I'm full up. Way up to here. I've taken just about all the shit I'm going to take from anybody today."

"Wow," said Frankie. "He sure is fucking mad, ain't he?"

"Dear me, yes," said Joe. "Like my Aunt Matilda used to say. Do my ears deceive me? Where have I heard that song before?"

"Before every ball game," said Frankie.

"What?" said Joe. "Was that our national anthem he was warbling so sweetly there? Damn it. I knew it sounded familiar."

"I guess he's a schmuck too for getting so sore. Right, Joe?"

"Well," said Joe. "It really does get rough sometimes."

"Gosh," said Frankie. "I just thought of it. With him so fucking mad at us, maybe now I'll be losing my lousy buck."

"Working or not," said Joe. "Either way. Sometimes you just can't seem to get the jump on the other guy. Even when you stand on your head and quote reams of old shake a spear."

"You think I should run up and get some cold water to throw on him?"

"Certainly not," said Joe. "It's only a passing cloud. The man hates the feel of water. Anybody can see that."

"Check," said Bert. "But remember, pal. From now on. Lay off."

"My dear fellow," said Joe. "After what happened, I wouldn't dream of doing anything else. By the way. Now that you're back to your old sparkling self. I forget now. Where did you say you were shipping the stuff?"

"I didn't."

"Then say."

"Jesus," said Bert. "Do you mind telling a guy? What does this monk do in his spare time? Flub his dub or something?"

"Oh," said Joe. "Don't mind him. He's always eating what he picks out of his nose. Some days it's a long time between meals. You were about to say?"

"Eech."

"What part of the country is that?"

"Up the old hole," said Bert. "Where in the hell do you think? Put that in your dome there and see what it does for you. Always such a fucking wiseguy, ain't you? Don't it bore the shit out of you sometimes? What in the hell are you holding me up for? You think I can change the fucking map of the world for you or something?"

"You don't really try," said Joe. "That's your whole trouble."

"Look," said Bert. "You want to know something? Then I'll tell you. Even when I can kick myself from here to Canarsie for some of the crummy things I have to pull off to get some butter to go with my bread. And don't worry, I kick myself, plenty. And even when I know at the same time that I'm getting rooked in a thousand different ways. And it happens, it happens. Even then. I don't give a damn how many times you grab me by the balls and how hard you squeeze. When I tell a customer I won't say, I don't say."

"Okay," said Joe. "I respect that."

"Ha. Who gives a shit if you do?"

"Fine," said Joe. "I respect that too."

"Hey, now," said Bert. "Wait a second. What in hell's going on here? Who ripped my fly open?"

"The wind," said Frankie. "I watched it all the way."

"What was that?" said Bert. "Come over here you. I swear. I'll cockalize him. Where did he go?"

"Upstairs," said Joe. "With the wind. Waiting for orders."

"Sonofabitch," said Bert. "You're driving me nuts. You lousy bastards. All of you."

"Well," said Joe. "Don't worry about it too much. Who knows? Maybe tomorrow it'll be just the opposite."

"Holy cripes," said Bert. "I just remembered. I got another pickup before lunch. My goddamn watch is busted. You think I'll make it?"

"Not this way you will."

"Of all the crap I ever heard," said Bert. "I swear. I still can't believe my ears. You look so pale to me, says he, like he was a real red Indian. Goddamn it, man, climb right up there in your old chariot and put her in high, says he, and zoom, shake yourself loose for a change. Git. You heard what I said me. Go. Get yourself lost out there in the wilds somewhere and sit down in the sun for a while like you were a little bunny rabbit. But keep your hat on. There may be woodpeckers. There's a nifty I'll have to file away. Hoo. You'll see a whole green bush like it was a new ladies hat, says he. You'll see moonlight on your mashed potatoes. I think. And blue butterflies in their cuckoo nests. And bunches of warts in bloom. I guess. And phlox like foxes galumping. And would you believe it, friends? I just stood there like a sponge and sopped it all up."

"I may be wrong," said Joe. "But I have a very strong feeling. I bet you're absolutely the very best Bert there is in your own age group."

"I'll do you a favor," said Bert. "I'll go to the library tomorrow and look it up for you."

"I must say," said Joe. "I really can't blame you. If I felt the way you do, I'd be stalling for time too."

"Stalling for time?" said Bert. "What in hell are you talking about? I was waiting on you, wasn't I?"

"Then I got a surprise for you," said Joe. "I'm right here, Bert. I arrived. Honest. And not only that. Now goddamn it. It's me waiting on you."

"And no pesty people, says he, like pine trees smelling like ducks lapping up the plums in the lazy waters. Now what the hell can that be? Is that my call sheet I gave you? Let's have a look at it a second. There's something there that bothers me."

"Check," said Joe. "But if I were you, I'd sure begin to pray."

"Right," said Bert. "I'll do that little thing for you. It says right here. Let me see."

"Watch it now," said Joe. "You better get going, Bert. They're closing in on you."

"Oh," said Maisie Dubrow. "What's the use? It's hopeless. I'm getting sick and tired of always having to beg people. Now don't keep pulling on me, please. I'm not your little blue poodle yet. Or is it a cocker spaniel this year? Or am I confusing you with two other guys? I have absolutely no right to ask the gentleman. And he has a perfect right to refuse."

"But that's silly," said Estelle Schneider. "When the ship is sinking, what has pride got to do with it? Anchors aweigh. Heave ho. Lower that mainsail. And get right up there on that poop deck. Land sakes. You should've heard how our dad used to drum that into our heads. Why, that's the first rule a good chairlady should follow. If you want to reach port safely, you just have to get down on your knees and pray the good lord to get the union to keep your feet from getting wet. Am I right?"

"Sure," said Maisie. "Right as rain. But you can be damn wrong sometimes too. And no two ways about it either."

"Uh-uh," said Estelle. "One demerit for you. You said damn."

"Yes," said Maisie. "And I'll say it again, if you don't shut up for a second and let me think."

"My gracious," said Estelle. "Look at that thing there. Now really. Why should you shake and tremble before an object like that? As far as I can see. And don't worry. I can see very far sometimes. If I want to. It's just another little glob of something or other in dirty old suspenders and pants."

"That's very interesting," said Bert. "Are you referring to me, lady?"

"If I can say even that much."

"Whew," said Bert. "There's a bedful of bones for you."

"Imagine," said Estelle. "Imagine the colossal nerve. Sneaking in on all four paws like this with his rotten old ropes and rags to wrap us all up ready for the cleaners in lumpy packages like I see back in there. The monster. Thank god I never found him under my bed."

"Lady," said Bert. "You can believe me. If you ever found a real live hunk of a man like me with the fluff under there, kerflop, you would drop down dead right on the spot."

"Now really," said Estelle. "Isn't it funny? One whiff and you can tell just like that. I bet he drinks beer a lot. And goes to the movies alone."

"Well," said Bert. "Not exactly. If it's a cool night, and I don't happen to have the gripes, I always take along with me a whole big bag of polly seeds. Since you look like one yourself. You know the kind I mean?"

"Rats," said Estelle. "Now look at this, will you? Why should this bun of mine always be falling apart on me lately? Oh, I can tell you. In Ulster County where I was born. I guess it gets so soft and silky sometimes when I rub in too much warm olive oil before I shampoo. We sure had a special name for the likes of him all right. Now don't all rush at once. But who here has a bobby pin she can spare? And if I weren't such a lady, I wouldn't hesitate a second to use it."

"Use your what where?" said Bert.

"Thank you, dear. Now let me see. What should I do now? Though it is a little bit bent. Should I say shoo? Or should I just haul off and swat him one?"

"Now, now," said Bert. "You should be very careful how you strain yourself, my dear. You're all mouth already."

"Oh, boy," said Estelle. "This is becoming my whole social life lately. Everywhere I go, I meet these great big polite and brilliant men. Yes, yes. You see now why I foam at the mouth? Go on, Maisie, dear. Speak to this sorry specimen. Settle his hash for him before he pollutes the air altogether. And if you happen to bite his head off while you're at it, why, don't you worry about it one bit. We'll just all chip in and mount it for him."

"And mazeltov to you too," said Bert.

"It's wasted. I happen to be a practicing Episcopalian."

"No kidding?" said Bert. "And here I was trying to guess. Is that what sticks out all over?"

"Why, you miserable thing."

"Guilty, your honor. But I swear. I didn't know it was loaded."

"Why," said Estelle. "After that. All I can say is. I pity you."

"Say it, say it. It's a damn good way to relieve yourself."

"I pity you from the bottom of my heart."

"Fine," said Bert. "If it's for free. I'll take a pound of that too. I'm a man who needs anything he can get."

"God help me," said Estelle. "Isn't this terrible? What is it with me anyway? I don't know why it is. But such creatures always bring out the worst in me."

"Well," said Bert. "Maybe that's because."

"Is it that my ears are too far apart? And that I always keep forgetting there's very little operating in between? That could be it in a nutshell. Don't you think? Of course if I were only a fat man, everybody in high or low places would love me dearly whether I had hair on my lip or not. And thank you all very much for listening. One thing I am beginning to realize. Every day in every way I'm becoming more and more like my married sister, Tess, who's vegetating in Mishawaka, Indiana of all places, who was always such an awful complainer. Even when as the eldest she inherited my mother's gold sapphire ring inlaid with simulated pearls which to my horror she, my sister, that is, always used to catch me when I was slipping it on and off. Maybe then. What I keep thinking is. Maybe it's all because I can't seem to control these long pale sensitive hands of mine, palms up or otherwise. Which is about all I ever inherited as my share from my slightly dippy female parent. All of a sudden I wake up in a great sweat, as so many of us do, and find my own fingers clawing and scratching right where the doctor said this lovely twittering thing I'm so afraid of decided to build itself a permanent nest. I've even tried washing my hands daily with fels naphtha. No fooling. And once even for a whole week with a solution of prune juice I cooked myself over a very slow fire. But. And there's always this horrid exception cropping up when you least expect it. It doesn't matter what I do. But nothing. Nothing seems to help."

"My dear lady," said Bert. "If I may have the honor of so addressing you. I can see you're really in there digging. And there's no question in my mind you have your whole heart in your work. But like Jesus said on the mountain top. That's all sheer tommytrot. And I was right there when he said it. If you're laying eggs, he said, stay in your coop. Watch your hem line where it hangs. Don't fly out so fast to tangle with barbed wire. You'll not only lose a lot of your tail feathers. You're liable to come up bleeding from the mouth with the bends. You get the point I'm driving at? Or are you going to leave me sitting on it all by myself?"

"Oh," said Estelle. "Shut up. Shut up already. I wasn't even talking to you in the first place."

"Ha," said Bert. "How do you like that? Now she tells me."

"As for you, Estelle, my own dear self. You vain stupid thing. You just had to have your own selfish little flare-up right out in public, didn't you? That was so very original, wasn't it? And what was the result? Why, you began real well, but you sure did dribble out fast, as usual. You thought you heard the call of the wild. You drifted off to

586

the warm magnetic south of a perfect stranger when you should have steered straight for the lonely icy north of your own heart where you knew you'd be absolutely cool and safe. As I remember. You went and slept all night on one side. You saw that morning sun come up. So like a real maniac, you flew to work in your sheerest outfit with both your petticoats to keep yourself from showing. And as soon as you heard the bad news, god, you had such visions of hunger that you flopped right down with a squawk on a tiny speck of corn. Merely a niblet. And of course, being you, you were immediately trapped in your own lime. As indeed you deserved. So bow out already. And stop that awful babbling, please. And for pete's sake, do try to take the sharp corners more slowly. And steel yourself for once to institute a search in your every pocket. Take stock. See where the real grass is growing. Piece yourself together, sister. It sure is time."

"That's funny," said Bert. "You know something? I once had a landlady out in Jamaica before I hooked up with Mae who used to give herself the pip like that. Only she had no teeth except what she could buy. And she was half black."

"I bite my lips. I counsel myself. I try to remember."

"Yeah," said Bert. "I sure know what you mean. It's like me and greasing my axle. I don't know. Maybe it's connected with taking a lousy bath. But I'll be damned if I don't keep forgetting."

"I keep saying to myself, even though there's always someone interrupting, as sure as there is a God in heaven, there's bound to be a hell here on earth for a least little schneider like you. Because why? Because his time is never your time. You're not the only flea in his ear. Why, the very second after you pray, you can hear our Almighty Father say, brace yourself, girlie, I have helped you all I possibly can, you are now absolutely on your own. You may ply, he tells me, your needle like a prim old pixie in pajama tops. You may snap up a sunflower seed like a saucy little titmouse in a picture book. Or pick up a green thread with all the grace of a gazelle in town for the races. But the cat's in the fire, woman. And that's the way the crockery crumbles."

"Well," said Bert. "Maybe that's because."

"So oolala," said Estelle. "And what the devil. Or some such smart-alecky thing."

"Check," said Bert. "You're right on the beam there, missus.

587

Chicken or not, you just have to try to be chipper or else. Or like that three-legged goofus with the sour grapes, who if I remember correct was terribly constipated for some seven-eleven years, and who had his bald gonk bashed in by a big square rock he was pushing up the hill with his schnoz as per agreement with the main cheese somewhere in the land of Greece, you'll never get out of this life alive."

"Ah," said Estelle. "I wish you hadn't said that."

"Why?" said Bert. "Did I blow on your face or something?"

"Why, it's fantastic," said Estelle. "Really. You must tell me before you go speeding away in your Stanley Steamer there. How in the world did you ever get to know such things? Did you pour over the Police Gazette while waiting for your next at the barber shop? Or did the little wifie push you into taking a home correspondence course in advanced plumbing with Price & Pitman?"

"Yea," said Bert. "Did you see what happened there? I bet I get a bronze medal for that. I finally made her crack her face."

"A clod," said Estelle. "Now admit it. You're a perfect clod, aren't you?"

"Well," said Bert. "I don't know about perfect."

"And yet," said Estelle. "There you are like any other boob in your heavy beard and seven-league boots. As big as life and twice as sassy."

"About that beard now. I know you won't believe this. But my face screams like hell if I shave every day."

"And mine," said Maisie Dubrow. "Mine always does when I don't."

"I guess," said Estelle. "It's just one of life's little mysteries."

"Sorry," said Maisie. "I know it's rude of me to be thinking aloud this way. But so far. Let me see. All I've been able to make out is this. He thinks he's well. And she knows she's not."

"But there it is," said Estelle. "Like a bright shining miracle that can blind you if you don't turn away. Oh, yes, my good man. You needn't drop your head that way. It's as plain as the nose on your face. And what could be plainer? You're all heart. You know how to reach out. That sure did look like a dime to me too until you just tested it with your foot. Who knows now? Maybe you were just born with it. But you sure do have the touch, don't you?"

"Oh," said Bert. "You know how it is. It's like I always say. To me everybody in this world is a person. And I don't care if it's a dog or a rat."

"And the strength," said Estelle. "And the patience of a good farm horse when it comes to taking guff from silly old hens like me. Is it that you never suffer from hangnails? How do you explain it all?"

"Easy," said Bert. "I don't crap around too much if I can help it. I roll with the punch. I try to handle people with silk gloves. I use my eyes. I move things. I get the kind of experience in my particular line of business you couldn't buy even if you had millions. Like today. You've got to stick with what's right there. And whop, before you know it, your nails are hard enough to play ticktacktoe, and you're voting the socialist ticket."

"Ah," said Estelle. "I see. So you recommend I shift weights around and travel more, is that it?"

"That," said Bert. "And maybe a little mineral oil too. It all depends on who your doctor is."

"Seigel."

"Seigel," said Bert. "Now how do you like that? Every place I go lately, I hear nothing but Seigel, Seigel. You have his phone number? He must be a real good man."

"He must," said Maisie. "She must. We all must. And you. Even you must too. I'm sorry to say."

"It could be," said Bert. "But I don't follow you."

"If you did," said Maisie. "I assure you. You would immediately find yourself a head shorter."

"Okay," said Bert. "What the hell. I guess you're next. But this'll have to be the last, folks. I'm running short of change."

"Believe me," said Maisie. "These are the days. When really. It becomes so painful for me to have to butt in this way and break up such a soulful affair just when it's beginning to show such progress. It's like killing off a baby before it gets born. I know it's a weakness of mine. But I really hate to do it."

"Jesus," said Bert. "If I knew what was good for me, I'd throw in the towel right now. These dames here are getting tougher to handle all the time."

"But I do want you two especially to understand why, after listening to you for so long, I have no other choice. I just have to stick my finger down my throat now to make myself vomit. Or so help me. I'll simply fade away and die."

"My dear miss," said Bert. "You think I was busted down to private

589

in the army for nothing? I'm a vet who happens to know his onions. I stand here ready to give you all the room you need to upchuck. Like my 2B teacher Mrs. Bumpington used to say. He who serves well serves last. So you just go right ahead and shoot to kill. Cousin Joe here will back me up on this. I just don't give a good goddamn any more what's in it for me. I'm here purely for your pleasure."

"How lovely," said Maisie. "The voice of the people again. Mind you. It's not that I don't appreciate what sounds like the genuwine article. And let's not get too snooty about it either. But all I really wanted to say was, oh, my poor head. But the trouble is. The last time I looked. So help me. I just couldn't locate it."

"Ha," said Bert. "You and me and the man on the corner. I'll tell you something, princess. If you'll be so kind as to invite me to one of your Saturday night shindigs, I'll be glad to shuffle in with my topper and tails on. My old bean here is beginning to conk out too."

"Great," said Maisie. "So much for that kind of noise. To turn now to what I understand a little better. I know you people will think I'm crazy when I tell you I really got to like the rattle and roar of those flipping machines because it gave me such a terrific sense of security. By the dawn's early light. And right on the dot too. It made my life hum so pleasantly as it skipped along getting fast nowhere. As I don't have to tell you. At the. I told you about my head. At the twilight's last gleaming. And o'er the ramparts we watch. But now. May those ratty things rot in hell with all their screwy attachments which never really worked right anyway. Together with our boss. May he never rest in peace. Him and his sheep's eyes. Flick. Ever since Monday. Of course now I understand. But I just couldn't figure out what he was trying to tell me with that tricky little finger of his every time he snuck by me. So that. Flick. Right where I sit on the softest part of me. As you can imagine. I was getting madder and madder all the time. If only I could somehow spit out what's still burning inside me like fire right here on the tip of my tongue."

"Say," said Bert. "You know something? I just now noticed it."

"Which is," said Maisie. "Why? Will someone here please tell me?"

"My Mae has a mouth something like that. But like I keep telling her. For cripes sake, Mae, you're not your frig, I mean, your slobby old lady. You're you. You got real class. Who in the hell tells you you have to smear it on so thick like that?"

590

"Why when it comes does love have to be the same old animule?"

"Oyoyoy," said Bert. "Like you people say."

"It's getting to be such a bore. It's positively sickening."

"Right," said Bert. "This is when I can tell. When a person talks to me like I'm some kind of an it, which a certain shamus in the Bronnix I once bunked into told me is even worse than being a schlemozzle, then right away I know I should run down to the ocean by the sea somewhere, and take a good duck for myself."

"Though why," said Maisie. "I should be so upset myself as to be yelling my head off is something a third party will have to tell me."

"It must be," said Bert. "I hang around you Jewish people so much. I swear. I'm beginning to sound just like one."

"What?" said Maisie. "Am I right, Joe? Wasn't it stupid of me to forget to bring my aggies today of all days? You once told me. You used to love to play farmer in the dell. As for me. All I have to do is to strike up the band with me, me, me. And right away I become you and you become me. The usual mix-up. Which means we could be just about anybody with a full crop of coarse hair, with a few crow's-feet thrown in, and two crunched ears all clogged up with the muck that words make. How about a quick game of odds and evens? Come on, boy, you're usually the champ around here. Guess which of my hands is holding the ice pick. Or why I should be the only one in my family who looks like she came straight out of Lapland instead of sweet old Bensonhurst. Which reminds me. Could any of you men here possibly give me some kind of estimate? What do you think every bit of me from my teensie-weensie waist up would fetch if I tried to auction it off? Just as a starter. And that of course would include what I boldly breast the waves with, since they stick so way out anyway, and my silky tanned arms which you should see how they can make at you in private like I was a real belly dancer from Egypt, and these slightly overlapping sparkling teeth of mine which once I sink them even into the hardest part of you, I warn you, watch out. And I guarantee you it's all untouched as yet by human hands. Male or otherwise. I really had to say to him. Papa, dear, you're wetting the bed again. You saw Mom when they dragged her out of here. Who's going to keep changing you now? Then turning to the other. Brud, I said. Always called my dear brother that. I swear, I said. You've become such an awful bitter seed. It should be written up in all the papers. First you go and switch pillows on me, and then you take another knot in my guts by telling me I've hit the jack pot with Pop because I happen to be the last daughter left, and then, to top it all off, you knock the checkerboard over with your snotty bessarabian elbow just when I was about to jump you twice. Damn you. Why? Why should it always be my fault when I never know who's on first? Or what clinging vine I never heard of has already jumped my claim to cloud nine? Or why, when I refuse to date again that stage-struck crony of yours who whistles through his nose until I'm fit to be tied, you have nerve enough to tell me it's bound to be the one mistake of my lifetime? Why? And that's the way she goes. In one head and out the other. Until I almost poked your eye out there, didn't I? Now isn't this hell? I know I was trying to get at something. Darn it. Now what was it I was trying to say?"

"That you're absolutely pooped," said Joe. "And you sure do feel the need for some kind of a pickup. Like say a nice good strong hot cup of java right down from the bottom of the boiler."

"Yes, yes," said Maisie. "And a powdered doughnut too. If there's any left this late. That's certainly part of it."

"Though actually," said Joe. "Just to show you who's the real wiseguy around here. I knew I was already at least a good half hour late. But something inside of me said, whoa, now, you never can tell, you better first pack yourself in a real big breakfast."

"Swell," said Maisie. "And where was I when you raised your knife and fork on high?"

"You?" said Joe. "You were gently creeping up like the gracious little dame you are on a certain kind of animal called death which is only too familiar and frightening to us all. And I have here a whole cigarette, plus a light no matter how many matches it takes, for the first one who can guess who the hell it is I'm trying to imitate now. And it's no use your looking at Judy or Tavia here. If they'll excuse me for dropping names. Whose faces positively shine now, I might as well tell you while I'm at it, because they are suddenly free to be slaves again in some other county at large. If they can possibly swing it. It can't be the two Black Crows. Whose real names, according to these same two kids, are actually Finkel and Schwartz. Or maybe I'm making like old Princess Pocahontas who traveled the ocean blue with Mr. Jake Smith, I think, whose name cropped up in a book I was reading the other day about some scotch lord who came to the new world to get the kinks

592

out of his stiff upper lip, which he kept bare of hair because he had his wind up about his swiss niece, or ít could be she was half eyetalian, who wandered all over the alps like a wombat about to drop its young, and jolly well shoot down in america the beautiful, this duke I mean, the wild turkey and the thundering buffalo. Good show. Does any of this protect you and give you a chance to breathe? Great. Or that. You know. That goofy guy in the movies with the pancake hat my sister loves so much because he never cracks his face, or ever gives you any hint in so many words what went wrong in the first place, though a trillion cops keep chasing him, or even bothers to send out a single S.O.S. in or out of a balloon so that if the people saw they would rush to the rescue, but just goes right down with his ship, still puffing away on that cold corncob pipe of his, and as the waters slowly cover him over, you're beginning to know who, two tiny words come up on the screen, and get larger and larger until we hate to admit it, but that's it, folks, that's the end, what he had to give us he gave us, there's no use hanging around any more, it's all over."

"Buster Keaton."

"Right," said Joe. "That's the bozo. I tell you, Dubromowitz."

"Do so," said Maisie. "Maybe you're the one who really can. Who knows?"

"Whoever now," said Joe. "And I don't care if it's the whole floating membership of your whole. And let me ask you now. Where the hell is that cuckoo thing keeping itself now that you need it so bad? Your whole good old spitting and spatting international ladies garment workers union. I assure you now. Whoever has the gall to say you're a real gone goose, and then tries to turn his rotten back on you, is going to have to hold his horses there a second and battle it out with me."

"My friend," said Maisie. "Well, now, aren't you nice?"

"But I mean," said Joe. "And it's no use batting your lashes at me that way. Because after all I like this nip in the air as much as you do. And I'm not going to let anyone shove me out of my good spot here until I can get myself aired out as I should. Because I assure you. When I finally get my gander up."

"Dander."

"That's it. I'm ready to wipe up the floor with anyone. And it could be the Manassa Mauler himself. Or old King Solomon who was so solly dear, as I guess you heard, after he shared his pup tent with the

Queen of Sheba. Or even that Himmelfarb union man of yours with murder in his eye you're always going into a huddle with. It makes no difference to me. I don't care who it is."

"Gee," said Maisie. "I hope I hear you right. You mean to say you're really going to jump right in there like George Hackenschmidt, or is it Strangler Lewis who's champ now, and fling all those half-dead bodies around just for the sake of poor little old insignificant me?"

"Yep," said Joe. "Until whop, whop. With one good crunching scissors and a nice clean body slam, either way, I pin them all to the mat, two straight falls out of three."

"Terrific," said Maisie. "And after which? What follows? Now take a good deep breath. And give us the rest of it."

"Since what the hell," said Joe. "I might as well. Since this may be my last chance to give my all. Because who knows what silly business will next take place? It's like. You know. It's like Karl the Marxist used to scribble on his yellow writing pepper when he felt particularly cold and hungry, which was exactly three times a day, my worker of the world, he used to say, first give that blue stranded nose of yours a preliminary wipe to see vas iz loose in the way of fluid assets, and if not a drop, then pop, flick out your feeble left, if you still got a face to save, to knock down the bosses, all covered over and blinded with blood, please check with Colish for color, you then cross over your crippled right, and all them rusty chains will suddenly fall from you with an awful clank, if you can stand the noise, I say. Ha. A little exercise always helps. I tell you, Mais. You've hardly begun to work up a real sweat yet. The hell with being so hard on yourself. All you have to do is compare yourself with a nogoodnik gym fighter like myself. And you will immediately see. You're right up there with the best of them."

"My gosh," said Maisie. "I know I said a deep breath. But I never dreamed you would make it that deep."

"I'm struggling," said Joe. "I don't know what I'm trying to say."

"How was it you were so smart? You saw it all coming, didn't you?"

"Saw it all coming?" said Joe. "What are you talking about? Are you looking for a punch in the eye or something? You mean to say you think that if I knew you were all going to be squeezed out of your jobs, I wouldn't have been the first one to warn you? I wasn't the only one who fell asleep at the switch. Hell. I'm right here. I'm not afraid to show myself. You don't see me running out on you like a dirty rat, do you?"

"Oh, sure," said Maisie. "I always knew I could count on you. Since you claim to be so honest and seem to have so much time on your hands. I wonder if you could take a quick look around for me and see if we already have enough people for a minyan. Before we all collapse like bowling balls one on top of the other. After all that's happened. Or do I mean pins? Look around you and tell me. Who is there I can trust? Is there anybody in this whole stinking. I'm no snob. I've always been willing to smell my share. Like our amazing truckman here who's just been investigating the state of his own armpits like the sly dog he is. Tell me. Is there anywhere a single creature left in this whole chiseling and chickenhearted world I can still believe in?"

"Why, yes," said Joe. "You. And no one else but you. That's who."

"Who?" said Maisie.

"You, you."

"Oh," said Maisie. "Ah, well. If that's the best you can do. Still it's nice to know you still give a hoot."

"Ye gods," said Joe. "Talk about running around in circles. How long can we expect to live if we keep it up this way? Who's going to bury who around here if we all die first?"

"Don't worry about it. I have a funny feeling I hit rock bottom way before you did."

"Sure, sure," said Joe. "But whatever happened. I can bet you this. You sure in hell have learned one thing."

"That I'm an absolute flop on the telephone."

"Oh," said Joe. "Worse. Much worse."

"Why is it? Can you tell me?"

"And that is," said Joe.

"Why is it that it always seems to work for everyone else but me?"

"And that is," said Joe. "That breaking bread and breaking silence are two distinct and different things."

"Ugh," said Maisie. "I can't even begin to tell you. Either. You hear? Either I get a great big buzz for my money. Or I keep getting a string of wrong numbers like cold chick-peas rolling off a knife. Or. If it so happens I finally manage like a witch to get the right party, it turns out to be such a bad connection, it just about drives me wild. I just can't seem to get through to that woman at the union office there. A honeymoon sandwich. Now what does she mean by a honeymoon sandwich?"

"Why, you poor thing. You mean to say you don't know?"

"No, you ninny. I don't know. Would I be asking you otherwise?"

"Oh, my," said Joe. "The same old cry. Lettuce alone."

"Aie," said Maisie. "Of course. Let us alone. What else? I knew it had to be something as goshawful as that. Wait. Don't turn away from me now. Listen. It'll only take another second. See if I'm right, Joe. The way I figure it is. That grand old mountain of blubber, that Mrs. Pepke there, that widow lady for life to the nuttiest local in the needle trade. Or as she likes to jump you lately, Pauline here, if you're not ringing me about shelling out at least one percent of your arrears, then you can jolly well hang yourself up right where you are, comrade. It suddenly dawned on me. She must've had a real nervous breakdown without her knowing it. Gosh, I know she sounds like she's got a great big hole in her wig. But gee, who isn't a little touched in the head these days? It's weird. Before I can even open up my mouth. I can't hear you, she says, speak louder. What sow? she says. You're falling me off way off from where? Now why, she says, should I care if your old mare has the colic? What ish as in tish? You want me to send you quick which what by who? Uh-uh, she says. Sorry, sweetie. If you've got your heart set on hooking Pearl the Mutter, it's no dice, that chirpy radical chap's gone south to take a flying to reorganize the richer runaway factories in his red little union suit. It's like a bale of cotton that's soon forgotten. I said, cotton, rotten. If there's one thing I refuse to consider, she says, it's them artificial lilies. Just you try to imagine how you would feel, she says, if you always had to sit in a pool of sweat, fanning your face with one hand, and holding back the ocean with the other. Of course, she says. I understand perfectly. I've had a cork up mine for years and years. That scratchy lace is what I call a damn disgrace. You've got a new shipment for me of what? Traps? What bundle of scraps? Sure I know longerine. I wore lawn, she says, before you were born. I said. You say you're sending it by what? On whose balaam's ass? What room? she says. Where? Are you trying to put me on? Doggone it, sis, what with some of the saddest and wildest operators in the whole flopping industry packed so solid in my hallway, they are even occupying my spittoons, with one cheery group actually carried piggyback up the stairs by certain sporty brother cutters looking for

596

pussy, as is their privilege, singing avalon with the darkies in the field under the spreading apple tree, with the bigger older bunch so deep in the dumps, they squat there like zombies, digging for dry coozies way up their nose canals, reading over and over again with their lips what it says there under the fire hose and the axe, waking up all of a sudden to tweak out hairs like wool and slap some roses into their cheeks as if they just heard christ was coming like a playboy on his little old pushmobile, and the whole damn mob howling like hyenas every time New Jersey explodes and makes a smell, wired glass is no protection, and with right in front of me as I speak, a real tough titty-high tripartite board of tuckers just laid off from Lapidus & Sons, with the babe in the middle so bursting with juices and so zoftik generally, you could pop her right in the oven as is, swinging their long flashy stems with every stocking a run in it with such a thumpety-thump from high up my file cabinets stuffed full of the usual crap about you and me, though my photo will show I used to be quite a slinky sleeve setter myself, and with, with some kind of a brownish spaniel, will you hold yourself in a second, all curled up in my out basket like one big movement addressed to God, and I swear to you, will you please let me finish, the biggest blonde mamma's baby of a machinist, snoring away in three colors right on the top of my old oaken rolltop here, where in the holy swearword do you think I can put it? Well. Of course I knew exactly where. But being so dainty myself. How could I tell her? I can't hear you, she says, speak louder. Now, now, she says. Don't be such a sorehead. If that's my kissie, then I shoot first. Are you kidding? How many times a day do you think I can come again? Maybe if I switch ears. Honestly, she says. You're just about one of the worst dumb doras. You sure have your nerve practicing your famous burial scene from Rigoletto on my precious time. I said, she says. You remind me of a bald button puncher I used to lunch with at Murph's who lived with her stunning twin sister and her slobbering spitz at the bottom of the well. If I meant basement, would I say well? That's right, booby. A small woubleyou as it appears in the middle of a ripe pear. Cheez, she says. No matter what ailed that dame, she just had to get it off her chest. Right down her old screechy sliding part. She was like my water going down when it meets my gas coming up. And that, as I don't have to tell you, that can really hurt. Oof, yeah. Talk about your stabbing pains, she says. I guess I must've been clobbered by a loose horseshoe the last time I had to go and look at the crops. Now my rah-rah corset is riding up and up again. And as far as I can tell, I have a lady here in the balcony. While up the lazy river. Ah, so whatski? So what, she says, if your darn garters go pop and your blotchy gums begin to bleed? So long as you're well read. And you're still damn good in bed. I swear I can hear you scratching yourself in the worst possible area. I'm full of like who is? I hope you're not saying. Oh, well. As for that. Let me tell you this, kiddo. Even if, as I think you're implying, I'm enough to make you resign from the human race, I'm afraid you'd still be, as I hear tell, just plain shit out of luck just the same, because you'd only find, all spruced up as you may be, that you're still completely surrounded by nobody else but yourself, with cheers, as the feller says, with your granny's spangled china silk hoop skirt thrown over your head, which had to be all nicely pinked and shirred where the raw seams were beginning to show, as I can well imagine, keeping it tucked under your armpit like a bird, since actually it's what happens in the daytime and not in the night that scares the pants off of us, but I mean, as you blubber to go bye-bye where your land would be dry land, because you're apt to lose patience with your own body when all that matter comes gushing out of you without your permission like a dam busted every bloody month, I have a knack for seeing such things, because, it's like I'm telling you, when a fact's really a fact, you always have to face it all alone, standing there like a yuckish, it's good talking to you anyway, trying to think back to the time when your immediate boss first snuck in with his little awl to scout your lily of the valley, just above where your thing begins, where the pot's always boiling, I see I'm having a fine rattle, with all the trimmings, from me to you, your willing slave, as all of a sudden he locates and sinks in hard, hi there, have a cigar, with his two very interesting tax-exempt compound six percent alternating front snaggle-toots. Hey? How do you like the way I sound like Spinoza? Booshwah is right. I better watch myself, she says. One careless moment and poof. Even without my specs, I can smell disaster coming. I really must give a good heave ho some weekend soon and get that blasted window to the fire escape unblocked. I said. Holy molasses. Excuse me a second, she says. I seem to have a fresh development here, taking advantage of me while I'm busy gabbing, trying to dive with his hooks and eyes right down into my bosom. I'll give him such a shove soon. Geh, go on, now. Blow, I said. Hoo. Wait until I adjust. Now where on East 14th three doors away from Ohrbach's did such a lazy-looking assistant sweeper just two days on the job ever learn how to leave his feet like that? Snapping in half my best pearl button. Look at lover boy there with his black eyes as big as bombs, reaching out for another feel like he was walking in his sleep. Christopho Columbo still doesn't believe it. That's right, hot stuff. You made the trip. You were there. You can bet your sweet ass they're real. Ah, now, you better watch it, bub. I know a plumb-ber's helper who once lost a whole arm that way. Hey? she says. You see now why I get so hot and bothered? Maybe you can tell me while you're lolling around there, waiting to catch the early show. What dopey higher-up was it who sent out such a rush order for, gosh, it'll just about kill my looks altogether if I have to go around with a clothespin over my nose, as I'm beginning to think, for so many mussed up, discarded samples of last year's style of people-knits in case some damn fool buyer comes hotfooting it in to scoop them all up for her next fire sale? It's like I'm dreaming. If them leftover workers had wings, they'd be first-class termites. Either they come buzzing and sucking around me like I was a free soup kitchen from down on the Bowery. Or whole gangs of them settle on me to stay like they thought I was their last big fat bundle of cutwork. Oh, I'm so worried about him. You have no idea. And I'm not even talking about those awful piles he's worked up ever since he became such a squirming sitting down exec. Or that case of colitis from his Thanksgiving turkey stuffing he fixed himself out of old chestnuts that left him looking like a crooked walking stick. But now they say it may be Parkinson's. Today he suddenly appears right on the dot for a change, all dolled up in his son's beanie, and the top half of his flowered perjumpers for a shirt. Go tell Ernie Bo-peep he's losing his sheep. There's a blackhead on the tip of his nose I'm dying to squeeze. And I notice one of his ears is bleeding. He holds up his hand to shut me off before I can really get going, and shuffles off to the men's to stick his head under the cold water faucet. It's like three years later when he comes sloshing back, carrying a mousetrap with a live thing in it, and in his great excitement, sprays me from head to foot. Mrs. Peepee, he says, it's happening, they're beginning to eat certain parts of people. Really? I say. Ugh. In which case, I say, backing away, I sure am glad to see you brought your lunch. With me, he says, it's like overnight and I have a full-grown boil and moustache. You should've seen the size of that kiss sore on the neck of that shrimp. I never know, he says, what my sugar count is between nine and twelve, but it's a real blessing my suspenders are always attached to my best patched pair. May I have your attention for just one second, please? Sure thing, I say, looking up from my hand mirror, that klutz, I tell him, from Charlie's Stationery called on his final price on them white bond pads and ring binders, and I have a note here to myself to ask again what precisely is the fine for any group showing of french pictures if it falls within the purview of this local, where I come from, we call that kind of a kiss sore a hickey. Now don't start thinking, he says, that I'm always saying yes when my head begins to shake up and down this way. Listen to the little bastard, he says. It's singing. What's a hair more or less? I can remember when I had teeth that could handle jelly apples. I keep having this awful feeling I'm about to make in my pants. I may be a little thicker behind than I used to be, but I can still feel it when I'm standing in my own draft. In the higher gusts. Are you the jane who percolates or drips it? Mrs. Peepee, as one Litvak to another, I call on you now to have courage. Snap that top fastener. Put your tweezers down and chalk this up on the board for me in your nice big round letters. From now on. Look at it. It's right up there on its toes, listening. You spik henglish, buster? From now on, if any member feels she has to croak from whatever cause from April through December, she'll just have to do it all on her own. You got that? I'm in no position any more to go around saying, be my guest. You tell them straight from me. No more funeral benefits this year. My old kitty and me, we're absolutely busted. Meeting adjourned. Did this mouse come with a hat on or not? If you hear screaming, forget it. I'm late as it is for my finger painting lesson. His ha-ha. I see, I said to her. Thank you, Mrs. Pepke. His ho-ho. Thank you so much for these belly laughs. Hee. I really must run now before I wet myself. Break, I says to her, break thou roaring ocean right upon the shingle of this she-she-sheety shore. Like my kid brother says when I try to get chummy with him, lay off or I'll monopolize you. In union there is solidarity? Is a pint still a pound the whole world around? Is this where I expect help to come to me? Maisie, not Daisy, Maisie Dubrow, speaking. Is this your idea of a game? I can't hear you, she says to me, you'll have to speak louder, louder. Have you lost your lushen altogether? You're driving me crazy with your crackling there. Are you sure your rattletrap is really open? Jiggle your hook for the operator. Maybe you're breathing wrong. Are you standing up or sitting down? What do you mean both? Don't be such a wiseguy. Come on, now, suck in that stomach. Make believe your chest's a drum. And give it all you got with your umlaut. Ready? Let's hear you loud and clear now. Oh, fine. Very good. If that's a heigh-ho, silver, then I'm the masked marvel. Say. Are you the comic who's always telling me she's calling from Capistrano? You're kidding. Is that with a Co. or an Inc.? Aha, I see. Nothing. Aren't you lovely now, trying to snub me? Do you realize how many people are waiting their next while I'm holding this line open for you? Aw, now. How would I know if I'm bragging or complaining? All I ask is, don't spit in my kasha, and I won't spit in yours. But of course, my dear. I understand. I know words aren't everything. If I could only tell you how I used to listen. How can anyone expect me to help even the smallest child when I'm still such a babe in the woods myself? I used to lay awake all night listening, and if I'd hear his lips go pop, or that low soft chrup of his, I'd begin to breathe again, and I'd doze off a little in between, and try to catch a few winks myself. Do you know what that bean pole in his shiny black at the parlor was so mean as to say to me? And all because I couldn't afford satin lining. My good woman, he said to me, with such a smile, not that it's any skin off my nose, but why the, I mean, why should you want to bury the poor bast, I mean of course, your dearly beloved with his hearing aid on for when you can so easily hock it yourself? So I said to him, my good sir, if I may call you such, that's the way the gentleman came when fully equipped, and I want him to be all ears down there in case he hears something to my advantage he might want to pass along, all depending on what, do you mind? Men. It's always a battle with those jocks all the way. The company doctor said to me, for a ship's carpenter who used to fence with the sea and fight mountains with a stick, his lower bowel is a howl, and his right kidney is a riot, and his babbling blood system has blipped off one million point two red corpuscles somewhere along the line between San Fran and the Solomon Isles, what kind of grub do you feed the guy after he pumps ship after he gets so red in the face on his shore leave which he says is killing him? Did you ever? Wherever I go, I get arguments. Oh, my darling Alphie, my beautiful Al. They say there's a knot at the end of the rope for everyone, but there wasn't

601

one for him. I know because I looked. I swooped down on it like a hawk. I picked it apart like it was oakum. I wound it around my neck and pulled. I carried it around in my mouth like a dog. I wore it for a belt until I got rope burns. I coiled it in my hair and played a thousand games of double solitaire, and a few hands of pisheh-payseh when I could, asking the marked cards to tell me. One time I was so off my nut, I found myself looking at the wrong end under gnu, but even there I had no luck. Is it that I'm too superstitious or what? It's all so weird, ain't it? How can a man with a size eighteen neck, and a chest on him like a beer barrel, who loved to strut around in immaculate wrestler's tights, break down so quick, and become such an awful bawlbaby? What is there in our bodies that can make us do that? Come home, quick, I'm dying. What time is it getting to be? I hope I'm not keeping you? Every day at twelve sharp when I phoned him from here to check, all I ever got was, come home, quick, I'm dying. Aw, now, I used to say to him. Of course you are. We all are, aren't we? All the time. I'm amazed I could say such things. But I had to say something, didn't I? How could I keep running home when I had to protect my job? Why, even when he punctured his dropsy and gangrene set in, I tried my very best to keep up his spirits. I used to say to him, Al, listen. Don't think about love. And stop thinking about sex. Just think about living. Living, Al, dear, only living. Use up your ass's skin. I'll wash between your toes tonight as soon as I come home from shopping. Try to see my side of it. But all he could ever say like a drunken man was, it's no use your talking, you better come home, quick, I'm dying. Until one day it got so on my nerves, I slammed down the receiver before I knew what I was doing, and I was so horrified at myself that I immediately called him right back, but it was too late, there was no answer. My ring finger is still bent like a fishhook where I caught it on the bedspring trying to lift his body back on. He does have one sister left, but she lives way the hell out in Seattle somewhere, so I'm the only one he can really count on to be at the unveiling. I sometimes wonder what he'll come back as. Ain't it lucky I know how to edge my own hankies? I don't know if the moon will be out tonight, but I'm suddenly so tired. Oh, dear. I hope I'm not blowing in your ear. I wish I knew where I could go to practice dying. I hate someone who sticks to you like glue, don't you? What's the matter with you there that you're so quiet? I know this call is costing you a mint. But don't you see now why I can't bring myself to hang up on anyone? I sure do pray you go on to finer things after this. Would you like to try for broke? What exactly was it you wanted? I said to Mrs. Pepke, to report a runaway, I said. A what? she said. I said, a complete collapse, I said of all my various castles in Spain. I'm sorry, she says. I can't hear you. You'll have to speak louder. Oh, I said. Oh. Oh, I said. I began to moan to myself and bow up and down like I was in the temple dovening. Oh, I said, oh. I knew I was elected. I almost began to giggle. I knew I was the little one who had to be the big one again and put that poor thing out of her misery instead of expecting her to put me out of mine. I said to myself, be gentle now, even if you don't feel it. So oh. I quietly hung up on her and just stood there. I felt like after praying to God while making water. I was still myself. A first generation female fool. I was such a great success. I was right back where I started from."

"And then," said Frankie. "I sat me down and wrote."

"Jesus," said Joe. "What can I say? They're sprinkling the street on our side. Maybe that'll help clean up the mess we're all in."

"Hey," said Frankie. "Wait till you hear me. I've been practicing like a maniac."

"Watch it," said Joe. "Look at that queer potato there with gloves on with the fingers cut off, holding up an open umbrella to keep the sky from caving in on him. We're crazy not to charge admission. Will you all please kindly step back a second before some innocent party here gets entirely swept away?"

"Poo-poo-pee-dpo," said Frankie. "And a hot-cha-cha. There's a fairy in my garden. And a red rose up my nose."

"Why not?" said Joe. "Knowing you, I was sure it had to happen sooner or later."

"It's a song," said Frankie. "You want to hear me toot it out on this harmonica?"

"Uh-uh. Sticky fingers. How do you do?"

"I didn't swipe it," said Frankie. "It's old Georgie's. Honest. He said I could schmooze around with it if I knocked out all the spit after I was finished. What a dumb cluck. I'm always forgetting. Is the top where it says Hohner? Where do you stick the tongue? Maybe mine is too pointy. You should see. I always have to sneak out and practice in the hall because right away I get so goddamn red in the face. I still don't know. What's the best way to blow? In or out?"

"Well," said Joe. "If it's Mozart you're trying to wah-wah, then I'd certainly have to say out."

"Really?" said Frankie. "Mozart? Is that on the hit parade? How's it go?"

"Oh, god. Oh, well."

"I'll be a snotnosed gazook," said Bert.

"All right," said Joe. "I don't mind. If it helps us out of this fix, I'm all for it."

"A dewdrop," said Bert. "A real wholesale manufacturer. Did you see what a pippin business came dripping out of me?"

"I was fascinated," said Joe. "I was wondering when it would flop."

"Plop," said Bert. "Before I even know it's happening. It just about drives me up the wall. Every time I get myself steamed up a little, my goddamn nose starts running."

"Really," said Joe. "I'm getting curious. Are you about to ask for my hand in marriage? Is this what you do when you're not frying ice? What in the hell keeps you anchored here?"

"Shit, man."

"Aw, now, that tells us something."

"But I mean," said Bert.

"I don't doubt that for a second."

"I keep thinking I'm my own boss," said Bert. "But look at me. Not only was I born without pockets, and so puckered up in the puss, my Pop said I looked older than him, but I was pulled out of there so rough and on the bias that I'm still kind of groggy."

"Hell," said Joe. "You were lucky. I had one front tooth showing, but absolutely no brains."

"That's what I've been saying," said Bert. "That's exactly what I've been saying there. You just got to rip off a few like that a couple of times a year or you'll bust altogether. Did you see the knockers on that one? I know I snuffle a lot. But you won't catch me giving my love letter a good smack in public before I mailed it like that fat little fuzzface there. How do you like me getting high on other people's troubles? I'll show you in a second the fake goatee I use to make me look like Uncle Sam when I'm crossing the state line with a hot load of peppercorns and applejack."

"Oh," said Joe. "That's okay. No great rush. I can see already I pushed the wrong button."

"But I'm only trying to show you," said Bert. "When you're absolutely desperate and dying to make it into tomorrow. It's a fact. Once you tuck yourself in for the night. Everthing in this fucked-up world from graves to jobs is up for grabs. How else do you think I take my vacation every year except in little bits like this?"

"I think I should warn you," said Joe. "This is just the kind of talk that grows warts."

"Warts," said Bert. "I didn't know that."

"I didn't think you did."

"Right," said Bert. "The ignorance of some people. It's like with this maroon here who didn't know Mozart is the kind of stuff you paint on walls. Look at them wide-open spaces on his mug. No wonder like krazy kat he gets himself conked right and left wherever he goes. He ain't got no proper eyes yet. He's still wearing his behind on his head."

"Well," said Joe. "At least it keeps him warm."

"Aardvark, ain't he? You think we should slap him in a cage?"

"I don't know," said Joe. "There's something familiar about you. Did you ever carry a banana, I mean a banner in a parade?"

"That's okay," said Bert. "Don't worry, kid. I'm no nut altogether. I know where I am. I'm keeping my finger right on the place."

"Where?" said Joe. "Show me."

"Here," said Bert. "See what it says right here on this sheet?"

"Shake well before using. Jesus saves."

"What?" said Bert. "Where the hell are you looking?"

"Wait," said Joe. "How can I read when you don't hold it straight? It's a good thing I know a little Yiddish mixed with goy. Scratch that. See Mack Ritter the tack spitter about breaking his blip is that for running his magic hammer up Mae. The cad. I should say. I have a rotten lob? My flush needs a new washer. My old heap a ring job. The guy's a poet and don't know it. It might pay to look into this. Am I cockeyed or merely stupid? It says here. Baby lima beans are best with the bells of St. Mary and four-lane highways. That's a pretty mess. I flashed. No. I smashed my 1 oz. eye drooper. Dropper. It really burns me bad in the corners when she stoops to bend and it all backs up. Sorry about that. If what? Wrong font. How can I read it when you pull? If rain resists? Ah, if pain persists, consult my heart at thy sweet voice? Cripes. Whatever you do, don't forget to take in the wash."

"No, no," said Bert. "Not up there. Right down here. See what it says? It says I'm supposed to pick up only your machine heads today. I tell you, pal. You people are still lucky. You must've all stepped in horseshit or something."

"Crazy," said Joe. "That's real crazy, man. And when are you supposed to come for the rest of our bodies?"

"Ah," said Bert. "That's it. Who knows? Maybe never. I like the way you said that. Maybe the sonofabitch will get religion and call it off the last second. I got a feeling maybe an angel will come down from heaven and tip his elbow and throw it all in reverse. Maybe it's like the doc says, you can pull up your pants now, son, that thing ain't terminal. I know it's costing me. But I just had to hang around and tell you."

"Oh," said Joe. "You're a brick all right."

"Ditto," said Bert. "I tell you what. If you're free some Thursday night, I'll take you down to the Y to watch how the real pros play four-wall handball."

"Better yet," said Joe. "Make it next Monday and maybe we'll do a little head-hunting together."

"I can't," said Bert. "I didn't tell you about those floating bone chips in my elbow yet, did I?"

"Shake," said Joe. "Since you're hurting, I won't squeeze too hard."

"It sure is tough trying to be a human being, ain't it?"

"So long as you can say it with a smile."

"I kind of overdid it, didn't I?"

"Hell," said Joe. "It's the only way."

"My fellow Americans," said Bert. "Of whatever nationality. Next time, I'll try something easier. Ain't she sweet walking down the street? Like having a baby or something. Aw, says she, why don't you dry up? Well, says I, it's like anything else. It's a day by day proposition. You know and I know there's a broken heart for every light on Broadway. River. Stay away from my door. I know you gals hate my guts for making tracks like a cat all over your nice clean kitchen floor. But today. Who's walked off with my hand truck? I know it's disgusting the way it spilled over on you. But today. How can I explain it? The way I feel. It's like. I can only make like this with both hands. Today the whole world's my family."

"You hear that?" said Joe. "I don't know what you people are complaining about? You may be losing an entire factory, but you sure in hell have gained a son."

606

"I don't know what it is," said Estelle. "It's not that I'm such a prude. Or anything like that. But somehow or other. I just can't kiss men."

"For real?" said Maisie. "Or just imagining?"

"Not that I'm exactly dying to. Seeing what choice I have."

"Maybe it's because your shade of lipstick isn't dark enough."

"You think so?" said Estelle. "To go with what?"

"With the color of your upset insides on this glorious red-letter day. Or with mine. It doesn't matter which."

"Oh, boy," said Estelle. "That would be rich."

"I should say," said Maisie. "And not only that. Here's me now with a fresh cold sore coming up on the corner of my mouth. It frazzles me. Ever since I was a kid. Always popping up on the exact same spot."

"Courage," said Estelle. "Let's kiss this world goodbye no matter how much it hurts. Let's zoom out there. Let's do it as a team. Let's try Macy's first."

"Good idea," said Maisie. "Now that my position has changed so all of a sudden, I could use a smaller change purse."

"And I," said Estelle. "I've been looking high and low like a crazy one for a hurricane lamp that really works."

"I'm forever blowing bubbles. Pretty bubbles in the air."

"Now don't start mocking," said Estelle.

"Vesta la goober," said Maisie. "Like in peanuts. Watch now. Watch how every little dope springs eternal."

"I'm serious," said Estelle. "How do you know what I mean?"

"And of course," said Maisie. "And like my dreams. They fade and die away. Estelle the solemn owl. Tickle, tickle. How much do you weigh on the hoof? Let me see if I can throw you over my shoulder like a hunk of beef."

"Is she dotty?" said Estelle. "All I'm trying to say is. Stop it, I said. I see it as a sputtering candle. Will someone please come and help me sit on her? And I'm always so afraid the merest puff will blow it out."

"Poof," said Maisie. "Where have you been all your life? Don't you know yet what's happened? It's gone. It's already went."

"I'm talking about my soul," said Estelle.

"Soul," said Maisie. "Job. Same old cute little thing. Now you see it. Now you don't. How would you like to pat some fresh peach powder on your dainty foghorn, ducks, and accompany me to our recent place of employment, and there to assist me with your fine pinpricked fingers in cleaning out my drawers?"

"Sorry, love. You would need a man for that."

"Why, Estelle."

"It isn't beginning to sprinkle, is it? You people never knew she was such a giggler, did you?"

"Ah, me," said Maisie. "With a one and a two. And a buckle your shoe. What's the use of me trying to show you how I can laugh it off like a good sport when you all know how much it really burns me up? Especially when I was just beginning to feel like a real solid citizen who was so proud to be paying income tax. Talk about being battered and all balled up. I can't even get silly for a second lately without feeling like an absolute wreck. I wonder what it is that's finally catching up with me? I thought if I had my ears pierced. Is my pancreas under my spleen? Or is it the other way around? I wish I had more of those red capsules racing around in my blood. Corpuscles. You're right. With a three and a four. And a good spit on the floor. Like my fierce papery Momkins used to say when she'd begin to reel. Bring that schmootzik wallpaper of roses nearer to me or I'll fall."

"Fine," said Estelle. "Just tell me how far. And which way. Not that I'm so perfectly steady on my pins myself. But I'm here to help all I can. I always knew I'd make a good hitching post."

"Everything," said Maisie. 'Everything is such a shock. My poor mother must've had some pleasure out of it."

"But think," said Estelle. "Think. Something else is already beginning to happen to you behind your back."

"Oh, god," said Maisie. "Don't tell me what. Even if you know."

"It's a fact," said Estelle. "Just turn around and you'll see. Look how this one big happy family is now breaking up into restless and worried little groups. They're sniffing around. They're looking for the right combination. They want to live. Their mouths are open like dried-up little birds. Can you hear them? Where's my daily bread? Where's my silks and sashes? Where are all the exciting options and possibilities we dream about until we are dizzy? I'm not saying it's progress. But they always keep changing on us, don't they? Look. No wonder our audience is shrinking. Look at the way this wild and wicked earth, for example, is flirting with that good-time Charlie the sun. How else do you think a new boss is born? You're smiling. But take that fat buck of a pigeon there strutting after his snooty opposite number to make more of the same. And yet no two ever come out exactly alike. Doesn't

608

that give you hope? Doesn't that curdle you? Isn't this music to your ears? Like say one night of love? And how all the horns and brakes of the whole metropolitan area are announcing a tremendous clearance sale of discards like you and seconds like me for the sake of the future with how shall I say? With such joi de vivre. If you'll pardon my upper Hudson River accent. And how in spite of all, the color at last is returning to my heart-shaped face. You have no idea how much a real fancy wedding with all the trimmings costs nowadays."

"Trot, trot," said Maisie. "I am only a clucking hen. Trying my best to follow you."

"The flowers alone. And the booze. And a four-piece band. Not to speak of the upkeep afterwards of a new apartment to the front if available. And heaps of pillowcases and jars of vaseline. And tons of cat food if both have. And prospective in-laws with their exorbitant demands waiting in the wings to pounce. Eech. I'd rather die first than expose myself to anything as awful as all that."

"I'm not saying which," said Maisie. "But one of us sounds like the noon whistle."

"Nonsense," said Estelle. "Your voice does get a little squeaky every now and then. But that's perfectly understandable. Considering the heavy load you had on your heart. And the way you had to let loose."

"Oh," said Maisie. "So you think it's me?"

"There," said Estelle. "You see what I mean? I hope it doesn't become permanent. If you ask me, what you need most of all right now is a long drink of water and a brisk walk around the block. That ought to shake up your liver for you."

"If I still have one."

"So," said Estelle. "If not, not. It's amazing what you can do without. If you're wild to howl in the wilderness, you'll always find a short cut. How about it, lost one? Are you coming or not?"

"I'm coming, mother, I'm coming."

"Isn't this nice?" said Estelle. "Arm in arm like two mouseketeers. It's like the flight from Egypt all over again, isn't it it?"

"Why, that's fantastic," said Maisie. "That's exactly what I was thinking myself. Let the other guy chase us for a change. If he has nothing better to do. As who has these days? Ta-ta, everyone. Now don't you girls be watching that birdie too long. Olive oil, my son. If old man Pharaoh ever asks for me, let him jolly well ask again."

"Do you mind?" said Estelle. "I'm kind of superstitious about this. If at all possible, I always try to walk south first."

"Oh," said Maisie. "Of course. I'm sorry. By all means. I guess I was a little too anxious to turn my slim beautiful back on the whole shooting match for a while. By the way. That reminds me. How's your neighbor's dog?"

"Which one?"

"You know," said Maisie. "That poor wiener schnitzel with the broken back and its hind legs up on wheels."

"Oh," said Estelle. "The dachshund. That rascal. Nothing ever fazes him much. He just goes spinning along. I'm in such a whirl. I can't for the life of me remember if I felt the stove this morning before I left to make sure the pilot light was still burning. I'm afraid that little beggar will have to go scratching on somebody else's door now for his lick of custard. How are you on the subject of butterscotch? Or are you strictly a jello person? Silent like the p in raspberry. Do you realize you've hardly taken three decent steps yet? It's a wonder to me you're not already a pillar of salt. The funny thing is it was the mister, as I'm sure I've told you before, who hauled off the day he lost his job laying unborn linoleum or some such slimy thing and booted him whang up against the wall and plop right into the washtub full of soaking clothes. Two points. Yet that screwy animal loves him and hates her. There's that something between men a woman resents, isn't there? Hi. You tell Father Divine for me, Judy, I think he's really on to something. Beautiful. May your iron always sizzle when you spit on it. Right. It was just as if God himself had slapped an injunction on that platinum blonde, saying, you can have a dog, male or otherwise, but children of any kind or color, absolutely not, and don't bother me. Sometimes even He can be as hard as nails. Don't ask me why. All I know is I've come down quite a bit in the world myself, so I have a pretty good idea what goes on in that poor mutt's mind every time my good friend Goldie jumps him to show him who's boss, trying to train him to climb up the steampipe while it's still hot, poopsie. Flop. What do you mean ouch? Roll, roll. Make like you're swimming on your back, sweets. Not on your belly, your back, you dumb dodo. Or driving him to do something dashing like dancing on one leg with his tail in his mouth. I must say one thing for him. Sometimes he comes awfully close. Last Sunday morning. You're sure I didn't tell you this before?

610

Just when I was about to settle down to a second cup of Salada, this time with saccharine, and a dilapidated copy of Better Homes & Gardens I scrounged out of the overflow when I pulled up the dumbwaiter on my Saturday night treasure hunt, my neighbor comes banging and busting in to drag me out in my battered robe and my hair pinned high on my head like a pile of you know what to make me listen. I couldn't believe my ears. Not once did that popeyed little Strassvogel slip up no matter how fast his Golden Goddess snapped out her commands. One bark for burglar. Two barks for fire. I had to shake them both by the paw. If people are happy and think they're a big success, what I say is, don't throw cold water, be a sport, swallow hard and try to go along with them. Until Tuesday night, was it? No, it was Wednesday because I distinctly remember medicating my pet bunion before hopping into bed. Ah, what's the use? One of these days, I'll just drop. And that'll be the end of me. At first, you know, I used to wake up shaking all over at the slightest squeak. Now I'm so blasé about it, I usually sleep right through their worst jiggling even if it happens more than twice. But three? I sat up and counted. What in the world did that crazy critter mean by barking three? Jeez, me beads. Oh, that awful bitchy day she accidentally on purpose spilled a whole packet of needles in his useless toolbox just a laying and a rusting there under the commode taking up precious space so he could keep his weather eye cocked on it. Buttermilk, Amelia. I keep preaching to you. Buttermilk is what will erase those shadows under your own gorgeous Neapolitan eyes exactly like your Mamma Mia's in that photo from the old country. I thought I smelled hooves burning. I was sure I heard that Taurus the Bull lumbering up and down the scale on a bassoon when I knew that the only instrument he could even half play was the uke. Otherwise he was about as good as I am at making paper crackle. Isn't this a rare day, Octavia? Isn't this a day for us? You voodoo you. You ought to be shot. You are so right when you say it always gets worse before it gets worser. Something very close to my flattened ear went phtt, phtt, like a bat's wings. Then boing like a Chinese gong. God, you have no idea how much I hate new sounds. What the devil is it that makes us think that real life, as it is called, is only what's happening on the other side of the wall? All of a sudden it dawned on me it was Goldie herself, our marathon dancer, who was doing the barking. What's that pun again she makes in Yiddish about a wet rag between her legs? Little pitchers have big ears, don't they? I ask you now. How on god's earth can you ever relax in the tub with your hair up in curlers and a cigarillo between your teeth, let's say, when people start knocking on the pipes to scare you out of your wits to keep you guessing? Some of us are real long shots, aren't we? Thank you, Frank, thank you so much for running interference for us. I understand he bled a lot at both ends. Thou hast the manners of a scholar and a gentleman. I guess I'm much like a chained dog myself. I always liked the idea of being married to my job. I'm afraid to look. I must be slobbering all over you. Ah, space, space. Free at last. And plowing ahead like the prow of a ship. If we only knew where and what for. Eh, Maisie, dear? Oh, it was all so different. It was even crazier than I imagined. What really happened was. Ah, you'll never believe this when you hear."

"Believe," said Octavia. "Jesus. She should try me. After all the crazy things I've heard today, there's nothing I don't believe."

"Mercy," said Judy. "You go in for large helpings too?"

"Huh," said Octavia. "And that poor me, poor everybody stuff. Who do they think they're kidding? It's not that I don't feel for them white folks. You know the lopsided way I'm built. Who really would if we didn't? Excuse me, said the lion to the mouse. Is that man rushing to throw up or something? There's a pretty putty color for you. Still has a lot of push left for an old gink, hasn't he? But honestly. Everybody but us, they mean."

"Skip it," said Judy. "You're only wasting your spit."

"Ah," said Octavia. "Don't worry. There's plenty more where that came from. If I ever run dry, all I have to do is slip off at night and lap up a mouthful of the white man's water from the toilet bowl."

"They talk about dogs," said Judy. "How about us coons?"

"Hey," said Frankie. "I know one."

"Oh, god," said Judy. "I must say. We sure did work our way up that old ladder of success, didn't we? Enough said. Why say more? From wet-nursing their babes and weeding their sugar beets to scrubbing their marble halls and pleating their silly pink slip-ups. Patience. Where does it all come from? And all in one generation too. Better to keep seeing red than playing dead. Is that how you say it? Gotcha. Somehow I feel. What's with that dream of yours of installing a new combination tumbler and toothbrush holder? Did you ever manage to

612

get paid up on that secondhand acid resisting sink? Worse than being a prisoner of love, ain't it? You remember the year you first came up that great big muddy stream with a red bandana on your head and a bundle in a bed sheet on your back and a great big lump in your throat? I hate to show it, but I'm kind of scared stiff myself. Quick. Let's have a look at your palm before the bugle sounds and I'm called back to the colors."

"Oh," said Octavia. "Don't bother. I know my fortune. I've seen the glory of what's never coming. I've squeezed my last melon. I'm a busted play. I'm wiped out."

"Good," said Judy. "I was hoping I'd see that. You have nothing to worry about really. Your hand is still dark enough to do any kind of dirty work."

"Oh, lead me to it, oh, kindly light."

"Gosh, yes," said Judy. "I can't say I blame you. Really, sonny. How do you expect a gal to fall for you if you keep chewing that awful juicy fruit? It's like the prophet says. It was only Ezekiel who saw that wheel. Hold back the waters and it bursts out like hell. Any time a sweet woman like you who loses her job what keeps her man where she can hear him snoring, she always feels best when she feels bitter."

"She do?" said Octavia. "You could be right. Just the same. I don't know what's got into me lately. I've become so suspicious, I can't even trust the ass I sit on."

"Yes," said Judy. "And whatever else ain't yet exposed."

"We never stop to think, do we? You mind if I tap on your head a little? You look like you've been poleaxed anyway. You still on a freedom train? Was it you who once got stuck like a cannonball in the torch arm of the Statue of Liberty? At least you have a bathtub in your kitchen. Now don't let them know I'm willing to sit in the back of the bus so long as it's headed straight for heaven. Don't give them the satisfaction. Please. I know you hate fuss. But pounding the sidewalk again ain't exactly your favorite turkey trot, is it? You know what the prophet, he also say. Losing your job is like losing your hands and feet. Including the full use of your own one and only glory hole. You're a strong one. Tell me the truth now. How far down do you feel it?"

"I don't know," said Judy. "How do you measure such things?"

"Hold this a second," said Frankie. "I'll show you."

"No," said Judy. "It can't be. I don't believe it."

"You take," said Frankie. "You're watching?"

"So this," said Judy. "So this is the Holy Grail. Imagine. A common ordinary feather duster."

"You take," said Frankie. "You take any piece of string you happen to have on you. Even if it has knots in it like this. And you start with it from the end of your nose. Plunk in the middle. I'm lucky I have a lot of bone there. And you. And you stretch it around until you hit the tip of your left ear. And hold it there. It has to be the left or it's no dice. And you. And you let the rest of it hang straight down. Depending on the wind. It's a good idea to wet your finger first. And you. And that's it exactly."

"It is?" said Judy. "You're sure you're not leaving anything out?"

"I don't know," said Frankie. "I forget now. What was I supposed to be doing?"

"Find six faces in this drawing of a spotted snoophound nosing around a lame duck by the name of. It may take you a whole week. But keep looking. And you get a free dancing lesson on how to do the dipsy-doodle."

"The dipsy," said Frankie. "Terrific. Sounds great. Say, I bet. Is that how you cats up in Harlem hop around at those rent parties who was it told me about?"

"Young people," said Octavia. "All-day bloodsuckers."

"You said it," said Frankie. "You should see. Every day like clockwork."

"It speaks," said Octavia. "But does it know what it's saying? It most certainly does not."

"Beep-beep," said Frankie. "And that's no bughouse either."

"Goddamn it," said Octavia. "Why us? Who wished him on us? What did we do to deserve this?"

"Beats me," said Frankie. "I'm no Bolshevik."

"Honestly," said Octavia. "It's worse than tangling with barbed wire."

"Knock wurst," said Frankie. "Excuse me for living. Get a load of him, will you? Ah, you mug, is all I hear. You poke me one more time that way, and so help me, I'll lay you out cold. Gang up on him. Squelch the little bastard. Smack him right into the loonybin. Some fun, eh, kid? If that's the way it's got to be, that's the way it's got to be. Who am I to object? Big word, big turd. Now you take Friday for instance. Hey, who let loose that paper airplane? Friday used to be a damn good day for me. Ha, I see you up there, Georgie. You can't hide from me, boy. Even he's entitled. He makes believe he's a kid again. It's the only way. Mamma mia, what a bottom. Catch me where the chicken got it. I'm sliding down a wave. I figure something like that has to be a girl or a married woman or both. So I always try to act accordingly. You know what I mean? Blink and I'll know you're alive. Aw, come on, Judy. You don't have to be such a sourpuss. You're not that old yet. Hell's bells. It's like Joe here says. Watch out, kid. Once this bastard world sees you break down and blubber, it dies laughing right on top of you."

"I should say," said Judy. "Tell me, sir. Were you born a regular screwtop? Or did you gradually work your way up to it?"

"You know," said Frankie. "It's funny you should ask."

"It sure is," said Judy. "I hope by tomorrow I'll have something better to do."

"Go on," said Frankie. "I dare you. Ask anybody around here. And I bet you anything you got I'm the only one here who didn't pray to be boss or take a real stiff physic last night."

"It's amazing," said Judy. "I've been working with you in the same place how long? I never knew you were so good at calling hogs."

"Gee," said Frankie. "Maybe so. But even a baby knows. There's more than one side to a box, isn't there? It's like. It's like when my Ma says to me, how's conditions in your place of business, is your boss from the old country, what sort of different types do you work with? And I say to her, I tell you, Ma, I say to her real quick because she's the kind who hates to wait around for an answer, even if my mouth is full of cabbage soup, so I say to her, as for the first, mostly beh–meh, sorry to say, and as for the second, boy, and how, is he a case, and as for the people you ask about, ah, you should see, Ma, I don't care what the weather is, we're all just like boys and girls together. Man, I sure do love them big sucking bones when I find them. And it has nothing to do with the cat is after the rat, which it can't spell anyhow, or that flat celery tonic and not fancy arithmetic. Ow, what a swat. You made me spill, Ma. I didn't know that was going to come out. Honest, the way I am, I can jump in anywhere, if I feel like it. And if I don't get slapped down, it really bucks me up. Especially. I always get such a great big bang out of kidding around with them peppy high-toned presser gals."

615

"Good grief," said Judy. "Talk about wishing on a star. Comes hard times. Jesus always saves the tiny bits and pieces, don't he? I must say. I haven't seen such all-out scratching in public since I was a pea weevil myself. Here. Say it ain't catching, son. You can take this thing back now and go out there and tickle the rest of the world. And see how goddamn silly it can get."

"Right," said Frankie. "Will do. And flickeroo to you too. Ha, fooled you that time, didn't I? You see how I did that? I tickled myself right under me own armpit. Ho, get away from me, you dog. Ha, see how fat I'm getting? The joke's on me. I'm giving myself the old brush-off. Ho, I'm really laughing it up. I'm busting my belly."

"Worse than that," said Octavia. "Your snappy little tail there is still wagging like sixty."

"Tail," said Frankie. "That's it. Thanks for reminding me. Now I know what I was going to say. Wait till you hear this one, Tavie. This'll knock you for a loop."

"That'll be a novelty."

"I hope," said Frankie. "Oops. That's okay. I'll get it. I'll have to ask Joe. How the hell do you balance such a light thing? I pick it up better than I drop it, don't I? Like I was telling you. This old Boston bull now from around my block. Scooter, they call him. Beats me why. He creeps along so slow with his legs spread apart like he's got a thermometer stuck up there. And it's saying, cold, cold as ice. Hell, I guess he figures he doesn't have to make a living, so why should he break his ass rushing around? It kind of gripes you looking at him. You feel like sneaking up behind him and giving him a good boot, but he always turns around just when you got your foot lifted and gives you that look, so you say to yourself, oh, well, some other time. I feel if you're fooling around with animals, you're real lucky if you break even. What a slippery mess. You know what that character does every day? He makes eh-eh right in the middle of where everybody's walking. And you know what? He never even once wipes himself."

"Pooh," said Octavia. "That's nothing."

"Nothing?" said Frankie. "Gee whiz. I mean. What the hell. If we all have to, why don't he?"

"But nothing," said Octavia. "But I mean. It doesn't even compare. I once had an experience with a toy poodle by the name of Cissy I received as a gift from the gods, meaning a certain sporty gentleman who happened to hit the numbers with his last two bits, to keep me company when I was a sleep-in cook with a reformed Hebrew family that still shakes me up when I think of it. Well, look a here. His master's voice again. You look exactly like my dear pet that once was when it used to turn its head to listen to me. Only you favor leaning into the wind when you cock an ear, don't you? Was that really the top thrill of your life when they first kicked you out of school? That's the lively look I like. Now why do you think I finally had to get rid of that pretty little puffball?"

"A he or a she?"

"I said, Cissy, remember?"

"Oh," said Frankie. "Well, then. It was because. Because. I know. She got herself knocked up when you wasn't looking."

"Don't be silly," said Octavia. "She couldn't. She was spayed."

"Aw," said Frankie. "Them mutts. Leave it to them. They always find a way."

"Sorry," said Octavia. "My fault. I started this swatch. And it's up to me to cut it short."

"Wait," said Frankie. "Hold them snippers. A bulb just lit up in my head. I bet you I know now. She had to wear one of those wigs. She was the wrong religion."

"She was," said Octavia. "She was born. She came oozing out into this particular world on the coo-coo west coast where every dumb beast, or otherwise, is a real biff-bang four-legged freethinker. The poor motherless child. She was shipped east in a wooden crate weeping all the way like a slave in irons to land right in the doghouse of my big fat dingy lovey-dovey arms. Kismet. What in hell does American or Portugoose ever tell us? Woof is the only language we really know. I couldn't bear to fool her. I just couldn't. I used to shampoo her so white, it hurt my eyes to look at her. I absolutely adored the princess in snow or rain or sleet when she did her duty so nicely on Central Park West until one dark of night it suddenly hit me. How could such a super-duper type be such a stupid cupid? It got to be so fantastic. She was so attached to me, I couldn't go to the can without her. She had to eat whatever I ate even if it made her throw up. She slept with me under the covers like a doll who never dreamed I could squash her if I rolled over. She could hardly live a single second without wanting to lick my hand. She was always, always looking up at me with such pure

617

love, it did things to me, I can tell you, besides positively tearing me apart. And yet. You know what? Like you say. It's hard to believe. She never even once caught on that I was black."

"Hey," said Frankie. "Yeah. Wow. I see what you mean."

"Oh, sure," said Joe. "And who doesn't? Plump them up, son. That's the way to kid the public. What a farce. And how about you yourself, Joey boy? What do you finally see from where you stand with your back foot in the bucket? I see, said he quietly chuckling to himself. Fantastic what a fool you can be without any help from anyone. I think, said he. I think that self-pity kills more people than cancer. No question about it. If I see so much more than I ever did before, I must kiss my hand to thee, oh, lord, wherever thou hast removed thy main plant and hot seat of thy anti-people operations. You don't say? And how's by you? If I may so ask? Aw, have a heart already, will you? Sure as hell, if I grew a full moustachio now, it would turn out absolutely grey. And thicker one side than the other."

"Don't quote me," said Felix. "But something seems to be bugging this gentleman."

"By jove," said Hymie. "And why not? The blighter was born with bare feet, weren't he?"

"And just think," said Joe. "Tomorrow's another day."

"Fastafazoo," said Felix. "How true. Since everything's going so smooth with me now, I'll tell you what I'll do for you, sucker, I'll back you up on that. How do you like the way the bum has it all figured out? Puffing away there on his old trusty Camel, inhaling the irony and bitterness of it all. How all of a sudden he realizes on this day of all days that it's curtains for the sweet little shepherd of this busy midtown block and his whole beat, pardon me while I burp, his whole bare-ass naked flock. And this, they tell me. This used to be such a fine figure of a man. I'm willing to make book the sonofabitch is bucking to be our next shoeshine boy. Shit. Look how easy to push. Up against the fire hydrant, citizen. If you feel a little rocky, that's the way it should be. It's better to be a dead cat than a deaf post. Or so I've been told. Or is it the other way around?"

"Around," said Hymie. "Definitely. And around. And once again, dear heart. Jeez. A Pavlova you're not. Lightly, you old fart, lightly. Let's bang it out nice and clear now. For why you hita my Ikey? My Ikey do nuttin to you."

618

"Right," said Felix. "I'm with you. I knew there'd be dancing in the streets. It don't surprise me in the least. Watch my bunion, boy. Hey. Not so bad for an old snorting bull. Shivering and sweating there with all the cockeyed excitement of being saved by the bell, ain't you? Okay, schlub, okay. Take five. Actually. Mind if I rub you down later? Actually I came tooling down here to see if I could give the needle to this great Joe we used to know, hero of the masses, yours and mine favorite friend of the family. Aie. I ask you now. Look at that open face. If he's making believe he's not the same old lousy floperoo, what sort of a stuck-up philosoph does he think he's disguised as now? Forget it, babe. You can't fool Papa. Woof. It's like I always say when I get to barking. Every goddamn kiyoodle has his day. And this one's mine. It's all mine, I tell you."

"Gee," said Hymie. "Just like the Count of Monte Cristo when he was on that island with all them jewels. You sure got talent, fella."

"He," said Felix. "Not me. He, he. Or whatever the hell else you want to call him. Who else would do what he does? Notice how he screws up his eyes to study the polluted area around his shoes. The ham what am. You can almost hear him say. I no understan. What prick make puddle here? If me, me. Then gee. The distance between me being me and me being God is wow. Listen to me catching his disease. The aggravating bastard. How is it possible he doesn't hear us? I'm sure if you'd ask him now what he was up to, he'd only say, just putting in my time, man, like everybody else. Like any other crippled wage slave. Shaking out his tingling fingers. Looking around like a real ruined man for relief. You watch. In a second, he'll be lifting up his third leg to pee. Quite a specimen there, ain't he?"

"Specimen," said Hymie. "My favorite gum."

"Rotten, miserable type," said Felix. "Sicker in the head than Uncle Tom aching for another session with the whip. Or. Jesus. I knew I'd go absolutely blooey, mucking around without my paisley scarf and white kid gloves with that goshawful mighty pimple there come to a head. I mean him, not you. You grinning nut. You look like you just had yourself a real nice taffy pull. Set the alarm for six. Maybe I'll wake up in time to save a dime on every dollar before my own stupid monkey business goes all to smash. That's why, ach-chew, when I don't hack, I have to hoick. Christ, man. Just don't stand there, picking all them female butterflies off your clothes. If you get what any of this means, tell me before I fizzle out like a wet firecracker, give it to me straight, fill me in. Shit as I like to say. Think how we all dream we can quit our jobs without dragging along a whole bunch of snotty bawling dependents in a mass shotgun suicide jump feet first in that lovely, god, yes, I've seen it, I've seen it light up the whole sky, in that terrible candle way of falling."

"Unbelievable," said Hymie.

"I can hear myself," said Felix. "Couldn't stop it if I stood on my head. Fine business. I talk like a man with a paper asshole. It's really fierce. All them good working blood vessels and brains spattering all over creation."

"I mean," said Hymie. "You live long enough, you hear everything."

"Stubborn bastard," said Felix. "Gets my goat. I've tried every goddamn which way I know to be friendly with him and warn him."

"You sure have," said Hymie. "Just like me lately when I get black in the face, schmoozing around with the impossible. Like when I try to eat broken glass and shit diamonds."

"Sad," said Felix. "To me it's the saddest story ever told. If that frigging apple of your eye there ain't suffering for the other guy, except me, of course, he don't feel well at all."

"And with you," said Hymie. "With you it's just the opposite. So what's the beef?"

"The beef," said Felix. "Can't you see? The beef is hanging right up there on a hook."

"Beautiful," said Hymie. "Beautiful beyond belief."

"Now don't break your fat neck showing us. We all know you have a whole flock of last year's hairs up your nose."

"How do you like that?" said Hymie. "Another sizzler right over the heart of the plate. This guy's got me groggy, whiffing at his dipsy-doos."

"Next time," said Felix. "I stick to pillow fights. That much I think I can handle."

"It's a shame," said Hymie. "Really. I bet if you only knew English a little better, you'd be able to give me the lowdown on why the hell it is there's this schmucky little dickybird in me which is always talking to myself."

"Well, now," said Felix. "I don't suppose it'll do me any good to tell

620

you to go fuck yourself. You do that all the time anyway, don't you?"

"Ho," said Hymie. "The feelthy fox. You see what a crap he take on me? Catch heem, catch heem. Ah, so, skinny spitta. What's you last name? You keepa you longa nosa clean? Who's a cooka you pop? At's a yousa kid who's a gotta da biggest pecker? Look who's looking so disgusted with me. I could smash his head like a light bulb. But I think I'll let him live and suffer. Yeah, I'll say. You sure do look like a real smoothie in your special red and black argyle socks, but without that solid color polished toothpick stuck in your puss, what kind of a pedigree putz do you think you'd be? What kind of a what, what? Starts to sizzle inside sliddle by slowly. Bugs out his eyes like he's pulling off in public. Kicks a mashed cigar butt into the next county. Takes a step back into his dummy act. Got all day to say he can't say. Well, boss. Since you've been axing me, I'll tell you. If you're running scared, you're not exactly flying high, are you? Now look. Don't start acting like you're dying because I'm trying to put in my own two cents. You no like me? I no like you. It's like Fu Manchu says. God save the kling. Lookee what I flind in fortune cookie. How come ellybody in stars and slipes have tong war, awlatime go chop-chop and no washee his bletter nature like such a hah, like such a flucken goldang jerkoff? Only the Shadow knows. You got to keep your hand in. It's a mystery even to me. Like why out of a clear blue sky a whole gang of good people gets wiped out. And a big bullshitter like me gets to keep his job because I guess somebody has to cut the goddamn goods what's left over. The lightning went zip all around me and zapped the other guy. You hear how I'm hollering? Who's got a tree here I can push over with my trunk? Wait till I get upstairs. I'll start my walking up and down again. Worrying, worrying. Hey? How about that, Joey kid? It's Daddy, Daddy. How do you like me knowing where my next million is coming from? You're not exactly here for your health either, are you? I always talk best to him when he's not looking at me. You think I'm showing myself too happy here in my baggy pants? Am I behaving like a louse and blowing out my candle, like you say? How can I hold it in? It's like what comes out of my ear the Doc calls a discharge. I just got to break out in a sweat and crow. It's the law of the land, ain't it?"

"Did you ever see?" said Joe. "As soon as I tighten one shoelace, the other one feels loose. Hell with it. I better give up. This can go on forever."

"You're joshing."

"No, I'm Joe. I'm sorry to say."

"What I mean is," said Hymie. "Just flash me the sign I'm way off base. And I'll pack up my dirty wash and sneak right back to the end of the line."

"So this," said Joe. "So this is what's waiting for me at the end of the rainbow."

"Flowing over," said Hymie. "A crock of the usual. Got a message for you."

"There's always a footprint in the sands of time."

"I was going to say. Some bird named Bert told me to tell you he'd be a little delayed."

"Bert," said Joe. "The sonofagun. Where is he? What happened to him?"

"He was suddenly caught short. He had to run and relieve himself."

"Oh, well," said Joe. "That's perfectly natural. I hope you showed him every courtesy."

"Me?" said Hymie. "Like what, for instance?"

"Like taking down his pants for him and wiping off the seat."

"Excuse me," said Hymie. "I thought of it. But the way that poor fish exploded, I was lucky to make it to the door."

"Exactly," said Joe. "And the door is not the floor. And that's about the size of it. And today's flop. How does it go again? And today's flop is tomorrow's smash. Looks like we're getting boxed in by traffic both ways. You hear that? I feel just like the last old clothesman, saying goombye to the commercial world, straying so far uptown, with his copper cowbell stretched out on a string, tinkalinking, me too, me too. That's precisely what I say to myself at the end of every day. I thought of it. I keep thinking of it. I thought of it. If I thought of it. So why didn't I do it?"

"It's Daddy," said Hymie. "I told you, didn't I? It's Daddy, Daddy."

"Wow, yes. And to think there was a time when I was known as Young Tom Watson."

"Lean on me, father, lean on me."

"I don't know," said Joe. "It worries me. I don't see the end of this, do you? If I'm so bushed, I'm practically deaf, dumb and blind, why am I still standing here, watching over nothing? Though I do understand. Some days you make too much. And some days, no matter how hard you squeeze, you can't produce even the smallest floater. It's really crazy. What in hell can begin or end with me? I'm too young. I haven't seen enough people die yet. Or pop up and out and get born. Like bread out of a toaster. It's so hard to see around a brickhouse like you. I can't make up my mind. Are you a waterfall or an avalanche? Hymie, of all people. Who appointed you? Can't say I blame you for trying to give me the business. If the whole world stinks, like you say, why can't I at least find the right match and tear it off and burn it to take off the smell a little?"

"You will, said the lamppost, you will. Keep poking in my ribs, Dad, I got a million of them. I got a feeling. Once you get past me, you'll be over the hump. You're always doubling up on your bets. You're just too goddamn smart for your own good. That's your trouble."

"I don't know," said Joe.

"You hear that? There's a hell of an echo around here."

"I don't know," said Joe.

"Balls," said Hymie. "Come on, boy. Get your feet planted right and start swinging away. You're still one of us. Tell us. We depend on you to come out with something new. Knock us over with a real live pipperoo. Send us all home happy."

"I don't know," said Joe. "I can't. I told you. Can't you see? I'm not through with the old yet."

16.

Like you know. Like say with that ancient and abominable dictum
which tells us that the moment any mere spittance of the truth attains a
certain modest basement height, in a real tizzy to enjoy its one lurk
and quirk of suspense, it doth forthwith break like a baroque inane
bubble as if it never wert. Like you know. Like the smart apes on the
stoop used to say, in the aura of radiant graffiti and rat droppings, if no
matter, no mind. So that naturally even a notorious smileface like you,
if you happen to be on the receiving end, may well be tempted to
sneer, ah, fug the whole fugging thing. Or less likely. Patience, pal, let
us give the same general rinky-dink idea another fast shuffle. Since the
invented of any such ilk of perimetric conceptuals is to the imagined as
the ace of spades is to the very lowest trump. Of a fellow. Which
certainly does sound like some prize indoor type palooka on the loose
here, entirely self-taught in his legendary sagacity, is as vastly under-
gifted as some poor pricks at large are vainly oversexed. As one would
venture to say if one were indeed as witty as all getout. As she is spoke
to show you again that the sheer oldness of what is new can be as weird
as it is fantabulous. Of what possible use is this world when every
single remark in it has already seen its best days? Such as that rich lulu
which reiterates that to be as old as Joe is to be older than God.

It says here. Like it or not. How mystifying to find that the slyest

cryptic saying as a fun thing has no staying power and is soon transformed into one of the most blatant and insipid artifacts of life, if one
may so to squeak. From which it surely flows as it follows that nothing sooner dejects a man than to learn that his finest thoughts are
already out of fashion. Such are the common blips that form in the
common brain.

Are you also in this life strictly for laughs? Are you as passionately
weary of making passes at the impalpable? What irresistible compulsion to impersonate a real live highbrow has increased your daily
quota of crying jags for the communal tear bottle? How often do we
have to be told that when the heart goes out of a man it is more than
likely to be an inside job? Or that its entire haunt is the asshole of
history? Or that your own slightest mental lapse can seem like my
deepest inspiration? Or that inclusive of this, if lumped together by
the lily imagination, we represent one pussy, one penis, one orgasm,
one set of wings?

The answer is, if not once, then a thousand times. And yet. So what
else is hardly new? And yet one of these dreamy days we shall all of us
have to take time out to die. And yet. Who dares say what sort of
sickly sufferance and cringing crap is this? All else being equal. You
just keep fagging your own end. And I will take the strap to mine.
And yet before we damn well do. Talk to us, talk to us, tell us. If
outside our thoughts there is only mist. If to wink at mindlessness is to
blink at murder in Brooklyn as in Blackpool. You name it. If logic as
in storming the heights of heaven is as ever the top unattainable. If the
illogical is the grand sum total of all that has already been thought. As
it idly picks its nose and reams out its ears. If the ripe idiot activity of
the body proper has only a squashed and snotgreen relation to the solid
and shimmery play of the whole mother wit of the world in its whale-
bone stays and rubber lifts. Then surely we must say with our next to
our last breath. It is still far better for a man to go down thinking.

"Oh, absolutely," said Artie. "I'm with you there. As far as my
credit will carry me. I don't think it'll get my socks washed. Or
anything as wonderful as all that. But maybe if we really turned the
juice on, it could set fire to some of the junk in this clubroom for us to
collect the insurance on it. If we had any. See if I kicked my other shoe
under your chair. How did you get here so early?"

"I skipped dessert," said Joe.

"Skipped dessert?" said Artie. "Why, that's mad. What was it?"

"Sliced peaches and cream, I think."

"Incredible. Where are you from, man? Another planet?"

"Sorry to say," said Joe. "Looks like you need some new laces here."

"Don't be so sorry," said Artie. "What I really needed, I think I got. Rest, rest. I'm amazed. This is the first time I've managed to hit the hay all day since my mother, god rest her whatever, used to powder me for diaper rash and clean the coozies out of my nose with styptic cotton."

"Rest," said Joe. "Escape. Same difference."

"Though I must say," said Artie. "I still feel so bushed, I don't know whether to puke now or vomit later."

"It'll come to you. Maybe you haven't heard yet. But I understand it ain't exactly healthy to sleep with all them clothes on."

"Don't be an ass. I took my tie off, didn't I?"

"Yes," said Joe. "That was smart, I admit. But I do think you're scrawny enough as it is to go all day without eating."

"What without eating?" said Artie. "Besides water. See the tufts of hog hair from this couch stuck between my teeth? They're a little dry. But I make out."

"Have a whole Life Saver anyway."

"Well," said Artie. "Just to please you."

"Now don't laugh," said Joe. "But after the kind of day I had, I do appreciate that. Nuts. What a screwy mechanism. Stupid light in this lamp is always kicking out, isn't it?"

"Yes," said Artie. "Among other things."

"Ah, well," said Joe. "That's the way she blows. I may be slow. But I'm beginning to learn. It's better not to see too much anyway."

"Now look what you've done," said Artie. "As soon as you said that, my feet began to swell up."

"Relax," said Joe. "At least it's not your head."

"Not your head, the man says. Jesus. If ever a guy was groggy, believe me, I'm right up there with the best of them. With the whole left side of my nose stuffed up. Whew. You're no breath of fresh air yourself, are you? Every little sniff is absolutely no answer. I suppose I'm still more where I was than I am where I am. And don't ask me where that is either. Christ. Some dreams never end, do they? I don't know what I was up to. Or what the hell the world was trying to tell

627

me in some six or seven languages. But so help me. I was in and out of that picture on the wall behind me a million times."

"I'll bet. No wonder it's hanging so crooked."

"I'm telling you," said Artie. "It's a damn good thing I have a tendency to roll to my right. This dear dirty wall saved me every time."

"There you are," said Joe. "You see? If you can still get red in the face when you bend over that way, it must mean there's a lot of life left in the old carcass yet."

"Well, yes," said Artie. "That was a pretty good one. What else is on your mind besides your hair?"

"I still have hair? Impossible. How can that be?"

"The hell with you," said Artie. "I don't see where you have such a problem. Goldarn it. You were right. There goes the rotten old shoelace."

"I thought," said Joe. "If I came down here."

"You would tie yourself up in more knots like me."

"That here at least."

"You would be safe for a while. In your own home. Your castle."

"Something like that."

"Dream on, old boy, dream on."

"And how many grey hairs did you grow overnight?"

"Hey, now," said Artie. "How about this? You never thought I would ever be able to hold up my chin again with my eyes flashing, did you? Of course you did. You're the one who always knew the glacier in us had to be moving. Even if the rest of us was sunk in shit. Lend us your comb there a second, will you?"

"Like me to give you a shampoo too?"

"Later, later. I've been laying here all day and thinking."

"Sorry I missed that."

"You're just jealous the seat of my pants is shinier than yours, that's all."

"Thinking about what?"

"Katzie," said Artie. "Or Rancid Fat as he was otherwise known as. On summer days especially when the humidity went shooting up. Blimy, says he. You should've heard him with his phony cockney accent. I'll be screwed by a spider, says he, if I ever go a futzing to pull off a job with you buggers again. Pig's eyes twinkling way back in his head. His idea of fun was to eat what he picked out of his sneezer.

His pants flapping all around him like sails. Loved fish heads for some strange reason. Had this dumb kid sister we used to call The Tiger Lady. Licking a little um, she would say, how can that hurt me? So we never told her. So what do you think happens? So one rainy Saturday night Katzie goes out on a date in his stiff Arrow collar with the short points and his pearl grey spats, did those swishy things ever come in any other color, and after the Elks Ball he crashed is over, feeling kind of teaed up, he decides to take this broad home in a cab, and just as it's pulling up to her house on Livonia, I got to know the kid pretty well afterwards, Katzie is so anxious to accommodate what looks like a sure lay, he starts to get out while the vehicle is still in motion, and smashes the door against an old tree trunk that happened to be standing there. Phtt. The next thing we know we're getting a picture postcard with a skull and crossbones in the middle and his tiny signature in the left-hand corner. After which I understand he held his breath until he conked out forever. He always claimed he could pull that trick off. All for a little thing like that. Another poor slob who didn't pan out. I've been ticking them off."

"That," said Joe. "That's arithmetic. That isn't thinking."

"Well," said Artie. "To each his own. What can you do?"

"Wipe a guy's comb before you hand it back."

"I told you," said Artie. "I'm still feeling my way."

"And what about me?" said Joe.

"Who?" said Artie.

"Did I make that list too?"

"Oh," said Artie. "You. Yesterday's news. Let me see. I did get a flash about you the first time I hopped off to take a pee. Ah. There he is. At last. Thank you, lord, thank you. Did you bring it? What in the hell took you so long?"

What a question, so clearly reduced to a dumb haggard likeness of his former expansive speaking self, Mel could only field it with a single weary backflip of his embittered hand. And this. His hatless oval head had the kind of slow every which way kind of shakes which people in shock are not ashamed to show. This is what I get on top of everything else. As I seem to remember. I used to be a creditable animal with glinting outrage for eyes and curved resistance for claws. If my whole gut aches with the utmost acids of alarm, what unsight-unseen terror was it I turned my back on that is now getting me in the end? I wish I had a better bumper. The wild arrow of my aspiration in its blunted flight has begun to wobble badly. My heart feels so cold, I am afraid it will freeze my balls off. My comrade in alms. I have been drummed out of the regiment of this rageous world for desertion of my own riled and ripped off body. What you see in me, you see in everyone. I have barely brought myself back alive. As expelling the last bit of his long imprisoned breath, Mel flopped down next to Artie, and without as much as glancing at him, handed him a package in the shape of a silver loving cup with two handles, all done up in wads of white tissue paper, and crisscrossed tightly with knotted threads of many colors. Though now his mission seemed to have been fairly successful, to judge by Artie's jubilant expression, the first button of Mel's grey thin wale corduroy jacket was still trapped rather sadly in the frayed loop of the second buttonhole.

"And all," said Artie. "For a little fun in bed. Hee-hee. Look at old Joe there, that desperate sonofabitch, studying us like we were some new batch of monkeys, pulling on a long white beard he hasn't got yet like he was his own great-grandfather the lumber king of Upper Silesia where like anywhere else the shit flies thick and fast. Busy little bugger. Always trying to crack something wide open. Always looking to see if there is a lump in the armpit. Sorry, pal. I don't play catch with this with no one. Since right now I feel like a real horse's ass. Go do me something. Right. I can hear him saying to himself. I know I've heard that one before. But what's the connection? The connection is. If you want to raise a cloud of dust, you punch one of these old cushions. But if you're looking for someone to listen to you, who's going to guarantee you that? It's like. Ha. It's like the man said to St. Peter as he puffed up to the gates of heaven with his own ashes in a stone jar. Jeez, said the man, as he waited for the red blinkers in the sleepy old gink's eyes to turn green. I don't mean to be inquisitive, said he, but who are these so-and-sos lounging around there in their birthday suits without no bushes on them or peckers? Is there room here for just people in plain white t-shirts and slim-jim work pants?"

"Aladdin's lamp," said Joe. "Of course. What else could it be?"

"And St. Peter said, whah? And the man said, is there room here? And St. Peter said, oh, I'm sorry. I didn't hear you. I was yawning."

"Ha," said Joe. "How true. If you mean me with my mouth wide open. And what else went down the drain today?"

"Was I talking to you?" said Artie. "I don't seem to remember."

"Aha," said Joe. "I see. That's okay. I get it. When you're not busy putting the screws on yourself, you're beating your brains out to put the other guy through the hoop. I hope it doesn't take too much out of you."

"I almost broke my pinky," said Mel.

"You know what I miss most sometimes?" said Artie. "A real nice quiet kid I could love."

"It's funny," said Mel. "I have a pretty good sense of direction otherwise. But every time I have to give my old lady a shot for her diabetes, I always manage to stick and mess her up in the wrong place."

"It wouldn't matter," said Artie. "She could even be a whole head taller than me or more. It wouldn't bother me in the least. It's no secret. I've been hunting all my life for someone I could look up to."

"I guess," said Mel. "It all depends on what kind of nature you've got. Some people like pissing in dark halls. But me. Place smells like bears have been sleeping here all winter. I'm not really happy until a perfect stranger takes one peep at me and slams the door in my face."

"In any case," said Artie.

"Or some knock-kneed creep from the old neighborhood who works with his Pop in crushable hats walks right by me crossing 34th at 6th with his putty nose stuck way up in the air."

"At least now," said Artie. "Whatever else happens. I have a beautiful pot for my wild petunias."

"No wonder then," said Mel. "With or without checking to see if I still have any backbone left. I can hardly remember any more what it means to sit up straight. Dear limp wrists. We don't have to ask how's by you, do we? The day before yesterday, I think it was, I started to count up to twelve like a damn fool and couldn't get past six. I had this piece of ruled paper in my sweaty hand with the exact name and address on it my Aunt Nita from the Hebrew Aid Society copied out for me in a great rush to do her a personal favor in her elegant Palmer penmanship. And I wandered up to this two-storey stuccoed house on Sutter with the last two gold numbers knocked off I felt had to be it. And there was this mixed crowd of some ten to fifteen ex-human beings blocking up the doorway. And three men of different sizes digging a hole in the street. And I looked from the hole to the house. And I wondered to myself. And I'll tell you another thing. If time is passing

631

while I'm laying an egg here, then I suppose I'll just have to say to it, so pass, so who cares? After all, what's it ever done for me that I should have to stand at attention now and salute its every snotty little second as it goes whizzing right by my own red running nose? Completely shot as I already am from staggering around in smaller and smaller circles. So I tapped this guy in front of me on the shoulder and I said to him, what's up, doc? So he turned around and looked up at me and he said, you wouldn't hit a world war veteran, would you? So I thought to myself, gee, I sure in hell wish I could be lying down sick for a while with just enough fever to make me drowsy and send me in and out of dreamland where the hearse parks and the pussy willows play. And all that sort of goofy relaxing stuff. And while I'm standing there and watching those three pick and shovel stiffs climb out of their hole and arrange themselves on the mound of dirt to have their lunch, this ancient female person comes trotting up to me with a whole lifetime of grabbing hold and letting go in her broken nails and knobby joints, and just a wee speck of light left in her bombed out eyes, and begins to tell me all that's been happening to that rotten apple the human heart since the year one in the greatest speech you ever heard without words. Sweet. I can tell. I always know when my feet are sticky when I realize my toes are bunching up in my shoes. So of course when the screams began, I looked for the coffin to come out. And sure enough out it came with such a strong onion and sausage smell. And I said out loud without knowing it, is that Aaron Gershberg, the umbrella repair man? I have a message for him. And a snippy little chap in knickers did a tumbletrick under my chin and stuck out his hand and said, yes, I'll take it. And I bit my lips and looked over his head. And what a terrific fight that Mrs. G. was putting up with her popeyed kids swinging from her skirts and bawling like crazy, mamma, please, to keep that cruel deaf and dumb corpse from sliding out of her life. That'll put a spoke in your wheel. Aw, now, stop your sniveling and let's be sewing up them black arm bands out of old bumbershoots. And I took my own step back into spit. And those three solid laborers sat there on the earth with their elbows resting on their knees and licked their fingers and took their swigs and tore off great big chunks with their bare teeth and wolfed down the whole scene. Including that zombie with the common cold I call me. I am always there. I smell my share. Whatever I see, it hurts. Dead or alive, you still have to eat. My beautiful city by the sea. You have no idea how bored I get sometimes. The last couple of days. All I have to do is close my eyes and my whole head begins to swim away."

"Tell him," said Doc. "It's only his ding-dang blood sugar."

"There you are," said Mel. "That's what gets me down."

"Tell him," said Doc. "If he wants."

"People come," said Mel. "And people go."

"I know an easy way to fix that."

"But some bastards hang around forever."

"You hear that?" said Doc. "That's a grown man there? That's an answer?"

"This is news to me," said Joe. "When did these two fall in love again?"

"Well," said Artie. "And I'm sick of saying well. When I'm not. It usually happens when the moon is full."

"Usually happens," said Doc. "Not bad. Not bad at all. As a matter of fact, it's got a pretty good ring to it. Hold it now. Wait a second while I drag a chair over and get up real close so we could touch noses to set off a little static electricity. Now. How was that again? How did the rest of it go? When was the who is what?"

"How do you like that?" said Artie. "Go know. This worm here is still wriggling."

"Weird," said Doc. "Isn't it? And not only that. You should have respect. Like you take Joe here. A worm too can be a separate nation."

"Nom de pip," said Joe.

"Hark," said Doc. "Is that a lark I hear?"

"I'm beginning to see," said Joe. "Every goddamn boob is got something boiling on the back burner."

"And me," said Doc. "Without a decent pot holder to my name. Ain't that typical?"

"Boy," said Mel. "And how. Which ought to tell him. Even when we see him, we don't believe him."

"But why?" said Doc. "Ask him. Whose creaky old knee did I tap that time? Just because I happen to be built like a brick shithouse and not like a breakable swizzle stick like him? He's no baby any more. He's got to understand. To a sea elephant, round shoulders are beautiful. But they are. I like the way he opens his mouth to laugh, but nothing comes out. Go on now. Ask him. Who says a limp carrot is

633

superior to a lumpy matzoh ball? Shakes his stubborn noodle. Can't swallow that. Okay, then. I'll tell him what I'll do. Since I came prepared in my sneakers, I'll race him two sewers any time. I may be getting a little bald on top, but I'm still a speedster compared to him. You should've seen. We were futzing around outside Epstein's candy store, and while old grump in there was fixing up a double malted payola for the new cop on the beat, I laid out the last copy of the Times on the stand and began to flip through it back to front, and just when I got to the help wanted page male, which didn't take long, this genius type friend of mine here grabs me by the wrist. He reads. He keeps reading. Every time I try to turn the page, he tightens his grip. For a whole half hour on the clock. I was ready to bust. He knew there was nothing there for him. I jerked my hand free and walked away in disgust. I never did get to find out what kind of a trade the Yankees pulled off with the Boston Red Sox for a left-handed relief pitcher. Or how the dramatic drop in prices of three of the nation's basic commodities of wheat, corn, and soybeans was affecting the pocketbook of the average consumer. Or if the embargo on swine movement due to hog cholera was easing off. These things are very important to me. I don't always like to be taking second place. So all right. So he catches up with me in his loping way and wraps his arm around my shoulder to slow me down in the noonday sun, his eyes like pin points, still lost somewhere way inside of him, chewing on the hind end of a kitchen match like he was a river boat gambler figuring out ways and means of beating the odds. That's the stuff. That's what I like about a cane chair. Every time it creaks, I know exactly what it means. Ask him. How the hell did I know something was building up in him? A vodka cocktail. Half a ripe muskmelon with just the right dash of salt and pepper. Thick Ukranian borscht. Thin slices of tender boiled beef with whole white onions and baby carrots and pot gravy on the side. A dried prune and sweet potato compote surrounding a stuffed chicken neck. A creamy napoleon topped with a layer of bitter chocolate. A splash of brandy to liven up the after-dinner mocha. A funky seegar. And a couple of new jewish jokes. I don't mind it when he mumbles about things like that. So I have a bite with him in imagination. What've I got to lose? I'll still be the same old fathead, won't I? But jesus, when he starts in nudging me to answer some of his crazy questions, that's when it really begins to get me. Would you say it was a Siamese cat

634

who first meowed out loud it was going to lick the world all by itself? How about it, old boy? Suppose now it began to rain in earnest, what part of the country would you say was that? You for instance. You keep telling me I cry wolf all the time. What do you think would happen if I began to cry ant, grasshopper? Don't make believe you're napping. Suppose I had to tack up a sign over my bed telling me it's a sin to do it with either hand. Would I be well within my rights to try it with my teeth instead or my toes? Who said any of this was supposed to be funny, bunny? Listen and ye shall hear. If he who prays remains on his knees, would standing on your head be a sure cure for cancer? Since you look so goddamn grim again. Let me present to you a case. This morning with great effort I produced a turd that curved a bit more to the left than it usually does. Now what exactly do you think it means? I said, hell, man, I said. I looked at him. I was sick of taking all that crap. I said to him. It has to be a boy or a girl. What else? Well, now. Did that do it. Did he proceed to blow his stack. Did he give it to me right and left on the corner of Pitkin and Stone where the traffic is heavy and crowds collect fast nosy as hell. Reminds me of the time when I bit my big brother Schlemmie's finger to the bone in our beloved kitchen when that bum almost broke a blood vessel trying to put me into an airplane spin. Just because he had to wear that awful looking hearing aid to school, he had to have someone he could take it out on. So he pinned me down and put our large tin washtub over on top of me and began to beat the hell out of the tub with the mixing stick. Well, my dear friends. What can I tell you? Ask him now. Isn't that the way we crawl out of bed these days, stunned to say the least, shaking the cobwebs out of our heads, stumbling around like we were trying to get under a tremendously high pop-up to the infield? Muttering to ourselves. Where am I? What hit me? What's going on? Hey, man? How do you like all the extra elbow room we have in this huge palace of ours? Can't get a rise out of him even when I poke him. Ain't it a goddamn lucky thing none of us bums here can possibly be late for anything any more?"

"And these," said Joe. "These when we look back at them."

"Are going to be," said Artie. "The good old days."

"Exactly," said Joe. "Only the next time. If you don't mind. Find something of your own to say. Don't go horning in on mine."

"Gee," said Artie. "I'm sorry. It slipped out before I knew it. But gosh. You'll have to admit. When will I ever get another chance to come out with anything so absolutely ordinary?"

"Easy," said Joe. "Just keep making with your mouth the usual umpteen times every hour on the hour. The law of averages is bound to catch up with you."

"There," said Artie. "That's the whole story of my life so far. Everywhere I go, I get an argument."

"Go where?" said Joe.

"I knew you'd say that. How about my trips under the bedclothes? Don't they count?"

"Up to five? Or up to ten?"

"The hell with you," said Artie.

"That's the second time tonight."

"I don't give a damn what you say. Travel is travel. Take you for instance."

"You'd be crazy to do so," said Joe. "But go on, go on."

"Now I ask you," said Artie. "Just by looking at you. Who would ever think you've already made a tremendous trip from A to B just by announcing to all your friendly enemies that you're going to use your precious job as a jumping-off-place?"

"It's plain as heck," said Joe. "This smartass is begging me to give him a big fat lip. If I only had my health. B. What in hell's B?"

"B," said Artie. "B is just before C. What else? The great dark deep. The bitter land of nowhere. The bottom of the chute, man. Resting, if that's the word, in the muck and mire of C. Sounds like a nice shyster law firm, don't it? If you can stand me piling it on a bit. Where the rest of us joblessniks are sliching and sliding, trying desperately to scramble back up again to B. What a spectacle. Scared shitless we'll be dragged down to D where we'll all be damn well dead. As for the rest of the alphabet. Forget it. Nothing but a fucking fairy tale. It's the truth. Don't give me that sleepy-eyed bored look stuff. The real action is right there on that shriveled up sliding scale. That's the kind of fantastic trek you're going to make to all the sweet and familiar places."

"Sounds great," said Joe. "I wonder what's delaying me?"

"It's in the cards," said Artie. "You can't lose. You're going to be a frigging hero even if you fall flat on your face."

"Oh, sure," said Joe. "Everything's possible. And yet. Just the same.

636

In spite of all them fine words. Here I am. The same old stupid lump. Still sitting on my hands."

"With every black nail broken," said Artie. "While slowly getting up your nerve. To say to us all. So loud and clear. Get out of my life, will you?"

"To say what?" said Joe. "What was that again?"

"How about that?" said Doc. "That's exactly what this screwball here kept saying to me."

"Speaking of the cost of living," said Mel.

"Out," said Doc. "Out, he said, out. Out how? Out where?"

"Outhouse," said Mel. "He must mean."

"Shit," said Doc. "We see it. We all know it. With your rotten heart ripped out of your chest because the good lord thinks it's best to allow more room for the rest of your pushy body to grow on less intake of cashews and chocolate chip cookies. And your empty bladder. Now, now. Don't let him try to tell me with his glary eyes I can't say what I say. I went and said it, didn't I? And your empty pockets always stuffed full of your own nervous useless hands. And the cracked sidewalks getting narrower with whole households of furniture and effects thrown out into the street. And a mixed chorus of kids to every folding bed propped up with old fat Manhattan phonebooks. Oh, don't let me fall, please. I'll throw up. I'll faint. And if you happen to lean a little to one side taking a leak, you hear immediately you're making somebody else wet. And cripes. If you bend over to kiss your mother on the cheek, you're bound to bite your father on the ass."

"I think," said Mel. "And I do believe."

"What then?" said Doc. "What in the hell is everyone batting about? What's the sense of chasing each other tied together the way we are? How can we separate so easy? Where can we run away? How do we disappear?"

"It would be very advisable to inform the lout."

"Honest," said Doc. "What a thing. I still can't get it into my head."

"If he has anything to say worth a damn," said Mel. "He better get it out fast. The minute is down to forty-five seconds."

"Jesus H. Christ," said Doc. "I knew it would happen. This poor bastard here is beginning to bleed again."

"Himmel," said Artie. "What Christ?"

"I never point," said Doc.

"Behold," said Artie. "Unto us an Irving is born."

But of course, said that particular sample of an upstart subspecies of flaming youth, how on god's constantly greening earth could it possibly be otherwise, supremely indifferent as he was for once to their cool cat stare, his conception as maculate as his animation was malapert, if only in the strict and little joe sense that each and every hunk of humanity is a blessed event which can occur only once. And a damn good thing too. And no two ways about it. They sure would have to produce more than a mere resounding fart before they could ever hope to gasphyxiate that crafty and elaborate quibble of his, though he was quick to admit, it has such a familiar stink to it, they could only react by sprawling everywhere in a sham faint which featured the whole furry red rag of their dismalest dumps and fondest dreams deferred totally hung out.

Like if you take anything and look at it right. Like his own slightly askew bran-new polka dot bow tie. It sure does boggle the mind. If a certain party present here in his diminished propositions was once inspired enough to declare that the one most alive is the one most in trouble, how come he too seems to be so entrapped in this fast multiplying subdivision of the prematurely pooped and past caring? While others, like Irving himself, are somehow so strangely on the upswing, they are inclined to be rude and run off at the mouth with their own crude and crack-of-doom answers. His burnished oxblood red loafers attested. His silky white shirt asseverated. Gold of his monogrammed cuff links confirmed that, just as it is not the fate of every generality to glitter, so every other prone underground person is foredoomed to become an unconscionable nit who would rather be acted upon than act.

You better all believe it. While your several boorish toenails do the grow in bit and blacken. If this most hazy and sapient air is not genesis but germination, how could they continue to crouch there so sere and smallish, with no discernible blood on their hands as yet, wracked by that cigarette cough which is such a drag, distinctly so dreamy and drained as they watch the cosmic in their time waste away, wander ing around in terrestrial circles, wetting its softening whistle, sporting its own useless street-smart smile? It is a well known fact that those who feel they are failing will always believe that silence is their best bet. As the r in Irving is hardening. You can take it from him. That squelched squirt who concludes he has but his own life to lay down on the line has already fallen flat on his face for each and every one of us. Saying which from his dizzy rhetorical height, the air-borne expounder found himself asked from all sides to come down out of the clouds and land on his can beside them for their closer inspection. A cockeyed wonder for sure. Anyone who seemed to be so on top of things had definitely earned a second look. It was as if the goose had become a hawk, the pismire ant a philosophical wolf.

"It's a sign," said Doc. "A real sign, I tell you."

"Be damned," said Artie. "Never thought I'd live to see the day."

"Yes, sir," said Doc. "Like that drag-assed Polski janitor of our creaky building says when he gets all steamed up about the good old country that never was. Wunderbar. If it can happen to a yuckish like Oiving, it can happen to anyone."

"I know it won't last," said Artie. "But right now. I don't know why. That same party there is my favorite breed of cat."

"It's a cinch," said Doc. "Nothing to it. All you have to do is grow a springy little appendage for extra balance and power on the tip of your spineola, or thereabouts, and ow, watch that lower limb, you're scoring big with the bananas, swinging."

"And yet," said Artie. "Even as I say that, I wonder if I mean it."

"Swinging," said Doc. "I hope to hell I can knock this one off before our snoozing prez there wakes up to rap me on the nut with his knuckles. Swinging like something all prick and kiss curls, if you can believe it, from one sappy tree of an idea to another through the whole tangle bush of a dime pocket dictionary. Hey, now. I sure hit the big time with that one, didn't I? Hold your fire, men, while I slap myself on the back until I am nice and round-shouldered, and fit to sit and sip wine with the gods."

"Well, well," said Artie. "I must say. That's pretty damn fancy for a plain ordinary dumbbell."

"Absolutely," said Doc. "No question about it. Only there's one thing that scares the shit out of me."

"It does?" said Artie. "Wait a second. Let me see. Swell. Since my nails are still pink, I'll take a chance and ask you. You? One of our true stouthearted men? Scared of what? How can that possibly be?"

"No kidding," said Doc. "You have no idea how blue I get sometimes when I think of it. It's the rotten truth and I know it. If I were any more stupid, I'd have to be you."

"Ha," said Artie. "You see now? You see what I mean? The bum is helping me out without knowing it. What the hell. This thing is beginning to make me jumpy. Did you see that light give a blink again? Keep your cuckoo message to yourself, you bastard. I don't give a damn who the joker is. I've lived long enough to know. Every man's world is flat until he can prove to you it's round."

"Rubbish," said Mel.

"Well, yes," said Artie. "That could wrap it up once and for all."

"Animal spirits," said Mel. "Sheer animal spirits."

"Too simple," said Artie. "Try again."

"In my condition?" said Mel. "Don't be ridiculous."

"That's the way it goes," said Artie. "Someone is always asking of me the impossible."

"Gosh, yes," said Mel. "Don't I know it. It's like with me and my left hand. Maybe I expect too much. But it ain't worth a hoot when it comes to stifling a yawn."

"I've noticed that," said Artie.

"So?" said Mel. "So what in the hell else have you got to do?"

"So," said Artie. "So I'll ask you. So if your wrong hand fails you, why in hell don't you try your right?"

"Can't," said Mel. "Use that to wipe myself."

"Of course," said Artie. "I'm sorry. I keep forgetting about that. Ah, well. No sense hanging your head in shame. You know what Rabbi Joe once said to the Bishop of Brownsville when they bumped heads in the men's room in the Saratoga Avenue station?"

"No," said Mel. "What did the good man say?"

"He say," said Artie. "Watch me mangle it, boy. He say. Now don't let this ruffle your hair too much. He say. Psst. Mercy, father, with all due respect. Your slip is showing. The frost is on my pumpkin. Consider what is writ upon this wall. Everybody has a kind of religion like everybody has a behind."

"Jesus," said Mel. "Another bad trip. And all pulled off without a single salted peanut or a swig of mountain dew. Nothing to get excited about. Wiping my lips this way with the back of my hand is merely a habit I have after swallowing a lot of hot air. Mostly my own. Believe me. I don't care if you call me Sniffles, but please, don't nag me to wear a flea collar. But what's the use? All I know is. Give any jerk enough lost chord and he's sure to hang himself from the highest clef.

640

Boing. Never knew I knew that. And that mammals, to begin with, are damn glad to nourish their young with milk. Okay, okay. So what's so funny? You lousy bummers. You may not know it, but I can blow you all to the outskirts of Peoria with one good sneeze. If and when it ever comes. It's maddening. And that a woman's piss is held in longer. And that rabbits hate moth balls. But god. With my whole heart I cry out. Where in which Woolworth Store will I ever find my million dollar baby? Why does my mouth go dry and my prick stand at attention when the moon comes over the mountain? I'm listening. But what do I hear? Nothing. What's the good of having an address when it never becomes a home? Hey? Pick, pock. How do you like me as water wearing away stone? Or would you moochers rather be smashed into triangles? Since I am only as smart as the next guy. And god knows. This may be the last time I will ever be the center of attraction. How now? How does a gink without work saddle up his ass? Who the shit was Balaam when he lifted up his eyes and made his nest in a rock?"

"Put, put," said Artie. "Not made. I think. And he began to bawl like a baby. And he hauled off and smote himself on both shins, opening up old scabs, like someone else we know rhyming with Joe who's been at it lately like a maniac, and whacked away at the grand entrance to his abode with his busted riding whip, like so, since I happened to be on the scene, supervising the delivery of a truckload of tinkling brass, until ploop, the end was, like with anyone who tries too hard, his bleeping mockie blood began to burble out like lava from his blistered bazoo and boiling mad noseholes."

"And how," said Doc. "I can back you up on that. It sure was something to see. Since I was right there behind you, lugging the junk. A real gutsy old gasbag, wasn't he? He didn't give a damn who was watching as he packed himself up to the hilt with what looked like to me wads of used monthly rags, and settled down on a slab of imitation onyx to slurp his tea-bag tea, and scratched in his crotch because he had to, and chuckled in his beard to think how, no matter what, there was always so much more room on the bottom than there was on top, and his watery eyes danced with his own shadow on the wall, and he burped like a bullfrog to show what a merry old soul was he. Let's see. I know it's hopeless. But I'm looking around. Who else qualifies as?"

"Hey," said Irving. "Remember me?"

"No," said Doc. "I don't remember you. Why should I remember you?"

"And so," said Artie. "So much for our part of it. Exquisite gentlemen all, aren't we? Still. When you get desperate for a little action, you have to take what comes and make the most of it. As for off-key Irv here who just piped up. I'll match him against a penny whistle any time. Fresh crumbs in me crappy old cuffs? It can't be. From what? Where the elite meet not to eat. Did we have a bed check yet? Who's out on the town tonight? Oh, well. Some animals are dumber than others. I used to be such a shy little thing, but look at me now. It's a slack time. So I'm coasting, just coasting. What it all boils down to. All of a sudden it hits him. Hot diggety dog. For the first time in his life he realizes. He knows now for sure. He happens to be alive. So he figures. He might as well take advantage of it."

"And they say," said Irving. "And I hear it all around. A miracle is something that used to happen."

"Oh," said Artie. "No need to get your shit hot. Some Fridays it's my turn to be the exception. And I'll just have to learn to live with it."

"It's fantastic," said Irving. "I'm really stumped. Am I dreaming here or what? What's wrong with you guys? You're taking me seriously."

"Bunk," said Artie. "All it is. We planned to pick out the nits tonight. And we're doing it."

"And a smashing fine job too," said Irving. "As far as that goes. I will always maintain. That is absolutely your one right and privilege."

"Don't feel hurt," said Artie. "But we knew that without you."

"As who wouldn't?" said Irving. "Even so. This is history, man. Don't you realize it? This is all history. Every grand and mean little bit of it. And imagine. Lucky me. Just because I happened to turn the right knob at the right time, here I am, bright as a new dollar, which is bright enough these days, helping you all make it. How is that for being really useful finally? Isn't that one of the great little pleasures?"

"Mary had a little lamb," said Doc. "And that was hers."

"I don't doubt that for a second," said Irving. "Hold it now. Let me peel it off. Ta-ra. Toot them tooters. Take a look. See what's fluttering in the breeze?"

"Holy cow," said Artie. "A ten-spot. Our own. Our native flag. May I inspect it to see if it's genuine?"

"No false pride now," said Irving. "And all that stupid stinking stuff. Just say the word, men. And I'll gladly foot the bill for a group picture. You know. Amid my souvenirs. Give me something to remember you by. And along lines like that. To leave behind us. Is it conceivable? When will we ever be more dear to ourselves? Some simple record of our common vital statistics. A pitiful collection of sorry-looking mugs totally unemployed. Retouched and tinted wherever necessary. Since they tell me every blasted thing in this life must be glamorized and faked. Otherwise who will ever give it a second look? For our children's children of whatever sex. Are you with me or not? For future colonies on the filthy moon. And all the other secondary planets that may be of a friendly nature."

"You goddamn disgusting plutocrat," said Doc. "Don't you know yet what money is for?"

"You mean for food?" said Irving. "For shelter?"

"Now, now," said Doc. "Would I be so vulgar as to say that?"

"A fine type like you?" said Irving. "I should say not. As for sinking so low as to believe. Never. I'm sure you know as anyone who has a button missing. There's one thing money can't buy. And that's love."

"Ha," said Doc. "Maybe not. But it sure in hell can encourage the frigging thing to sit up and beg a little, eh, boy? We already know a few dirty tricks about that lovely operation, don't we?"

"Said he," said Irving. "With such a funny smile. It couldn't possibly be you were actually there? You weren't hiding in the next booth and listening in on me, were you?"

"Okay, son," said Doc. "You've been futzing around with it long enough. Mind passing it along so someone else can get a feel of it?"

"Aie," said Artie. "I hate to have to say it. Since it ain't mine. But it's the real red-hot stuff, all right. A fresh live crackly double finn. Och. Me heart is thumping like mad. One last smell ere we part. What happened out there in the cold cruel world while the rest of us were wrapt up in our own dreams and merrily jerking off? Did your old man foreclose another mortgage on a dust farm in old Ioway? Or did he sell some poor stiff down on the Bowery a pink little pig in a poke?"

"He has his ways," said Irving. "He has his ways. As I've discovered. We can all be a little cunning and sneaky in our family. Especially on the male side."

"Whoa now," said Artie. "Don't come crying on my shoulder. If that is what it produces. By the way. Can anyone put me wise? Since

643

I'm in the proper company. I know what a pig is. But what in hell's a poke?"

"A poke," said Mel. "A poke is what we will all have to stick our heads into when the time comes."

"What?" said Doc. "What was that? What did the man say there?"

"Hear ye," said Irving. "Hear ye. Lady with a baby. Squalls sighted in vicinity of too close for crying out loud. Sucking on thumbs painted with iodine to be suspended immediately. Request remove all imperfect condoms from sticky handles of semibald broomsticks. Suggest military police goose lower grades to get the lead out and tighten drawstrings. Black looks, black looks. Most urgently advise any clean idea hiding in the hold to crawl back on deck on belly in best yellow slickers. Nice day for ducks coming up. Hear ye. The groggy glass is falling fast. The humped up heart has done its part. No more arguments. Please. You hear ye? All umbilical cords absent without leave report at once to the nearest navel station."

"Nearest," said Artie. "Aha. I don't see why not. If you'll wait until I bite off this pesty hangnail, I'll hop right into my four-poster and do that very thing."

"And then what?" said Irving. "What in the name of King Tut do you think happened to me next? Can you imagine how I felt when I finally decided to look it up in my old Funk & Wagnalls and discovered what the axilla was?"

"Axilla," said Artie. "Axilla. A fleet of sailing vessels?"

"The armpit, man, the armpit."

"Mind if I tell you to go fuck yourself?"

"Me?" said Irving. "Deprive you of your birthright? Not while the North Star and the Lesser Dog are still where I can find them. No, sir. Not me."

"If only because," said Artie. "I'm really sorry about this. But even when I understand what you're saying, I don't know what in hell you're talking about."

"And which mental giant among us?" said Irving. "And where in what far-gone section of America? And what exactly would spendable money or moonshine? Ain't it the devil now? What a drag. Just when you think you've snuck under the barbed wire of a great stretch of one bitchy why, you snag yourself smack on the rusty spikes of its twangy blood brother wherefore. Surprise and consternation. How do you like that for a snappy piece for our drum and bugle corps when next it meets? To arms, to arms. You offbeat Brooklyn improvisers. Protect yourself at all times. And come out fighting. I say to you people this whole nasty business of nosing around to see where the feet grow, as if meaning can be found only between the toes, is sheer bullshit in a bottomless pit when you're a hopeless wallflower like me. And a brooding scavenger to boot. What does his highness Mister Joe say, whose eyes are closed though he is not asleep? Look and ye shall find. Every baby does a lot of cribbing. And a tyro is he who has not even begun to learn how to unlearn. Though I can assure you that at the present time my polyphony is always very plump. And my arabesques can best be described as clouds of incense. And I can change keys like I change my underwear. But I must admit I still have immense difficulty in ascending with perfect pitch to your high group level here of instantaneous response, crackling counterpoint, clanging triads of exquisite afterclap, and tickled pink part singing of heaven-storming and hi-there harmony. Not exactly your own particular brand of universal language, is it? Talk about being uppity. You may now all shift your idling peenies into second and proceed to stabat your own maters. No one has to crown me with a tuning fork. I know a classic put-down when I see one. Like I have here in my vest pocket on my heart side a crumpled note addressed to myself and postdated the first of January of the year two thousand which reads. This is the agenda for today. And you are not on it. Period. Ah, but the soul. There is where I know I reign supreme. The way I look at it. I feel if I can scratch my leg, I can fix the damn thing. But that other business. The body. Oh, that body, men, that body. May stink and rot. Why am I rushing to stick my nose into this? Is anyone asking me? May absolute ruination visit this fearful apparatus I have here which before I know it is hard as a rock and standing up. For Jesus, I almost said. Who in god's name picked it to be the boss? Where in hell did it get the right to force me to make a religion out of it? There is no room for all that in my pants. It hurts. What else but as a complete and entire prick am I speaking to you when I say? Fun is when you do it in your handkerchief. Happiness is when you use your bare hand. See what you think is a rash on it and you break out in a cold sweat. My rabbit ears tell me. When the body is in heat, the mind is in a haze. Now you take Becky from down on my block. Becky has such a soft sweet smile and two of the most shimmering pale blue eyes and gentile hair like spun gold, and may she roast in hell, this great big solid wiggle-waggling metronome and miracle of a behind. Ass me, ass me. This is how we all become equal under god. Sex is in the air. Sex is everywhere. You feel life is not worth living unless you can lick and nibble on those perfect yummy biscuits. The whole world stops turning and waits. You jump fantastic puddles. You knock aside the bulkiest people. And just when you get within ten feet of this glowing girl, this gorgeous human being, she whips around and snaps at you, buzz off, will you? I stop dead in my tracks. Was that me doing that again? Ye gods. What's going on in this dopey mind of mine? Is it possible I will never grow up? Is this going to be my sole mission in life to land on top of her like a fly? And yet when I received that mystery call, I dashed out like a crazy man to do exactly what it told me. Listen carefully, it said. This is absolutely on the up and up. Utmost secrecy is called for. Sneak out to the most private phone booth you can find and call this number and ask for Bella Donna and I guarantee you will hear something that will make you piss with joy. Budapest? she said. What quartet? Are you asking me to go abroad? Was I asking her. Who knows? Maybe this is it. Maybe this is what will free me. I felt so high after fixing a time and place for a date, I had to lie down when I got home and put a cold compress on my head. If this doesn't work out. I see now the best way to die healthy is to die young. I sure have my nerve tackling that two-papa mama. Every slimy mind goes wandering all over the map. Boy. Was I surprised to find this little plug of wax on my pillow that had oozed out of my right ear which has the smaller opening. How is that for laying something down on the line? What's the good of living if you're afraid to take a chance? Funny thing. Lately my bladder has stepped up its signals to every hour on the hour. Ow. Sorry. I must run now and relieve myself. Hold everything until I get back. I promise I'll keep my trap shut. I'm still so hungry to hear something good."

"I'll be laid by a leaping lizard," said Artie.

"As a one time thing?" said Doc. "Or on a daily basis?"

"I'm ruined," said Artie. "Another broken nail."

"You're bugs," said Doc. "That was no broken nail."

"Look at me," said Artie. "Before I even know it. My underwear is all pasted to my private parts. I guess I can't take it any more. I begin to steam no matter what happens."

"That," said Doc. "That was a real jazzy person there. No question about it."

"All this howling," said Artie. "That's what gets me. Every little cocker in this world howling all the time. With his fly wide open. Married to himself. And always for worse and worse."

"Till death do him part," said Doc. "And even then."

"And here I thought," said Artie. "I was hoping we had all that stupid baby stuff behind us. For at least one night this week. Did anyone clock him? If I weren't so goddamn lazy, I'd scour that crummy breakfast bowl back there and sponge myself off a bit with a dash of rusty water. He sure spoke a whole book that time, didn't he?"

"His absolute best yet," said Doc. "Fat as a bible with both the old and the new. It's like I always say. If you listen, you find out. It don't matter who."

"Doesn't," said Artie.

"Doesn't what?"

"Never mind," said Artie. "It don't matter."

"What don't?"

"Holy mackerel," said Artie. "How did I ever get myself all tangled up with that ball of thick wool?"

"Then why the hell interrupt me?" said Doc. "Now I forgot what I was going to say."

"I'm sure," said Artie. "It's such a great loss to humanity, I've already ordered a snazzy mouseoleum for it."

"It's incredible," said Doc. "The people you have to ignore. All I was going to say. If I may be so permitted. There comes a time. The time comes to everyone that whatever is bottled up inside of him, he's got to let loose and eliminate."

"Like in number one or number two?"

"That's for you to decide," said Doc. "I'm neutral."

"Boy," said Artie. "I don't mind telling you. There was so much in what that Irving kiddo rattled off. I was really getting scared. For a few seconds there, I could feel myself beginning to like him."

"Ha," said Doc. "Still all wet, aren't you?"

"I'm improving the situation."

"Like him, my foot," said Doc. "Explain that last statement. I demand a hearing."

"Because," said Artie. "Because the dear boy came to us as an only child, you dummy."

"Only child, my ass."

"And do you be telling me?" said Artie. "And is it elegant speechifying you are practicing? And why should a blah-faced boyo like you with blue stubble on his chin and a turnip for a nose be introducing his grey bulky ass into this lovely green commotion?"

"My god, man," said Doc. "Don't you know?"

"I have a feeling I will," said Artie. "As soon as I blow my nose."

"I'm Mr. Buttinski of Brooklyn for the month of April," said Doc. "It's my bounden duty."

"Then bounden over a little closer," said Artie. "And tell me. You still have that ten bucks?"

"What ten bucks?" said Doc. "Eddie, tahteleh. What a pleasant surprise. Where did you come from?"

"Huh," said Eddie. "Don't ask. I might tell you."

"Shoot," said Artie. "How do you like that for luck? At last. Here's a real sight for you. Only right now my dear sweet eyes aren't sore."

"How nice," said Eddie. "Isn't this ducky? Somebody's been keeping this chair warm for me."

"That's the way," said Artie. "Spread out, my boy. Blow the lid off. Make waves. You're exactly what we've been aching for. Another weary man of the world."

"Luck," said Eddie. "What do you know about luck? All I do lately is go from one seat to another."

"And in between," said Artie. "Play a little gitchy where the gitchy is good. Give. What bold creature by the name of Honey has been running her electric hands through that overgrown mop of yours? You look all ruffled up like an old rooster that's been caught sliding into the wrong base."

"Did," said Eddie. "Ancient history. Went right on up from there. Until now. Proud to say. New idea. Never felt more like a straw mattress that's been pissed on and slashed open. Ought to give it a whirl yourself some day when you learn to turn your face away before you belch."

"Excuse me," said Doc.

"Certainly," said Eddie. "I'm agreeable. Only a gentleman would put on white gloves before he raps on me like I was a closed door."

"Sorry," said Doc. "Emergency. I don't know if you realize it yet. But as far as I can see in all this smog, you came straggling in here all alone."

"Ah," said Eddie. "Is that what felt so funny?"

"It can't be," said Doc. "When did this ever happen before? Where's your old sidekick?"

"He can't make it," said Eddie. "His face blew up."

"His face did what?" said Joe. "Hi. Are you talking about Dave?"

"And yet," said Eddie. "If I hear right. It's really touching. Life goes on just the same. Someone is back in there flushing his precious mix of pee water and grunt down the old toilet and out to sea."

"I guess," said Joe. "Like someone is always in the kitchen with what's her name. What's this about Dave?"

"Don't shoot," said Eddie. "You got me covered like a blanket. I know when I'm licked. I surrender, dear."

"Later," said Joe. "When I'm more in the mood."

"There," said Eddie. "That's what kills me. My pockets are hanging way down stuffed full of rocks. And I'm about to take my last serious walk out into the Atlantic. And all I get is, later, later."

"Be damned," said Joe. "Nothing changes. As soon as I begin to wander in the woods again to gather me some wild flowers if I can, I bump right up against some kind of rambling nut."

"And one makes two," said Eddie.

"My dear fellow," said Joe.

"Swell," said Eddie. "I'm so glad we're going formal."

"Maybe," said Joe. "Maybe it ain't possible any more. Wake up, you bum. Lazy left leg fell asleep without asking. But really. I wish to hell you would try to listen. I'm not asking you to take a stiff civil service exam for temporary assistant substitute clerk. All I want from you is one simple answer."

"It's sad," said Eddie. "What can I say?"

"Say," said Joe. "Say the dew is on the drainpipes. Or something. Say. Say there's the same dirty ring around the moon and that elegant bathtub of yours with claws for feet. Anything to make my head swim and see double."

"I don't know," said Eddie. "It's like. It's like a blood vessel got busted in my head. I don't understand it."

"Not from where I sit," said Joe. "I don't have any trouble."

"No kidding," said Eddie. "It really scares me. I can remember. There was a time when I used to get mad and stay mad. Now I peter out before it can do me any good."

"Sorry to hear that," said Joe. "Have a smoke anyway."

"Even though," said Eddie. "You know and I know. It definitely ain't good for what ails me. I need a handout like a dog needs fleas. Another brilliant remark. Coming out of me feet first and covered with a flock of moth balls. Oh, boy. See what I mean? Whatever else. I sure got the old dropsy today. A real jerk. Can't even pick it up without crumpling it. Been watching myself. You get soft, you get clumsy. Stump, stump. If I had a waxed number three wooden leg like you feel you have, I know I would make much better time getting nowhere fast. At least. I don't get the feeling anyone is rushing us around here, do you? How about these crazy motes? Couldn't care less if time went backwards or forwards. Ever hear anything so quiet as they come lazily drifting down? Freeze a second while I blow a zillion or so off the top of your cool and luffly head of hair there. Since I owe this great appointment to you. I give you Ed Lapolsky, worst janitor for the week. Puff, puff. Hands are raw. Running out of rags. Can't believe the cobwebs. Stickiest kind of crud like from the next world collecting like black honey right in the point of every corner. I consider that holy. That kind of goop I never touch. Like something also tells me to steer away from those little heaps of plaster bits piling up in certain places. My share of rainbows and shooting stars. Wow. What a shot in the arm. As for plain dust, I use that only for sneezing. But them grease spots over both sofas we started with our own itchy and pushy heads, I want to tell you, they're spreading out into such a funny map, into such a whole life history of all the stupid fucking things we've ever done, it just about wipes up the floor with me. Can't make up my mind. Was that a laugh or a snort? Never expected me to sound like a cranky bastard with a bad case of crabs, did you? Just the same. Scratch on the bump of my schnoz or no scratch. Sweaty or not sweaty as my armpits may be from being laid off so long. I'm still the same sweet little old me. Only more so. I know it's hard to believe. But I swear. I'm getting to be such a horse's ass about people, I'm absolutely impossible. I want nothing but good. Nothing but good for everybody."

"Including," said Joe. "Lots of iodine. When did you start using that stuff for war paint?"

"When did I start doing what?" said Eddie.

"Crack," said Joe. "Like a pistol shot. Right between the eyes."

"Really?" said Eddie. "Am I boring you, dear? What's wrong? You're not happy with what I said?"

"Happy?" said Joe. "Hilarious. Higher than a kite. Merry as a cricket. Absolutely groggy with joy."

"Go to hell," said Eddie. "Okay? Do me a favor. Go to hell. You and you and you. The whole goddamn bunch of you. Go to hell. And I don't give a shit how you goofy grinning gripers get there. Indian file. Lock step. Daisy chain. In snoods. Nose bags. In a pyramid like a stack of out of shape acrobats from way out the sticks like Flushing Meadow or Far Rockaway. You arrange it. I'm too frigging busy these days trying to pick my own brains without poking my own elbow in my own stupid bleary eye. And I'm one clumsy yak who can tell you. It can't be done. It's like. Floating. A lost fart again. On a flying trip through the Smokies. Landing in some sucking fucking quicksand. Blood banging out the same lovely message in my head that's so low on amps and voltage. Stop, you dippy little dead beat, or I'll shoot. So there I find myself finally jackknifed over knees absolutely straight like Honey is such a crackerjack at, love-making with that's life for you upside-down through my legs. Trying to get an angle on it. I get mad. And I wonder. If I was a whole twelve months younger last year at this time, why is it I still don't have a single bank account? How can you expect a guy to wipe his antisocial ass with a slick page from his family doctor's waiting room copy of the Saturday Evening Post advertising ask the man who owns one? Well, says she, it so happens to be my own luscious body, and I'll do with it what I damn well please, if you don't mind. Mind? says I. You silly broad. Why should I mind so long as you let me watch? And hang around while I buff my nails and check my fly and prepare myself generally until you are in the proper mood to lay down your frame and allow this particular prick to take a good hefty crack at it? How do I know why I love you? You all bush and no brains. You catch what I dig me? Who cares who's on first? The question is who's on top? America, America. You make me dizzy. You give with one hand and take away with the other. Where did I lose you? Which way did you go? The smells I make. The way I am scared shitless to peep out of my pothole. Every day the yellow mellow sun goes down like it's been hitting the bottle. And my lower bowel lives all by itself way off there somewhere. Kvetching. What a nutty business. What fantastic noodlework. What a stinking mess. Like a stopped-up sewer after a heavy rain. Watch it, buster. The first thing that dopey cat of Dave's does in the hall when it spies me sprinting up the stairs humming I Love Louisa is scoot up the ladder to the

651

trap door to the roof and start pissing down like it's been holding it in for years. I did a quick ballet step. I lifted up my nose. Holy rat turds and rotten underwear. What did I run into this time? Well, thanks a lot. It's a damn good thing I'm wearing my Uncle Sy's old army boots today. That's okay, son, I understand perfectly. If you're Irving, you're stuck. You have to try to squeeze in somewhere. And to hell with who gets his lumps. How's the ringing in the ears? Maybe later we can harmonize. So naturally. So I was pretty darn careful how I pushed open that screwy door that sings like a mouse with itchy pants whose spring lock's been busted for years because I once had a whole bucket of freeezing water dumped right down on top of me. And I was expecting Dr. Pepper. Hey, Joe? Remember me telling you about that? What do you mean you don't remember? Are you dumb all of a sudden or what? I told you. He was trying to get back at me for plugging up his old clay pipe I dug out of his garbage and scoured with steel wool and switched for the new one he claims he swiped off a pushcart on Blake with a bit of putty at the bowl end. As I swore later. To save him from getting a hole in his tongue like it shows in the medical books from smoking crap like that awful Prince Albert his worst enemy he was always telling mister old softy himself Snuffsaid Sternweis the tobacconist his fancy title for his lifetime in his floppy fedora to keep off the chill in his dingy 40 watt bulb stationery and notions layout with a lot of old crummy games and toys for the next crop of kids to mangle with a gas burner in the back for boiling milk and a folding cot for resting his bones in real dutch with that weird Paget's disease a slow grower in his greasy leather vest sure to outlast him a most interesting thin-skin hangover type from a time we should thank god we never had to suffer all scrunched over behind his sticky glass top counter like the hunchback of Notre Dame to chalk it up because in the long run you can bet your bottom dollar in this bear market that credit is the best fiscal policy for no matter who like say those lazy dog-hungry Tamales toasting their dusty toes in the sun and passing out of life so quiet you can hardly hear it underneath their beautiful sombreros or their brown and wrinkled brother Incadoos at fourteen thousand elevation squatting on a rock there kind of cokey from them nuts they chew to keep from thinking how long they've been so fucking down and out in their dunce caps and gorgeous serapes or like you know any other spot on this banged and beat-up

652

globe you can put your finger on and shout out loud as you knock it down to the highest bidder with a great big clap, sold american. Bite my ear, says Dave to Sternweis. Bugger my crabby clapper. What am I doing wasting my body heat in this dump you have to pump daylight in to make it look like morning? Is that the way for one human being to make contact with another? Who brung you his best sawed-off pool stick to protect your last broken glass vending machine outside from the gang of gumball fiends? Who else is willing to waltz with you in the inner city of my heart? I have muscles I haven't used yet I am prepared to lay at your feet. You see something crawling? Where are you looking in the middle of my eyes? What a big fat bore. How long do I have to wait for you to come across? Come on, pappy, make it snappy. This is no little thing. Before I conk out in this funk hole for want of a wee bit of the weed. Cut the cackle. And toss me a can, man. Gimme, gimme. And he got. I once heard an ordinary guy say. Unbelievable. Let's hear it loud and clear now. Is our boy Doodie a real hopped up pro with the hot air or ain't he? Crazy sonofabitchin bum with his lousy yankee-doodle slapstick tricks. I love the guy. I really do. It's a funny thing with me. It doesn't take much. I can be sad a lot. But I can be very happy too. Sure enough, yea, there was that old stinker in his Erasmus High sweat shirt he never went to, with his tongue hanging out kind of sideways, scratching out his last will and testicles with his trusty steel pen point and wooden holder with its trillion built-in blots in a space he cleared on the kitchen table piled high with those cheap shiny ribbons and other junky material his Mom slaps together to make them tiny celluloid fans piecework for something like a jitney per thousand, jesus, no wonder, you come into her house, house they call it, that dilapidated, peewee two-room flat as dark as the inside of a black cat, you skip in there, and she gives you one stab with her sharp bitter eyes, so fierce and young-looking yet, with such a cute kisser on her, and skin like fresh snow, and such a happy head of hair, and lips, but don't worry, that old tramp mother nature and her steady sweetheart hard times are already doing a pretty fair hurry-up job on her, Jenny, I used to call her until, rips the heart right out of you like she was saying, yes, I can see, we all have shoes, but we're so empty inside, so what hope is there, and she's so right, because if you take me, what can I give her, how can I help, what do I have control of, what can I change? My diaper. Right. And what? Gee.

Hope you don't mind if I ask. Is what you two big brains there whispering about strictly confidential? Or can any boob get in on it? So okay. So all right. So how could I know? So I snuck up on him and gave him a good whack on the back, and said, hey, I know you can read a little if the stuff is all in caps, but when the hell did you learn how to write? Oh, god. Oh, what a terrible feeling that is. No one has to tell me. It just about tears you apart when some babe who's crept into your bones without your realizing it gets the jump on you and ditches you before you can dump her. Oh, does that hurt. Either way. All of a sudden, it's you who's down on your jelly knees, squealing like a stuck pig, you can't do this to me, how can you do this to me? He was like someone crazy. Dave. Our Dave with his crap shooter's luck. The first time it ever really happened to him. Kissed off. Getting the axe just like any other ordinary limp cock from a bitchy two-timing bundle all pair of titties like Belle. Big beeswax. Little wreck-tangle. Dismal flops everywhere. Like it comes to all men. Ran to the clinic with his horrible blown up face to wait on that hard bench, and after squirming and chewing on his green ticket for three hundred years, the Doc there takes one look at him and says, nerves, son, next. Air. Give me all the air you can. Before I knew it, the poor guy, he was all over me like a ton of bricks, reaching for my neck with his neglected nails, and me yelling like a nut, hold it, hold it, if this is a rape, I'm not resisting, I'm not resisting. Cost me a nice hunk of meat out of my snoot before I could calm him down. Had to drag me into the toilet to hand it to me. Sure, I said to him, sure, you can depend on me, I'll deliver your fucking begging billy-do to that fucking dame personally. Bull. As soon as I got out into the street, I had me a ball. I made confetti out of it. Hello? Is that you, Honeybunch? Tell me truly. Are we still in this together? How's your bouncy little fanny I so dearly love? Are you minding your precious old p's and q's? That was a lovely screech. What's biting you now? I guess I'm worried. So I'm imagining things. I was sure I had me a nickel somewhere to make a quick call. If I felt any more rotten, I'd be plumb dead. What is today? Is today still Friday?"

"Oh, no," said Joe. "No, sir. Don't look at me. I didn't hear a word you said. I don't want any part of this."

"Cold," said Eddie. "Like a dead man his head."

"Get your filthy paws off of me."

654

"My pal," said Eddie. "At least. If I had to eat all them words, I'd never go hungry, would I?"

"Women," said Joe. "What a mystery. What's wrong with us anyway? Why are we always messing it up? Why can't it be a happy thing?"

"And that," said Eddie. "That's why a chicken crosses the road."

"Just the same," said Joe. "I swear. I'm no hotshot myself when it comes to fooling around with them funny ducks. But I'll be damned if I'd ever let a thing like that knock me for a loop. Or make me want to kiss myself goodbye and go over Niagara Falls in a barrel. Not in a million years. Never."

"And my country tis of thee," said Artie. "And cannon to the right of him. And cannon to the left. And the flag was still there."

"Huh," said Eddie. "My country."

"I don't know why," said Joe. "I could smell it coming."

"Wow, yes," said Artie. "And come it sure did. To Dave. Dovidle baby. Our A number 1 laughing-boy high-water pants lady-killer. Even with your nose. It sure is hard to believe."

"I warned him," said Joe. "I kept warning him all I knew how."

"And zing," said Doc. "And give us a little room here. With a spear in the ribs. And an arrow to the gizzard. And guggle-muggle. When it's nighttime on the reservation. When the East Flatbush Bellyaching Braves meet the East New York Bellybumping Squaws. And fuck everyone who's not listening to me. And another cunt crazy bastard bites the dust."

"I'm listening to him," said Mel. "Do I have to look at him to listen to him?"

"Horse apples," said Doc. "And a crock of shit on top of that. How many fat asses weighing a ton do we need in this fucking world?"

"Well, yes," said Mel. "Looks like you got something there, son. So long as the whole world keeps screwing like rabbits day and night. And no time off on Sundays. It's absolutely hopeless, ain't it?"

"Your fucking jacket is buttoned wrong."

"What gets me is," said Mel. "What was I so busy with? It seems to me I remember. I did get a whiff of her once or twice. What's the name of them little brown things our fellow Americans stick in a ham? Could be eaten. Eh, what? Awfully sweet walking down the street, wasn't she? With a sticklebur under her tail. My sweet embraceable you. The way she would flop herself down all in one solid piece. Broken springs or not. Back as straight as a broomstick. And pick apart the premises with her magic mirror eyes for more man-meat to eat. You thought she was smiling at you, but she was already looking over your head. Ring out them Belles. Can't be she was only a witch. What's with them babes anyway? Why can't they just be people? Ho. Listen to this hunk of crap. As if I were a fully paid-up member of the human race myself. Oof. As of right now. I must say. Disgusted as I am with the whole boiling works. I'm with Joe there. You turn them all upside down. And what've you got?"

"My country," said Eddie. "Yeah. Sure. Look at it. It keeps sticking out its chest. It sweats but never stinks. It thinks it's so great. Well, it's not. It better start thinking all over again."

"Boing," said Doc. "Down with up. There's a real biggie for you."

"I'll say," said Artie. "With a dagger over the dot. And close them quotes. But quick. Excuse me, sir. Will that be in the form of a letter or a telegram?"

"Oh," said Eddie. "Don't knock yourself out. Just brand it on your pecker with a glowing butt the next time you sneak off to the piss-house to do your little thing."

"And he went," said Artie. "And he blamed it on the mountain. And the mountain looked at him with such sad eyes and said. When the hell did you become such a goddamn sorehead?"

"Same old story," said Eddie. "I was born stupid. And I'll die stupid. I don't know what gets into me sometimes. I come hippety-hopping down here like I usually do. And all of a sudden. Before I know what I'm doing, I'm dropping my pants all over the place. I show my all. I talk my heart out. I shoot the works. And what happens? Nix. A great big bunch of nothing. You little shit-ass. You think I get these cramps thinking only about myself? It's you I'm worried about. About all of you fine-looking permanent flops. I'm telling you, men. You better be ready to duck and run. That man has had it. He's had it way up to where he can't even reach. Push, push. How far can you push an ordinary piece of humanity? What's wrong? You never saw such a look on my face? Watch out now. I'm warning you. As soon as that crazy guy Dave can see around the corner, he's going to run out and kill. Kill, kill. Right and left. Left and right. It could be anybody. Anybody. Jesus. Who knows who it's going to be?"

"Me," said Irving. "If what you say is true. It has to be me. Who else?"

"Whack," said Eddie. "With one side of his hand. Like this. What a nut. That Dave. Who the hell does he think he is? It kills him to feel the world has no use for him whatsoever. He's a little slow there. He has to imagine there's still some power for good left in him or else. So ha. Before you know it. Since as it happens the man is temporarily out of funds for finding a cure for dry rot of the jobs available situation in his field. Whop. There he is. Whanging away at old pieces of crate and picture frames until he has it down pat. Caught him once eyeing that crazy cat of his when it was licking itself all over, like he was thinking, hey, if I can only get that filthy beast cornered, here's a chance to take a crack at something warm and still kicking. Boom. One time. I'll never forget it. Remember that hotcha time a couple of months ago, Joe, at that fake surprise party for that klutzy kid whose dad deals in cut flowers wholesale, who will buy from me my smelly bunch of Violette, when old Davey boy there, I love the guy, I really do, laid out his own big dame hunting cousin, Fascinating Fred, as he was known, with his how's every little thing and fancy nose job, who kept goosing him trying to cut in on him with Belle so flat, we all just stood there like perfect dummies with our mouths open, looking down at what used to be a pretty solid curly-headed wide-awake person? What do you mean if what I say is true?"

"I'm sick," said Irving. "What's the use? I'm dead already. It can't be. How can it be? I swear to you guys. It was Dave. It was Dave himself who called me up and gave me permission and told me what to do. He knew I knew who he was. He knew he wasn't fooling me by covering the mouthpiece with his best flour-sack hanky or babushka out of ticking to protect his scalp rash from the poisons in the air or that flowing color-blind taffeta tie of his or whatever the hell else he had on his royal person. It had to mean he was itching to shake her off and picked me to be the fall guy to get him off the hook. And not the other way around like Eddie's been telling us. Ah, now, please. What kind of a look is that? You think I'm batty altogether? You think I'd ever have nerve enough to try to date that nutty muscleman's girl friend behind his back? Me? Little old lanky jelly bean Irving? Fat chance. You think I'm that tired of living yet? What's the matter with you guys? Wasn't anybody listening? Goddamn it. Don't keep looking at me that way. I

657

told you. It's the truth. I swear to you. That's exactly the way it happened."

"Of all the stupid things," said Joe. "This has to happen to us."

"Ho, ho," said Artie. "Clogged nose and all. Seems to me I definitely smell a rat."

"And a bottle of bay rum," said Doc. "Who would've thunk it? What a break. Thank you, lord, thank you. This is going to be a real pleasure.".

"That's my pal," said Mel. "Now I remember. And this used to be such a plain old knucklehead. I love it when he gets all fired up that way. You can rub your crackling hands for me too, bub. Like old Simple Simon the pattern maker used to say. We sure got our work cut out for us. And you can bet your bottom dollar. And your top one too if you happen to have one on you. It won't take us but half a mo."

"Yeah," said Doc. "Our next Pres for sure. Take over, take over. You're piping hot right there, boy. Maybe he doesn't know it yet. But there's one cluck who's never going to live long enough to see his kids through college."

"Of course," said Irving. "What a ninny. When will I ever learn? How on earth could I expect such highly cultured gentlemen to believe a low-down awful nitwit like me?"

"I'm wondering," said Eddie. "Should I tap out a message and warn him? Or should I just make a tight little fist and bash his fucking head in?"

"My, my," said Irving. "Isn't this positively ducky? I really am amazed. Such enthusiasm everywhere."

"That's it," said Eddie. "I got it now. It's going to be my life's work. I'm going to bash his fucking head in. And have enough left over for gas and rent."

"One thing," said Irving.

"Make it two," said Eddie. "And see if I care."

"Maybe it looked like it," said Irving. "But I wasn't hunched over there for a second with my head in my hands because my teeth were chattering and I was shivering in my boots."

"He speaks," said Artie. "He curls his lip like he was very knowledgeable about the fine art of fisticuffs."

"Now, now," said Mel. "No violence, please. We'll handle this in the proper way."

658

"Oh," said Irving. "Indubitably. I guess I don't have to wet my finger to see which way the wind is blowing, do I?"

"My dear man," said Artie. "I hope you realize it. You are now marked lousy for life."

"Is that a fact?" said Irving. "Well, I must confess. It doesn't surprise me in the least. I always knew it was my inescapable destiny. As a matter of fact. I can remember way back to the day I was born. The doctor took one look at me and said, he's in trouble."

"Shame on you," said Mel. "You naughty boy. You know what you did, don't you?"

"Do I know what I did?" said Irving. "Oh, boy. I sure do. In spades. And the joker wild. According to you. The unwritten constitution, it say. I broke the only law you people respect around here. I ratted on a clubmember. I wasn't on the square with a pal."

"Exactly," said Mel. "Smack on the button. You get A plus. And you know what that means, don't you?"

"It means," said Irving. "Let me spare you the trouble and expense of printing up a fancy ballot and voting me out. Here's my key."

"Whoa, now," said Joe. "Wait a minute. Not so fast. What do you think you're doing? You mean to say you're going to quit just like that without fighting back?"

"Fighting back," said Irving. "Yeah, yeah. Fight your father. Fight your mother. Put your shitty shoe on the nearest born loser's neck and keep it there. Grind, grind. Squash the squishy guilt out of his skull. Bleed the sissy non-fucking animal until he makes in his pants and passes out. That'll learn him. It's so healthy for him to know that if he makes one single mistake, that's it, he might as well pack up and get lost permanently. But quit. Ah, I'm afraid you have me there. That's about the nastiest four-letter word in these hairy spectacular States of America the Beautiful, ain't it? Sorry I didn't consult with you on that. Since you're such a great specialist on quitting. Hey, now, says he. What the hell is this? Don't get fresh with me. I'm only trying to help you. Is that what's bubbling on your lips? Will you listen to me a second? Will you listen to me? Fine. Fire away while I go the route and pat my pockets. I know I suffered some great loss all of a sudden. So I can't possibly leave with everything I came with, can I? No, no. I didn't mean that. You keep that crackling ten dollar bill, Doc old boy old kid. That's for closing fees. Spread it around. Have a wake on me.

659

Famous last words. I'm innocent, I tell you, I'm innocent. I'm really shocked. What a terrible thing to do to a man. The only way I could be dirtier in your eyes would be to be bigger. Strange. It doesn't really matter a hoot who's been telling the truth around here, does it? Ah, well. Up we go. I've been down on my knees so long, I hope to hell I still know how to walk. Easy as in Fox. Beep, beep. Ahoy the forecastle and scuttlebutts. Congrats to the whole Atlantic force. Enemy has been sighted and disposed of. Like the man says. When his heart's not in it. It's been nice knowing you all. I think."

"Sit down," said Joe.

"Well," said Irving. "I can't say thanks for the push."

"Hey, you," said Joe. "Give it back to him."

"First of all," said Mel. "Hay is for horses. I thought you knew that. And second. For us. For us here it sure has been one great big mess after another. So keep a tight asshole. Don't let the smoke get in your eyes. Be a man. You just let us chickens here try to clear this one up without you for a change. If it won't kill you altogether."

"Kill me," said Joe. "Who cares? I don't know what the hell it is you have against me. But please. I beg you. Don't take it out on him. It's wrong. Why gang up on the poor guy? Is anyone here building his nest yet? What's the great offense? At this time of your stupid unsettled lives. Women come. And women go. Can't you all see how petty it is? Give him back his key. Let him live. Jesus. You don't need me to tell you. At any time. And no matter what. It's not good for your soul to be so hard."

"What hard?" said Mel. "Another insult. You were here. You saw what happened. No one twisted his arm. The kid himself gave me the goddamn thing. And being the fine gentleman that I am, I accepted it as politely as I could. And if god in his ignorance spares me. I intend to hold on to it until I too go over the dam with my eyes closed and holding my nose all the way. Oh, sure. It's sad. And really. It's such a shame. But there it is. Why the hell do we have to discuss it until our tongues are hanging out? Somehow or other. I'm sorry to say. The damn fool went and done himself in. He knows it. We all know it. He's out."

"He is, is he?" said Joe. "And since when are you so in?"

"Oh, the sonofabitch," said Mel. "Did you hear that sly little piece of whatever there? No wonder I'd go to hell on a red-hot poker for such a brainy smalltime big shot. Excuse me a second. Hey, Doc. Doc baby? Hey, I'm talking to you. Will you stop twanging away on that crummy old rubber band? Never still a second. Makes me so goddamn nervous. Another dreamer in this dump. Grabs hold of it in his teeth. Pulls and picks on it. And thinks he's making music. Happy with his little fortune nicely folded and tucked away. Remember, bud, that ten bucks is for all of us. For you. Let me guess. For you a big pound bag of peppermint bull's-eyes. And for me. Huh. Since when am I so in. That's a good one. That'll last me for a while. Impossible to imagine. Was there ever such a wiseguy since the world began? The next thing you know he'll be saying to me. See the earth. It's a dilly and a dumpling. It turns only one way. On its blow bubbles. On its bare ass in the air what's called its axle. And so long as it keeps wobbling and spinning that way, pretty soon, there's going to be a new lock on that door, and none of us is going to have a key to it."

"Aie, aie, aie," said Doc. "Was that ever beautiful. May I be the first to shake your hand?"

"Sure," said Mel. "Only if you chop that big ham of yours off at the wrist and scrub it first."

"I hope," said Joe. "I hope when I grow up, I'll never be such a tough egg. Or think I am. And have to act up to it."

"Aw, now," said Artie. "You? Our tiptop esteemed rabbi? Handing us such tired old crap? I don't believe it. Come on, boy. You can do better than that. What's ailing you, man? What's happened to the old zip? You're not the bloke who wrote the blues. Why be so downhearted? Look how I'm snapping out of it when I think that for me it's going to be a succulent blue plate of salami and eggs. Yum, yum. I'm already reordering. It's like my goofy big toe sticking through me cuckoo mismatched sock. What's a little trouble between friends? Can we avoid it? Can we ever live without it? I say no. I say trouble is what tears and rips us apart. And trouble is what patches us up together again. Patches us up. Um. Not bad. Not bad at all. Did you catch that sizzling line drive barehanded? What's your feeling about it?"

"Simple," said Joe. "There are some jokers in this world who think they can solve the riddle of the universe just by scratching their balls."

"That's the ticket," said Artie. "That's the way to go. Who ever said you were on your last legs? Sitting as pretty as you are. Orchids to you, me boy. If you're imitating a corkscrew. Relax. You got it made.

661

You who are about to be a bum. Who by this time would know better than you? For some goddamn reason. I don't know why. But no one. No one ever looks good when he's trying to do what he thinks is the right thing. Even when he's absolutely sure of it. Which who the hell ever is?"

"Ah," said Eddie. "Thank you, Art. Thank you for saying that. That's exactly the way it is with me. I don't care what happened. All I know is. He made Dave suffer. And that's enough for me. As far as I'm concerned. He's all washed up. He's cooked. How did he wander in here anyway? Who forced him on us? We were so comfortable. We were so happy without him. He knew he didn't belong. What was he looking for? What did he expect?"

"And you," said Joe. "You were the one who said. I want nothing but good. Nothing but good for everybody."

"I know," said Eddie. "I know I'm a case. But that's my nature. I can't help it. I know I sound like a shit. But after what happened. It hurts to have to say it. I can't look him in the face. I can't stand to have him around any more."

"Hey," said Doc. "Did you hear that bugle call? Real snappy, wasn't it? Didn't sound like taps to me. If that Irv with a lot of nerve can still blow his nose that way. That's his way of telling us. No problem, men. Nothing to worry about. He's emptying his bilge. He's shaking it off. He's getting himself set for the next move. He'll get over it. He'll make it."

"Right as rain," said Joe. "As usual."

"You betcha my life," said Doc. "I may be a little too square where I should be a lot more round. But I'm no fusspot. I'm for what is. I'm for what happens."

"Great," said Joe. "Sounds real smart. And me. I'm for nothing but blue skies. Since I'm for what's never going to happen."

"And why not?" said Doc. "That's very possible. Since it ain't."

"Extremely so," said Joe. "How's the head you left at home? Does it still fit?"

"Squashed," said Doc. "Terrible shape. My Pop's been carrying it around under his arm."

"Saying, I suppose," said Joe. "Get a load of him."

"Gee," said Doc. "Maybe so. I'll tune in the next time on my trusty crystal set and let you know."

"Fine," said Joe. "That puts the cap on that bit. Serves me right for trying to break in through the back door."

"Ah," said Doc. "You old goat. You're still my favorite crossword puzzle. You're just as scrambled and screwy sideways as you are up and down. But I wonder if you know it. You always do better when you talk to yourself."

"Yep," said Joe. "You sure rang the bell that time. And so. Since I see it's absolutely hopeless. Since I'm dealing with a bunch of goddamn stubborn boobs. We come to the end of a nice evening's enjoyment. Or did I already say that?"

"Going my way?" said Irving.

"Ha," said Joe. "I don't know. It all depends. Which way is that?"

"Out," said Irving. "Out of this whacky beat-up wilderness. To hack my way to the glory road. Pouring it on until I reach the promised land. Since I've shown myself to be such a positively superior being. Why should I settle for less?"

"Watch it, son," said Joe. "You're spilling things."

"My mother is right," said Irving. "I should keep my hands out of my pockets."

"And your mighty person," said Joe. "Out of revolving doors. I should know. I'm caught in one myself. No wonder I feel a little rocky. I've been trying to figure it out. What was that about Budapest?"

"Budapest," said Irving. "A quartet."

"Barbershop?" said Joe.

"No, no," said Irving. "String. Four strings."

"Strings," said Joe. "Sounds like a hanging committee to me."

"Oh," said Irving. "It does, does it? And where have you been keeping yourself? Isn't it time you stopped playing dumb?"

"I should say," said Joe. " I swear to god. I can hardly wait for the day. But until then. What's the sense of kidding you? I am dumb. I am still an unfinished person. Oh, sure. I may know a thing or two. Such accidents will happen. Like I think I know the sound of chamber pot music when I hear it. Or what a bib is. But then I have to scratch my head. What in hell's a tucker? I mean to say. I'm only thinking out loud. But what's my responsibility here? What's wrong in coming to my own rescue? If I catch you smiling, does that mean my day's work is done? Good. Because when I go out of here, I'm going out alone. I have to cut it short. I have to rest up. Tomorrow's a tremendous day for

663

me. God knows which way I'll swing. Or what kind of a human being I'll turn out to be. Don't look so sad, you twerp. I still think you're just as important as I am. Would you like to make a dash for the door before me? Yes? No? Okay, then. Like Artie would say. To horse. Imagine having to listen to yourself saying a thing like that. Be seeing you, guys. Don't talk about me when I'm gone. I've told every little star. But I know you will never believe this. The whole wide world is waiting for me with open arms."

17.

Great and good god, however marvelous in heat the all too human in him, like in so many of us brainstorming male brutes shedding our quickie ideas like short hairs and growing beer bellies, and them bubbly companion babes with their sassy lilac notions and tidal waves of flinging woo with such a wild rosy mystical compassion for their ultimate comeuppance as miraculous yet mere mortals suffusing their boy-crazy faces, good grief, however much it thrilled as it ploughed up his heart when he realized that every bridge ever built was meant to be burned behind him, even so, what a truly turned-on transfixed of the mock-heroic, what a shut-in snip of self-assertion so snapped out of place, what a flip windup of his flaming goodbye for now if not forever, in his unmannerly haste to leave the people flat as he hoped to leave them laughing at, as if in its hello again and heads up, its april and inapprehensible, its improbable red-hot molten core, its pastel and elegant periodic greening, its beard-lifting tremors and upheavals to burp itself, its constant bolting from the blue, its windy penchant for pulling fast ones, its cool misty-moisty ishkabibble isness, this dear and drat it inconceivability, this oblate spoof, this witless spinoff from the whole entire reluctant universe, this relative pinprick of a world was one great thought, and he was thinking it.

Terrifying. You have to be crazier than a bedbug to believe that. If by now. Are you also as afflicted and afraid to take a good look squarely in your own eyes? As anyone can see. You are so tiny when all tied up in knots. A sort of apostrophical ass on the loose on a lurid moonscape of dusty and infatuated half-truths and poorly limned ill-becomes you semi-lies. And as it may no doubt seem to many of our most pushy and self-purging pundits who love the word when least written, much more hyphenated and loquacious than need be in this your stutter-step and steppingstone translation from the creepy forest murmurs of some way out of sight here to the blazing sahara of some stark-staring where. As from true chaos to as true a clarity is scarcely one short flea leap in the dark. Not forgetting for a moment that in these dotty head-swimming days any blooming young hopeful who rushes his slightest part-time supraliminal noodling is simply ripping himself off. If by this time you are not as crazy ambitious and hipped as he is to hit the high spots only. Having somehow arrived after blundering down the low road at the very fringes of the unreachable with your squinty conglomerate eyes and symbolical crooked feet. So charmed by your own silly smile as you contemplate the immense sunny with passing puffball clouds of the tragicomic complexity of any and every crossroad you hang back from. If by this time. If by now you are not as utterly wiped out and are still at it with him for this one last time.

For this one last what? What last? Is it possible? What are you saying? Exactly what was said? This tag reads. Take your hand away and let me see. Beware of the dog. Neglected myths grow nettles. Elderly fables gather acorns and mind cows. Wingless termites with tenure are assured of getting to heaven without dying. After a mere drench of sleep. Every simplistic and inscape person ups and says to himself. Git. Will you please mind your own beeswax? Not every road is good which arrives. The eternal boob pees in his pants when god tackles him from the blind side. Even the wisest flashy youngster can bust a gut laughing and never know why. There are times. What does it all mean? Some are so glad to be interred by success. Other idealists sweat like hell to achieve their own unhappy ending. Nothing ever gets less difficult. The lowliest form of human life is like a mountain which is a huge compression of matter. As an estuary. To fail is to sink. How much more of this can I take? As an estuary is a drowned river mouth. And an ocean is all water. And any truth. Any truth at all is better than any kind of make-believe. Believe, believe. To hear is to take heart. And no longer take umbrage. What a fresh analeptic breeze recharging our exchangeable offbeat see-through heads. What a wicked way of shuffling off a large portion of the unbearable weight. What a dazzler of a day. More light, more light. The end is in sight.

And the voice said, cry. And old Joe said, what shall I cry? My time is up. My day is over. I have run out of havocs. I am no longer in line to use the wailing wall. Though this day too may be one of trouble and of treading down. I am afraid to mention I have a heart. Sometimes it is as slippery as a lemon seed. And sometimes as large and upright as a cabbage rose. I love to look at what is just as it is. I was born to be a listener. I shall always be of two minds. Peel and all. Both of which natural enemies so clashingly aware of. Think. If everything has been thought of before, how difficult it is to think of it again. And the voice said, ditto and glad tidings, the difficulty is as rife as bloodstroke and the falling sickness. You may be as comic as a basket case. And you are inclined to sum up before a sea of empty faces. But it seems to be a fact that you do often feel a sensation which reminds you that you have a head. So grab hold of yourself. You hear what immediately means? Only chickens come to definite conclucksions. As cowards dream of being fastened as a nail to a sure place. Are you merely a tail which wags every which way? Are you as an apple corrected for wind? Are you like a snake with no movable eyelids? Blink. And you will see. See how far-advanced to far-gone you are in one ordinary stupendous week. Bother all them blooming put downs and bum raps. If this is your deepest drag yet on your next to last cigarette. The tide what runs out will run in again. Glory be to any man who can stretch his attention span. And Joe said, it is you who say it.

And what else are you ignorant of? And where, said Joe, where did you get the idea I was a sort of luminous heavenly body on whose nebulous tail you could take such a ripping joy ride? And who else but a sponge and tagalong like you would be able to tell me who first cracked likewise so tripping and cribbing off the topmost tip of his tumultuous head? And when it comes down to it. As come down it must. Who in this vale of tearless dishonesty and dreadful distortion and demonic vandalism do you think I think I am? As told to wait, I feel as confined and confounded as ever as I sit here in this chicken

667

coop Mr. Colish calls his private office, elevated to a fine state of unbalance by a broken spring, existing as best as I can at arm's length with my highly excited ur-self, praying I would finally become addicted to plainer speaking, crossing and recrossing my legs to keep them limber for beating the lights to get to the other side with all my marbles intact and clicking, anxious to abate, since I cannot get rid of the pain of being a man, terrified of turning overnight into one hock-tuey after another of a bald lumpy alter cocker, sensing that my vague and uneasy yearning after the pitiful cushion of severance pay means that my old spirit is already in danger of beginning to stink on ice, somehow so cocksure that I have an eternity of time before me, yet scarcely knowing where my next minute is coming from.

Not knowing. It surely is to laugh. How I did hope otherwise. After suffering a whole week this superlative rush of brains to my head, I see I have shot up from the common level of absolute idiot to the unique plateau of certified ignorant cuss. Yet sickly wondering. Will the time for such sprees of slashing and scoffing at one's own poor spluttering and skulking self ever be other than now? Even if I always keep my afterimages in the open position? Is it reasonable to believe that only the bowels can be fully aware of what a real movement means? Can a bad idea become a good one if I take and wring its neck? Will the number of my revengeful neuroses be visibly reduced by a multiple listing? When did clever me first begin to suspect that to be hooked on fantasy, in an open fly orgasmic flap over every foul and induced experience that flows from it, is far more dangerous than being addicted to pot cheese or nose candy? And god. What if. I am waiting to be told. What if the truth turns out to be true? Would it petrify? Would it entirely destroy me?

Anything to be different. Is this not as pure and pretty a praeludium as can be plucked and luted in these harsh dumdum indelicate days? Mighty generous of you to say no. As clearly it is up to me to speak up before I run out of time. Damn me. How I wish I knew something. I sure do wish I knew just enough to. Let me take a second now to feel myself all over to see if trying to squeeze in so much has taken some of the squeak out of my soul. Dished again. In no way whatsoever. Such sorrow. How I hate to wait. Yet I am happier than most. Is this what I mean when I say that being born is merely the first frustration? It is curious that every time I drive myself up the wall, I find I have plenty of company. When will I stop bothering the people? What is this daffy wrestling of mine with that old granny concept of freedom of choice when, as some sharpie who saw so straight as to sound brutal once said, all it boils down to is whether you choose to be clobbered by the left or right hand of fate? I takes my lumps, but I never likes it. There is dirt under my fingernails from probing a certain crack right down my middle. I know a man is worthless unless he works. But job. Job is the one frightful man-made false bottom which has me fazed. I see that necessity is stocked on the lowest shelf. But it comes in giant size only. Because pride goes before price, I refuse to bend. The last time around for anyone is an agony. Why should my countless superiors be queueing up to push me around? Any total commitment to any resounding yes or no is rousing music to me. Not to try is to die. If I waver now, I am as the worm is to the butterfly. Who are these untold millions on a massive sneering jeering sitdown strike against any real act? Who are they to be shouting at me? Wrong way. Go back, go back. I try not to listen, but it shakes me up. I am so afraid of ending up alone. So self-suspicious of. My stars. Did you see that? How can I explain it? Here I am about to enter into a furious tickle fight with the fierce unbeatable future. And I am absolutely amazed to catch myself smiling at myself. Perhaps it may be. I can only guess. Perhaps. After all is said and done unto death. For me at least. It still feels so funny to be alive.

"Still alive," said Mr. Colish. "Still alive. What's all this screaming so happy about still alive? That all of a sudden a solid person I know all my life is like soft meat not fit to eat? With eyes like glass that shines without seeing? With that ich, that awful catchum shoved up his so he can make water? Don't tell me no. If he's afraid, I'm afraid, you're afraid. Only my dear sweet wife knows how to fold a handkerchief so five points are showing. Was it last Thursday or Friday poor Miss Fatstuff from Filene's bent my ear a whole hour with the same story? Who needs another losing proposition in the middle of the night? So quiet. I run out in my slipslappers. Taxi, taxi. I pick him up like a sack and plop him back in bed. I never dreamed my Papa was so light. A markdown on my hands. I should have a fire sale for my stupid heart that's always working overtime. First it makes like a fist. Then it flops around like a fish. A bull. A bumblebee would behave better. On your knees, you bummer. I begin to slap and shake him. I can hear myself crying like an old yenteh. Why do you pick on now? How can you do this to me? But he can't hear. He doesn't recognize. Rolling around in his own manure. A new expense. I thought a shorter haircut. I will never listen to another doctor. I can soap myself all over a million times, but there is something only I can smell that is stuck to me. I say. I say some day I will kill. So? So what's the matter with now? Will I ever have a minute for myself? Who's in charge of moles? A new one should be where no one can see. Now where the hell's that bill for all that trucking I just put here? You been poking in my papers? You can't rock in that. What's the message? You have to pee? What are you doing here?"

"Dovening," said Joe. "As if for the first time. Rough. And losing my patience. Just like you."

"Patience?" said Mr. Colish. "What patience? How can I lose what I never had?"

"I must say," said Joe. "With all due respect. If I had your shyster of a lawyer. I would sue you blind for my sore behind for making me sit here for seven centuries."

"Another fly buzzing around me."

"And forty-three minutes."

"Ah," said Mr. Colish. "So there you are. You little piece of dreck. With me, if I touch something, right away it grows feet. What I'll do is take ten percent right off the top. He can sue me too."

"Who's been rolling around in what do you call it?"

"My father, my father."

"Your father?" said Joe. "What happened?"

"Chop," said Mr. Colish. "A stroke. Just like that. God with his golden hatchet he got wholesale from a second cousin of that hustler his foreman Mr. Benjamin Beelzebub. What a thing. What a business. And who do you think is next? Me. It runs in the family. But runs."

"Oh," said Joe. "That's terrible. I don't like that."

"Terrible," said Mr. Colish. "I can't figure it out. What's happening to me? I used to be so in control of myself. So in charge. Now I catch myself thinking. Maybe I'll take a side trip Monday from the new factory to Miami. And hide there until it happens. I can't. I won't hang around like a dummy with spit coming out of my mouth. Something in me won't let me. I can't. I won't watch him die."

"Aie," said Joe. "There it is again. The lousy rotten thing."

"He's dying," said Mr. Colish. "He's getting ready to be dead."

"Dead," said Joe. "To be dead. I pass. Who can understand it?"

"When did my middle all around me begin to burn and itch? What is this starting up with me now? You hear anything?"

"Hear anything?" said Joe. "What's there to hear?"

"Sounds quiet."

"Sounds like the same old racket to me."

"The door is closed," said Mr. Colish. "It is five o'clock. My business for the day is finished. Join me. On our holy sabbath that once was. Be my partner. Up with the head. Let us howl like wolves."

"Just the same," said Joe. "Just the same."

"I'm looking," said Mr. Colish. "I'm listening."

"That sure was a dirty trick you played on me."

"Which one?"

"They blamed me," said Joe. "They thought I knew. Why did you keep it such a secret? Why didn't you let me know?"

"Because," said Mr.Colish. "I know my customers. You're just like my Aunt Emmie who used to say to Babe her youngest. Go out and see what your brother Hershie is doing and tell him to stop it."

"Some joke," said Joe.

"Your loss if you don't appreciate."

"It was their jobs, Mr. Colish. Their jobs. How could you be so cruel? You took their jobs right out from under them."

"The door is closed," said Mr. Colish. "It is now. It is now exactly five after five."

"Oh, no," said Joe. "No, sir. I refuse to believe that. You mean to say we're all that helpless? That no matter what happens all we can do is sit here and howl?"

"Cruel," said Mr. Colish. "Cruel, he says. What's with you? You didn't sleep a single wink last night? Is sawdust all you have left in your head? Cruel. Of course it's cruel. What's so special about being selfish? If you come first, and the other momzer second, that's it. You can take the best lies about it you have in stock and stitch them to the best words you can buy on the market. And what have you got? A botch. A baby not born yet knows. It is always a sin. It is always a crime."

"Even if," said Joe.

"And believe me," said Mr. Colish. "I should know. I punched. I pushed. I yelled louder. I was quicker. I was more alive. I became a

671

boss. I loved it. If you want to know how to eat people with or without ketchup, come to me. I've had a thousand times more experience as a plain animal than a real human being."

"Even if," said Joe. "Even if it's only a lot of nothing? Like something really innocent? Like me quitting my job? Even if all I want to do is to be free for a while to lift up my eyes and look?"

"I also chew toothpicks," said Mr. Colish. "What do you do?"

"Me?" said Joe. "Ha. That's easy. You just saw. I always make sure I finish second. I'm pretty damn good at it, ain't I?"

"Maybe it's a sickness."

"Well," said Joe. "If so. At least I'm sick in my way. Not yours."

"And that's success?" said Mr. Colish. "I'll kill that fresh Miss Golschman. What is this? Am I asking her to take out the garbage? It's such a little thing. I keep telling her and telling her. She spreads her skirt. She bows. She says, yes, your royal catnip. She knows. But she won't listen. If the pencil is too sharp, the point will break."

"Oops," said Joe. "There goes another one. I don't mean to mix in. But you better watch it. You'll never live long that way."

"Live long," said Mr. Colish. "Live long. What's this with you and live long? You been practicing the subject in the toilet all night, making the sign of the red circle on your skinny rumpadoodle? Did you squeeze there so brokenhearted and only did what you know what? Was the light switched off? Was the dark too cold? When did you become such a Johnny one whistle? You don't wear glasses yet. You got twenty-twenty. Look. You're not looking. I'm nothing but a tight collar. I'm an empty suit. I'm the flop. I've already lived longer than you."

"Ah, yes," said Joe. "You're so right. At least there I'm still lucky. It sure does take a lot of time, doesn't it? You really have to learn how to look. Mind if I ask you? How come you can make such beautiful capital letters? Are you like me? I can't remember when I first learned our grand numbers and glorious alphabet. It just happened. I really feel it in every part of me. How long can I fool around like this without flying apart? I have to. I know I'm going to die young."

"All the young say that."

"Ha," said Joe. "Hoping otherwise."

"Two people," said Mr. Colish. "In the same elevator. One is going up. The other is going down."

672

"Yes," said Joe. "Up and down. Smelling of smoke. Doors never opening. Stuck between floors. You sure hit it right on the button that time. The question is. Which one is which?"

"If I drop off," said Mr.Colish. "If I tell you how sad it makes me to listen to you, you will know which. My situation is this. My whole lunch of spinach and spanish omelette wants to come up and say hello. My head from last year is like a balloon. The cuckoo clock keeps skipping back. The day is stretching out so long. I am so pooped. Sleep. Sleep is all I want. It would be so wonderful to be able to sleep."

"Not me," said Joe. "I hate it. I'm always afraid I'll never wake up. And be dead. And never know it."

"I was told," said Mr. Colish. "I mustn't forget. Remind me. Before you go. I have a gorgeous present for you."

"I can tell you now," said Joe. "If it's a house, wife and a car, I don't want it."

"I am surprised," said Mr. Colish. "I thought you were an American."

"Absolutely," said Joe. "And not only that. I am every inch of me a typical member of the human race. A second-string quarterback aching to get in there and turn the game around. I was hoping. I was praying you would beg me to stay."

"I was thinking," said Mr.Colish.

"Just to see," said Joe. "Just to see if I have nerve enough to say no again."

"What a wonderful day for cutting up old dish towels."

"Yes," said Joe. "Ain't it though? And so perfect for throwing the old nostrils into the air. Um, boy. It is incredible, isn't it? So many clear dry glorious days in a row. I wonder what it means. You think when it finally rains, everything will be rearranged? You on the bottom? And me on top?"

"Forget it," said Mr. Colish. "Won't work. Too slippery up there for a luftmensch with two left feet like you."

"Foiled again," said Joe.

"It happens," said Mr. Colish. "And now. If you please. I want you to take. Here. Beautiful dreamer that you are. Wear it in good health. The last thing he wrapped up with his poor crooked fingers. My old father's number two tuxedo."

"Ah," said Joe. "So that's what it is?"

673

"Now you can dress up."

"He remembered," said Joe. "Isn't that sweet? Somebody was thinking about me. I really appreciate that."

"Now you can go to the dogs formal."

"What the hell," said Joe. "At least I will look rich. How I hate to wear someone's dead clothes."

"Not a Bolshevik," said Mr. Colish. "But already so bitter."

"Oh, no," said Joe. "Not true. Not true at all. It's only that. You try it and see. No one likes to get the bum's rush. Even the last cockroach I chased who beat me to the crack in the wall. So sly and shiny. Such a marvelous smeller. Assigned to the business district. It's funny. I get so excited. And I think I know why. I have this strange feeling in my gut that my new life will turn out to be exactly like my old. I have my nerve. I'm the one who's running out on you. Yet it kind of hurts to know you have no more use for me. Freiheit. Freiheit. It has to be more than the name of a newpaper. Pipe this. Tomorrow I'm going to have a tremendous mailing. Every living thing in this land will receive from me a postcard where I sign away with my stamped x all my rights to my piece of the pie. I want my mouth to be free. I want my apple to remain on the tree. Easy on the corn. Let's hear one from the brass section. I wonder. Do you happen to have any good tips on how I can finish out my life in some spectacular way without causing too much damage to man or beast? You don't know. You refuse to say. How about all this big talk I keep hearing about security? And all the true love lost while making whoopee? And otherwise bugging out your eyes and swallowing your tongue so as not to spill the beans and play it safe? What? Was that me saying what? What is this silence that I hear? I feel so put down I wonder if I am still where I am. I sure do hope for your sake you have a lot of dough stashed away. One sniff should tell me. There will never be enough air in here to burn a candle in my memory. I guess we all listen better with our eyes closed. Oh, my elders. Aren't they really? Aren't they the pip?"

"Ah," said Mr. Colish. "Thank god."

"I'm willing," said Joe. "If I only knew for what."

"I took a big pill. I am beginning to feel it."

"A pill," said Joe. "I should say. Look at that lovely expression. Is that what it does? Some people have all the luck."

"Wonderful," said Mr. Colish. "I weigh nothing. I can look right in

674

the sun. What is bluing to me? The birds also do it. Nothing lasts. I like things fast, fast, fast. I remember. I was told. Want two friends? Bite a snake in half. Like you I want every human lump to love me. But not to touch. It is you. It is you who makes me see. These are my own eyes. This is my own nose. I must try to be happy to be nobody but me. Scoot. Take off. Paddle your own canoe. Study the books. Pray for me. What are you downstairs here in the dirt but a pest? Too bright. Too full of blood. Too good, too good. But high upstairs where the whole sky is black? Who knows? Take with you plenty of kitchen matches. Light for me a way. Reserve for me a place in the last row. Pray for me. I'm an old discontinued model. I can float so much better than I can swim. Watch how. I am starting to bounce down the steps. Some days it takes so long to get dark. When I snooze where I sit, I will stand in the doorway and watch a woman crack pistachio nuts and separate the whites from the yolks. If I was next to the last man, I would shoot you all full of holes."

"And then," said Joe. "You would reload. And turn the flaming pistol on yourself."

"And poof," said Mr. Colish. "A little smoke. And all. All would be so quiet."

"Like on the moon," said Joe. "At last. All kaput. All dead. And god would have to rush back to the drawing board, holding up his pants with one hand."

"Someone is knocking?"

"Knocking?" said Joe. "I don't hear anything."

"Give me your hand."

"Ow," said Joe. "That hurts."

"Soon," said Mr. Colish. "You will close the door on me. You will be on the other side."

"Trick of the week," said Joe. "That's what doors are for."

"Pray for me."

"Impossible," said Joe. "I don't know how."

"You hear that knocking?"

"What knocking?" said Joe. "Where?"

"Aie," said Mr. Colish. "When I hear that knocking, I know it is the end."

"What end?" said Joe. "Can't you see? Here we are. Until we come together again somewhere. Just two more people saying goodbye."

"The devil," said Mr. Colish. "You hear it? Someone is knocking."

"Ah," said Joe. "Maybe. Maybe it's only the thumping of your heart and mine. What else?"

"Heart?" said Mr. Colish.

"Right," said Joe. "That's the way. That's a good way to rest. With your head in your arms."

"Rest," said Mr. Colish.

"It's enough," said Joe.

"Enough," said Mr. Colish.

"When all is said and done."

"Done," said Mr. Colish.

"It's enough to have lived."

"Lived," said Mr. Colish.

"Yes," said Joe. "And that. Oh, how immense. And wonderful enough. That. As of now. That is our only. That is our whole story."

Flatiron Book Distributors Inc., 175 Fifth Avenue (Suite 814), NYC 10010